W9-BXQ-365

CASTLE RICHMOND

BY
Anthony Trollope

Dover Publications,Inc.
New York

Published in Canada by General Publishing Company, Ltd., 30
Lesmill Road, Don Mills, Toronto, Ontario.
Published in the United Kingdom by Constable and Company,
Ltd., 10 Orange Street, London WC2H 7EG.

This Dover edition, first published in 1984 is an unabridged and
unaltered republication of the work as first published by Chapman &
Hall, London, in 1860.

Manufactured in the United States of America
Dover Publications, Inc., 31 East 2nd Street, Mineola, N.Y.
11501.

International Standard Book Number 0-486-24760-0

Library of Congress Cataloging in Publication Data

Trollope, Anthony, 1815–1882.
  Castle Richmond.

  Includes bibliographical references.
  I. Title.
PR5684.C3   1984   823'.8   84-8021
ISBN 0-486-24760-0

CONTENTS.

iv   CONTENTS.

CASTLE RICHMOND.

CHAPTER I.

THE BARONY OF DESMOND.

I WONDER whether the novel-reading world—that part of it, at least, which may honour my pages—will be offended if I lay the plot of this story in Ireland! That there is a strong feeling against things Irish it is impossible to deny. Irish servants need not apply; Irish acquaintances are treated with limited confidence; Irish cousins are regarded as being decidedly dangerous; and Irish stories are not popular with the booksellers.

For myself, I may say that if I ought to know anything about any place, I ought to know something about Ireland; and I do strongly protest against the injustice of the above conclusions. Irish cousins I have none. Irish acquaintances I have by dozens; and Irish friends, also, by twos and threes, whom I can love and cherish—almost as well, perhaps, as though they had been born in Middlesex. Irish servants I have had some in my house for years, and never had one that was faithless, dishonest, or intemperate. I have travelled all over Ireland, closely as few other men can have done, and have never had my portmanteau robbed or my pocket picked. At hotels I have seldom locked up my belongings, and my carelessness has never been punished. I doubt whether as much can be said for English inns.

Irish novels were once popular enough. But there is a fashion in novels, as there is in colours and petticoats; and now I fear they are drugs in the market. It is hard to say why a good story should not have a fair chance of success whatever may be its bent; why it should not be reckoned to be good by its own intrinsic merits alone; but such is by no means the case. I was waiting once, when I was young at the work, in the back parlour of an eminent publisher, hoping to see his eminence on a small matter of business touching a three-volumed manuscript which I

held in my hand.   The eminent publisher, having probably larger
fish to fry, could not see me, but sent his clerk or foreman to
arrange the business.

' A novel, is it, sir?' said the foreman.

' Yes,' I answered; ' a novel.'

' It depends very much on the subject,' said the foreman, with a
thoughtful and judicious frown—' upon the name, sir, and the subject;—daily life, sir; that's what suits us; daily English life. Now
your historical novel, sir, is not worth the paper it's written on.'

I fear that Irish character is in these days considered almost as
unattractive as historical incident; but, nevertheless, I will make
the attempt.   I am now leaving the Green Isle and my old
friends, and would fain say a word of them as I do so. If I do
not say that word now it will never be said.

The readability of a story should depend, one would say, on
its intrinsic merit rather than on the site of its adventures.   No
one will think that Hampshire is better for such a purpose than
Cumberland, or Essex than Leicestershire.   What abstract
objection can there then be to the county Cork?

Perhaps the most interesting, and certainly the most beautiful
part of Ireland is that which lies down in the extreme south-
west, with fingers stretching far out into the Atlantic Ocean.
This consists of the counties Cork and Kerry, or a portion,
rather, of those counties.   It contains Killarney, Glengarriffe,
Bantry, and Inchigeela; and is watered by the Lee, the Blackwater, and the Flesk.   I know not where is to be found a land
more rich in all that constitutes the loveliness of scenery.

Within this district, but hardly within that portion of it which
is most attractive to tourists, is situated the house and domain of
Castle Richmond.   The river Blackwater rises in the county
Kerry, and running from west to east through the northern part
of the county Cork, enters the county Waterford beyond Fermoy.
In its course it passes near the little town of Kanturk, an
through the town of Mallow: Castle Richmond stands close upon
its banks, within the barony of Desmond, and in that Kanturk
region through which the Mallow and Killarney railway now
passes, but which some thirteen years since knew nothing of the
navvy's spade, or even of the engineer's theodolite.

Castle Richmond was at this period the abode of Sir Thomas
Fitzgerald, who resided there, ever and always, with his wife,
Lady Fitzgerald, his two daughters, Mary and Emmeline Fitzgerald, and, as often as purposes of education and pleasure suited,
with his son Herbert Fitzgerald.   Neither Sir Thomas nor Sir
Thomas's house had about them any of those interesting pictu-
resque faults which are so generally attributed to Irish landlords

and Irish castles. He was not out of elbows, nor was he an absentee. Castle Richmond had no appearance of having been thrown out of its own windows. It was a good, substantial, modern family residence, built not more than thirty years since by the late baronet, with a lawn sloping down to the river, with kitchen gardens and walls for fruit, with ample stables, and a clock over the entrance to the stable yard. It stood in a well-timbered park duly stocked with deer,—and with foxes also, which are agricultural animals much more valuable in an Irish county than deer. So that, as regards its appearance Castle Richmond might have been in Hampshire or Essex; and as regards his property, Sir Thomas Fitzgerald might have been a Leicestershire baronet.

Here, at Castle Richmond, lived Sir Thomas with his wife and daughters; and here, taking the period of our story as being exactly thirteen years since, his son Herbert was staying also in those hard winter months; his Oxford degree having been taken, and his English pursuits admitting of a temporary sojourn in Ireland.

But Sir Thomas Fitzgerald was not the great man of that part of the country—at least, not the greatest man; nor was Lady Fitzgerald by any means the greatest lady. As this greatest lady, and the greatest man also, will, with their belongings, be among the most prominent of our dramatis personæ, it may be well that I should not even say a word of them.

All the world must have heard of Desmond Court. It is the largest inhabited residence known in that part of the world, where rumours are afloat of how it covers ten acres of ground; how in hewing the stones for it a whole mountain was cut away; how it should have cost hundreds of thousands of pounds, only that the money was never paid by the rapacious, wicked, blood-thirsty old earl who caused it to be erected:—and how the cement was thickened with human blood. So goes rumour with the more romantic of the Celtic tale-bearers.

It is a huge place—huge, ungainly, and uselessly extensive; built at a time when, at any rate in Ireland, men considered neither beauty, aptitude, nor economy. It is three stories high, and stands round a quadrangle, in which there are two entrances opposite to each other. Nothing can be well uglier than that great paved court, in which there is not a spot of anything green, except where the damp has produced an unwholesome growth upon the stones; nothing can well be more desolate. And on the outside of the building matters are not much better. There are no gardens close up to the house, no flower-beds in the nooks and corners, no sweet shrubs peeping in at the square windows. Gardens there are, but they are away, half a mile off;

and the great hall door opens out upon a flat, bleak park, with hardly a scrap around it which courtesy can call a lawn.

Here, at this period of ours, lived Clara, Countess of Desmond, widow of Patrick, once Earl of Desmond, and father of Patrick, now Earl of Desmond. These Desmonds had once been mighty men in their country, ruling the people around them as serfs, and ruling them with hot iron rods. But those days were now long gone, and tradition told little of them that was true. How it had truly fared either with the earl, or with their serfs, men did not well know; but stories were ever being told of walls built with human blood, and of the devil bearing off upon his shoulder a certain earl who was in any other way quite unbearable, and depositing some small unburnt portion of his remains fathoms deep below the soil in an old burying-ground near Kanturk. And there had been a good earl, as is always the case with such families; but even his virtues, according to tradition, had been of a useless namby-pamby sort. He had walked to the shrine of St. Finbar, up in the little island of the Gougane Barra, with unboiled peas in his shoes; had forgiven his tenants five years' rent all round, and never drank wine or washed himself after the death of his lady wife.

At the present moment the Desmonds were not so potent either for good or ill. The late earl had chosen to live in London all his life, and had sunk down to be the toadying friend, or perhaps I should more properly say the bullied flunky, of a sensual, wine-bibbing, gluttonous —— king. Late in life, when he was broken in means and character, he had married. The lady of his choice had been chosen as an heiress; but there had been some slip between that cup of fortune and his lip; and she, proud and beautiful—for such she had been—had neither relieved nor softened the poverty of her profligate old lord.

She was left at his death with two children, of whom the eldest, Lady Clara Desmond, will be the heroine of this story. The youngest, Patrick, now Earl of Desmond, was two years younger than his sister, and will make our acquaintance as a lad fresh from Eton.

In these days money was not plentiful with the Desmonds. Not but that their estates were as wide almost as their renown, and that the Desmonds were still great people in the country's estimation. Desmond Court stood in a bleak, unadorned region, almost among the mountains, half way between Kanturk and Maccoom, and the family had some claim to possession of the land for miles around. The earl of the day was still the head landlord of a huge district extending over the whole barony of Desmond, and half the adjacent baronies of

Muskerry and Duhallow; but the head landlord's rent in m
cases hardly amounted to sixpence an acre, and even those
sixpences did not always find their way into the earl's pocket.
When the late earl had attained his sceptre, he might probably
have been entitled to spend some ten thousand a year; but
when he died, and during the years just previous to that, he
had hardly been entitled to spend anything.

But, nevertheless, the Desmonds were great people, and owned
a great name. They had been kings once over those wild
mountains; and would be still, some said, if every one had
his own. Their grandeur was shown by the prevalence of their
name. The barony in which they lived was the barony of
Desmond. The river which gave water to their cattle was
the river Desmond. The wretched, ragged, poverty-stricken
village near their own dismantled gate was the town of Desmond. The earl was Earl of Desmond—not Earl Desmond,
mark you; and the family name was Desmond. The grand-
father of the present earl, who had repaired his fortune by
selling himself at the time of the Union, had been Desmond
Desmond, Earl of Desmond.

The late earl, the friend of the most illustrious person in
the kingdom, had not been utterly able to rob his heir of
everything, or he would undoubtedly have done so. At the
age of twenty-one the young earl would come into possession
of the property, damaged certainly, as far as an actively evil
father could damage it by long leases, bad management, lack
of outlay, and rack-renting;—but still into the possession of a
considerable property. In the mean time it did not fare very
well, in a pecuniary way, with Clara, the widowed countess,
or with the Lady Clara, her daughter. The means at the
widow's disposal were only those which the family trustees
would allow her as the earl's mother: on his coming of age
she would have almost no means of her own; and for her
daughter no provision whatever had been made.

As this first chapter is devoted wholly to the locale of my story,
I will not stop to say a word as to the persons or characters
of either of these two ladies, leaving them, as I did the Castle
Richmond family, to come forth upon the canvas as opportunity may offer. But there is another homestead in this same
barony of Desmond, of which and of its owner—as being its
owner—I will say a word.

Hap House was also the property of a Fitzgerald. It had
originally been built by an old Sir Simon Fitzgerald, for the
use and behoof of a second son, and the present owner of it
was the grandson of that man for whom it had been built.

And old Sir Simon had given his offspring not only a house—
he had endowed the house with a comfortable little slice of
land, either cut from the large patrimonial loaf, or else, as was
more probable, collected together and separately baked for
this younger branch of the family. Be that as it may, Hap
House had of late years been always regarded as conferring
some seven or eight hundred a year upon its possessor, and
when young Owen Fitzgerald succeeded to this property, on
the death of an uncle in the year 1843, he was regarded as a
rich man to that extent.

At that time he was some twenty-two years of age, and he
came down from Dublin, where his friends had intended that
he should practise as a barrister, to set up for himself as a
country gentleman. Hap House was distant from Castle
Richmond about four miles, standing also on the river Blackwater, but nearer to Mallow. It was a pleasant, comfortable
residence, too large no doubt for such a property, as is so
often the case in Ireland; surrounded by pleasant grounds
and pleasant gardens, with a gorse fox covert belonging to the
place within a mile of it, with a slated lodge, and a pretty
drive along the river. At the age of twenty-two, Owen
Fitzgerald came into all this; and as he at once resided upon
the place, he came in also for the good graces of all the
mothers with unmarried daughters in the county, and for the
smiles also of many of the daughters themselves.

Sir Thomas and Lady Fitzgerald were not his uncle and
aunt, but nevertheless they took kindly to him:—very kindly
at first, though that kindness after a while became less warm.
He was the nearest relation of the name; and should anything
happen—as the fatal death-foretelling phrase goes—to young
Herbert Fitzgerald, he would become the heir of the family title
and of the family place.

When I hear of a young man sitting down by himself as
the master of a household, without a wife, or even without a
mother or sister to guide him, I always anticipate danger.
If he does not go astray in any other way, he will probably
mismanage his money matters. And then there are so many
other ways. A house, if it be not made pleasant by domestic
pleasant things, must be made pleasant by pleasure. And a
bachelor's pleasures in his own house are always dangerous.
There is too much wine drunk at his dinner parties. His
guests sit too long over their cards. The servants know that
they want a mistress; and, in the absence of that mistress, the
language of the household becomes loud and harsh—and sometimes improper. Young men among us seldom go quite straight

in their course, unless they are, at any rate occasionally, brought under the influence of tea and small talk.

There was no tea and small talk at Hap House, but there were hunting-dinners. Owen Fitzgerald was soon known for his horses and his riding. He lived in the very centre of the Duhallow hunt; and before he had been six months owner of his property had built additional stables, with half a dozen loose boxes for his friends' nags. He had an eye, too, for a pretty girl—not always in the way that is approved of by mothers with marriageable daughters; but in the way of which they so decidedly disapprove.

And thus old ladies began to say bad things. Those pleasant hunting-dinners were spoken of as the Hap House orgies. It was declared that men slept there half the day, having played cards all the night; and dreadful tales were told. Of these tales one-half was doubtless false. But, alas, alas! what if one-half were also true?

It is undoubtedly a very dangerous thing for a young man of twenty-two to keep house by himself, either in town or country.

CHAPTER II.

OWEN FITZGERALD.

I HAVE tied myself down to thirteen years ago as the time of my story; but I must go back a little beyond this for its first scenes, and work my way up as quickly as may be to the period indicated. I have spoken of a winter in which Herbert Fitzgerald was at home at Castle Richmond, having then completed his Oxford doings; but I must say something of two years previous to that, of a time when Herbert was not so well known in the county as was his cousin of Hap House.

It was a thousand pities that a bad word should ever have been spoken of Owen Fitzgerald; ten thousand pities that he should ever have given occasion for such bad word. He was a fine, high-spirited, handsome fellow, with a loving heart within his breast, and bright thoughts within his brain. It was utterly wrong that a man constituted as he was should commence life by living alone in a large country house. But those who spoke ill of him should have remembered that this was his misfortune rather than his fault. Some greater endeavour might perhaps have been made to rescue him from evil ways. Very little such endeavour was made at all. Sir Thomas once or twice spoke to him; but Sir Thomas was not an energetic man; and as for

Lady Fitzgerald, though she was in many things all that was
excellent, she was far too diffident to attempt the reformation of a
headstrong young man, who after all was only distantly connected
with her.

And thus there was no such attempt, and poor Owen became
the subject of ill report without any substantial effort having been
made to save him.   He was a very handsome man—tall, being
somewhat over six feet in height—athletic, almost more than in
proportion—with short, light chestnut-tinted hair, blue eyes, and
a mouth perfect as that of Phœbus.   He was clever, too, though
perhaps not educated as carefully as might have been: his speech
was usually rapid, hearty, and short, and not seldom caustic and
pointed.   Had he fallen among good hands, he might have done
very well in the world's fight; but with such a character, and
lacking such advantages, it was quite as open to him to do ill.
Alas! the latter chance seemed to have fallen to him.

For the first year of his residence at Hap House, he was popular
enough among his neighbours.   The Hap House orgies were not
commenced at once, nor when commenced did they immediately
become a subject of scandal; and even during the second year he
was tolerated;—tolerated by all, and still flattered by some.

Among the different houses in the country at which he had
become intimate was that of the Countess of Desmond.   The
Countess of Desmond did not receive much company at Desmond
Court.   She had not the means, nor perhaps the will, to fill the
huge old house with parties of her Irish neighbours—for she
herself was English to the backbone.   Ladies of course made
morning calls, and gentlemen too, occasionally; but society at
Desmond Court was for some years pretty much confined to this
cold formal mode of visiting.   Owen Fitzgerald, however, did
obtain admittance into the precincts of the Desmond barracks.

He went there first with the young earl, who, then quite a boy,
had had an ugly tumble from his pony in the hunting-field.
The countess had expressed herself as very grateful for young
Fitzgerald's care, and thus an intimacy had sprung up.   Owen
had gone there once or twice to see the lad, and on those occasions had dined there; and on one occasion, at the young earl's
urgent request, had stayed and slept.

And then the good-natured people of Muskerry, Duhallow, and
Desmond began, of course, to say that the widow was going to
marry the young man.   And why not? she was still a beautiful
woman; not yet forty by a good deal, said the few who took her
part; or at any rate, not much over, as was admitted by the many
who condemned her.   We, who have been admitted to her
secrets, know that she was then in truth only thirty-eight.   She

was beautiful, proud, and clever; and if it would suit her to marry a handsome young fellow with a good house and an unembarrassed income of eight hundred a year, why should she not do so? As for him, would it not be a great thing for him to have a countess for his wife, and an earl for his stepson?

What ideas the countess had on this subject we will not just now trouble ourselves to inquire. But as to young Owen Fitzgerald, we may declare at once that no thought of such a wretched alliance ever entered his head. He was sinful in many things, and foolish in many things. But he had not that vile sin, that unmanly folly, which would have made a marriage with a widowed countess eligible in his eyes, merely because she was a countess, and not more than fifteen years his senior. In a matter of love he would as soon have thought of paying his devotions to his far-away cousin, old Miss Barbara Beamish, of Ballyclahassan, of whom it was said that she had set her cap at every unmarried man that had come into the west riding of the county for the last forty years. No; it may at any rate be said of Owen Fitzgerald, that he was not the man to make up to a widowed countess for the sake of the reflected glitter which might fall on him from her coronet.

But the Countess of Desmond was not the only lady at Desmond Court. I have before said that she had a daughter, the Lady Clara, the heroine of this coming story; and it may be now right that I should attempt some short description of her: her virtues and faults, her merits and defects. It shall be very short; for let an author describe as he will, he cannot by such course paint the characters of his personages on the minds of his readers. It is by gradual, earnest efforts that this must be done—if it be done. Ten, nay, twenty pages of the finest descriptive writing that ever fell from the pen of a novelist will not do it.

Clara Desmond, when young Fitzgerald first saw her, had hardly attained that incipient stage of womanhood which justifies a mother in taking her out into the gaieties of the world. She was then only sixteen; and had not in her manner and appearance so much of the woman as is the case with many girls of that age. She was shy and diffident in manner, thin and tall in person. If I were to say that she was angular and bony, I should disgust my readers, who, disliking the term, would not stop to consider how many sweetest girls are at that age truly subject to those epithets. Their undeveloped but active limbs are long and fleshless, the contour of their face is the same, their elbows and shoulders are pointed, their feet and hands seem to possess length without breadth. Birth and breeding have given

them the frame of beauty, to which coming years will add the
soft roundness of form, and the rich glory of colour. The plump,
rosy girl of fourteen, though she also is very sweet, never rises
to such celestial power of feminine grace as she who is angular
and bony, whose limbs are long, and whose joints are sharp.

Such was Clara Desmond at sixteen. But still, even then, to
those who were gifted with the power of seeing, she gave promise
of great loveliness. Her eyes were long and large, and wonderfully clear. There was a liquid depth in them which enabled
the gazer to look down into them as he would into the green,
pellucid transparency of still ocean water. And then they said
so much—those young eyes of hers: from her mouth in those
early years words came but scantily, but from her eyes questions
rained quicker than any other eyes could answer them. Questions of wonder at what the world contained—of wonder as to
what men thought and did; questions as to the inmost heart,
and truth, and purpose of the person questioned. And all this
was asked by a glance now and again; by a glance of those
long, shy, liquid eyes, which were ever falling on the face of
him she questioned, and then ever as quickly falling from it.

Her face, as I have said, was long and thin, but it was the
longness and thinness of growing youth. The natural lines of it
were full of beauty, of pale silent beauty, too proud in itself to
boast itself much before the world, to make itself common among
many. Her hair was already long and rich, but was light in
colour, much lighter than it grew to be when some four or five more
years had passed over her head. At the time of which I speak
she wore it in simple braids brushed back from her forehead,
not having as yet learned that majestic mode of sweeping it
from her face which has in subsequent years so generally prevailed.

And what then of her virtues and her faults—of her merits
and defects? Will it not be better to leave them all to time and
the coming pages? That she was proud of her birth, proud
of being an Irish Desmond, proud even of her poverty, so much
I may say of her, even at that early age. In that she was
careless of the world's esteem, fond to a fault of romance, poetic
in her temperament, and tender in her heart, she shared the ordinary—shall I say foibles or virtues?—of so many of her sex.
She was passionately fond of her brother, but not nearly equally
so of her mother, of whom the brother was too evidently the
favoured child.

She had lived much alone; alone, that is, with her governess,
and with servants at Desmond Court. Not that she had been
neglected by her mother, but she had hardly found herself to be

her mother's companion; and other companions there she had had
none. When she was sixteen her governess was still with her:
but a year later than that she was left quite alone, except inas-
much as she was with her mother.

She was sixteen when she first began to ask questions of
Owen Fitzgerald's face with those large eyes of hers; and she
saw much of him, and he of her, for the twelve months immediately after that. Much of him, that is, as much goes in this
country of ours, where four or five interviews in as many months
between friends is supposed to signify that they are often together. But this much-seeing occurred chiefly during the young
earl's holidays. Now and again he did ride over in the long
intervals, and when he did do so was not frowned upon by the
countess; and so, at the end of the winter holidays subsequent
to that former winter in which the earl had had his tumble, people
through the county began to say that he and the countess were
about to become man and wife.

It was just then that people in the county were also beginning
to talk of the Hap House orgies; and the double scandal reached
Owen's ears, one shortly after the other. That orgies scandal
did not hurt him much. It is, alas! too true that consciousness
of such a reputation does not often hurt a young man's feelings.
But the other rumour did wound him. What! he sell himself to
a widowed countess almost old enough to be his mother; or bestow
himself rather,—for what was there in return that could be
reckoned as a price? At any rate, he had given no one cause to
utter such falsehood, such calumny as that. No; it certainly
was not probable that he should marry the countess.

But this set him to ask himself whether it might or might not
be possible that he should marry some one else. Might it not be
well for him if he could find a younger bride at Desmond Court?
Not for nothing had he ridden over there through those bleak
mountains; not for nothing, nor yet solely with the view of
tying flies for the young earl's summer fishing, or preparing
the new nag for his winter's hunting. Those large bright eyes
had asked him many questions. Would it not be well that he
should answer them?

For many months of that year Clara Desmond had hardly
spoken to him. Then, in the summer evening, as he and her
brother would lie sprawling together on the banks of the little
Desmond river, while the lad was talking of his fish, and his
school, and his cricket club, she would stand by and listen,
and so gradually she learned to speak.

And the mother also would sometimes be there; or else she
would welcome Fitzgerald in to tea, and let him stay there

talking as though they were all at home, till he would have to make a midnight ride of it before he reached Hap House. It seemed that no fear as to her daughter had ever crossed the mother's mind ; that no idea had ever come upon her that her favoured visitor might learn to love the young girl with whom he was allowed to associate on so intimate a footing. Once or twice he had caught himself calling her Clara, and had done so even before her mother ; but no notice had been taken of it. In truth, Lady Desmond did not know her daughter, for the mother took her absolutely to be a child, when in fact she was a child no longer.

'You take Clara round by the bridge,' said the earl to his friend one August evening, as they were standing together on the banks of the river, about a quarter of a mile distant from the sombre old pile in which the, family lived. 'You take Clara round by the bridge, and I will get over the stepping-stones.' And so the lad, with his rod in his hand, began to descend the steep bank.

'I can get over the stepping-stones, too, Patrick,' said she.

'Can you though, my gay young woman? You'll be over your ankles if you do. That rain didn't come down yesterday for nothing.'

Clara as she spoke had come up to the bank, and now looked wistfully down at the stepping-stones. She had crossed them scores of times, sometimes with her brother, and often by her-self. Why was it that she was so anxious to cross them now?

'It's no use your trying,' said her brother, who was now half across, and who spoke from the middle of the river. 'Don't you let her, Owen. She'll slip in, and then there will be no end of a row up at the house.'

'You had better come round by the bridge,' said Fitzgerald. 'It is not only that the stones are nearly under water, but they are wet, and you would slip.'

So cautioned, Lady Clara allowed herself to be persuaded, and turned upwards along the river by a little path that led to a foot bridge. It was some quarter of a mile thither, and it would be the same distance down the river again before she regained her brother.

'I needn't bring you with me, you know,' she said to Fitz-gerald. 'You can get over the stones easily, and I can go very well by myself.'

But it was not probable that he would let her do so. 'Why should I not go with you?' he said. 'When I get there I have nothing to do but see him fish. Only if we were to leave him by himself he would not be happy.'

'Oh, Mr. Fitzgerald, how very kind you are to him! I do

so often think of it.   How dull his holidays would be in this place
if it were not for you !'

'And what a godsend his holidays are to me !' said Owen.
'When they come round I can ride over here and see him, end
you—and your mother.   Do you think that I am not dull also,
living alone at Hap House, and that this is not an infinite
blessing to me ?'

He had named them all—son, daughter, and mother; but
there had been a something in his voice, an almost inappreci-
able something in his tone, which had seemed to mark to
Clara's hearing that she herself was not the least prized of the
three attractions.   She had felt this rather than realized it,
and the feeling was not unpleasant.

' I only know that you are very goodnatured,' she continued, ' and that Patrick is very fond of you.   Sometimes
I think he almost takes you for a brother.'   And then a
sudden thought flashed across her mind, and she said hardly
a word more to him that evening.

This had been at the close of the summer holidays.   After
that he had been once or twice at Desmond Court, before the
return of the boy from Eton ; but on these occasions he had
been more with the countess than with her daughter.   On the
last of these visits, just before the holidays commenced, he
had gone over respecting a hunter he had bought for Lord
Desmond, and on this occasion he did not even see Clara.

The countess, when she had thanked him for his trouble in
the matter of the purchase, hesitated a moment, and then went
on to speak of other matters.

'I understand, Mr. Fitzgerald,' said she, 'that you have
been very gay at Hap House since the hunting commenced.'

'Oh, I don't know,' said Owen, half laughing and half
blushing.   'It's a convenient place for some of the men, and
one must be sociable.'

'Sociable! yes, one ought to be sociable certainly.   But I
am always afraid of the sociability of young men without ladies.
Do not be angry with me if I venture as a friend to ask you
not to be too sociable.'

' I know what you mean, Lady Desmond.   People have been
accusing us of—of being rakes.   Isn't that it ?'

' Yes, Mr. Fitzgerald, that is it.   But then I know that I
have no right to speak to you on such a—such a subject.'

'Yes, yes ; you have every right,' said he, warmly ; 'more
right than any one else.'

' Oh, no ; Sir Thomas, you know—'

' Well, yes, Sir Thomas.   Sir Thomas is very well, and so

also is Lady Fitzgerald ; but I do not feel the same interest about them that I do about you. And they are such humdrum, quiet-going people. As for Herbert, I'm afraid he'll turn out a prig.'

'Well, Mr. Fitzgerald, if you give me the right I shall use it.' And getting up from her chair, and coming to him where he stood, she looked kindly into his face. It was a bonny, handsome face for a woman to gaze on, and there was much kindness in hers as she smiled on him. Nay, there was almost more than kindness, he thought, as he caught her eye. It was like,—almost like the sweetness of motherly love. 'And I shall scold you,' she continued. 'People say that for two or three nights running men have been playing cards at Hap House till morning.'

'Yes, I had some men there for a week. I could not take their candles away, and put them to bed ; could I, Lady Desmond ?'

'And there were late suppers, and drinking of toasts, and headaches in the morning, and breakfast at three o'clock, and gentlemen with very pale faces when they appeared rather late at the meet—eh, Mr. Fitzgerald ?' And she held up one finger at him, as she upbraided him with a smile. The smile was so sweet, so unlike her usual look ; that, to tell the truth, was often too sad and careworn for her age.

'Such things do happen, Lady Desmond.'

'Ah, yes ; they do happen. And with such a one as you, heaven knows I do not begrudge the pleasure, if it were but now and then,—once again and then done with. But you are too bright and too good for such things to continue.' And she took his hand and pressed it, as a mother or a mother's dearest friend might have done. ' It would so grieve me to think that you should be even in danger of shipwreck.

'You will not be angry with me for taking this liberty ?' she continued.

'Angry ! how could any man be angry for such kindness ?'

'And you will think of what I say. I would not have you unsociable, or morose, or inhospitable ; but——'

'I understand, Lady Desmond ; but when young men are together, one cannot always control them.'

'But you will try. Say that you will try because I have asked you.'

He promised that he would, and then went his way, proud in his heart at this solicitude. And how could he not be proud ? was she not high in rank, proud in character, beautiful withal, and the mother of Clara Desmond ? What sweeter friend could a man have; what counsellor more potent to avert those dangers which now hovered round his head?

And as he rode home he was half in love with the countess. Where is the young man who has not in his early years been half in love with some woman older, much older than himself, who has half conquered his heart by her solicitude for his welfare?—with some woman who has whispered to him while others were talking, who has told him in such gentle, loving tones of his boyish follies, whose tenderness and experience together have educated him and made him manly? Young men are so proud, proud in their inmost hearts, of such tenderness and solicitude, as long as it remains secret and wrapt as it were in a certain mystery. Such liaisons have the interests of intrigue without—I was going to say without its dangers. Alas! it may be that it is not always so.

Owen Fitzgerald as he rode home was half in love with the countess. Not that his love was of a kind which made him in any way desirous of marrying her, or of kneeling at her feet and devoting himself to her for ever; not that it in any way interfered with the other love which he was beginning to feel for her daughter. But he thought with pleasure of the tone of her voice, of the pressure of her hand, of the tenderness which he had found in her eye.

It was after that time, as will be understood, that some good-natured friend had told him that ho was regarded in the county as the future husband of Lady Desmond. At first he laughed at this as being—as he himself said to himself—too good a joke. When the report first reached him, it seemed . to be a joke which he could share so pleasantly with the countess. For men of three-and-twenty, though they are so fond of the society of women older than themselves, understand so little the hearts and feelings of such women. In his ideas there was an interval as of another generation between him and the countess. In her thoughts the interval was probably much less striking.

But the accusation was made to him again and again till it wounded him, and he gave up that notion of a mutual joke with his kind friend at Desmond Court. It did not occur to him that she could ever think of loving him as her lord and master; but it was brought home to him that other people thought so.

A year had now passed by since those winter holidays in which Clara Desmond had been sixteen, and during which she was described by epithets which will not, I fear, have pleased my readers. Those epithets were now somewhat less deserved, but still the necessity of them had not entirely passed away. Her limbs were still thin and long, and her shoulders pointed;

but the growth of beauty had commenced, and in Owen's eyes she was already very lovely.

At Christmas-time during that winter a ball was given at Castle Richmond, to celebrate the coming of age of the young heir. It was not a very gay affair, for the Castle Richmond folk, even in those days, were not very gay people. Sir Thomas, though only fifty, was an old man for his age; and Lady Fitzgerald, though known intimately by the poor all round her, was not known intimately by any but the poor. Mary and Emmeline Fitzgerald, with whom we shall become better acquainted as we advance in our story, were nice, good girls, and handsome withal; but they had not that special gift which enables some girls to make a party in their own house bright in spite of all obstacles.

We should have but little to do with this ball, were it not that Clara Desmond was here first brought out, as the term goes. It was the first large party to which she had been taken, and it was to her a matter of much wonder and inquiry with those wondering, speaking eyes.

And Owen Fitzgerald was there;—as a matter of course, the reader will say. By no means so. Previous to that ball Owen's sins had been commented upon at Castle Richmond, and Sir Thomas had expostulated with him. These expostulations had not been received quite so graciously as those of the handsome countess, and there had been anger at Castle Richmond.

Now there was living in the house of Castle Richmond one Miss Letty Fitzgerald, a maiden sister of the baronet's, older than her brother by full ten years. In her character there was more of energy, and also much more of harsh judgment, and of consequent ill-nature, than in that of her brother. When the letters of invitation were being sent out by the two girls, she had given a decided opinion that the reprobate should not be asked. But the reprobate's cousins, with that partiality for a rake which is so common to young ladies, would not abide by their aunt's command, and referred the matter both to mamma and papa. Mamma thought it very hard that their own cousin should be refused admittance to their house, and very dreadful that his sins should be considered to be of so deep a dye as to require so severe a sentence; and then papa, much balancing the matter, gave final orders that the prodigal cousin should be admitted.

He was admitted, and dangerously he used the privilege. The countess, who was there, stood up to dance twice, and twice only. She opened the ball with young Herbert Fitzgerald the heir; and in about an hour afterwards she danced again with Owen. He did not ask her twice; but he asked her daughter

three or four times, and three or four times he asked her success-
fully.

'Clara,' whispered the mother to her child, after the last of
these occasions, giving some little pull or twist to her girl's
frock as she did so, 'you had better not dance with Owen Fitzgerald again to-night. People will remark about it.'

'Will they?' said Clara, and immediately sat down, checked in
her young happiness.

Not many minutes afterwards, Owen came up to her again.
'May we have another waltz together, I wonder?' he said.

'Not to-night, I think. I am rather tired already.' And so
she did not waltz again all the evening, for fear she should offend
him.

But the countess, though she had thus interdicted her daughter's
dancing with the master of Hap House, had not done so through
any absolute fear. To her, her girl was still a child; a child
without a woman's thoughts, or any of a woman's charms. And
then it was so natural that Clara should like to dance with
almost the only gentleman who was not absolutely a stranger
to her. Lady Desmond had been actuated rather by a feeling
that it would be well that Clara should begin to know other
persons.

By that feeling,—and perhaps unconsciously by another, that
it would be well that Owen Fitzgerald should be relieved from
his attendance on the child, and enabled to give it to the mother.
Whether Lady Desmond had at that time realized any ideas as to
her own interest in this young man, it was at any rate true that
she loved to have him near her. She had refused to dance a
second time with Herbert Fitzgerald; she had refused to stand
up with any other person who had asked her; but with Owen
she would either have danced again, or have kept him by her
side, while she explained to him with flattering frankness that
she could not do so lest others should be offended.

And Owen was with her frequently through the evening.
She was taken to and from supper by Sir Thomas, but any
other takings that were incurred were done by him. He led her
from one drawing-room to another; he took her empty coffee-
cup; he stood behind her chair, and talked to her; and he
brought her the scarf which she had left elsewhere; and finally,
he put a shawl round her neck while old Sir Thomas was waiting to hand her to her carriage. Reader, good-natured, middle-
aged reader, remember that she was only thirty-eight, and that
hitherto she had known nothing of the delights of love. By
the young, any such hallucination on her part, at her years, will
be regarded as lunacy, or at least frenzy.

Owen Fitzgerald drove home from that ball in a state of mind that was hardly satisfactory. In the first place, Miss Letty had made a direct attack upon his morals, which he had not answered in the most courteous manner.

'I have heard a great deal of your doings, Master Owen,' she said to him. 'A fine house you're keeping'

'Why don't you come and join us, Aunt Letty?' he replied. 'It would be just the thing for you.'

'God forbid!' said the old maid, turning up her eyes to heaven.

'Oh, you might do worse, you know. With us you'd only drink and play cards, and perhaps hear a little strong language now and again. But what's that to slander, and calumny, and bearing false witness against one's neighbour? and so saying he ended that interview—not in a manner to ingratiate himself with his relative, Miss Letty Fitzgerald.

After that, in the supper-room, more than one wag of a fellow had congratulated him on his success with the widow. 'She's got some sort of a jointure, I suppose,' said one. 'She's very young-looking, certainly, to be the mother of that girl,' declared another. 'Upon my word, she's a handsome woman still,' said a third. 'And what title will you get when you marry her, Fitz?' asked a fourth, who was rather ignorant as to the phases under which the British peerage develops itself.

Fitzgerald pshawed, and pished, and poohed; and then, breaking away from them, rode home. He felt that he must at any rate put an end to this annoyance about the countess, and that he must put an end also to his state of doubt about the countess's daughter. Clara had been kind and gracious to him in the first part of the evening; nay, almost more than gracious. Why had she been so cold when he went up to her on that last occasion? why had she gathered herself like a snail into its shell for the rest of the evening?

The young earl had also been at the party, and had exacted a promise from Owen that he would be over at Desmond Court on the next day. It had almost been on Owen's lips to tell his friend, not only that he would be there, but what would be his intention when he got there. He knew that the lad loved him well; and almost fancied that, earl as he was, he would favour his friend's suit. But a feeling that Lord Desmond was only a boy, restrained him. It would not be well to induce one so young to agree to an arrangement of which in after and more mature years he would so probably disapprove.

But not the less did Fitzgerald, as he drove home, determine that on the next day he would know something of his fate: and with this resolve he endeavoured to comfort himself as he drove up into his own avenue, and betook himself to his own solitary home.

CHAPTER III.

CLARA DESMOND.

It had been Clara Desmond's first ball, and on the following morning she had much to occupy her thoughts. In the first place, had she been pleased or had she not? Had she been most gratified or most pained?

Girls when they ask themselves such questions seldom give themselves fair answers. She had liked dancing with Owen Fitzgerald; oh, so much! She had liked dancing with others too, though she had not known them, and had hardly spoken to them. The mere act of dancing, with the loud music in the room, and the gay dresses and bright lights around her, had been delightful. But then it had pained her—she knew not why, but it had pained her—when her mother told her that people would make remarks about her. Had she done anything improper on this her first entry into the world? Was her conduct to be scanned, and judged, and condemned, while she was flattering herself that no one had noticed her but him who was speaking to her?

Their breakfast was late, and the countess sat, as was her wont, with her book beside her teacup, speaking a word every now and again to her son.

'Owen will be over here to-day,' said he. 'We are going to have a schooling match down on the Callows.' Now in Ireland a schooling match means the amusement of teaching your horses to jump.

'Will he?' said Lady Desmond, looking up from her book for a moment. 'Mind you bring him in to lunch; I want to speak to him.'

'He doesn't care much about lunch, I fancy,' said he; 'and, maybe, we shall be half way to Millstreet by that time.'

'Never mind, but do as I tell you. You expect everybody to be as wild and wayward as yourself.' And the countess smiled on her son in a manner which showed that she was proud even of his wildness and his waywardness.

Clara had felt that she blushed when she heard that Mr. Fitzgerald was to be there that morning. She felt that her own manner became constrained, and was afraid that her mother should look at her. Owen had said nothing to her about love;

and she, child as she was, had thought nothing about love. But she was conscious of something, she knew not what. He had touched her hand during those dances as it had never been touched before; he had looked into her eyes, and her eyes had fallen before his glance; he had pressed her waist, and she had felt that there was tenderness in the pressure. So she blushed, and almost trembled, when she heard that he was coming, and was glad in her heart when she found that there was neither anger nor sunshine in her mother's face.

Not long after breakfast, the earl went out on his horse, and met Owen at some gate or back entrance. In his opinion the old house was stupid, and the women in it were stupid companions in the morning. His heart for the moment was engaged on the thought of making his animal take the most impracticable leaps which he could find, and it did not occur to him at first to give his mother's message to his companion. As for lunch, they would get a biscuit and glass of cherry-brandy at Wat M'Carthy's, of Drumban; and as for his mother having anything to say, that of course went for nothing.

Owen would have been glad to have gone up to the house, but in that he was frustrated by the earl's sharpness in catching him. His next hope was to get through the promised lesson in horse-leaping as quickly as possible, so that he might return to Desmond Court, and take his chance of meeting Clara. But in this he found the earl very difficult to manage.

'Oh, Owen, we won't go there,' he said, when Fitzgerald proposed a canter through some meadows down by the river-side. 'There are only a few gripes'—Irish for small ditches—'and I have ridden Fireball over them a score of times. I want you to come away towards Drumban.'

'Drumban! why Drumban's seven miles from here.'

'What matter? Besides, it's not six the way I'll take you. I want to see Wat M'Carthy especially. He has a litter of puppies there, out of that black bitch of his, and I mean to make him give me one of them.'

But on that morning, Owen Fitzgerald would not allow himself to be taken so far a-field as Drumban, even on a mission so important as this. The young lord fought the matter stoutly; but it ended by his being forced to content himself with picking out all the most dangerous parts of the fences in the river meadows.

'Why, you've hardly tried your own mare at all,' said the lad, reproachfully.

'I'm going to hunt her on Saturday,' said Owen; 'and she'll have quite enough to do then.'

'Well, you're very slow to-day. You're done up with the dancing, I think. And what do you mean to do now?'

'I'll go home with you, I think, and pay my respects to the countess.'

'By-the-by, I was to bring you in to lunch. She said she wanted to see you. By jingo, I forgot all about it! But you've all become very stupid among you, I know that.' And so they rode back to Desmond Court, entering the demesne by one of the straight, dull, level roads which led up to the house.

But it did not suit the earl to ride on the road while the grass was so near him; so they turned off with a curve across what was called the park, thus prolonging their return by about double the necessary distance.

As they were cantering on, Owen saw her of whom he was in quest walking in the road which they had left. His best chance of seeing her alone had been that of finding her outside the house. He knew that the countess rarely or never walked with her daughter, and that, as the governess was gone, Clara was driven to walk by herself.

'Desmond,' he said, pulling up his horse, 'do you go on and tell your mother that I will be with her almost immediately.'

'Why, where are you off to now?'

'There is your sister, and I must ask her how she is after the ball;' and so saying he trotted back in the direction of the road.

Lady Clara had seen them; and though she had hardly turned her head, she had seen also how suddenly Mr. Fitzgerald had stopped his horse, and turned his course when he perceived her. At the first moment she had been almost angry with him for riding away from her, and now she felt almost angry with him because he did not do so.

He slackened his pace as he came near her, and approached her at a walk. There was very little of the faint heart about Owen Fitzgerald at any time, or in anything that he attempted. He had now made up his mind fairly to tell Clara Desmond that he loved her, and to ask for her love in return. He had resolved to do so, and there was very little doubt but that he would carry out his resolution. But he had in nowise made up his mind how he should do it, or what his words should be. And now that he saw her so near him he wanted a moment to collect his thoughts.

He took off his hat as he rode up, and asked her whether she was tired after the ball; and then dismounting, he left his mare to follow as she pleased.

'Oh, Mr. Fitzgerald, won't she run away?' said Clara, as she gave him her hand.

'Oh, no; she has been taught better than that. But you don't tell me how you are. I thought you were tired last night when I saw that you had altogether given over dancing.' And then he walked on beside her, and the docile mare followed them like a dog.

'No, I was not tired; at least, not exactly,' said Clara, blushing again and again, being conscious that she blushed. 'But—but—you know it was the first ball I was ever at.'

'That is just the reason why you should have enjoyed it the more, instead of sitting down as you did, and being dull and unhappy. For I know you were unhappy; I could see it.'

'Was I?' said Clara, not knowing what else to say.

'Yes; and I'll tell you what. I could see more than that; it was I that made you unhappy.'

'You, Mr. Fitzgerald!'

'Yes, I. You will not deny it, because you are so true. I asked you to dance with me too often. And because you refused me, you did not like to dance with any one else. I saw it all. Will you deny that it was so?'

'Oh, Mr. Fitzgerald!' Poor girl! She did not know what to say; how to shape her speech into indifference; how to assure him that he made himself out to be of too much consequence by far; how to make it plain that she had not danced because there was no one there worth dancing with. Had she been out for a year or two, instead of being such a novice, she would have accomplished all this in half a dozen words. As it was, her tell-tale face confessed it all, and she was only able to ejaculate, 'Oh, Mr. Fitzgerald!'

'When I went there last night,' he continued, 'I had only one wish—one hope. That was, to see you pleased and happy. I knew it was your first ball, and I did so long to see you enjoy it.'

'And so I did, till——'

'Till what? Will you not let me ask?'

'Mamma said something to me, and that stopped me from dancing.'

'She told you not to dance with me. Was that it?'

How was it possible that she should have had a chance with him; innocent, young, and ignorant as she was? She did not tell him in words that so it had been; but she looked into his face with a glance of doubt and pain that answered his question as plainly as any words could have done.

'Of course she did; and it was I that destroyed it all. I that should have been satisfied to stand still and see you happy. How you must have hated me!'

'Oh, no; indeed I did not. I was not at all angry with you.

Indeed, why snould I have been? It was so kind of you, wishing to dance with me.'

'No; it was selfish—selfish in the extreme. Nothing but one thing could excuse me, and that excuse——'

'I'm sure you don't want any excuse, Mr. Fitzgerald.'

'And that excuse, Clara, was this: that I love you with all my heart. I had not strength to see you there, and not long to have you near me—not begrudge that you should dance with another. I love you with all my heart and soul. There, Lady Clara, now you know it all.'

The manner in which he made his declaration to her was almost fierce in its energy. He had stopped in the pathway, and she, unconscious of what she was doing, almost unconscious of what she was hearing, had stopped also. The mare, taking advantage of the occasion, was cropping the grass close to them. And so, for a few seconds, they stood in silence.

'Am I so bold, Lady Clara,' said he, when those few seconds had gone by—'Am I so bold that I may hope for no answer?' But still she said nothing. In lieu of speaking she uttered a long sigh; and then Fitzgerald could hear that she was sobbing.

'Oh, Clara, I love you so fondly, so dearly, so truly!' said he in an altered voice and with sweet tenderness. 'I know my own presumption in thus speaking. I know and feel bitterly the difference in our rank.'

'I—care—nothing—for rank,' said the poor girl, sobbing through her tears. He was generous, and she at any rate would not be less so. No; at that moment, with her scanty seventeen years of experience, with her ignorance of all that the world had in it of grand and great, of high and rich, she did care nothing for rank. That Owen Fitzgerald was a gentleman of good lineage, fit to mate with a lady, that she did know; for her mother, who was a proud woman, delighted to have him in her presence. Beyond this she cared for none of the conventionalities of life. Rank! If she waited for rank, where was she to look for friends who would love her? Earls and countesses, barons and their baronesses, were scarce there where fate had placed her, under the shadow of the bleak mountains of Muskerry. Her want, her undefined want, was that some one should love her. Of all men and women whom she had hitherto known, this Owen Fitzgerald was the brightest, the kindest, the gentlest in his manner, the most pleasant to look on. And now he was there at her feet, swearing that he loved her;—and then drawing back as it were in dread of her rank. What did she care for rank?

'Clara, Clara, my Clara! Can you learn to love me?'

She had made her one little effort at speaking when she attempted to repudiate the pedestal on which he affected to place her; but after that she could for a while say no more. But she still sobbed, and still kept her eyes fixed upon the ground.

'Clara, say one word to me. Say that you do not hate me.' But just at that moment she had not one word to say.

'If you will bid me do so, I will leave this country altogether. I will go away, and I shall not much care whither. I can only stay now on condition of your loving me. I have thought of this day for the last year past, and now it has come.'

Every word that he now spoke was gospel to her. Is it not always so,—should it not be so always, when love first speaks to loving ears? What! he had loved her for that whole twelve-month that she had known him; loved her in those days when she had been wont to look up into his face, wondering why he was so nice, so much nicer than any one else that came near her! A year was a great deal to her; and had he loved her through all those days? and after that should she banish him from her house, turn him away from his home, and drive him forth un-happy and wretched? Ah, no! She could not be so unkind to him;—she could not be so unkind to her own heart. But still she sobbed; and still she said nothing.

In the mean time they had turned, and were now walking back towards the house, the gentle-natured mare still following at their heels. They were walking slowly—very slowly back—just creeping along the path, when they saw Lady Desmond and her son coming to meet them on the road.

'There is your mother, Clara. Say one word to me before we meet them.'

'Oh, Mr. Fitzgerald; I am so frightened. What will mamma say?'

'Say about what? As yet I do not know what she may have to say. But before we meet her, may I not hope to know what her daughter will say? Answer me this, Clara. Can you, will you love me?'

There was still a pause, a moment's pause, and then some sound did fall from her lips. But yet it was so soft, so gentle, so slight, that it could hardly be said to reach even a lover's ear. Fitzgerald, however, made the most of it. Whether it were Yes, or whether it were No, he took it as being favourable, and Lady Clara Desmond gave him no sign to show that he was mistaken.

'My own, own, only loved one,' he said, embracing her as it were with his words, since the presence of her approaching mother forbade him even to take her hand in his, 'I am happy now, whatever may occur; whatever others may say; for I know that you will be true to me. And remember this—whatever others may say, I also will be true to you. You will think of that, will you not, love?'

This time she did answer him, almost audibly. 'Yes,' she said. And then she devoted herself to a vain endeavour to remove the traces of her tears before her mother should be close to them.

Fitzgerald at once saw that such endeavour must be vain. At one time he had thought of turning away, and pretending that they had not seen the countess. But he knew that Clara would not be able to carry out any such pretence; and he reflected also that it might be just as well that Lady Desmond should know the whole at once. That she would know it, and know it soon, he was quite sure. She could learn it not only from Clara, but from himself. He could not now be there at the house without showing that he both loved and knew that he was beloved. And then why should Lady Desmond not know it? Why should he think that she would set herself against the match? He had certainly spoken to Clara of the difference in their rank; but, after all, it was no uncommon thing for an earl's daughter to marry a commoner. And in this case the earl's daughter was portionless, and the lover desired no portion. Owen Fitzgerald at any rate might boast that he was true and generous in his love.

So he plucked up his courage, and walked on with a smiling face to meet Lady Desmond and her son; while poor Clara crept beside him with eyes downcast, and in an agony of terror.

Lady Desmond had not left the house with any apprehension that there was ought amiss. Her son had told her that Owen had gone off ' to do the civil to Clara;' and as he did not come to the house within some twenty minutes after this, she had proposed that they would go and meet him.

' Did you tell him that I wanted him?' said the countess.

' Oh, yes, I did; and he is coming, only he would go away to Clara.'

' Then I shall scold him for his want of gallantry,' said Lady Desmond, laughing, as they walked out together from beneath the huge portal.

But as soon as she was near enough to see the manner of their gait, as they slowly came on towards her, her woman's tact told her that something was wrong;—and whispered to her also what might too probably be the nature of that something. Could it be possible, she asked herself, that such a man as Owen Fitzgerald should fall in love with such a girl as her daughter Clara?

'What shall I say to mamma?' whispered Clara to him, as they all drew near together.

'Tell her everything.'

'But, Patrick——'

'I will take him off with me if I can.' And then they were all together, standing in the road.

'I was coming to obey your behests, Lady Desmond,' said Fitzgerald, trying to look and speak as though he were at his ease.

'Coming rather tardily, I think,' said her ladyship, not altogether playfully.

'I told him you wanted him, as we were crossing to the house,' said the earl. 'Didn't I, Owen?'

'Is anything the matter with Clara?' said Lady Desmond, looking at her daughter.

'No, mamma,' said Clara; and she instantly began to sob and cry.

'What is it, sir?' And as she asked she turned to Fitzgerald; and her manner now at least had in it nothing playful.

'Lady Clara is nervous and hysterical. The excitement of the ball has perhaps been too much for her. I think, Lady Desmond, if you were to take her in with you it would be well.'

Lady Desmond looked up at him; and he then saw, for the first time, that she could if she pleased look very stern. Hitherto her face had always worn smiles, had at any rate always been pleasing when he had seen it. He had never been intimate with her, never intimate enough to care what her face was like, till that day when he had carried her son up from the hall door to his room. Then her countenance had been all anxiety for her darling; and afterwards it had been all sweetness for her darling's friend. From that day to this present one, Lady Desmond had ever given him her sweetest smiles.

But Fitzgerald was not a man to be cowed by any woman's looks. He met hers by a full, front face in return. He did not allow his eye for a moment to fall before hers. And yet he did not look at her haughtily, or with defiance, but with an aspect which showed that he was ashamed of nothing that he had done,—whether he had done anything that he ought to be ashamed of or no.

'Clara,' said the countess, in a voice which fell with awful severity on the poor girl's ears, 'you had better return to the house with me.'

'Yes, mamma.'

'And shall I wait on you to-morrow, Lady Desmond?' said Fitzgerald, in a tone which seemed to the countess to be, in the present state of affairs, almost impertinent. The man had certainly been misbehaving himself; and yet there was not about him the slightest symptom of shame.

'Yes; no,' said the countess. 'That is, I will write a note to you if it be necessary. Good morning.'

'Good bye, Lady Desmond,' said Owen. And as he took off his hat with his left hand, he put out his right to shake hands with her, as was customary with him. Lady Desmond was at first inclined to refuse the courtesy; but she either thought better of such intention, or else she had not courage to maintain it; for at parting she did give him her hand.

'Good-bye, Lady Clara;' and he also shook hands with her, and it need hardly be said that there was a lover's pressure in the grasp.

'Good-bye,' said Clara, through her tears, in the saddest, soberest tone. He was going away, happy, light hearted, with nothing to trouble him. But she had to encounter that fearful task of telling her own crime. She had to depart with her mother;—her mother, who, though never absolutely unkind, had so rarely been tender with her. And then her brother——!

'Desmond,' said Fitzgerald, 'walk as far as the lodge with me like a good fellow. I have something that I want to say to you.'

The mother thought for a moment that she would call her son back; but then she bethought herself that she also might as well be without him. So the young earl, showing plainly by his eyes that he knew that much was the matter, went back with Fitzgerald towards the lodge.

'What is it you have done now?' said the earl. The boy had some sort of an idea that the offence committed was with reference to his sister; and his tone was hardly as gracious as was usual with him.

This want of kindliness at the present moment grated on Owen's ears; but he resolved at once to tell the whole story out, and then leave it to the earl to take it in dudgeon or in brotherly friendship as he might please.

'Desmond,' said he, 'can you not guess what has passed between me and your sister?'

'I am not good at guessing,' he answered, brusquely.

'I have told her that I loved her, and would have her for my wife; and I have asked her to love me in return.'

There was an open manliness about this which almost disarmed the earl's anger. He had felt a strong attachment to Fitzgerald, and was very unwilling to give up his friendship; but, nevertheless, he had an idea that it was presumption on the part of Mr. Fitzgerald of Hap House to look up to his sister. Between himself and Owen the earl's coronet never weighed a feather; he could not have abandoned his boy's heart to the man's fellowship more thoroughly had that man been an earl as well as himself. But he could not get over the feeling that Fitzgerald's worldly position was beneath that of his sister ;—that such a marriage on his sister's part would be a mesalliance. Doubting, therefore, and in some sort dismayed—and in some sort also angry—he did not at once give any reply.

'Well, Desmond, what have you to say to it? You are the head of her family, and young as you are, it is right that I should tell you.'

'Tell me! of course you ought to tell me. I don't see what youngness has to do with it. What did she say?'

'Well, she said but little ; and a man should never boast that a lady has favoured him. But she did not reject me.' He paused a moment, and then added, 'After all, honesty and truth are the best. I have reason to think that she loves me.'

The poor young lord felt that he had a double duty, and hardly knew how to perform it. He owed a duty to his sister which was paramount to all others ; but then he owed a duty also to the friend who had been so kind to him. He did not know how to turn round upon him and tell him that he was not fit to marry his sister.

'And what do you say to it, Desmond?'

'I hardly know what to say. It would be a very bad match for her. You, you know, are a capital fellow ; the best fellow going. There is nobody about anywhere that I like so much.'

'In thinking of your sister, you should put that out of the question.'

'Yes; that's just it. I like you for a friend better than any one else. But Clara ought—ought—ought——'

'Ought to look higher, you would say.'

'Yes; that's just what I mean. I don't want to offend you, you know.'

'Desmond, my boy, I like you the better for it. You are a fine fellow, and I thoroughly respect you. But let us talk sensibly about this. Though your sister's rank is high——'

'Oh, I don't want to talk about rank. That's all bosh, and I don't care about it. But Hap House is a small place, and Clara wouldn't be doing well ; and what's more, I am quite sure the countess will not hear of it.'

'You won't approve then?'

'No, I can't say I will.'

'Well, that is honest of you. I am very glad that I have told you at once. Clara will tell her mother, and at any rate there will be no secrets. Good-bye, old fellow.'

' Good-bye,' said the earl. Then they shook hands, and Fitz-gerald rode off towards Hap House. Lord Desmond pondered over the matter some time, standing alone near the lodge ; and then walked slowly back towards the mansion. He had said that rank was all bosh ; and in so saying had at the moment spoken out generously the feelings of his heart. But that feeling re-garded himself rather than his sister ; and if properly analyzed would merely have signified that, though proud enough of his own rank, he did not require that his friends should be of the same standing. But as regarded his sister, he certainly would not be well pleased to see her marry a small squire with a small income.

CHAPTER IV.

THE COUNTESS.

THE countess, as she walked back with her daughter towards the house, had to bethink herself for a minute or two as to how she should act, and what she would say. She knew, she felt that she knew, what had occurred. If her daughter's manner had not told her, the downcast eyes, the repressed sobs, the mingled look of shame and fear ;—if she had not read the truth from these, she would have learned it from the tone of Fitzgerald's voice, and the look of triumph which sat upon his countenance.

And then she wondered that this should be so, seeing that she had still regarded Clara as being in all things a child ; and as she thought further, she wondered at her own fatuity, in that she had allowed herself to be so grossly deceived.

' Clara,' said she, ' what is all this ?'

' Oh, mamma !'

' You had better come on to the house, my dear, and speak to me there. In the mean time, collect your thoughts, and re-member this, Clara, that you have the honour of a great family to maintain.'

Poor Clara ! what had the great family done for her, or how had she been taught to maintain its honour ? She knew that she was an earl's daughter, and that people called her Lady Clara ; whereas other young ladies were only called Miss So-and-So. But she had not been taught to separate herself from the ordinary throng of young ladies by any other distinction. Her great family had done nothing special for her, nor placed before her for example any grandly noble deeds. At that old house at Desmond Court company was scarce, money was scarce, servants were scarce. She had been confided to the care of a very ordinary governess; and if there was about her anything that was great or good, it was intrinsically her own, and by no means due to intrinsic advantages derived from her grand family. Why should she not give what was so entirely her own to one whom she loved, to one by whom it so pleased her to be loved?

And then they entered the house, and Clara followed her mother to the countess's own small up-stairs sitting-room. The daughter did not ordinarily share this room with her mother, and when she entered it, she seldom did so with pleasurable emotion. At the present moment she had hardly strength to close the door after her.

'And now, Clara, what is all this?' said the countess, sitting down in her accustomed chair.

'All which, mamma?' Can any one blame her in that she so far equivocated?

'Clara, you know very well what I mean. What has there been between you and Mr. Fitzgerald?'

The guilt-stricken wretch sat silent for a while, sustaining the scrutiny of her mother's gaze; and then falling from her chair on to her knees, she hid her face in her mother's lap, exclaiming, 'Oh, mamma, mamma, do not look at me like that!'

Lady Desmond's heart was somewhat softened by this appeal; nor would I have it thought that she was a cruel woman, or an unnatural mother. It had not been her lot to make an absolute, dearest, heartiest friend of her daughter, as some mothers do; a friend between whom and herself there should be, nay, could be, no secrets. She could not become young again in sharing the romance of her daughter's love, in enjoying the gaieties of her daughter's balls, in planning dresses, amusements, and triumphs with her child. Some mothers can do this; and they, I think, are the mothers who enjoy most fully the delights of maternity. This was not the case with Lady Desmond; but yet she loved her child, and would have made any reasonable sacrifice for what she regarded as that child's welfare.

'But, my dear,' she said, in a softened tone, 'you must tell me what has occurred. Do you not know that it is my duty to ask, and yours to tell me? It cannot be right that there should be any secret understanding between yourself and Mr. Fitzgerald. You know that, Clara, do you not?'

'Yes, mamma,' said Clara, remembering that her lover had bade her tell her mother everything.

'Well, my love?'

Clara's story was very simple, and did not, in fact, want any telling. It was merely the old well-worn tale, so common through all the world. 'He had laughed on the lass with his bonny black eye!' and she,—she was ready to go 'to the mountain to hear a love-tale!' One may say that an occurrence so very common could not want much telling.

'Mamma; he says——'

'Well, my dear?'

'He says—. Oh, mamma! I could not help it.'

'No, Clara; you certainly could not help what he might say to you. You could not refuse to listen to him. A lady in such a case, when she is on terms of intimacy with a gentleman, as you were with Mr. Fitzgerald, is bound to listen to him, and to give him an answer. You could not help what he might say, Clara. The question now is, what answer did you give to what he said?'

Clara, who was still kneeling, looked up piteously into her mother's face, sighed bitterly, but said nothing.

'He told you that he loved you, I suppose?'

'Yes, mamma.'

'And I suppose you gave him some answer? Eh! my dear?'

The answer to this was another long sigh.

'But, Clara, you must tell me. It is absolutely necessary that I should know whether you have given him any hope, and if so, how much. Of course the whole thing must be stopped at once. Young as you are, you cannot think that a marriage with Mr. Owen Fitzgerald would be a proper match for you to make. Of course the whole thing must cease at once—at once.' Here there was another piteous sigh. 'But before I take any steps, I must know what you have said to him. Surely you have not told him that you have any feeling for him warmer than ordinary regard?'

Lady Desmond knew what she was doing very well. She was perfectly sure that her daughter had pledged her troth to Owen Fitzgerald. Indeed, if she made any mistake in the matter, it was in thinking that Clara had given a more absolute assurance of love than had in truth been extracted from her. But she calculated, and calculated wisely, that the surest way of talking her daughter out of all hope, was to express herself as unable to believe that a child of hers would own to love for one so much beneath her, and to speak of such a marriage as a thing absolutely impossible. Her method of acting in this manner had the effect which she desired. The poor girl was utterly frightened, and began to fear that she had disgraced herself, though she knew that she dearly loved the man of whom her mother spoke so slightingly.

'Have you given him any promise, Clara?'

'Not a promise, mamma.'

'Not a promise! What then? Have you professed any regard for him?' But upon this Clara was again silent.

'Then I suppose I must believe that you have professed a regard for him—that you have promised to love him?'

'No, mamma; I have not promised anything. But when he asked me, I—I didn't—I didn't refuse him.'

It will be observed that Lady Desmond never once asked her daughter what were her feelings. It never occurred to her to inquire, even within her own heart, as to what might be most conducive to her child's happiness. She meant to do her duty by Clara, and therefore resolved at once to put a stop to the whole affair. She now desisted from her interrogatories, and sitting silent for a while, looked out into the extent of flat ground before the house. Poor Clara the while sat silent also, awaiting her doom.

'Clara,' said the mother at last, 'all this must of course be made to cease. You are very young, very young indeed, and therefore I do not blame you. The fault is with him—with him entirely.'

'No, mamma.'

'But I say it is. He has behaved very badly, and has betrayed the trust which was placed in him when he was admitted here so intimately as Patrick's friend.'

'I am sure he has not intended to betray any trust,' said Clara, through her sobs. The conviction was beginning to come upon her that she would be forced to give up her lover; but she could not bring herself to hear so much evil spoken of him.

'He has not behaved like a gentleman,' continued the countess, looking very stern. 'And his visits here must of course be altogether discontinued. I am sorry on your brother's account, for Patrick was very fond of him——'

'Not half so fond as I am,' thought Clara to herself. But she did not dare to speak her thoughts out loud.

'But I am quite sure that your brother, young as he is, will not continue to associate with a friend who has thought so slightly of his sister's honour. Of course I shall let Mr. Fitzgerald know that he can come here no more; and all I want from you is a promise that you will on no account see him again, or hold any correspondence with him.'

That was all she wanted. But Clara, timid as she was, hesitated before she could give a promise so totally at variance with the pledge which she felt that she had given, hardly an hour since, to Fitzgerald. She knew and acknowledged to herself that she had given him a pledge, although she had given it in silence. How then was she to give this other pledge to her mother?

'You do not mean to say that you hesitate?' said Lady Desmond, looking as though she were thunderstruck at the existence of such hesitation. 'You do not wish me to suppose that you intend to persevere in such insanity? Clara, I must have from you a distinct promise,—or——'

What might be the dreadful alternative the countess did not at that minute say. She perhaps thought that her countenance might be more effective than her speech, and in thinking so she was probably right.

It must be remembered that Clara Desmond was as yet only seventeen, and that she was young even for that age. It must be remembered, also, that she knew nothing of the world's ways, of her own privileges as a creature with a soul and heart of her own, or of what might be the true extent of her mother's rights over her. She had not in her enough of matured thought to teach her to say that she would make no promise that should bind her for ever; but that for the present, in her present state, she would obey her mother's orders. And thus the promise was exacted and given.

'If I find you deceiving me, Clara,' said the countess, 'I will never forgive you.'

Hitherto, Lady Desmond may probably have played her part well;—well, considering her object. But she played it very badly in showing that she thought it possible that her daughter should play her false. It was now Clara's turn to be proud and indignant.

'Mamma!' she said, holding her head high, and looking at her mother boldly through her tears, 'I have never deceived you yet.'

'Very well, my dear. I will take steps to prevent his intruding on you any further. There may be an end of the matter now. I have no doubt that he has endeavoured to use his influence with Patrick; but I will tell your brother not to speak of the matter further.' And so saying, she dismissed her daughter.

Shortly afterwards the earl came in, and there was a conference between him and his mother. Though they were both agreed on the subject, though both were decided that it would not do for Clara to throw herself away on a county Cork squire with eight hundred a year, a cadet in his family, and a man likely to rise to nothing, still the earl would not hear him abused.

'But, Patrick, he must not come here any more,' said the countess.

'Well, I suppose not. But it will be very dull, I know that. I wish Clara hadn't made herself such an ass;' and then the boy went away, and talked kindly over the matter to his poor sister.

But the countess had another task still before her. She must make known the family resolution to Owen Fitzgerald. When her children had left her, one after the other, she sat at the window for an hour, looking at nothing, but turning over her own thoughts in her mind. Hitherto she had expressed herself as being very angry with her daughter's lover; so angry that she had said that he was faithless, a traitor, and no gentleman. She had called him a dissipated spendthrift, and had threatened his future wife, if ever he should have one, with every kind of misery that could fall to a woman's lot; but now she began to think of him perhaps more kindly.

She had been very angry with him;—and the more so because she had such cause to be angry with herself;—with her own lack of judgment, her own ignorance of the man's character, her own folly with reference to her daughter. She had never asked herself whether she loved Fitzgerald—had never done so till now. But now she knew that the sharpest blow she had received that day was the assurance that he was indifferent to herself.

She had never thought herself too old to be on an equality with him,—on such an equality in point of age as men and women feel when they learn to love each other; and therefore it had not occurred to her that he could regard her daughter as other than a child. To Lady Desmond, Clara was a child; how then could she be more to him? And yet now it was too plain that he had looked on Clara as a woman. In what light then must he have thought of that woman's mother? And so, with saddened heart, but subdued anger, she continued to gaze through the window till all without was dusk and dark.

There can be to a woman no remembrance of age so strong as that of seeing a daughter go forth to the world a married woman. If that does not tell the mother that the time of her own youth has passed away, nothing will ever bring the tale home. It had not quite come to this with Lady Desmond;—Clara was not going forth to the world as a married woman. But here was one now who had judged her as fit to be so taken; and this one was the very man of all others in whose estimation Lady Desmond would have wished to drop a few of the years that encumbered her.

She was not, however, a weak woman, and so she performed her task. She had candles brought to her, and sitting down, she wrote a note to Owen Fitzgerald, saying that she herself would call at Hap House at an hour named on the following day.

She had written three or four letters before she had made up her mind exactly as to the one she would send. At first she had desired him to come to her there at Desmond Court; but then

she thought of the danger there might be of Clara seeing him ;—
of the danger, also, of her own feelings towards him when he
should be there with her, in her own house, in the accustomed
way. And she tried to say by letter all that it behoved her to
say, so that there need be no meeting. But in this she failed.
One letter was stern and arrogant, and the next was soft-hearted,
so that it might teach him to think that his love for Clara might
yet be successful. At last she resolved to go herself to Hap
House ; and accordingly she wrote her letter and despatched it.

Fitzgerald was of course aware of the subject of the threatened
visit. When he determined to make his proposal to Clara, the
matter did not seem to him to be one in which all chances of
success were desperate. If, he thought, he could induce the girl
to love him, other smaller difficulties might be made to vanish
from his path. He had now induced the girl to own that she
did love him; but not the less did he begin to see that the difficulties were far from vanishing. Lady Desmond would never
have taken upon herself to make a journey to Hap House, had
not a sentence of absolute banishment from Desmond Court been
passed against him.

'Mr. Fitzgerald,' she began, as soon as she found herself alone
with him, 'you will understand what has induced me to seek you
here. After your imprudence with Lady Clara Desmond, I
could not of course ask you to come to Desmond Court.'

'I may have been presumptuous, Lady Desmond, but I do not
think that I have been imprudent. I love your daughter dearly,
and I told her so. Immediately afterwards I told the same to her
brother ; and she, no doubt, has told the same to you.'

'Yes, she has, Mr. Fitzgerald. Clara, as you are well aware,
is a child, absolutely a child ; much more so than is usual with
girls of her age. The knowledge of this should, I think, have
protected her from your advances.'

'But I absolutely deny any such knowledge. And more than
that, I think that you are greatly mistaken as to her character.'

'Mistaken, sir, as to my own daughter ?'

'Yes, Lady Desmond ; I think you are. I think——'

'On such a matter, Mr. Fitzgerald, I need not trouble you for
an expression of your thoughts. Nor need we argue that subject
any further. You must of course be aware that all ideas of any
such marriage as this must be laid aside.'

'On what grounds, Lady Desmond ?'

Now this appeared to the countess to be rather impudent on
the part of the young squire. The reasons why he, Owen Fitzgerald of Hap House, should not marry a daughter of an Earl of
Desmond, seemed to her to be so conspicuous and conclusive,

that it could hardly be necessary to enumerate them. And such as they were, it might not be pleasant to announce them in his hearing. But though Owen Fitzgerald was so evidently an unfit suitor for an earl's daughter, it might still be possible that he should be acceptable to an earl's widow. Ah! if it might be possible to teach him the two lessons at the same time!

'On what grounds, Mr. Fitzgerald!' she said, repeating his question; 'surely I need hardly tell you. Did not my son say the same thing to you yesterday, as he walked with you down the avenue?'

'Yes; he told me candidly that he looked higher for his sister; and I liked him for his candour. But that is no reason that I should agree with him; or, which is much more important, that his sister should do so. If she thinks that she can be happy in such a home as I can give her, I do not know why he, or why you should object.'

'You think, then, that I might give her to a blacksmith, if she herself were mad enough to wish it?'

'I thank you for the compliment, Lady Desmond.'

'You have driven me to it, sir.'

'I believe it is considered in the world,' said he,—'that is, in our country, that the one great difference is between gentlemen and ladies, and those who are not gentlemen or ladies. A lady does not degrade herself if she marry a gentleman, even though that gentleman's rank be less high than her own.'

'It is not a question of degradation, but of prudence;—of the ordinary caution which I, as a mother, am bound to use as regards my daughter. Oh, Mr. Fitzgerald!' and she now altered her tone as she spoke to him; 'we have all been so pleased to know you, so happy to have you there; why have you destroyed all this by one half-hour's folly?'

'The folly, as you call it, Lady Desmond, has been pre-meditated for the last twelve months.'

'For twelve months!' said she, taken absolutely by surprise, and in her surprise believing him.

'Yes, for twelve months. Ever since I began to know your daughter, I have loved her. You say that your daughter is a child. I also thought so this time last year, in our last winter holidays. I thought so then; and though I loved her as a child, I kept it to myself. Now she is a woman, and so thinking I have spoken to her as one. I have told her that I loved her, as I now tell you that come what may I must continue to do so. Had she made me believe that I was indifferent to her, absence, perhaps, and distance might have taught me to forget her. But such, I think, is not the case.'

'And you must forget her now.'

'Never, Lady Desmond.'

'Nonsense, sir. A child that does not know her own mind, that thinks of a lover as she does of some new toy, whose first appearance in the world was only made the other night at your cousin's house! you ought to feel ashamed of such a passion, Mr. Fitzgerald.'

'I am very far from being ashamed of it, Lady Desmond.'

'At any rate, let me tell you this. My daughter has promised me most solemnly that she will neither see you again, nor have any correspondence with you. And this I know of her, that her word is sacred. I can excuse her on account of her youth; and, young as she is, she already sees her own folly in having allowed you so to address her. But for you, Mr. Fitzgerald, under all the circumstances I can make no excuse for you. Is yours, do you think, the sort of house to which a young girl should be brought as a bride? Is your life, are your companions of that kind which could most profit her? I am sorry that you drive me to remind you of these things.'

His face became very dark, and his brow stern as his sins were thus cast into his teeth.

'And from what you know of me, Lady Desmond,' he said,— and as he spoke he assumed a dignity of demeanour which made her more inclined to love him than ever she had been before, —'do you think that I should be the man to introduce a young wife to such companions as those to whom you allude? Do you not know, are you not sure in your own heart, that my marriage with your daughter would instantly put an end to all that?'

'Whatever may be my own thoughts, and they are not likely to be unfavourable to you—for Patrick's sake, I mean; but whatever may be my own thoughts, I will not subject my daughter to such a risk. And, Mr. Fitzgerald, you must allow me to say, that your income is altogether insufficient for her wants and your own. She has no fortune——'

'I want none with her.'

'And—— but I will not argue the matter with you. I did not come to argue it, but to tell you, with as little offence as may be possible, that such a marriage is absolutely impossible. My daughter herself has already abandoned all thoughts of it.'

'Her thoughts then must be wonderfully under her own control. Much more so than mine are.'

'Lord Desmond, you may be sure, will not hear of it.'

'Lord Desmond cannot at present be less of a child than his sister.'

'I don't know that, Mr. Fitzgerald.'

'At any rate, Lady Desmond, I will not put my happiness, nor as far as I am concerned in it, his sister's happiness, at his disposal. When I told her that I loved her, I did not speak, as you seem to think, from an impulse of the moment. I spoke because I loved her; and as I love her, I shall of course try to win her. Nothing can absolve me from my engagement to her but her marriage with another person.'

The countess had once or twice made small efforts to come to terms of peace with him; or rather to a truce, under which there might still be some friendship between them,—accompanied, however, by a positive condition that Clara should be omitted from any participation in it. She would have been willing to say, 'Let all this be forgotten, only for some time to come you and Clara cannot meet each other.' But Fitzgerald would by no means agree to such terms; and the countess was obliged to leave his house, having in effect only thrown down a gauntlet of battle; having in vain attempted to extend over it an olive-branch of peace.

He helped her, however, into her little pony carriage, and at parting she gave him her hand. He just touched it, and then, taking off his hat, bowed courteously to her as she drove from his door.

CHAPTER V.

THE FITZGERALDS OF CASTLE RICHMOND.

WHAT idea of carrying out his plans may have been prevalent in Fitzgerald's mind when he was so defiant of the countess, it may be difficult to say. Probably he had no idea, but felt at the spur of the moment that it would be weak to yield. The consequence was, that when Lady Desmond left Hap House, he was obliged to consider himself as being at feud with the family.

The young lord he did see once again during the holidays, and even entertained him at Hap House; but the earl's pride would not give way an inch.

'Much as I like you, Owen, I cannot do anything but oppose it. It would be a bad match for my sister, and so you'd feel if you were in my place.' And then Lord Desmond went back to Eton.

After that they none of them met for many months. During this time life went on in a very triste manner at Desmond Court. Lady Desmond felt that she had done her duty by her daughter; but her tenderness to Clara was not increased by the fact that her foolish attachment had driven Fitzgerald from the place.

As for Clara herself, she not only kept her word, but rigidly resolved to keep it. Twice she returned unopened, and without a word of notice, letters which Owen had caused to be conveyed to her hand. It was not that she had ceased to love him, but she had high ideas of truth and honour, and would not break her word. Perhaps she was sustained in her misery by the remembrance that heroines are always miserable.

And then the orgies at Hap House became hotter and faster. Hitherto there had perhaps been more smoke than fire, more calumny than sin. And Fitzgerald, when he had intimated that the presence of a young wife would save him from it all, had not boasted falsely. But now that his friends had turned their backs upon him, that he was banished from Desmond Court, and twitted with his iniquities at Castle Richmond, he threw off all restraint, and endeavoured to enjoy himself in his own way. So the orgies became fast and furious; all which of course reached the ears of poor Clara Desmond.

During the summer holidays, Lord Desmond was not at home, but Owen Fitzgerald was also away. He had gone abroad, perhaps with the conviction that it would be well that he and the Desmonds should not meet; and he remained abroad till the hunting season again commenced. Then the winter came again, and he and Lord Desmond used to meet in the field. There they would exchange courtesies, and, to a certain degree, show that they were intimate. But all the world knew that the old friendship was over. And, indeed, all the world—all the county Cork world—soon knew the reason. And so we are brought down to the period at which our story was to begin.

We have hitherto said little or nothing of Castle Richmond and its inhabitants; but it is now time that we should do so, and we will begin with the heir of the family. At the period of which we are speaking, Herbert Fitzgerald had just returned from Oxford, having completed his affairs there in a manner very much to the satisfaction of his father, mother, and sisters: and to the unqualified admiration of his aunt, Miss Letty. I am not aware that the heads of colleges, and supreme synod of Dons had signified by any general expression of sentiment, that Herbert Fitzgerald had so conducted himself as to be a standing honour and perpetual glory to the University; but at Castle Richmond it was all the same as though they had done so. There are some kindly-hearted, soft-minded parents, in whose estimation not to have fallen into disgrace shows the highest merit on the part of their children. Herbert had not been rusticated; had not got into debt, at least not to an extent that had been offensive to his father's pocket; he had not been plucked.

Indeed, he had taken honours, in some low unnoticed degree ;—
unnoticed, that is, at Oxford; but noticed at Castle Richmond
by an ovation—almost by a triumph.

But Herbert Fitzgerald was a son to gladden a father's heart
and a mother's eye. He was not handsome, as was his cousin
Owen; not tall and stalwart and godlike in his proportions, as
was the reveller of Hap House; but nevertheless, and perhaps
not the less, was he pleasant to look on. He was smaller and
darker than his cousin; but his eyes were bright and full of
good humour. He was clean looking and clean made; pleasant
and courteous in all his habits; attached to books in a moderate,
easy way, but no bookworm ; he had a gentle affection for bind
ings and title-pages; was fond of pictures, of which it might be
probable that he would some day know more than he did at
present; addicted to Gothic architecture, and already proprietor
of the germ of what was to be a collection of coins.

Owen Fitzgerald had called him a prig; but Herbert was no
prig. Nor yet was he a pedant; which word might, perhaps,
more nearly have expressed his cousin's meaning. He liked
little bits of learning, the easy outsides and tags of classical acquirements, which come so easily within the scope of the memory
when a man has passed some ten years between a public school
and a university. But though he did love to chew the cud of
these morsels of Attic grass which he had cropped, certainly
without any great or sustained effort, he had no desire to be
ostentatious in doing so, or to show off more than he knew. Indeed, now that he was away from his college friends, he was
rather ashamed of himself than otherwise when scraps of quota-
tions would break forth from him in his own despite. Looking
at his true character, it was certainly unjust to call him either a
prig or a pedant.

He was fond of the society of ladies, and was a great favourite
with his sisters, who thought that every girl who saw him must
instantly fall in love with him. He was goodnatured, and, as
the only son of a rich man, was generally well provided with
money. Such a brother is usually a favourite with his sisters.
He was a great favourite too with his aunt, whose heart, however,
was daily sinking into her shoes through the effect of one great
terror which harassed her respecting him. She feared that he
had become a Puseyite. Now that means much with some ladies
in England ; but with most ladies of the Protestant religion in
Ireland, it means, one may almost say, the very Father of Mischief himself.   In their minds, the pope, with his lady of Babylon,
his college of cardinals, and all his community of pinchbeck saints,
holds a sort of second head-quarters of his own at Oxford. And

there his high priest is supposed to be one wicked infamous Pusey, and his worshippers are wicked infamous Puseyites. Now, Miss Letty Fitzgerald was strong on this subject, and little inklings had fallen from her nephew which robbed her of much of her peace of mind.

It is impossible that these volumes should be graced by any hero, for the story does not admit of one. But if there were to be a hero, Herbert Fitzgerald would be the man.

Sir Thomas Fitzgerald at this period was an old man in appearance, though by no means an old man in years, being hardly more than fifty. Why he should have withered away as it were into premature grayness, and loss of the muscle and energy of life, none knew; unless, indeed, his wife did know. But so it was. He had, one may say, all that a kind fortune could give him. He had a wife who was devoted to him; he had a son on whom he doted, and of whom all men said all good things; he had two sweet, happy daughters; he had a pleasant house, a fine estate, position and rank in the world. Had it so pleased him, he might have sat in Parliament without any of the trouble, and with very little of the expense, which usually attends aspirants for that honour. And, as it was, he might hope to see his son in Parliament within a year or two. For among other possessions of the Fitzgerald family was the land on which stands the borough of Kilcommon, a borough to which the old Reform Bill was merciful, as it was to so many others in the south of Ireland.

Why, then, should Sir Thomas Fitzgerald be a silent, melancholy man, confining himself for the last year or two almost entirely to his own study; giving up to his steward the care even of his own demesne and farm; never going to the houses of his friends, and rarely welcoming them to his; rarely as it was, and never as it would have been, had he been always allowed to have his own way?

People in the surrounding neighbourhood had begun to say that Sir Thomas's sorrow had sprung from shortness of cash, and that money was not so easily to be had at Castle Richmond nowa-days as was the case some ten years since. If this were so, the dearth of that very useful article could not have in any degree arisen from extravagance. It was well known that Sir Thomas's estate was large, being of a value, according to that public and well-authenticated rent-roll which the neighbours of a rich man always carry in their heads, amounting to twelve or fourteen thousand a year. Now Sir Thomas had come into the unencumbered possession of this at an early age, and had never been extravagant himself or in his family. His estates were strictly entailed, and therefore, as he had only a life interest in them, it of course was necessary that he should save money and insure his life, to make provision for his daughters.   But by a man of his habits and his property, such a burden as this could hardly have been accounted any burden at all.   That he did, however, in this mental privacy of his carry some heavy burden, was made plain enough to all who knew him.

And Lady Fitzgerald was in many things a counterpart of her husband, not in health so much as in spirits.   She, also, was old for her age, and woebegone, not only in appearance, but also in the inner workings of her heart.   But then it was known of her that she had undergone deep sorrows in her early youth, which had left their mark upon her brow, and their trace upon her inmost thoughts.   Sir Thomas had not been her first husband. When very young, she had been married, or rather, given in marriage, to a man who in a very few weeks after that ill-fated union had shown himself to be perfectly unworthy of her.

Her story, or so much of it as was known to her friends, was this.   Her father had been a clergyman in Dorsetshire, burdened with a small income, and blessed with a large family.   She who afterwards became Lady Fitzgerald was his eldest child ; and, as Miss Wainwright—Mary Wainwright—had grown up to be the possessor of almost perfect female loveliness.   While she was yet very young, a widower with an only boy, a man who at that time was considerably less than thirty, had come into her father's parish, having rented there a small hunting-box.   This gentleman —we will so call him, in lack of some other term—immediately became possessed of an establishment, at any rate eminently respectable.   He had three hunters, two grooms, and a gig ; and on Sundays went to church with a prayer-book in his hand, and a black coat on his back.   What more could be desired to prove his respectability ?

He had not been there a month before he was intimate in the parson's house.   Before two months had passed he was engaged to the parson's daughter.   Before the full quarter had flown by, he and the parson's daughter were man and wife ; and in five months from the time of his first appearance in the Dorsetshire parish, he had flown from his creditors, leaving behind him his three horses, his two grooms, his gig, his wife, and his little boy.

The Dorsetshire neighbours, and especially the Dorsetshire ladies, had at first been loud in their envious exclamations as to Miss Wainwright's luck.   The parson and the parson's wife, and poor Mary Wainwright herself, had according to the sayings of that moment prevalent in the county, used most unjustifiable wiles in trapping this poor rich stranger.   Miss Wainwright, as they

all declared, had not clothes to her back when she went to him.
The matter had been got up and managed in most indecent
hurry, so as to rob the poor fellow of any chance of escape.
And thus all manner of evil things were said, in which envy of
the bride and pity of the bridegroom were equally com-
mingled.

But when the sudden news came that Mr. Talbot had bolted,
and when after a week's inquiry no one could tell whither Mr.
Talbot had gone, the objurgations of the neighbours were expressed in a different tone. Then it was declared that Mr.
Wainwright had sacrificed his beautiful child without making
any inquiry as to the character of the stranger to whom he had
so recklessly given her. The pity of the county fell to the
share of the poor beautiful girl, whose welfare and happiness
were absolutely ruined ; and the parson was pulled to pieces for
his sordid parsimony in having endeavoured to rid himself in so
disgraceful a manner of the charge of one of his children.

It would be beyond the scope of my story to tell here of the
anxious family councils which were held in that parsonage parlour, during the time of that daughter's courtship. There had
been misgivings as to the stability of the wooer ; there had been an
anxious wish not to lose for the penniless daughter the advantage
of a wealthy match ; the poor girl herself had been much cross-
questioned as to her own feelings. But let them have been
right, or let them have been wrong at that parsonage, the matter
was settled, very speedily as we have seen ; and Mary Wainwright became Mrs. Talbot when she was still almost a child.

And then Mr. Talbot bolted ; and it became known to the
Dorsetshire world that he had not paid a shilling for rent, or
for butcher's meat for his human family, or for oats for his
equine family, during the whole period of his sojourn at Chevy-
chase Lodge. Grand references had been made to a London
banker, which had been answered by assurances that Mr. Talbot
was as good as the Bank of England. But it turned out that the
assurances were forged, and that the letter of inquiry addressed
to the London banker had been intercepted. In short, it was
all ruin, roguery, and wretchedness.

And very wretched they all were, the old father, the young
bride, and all that parsonage household. After much inquiry
something at last was discovered. The man had a sister whose
whereabouts was made out ; and she consented to receive the
child—on condition that the bairn should not come to her
empty-handed. In order to get rid of this burden, Mr. Wainwright with great difficulty made up thirty pounds.

And then it was discovered that the man's name was not

Talbot. What it was did not become known in Dorsetshire, for the poor wife resumed her maiden name—with very little right to do so, as her kind neighbours observed—till fortune so kindly gave her the privilege of bearing another honourably before the world.

And then other inquiries, and almost endless search was made with reference to that miscreant—not quite immediately—for at the moment of the blow such search seemed to be but of little use; but after some months, when the first stupor arising from their grief had passed away, and when they once more began to find that the fields were still green, and the sun warm, and that God's goodness was not at an end.

And the search was made not so much with reference to him as to his fate, for tidings had reached the parsonage that he was no more. The period was that in which Paris was occupied by the allied forces, when our general, the Duke of Wellington, was paramount in the French capital, and the Tuileries and Champs Elysées were swarming with Englishmen.

Report at the time was brought home that the soi-disant Talbot, fighting his battles under the name of Chichester, had been seen and noted in the gambling-houses of Paris; that he had been forcibly extruded from some such chamber for non-payment of a gambling debt; that he had made one in a violent fracas which had subsequently taken place in the French streets; and that his body had afterwards been identified in the Morgue.

Such was the story which bit by bit reached Mr. Wainwright's ears, and at last induced him to go over to Paris, so that the absolute and proof-sustained truth of the matter might be ascertained, and made known to all men. The poor man's search was difficult and weary. The ways of Paris were not then so easy to an Englishman as they have since become, and Mr. Wainwright could not himself speak a word of French. But nevertheless he did learn much; so much as to justify him, as he thought, in instructing his daughter to wear a widow's cap. That Talbot had been kicked out of a gambling-house in the Rue Richelieu was absolutely proved. An acquaintance who had been with him in Dorsetshire on his first arrival there had seen this done; and bore testimony of the fact that the man so treated was the man who had taken the hunting-lodge in England. This same acquaintance had been one of the party adverse to Talbot in the row which had followed, and he could not, therefore, be got to say that he had seen him dead. But other evidence had gone to show that the man who had been so extruded was the man who had perished; and the French lawyer whom Mr. Wainwright had employed, at last assured the poor broken-hearted clergyman that he might look upon it as proved. ' Had he not been dead,' said the lawyer, ' the inquiry which has been made would have traced him out alive.' And thus his daughter was instructed to put on her widow's cap, and her mother again called her Mrs. Talbot.

Indeed, at that time they hardly knew what to call her, or how to act in the wisest and most befitting manner. Among those who had truly felt for them in their misfortunes, who had really pitied them and encountered them with loving sympathy, the kindest and most valued friend had been the vicar of a neighbouring parish. He himself was a widower without children, but living with him at that time, and reading with him, was a young gentleman whose father was just dead, a baronet of large property, and an Irishman. This was Sir Thomas Fitzgerald.

It need not now be told how this young man's sympathies were also excited, or how sympathy had grown into love. In telling our tale we fain would not dwell much on the cradledom of our Meleager. The young widow in her widow's cap grew to be more lovely than she had ever been before her miscreant husband had seen her. They who remembered her in those days told wondrous tales of her surprising loveliness;—how men from London would come down to see her in the parish church; how she was talked of as the Dorsetshire Venus, only that unlike Venus she would give a hearing to no man; how sad she was as well as lovely ; and how impossible it was found to win a smile from her.

But though she could not smile, she could love ; and at last she accepted the love of the young baronet. And then the father, who had so grossly neglected his duty when he gave her in marriage to an unknown rascally adventurer, endeavoured to atone for such neglect by the severest caution with reference to this new suitor. Further inquiries were made. Sir Thomas went over to Paris himself with that other clergyman. Lawyers were employed in England to sift out the truth ; and at last, by the united agreement of some dozen men, all of whom were known to be worthy, it was decided that Talbot was dead, and that his widow was free to choose another mate. Another mate she had already chosen, and immediately after this she was married to Sir Thomas Fitzgerald.

Such was the early life-story of Lady Fitzgerald ; and as this was widely known to those who lived around her—for how could such a life-story as that remain untold?—no one wondered why she should be gentle and silent in her life's course. That she had been an excellent wife, a kind and careful mother, a loving neighbour to the poor, and courteous neighbour to the rich, all the county Cork admitted. She had lived down envy by her gentleness and soft humility, and every one spoke of her and her retiring habits with sympathy and reverence.

But why should her husband also be so sad—nay, so much sadder? For Lady Fitzgerald, though she was gentle and silent, was not a sorrowful woman—otherwise than she was made so by seeing her husband's sorrow. She had been to him a loving partner, and no man could more tenderly have returned a wife's love than he had done. One would say that all had run smoothly at Castle Richmond since the house had been made happy, after some years of waiting, by the birth of an eldest child and heir. But, nevertheless, those who knew most of Sir Thomas saw that there was a peacock on the wall.

It is only necessary to say further a word or two as to the other ladies of the family, and hardly necessary to say that. Mary and Emmeline Fitzgerald were both cheerful girls. I do not mean that they were boisterous laughers, that in waltzing they would tear round a room like human steam-engines, that they rode well to hounds as some young ladies now-a-days do—and some young ladies do ride very well to hounds; nor that they affected slang, and decked their persons with odds and ends of masculine costume. In saying that they were cheerful, I by no means wish it to be understood that they were loud.

They were pretty, too, but neither of them lovely, as their mother had been—hardly, indeed, so lovely as that pale mother was now, even in these latter days. Ah, how very lovely that pale mother was, as she sat still and silent in her own place on the small sofa by the slight, small table which she used! Her hair was gray, and her eyes sunken, and her lips thin and blood-less; but yet never shall I see her equal for pure feminine beauty, for form and outline, for passionless grace, and sweet, gentle, womanly softness. All her sad tale was written upon her brow; all its sadness and all its poetry. One could read there the fear-ful, all but fatal danger to which her childhood had been exposed, and the daily thanks with which she praised her God for having spared and saved her.

But I am running back to the mother in attempting to say a word about her children. Of the two, Emmeline, the younger, was the more like her; but no one who was a judge of outline could imagine that Emmeline, at her mother's age, would ever have her mother's beauty. Nevertheless, they were fine, hand-some girls, more popular in the neighbourhood than any of their neighbours, well educated, sensible, feminine, and useful; fitted to be the wives of good men.

And what shall I say of Miss Letty? She was ten years older than her brother, and as strong as a horse. She was great at walking, and recommended that exercise strongly to all young ladies as an antidote to every ill, from love to chilblains. She was short and dapper in person; not ugly, excepting that her nose was long, and had a little bump or excrescence at the end of it. She always wore a bonnet, even at meal times; and was supposed, by those who were not intimately acquainted with the mysteries of her toilet, to sleep in it; often, indeed. she did sleep in it, and gave unmusical evidence of her doing so. She was not illnatured; but so strongly prejudiced on many points as to be equally disagreeable as though she were so. With her, as with the world in general, religion was the point on which those prejudices were the strongest; and the peculiar bent they took was horror and hatred of popery. As she lived in a country in which the Roman Catholic was the religion of all the poorer classes, and of very many persons who were not poor, there was ample scope in which her horror and hatred could work. She was charitable to a fault, and would exercise that charity for the good of Papists as willingly as for the good of Protestants; but in doing so she always remembered the good cause. She always clogged the flannel petticoat with some Protestant teaching, or burdened the little coat and trousers with the pains and penalties of idolatry.

When her brother had married the widow Talbot, her anger with him and her hatred towards her sister-in-law had been extreme. But time and conviction had worked in her so thorough a change, that she now almost worshipped the very spot in which Lady Fitzgerald habitually sat. She had the faculty to know and recognize goodness when she saw it, and she had known and recognized it in her brother's wife.

Him also, her brother himself, she warmly loved and greatly reverenced. She deeply grieved over his state of body and mind, and would have given all she ever had, even her very self, to restore him to health and happiness.

The three children of course she loved, and petted, and scolded; and as children bothered them out of all their peace and quietness. To the girls she was still almost as great a torment as in their childish days. Nevertheless, they still loved and sometimes obeyed her. Of Herbert she stood somewhat more in awe. He was the future head of the family, and already a Bachelor of Arts. In a very few years he would probably assume the higher title of a married man of arts, she thought; and perhaps the less formidable one of a member of Parliament also. Him, therefore, she treated with deference. But, alas! what if he should become a Puseyite!

CHAPTER VI.

THE KANTURK HOTEL, SOUTH MAIN STREET, CORK.

ALL the world no doubt knows South Main Street in the city of Cork. In the 'ould' ancient days, South and North Main Streets formed the chief thoroughfare through the city, and hence of course they derived their names. But now, since Patrick Street, and Grand Parade, and the South Mall have grown up, Main Street has but little honour. It is crowded with second-rate tobacconists and third-rate grocers; the houses are dirty, and the street is narrow; fashionable ladies never visit it for their shopping, nor would any respectable commercial gent stop at an inn within its purlieus.

But here in South Main Street, at the time at which I am writing, there was an inn, or public-house, called the Kanturk Hotel. In dear old Ireland they have some foibles, and one of them is a passion for high nomenclature. Those who are accustomed to the sort of establishments which are met with in England, and much more in Germany and Switzerland, under the name of hotels, might be surprised to see the place in South Main Street which had been dignified with the same appellation. It was a small, dingy house of three stories, the front door of which was always open, and the passage strewed with damp, dirty straw. On the left-hand side as you entered was a sitting-room, or coffee-room as it was announced to be by an appellation painted on the door. There was but one window to the room, which looked into the street, and was always clouded by a dingy-red curtain. The floor was uncarpeted, nearly black with dirt, and usually half covered with fragments of damp straw brought into it by the feet of customers. A strong smell of hot whisky and water always prevailed, and the straggling mahogany table in the centre of the room, whose rickety legs gave way and came off whenever an attempt was made to move it, was covered by small greasy circles, the impressions of the bottoms of tumblers which had been made by the overflowing tipple. Over the chimney there was a round mirror, the framework of which was bedizened with all manner of would-be gilt ornaments, which had been cracked, and twisted, and mended till it was impossible to know what they had been intended to represent; and the whole affair had become a huge receptacle of dust, which fell in flakes upon the chimney-piece when it was invaded. There was a second table opposite the window, more rickety than that in the centre; and against the wall opposite to the fireplace there was an old sideboard, in the drawers of which Tom, the one-eyed waiter, kept knives and forks, and candle-ends, and bits of bread, and dusters. There was a sour smell, as of old rancid butter, about the place, to which the guests sometimes objected, little inclined as they generally were to be fastidious. But this was a tender subject, and not often alluded to by those who wished to stand well in the good graces of Tom. Many things much annoyed Tom; but nothing annoyed him so fearfully as any assertion that the air of the Kanturk Hotel was not perfectly sweet and wholesome.

Behind the coffee-room was the bar, from which Fanny O'Dwyer dispensed dandies of punch and goes of brandy to her father's customers from Kanturk. For at this, as at other similar public-houses in Irish towns, the greater part of the custom on which the publican depends came to him from the inhabitants of one particular country district. A large four-wheeled vehicle, called a long car, which was drawn by three horses, and travelled over a mountain road at the rate of four Irish miles an hour, came daily from Kanturk to Cork, and daily returned. This public conveyance stopped in Cork at the Kanturk Hotel, and was owned by the owner of that house, in partnership with a brother in the same trade located in Kanturk. It was Mr. O'Dwyer's business to look after this concern, to see to the passengers and the booking, the oats, and hay, and stabling, while his well-known daughter, the charming Fanny O'Dwyer, took care of the house, and dispensed brandy and whisky to the customers from Kanturk.

To tell the truth, the bar was a much more alluring place than the coffee-room, and Fanny O'Dwyer a more alluring personage than Tom, the one-eyed waiter. This Elysium, however, was not open to all comers—not even to all comers from Kanturk. Those who had the right of entry well knew their privilege; and so also did they who had not. This sanctum was screened off from the passage by a window, which opened upwards conveniently, as is customary with bar-windows; but the window was blinded inside by a red curtain, so that Fanny's stool near the counter, her father's wooden arm-chair, and the old horsehair sofa on which favoured guests were wont to sit, were not visible to the public at large.

Of the upstair portion of this establishment it is not necessary to say much. It professed to be an hotel, and accommodation for sleeping was to be obtained there; but the well-being of the house depended but little on custom of this class.

Nor need I say much of the kitchen, a graphic description of which would not be pleasing. Here lived a cook, who, together with Tom the waiter, did all that servants had to do at the Kanturk Hotel. From this kitchen lumps of beef, mutton chops, and potatoes did occasionally emanate, all perfumed with plenteous onions; as also did fried eggs, with bacon an inch thick, and other culinary messes too horrible to be thought of. But drinking rather than eating was the staple of this establishment. Such was the Kanturk Hotel in South Main Street, Cork.

It was on a disagreeable, cold, sloppy, raw, winter evening—an evening drizzling sometimes with rain, and sometimes with sleet—that an elderly man was driven up to the door of the hotel on a one-horse car—or jingle, as such conveniences were then called in the south of Ireland. He seemed to know the house, for with his outside coat all dripping as it was he went direct to the bar-window, and as Fanny O'Dwyer opened the door he walked into that warm precinct. There he encountered a gentleman, dressed one would say rather beyond the merits of the establishment, who was taking his ease at full length on Fanny's sofa, and drinking some hot compound which was to be seen in a tumbler on the chimney-shelf just above his head. It was now six o'clock in the evening, and the gentleman no doubt had dined.

'Well, Aby; here I am, as large as life, but as cold as death. Ugh; what an affair that coach is! Fanny, my best of darlings, give me a drop of something that's best for warming the cockles of an old man's heart.'

'A young wife then is the best thing in life to do that, Mr. Mcllett, 'said Fanny, sharply, preparing, however, at the same time, some mixture which might be taken more instantaneously.

'The governor's had enough of that receipt already,' said the man on the sofa; or rather the man now off the sofa, for he had slowly arisen to shake hands with the new comer.

This latter person proceeded to divest himself of his dripping greatcoat. 'Here, Tom,' said he, 'bring your old Cyclops eye to bear this way, will you. Go and hang that up in the kitchen; not too near the fire now; and get me something to eat; none of your mutton chops; but a beefsteak if there is such a thing in this benighted place. Well, Aby, how goes on the war?'

It was clear that the elderly gentleman was quite at home in his present quarters; for Tom, far from resenting such impertinence, as he would immediately have done had it proceeded from an ordinary Kanturk customer, declared 'that he would do his nonour's bidding av there was such a thing as a beefsteak to be had anywhere's in the city of Cork.'

And indeed the elderly gentleman was a person of whom one might premise, judging by his voice and appearance, that he would probably make himself at home anywhere. He was a hale hearty man, of perhaps sixty years of age, who had certainly been handsome, and was even now not the reverse. Or rather, one may say, that he would have been so were it not that there was a low, restless, cunning legible in his mouth and eyes, which robbed his countenance of all manliness. He was a hale man, and well preserved for his time of life; but nevertheless, the extra rubicundity of his face, and certain incipient pimply excrescences about his nose, gave tokens that he lived too freely. He had lived freely; and were it not that his constitution had been more than ordinarily strong, and that constant exercise and exposure to air had much befriended him, those pimply excrescences would have shown themselves in a more advanced stage. Such was Mr. Mollett senior—Mr. Matthew Mollett, with whom it will be soon our fate to be better acquainted.

The gentleman who had slowly risen from the sofa was his son, Mr. Mollett junior—Mr. Abraham Mollett, with whom also we shall become better acquainted. The father has been represented as not being exactly prepossessing; but the son, according to my ideas, was much less so. He also would be considered handsome by some persons—by women chiefly of the Fanny O'Dwyer class, whose eyes are capable of recognizing what is good in shape and form, but cannot recognize what is good in tone and character. Mr. Abraham Mollett was perhaps some thirty years of age, or rather more. He was a very smart man, with a profusion of dark, much-oiled hair, with dark, copious mustachoes—and mustachoes being then not common as they are now, added to his otherwise rakish, vulgar appearance—with various rings on his not well-washed hands, with a frilled front to his not lately washed shirt, with a velvet collar to his coat, and patent-leather boots upon his feet.

Free living had told more upon him, young as he was, than upon his father. His face was not yet pimply, but it was red and bloated; his eyes were bloodshot and protruding; his hand on a morning was unsteady; and his passion for brandy was stronger than that for beefsteaks; whereas his father's appetite for solid food had never flagged. Those who were intimate with the family, and were observant of men, were wont to remark that the son would never fill the father's shoes. These family friends, I may perhaps add, were generally markers at billiard-tables, head grooms at race-courses, or other men of that sharp, discerning class.

Seeing that I introduce these gentlemen to my readers at the Kanturk Hotel, in South Main Street, Cork, it may be perhaps as well to add that they were both Englishmen; so that mistakes on that matter may be avoided.

The father, as soon as he had rid himself of his upper coat, his dripping hat, and his goloshes, stood up with his back to the bar-room fire, with his hands in his trousers-pockets, and the tails of his coat stuck inside his arms.

'I tell you, Aby, it was cold enough outside that infernal coach. I'm blessed if I've a morsel of feeling in my toes yet. Why the d—— don't they continue the railway on to Cork? It's as much as a man's life is worth to travel in that sort of way at this time of the year.'

'You'll have more of it then if you intend going out of town to-morrow,' said the son.

'Well, I don't know that I shall. I shall take a day to consider of it I think.'

'Consideration be bothered,' said Mollett junior; 'strike when the iron's hot; that's my motto.'

The father here turned half round to his son and winked at him, nodding his head slightly towards the girl, thereby giving token that, according to his ideas, the conversation could not be discreetly carried on before a third person.

'All right,' said the son, lifting his joram of brandy and water to his mouth; an action in which he was immediately imitated by his father, who had now received the means of doing so from the hands of the fair Fanny.

'And how about a bed, my dear?' said Mollett senior; 'that's a matter of importance too; or will be when we are getting on to the little hours.'

'Oh, we won't turn you out, Mr. Mollett,' said Fanny; 'we'll find a bed for you, never fear.'

'That's all right then, my little Venus. And now if I had some dinner I'd sit down and make myself comfortable for the evening.'

As he said this, Fanny slipped out of the room, and ran down into the kitchen to see what Tom and the cook were doing. The Molletts, father and son, were rather more than ordinary good customers at the Kanturk Hotel, and it was politic therefore to treat them well. Mr. Mollett junior, moreover, was almost more than a customer; and for the sake of the son, Fanny was anxious that the father should be well treated.

'Well, governor, and what have you done?' said the younger man in a low voice, jumping up from his seat as soon as the girl had left them alone.

'Well, I've got the usual remittance from the man in Bucklers-bury. That was all as right as a trivet.'

'And no more than that? Then I tell you what it is; we must be down on him at once.'

'But you forget that I got as much more last month, out of the usual course. Come, Aby, don't you be unreasonable.'

'Bother—I tell you, governor, if he don't——' And then Miss O'Dwyer returned to her sanctum, and the rest of the conversation was necessarily postponed.

'He's managed to get you a lovely steak, Mr. Mollett,' said Fanny, pronouncing the word as though it were written 'steek.' 'And we've beautiful pickled walnuts; haven't we, Mr. Aby? and there'll be kidneys biled' (meaning potatoes) 'by the time the " steek's " ready. You like it with the gravy in, don't you, Mr. Mollett?' And as she spoke she drew a quartern of whisky for two of Beamish and Crawford's draymen, who stood outside in the passage and drank it at the bar.

The lovely 'steek' with the gravy in it—that is to say, nearly raw—was now ready, and father and son adjourned to the next room. 'Well, Tom, my lad of wax; and how's the world using you?' said Mr. Mollett senior.

'There ain't much difference then,' said Tom; 'I ain't no younger, nor yet no richer than when yer honour left us—and what is't to be, sir?—a pint of stout, sir?'

As soon as Mr. Mollett senior had finished his dinner, and Tom had brought the father and son materials for making whisky-punch, they both got their knees together over the fire, and commenced the confidential conversation which Miss O'Dwyer had interrupted on her return to the bar-room. They spoke now almost in a whisper, with their heads together over the fender, knowing from experience that what Tom wanted in eyes he made up in ears.

'And what did Prendergast say when he paid you the rhino?' asked the son.

'Not a word,' said the other. 'After all, I don't think he knows any more than a ghost what he pays it for: I think he gets fresh instructions every time. But, any ways, there it was, all right.'

'Hall right, indeed! I do believe you'd be satisfied to go on getting a few dribblets now and then like that. And then if anything 'appened to you, why I might go fish.'

'How, Aby, look here——'

'It's hall very well, governor; but I'll tell you what. Since you started off I've been thinking a good deal about it, and I've made up my mind that this shilly-shallying won't do any good : we must strike a blow that'll do something for us.'

'Well, I don't think we've done so bad already, taking it all in-all.'

'Ah, that's because you haven't the pluck to strike a good blow. Now I'll just let you know what I propose—and I tell you fairly, governor, if you'll not hear reason, I'll take the game into my own hands.'

The father looked up from his drink and scowled at his son, but said nothing in answer to this threat.

'By G— I will!' continued Aby. 'It's no use 'umbugging, and I mean to make myself understood. While you've been gone I've been down to that place.'

'You 'aven't seen the old man?'

'No; I 'aven't taken that step yet; but I think it's very likely I may before long if you won't hear reason.'

'I was a d—— fool, Aby, ever to let you into the affair at all. It's been going on quiet enough for the last ten years, till I let you into the secret.'

'Well, never mind about that. That mischief's done. But I think you'll find I'll pull you through a deal better than hever you'd have pulled through yourself. You're already making twice more out of it than you did before I knew it. As I was saying, I went down there; and in my quiet way I did just venture on a few hinquiries.'

'I'll be bound you did. You'll blow it all in about another month, and then it'll be all up with the lot of us.'

'It's a beautiful place: a lovely spot; and hall in prime horder. They say it's fifteen thousand a year, and that there's not a shilling howing on the whole property. Even in these times the tenants are paying the rent, when no one else, far and near, is getting a penny out of them. I went by another place on the road—Castle Desmond they call it, and I wish you'd seen the difference. The old boy must be rolling in money.'

'I don't believe it. There's one as I can trust has told me he's hard up enough sometimes. Why, we've had twelve hundred in the last eight months.'

'Twelve hundred! and what's that? But, dickens, governor, where has the twelve hundred gone? I've only seen three of it, and part of that——. Well; what do you want there, you long-eared shark, you?' These last words were addressed to Tom, who had crept into the room, certainly without much preparatory noise.

'I was only wanting the thingumbob, yer honour,' said Tom, pretending to search diligently in the drawer for some required article.

'Then take your thingumbob quickly out of that, and be d——

to you. And look here; if you don't knock at the door when next you come in, by heavens I'll throw this tumbler at your yead.

' Sure and I will, yer honour,' said Tom, withdrawing.

' And where on hearth has the twelve hundred pounds gone ?' asked the son, looking severely at the father.

Old Mr. Mollett made no immediate answer in words, but putting his left hand to his right elbow, began to shake it.

' I do wonder that you kept hon at that work,' said Mollett junior, reproachfully. ' You never by any chance have a stroke of luck.'

' Well, I have been unfortunate lately; but who knows what's coming ? And I was deucedly sold by those fellows at the October meeting. If any chap ever was safe, I ought to have been safe then; but hang me if I didn't drop four hundred of Sir Thomas's shiners coolly on the spot. That was the only big haul I've had out of him all at once ; and the most of it went like water through a sieve within forty-eight hours after I touched it.' And then, having finished this pathetical little story of his misfortune, Mr. Mollett senior finished his glass of toddy.

' It's the way of the world, governor ; and it's no use sighing after spilt milk. But I'll tell you what I propose ; and if you don't like the task yourself, I have no hobjection in life to take it into my own hands. You see the game's so much our own that there's nothing on hearth for us to fear.'

' I don't know that. If we were all blown, where should we be——'

' Why, she's your own——'

' H-h-sh, Aby. There's that confounded long-eared fellow at the keyhole, as sure as my name's Matthew ; and if he hears you, the game's all up with a vengeance.'

' Lord bless you, what could he hear ? Besides, talking as we are now, he wouldn't catch a word even if he were in the room itself. And now I'll tell you what it is ; do you go down yourself, and make your way into the hold gentleman's room. Just send your own name in boldly. Nobody will know what that means, except himself.'

' I did that once before ; and I never shall forget it.'

' Yes, you did it once before, and you have had a steady income to live on ever since ; not such an income as you might have had Not such an income as will do for you and me, now that we both know so well what a fine property we have under our thumbs. But, nevertheless, that little visit has been worth something to you.'

' Upon my word, Aby, I never suffered so much as I did that day. I didn't know till then that I had a soft heart.'

'Soft heart! Oh, bother. Such stuff as that always makes me sick. If I 'ate anything, it's maudlin. Your former visit down there did very well, and now you must make another, or else, by the holy poker! I'll make it for you.'

'And what would you have me say to him if I did manage to see him?'

'Perhaps I'd better go——'

'That's out of the question. He wouldn't see you, or understand who you were. And then you'd make a row, and it would all come out, and the fat would be in the fire.'

'Well, I guess I should not take it quite quiet if they didn't treat me as a gentleman should be treated. I ain't always over-quiet if I'm put upon.'

'If you go near that house at all I'll have done with it. I'll give up the game.'

'Well, do you go, at any rate first. Perhaps it may be well that I should follow after with a reminder. Do you go down, and just tell him this, quite coolly, remember——'

'Oh, I shall be cool enough.'

'That, considering hall things, you think he and you ought to——'

'Well?'

'Just divide it between you; share and share alike. Say it's fourteen thousand—and it's more than that—that would be seven for him and seven for you. Tell him you'll agree to that, but you won't take one farthing less.'

'Aby!' said the father, almost overcome by the grandeur of his son's ideas.

'Well; and what of Haby? What's the matter now?'

'Expect him to shell out seven thousand pounds a year!'

'And why not? He'll do a deal more than that, I expect, if he were quite sure that it would make all things serene. But it won't; and therefore you must make him another hoffer.'

'Another offer!'

'Yes. He'll know well enough that you'll be thinking of his death. And for all they do say he might pop off any day.'

'He's a younger man than me, Aby, by full ten years.'

'What of that? You may pop off any day too, mayn't you? I believe you old fellows don't think of dying nigh as hoften as we young ones.'

'You young ones are always looking for us old ones to go. we all know that well enough.'

'That's when you've got anything to leave behind you, which hain't the case with you, governor, just at present. But what I was saying is this. He'll know well enough that you can split upon his son hafter he's gone, every bit as well as you can split on him now.'

'Oh, I always looked to make the young gentleman pay up handsome, if so be the old gentleman went off the hooks. And if so be he and I should go off together like, why you'd carry on, of course. You'll have the proofs, you know.'

'Oh, I should, should I? Well, we'll look to them by-and by. But I'll tell you what, governor, the best way is to make all that safe. We'll make him another hoffer—for a regular substantial family harrangement——'

'A family arrangement, eh?'

'Yes; that's the way they always manage things when great family hinterests is at stake. Let him give us a cool seven thousand a year between us while he's alive; let him put you down for twenty thousand when he's dead—that'd come out of the young gentleman's share of the property, of course—and then let him give me his daughter Hemmeline, with another twenty thousand tacked on to her skirt-tail. I should be mum then for hever for the honour of the family.'

The father for a moment or two was struck dumb by the magnitude of his son's proposition. 'That's what I call playing the game firm,' continued the son. 'Do you lay down your terms before him, substantial, and then stick to 'em. "Them's my terms, Sir Thomas," you'll say. "If you don't like 'em, as I can't halter, why in course I'll go elsewhere." Do you be firm to that, and you'll see how the game'll go.'

'And you think he'll give you his daughter in marriage?'

'Why not? I'm honest born, hain't I? And she's a bastard.'

'But, Aby, you don't know what sort of people these are. You don't know what her breeding has been.'

'D—— her breeding. I know this: she'd get a deuced pretty fellow for her husband, and one that girls as good as her has hankered hafter long enough. It won't do, governor, to let people as is in their position pick and choose like. We've the hupper hand, and we must do the picking and choosing.'

'She'd never have you, Aby; not if her father went down on his knees to her to ask her.'

'Oh, wouldn't she? By heaven, then, she shall, and that without any kneeling at all. She shall have me, and be deuced glad to take me. What! she'd refuse a fellow like me when she knows that she and all belonging to her'd be turned into the streets if she don't have me! I'm clear of another way of thinking, then. My opinion is she'd come to me jumping. I'll tell you what, governor, you don't know the sex.'

Mr. Mollett senior upon this merely shook his head. Perhaps

the fact was that he knew the sex somewhat better than his son. It had been his fate during a portion of his life to live among people who were, or ought to have been, gentlemen. He might have been such himself had he not gone wrong in life from the very starting-post. But his son had had no such opportunities. He did know and could know nothing about ladies and gentlemen.

'You're mistaken, Aby,' said the old man. 'They'd never suffer you to come among them on such a footing as that. They'd sooner go forth to the world as beggars.'

'Then, by G——! they shall go forth as beggars. I've said it now, father, and I'll stick to it. You know the stuff I'm made of.' As he finished speaking, he swallowed down the last half of a third glass of hot spirits and water, and then glared on his father with angry, bloodshot eyes, and a red, almost lurid face. The unfortunate father was beginning to know the son, and to feel that his son would become his master.

Shortly after this they were interrupted; and what further conversation they had on the matter that night took place in their joint bedroom ; to which uninviting retreat it is not now necessary that we should follow them.

CHAPTER VII.

THE FAMINE YEAR.

THEY who were in the south of Ireland during the winter of 1846-47 will not readily forget the agony of that period. For many, many years preceding and up to that time, the increasing swarms of the country had been fed upon the potato, and upon the potato only ; and now all at once the potato failed them and the greater part of eight million human beings were left without food.

The destruction of the potato was the work of God; and it was natural to attribute the sufferings which at once overwhelmed the unfortunate country to God's anger—to his wrath for the misdeeds of which that country had been guilty. For myself, I do not believe in such exhibitions of God's anger. When wars come, and pestilence, and famine ; when the people of a land are worse than decimated, and the living hardly able to bury the dead, I cannot coincide with those who would deprecate God's wrath by prayers. I do not believe that our God stalks darkly along the clouds, laying th usands low with the arrows of death, and those thousands the most ignorant, because men who are not ignorant have displeased Him. Nor, if in his wisdom He did do so, can I think that men's prayers would hinder that which his wisdom had seen to be good and right.

But though I do not believe in exhibitions of God's anger, I do believe in exhibitions of his mercy. When men by their folly and by the shortness of their vision have brought upon themselves penalties which seem to be overwhelming, to which no end can be seen, which would be overwhelming were no aid coming to us but our own, then God raises his hand, not in anger, but in mercy, and by his wisdom does for us that for which our own wisdom has been insufficient.

But on no Christian basis can I understand the justice or acknowledge the propriety of asking our Lord to abate his wrath in detail, or to alter his settled purpose. If He be wise, would we change his wisdom? If He be merciful, would we limit his mercy? There comes upon us some strange disease, and we bid Him to stay his hand. But the disease, when it has passed by, has taught us lessons of cleanliness, which no master less stern would have made acceptable. A famine strikes us, and we again beg that that hand may be stayed;—beg as the Greeks were said to beg when they thought that the anger of Phœbus was hot against them because his priest had been dishonoured. We so beg, thinking that God's anger is hot also against us. But, lo! the famine passes by, and a land that had been brought to the dust by man's folly is once more prosperous and happy.

If this was ever so in the world's history, it was so in Ireland at the time of which I am speaking. The country, especially in the south and west, had been brought to a terrible pass;—not as so many said and do say, by the idolatry of popery, or by the sedition of demagogues, or even mainly by the idleness of the people. The idolatry of popery, to my way of thinking, is bad; though not so bad in Ireland as in most other Papist countries that I have visited. Sedition also is bad; but in Ireland, in late years, it has not been deep-seated—as may have been noted at Ballingarry and other places, where endeavour was made to bring sedition to its proof. And as for the idleness of Ireland's people, I am inclined to think they will work under the same compulsion and same persuasion which produce work in other countries.

The fault had been the lowness of education and consequent want of principle among the middle classes; and this fault had been found as strongly marked among the Protestants as it had been among the Roman Catholics. Young men were brought up to do nothing. Property was regarded as having no duties attached to it. Men became rapacious, and determined to extract the uttermost farthing out of the land within their power, let the consequences to the people on that land be what they might.

We used to hear much of absentees. It was not the absence of the absentees that did the damage, but the presence of those they left behind them on the soil. The scourge of Ireland was the existence of a class who looked to be gentlemen living on their property, but who should have earned their bread by the work of their brain, or, failing that, by the sweat of their brow. There were men to be found in shoals through the country speaking of their properties and boasting of their places, but who owned no properties and had no places when the matter came to be properly sifted.

Most Englishmen have heard of profit-rent. In Ireland the term is so common that no man cannot have heard of it. It may, of course, designate a very becoming sort of income. A man may, for instance, take a plot of land for one hundred pounds a year, improve and build on it till it be fairly worth one thousand pounds a year, and thus enjoy a profit-rent of nine hundred pounds. Nothing can be better or fairer. But in Ireland the management was very different. Men there held tracts of ground, very often at their full value, paying for them such proportion of rent as a farmer could afford to pay in England and live. But the Irish tenant would by no means consent to be a farmer. It was needful to him that he should be a gentleman, and that his sons should be taught to live and amuse themselves as the sons of gentlemen—barring any such small trifle as education. They did live in this way; and to enable them to do so, they underlet their land in small patches, and at an amount of rent to collect which took the whole labour of their tenants, and the whole produce of the small patch, over and above the quantity of potatoes absolutely necessary to keep that tenant's body and soul together.

And thus a state of things was engendered in Ireland which discouraged labour, which discouraged improvements in farming, which discouraged any produce from the land except the potato crop; which maintained one class of men in what they considered to be the gentility of idleness, and another class, the people of the country, in the abjectness of poverty.

It is with thorough rejoicing, almost with triumph, that I declare that the idle, genteel class has been cut up root and branch, has been driven forth out of its holding into the wide world, and has been punished with the penalty of extermination. The poor cotter suffered sorely under the famine, and under the pestilence which followed the famine; but he, as a class, has risen from his bed of suffering a better man. He is thriving as a labourer either in his own country or in some newer—for him better—land to which he has emigrated. He, even in Ireland, can now get eight and nine shillings a week easier and with more constancy than he could get four some fifteen years since. But the other man has gone, and his place is left happily vacant.

There are an infinite number of smaller bearings in which this question of the famine, and of agricultural distress in Ireland, may be regarded, and should be regarded by those who wish to understand it. The manner in which the Poor Law was first rejected and then accepted, and then, if one may say so, swallowed whole by the people ; the way in which emigration has affected them ; the difference in the system of labour there from that here, which in former days was so strong that an agricultural labourer living on his wages and buying food with them, was a person hardly to be found : all these things must be regarded by one who would understand the matter. But seeing that this book of mine is a novel, I have perhaps already written more on a dry subject than many will read.

Such having been the state of the country, such its wretchedness, a merciful God sent the remedy which might avail to arrest it ; and we—we deprecated his wrath. But all this will soon be known and acknowledged ; acknowledged as it is acknowledged that new cities rise up in splendour from the ashes into which old cities have been consumed by fire. If this beneficent agency did not from time to time disencumber our crowded places, we should ever be living in narrow alleys with stinking gutters, and supply of water at the minimum.

But very frightful are the flames as they rush through the chambers of the poor, and very frightful was the course of that violent remedy which brought Ireland out of its misfortunes. Those who saw its course, and watched its victims, will not readily forget what they saw.

Slowly, gradually, and with a voice that was for a long time discredited, the news spread itself through the country that the food of the people was gone. That his own crop was rotten and useless each cotter quickly knew, and realized the idea that he must work for wages if he could get them, or else go to the poorhouse. That the crop of his parish or district was gone became evident to the priest, and the parson, and the squire ; and they realized the idea that they must fall on other parishes or other districts for support. But it was long before the fact made itself known that there was no food in any parish, in any district.

When this was understood, men certainly did put their shoulders to the wheel with a great effort. Much abuse at the time was thrown upon the government ; and they who took upon themselves the management of the relief of the poor in the south-west were taken most severely to task. I was in the country, travelling always through it, during the whole period, and I have to say—as I did say at the time with a voice that was not very audible—that in my opinion the measures of the government were prompt, wise, and beneficent; and I have to say also that the efforts of those who managed the poor were, as a rule, unremitting, honest, impartial, and successful.

The feeding of four million starving people with food, to be brought from foreign lands, is not an easy job. No government could bring the food itself; but by striving to do so it might effectually prevent such bringing on the part of others. Nor when the food was there, on the quays, was it easy to put it, in due proportions, into the four million mouths. Some mouths, and they, alas! the weaker ones, would remain unfed. But the opportunity was a good one for slashing philanthropical censure; and then the business of the slashing, censorious philanthropist is so easy, so exciting, and so pleasant!

I think that no portion of Ireland suffered more severely during the famine than the counties Cork and Kerry. The poorest parts were perhaps the parishes lying back from the sea and near to the mountains; and in the midst of such a district Desmond Court was situated. The region immediately round Castle Richmond was perhaps better. The tenants there had more means at their disposal, and did not depend so absolutely on the potato crop; but even round Castle Richmond the distress was very severe.

Early in the year relief committees were formed, on one of which young Herbert Fitzgerald agreed to act. His father promised, and was prepared to give his best assistance, both by money and countenance; but he pleaded that the state of his health hindered him from active exertion, and therefore his son came forward in his stead on this occasion, as it appeared probable that he would do on all others having reference to the family property.

This work brought people together who would hardly have met but for such necessity. The priest and the parson of a parish, men who had hitherto never been in a room together, and between whom neither had known anything of the other but the errors of his doctrine, found themselves fighting for the same object at the same board, and each for the moment laid aside his religious ferocity. Gentlemen, whose ancestors had come over with Strongbow, or maybe even with Milesius, sat cheek by jowl with retired haberdashers, concerting new soup-kitchens, and learning on what smallest modicum of pudding made from Indian corn a family of seven might be kept alive, and in such condition that the father at least might be able to stand upright.

The town of Kanturk was the head-quarters of that circle to which Herbert Fitzgerald was attached, in which also would have been included the owner of Desmond Court, had there been an owner of an age to undertake such work. But the young earl was still under sixteen, and the property was represented, as far as any representation was made, by the countess.

But even in such a work as this, a work which so strongly brought out what there was of good among the upper classes, there was food for jealousy and ill will. The name of Owen Fitzgerald at this time did not stand high in the locality of which we are speaking. Men had presumed to talk both to him and of him, and he replied to their censures by scorn. He would not change his mode of living for them, or allow them to believe that their interference could in any way operate upon his conduct. He had therefore affected a worse character for morals than he had perhaps truly deserved, and had thus thrown off from him all intimacy with many of the families among whom he lived.

When, therefore, he had come forward as others had done, offering to join his brother-magistrates and the clergyman of the district in their efforts, they had, or he had thought that they had, looked coldly on him. His property was half way between Kanturk and Mallow; and when this occurred he turned his shoulder upon the former place, and professed to act with those whose meetings were held at the latter town. Thus he became altogether divided from that Castle Richmond neighbourhood to which he was naturally attached by old intimacies and family ties.

It was a hard time this for the poor countess. I have endeavoured to explain that the position in which she had been left with regard to money was not at any time a very easy one. She possessed high rank and the name of a countess, but very little of that wealth which usually constitutes the chief advantage of such rank and name. But now such means as had been at her disposal were terribly crippled. There was no poorer district than that immediately around her, and none, therefore, in which the poor rates rose to a more fearful proportion of the rent. The country was, and for that matter still is, divided, for purposes of poor-law rating, into electoral districts. In ordinary times a man, or at any rate a lady, may live and die in his or her own house without much noticing the limits or peculiarities of each district. In one the rate may be one and a penny in the pound, in another only a shilling. But the difference is not large enough to create inquiry. It is divided between the landlord and the tenant, and neither perhaps thinks much about it. But

when the demand made rises to seventeen or eighteen shillings
in the pound—as was the case in some districts in those days,—
when out of every pound of rent that he paid the tenant claimed
to deduct nine shillings for poor rates, that is, half the amount
levied—then a landlord becomes anxious enough as to the peculiarities of his own electoral division.

In the case of Protestant clergymen, the whole rate had to be
paid by the incumbent. A gentleman whose half-yearly rent-
charge amounted to perhaps two hundred pounds might have
nine-tenths of that sum deducted from him for poor rates.
I have known a case in which the proportion has been higher
than this.

And then the tenants in such districts began to decline to pay
any rent at all—in very many cases could pay no rent at all.
They, too, depended on the potatoes which were gone; they,
too, had been subject to those dreadful demands for poor rates;
and thus a landlord whose property was in any way embarrassed
had but a bad time of it. The property from which Lady Desmond drew her income had been very much embarrassed; and
for her the times were very bad.

In such periods of misfortune, a woman has always some
friend. Let her be who she may, some pair of broad shoulders
is forthcoming on which may be laid so much of the burden as is
by herself unbearable. It is the great privilege of womanhood,
that which compensates them for the want of those other privileges which belong exclusively to manhood—sitting in Parliament, for instance, preaching sermons, and going on 'Change.

At this time Lady Desmond would doubtless have chosen the
shoulders of Owen Fitzgerald for the bearing of her burden, had
he not turned against her, as he had done. But now there was
no hope of that. Those broad shoulders had burdens of their
own to bear of another sort, and it was at any rate impossible
that he should come to share those of Desmond Court.

But a champion was forthcoming; one, indeed, whose shoulders
were less broad; on looking at whose head and brow Lady
Desmond could not forget her years as she had done while Owen
Fitzgerald had been near her;—but a champion, nevertheless,
whom she greatly prized. This was Owen's cousin, Herbert
Fitzgerald.

'Mamma,' her daughter said to her one evening, as they were
sitting together in the only room which they now inhabited,
'Herbert wants us to go to that place near Kilcommon to-
morrow, and says he will send the car at two. I suppose I
can go?'

There were two things that Lady Desmond noticed in this:

first, that her daughter should have called young Mr. Fitzgerald by his Christian name; and secondly, that it should have come to that with them, that a Fitzgerald should send a vehicle for a Desmond, seeing that the Desmond could no longer provide a vehicle for herself.

'You could have had the pony-chair, my dear.'

'Oh, no, mamma; I would not do that.' The pony was now the only quadruped kept for the countess's own behoof; and the young earl's hunter was the only other horse in the Desmond Court stables. 'I wouldn't do that, mamma; Mary and Emmeline will not mind coming round.'

'But they will have to come round again to bring you back.'

'Yes, mamma. Herbert said they wouldn't mind it. We want to see how they are managing at the new soup kitchen they have there. That one at Clady is very bad. The boiler won't boil at all.'

'Very well, my dear; only mind you wrap yourself up.'

'Oh, yes; I always do.'

'But, Clara—' and Lady Desmond put on her sweetest, smoothest smile as she spoke to her daughter.

'Yes, mamma.'

'How long have you taken to call young Mr. Fitzgerald by his Christian name?'

'Oh, I never do, mamma,' said Clara, with a blush all over her face; 'not to himself, I mean. You see, Mary and Emmeline are always talking about him.'

'And therefore you mean always to talk about him also.'

'No, mamma. But one can't help talking about him; he is doing so much for these poor people. I don't think he ever thinks about anything else from morning to night. Emmeline says he always goes to it again after dinner. Don't you think he is very good about it, mamma?'

'Yes, my dear; very good indeed; almost good enough to be called Herbert.'

'But I don't call him so; you know I don't,' protested Clara, very energetically.

'He is very good,' continued the countess; 'very good indeed. I don't know what on earth we should do without him. If he were my own son, he could hardly be more attentive to me.'

'Then I may go with the girls to that place? I always forget the name.'

'Gortnaclough, you mean.'

'Yes, mamma. It is all Sir Thomas's property there; and they have got a regular kitchen, beautifully built. Her— Mr.

Fitzgerald says, with a regular cook. I do wish we could have one at Clady.'

'Mr. Fitzgerald will be here to-morrow morning, and I will talk to him about it. I fear we have not sufficient funds there.'

'No; that's just it. I do wish I had some money now. You won't mind if I am not home quite early? We all mean to dine there at the kitchen. The girls will bring something, and then we can stay out the whole afternoon.'

'It won't do for you to be out after nightfall, Clara.'

'No, I won't, mamma. They did want me to go home with them to Castle Richmond for to-morrow night; but I declined that,' and Clara uttered a slight sigh, as though she had declined something that would have been very pleasant to her.

'And why did you decline it?'

'Oh, I don't know. I didn't know whether you would like it; and besides—'

'Besides what?'

'You'd be here all alone, mamma.'

The countess got up from her chair and coming over to the place where her daughter was sitting, kissed her on her forehead. 'In such a matter as that, I don't want you to think of me, my dear. I would rather you went out. I must remain here in this horrid, dull, wretched place; but that is no reason why you should be buried alive. I would much rather that you went out sometimes.'

'No, mamma; I will remain with you.'

'It will be quite right that you should go to Castle Richmond to-morrow. If they send their carriage round here for you—'

'It'll only be the car.'

'Well, the car; and if the girls come all that way out of their road in the morning to pick you up, it will be only civil that you should go back by Castle Richmond, and you would enjoy an evening there with the girls very much.'

'But I said decidedly that I would not go.'

'Tell them to-morrow as decidedly that you have changed your mind, and will be delighted to accept their invitation. They will understand that it is because you have spoken to me.'

'But, mamma—'

'You will like going; will you not?'

'Yes; I shall like it.'

And so that matter was settled. On the whole, Lady Desmond was inclined to admit within her own heart that her daughter had behaved very well in that matter of the banishment of Owen Fitzgerald. She knew that Clara had never seen him, and had refused to open his letters. Very little had been said upon the subject between the mother and daughter. Once or twice Owen's name had been mentioned; and once, when it had been mentioned, with heavy blame on account of his alleged sins, Clara had ventured to take his part.

'People delight to say ill-natured things,' she had said; 'but one is not obliged to believe them all.'

From that time Lady Desmond had never mentioned his name, rightly judging that Clara would be more likely to condemn him in her own heart if she did not hear him condemned by others : and so the mother and daughter had gone on, as though the former had lost no friend, and the latter had lost no lover.

For some time after the love adventure, Clara had been pale and drooping, and the countess had been frightened about her ; but latterly she had got over this. The misfortune which had fallen so heavily upon them all seemed to have done her good. She had devoted herself from the first to do her little quota of work towards lessening the suffering around her, and the effort had been salutary to her.

Whether or no in her heart of hearts she did still think of Owen Fitzgerald, her mother was unable to surmise. From the fire which had flashed from her eyes on that day when she accused the world of saying ill-natured things of him, Lady Desmond had been sure that such was the case. But she had never ventured to probe her child's heart. She had given very little confidence to Clara, and could not, therefore, and did not expect confidence in return.

Nor was Clara a girl likely in such a matter to bestow confidence on any one. She was one who could hold her heart full, and yet not speak of her heart's fulness. Her mother had called her a child, and in some respects she then was so; but this childishness had been caused, not by lack of mental power, but want of that conversation with others which is customary to girls of her age. This want had in some respects made her childish; for it hindered her from expressing herself in firm tones, and caused her to blush and hesitate when she spoke. But in some respects it had the opposite effect, and made her older than her age, for she was thoughtful, silent, and patient of endurance.

Latterly, since this dreary famine-time had come upon them, an intimacy had sprung up between Clara and the Castle Richmond girls, and in a measure, too, between Clara and Herbert Fitzgerald. Lady Desmond had seen this with great pleasure. Though she had objected to Owen Fitzgerald for her daughter, she had no objection to the Fitzgerald name. Herbert was his father's only son, and heir to the finest property in the county—at any rate, to the property which at present was the best circumstanced. Owen Fitzgerald could never be more than a little squire, but Herbert would be a baronet. Owen's utmost ambition would be to live at Hap House all his life, and die the oracle of the Duhallow hunt; but Herbert would be a member of Parliament, with a house in London. A daughter of the house of Desmond might marry the heir of Sir Thomas Fitzgerald, and be thought to have done well; whereas, she would disgrace herself by becoming the mistress of Hap House. Lady Desmond, therefore, had been delighted to see this intimacy.

It had been in no spirit of fault-finding that she had remarked to her daughter as to her use of that Christian name. What would be better than that they should be to each other as Herbert and Clara? But the cautious mother had known how easy it would be to frighten her timid, fawn-like child. It was no time, no time, as yet, to question her heart about this second lover—if lover he might be. The countess was much too subtle in her way to frighten her child's heart back to its old passion. That passion doubtless would die from want of food. Let it be starved and die; and then this other new passion might spring up.

The Countess of Desmond had no idea that her daughter, with severe self-questioning, had taken her own heart to task about this former lover; had argued with herself that the man who could so sin, could live such a life, and so live in these fearful times, was unworthy of her love, and must be torn out of her heart, let the cost be what it might. Of such high resolves on her daughter's part, nay, on the part of any young girl, Lady Desmond had no knowledge.

Clara Desmond had determined, slowly determined, to give up the man whom she had owned to love. She had determined that duty and female dignity required her to do so. And in this manner it had been done; not by the childlike forgetfulness which her mother attributed to her.

And so it was arranged that she should stay the following night at Castle Richmond.

CHAPTER VIII.

GORTNACLOUGH AND BERRYHILL.

AND now at last we will get to Castle Richmond, at which place, seeing that it gives the title to our novel, we ought to have arrived long since.

As had been before arranged, the two Miss Fitzgeralds did call at Desmond Court early on the following day, and were delighted at being informed by Lady Desmond that Clara had changed her mind, and would, if they would now allow her, stay the night at Castle Richmond.

'The truth was, she did not like to leave me,' said the countess, whispering prettily into the ear of the eldest of the two girls; 'but I am delighted that she should have an opportunity of getting out of this dull place for a few hours. It was so good of you to think of her.'

Miss Fitzgerald made some civil answer, and away they all went. Herbert was on horseback, and remained some minutes after them to discuss her own difficulties with the countess, and to say a few words about that Clady boiler that would not boil. Clara on this subject had opened her heart to him, and he had resolved that the boiler should be made to boil. So he said that he would go over and look at it, resolving also to send that which would be much more efficacious than himself, namely, the necessary means and workmen for bringing about so desirable a result. And then he rode after the girls, and caught the car just as it reached Gortnaclough.

How they all spent their day at the soup-kitchen, which however, though so called, partook quite as much of the character of a bake-house; how they studied the art of making yellow Indian meal into puddings; how the girls wanted to add milk and sugar, not understanding at first the deep principles of political economy, which soon taught them not to waste on the comforts of a few that which was so necessary for the life of many; how the poor women brought in their sick ailing children, accepting the proffered food, but bitterly complaining of it as they took it, —complaining of it because they wanted money, with which they still thought that they could buy potatoes—all this need not here or now be described. Our present business is to get them all back to Castle Richmond.

There had been some talk of their dining at Gortnaclough, because it was known that the ladies at Desmond Court dined early; but now that Clara was to return to Castle Richmond, that idea was given up, and they all got back to the house in time for the family dinner.

'Mamma,' said Emmeline, walking first into the drawing-room, 'Lady Clara has come back with us after all, and is going to stay here to-night; we are so glad!'

Lady Fitzgerald got up from her sofa, and welcomed her young guest with a kiss.

'It is very good of you to come,' she said; 'very good indeed.

You won't find it dull, I hope, because I know you are thinking about the same thing as these children.'

Lady Clara muttered some sort of indistinct little protest as to the impossibility of being dull with her present friends.

'Oh, she's as full of corn meal and pints of soup as any one,' said Emmeline; 'and knows exactly how much turf it takes to boil fifteen stone of pudding; don't you, Clara? But come up-stairs, for we haven't long, and I know you are frozen. You must dress with us, dear; for there will be no fire in your own room, as we didn't expect you.'

'I wish we could get them to like it,' said Clara, standing with one foot on the fender, in the middle of the process of dress-ing, so as to warm her toes; and her friend Emmeline was standing by her, with her arm round her waist.

'I don't think we shall ever do that,' said Mary, who was sitting at the glass brushing her hair; 'it's so cold, and heavy, and uncomfortable when they get it.'

'You see,' said Emmeline, 'though they did only have potatoes before, they always had them quite warm; and though a dinner of potatoes seems very poor, they did have it all together, in their own houses, you know; and I think the very cooking it was some comfort to them.'

'And I suppose they couldn't be taught to cook this them-selves, so as to make it comfortable in their own cabins?' said Clara, despondingly.

'Herbert says it's impossible,' said Mary.

'And I'm sure he knows,' said Clara.

'They would waste more than they would eat,' said Emmeline. 'Besides, it is so hard to cook it as it should be cooked; some-times it seems impossible to make it soft.'

'So it does,' said Clara, sadly; 'but if we could only have it hot for them when they come for it, wouldn't that be better?'

'The great thing is to have it for them at all,' said Mary the wise (for she had been studying the matter more deeply than her friend); 'there are so many who as yet get none.'

'Herbert says that the millers will grind up the husks and all at the mills, so as to make the most of it; that's what makes it so hard to cook,' said Emmeline.

'How very wrong of them!' protested Clara; 'but isn't Her-bert going to have a mill put up of his own?'

And so they went on, till I fear they kept the Castle Richmond dinner waiting for full fifteen minutes.

Castle Richmond, too, would have been a dull house, as Lady Fitzgerald had intimated, had it not been that there was a com-mon subject of such vital interest to the whole party. On that subject they were all intent, and on that subject they talked the whole evening, planning, preparing, and laying out schemes; devising how their money might be made to go furthest; discussing deep questions of political economy, and making, no doubt, many errors in their discussions.

Lady Fitzgerald took a part in all this, and so occasionally did Sir Thomas. Indeed, on this evening he was more active than was usual with him. He got up from his arm-chair, and came to the table, in order that he might pore over the map of the estate with them; for they were dividing the property into districts, and seeing how best the poor might be visited in their own localities.

And then, as he did so, he became liberal. Liberal, indeed, he always was; but now he made offers of assistance more than his son had dared to ask; and they were all busy, contented, and in a great degree joyous—joyous, though their work arose from the contiguity of such infinite misery. But what can ever be more joyous than efforts made for lessening misery?

During all this time Miss Letty was fast asleep in her own arm-chair. But let no one on that account accuse her of a hard heart; for she had nearly walked her old legs off that day in going about from cabin to cabin round the demesne.

'But we must consult Somers about that mill,' said Sir Thomas.

'Oh, of course,' said Herbert; 'I know how to talk Somers over.'

This was added *sotto voce* to his mother and the girls. Now Mr. Somers was the agent on the estate.

This mill was to be at Berryhill, a spot also on Sir Thomas's property, but in a different direction from Gortnaclough. There was there what the Americans would call a water privilege, a stream to which some fall of land just there gave power enough to turn a mill; and it was now a question how they might utilize that power.

During the day just past Clara had been with them, but they were now talking of what they would do when she would have left them. This created some little feeling of awkwardness, for Clara had put her whole heart into the work at Gortnaclough, and it was evident that she would have been so delighted to continue with them.

'But why on earth need you go home to-morrow, Lady Clara?' said Herbert.

'Oh, I must; mamma expects me, you know.'

'Of course we should send word. Indeed, I must send to Clady to-morrow, and the man must pass by Desmond Court gate.'

'Oh, yes, Clara; and you can write a line. It would be such a pity that you should not see all about the mill, now that we have talked it over together. Do tell her to stay, mamma.'

'I am sure I wish she would,' said Lady Fitzgerald. 'Could not Lady Desmond manage to spare you for one day?'

'She is all alone, you know,' said Clara, whose heart, however, was bent on accepting the invitation.

'Perhaps she would come over and join us,' said Lady Fitzgerald, feeling, however, that the subject was not without danger. Sending a carriage for a young girl like Lady Clara did very well, but it might not answer if she were to offer to send for the Countess of Desmond.

'Oh, mamma never goes out.'

'I'm quite sure she'd like you to stay,' said Herbert. 'After you were all gone yesterday, she said how delighted she was to have you go away for a little time. And she did say she thought you could not go to a better place than Castle Richmond.'

'I am sure that was very kind of her,' said Lady Fitzgerald.

'Did she?' said Clara, longingly.

And so after a while it was settled that she should send a line to her mother, saying that she had been persuaded to stay over one other night, and that she should accompany them to inspect the site of this embryo mill at Berryhill.

'And I will write a line to the countess,' said Lady Fitzgerald, 'telling her how impossible it was for you to hold your own intention when we were all attacking you on the other side.'

And so the matter was settled.

On the following day they were to leave home almost immediately after breakfast; and on this occasion Miss Letty insisted on going with them.

'There's a seat on the car, I know, Herbert,' she said; 'for you mean to ride; and I'm just as much interested about the mill as any of you.'

'I'm afraid the day would be too long for you, Aunt Letty,' said Mary: 'we shall stay there, you know, till after four.'

'Not a bit too long. When I'm tired I shall go into Mrs. Townsend's; the glebe is not ten minutes' drive from Berryhill.'

The Rev. Æneas Townsend was the rector of the parish, and he, as well as his wife, were fast friends of Aunt Letty. As we get on in the story we shall, I trust, become acquainted with the Rev. Æneas Townsend and his wife. It was ultimately found that there was no getting rid of Aunt Letty, and so the party was made up.

They were all standing about the hall after breakfast, looking up their shawls and cloaks and coats, and Herbert was in the act of taking special and very suspicious care of Lady Clara's throat, when there came a ring at the door. The visitor, who-ever he might be, was not kept long waiting, for one servant was in the hall, and another just outside the front door with the car, and a third holding Herbert's horse.

'I wish to see Sir Thomas,' said a man's voice as soon as the door was opened; and the man entered the hall, and then seeing that it was full of ladies, retreated again into the doorway. He was an elderly man, dressed almost more than well, for there was about him a slight affectation of dandyism; and though he had for the moment been abashed, there was about him also a slight swagger. 'Good morning, ladies,' he said, re-entering again, and bowing to young Herbert, who stood looking at him; 'I believe Sir Thomas is at home; would you send your servant in to say that a gentleman wants to see him for a minute or so, on very particular business? I am a little in a hurry like.'

The door of the drawing-room was ajar, so that Lady Fitz-gerald, who was sitting there tranquilly in her own seat, could hear the voice. And she did hear it, and knew that some stranger had come to trouble her husband. But she did not come forth; why should she? was not Herbert there—if, indeed, even Herbert could be of any service?

'Shall I take your card into Sir Thomas, sir?' said one of the servants, coming forward.

'Card!' said Mollett senior out loud; 'well, if it is necessary, I believe I have a card.' And he took from his pocket a greasy pocket-book, and extracted from it a piece of pasteboard on which his name was written. 'There; give that to Sir Thomas. I don't think there's much doubt but that he'll see me.' And then, uninvited, he sat himself down in one of the hall chairs.

Sir Thomas's study, the room in which he himself sat, and in which indeed he might almost be said to live at present,—for on many days he only came out to dine, and then again to go to bed, —was at some little distance to the back of the house, and was approached by a passage from the hall. While the servant was gone, the ladies finished their wrapping, and got up on the car.

'Oh, Mr. Fitzgerald,' said Clara, laughing, 'I shan't be able to breathe with all that on me.'

'Look at Mary and Emmeline,' said he; 'they have got twice as much. You don't know how cold it is.'

'You had better have the fur close to your body,' said Aunt Letty; 'look here;' and she showed that her gloves were lined with fur, and her boots, and that she had gotten some nondescript furry article of attire stuck in underneath the body of her dress.

'But you must let me have them a little looser, Mr. Fitzgerald,'
said Clara; 'there, that will do ;' and then they all got upon the
car and started. Herbert was perhaps two minutes after them
before he mounted; but when he left the hall the man was still
sitting there; for the servant had not yet come back from his
father's room.

But the clatter of his horse's hoofs was still distinct enough at
the hall door when the servant did come back, and in a serious
tone desired the stranger to follow him. 'Sir Thomas will see
you,' said the servant, putting some stress on the word will.

'Oh, I did not doubt that the least in the world,' said Mr.
Mollett, as he followed the man along the passage.

The morning was very cold. There had been rainy weather,
but it now appeared to be a settled frost. The roads were rough
and hard, and the man who was driving them said a word now
and again to his young master as to the expediency of getting
frost nails put into the horse's shoes. 'I'd better go gently, Mr.
Herbert; it may be he might come down at some of these
pitches.' So they did go gently, and at last arrived safely at
Berryhill.

And very busy they were there all day. The inspection of
the site for the mill was not their only employment. Here also
was an establishment for distributing food, and a crowd of poor
half-fed wretches were there to meet them. Not that at that
time things were so bad as they became afterwards. Men were
not dying on the road-side, nor as yet had the apathy of want
produced its terrible cure for the agony of hunger. The time
had not yet come when the famished living skeletons might be
seen to reject the food which could no longer serve to prolong
their lives.

Though this had not come as yet, the complaints of the
women with their throngs of children were bitter enough; and
it was heart-breaking too to hear the men declare that they had
worked like horses, and that it was hard upon them now to see
their children starve like dogs. For in this earlier part of the
famine the people did not seem to realize the fact that this
scarcity and want had come from God. Though they saw the
potatoes rotting in their own gardens, under their own eyes, they
still seemed to think that the rich men of the land could stay the
famine if they would; that the fault was with them; that the
famine could be put down if the rich would but stir themselves
to do it. Before it was over they were well aware that no
human power could suffice to put it down. Nay, more than
that; they had almost begun to doubt the power of God to bring
back better days.

They strove, and toiled, and planned, and hoped at Berryhill that day. And infinite was the good that was done by such efforts as these. That they could not hinder God's work we all know ; but much they did do to lessen the sufferings around, and many were the lives that were thus saved.

They were all standing behind the counter of a small store that had been hired in the village—the three girls at least, for Aunt Letty had already gone to the glebe, and Herbert was still down at the 'water privilege,' talking to a millwright and a carpenter. This was a place at which Indian corn flour, that which after a while was generally termed 'meal' in those famine days, was sold to the poor. At this period much of it was absolutely given away. This plan, however, was soon found to be injurious ; for hundreds would get it who were not absolutely in want, and would then sell it ;—for the famine by no means improved the morals of the people.

And therefore it was found better to sell the flour ; to sell it at a cheap rate, considerably less sometimes than the cost price ; and to put the means of buying it into the hands of the people by giving them work, and paying them wages. Towards the end of these times, when the full weight of the blow was understood, and the subject had been in some sort studied, the general rule was thus to sell the meal at its true price, hindering the exorbitant profit of hucksters by the use of large stores, and to require that all those who could not buy it should seek the means of living within the walls of workhouses. The regular established workhouses,—unions as they were called,—were not as yet numerous, but supernumerary houses were provided in every town, and were crowded from the cellars to the roofs.

It need hardly be explained that no general rule could be established and acted upon at once. The numbers to be dealt with were so great, that the exceptions to all rules were overwhelming. But such and such like were the efforts made, and these efforts ultimately were successful.

The three girls were standing behind the counter of a little store which Sir Thomas had hired at Berryhill, when a woman came into the place with two children in her arms and followed by four others of different ages. She was a gaunt tall creature, with sunken cheeks and hollow eyes, and her clothes hung about her in unintelligible rags. There was a crowd before the counter, for those who had been answered or served stood staring at the three ladies, and could hardly be got to go away ; but this woman pressed her way through, pushing some and using harsh language to others, till she stood immediately opposite to Clara.

'Look at that, madam,' she cried, undoing an old handkerchief which she held in her hand, and displaying the contents on the counter ; ' is that what the likes of you calls food for poor people ? is that fit 'ating to give to children ? Would any av ye put such stuff as that into the stomachs of your own bairns ?' and she pointed to the mess which lay revealed upon the handkerchief.

The food as food, was not nice to look at; and could not have been nice to eat, or probably easy of digestion when eaten.

' Feel of that.' And the woman rubbed her forefinger among it to show that it was rough and hard, and that the particles were as sharp as though sand had been mixed with it. The stuff was half-boiled Indian meal, which had been improperly subjected at first to the full heat of boiling water : and in its present state was bad food either for children or grown people. ' Feel of that,' said the woman; ' would you like to be 'ating that yourself now ?'

' I don't think you have cooked it quite enough,' said Clara, looking into the woman's face, half with fear and half with pity, and putting, as she spoke, her pretty delicate finger down into the nasty daubed mess of parboiled yellow flour.

' Cooked it!' said the woman scornfully. ' All the cooking on 'arth wouldn't make food of that fit for a Christian—feel of the roughness of it '—and she turned to another woman who stood near her; ' would you like to be putting sharp points like that into your children's bellies ?'

It was quite true that the grains of it were hard and sharp, so as to give one an idea that it would make good eating neither for women nor children. The millers and dealers, who of course made their profits in these times, did frequently grind up the whole corn without separating the grain from the husks, and the shell of a grain of Indian corn does not, when ground, become soft flour. This woman had reason for her complaints, as had many thousands reason for similar complaints.

' Don't be throubling the ladies, Kitty,' said an old man standing by ; ' sure and weren't you glad enough to be getting it?'

' She'd be axing the ladies to go home wid her and cook it for her after giving it her,' said another.

' Who says it war guv' me ?' said the angry mother. ' Didn't I buy it, here at this counter, with Mike's own hard-'arned money? and it's chaiting us they are. Give me back my money.' And she looked at Clara as though she meant to attack her across the counter.

' Mr. Fitzgerald is going to put up a mill of his own, and then the corn will be better ground,' said Emmeline Fitzgerald, deprecating the woman's wrath.

' Put up a mill !' said the woman, still in scorn. ' Are you going to give me back my money ; or food that my poor bairns can ate ?'

This individual little difficulty was ended by a donation to the angry woman of another lot of meal, in taking away which she was careful not to leave behind her the mess which she had brought in her handkerchief. But she expressed no thanks on being so treated.

The hardest burden which had to be borne by those who exerted themselves at this period was the ingratitude of the poor for whom they worked ;—or rather I should say thanklessness. To call them ungrateful would imply too deep a reproach, for their convictions were that they were being ill used by the upper classes. When they received bad meal which they could not cook, and even in their extreme hunger could hardly eat half-cooked ; when they were desired to leave their cabins and gardens, and flock into the wretched barracks which were prepared for them ; when they saw their children wasting away under a suddenly altered system of diet, it would have been unreasonable to expect that they should have been grateful. Grateful for what? Had they not at any rate a right to claim life, to demand food that should keep them and their young ones alive ? But not the less was it a hard task for delicate women to work hard, and to feel that all their work was unappreciated by those whom they so thoroughly commiserated, whose sufferings they were so anxious to relieve.

It was almost dark before they left Berryhill, and then they had to go out of their way to pick up Aunt Letty at Mr. Townsend's house.

'Don't go in whatever you do, girls,' said Herbert ; 'we should never get away.'

' Indeed we won't unpack ourselves again before we get home ; will we, Clara?'

'Oh, I hope not. I'm very nice now, and so warm. But, Mr. Fitzgerald, is not Mrs. Townsend very queer ?'

' Very queer indeed. But you mustn't say a word about her before Aunt Letty. They are sworn brothers-in-arms.'

' I won't of course. But, Mr. Fitzgerald, she's very good, is she not?'

' Yes, in her way. Only it's a pity she's so prejudiced.'

' You mean about religion ?'

' I mean about everything. If she wears a bonnet on her head, she'll think you very wicked because you wear a hat.'

' Will she? what a very funny woman ! But, Mr. Fitzgerald, I shan't give up my hat, let her say what she will.'

' I should rather think not.'

'And Mr. Townsend? we know him a little; he's very good too, isn't he?'

'Do you mean me to answer you truly, or to answer you according to the good-natured idea of never saying any ill of one's neighbour?'

'Oh, both; if you can.'

'Oh both; must I? Well, then, I think him good as a man, but bad as a clergyman.'

'But I thought he worked so very hard as a clergyman?'

'So he does. But if he works evil rather than good, you can't call him a good clergyman. Mind, you would have my opinion; and if I talk treason and heterodoxy and infidelity and papistry, you must only take it for what it's worth.'

'I'm sure you won't talk infidelity.'

'Nor yet treason; and then, moreover, Mr. Townsend would be so much better a clergyman, to my way of thinking, if he would sometimes brush his hair, and occasionally put on a clean surplice. But, remember, not a word of all this to Aunt Letty.'

'Oh dear, no; of course not.'

Mr. Townsend did come out of the house on the little sweep before the door to help Miss Letty up on the car, though it was dark and piercingly cold.

'Well, young ladies, and won't you come in now and warm yourselves?'

They all of course deprecated any such idea, and declared that they were already much too late.

'Richard, mind you take care going down Ballydahan Hill,' said the parson, giving a not unnecessary caution to the servant. 'I came up it just now, and it was one sheet of ice.'

'Now, Richard, do be careful,' said Miss Letty.

'Never fear, miss,' said Richard.

'We'll take care of you,' said Herbert. 'You're not frightened, Lady Clara, are you?'

'Oh, no,' said Clara; and so they started.

It was quite dark and very cold, and there was a sharp hard frost. But the lamps of the car were lighted, and the horse seemed to be on his mettle, for he did his work well. Ballydahan Hill was not above a mile from the glebe, and descending that, Richard, by his young master's orders, got down from his seat and went to the animal's head. Herbert also himself got off, and led his horse down the hill. At first the girls were a little inclined to be frightened, and Miss Letty found herself obliged to remind them that they couldn't melt the frost by screaming. But they all got safely down, and were soon chattering as fast as though they were already safe in the drawing-room of Castle Richmond.

They went on without any accident, till they reached a turn in the road, about two miles from home; and there, all in a moment, quite suddenly, when nobody was thinking about the frost or the danger, down came the poor horse on his side, his feet having gone quite from under him, and a dreadful cracking sound of broken timber gave notice that a shaft was smashed. A shaft at least was smashed; if only no other harm was done.

It can hardly be that Herbert Fitzgerald cared more for such a stranger as Lady Clara Desmond than he did for his own sisters and aunt; but nevertheless, it was to Lady Clara's assistance that he first betook himself. Perhaps he had seen, or fancied that he saw, that she had fallen with the greatest violence.

'Speak, speak,' said he, as he jumped from his horse close to her side. 'Are you hurt? do speak to me.' And going down on his knees on the hard ground, he essayed to lift her in his arms.

'Oh dear, oh dear!' said she. 'No; I am not hurt; at least I think not—only just my arm a very little. Where is Emmeline? Is Emmeline hurt?'

'No,' said Emmeline, picking herself up. 'But, oh dear, dear, I've lost my muff, and I've spoiled my hat! Where are Mary and Aunt Letty?'

After some considerable confusion it was found that nothing was much damaged except the car, one shaft of which was broken altogether in two. Lady Clara's arm was bruised and rather sore, but the three other ladies had altogether escaped. The quantity of clothes that had been wrapped round them had no doubt enabled them to fall softly.

'And what about the horse, Richard?' asked young Fitzgerald.

'He didn't come upon his knees at all at all, Master Herbert,' said Richard, scrutinizing the animal's legs with the car lamp in his hand. 'I don't think he's a taste the worse. But the car, Master Herbert, is clane smashed.'

Such being found to be undoubtedly the fact, there was nothing for it but that the ladies should walk home. Herbert again forgot that the age of his aunt imperatively demanded all the assistance that he could lend her, and with many lamentations that fortune and the frost should have used her so cruelly, he gave his arm to Clara.

'But do think of Miss Fitzgerald,' said Clara, speaking gently into his ear.

'Who? oh, my aunt. Aunt Letty never cáres for anybody's arm; she always prefers walking alone.'

'Fie, Mr. Fitzgerald, fie! It is impossible to believe such an assertion as that.' And yet Clara did seem to believe it; for she took his proffered arm without further objection.

It was half-past seven when they reached the hall door, and at that time they had all forgotten the misfortune of the car in the fun of the dark frosty walk home. Herbert had found a boy to lead his horse, and Richard was of course left with the ruins in the road.

'And how's your arm now?' asked Herbert, tenderly, as they entered in under the porch.

'Oh, it does not hurt me hardly at all. I don't mind it in the least.' And then the door was opened for them.

They all flocked into the hall, and there they were met by Lady Fitzgerald.

'Oh, mamma,' said Mary, 'I know you're quite rrightened out of your life! But there's nothing the matter. The horse tumbled down; but there's nobody hurt.'

'And we had to walk home from the turn to Ballyclough,' said Emmeline. 'But, oh mamma, what's the matter?' They all now looked up at Lady Fitzgerald, and it was evident enough that something was the matter; something to be thought of infinitely more than that accident on the road.

'Oh, Mary, Mary, what is it?' said Aunt Letty, coming forward and taking hold of her sister-in-law's hand. 'Is my brother ill?'

'Sir Thomas is not very well, and I've been waiting for you so long. Where's Herbert? I must speak to Herbert.' And then the mother and son left the hall together.

There was then a silence among the four ladies that were left there standing. At first they followed each other into the drawing-room, all wrapped up as they were, and sat on chairs apart, saying nothing to each other. At last Aunt Letty got up.

'You had better go up-stairs with Lady Clara,' said she; 'I will go to your mamma.'

'Oh, Aunt Letty, do send us word; pray send us word,' said Emmeline.

Mary now began to cry. 'I know he's very ill. I'm sure he's very ill. Oh, what shall we do?'

'You had better go up-stairs with Lady Clara,' said Aunt Letty. 'I will send you up word immediately.'

'Oh, don't mind me; pray don't mind me,' said Clara. 'Pray, pray, don't take notice of me;' and she rushed forward, and throwing herself on her knees before Emmeline, began to kiss her.

They remained here, heedless of Aunt Letty's advice, for some ten minutes, and then Herbert came to them. The two girls flew at him with questions; while Lady Clara stood by the window, anxious to learn, but unwilling to thrust herself into their family matters.

'My father has been much troubled to-day, and is not well,' said Herbert. 'But I do not think there is anything to frighten us. Come; let us go to dinner.'

The going to dinner was but a sorry farce with any of them; but nevertheless, they went through the ceremony, each for the sake of the others.

'Mayn't we see him?' said the girls to their mother, who did come down into the drawing-room for one moment to speak to Clara.

'Not to-night, loves. He should not be disturbed.' And so that day came to an end; not satisfactorily.

CHAPTER IX.

FAMILY COUNCILS.

WHEN the girls and Aunt Letty went to their chambers that night, Herbert returned to his mother's own dressing-room, and there, seated over the fire with her, discussed the matter of his father's sudden attack. He had been again with his father, and Sir Thomas had seemed glad to have him there; but now he had left him for the night.

'He will sleep now, mother,' said the son; 'he has taken laudanum.'

'I fear he takes that too often now.'

'It was good for him to have it to-night. He did not get too much, for I dropped it for him.' And then they sat silent for a few moments together.

'Mother,' said Herbert, 'who can this man have been?'

'I have no knowledge—no idea—no guess even,' said Lady Fitzgerald.

'It is that man's visit that has upset him.'

'Oh, certainly. I think there is no doubt of that. I was waiting for the man to go, and went in almost before he was out of the house.'

'Well?'

'And I found your father quite prostrated.'

'Not on the floor?'

'No, not exactly on the floor. He was still seated on his chair, but his head was on the table, over his arms.'

'I have often found him in that way, mother.'

'But you never saw him looking as he looked this morning, Herbert. When I went in he was speechless, and he remained so, I should say, for some minutes.'

'Was he senseless?'

'No; he knew me well enough, and grasped me by the hand; and when I would have gone to the bell to ring for assistance, he would not let me. I thought he would have gone into a fit when I attempted it.'

'And what did you do?'

'I sat there by him, with his hand in mine, quite quietly And then he uttered a long, deep sigh, and—oh, Herbert!'

'Well, mother?'

'At last, he burst into a flood of tears, and sobbed and cried like a child.'

'Mother!'

'He did, so that it was piteous to see him. But it did him good, for he was better after it. And all the time he never let go my hand, but held it and kissed it. And then he took me by the waist, and kissed me, oh, so often. And all the while his tears were running like the tears of a girl.' And Lady Fitzgerald, as she told the story, could not herself refrain from weeping.

'And did he say anything afterwards about this man?'

'Yes; not at first, that is. Of course I asked him who he was as soon as I thought he could bear the question. But he turned away, and merely said that he was a stupid man about some old London business, and that he should have gone to Prendergast. But when, after a while, I pressed him, he said that the man's name was Mollett, and that he had, or pretended to have, some claim upon the city property.'

'A claim on the city property! Why, it's not seven hundred a year altogether. If any Mollett could run away with it all, that loss would not affect him like that.'

'So I said, Herbert; not exactly in those words, but trying to comfort him. He then put it off by declaring that it was the consciousness of his inability to see any one on business which affected him so grievously.'

'It was that he said to me.'

'And there may be something in that, Herbert.'

'Yes; but then what should make him so weak, to begin with? If you remember, mother, he was very well,—more like himself than usual last night.'

'Oh, I observed it. He seemed to like having Clara Desmond there.'

'Didn't he, mother? I observed that too. But then Clara Desmond is such a sweet creature.' The mother looked at her son as he said this, but the son did not notice the look. 'I do wonder what the real truth can be,' he continued. 'Do you think there is anything wrong about the property in general? About this estate, here?'

'No, I don't think that,' said the mother, sadly.

'What can it be then?' But Lady Fitzgerald sat there, and did not answer the question. 'I'll tell you what I will do, mother; I'll go up to London, and see Prendergast, and consult him.'

'Oh, no; you mustn't do that. I am wrong to tell you all this, for he told me to talk to no one. But it would kill me if I didn't speak of it to you.'

'All the same, mother; I think it would be best to consult Prendergast.'

'Not yet, Herbert. I dare say Mr. Prendergast may be a very good sort of man, but we none of us know him. And if, as is very probable, this is only an affair of health, it would be wrong in you to go to a stranger. It might look——'

'Look what, mother?'

'People might think——he, I mean—that you wanted to interfere.'

'But who ought to interfere on his behalf if I don't?'

'Quite true, dearest; I understand what you mean, and know how good you are. But perhaps Mr. Prendergast might not. He might think you wanted——'

'Wanted what, mother? I don't understand you.'

'Wanted to take the things out of your father's hands.'

'Oh, mother!'

'He doesn't know you. And, what is more, I don't think he knows much of your father. Don't go to him yet.' And Herbert promised that he would not.

'And you don't think that this man was ever here before?' he asked.

'Well, I rather think he was here once before; many years ago—soon after you went to school.'

'So long ago as that?'

'Yes; not that I remember him, or, indeed, ever knew of his coming then, if he did come. But Jones says that she thinks she remembers him.'

'Did Jones see him now?'

'Yes; she was in the hall as he passed through on his way out. And it so happened that she let him in and out too when he came before. That is, if it is the same man.'

'That's very odd.'

'It did not happen here. We were at Tenby for a few weeks in the summer.'

'I remember; you went there with the girls just when I went back to school.'

'Jones was with us, and Richard. We had none other of our own servants. And Jones says that the same man did come then; that he stayed with your father for an hour or two; and that when he left, your father was depressed—almost as he was yesterday. I well remember that. I know that a man did come to him at Tenby; and—oh, Herbert!'

'What is it, mother? Speak out at any rate to me.'

'Since that man came to him at Tenby he has never been like what he was before.'

And then there was more questioning between them about Jones and her remembrances. It must be explained that Jones was a very old and very valued servant. She had originally been brought up as a child by Mrs. Wainwright, in that Dorsetshire parsonage, and had since remained firm to the fortunes of the young lady, whose maid she had become on her first marriage. As her mistress had been promoted, so had Jones. At first she had been Kitty to all the world, now she was Mrs. Jones to the world at large, Jones to Sir Thomas and her mistress and of late years to Herbert, and known by all manner of affectionate sobriquets to the young ladies. Sometimes they would call her Johnny, and sometimes the Duchess; but doubtless they and Mrs. Jones thoroughly understood each other. By the whole establishment Mrs. Jones was held in great respect, and by the younger portion in extreme awe. Her breakfast and tea she had in a little sitting-room by herself; but the solitude of this was too tremendous for her to endure at dinner-time. At that meal she sat at the head of the table in the servants' hall, though she never troubled herself to carve anything except puddings and pies, for which she had a great partiality, and of which she was supposed to be the most undoubted and severe judge known of anywhere in that part of the country.

She was supposed by all her brother and sister servants to be a very Crœsus for wealth; and wondrous tales were told of the money she had put by. But as she was certainly honest, and supposed to be very generous to certain poor relations in Dorsetshire, some of these stories were probably mythic. It was known, however, as a fact, that two Castle Richmond butlers, one out-door steward, three neighbouring farmers, and one wickedly ambitious coachman, had endeavoured to tempt her to matrimony—in vain. 'She didn't want none of them,' she told her mistress. 'And, what was more, she wouldn't have none of them.' And therefore she remained Mrs. Jones, with brevet rank.

It seemed, from what Lady Fitzgerald said, that Mrs. Jones's manner had been somewhat mysterious about this man, Mollett. She had endeavoured to reassure and comfort her mistress, saying that nothing would come of it as nothing had come of that other Tenby visit, and giving it as her counsel that the ladies should allow the whole matter to pass by without further notice. But at the same time Lady Fitzgerald had remarked that her manner had been very serious when she first said that she had seen the man before.

'Jones,' Lady Fitzgerald had said to her, very earnestly, 'if you know more about this man than you are telling me, you are bound to speak out, and let me know everything.'

'Who—I, my lady? what could I know? Only he do look to me like the same man, and so I thought it right to say to your ladyship.'

Lady Fitzgerald had seen that there was nothing more to be gained by cross-questioning, and so she had allowed the matter to drop. But she was by no means satisfied that this servant whom she so trusted did not know more than she had told. And then Mrs. Jones had been with her in those dreadful Dorsetshire days, and an undefined fear began to creep over her very soul.

'God bless you, my child!' said Lady Fitzgerald, as her son got up to leave her. And then she embraced him with more warmth even than was her wont. 'All that we can do at present is to be gentle with him, and not to encourage people around him to talk of his illness.'

On the next morning Lady Fitzgerald did not come down to breakfast, but sent her love to Clara, and begged her guest to excuse her on account of headache. Sir Thomas rarely came in to breakfast, and therefore his absence was not remarkable. His daughters, however, went up to see him, as did also his sister; and they all declared that he was very much better.

'It was some sudden attack, I suppose?' said Clara.

'Yes, very sudden; he has had the same before,' said Herbert. 'But they do not at all affect his intellect or bodily powers. Depression is, I suppose, the name that the doctors would call it.'

And then at last it became noticeable by them that Lady Clara did not use her left arm. 'Oh, Clara!' said Emmeline, 'I see now that you are hurt. How selfish we have been! Oh

dear, oh dear!' And both Emmeline and Mary immediately
surrounded her, examining her arm, and almost carrying her to
the sofa.

'I don't think it will be much,' said Clara. 'It's only a little
stiff.'

'Oh, Herbert, what shall we do? Do look here; the inside
of her arm is quite black.'

Herbert, gently touching her hand, did examine the arm, and
declared his opinion that she had received a dreadfully violent
blow. Emmeline proposed to send for a doctor to pronounce
whether or no it were broken. Mary said that she didn't think
it was broken, but that she was sure the patient ought not to be
moved that day, or probably for a week. Aunt Letty, in the
mean time, prescribed a cold-water bandage with great authority,
and bounced out of the room to fetch the necessary linen and
basin of water.

'It's nothing at all,' continued Clara. 'And indeed I shall go
home to-day; indeed I shall.'

'It might be very bad for your arm that you should be moved,'
said Herbert.

'And your staying here will not be the least trouble to us.
We shall all be so happy to have you; shall we not, Mary?'

'Of course we shall; and so will mamma.'

'I am so sorry to be here now,' said Clara, 'when I know you
are all in such trouble about Sir Thomas. But as for going,
I shall go as soon as ever you can make it convenient to send
me. Indeed I shall.' And so the matter was discussed between
them, Aunt Letty in the mean time binding up the bruised arm
with cold-water appliances.

Lady Clara was quite firm about going, and, therefore, at
about twelve she was sent. I should say taken, for Emmeline
insisted on going with her in the carriage. Herbert would have
gone also, but he felt that he ought not to leave Castle Richmond that day, on account of his father. But he would certainly ride over, he said, and learn how her arm was the next
morning.

'And about Clady, you know,' said Clara.

'I will go on to Clady also. I did send a man there yesterday to see about the flue. It's the flue that's wrong, I know.'

'Oh, thank you; I am so much obliged to you,' said Clara.
And then the carriage drove off, and Herbert returned into the
morning sitting-room with his sister Mary.

'I'll tell you what it is, Master Herbert,' said Mary.

'Well—what is it?'

'You are going to fall in love with her young ladyship.'

'Am I? Is that all you know about it? And who are you going to fall in love with pray?'

'Oh! his young lordship, perhaps; only he ought to be about ten years older, so that I'm afraid that wouldn't do. But Clara is just the age for you. It really seems as though it were all prepared ready to your hand.'

'You girls always do think that those things are ready prepared;' and so saying, Herbert walked off with great manly dignity to some retreat among his own books and papers, there to meditate whether this thing were in truth prepared for him. It certainly was the fact that the house did seem very blank to him now that Clara was gone; and that he looked forward with impatience to the visit which it was so necessary that he should make on the following day to Clady.

The house at Castle Richmond was very silent and quiet that day. When Emmeline came back, she and her sister remained together. Nothing had been said to them about Mollett's visit, and they had no other idea than that this lowness of spirits on their father's part, to which they had gradually become accustomed, had become worse and more dangerous to his health than ever.

Aunt Letty talked much about it to Herbert, to Lady Fitzgerald, to Jones, and to her brother, and was quite certain that she had penetrated to the depth of the whole matter. That nasty city property, she said, which had come with her grandmother, had always given the family more trouble than it was worth. Indeed, her grandmother had been a very troublesome woman altogether; and no wonder, for though she was a Protestant herself, she had had Papist relations in Lancashire. She distinctly remembered to have heard that there was some flaw in the title of that property, and she knew that it was very hard to get some of the tenants to pay any rent. That she had always heard. She was quite sure that this man was some person laying a claim to it, and threatening to prosecute his claim at law. It was a thousand pities that her brother should allow such a trifle as this—for after all it was but a trifle—to fret his spirits and worry him in this way. But it was the wretched state of his health: were he once himself again, all such annoyances as that would pass him by like the wind.

It must be acknowledged that Aunt Letty's memory in this respect was not exactly correct; for, as it happened, Sir Thomas held his little property in the city of London by as firm a tenure as the laws and customs of his country could give him; and seeing that his income thence arising came from ground rents near the river, on which property stood worth some hundreds of thousands, it was not very probable that his tenants should be in arrear. But what she said had some effect upon Herbert. He was not quite sure whether this might not be the cause of his father's grief; and if the story did not have much effect upon Lady Fitzgerald, at any rate it did as well as any other to exercise the ingenuity and affection of Aunt Letty.

Sir Thomas passed the whole of that day in his own room; but during a great portion of the day either his wife, or sister, or son was with him. They endeavoured not to leave him alone with his own thoughts, feeling conscious that something preyed upon his mind, though ignorant as to what that something might be.

He was quite aware of the nature of their thoughts; perfectly conscious of the judgment they had formed respecting him. He knew that he was subjecting himself, in the eyes not only of his own family but of all those around him, to suspicions which must be injurious to him, and yet he could not shake off the feeling that depressed him.

But at last he did resolve to make an attempt at doing so. For some time in the evening he was altogether alone, and he then strove to force his mind to work upon the matter which occupied it,—to arrange his ideas, and bring himself into a state in which he could make a resolution. For hours he had sat,—not thinking upon this subject, for thought is an exertion which requires a combination of ideas and results in the deducing of conclusions from premises; and no such effort as that had he hitherto made,—but endeavouring to think while he allowed the matter of his grief to lie ever before his mind's eye.

He had said to himself, over and over again, that it behoved him to make some great effort to shake off this incubus that depressed him; but yet no such effort had hitherto been even attempted. Now at last he arose and shook himself, and promised to himself that he would be a man. It might be that the misfortune under which he groaned was heavy, but let one's sorrow be what it may, there is always a better and a worse way of meeting it. Let what trouble may fall on a man's shoulders, a man may always bear it manfully. And are not troubles when so borne half cured? It is the flinching from pain which makes pain so painful.

This truth came home to him as he sat there that day, thinking what he should do, endeavouring to think in what way he might best turn himself. But there was this that was especially grievous to him, that he had no friend whom he might consult in this matter. It was a sorrow, the cause of which he could not explain to his own family, and in all other troubles he had sought assistance and looked for counsel there and there only. He had had one best, steadiest, dearest, truest counsellor, and now it had come to pass that things were so placed that in this great trouble he could not go to her.

And now a friend was so necessary to him! He felt that he was not fit to judge how he himself should act in this terrible emergency; that it was absolutely necessary for him that he should allow himself to be guided by some one else. But to whom should he appeal?

'He is a cold man,' said he to himself, as one name did occur to him, 'very cold, almost unfeeling; but he is honest and just.' And then again he sat and thought. 'Yes, he is honest and just; and what should I want better than honesty and justice?' And then, shuddering as he resolved, he did resolve that he would send for this honest and just man. He would send for him; or, perhaps better still, go to him. At any rate, he would tell him the whole truth of his grief, and then act as the cold, just man should bid him.

But he need not do this yet—not quite yet. So at least he said to himself, falsely. If a man decide with a fixed decision that his tooth should come out, or his leg be cut off, let the tooth come out or the leg be cut off on the earliest possible opportunity. It is the flinching from such pain that is so grievously painful.

But it was something to have brought his mind to bear with a fixed purpose upon these things, and to have resolved upon what he would do, though he still lacked strength to put his resolution immediately to the proof.

Then, later in the evening, his son came and sat with him, and he was able in some sort to declare that the worst of that evil day had passed from him. 'I shall breakfast with you all to-morrow,' he said, and as he spoke a faint smile passed across his face.

'Oh! I hope you will,' said Herbert; 'we shall be so delighted; but, father, do not exert yourself too soon.'

'It will do me good, I think.'

'I am sure it will, if the fatigue be not too much.'

'The truth is, Herbert, I have allowed this feeling to grow upon me till I have become weak under it. I know that I ought to make an exertion to throw it off, and it is possible that I may succeed.'

Herbert muttered some few hopeful words, but he found it very difficult to know what he ought to say. That his father had some secret he was quite sure; and it is hard to talk to a man about his secret, without knowing what that secret is.

'I have allowed myself to fall into a weak state,' continued Sir Thomas, speaking slowly, 'while by proper exertion I might have avoided it.'

'You have been very ill, father,' said Herbert.

'Yes, I have been ill, very ill, certainly. But I do not know that any doctor could have helped me.'

'Father——'

'No, Herbert; do not ask me questions; do not inquire; at any rate, not at present. I will endeavour—now at least I will endeavour—to do my duty. But do not urge me by questions, or appear to notice me if I am infirm.'

'But, father,—if we could comfort you?'

'Ah! if you could. But, never mind, I will endeavour to shake off this depression. And, Herbert, comfort your mother; do not let her think much of all this, if it can be helped.?'

'But how can it be helped?'

'And tell her this: there is a matter that troubles my mind.'

'Is it about the property, father?'

'No—yes; it certainly is about the property in one sense.'

'Then do not heed it; we shall none of us heed it. Who has so good a right to say so as I?'

'Bless you, my darling boy! But, Herbert, such things must be heeded—more or less, you know: but you may tell your mother this, and perhaps it may comfort her. I have made up my mind to go to London and to see Prendergast; I will explain the whole of this thing to him, and as he bids me so will I act.'

This was thought to be satisfactory to a certain extent both by the mother and son. They would have been better pleased had he opened his heart to them and told them everything; but that it was clear he could not bring himself to do. This Mr. Prendergast, they had heard, was a good man; and in his present state it was better that he should seek counsel of any man than allow his sorrow to feed upon himself alone.

CHAPTER X.

THE RECTOR OF DRUMBARROW AND HIS WIFE.

HERBERT FITZGERALD, in speaking of the Rev. Æneas Townsend to Lady Clara Desmond, had said that in his opinion the reverend gentleman was a good man, but a bad clergyman. But there were not a few in the county Cork who would have said just the reverse, and declared him to be a bad man, but a good clergyman. There were others, indeed, who knew him well, who would have declared him to be perfect in both respects, and others again who thought him in both respects to be very bad. Amidst these great diversities of opinion I will venture on none of my own, but will attempt to describe him.

In Ireland stanch Protestantism consists too much in a hatred of Papistry—in that rather than in a hatred of those errors against which we Protestants are supposed to protest. Hence the cross—which should, I presume, be the emblem of salvation to us all—creates a feeling of dismay and often of disgust instead of love and reverence ; and the very name of a saint savours in Irish Protestant ears of idolatry, although Irish Protestants on every Sunday profess to believe in a communion of such. These are the feelings rather than the opinions of the most Protestant of Irish Protestants, and it is intelligible that they should have been produced by the close vicinity of Roman Catholic worship in the minds of men who are energetic and excitable, but not always discreet or argumentative.

One of such was Mr. Townsend, and few men carried their Protestant fervour further than he did. A cross was to him what a red cloth is supposed to be to a bull ; and so averse was he to the intercession of saints, that he always regarded as a wolf in sheep's clothing a certain English clergyman who had written to him a letter dated from the feast of St. Michael and All Angels. On this account Herbert Fitzgerald took upon himself to say that he regarded him as a bad clergyman : whereas, most of his Protestant neighbours looked upon this enthusiasm as his chief excellence.

And this admiration for him induced his friends to overlook what they must have acknowledged to be defects in his character. Though he had a good living—at least, what the laity in speaking of clerical incomes is generally inclined to call a good living, we will say amounting in value to four hundred pounds a year— he was always in debt. This was the more inexcusable as he had no children, and had some small private means.

And nobody knew why he was in debt—in which word nobody he himself must certainly be included. He had no personal expenses of his own ; his wife, though she was a very queer woman, as Lady Clara had said, could hardly be called an extravagant woman ; there was nothing large or splendid about the way of living at the glebe ; anybody who came there, both he and she were willing to feed as long as they chose to stay, and a good many in this way they did feed ; but they never invited guests ; and as for giving regular fixed dinner-parties, as parish

rectors do in England, no such idea ever crossed the brain of
either Mr. or Mrs. Townsend.

That they were both charitable all the world admitted; and
their admirers professed that hence arose all their difficulties.
But their charities were of a most indiscreet kind. Money they
rarely had to give, and therefore they would give promises to
pay. While their credit with the butcher and baker was good
they would give meat and bread; and both these functionaries
had by this time learned that, though Mr. Townsend might not
be able to pay such bills himself, his friends would do so, sooner
or later, if duly pressed. And therefore the larder at Drumbarrow
Glebe—that was the name of the parish—was never long empty,
and then again it was never long full.

But neither Mr. nor Mrs. Townsend were content to bestow
their charities without some other object than that of relieving
material wants by their alms. Many infidels, Mr. Townsend
argued, had been made believers by the miracle of the loaves
and fishes; and therefore it was permissible for him to make use
of the same means for drawing over proselytes to the true church.
If he could find hungry Papists and convert them into well-fed
Protestants by one and the same process, he must be doing a
double good, he argued;—could by no possibility be doing an
evil.

Such being the character of Mr. Townsend, it will not be
thought surprising that he should have his warm admirers and
his hot detractors. And they who were inclined to be among
the latter were not slow to add up certain little disagreeable
eccentricities among the list of his faults,—as young Fitzgerald
had done in the matter of the dirty surplices.

Mr. Townsend's most uncompromising foe for many years had
been the Rev. Bernard M'Carthy, the parish priest for the same
parish of Drumbarrow. Father Bernard, as he was called by his
own flock, or Father Barney, as the Protestants in derision were
delighted to name him, was much more a man of the world than
his Protestant colleague. He did not do half so many absurd
things as did Mr. Townsend, and professed to laugh at what he
called the Protestant madness of the rector. But he also had
been an eager, I may also say, a malicious antagonist. What he
called the 'souping' system of the Protestant clergyman stank in
his nostrils—that system by which, as he stated, the most ignorant of men were to be induced to leave their faith by the hope
of soup, or other food. He was as firmly convinced of the inward,
heart-destroying iniquity of the parson as the parson was of that
of the priest. And so these two men had learned to hate each
other. And yet neither of them were bad men.

I do not wish it to be understood that this sort of feeling always prevailed in Irish parishes between the priest and the parson even before the days of the famine. I myself have met a priest at a parson's table, and have known more than one parish in which the Protestant and Roman Catholic clergymen lived together on amicable terms. But such a feeling as that above represented was common, and was by no means held as proof that the parties themselves were quarrelsome or malicious. It was a part of their religious convictions, and who dares to interfere with the religious convictions of a clergyman?

On the day but one after that on which the Castle Richmond ladies had been thrown from their car on the frosty road, Mr. Townsend and Father Bernard were brought together in an amicable way, or in a way that was intended to be amicable, for the first time in their lives. The relief committee for the district in which they both lived was one and the same, and it was of course well that both should act on it. When the matter was first arranged, Father Bernard took the bull by the horns and went there; but Mr. Townsend, hearing this, did not do so. But now that it had become evident that much work, and for a long time, would have to be performed at these committees, it was clear that Mr. Townsend, as a Protestant clergyman, could not remain away without neglecting his duty. And so, after many mental struggles and questions of conscience, the parson agreed to meet the priest.

The point had been very deeply discussed between the rector and his wife. She had given it as her opinion that priest M'Carthy was pitch, pitch itself in its blackest turpitude, and as such could not be touched without defilement. Had not all the Protestant clergymen of Ireland in a body, or, at any rate, all those who were worth anything, who could with truth be called Protestant clergymen, had they not all refused to enter the doors of the National schools because they could not do so without sharing their ministration there with papist priests; with priests of the altar of Baal, as Mrs. Townsend called them? And should they now yield, when, after all, the assistance needed was only for the body—not for the soul?

It may be seen from this that the lady's mind was not in its nature logical; but the extreme absurdity of her arguments, though they did not ultimately have the desired effect, by no means came home to the understanding of her husband. He thought that there was a great deal in what she said, and almost felt that he was yielding to instigations from the evil one; but public opinion was too strong for him; public opinion and the innate kindness of his own heart. He felt that at this very moment he ought to labour specially for the bodies of these poor people, as at other times he would labour specially for their souls; and so he yielded.

'Well,' said his wife to him as he got off his car' at his own door after the meeting, 'what have you done?' One might have imagined from her tone of voice and her manner that she expected, or at least hoped to hear that the priest had been absolutely exterminated and made away with in the good fight.

Mr. Townsend made no immediate answer, but proceeded to divest himself of his rusty outside coat, and to rub up his stiff, grizzled, bristly, uncombed hair with both his hands, as was his wont when he was not quite satisfied with the state of things.

'I suppose he was there?' said Mrs. Townsend.

''Oh, yes, he was there. He is never away, I take it, when there is any talking to be done.' Now Mr. Townsend dearly loved to hear himself talk, but no man was louder against the sins of other orators. And then he began to ask how many minutes it wanted to dinner-time.

Mrs. Townsend knew his ways. She would not have a ghost of a chance of getting from him a true and substantial account of what had really passed if she persevered in direct questions to the effect. So she pretended to drop the matter, and went and fetched her lord's slippers, the putting on of which constituted his evening toilet; and then, after some little hurrying inquiry in the kitchen, promised him his dinner in fifteen minutes.

'Was Herbert Fitzgerald there?'

'Oh yes; he is always there. He's a nice young fellow; a very fine young fellow; but——'

'But what?'

'He thinks he understands the Irish Roman Catholics, but he understands them no more than—than—than this slipper,' he said, having in vain cudgelled his brain for a better comparison.

''You know what Aunt Letty says about him. She doubts he isn't quite right, you know.'

Mrs. Townsend by this did not mean to insinuate that Herbert was at all afflicted in that way which we attempt to designate, when we say that one of our friends is not all right, and at the same time touch our heads with our forefinger. She had intended to convey an impression that the young man's religious ideas were not exactly of that stanch, true-blue description which she admired.

'Well, he has just come from Oxford, you know,' said Mr. Townsend: 'and at the present moment Oxford is the most dangerous place to which a young man can be sent.'

'And Sir Thomas would send him there, though I remember

telling his aunt over and over again how it would be.' And Mrs. Townsend as she spoke, shook her head sorrowfully.

'I don't mean to say, you know, that he's absolutely bitten.'

'Oh, I know—I understand. When they come to crossings and candlesticks, the next step to the glory of Mary is a very easy one. I would sooner send a young man to Rome than to Oxford. At the one he might be shocked and disgusted; but at the other he is cajoled, and cheated, and ruined.' And then Mrs. Townsend threw herself back in her chair, and threw her eyes up towards the ceiling.

But there was no hypocrisy or pretence in this expression of her feelings. She did in her heart of hearts believe that there was some college or club of papists at Oxford, emissaries of the Pope or of the Jesuits. In her moments of sterner thought the latter were the enemies she most feared; whereas, when she was simply pervaded by her usual chronic hatred of the Irish Roman Catholic hierarchy, she was wont to inveigh most against the Pope. And this college, she maintained was fearfully successful in drawing away the souls of young English students. Indeed, at Oxford a man had no chance against the devil. Things were better at Cambridge; though even there there was great danger. Look at A—— and Z——; and she would name two perverts to the Church of Rome, of whom she had learned that they were Cambridge men. But, thank God, Trinity College still stood firm. Her idea was, that if there were left any real Protestant truth in the Church of England, that Church should look to feed her lambs by the hands of shepherds chosen from that seminary, and from that seminary only.

'But isn't dinner nearly ready?' said Mr. Townsend, whose ideas were not so exclusively Protestant as were those of his wife. 'I haven't had a morsel since breakfast.' And then his wife, who was peculiarly anxious to keep him in a good humour that all might come out about Father Barney, made another little visit to the kitchen.

At last the dinner was served. The weather was very cold, and the rector and his wife considered it more cosy to use only the parlour, and not to migrate into the cold air of a second room. Indeed, during the winter months the drawing-room of Drumbarrow Glebe was only used for visitors, and for visitors who were not intimate enough in the house to be placed upon the worn chairs and threadbare carpet of the dining-parlour. And very cold was that drawing-room found to be by each visitor.

But the parlour was warm enough; warm and cosy, though perhaps at times a little close; and of evenings there would pervade it a smell of whisky punch, not altogether acceptable to unaccustomed nostrils. Not that the rector of Drumbarrow was by any means an intemperate man. His single tumbler of whisky toddy, repeated only on Sundays and some other rare occasions, would by no means equal, in point of drinking, the ordinary port of an ordinary English clergyman. But whisky punch does leave behind a savour of its intrinsic virtues, delightful no doubt to those who have imbibed its grosser elements, but not equally acceptable to others who may have been less fortunate.

During dinner there was no conversation about Herbert Fitzgerald, or the committee, or Father Barney. The old gardener, who waited at table with all his garden clothes on him, and whom the neighbours, with respectful deference, called Mr. Townsend's butler, was a Roman Catholic; as, indeed, were all the servants at the glebe, and as are, necessarily, all the native servants in that part of the country. And though Mr. and Mrs. Townsend put great trust in their servant Jerry as to the ordinary duties of gardening, driving, and butlering, they would not knowingly trust him with a word of their habitual conversation about the things around them. Their idea was, that every word so heard was carried to the priest, and that the priest kept a book in which every word so uttered was written down. If this were so through the parish, the priest must in truth have had something to do, both for himself and his private secretary; for, in spite of all precautions that were taken, Jerry and Jerry's brethren no doubt did hear much of what was said. The repetitions to the priest, however, I must take leave to doubt.

But after dinner, when the hot water and whisky were on the table, when the two old arm-chairs were drawn cosily up on the rug, each with an old footstool before it; when the faithful wife had mixed that glass of punch—or jug rather, for, after the old fashion, it was brewed in such a receptacle; and when, to inspire increased confidence, she had put into it a small extra modicum of the eloquent spirit, then the mouth of the rector was opened, and Mrs. Townsend was made happy.

'And so Father Barney and I have met at last,' said he, rather cheerily, as the hot fumes of the toddy regaled his nostrils.

'And how did he behave now?'

'Well, he was decent enough—that 'is, as far as absolute behaviour went. You can't have a silk purse from off a sow's ear, you know.'

'No, indeed; and goodness knows there's plenty of the sow's ear about him. But now, Æneas, dear, do tell me how it all was, just from the beginning.'

'He was there before me,' said the husband.

'Catch a weasel asleep!' said the wife.

'I didn't catch him asleep at any rate,' continued he. 'He was there before me; but when I went into the little room where they hold the meeting——'

'It's at Berryhill, isn't it?'

'Yes, at the Widow Casey's. To see that woman bowing and scraping and curtsying to Father Barney, and she his own mother's brother's daughter, was the best thing in the world.'

'That was just to do him honour before the quality, you know.'

'Exactly. When I went in, there was nobody there but his reverence and Master Herbert.'

'As thick as possible, I suppose. Dear, dear; isn't it dreadful?——Did I put sugar enough in it, Æneas?'

'Well, I don't know; perhaps you may give me another small lump. At any rate, you didn't forget the whisky.'

'I'm sure it isn't a taste too strong—and after such work as you've had to-day.——And so young Fitzgerald and Father Barney——'

'Yes, there they were with their heads together. It was something about a mill they were saying.'

'Oh, it's perfectly dreadful!'

'But Herbert stopped, and introduced me at once to Father Barney.'

'What! a regular introduction? I like that, indeed.'

'He didn't do it altogether badly. He said something about being glad to see two gentlemen together——'

'A gentleman, indeed!'

'——who were both so anxious to do the best they could in the parish, and whose influence was so great—or something to that effect. And then we shook hands.'

'You did shake hands?'

'Oh, yes; if I went there at all, it was necessary that I should do that.'

'I'm very glad it was not me, that's all. I don't think I could shake hands with Father Barney.'

'There's no knowing what you can do, my dear, till you try.'

'H—m,' said Mrs. Townsend, meaning to signify thereby that she was still strong in the strength of her own impossibilities.

'And then there was a little general conversation about the potato, for no one came in for a quarter of an hour or so. The priest said that they were as badly off in Limerick and Clare as we are here. Now, I don't believe that; and when I asked him how he knew, he quoted the "Freeman."'

'The "Freeman," indeed! Just like him. I wonder it wasn't

the "Nation."' In Mrs. Townsend's estimation, the parish priest was much to blame because he did not draw his public information from some newspaper specially addicted to the support of the Protestant cause.

'And then Somers came in, and he took the chair. I was very much afraid at one time that Father Barney was going to seat himself there.'

'You couldn't possibly have stood that?'

'I had made up my mind what to do. I should have walked about the room, and looked on the whole affair as altogether irregular,—as though there was no chairman. But Somers was of course the proper man.'

'And who else came?'

'There was O'Leary, from Boherbue.'

'He was another Papist?'

'Oh, yes; there was a majority of them. There was Greilly, the man who has got that large take of land over beyond Banteer; and then Father Barney's coadjutor came in.'

'What! that wretched-looking man from Gortnaclough?'

'Yes; he's the curate of the parish, you know.'

'And did you shake hands with him too?'

'Indeed I did; and you never saw a fellow look so ashamed of himself in your life.'

'Well, there isn't much shame about them generally.'

'And there wasn't much about him by-and-by. You never heard a man talk such trash in your life, till Somers put him down.'

'Oh, he was put down? I'm glad of that.'

'And to do Father Barney justice, he did tell him to hold his tongue. The fool began to make a regular set speech.'

'Father Barney, I suppose, didn't choose that anybody should do that but himself.'

'He did enough for the two, certainly. I never heard a man so fond of his own voice. What he wants is to rule it all just his own way.'

'Of course he does; and that's just what you won't let him do. What other reason can there be for your going there?'

And so the matter was discussed. What absolute steps were taken by the committee; how they agreed to buy so much meal of such a merchant, at such a price, and with such funds; how it was to be resold, and never given away on any pretext; how Mr. Somers had explained that giving away their means was killing the goose that laid the golden eggs, when the young priest, in an attitude for oratory, declared that the poor had no money with which to make the purchase; and how in a few

weeks' time they would be able to grind their own flour at
Herbert Fitzgerald's mill;—all this was also told. But the telling did not give so much gratification to Mrs. Townsend as the
sly hits against the two priests.

And then, while they were still in the middle of all this; when
the punch-jug had given way to the teapot, and the rector was
beginning to bethink himself that a nap in his arm-chair would
be very refreshing, Jerry came into the room to announce that
Richard had come over from Castle Richmond with a note for
' his riverence.' And so Richard was shown in.

Now Richard might very well have sent in his note by Jerry,
which after all contained only some information with reference
to a list of old women which Herbert Fitzgerald had promised to
send over to the glebe. But Richard knew that the minister
would wish to chat with him, and Richard himself had no indis-
position for a little conversation.

' I hope yer riverence is quite well then,' said Richard, as he
tendered his note, making a double bow, so as to include them
both.

' Pretty well, thank you,' said Mrs. Townsend. ' And how's
all the family?'

' Well, then, they're all rightly, considhering. The Masther's
no just what he war, you know, ma'am.'

' I'm afraid not—I'm afraid not,' said the rector. ' You'll not
take a glass of spirits, Richard?'

' Yer riverence knows I never does that,' said Richard, with
somewhat of a conscious look of high morality, for he was a rigid
teetotaller.

' And do you mean to say that you stick to that always?' said
Mrs. Townsend, who firmly believed that no good could come
out of Nazareth, and that even abstinence from whisky must be
bad if accompanied by anything in the shape of a Roman Catholic ceremony.

' I do mean to say, ma'am, that I never touched a dhrop of
anything sthronger than wather, barring tay, since the time I
got the pledge from the blessed apostle.' And Richard boldly
crossed himself in the presence of them both. They knew well
whom he meant by the blessed apostle: it was Father Mathew.

' Temperance is a very good thing, however we may come by
it,' said Mr. Townsend, who meant to imply by this that Richard's
temperance had been come by in the worst way possible.

' That's thrue for you, sir,' said Richard; ' but I never knew
any pledge kept, only the blessed apostle's.' By which he meant
to imply that no sanctity inherent in Mr. Townsend's sacerdotal
proceedings could be of any such efficacy.

And then Mr. Townsend read the note. 'Ah, yes,' said he; 'tell Mr. Herbert that I'm very much obliged to him. There will be no other answer necessary.'

'Very well, yer riverence, I'll be sure to give Mr. Herbert the message.' And Richard made a sign as though he were going.

'But tell me, Richard,' said Mrs. Townsend, 'is Sir Thomas any better? for we have been really very uneasy about him.'

'Indeed and he is, ma'am; a dail betther this morning, the Lord be praised.'

'It was a kind of a fit, wasn't it, Richard?' asked the parson.

'A sort of a fit of illness of some kind, I'm thinking,' said Richard, who had no mind to speak of his family's secrets out of doors. Whatever he might be called upon to tell the priest, at any rate he was not called on to tell anything to the parson.

'But it was very sudden this time, wasn't it, Richard?' asked the lady; 'immediately after that strange man was shown into his room—eh?'

'I'm sure, ma'am, I can't say; but I don't think he was a ha'porth worse than ordinar, till after the gentleman went away. I did hear that he did his business with the gentleman, just as usual like.'

'And then he fell into a fit, didn't he, Richard?'

'Not that I heard of, ma'am. He did a dail of talking about some law business, I did hear our Mrs. Jones say; and then afther he warn't just the betther of it.'

'Was that all?'

'And I don't think he's none the worse for it neither, ma'am; for the masther do seem to have more life in him this day than I'se seen this many a month. Why, he's been out and about with her ladyship in the pony-carriage all the morning.'

'Has he now? Well, I'm delighted to hear that. It is some trouble about the English estates, I believe, that vexes him?'

'Faix, then, ma'am, I don't just know what it is that ails him, unless it be just that he has too much money for to know what to do wid it. That'd be the sore vexation to me, I know.'

'Well; ah, yes; I suppose I shall see Mrs. Jones to-morrow, or at latest the day after,' said Mrs. Townsend, resolving to pique the man by making him understand that she could easily learn all that she wished to learn from the woman: 'a great comfort Mrs. Jones must be to her ladyship.'

'Oh yes, ma'am; 'deed 'an she is,' said Richard; ''specially in the matter of puddins and pies, and such like.'

He was not going to admit Mrs. Jones's superiority, seeing that he had lived in the family long before his present mistress's marriage.

'And in a great many other things too, Richard. She's quite a confidential servant. That's because she's a Protestant, you know.'

Now of all men, women, and creatures living, Richard the coachman of Castle Richmond was the most good-tempered. No amount of anger or scolding, no professional misfortune—such as the falling down of his horse upon the ice, no hardship—such as three hours' perpetual rain when he was upon the box—would make him cross. To him it was a matter of perfect indifference if he were sent off with his car just before breakfast, or called away to some stable work as the dinner was about to smoke in the servants' hall. He was a great eater, but what he didn't eat one day he could eat the next. Such things never ruffled him, nor was he ever known to say that such a job wasn't his work. He was always willing to nurse a baby, or dig potatoes, or cook a dinner, to the best of his ability, when asked to do so; but he could not endure to be made less of than a Protestant; and of all Protestants he could not endure to be made less of than Mrs. Jones.

''Cause she's a Protestant, is it, ma'am?'

'Of course, Richard: you can't but see that Protestants are more trusted, more respected, more thought about than Romanists, can you?'

''Deed then I don't know, ma'am.'

'But look at Mrs. Jones.'

'Oh, I looks at her often enough; and she's well enough too for a woman. But we all know her weakness.'

'What's that, Richard?' asked Mrs. Townsend, with some interest expressed in her tone; for she was not above listening to a little scandal, even about the servants of her great neighbours.

'Why, she do often talk about things she don't understand. But she's a great hand at puddins and pies, and that's what one mostly looks for in a woman.'

This was enough for Mrs. Townsend for the present, and so Richard was allowed to take his departure, in full self-confidence that he had been one too many for the parson's wife.

'Jerry,' said Richard, as they walked out into the yard together to get the Castle Richmond pony, 'does they often thry to make a Prothestant of you now?'

'Prothestants be d——,' said Jerry, who by no means shared in Richard's good gifts as to temper.

'Well, I wouldn't say that; at laist, not of all of 'em.'

'The likes of them's used to it,' said Jerry.

And then Richard, not waiting to do further battle on behalf of his Protestant friends, trotted out of the yard.

CHAPTER XI.

SECOND LOVE.

On the day after Clara's departure, Herbert did, as a matter of course, make his promised visit at Desmond Court. It was on that day that Sir Thomas had been driving about in the pony-carriage with Lady Fitzgerald, as Richard had reported. Herbert had been with his father in the morning, and then having seen him and his mother well packed up in their shawls and cloaks, had mounted his horse and ridden off.

'I may be kept some time,' said he, 'as I have promised to go on to Clady, and see after that soup kitchen.'

'I shouldn't wonder if Herbert became attached to Clara Desmond,' said the mother to Sir Thomas, soon after they had begun their excursion.

'Do you think so?' said the baronet; and his tone was certainly not exactly that of approbation.

'Well, yes; I certainly do think it probable. I am sure he admires her, and I think it very likely to come to more. Would there be any objection?'

'They are both very young,' said Sir Thomas.

'But in Herbert's position will not a young marriage be the best thing for him?'

'And she has no fortune; not a shilling. If he does marry young, quite young you know, it might be prudent that his wife should have something of her own.'

'They'd live here,' said Lady Fitzgerald, who knew that of all men, her husband was usually most free from mercenary feelings and an over-anxiety as to increased wealth, either for himself or for his children; 'and I think it would be such a comfort to you. Herbert, you see, is so fond of county business, and so little anxious for what young men generally consider pleasure.'

There was nothing more said about it at that moment; for the question in some measure touched upon money matters and considerations as to property, from all of which Lady Fitzgerald at present wished to keep her husband's mind free. But towards the end of the drive he himself again referred to it.

'She is a nice girl, isn't she?'

'Very nice, I think; as far as I've seen her.'

'She is pretty, certainly.'

'Very pretty; more than pretty; much more. She will be beautiful.'

'But she is such a mere child. You do not think that anything will come of it immediately;—not quite immediately?'

'Oh no; certainly not quite immediately. I think Herbert is not calculated to be very sudden in any such feelings, or in the expression of them: but I do think such an event very probable before the winter is over.'

In the mean time Herbert spent the whole day over at Desmond Court, or at Clady. He found the countess delighted to see him, and both she and Lady Clara went on with him to Clady. It was past five, and quite dark, before he reached Castle Richmond, so that he barely got home in time to dress for dinner.

The dinner-party that evening was more pleasant than usual. Sir Thomas not only dined with them, but came into the drawing-room after dinner, and to a certain extent joined in their conversation. Lady Fitzgerald could see that this was done by a great effort; but it was not remarked by Aunt Letty and the others, who were delighted to have him with them, and to see him once more interested about their interests.

And now the building of the mill had been settled, and the final orders were to be given by Herbert at the spot on the following morning.

'We can go with you to Berryhill, I suppose, can't we?' said Mary.

'I shall be in a great hurry,' said Herbert, who clearly did not wish to be encumbered by his sisters on this special expedition.

'And why are you to be in such a hurry to-morrow?' asked Aunt Letty.

'Well, I shall be hurried; I have promised to go to Clady again, and I must be back here early, and must get another horse.'

'Why, Herbert, you are becoming a Hercules of energy,' said his father, smiling: 'you will have enough to do if you look to all the soup kitchens on the Desmond property as well as our own.'

'I made a sort of promise about this particular affair at Clady, and I must carry it out,' said Herbert.

'And you'll pay your devoirs to the fair Lady Clara on your way home of course,' said Mary,

'More then probable,' he replied.

'And stay so late again that you'll hardly be here in time for

dinner,' continued Mary : to which little sally her brother
vouchsafed no answer.

But Emmeline said nothing. Lady Clara was specially her
friend, and she was too anxious to secure such a sister-in-law to
make any joke upon such a subject.

On that occasion nothing more was said about it; but Sir
Thomas hoped within his heart that his wife was right in
prophesying that his son would do nothing sudden in this
matter.

On the following morning young Fitzgerald gave the necessary
orders at Berryhill very quickly, and then coming back remounted another horse without going into the house. Then he
trotted off to Clady, passing the gate of Desmond Court without
calling; did what he had promised to do at Clady, or rather that
which he had made to stand as an excuse for again visiting that
part of the world so quickly; and after that, with a conscience
let us hope quite clear, rode up the avenue at Desmond Court.
It was still early in the day when he got there, probably not
much after two o'clock; and yet Mary had been quite correct in
foretelling that he would only be home just in time for dinner.

But, nevertheless, he had not seen Lady Desmond. Why or
how it had occurred that she had been absent from the drawing-
room the whole of the two hours which he had passed in the
house, it may be unnecessary to explain. Such, however, had been
the fact. The first five minutes had been passed in inquiries after
the bruise, and, it must be owned, in a surgical inspection of the
still discoloured arm. 'It must be very painful,' he had said,
looking into her face, as though by doing so he could swear that
he would so willingly bear all the pain himself, if it were only
possible to make such an exchange.

'Not very,' she had answered, smiling. 'It is only a little
stiff. I can't quite move it easily.'

And then she lifted it up, and afterwards dropped it with a
little look of pain that ran through his heart.

The next five minutes were taken up in discussing the case
of the recusant boiler, and then Clara discovered that she had
better go and fetch her mother. But against the immediate
taking of this step he had alleged some valid reason, and so
they had gone on, till the dark night admonished him that he
could do no more than save the dinner hour at Castle Richmond.

The room was nearly dark when he left her, and she got up
and stood at the front window, so that, unseen, she might see
his figure as he rode off from the house. He mounted his horse
within the quadrangle, and coming out at the great old-fashioned

ugly portal, galloped off across the green park with a loose
rein and a happy heart.   What is it the song says ?

'Oh, ladies, beware of a gay young knight
Who loves and who rides away.'

There was at Clara's heart, as she stood there at the window,
some feeling of the expediency of being beware, some shadow
of doubt as to the wisdom of what she had done.   He rode away
gaily, with a happy spirit, for he had won that on the winning
of which he had been intent.   No necessity for caution presented
itself to him.   He had been seen and loved ; had then asked, and
had not asked in vain.

She stood gazing after him, as long as her straining eye could
catch any outline of his figure as it disappeared through the gloom
of the evening.   As long as she could see him, or even fancy that
she still saw him, she thought only of his excellence ; of his high
character, his kind heart, his talents—which in her estimation
were ranked perhaps above their real value—his tastes, which
coincided so well with her own, his quiet yet manly bearing, his
useful pursuits, his gait, appearance, and demeanour.   All these
were of a nature to win the heart of such a girl as Clara Desmond ; and then, probably, in some indistinct way, she remembered the broad acres to which he was the heir, and comforted herself by reflecting that this at least was a match which none would
think disgraceful for a daughter even of an Earl of Desmond.

But sadder thoughts did come when that figure had wholly
disappeared.   Her eye, looking out into the darkness, could not
but see another figure on which it had often in past times
delighted almost unconsciously to dwell.   There, walking on that
very road, another lover, another Fitzgerald, had sworn that he
loved her ; and had truly sworn so, as she well knew.   She had
never doubted his truth to her, and did not doubt it now ;—and
yet she had given herself away to another.

And in many things he too, that other lover, had been noble
and gracious, and fit for a woman to love.   In person he exceeded
all that she had ever seen or dreamed of ; and why should we
think that personal excellence is to count for nothing in female
judgment, when in that of men it ranks so immeasurably above
all other excellences ?   His bearing, too, was chivalrous and
bold, his language full of poetry, and his manner of loving
eager, impetuous, and of a kin to worship.   Then, too, he was
now in misfortune ; and when has that failed to soften even the
softness of a woman's heart ?

It was impossible that she should not make comparisons,
comparisons that were so distasteful to her ; impossible, also,

that she should not accuse herself of some falseness to that first
lover. The time to us, my friends, seems short enough since
she was walking there, and listening with childish delight to
Owen's protestations of love. It was but little more than
one year since : but to her those months had been very long.
And, reader, if thou hast arrived at any period of life which
enables thee to count thy past years by lustrums; if thou art at
a time of life, past thirty we will say, hast thou not found that
thy years, which are now short enough, were long in those by-
gone days?

Those fourteen months were to her the space almost of a
second life, as she now looked back upon them. When those
earlier vows were made, what had she cared for prudence, for
the world's esteem, or an alliance that might be becoming to
her? That Owen Fitzgerald was a gentleman of high blood and
ancient family, so much she had cared to know; for the rest, she
had only cared to feel this, that her heart beat high with pleasure when he was with her.

Did her heart beat as high now, when his cousin was beside
her? No; she felt that it did not. And sometimes she felt, or
feared to feel, that it might beat high again when she should
again see the lover whom her judgment had rejected.

Her judgment had rejected him altogether long before an
idea had at all presented itself to her that Herbert Fitzgerald could
become her suitor. Nor had this been done wholly in obedience
to her mother's mandate. She had realized in her own mind
the conviction that Owen Fitzgerald was not a man with whom
any girl could at present safely link her fortune. She knew
well that he was idle, dissipated, and extravagant; and she
could not believe these vices had arisen only from his banishment from her, and that they would cease and vanish whenever
that banishment might cease.

Messages came to her, in underhand ways—ways well understood in Ireland, and not always ignored in England—to the
effect that all his misdoings arose from his unhappiness; that he
drank and gambled only because the gates of Desmond Court
were no longer open to him. There was that in Clara's heart
which did for a while predispose her to believe somewhat of this,
to hope that it might not be altogether false. Could any girl
loving such a man not have had some such hope? But then the
stories of these revelries became worse and worse, and it was
dinned into her ears that these doings had been running on in
all their enormity before that day of his banishment. And so,
silently and sadly, with no outspoken word either to mother or
brother, she had resolved to give him up.

There was no necessity to her for any outspoken word. She had promised her mother to hold no intercourse with the man; and she had kept and would keep her promise. Why say more about it? How she might have reconciled her promise to her mother with an enduring engagement, had Owen Fitzgerald's conduct allowed her to regard her engagement as enduring,—that had been a sore trouble to her while hope had remained; but now no hope remained, and that trouble was over.

And then Herbert Fitzgerald had come across her path, and those sweet, loving, kind Fitzgerald girls, who were always ready to cover her with such sweet caresses, with whom she had known more of the happiness of friendliness than ever she had felt before. They threw themselves upon her like sisters, and she had never before enjoyed sisterly treatment. He had come across her path; and from the first moment she had become conscious of his admiration.

She knew herself to be penniless, and dreaded that she should be looked upon as wishing to catch the rich heir. But every one had conspired to throw them together. Lady Fitzgerald had welcomed her like a mother, with more caressing soft tenderness than her own mother usually vouchsafed to her; and even Sir Thomas had gone out of his usual way to be kind to her.

That her mother would approve of such a marriage she could not doubt. Lady Desmond in these latter days had not said much to her about Owen; but she had said very much of the horrors of poverty. And she had been too subtle to praise the virtues of Herbert with open plain words; but she had praised the comforts of a handsome income and well-established family mansion. Clara at these times had understood more than had been intended, and had, therefore, put herself on her guard against her mother's worldly wisdom; but, nevertheless, the dropping of the water had in some little measure hollowed the stone beneath.

And thus, thinking of these things, she stood at the window for some half-hour after the form of her accepted lover had become invisible in the gathering gloom of the evening.

And then her mother entered the room, and candles were brought. Lady Desmond was all smiles and benignity, as she had been for this last week past, while Herbert Fitzgerald had been coming and going almost daily at Desmond Court. But Clara understood this benignity, and disliked it.

It was, however, now necessary that everything should be told. Herbert had declared that he should at once inform his father and mother, and obtain their permission for his marriage. He spoke of it as a matter on which there was no occasion for any doubt or misgiving. He was an only son, he said, and trusted and loved in everything. His father never opposed him on any subject whatever; and would, he was sure, consent to any match he might propose. 'But as to you,' he added, with a lover's flattering fervour, 'they are all so fond of you, they all think so much of you, that my only fear is that I shall be jealous. They'll all make love to you, Aunt Letty included.'

It was therefore essential that she should at once tell her mother, and ask her mother's leave. She had once before confessed a tale of love, and had done so with palpitation of the heart, with trembling of the limbs, and floods of tears. Then her tale had been received with harsh sternness. Now she could tell her story without any trembling, with no tears; but it was almost indifferent to her whether her mother was harsh or tender.

'What! has Mr. Fitzgerald gone?' said the countess, on entering the room.

'Yes, mamma; this half-hour,' said Clara, not as yet coming away from the window.

'I did not hear his horse, and imagined he was here still. I hope he has not thought me terribly uncivil, but I could not well leave what I was doing.'

To this little make-believe speech Clara did not think it necessary to return any answer. She was thinking how she would begin to say that for saying which there was so strong a necessity, and she could not take a part in small false badinage on a subject which was so near her heart.

'And what about that stupid mason at Clady?' asked the countess, still making believe.

'Mr. Fitzgerald was there again to-day, mamma; and I think it will be all right now; but he did not say much about it.'

'Why not? you were all so full of it yesterday.'

Clara, who had half turned round towards the light, now again turned herself towards the window. This task must be done; but the doing of it was so disagreeable! How was she to tell her mother that she loved this man, seeing that so short a time since she had declared that she loved another?

'And what was he talking about, love?' said the countess, ever so graciously. 'Or, perhaps, no questioning on the matter can be allowed. May I ask questions, or may I not? eh, Clara?' and then the mother, walking up towards the window, put her fair white hands upon her daughter's two shoulders.

'Of course you may inquire,' said Clara.

'Then I do inquire—immediately. What has this *preux chevalier* been saying to my Clara, that makes her stand thus solemn and silent, gazing out into the dark night?'

' Mamma !'

' Well, love?'

' Herbert Fitzgerald has—has asked me to be his wife. He has proposed to me.'

The mother's arm now encircled the daughter lovingly, and the mother's lips were pressed to the daughter's forehead. ' Herbert Fitzgerald has asked you to be his wife, has he ? And what answer has my bonny bird deigned to make to so audacious a request?'

Lady Desmond had never before spoken to her daughter in tones so gracious, in a manner so flattering, so caressing, so affectionate. But Clara would not open her heart to her mother's tenderness. She could not look into her mother's face, and welcome her mother's consent with unutterable joy, as she would have done had that consent been given a year since to a less prudent proposition. That marriage for which she was now to ask her mother's sanction would of course be sanctioned. She had no favour to beg; nothing for which to be grateful. With a slight motion, unconsciously, unwillingly, but not the less positively, she repulsed her mother's caress as she answered her question.

' I have accepted him, mamma ; that is, of course, if you do not object.'

' My own, own child !' said the countess, seizing her daughter in her arms, and pressing her to her bosom. And in truth Clara was, now probably for the first time, her own heart's daughter. Her son, though he was but a poor earl, was Earl of Desmond. He too, though in truth but a poor earl, was not absolutely destitute,—would in truth be blessed with a fair future. But Lady Clara had hitherto been felt only as a weight. She had been born poor as poverty itself, and hitherto had shown so little disposition to find for herself a remedy for this crushing evil ! But now—now matters were indeed changed. She had obtained for herself the best match in the whole country round, and, in doing so, had sacrificed her heart's young love. Was she not entitled to all a mother's tenderness? Who knew, who could know the miseries of poverty so well as the Countess of Desmond ? Who then could feel so much gratitude to a child for prudently escaping from them? Lady Desmond did feel grateful to her daughter.

' My own, own child ; my happy girl !' she repeated. ' He is a man to whom any mother in all the land would be proud to see her daughter married. Never, never did I see a young man so perfectly worthy of a girl's love. He is so thoroughly well educated, so thoroughly well conducted, so good-looking, so warm-hearted, so advantageously situated in all his circumstances. Of course he will go into Parliament, and then any course is open to him. The property is, I believe, wholly unembarrassed, and there are no younger brothers. You may say that the place is his own already, for old Sir Thomas is almost nobody. I do wish you joy, my own dearest, dearest Clara!' After which burst of maternal eloquence, the countess pressed her lips to those of her child, and gave her a mother's warmest kiss.

Clara was conscious that she was thoroughly dissatisfied with her mother, but she could not exactly say why it was so. She did return her mother's kiss, but she did it coldly, and with lips that were not eager.

'I'm glad you think that I have done right, mamma.'

'Right, my love! Of course I think that you have done right : only I give you no credit, dearest; none in the least; for how could you help loving one so lovable in every way as dear Herbert ?'

'Credit! no, there is no credit,' she said, not choosing to share her mother's pleasantry.

'But there is this credit. Had you not been one of the sweetest girls that ever was born, he would not have loved you.'

'He has loved me because there was no one else here,' said Clara.

'Nonsense! No one else here, indeed! Has he not the power if he pleases to go and choose whomever he will in all London. Had he been mercenary, and wanted money,' said the countess, in a tone which showed how thoroughly she despised any such vice, 'he might have had what he would. But then he could not have had my Clara. But he has looked for beauty and manners and high-bred tastes, and an affectionate heart; and, in my opinion, he could not have been more successful in his search.' After which second burst of eloquence, she again kissed her daughter.

'Twas thus, at that moment, that she congratulated the wife of the future Sir Herbert Fitzgerald ; and then she allowed Clara to go up to her own room, there to meditate quietly on what she had done, and on that which she was about to do. But late in the evening, Lady Desmond, whose mind was thoroughly full of the subject, again broke out into triumph.

'You must write to Patrick to-morrow, Clara. He must hear the good news from no one but yourself.'

'Had we not better wait a little, mamma?'

'Why, my love? You hardly know how anxious your brother is for your welfare.'

'I knew it was right to tell you, mamma——'

'Right to tell me! of course it was. You could not have had the heart to keep it from me for half a day.'

'But perhaps it may be better not to mention it further till we know——'

'Till we know what?' said the countess with a look of fear about her brow.

'Whether Sir Thomas and Lady Fitzgerald will wish it. If they object——'

'Object! why should they object? how can they object? They are not mercenary people; and you are an earl's daughter. And Herbert is not like a girl. The property is his own, entailed on him, and he may do as he pleases.'

'In such a matter I am sure he would not wish to displease either his father or his mother.'

'Nonsense, my dear; quite nonsense; you do not at all see the difference between a young man and a girl. He has a right to do exactly as he likes in such a matter. But I am quite sure that they will not object. Why should they? How can they?'

'Mr. Fitzgerald says that they will not,' Clara admitted, almost grudgingly.

'Of course they will not. I don't suppose they could bring themselves to object to anything he might suggest. I never knew a young man so happily situated in this respect. He is quite a free agent. I don't think they would say much to him if he insisted on marrying the cook-maid. Indeed, it seems to me that his word is quite paramount at Castle Richmond.'

'All the same, mamma; I would rather not write to Patrick till something more has been settled.'

'You are wrong there, Clara. If anything disagreeable should happen, which is quite impossible, it would be absolutely necessary that your brother should know. Believe me, my love, I only advise you for your own good.'

'But Mr. Fitzgerald will probably be here to-morrow; or if not to-morrow, next day.'

'I have no doubt he will, love. But why do you call him Mr. Fitzgerald? You were calling him Herbert the other day. Don't you remember how I scolded you? I should not scold you now.'

Clara made no answer to this, and then the subject was allowed to rest for that night. She would call him Herbert, she said to herself; but not to her mother. She would keep the use of that name till she could talk with Emmeline as a sister. Of all her anticipated pleasures, that of having now a real sister was perhaps the greatest; or, rather, that of being able to talk about

Herbert with one whom she could love and treat as a sister. But Herbert himself would exact the use of his own Christian name, for the delight of his own ears; that was a matter of course; that, doubtless, had been already done.

And then mother and daughter went to bed. The countess, as she did so, was certainly happy to her heart's core. Could it be that she had some hope, unrecognized by herself, that Owen Fitzgerald might now once more be welcomed at Desmond Court? that something might now be done to rescue him from that slough of despond?

And Clara too was happy, though her happiness was mixed. She did love Herbert Fitzgerald. She was sure of that. She said so to herself over and over again. Love him! of course she loved him, and would cherish him as her lord and husband to the last day of her life, the last gasp of her breath.

But still, as sleep came upon her eyelids, she saw in her memory the bright flash of that other lover's countenance, when he first astonished her with the avowal of his love, as he walked beside her under the elms, with his horse following at his heels.

CHAPTER XII.

DOUBTS.

I BELIEVE there is no period of life so happy as that in which a thriving lover leaves his mistress after his first success. His joy is more perfect then that at the absolute moment of his own eager vow, and her half-assenting blushes. Then he is thinking mostly of her, and is to a certain degree embarrassed by the effort necessary for success. But when the promise has once been given to him, and he is able to escape into the domain of his own heart, he is as a conqueror who has mastered half a continent by his own strategy.

It never occurs to him, he hardly believes, that his success is no more than that which is the ordinary lot of mortal man. He never reflects that all the old married fogies whom he knows and despises, have just as much ground for pride, if such pride were enduring; that every fat, silent, dull, somnolent old lady whom he sees and quizzes, has at some period been deemed as worthy a prize as his priceless galleon; and so deemed by as bold a captor as himself.

Some one has said that every young mother, when her first child is born, regards the babe as the most wonderful production of that description which the world has yet seen. And this too is true. But I doubt even whether that conviction is so strong as the conviction of the young successful lover, that he has achieved a triumph which should ennoble him down to late generations. As he goes along he has a contempt for other men; for they know nothing of such glory as his. As he pores over his 'Blackstone,' he remembers that he does so, not so much that he may acquire law, as that he may acquire Fanny; and then all other porers over 'Blackstone' are low and mean in his sight—are mercenary in their views and unfortunate in their ideas, for they have no Fanny in view.

Herbert Fitzgerald had this proud feeling strong within his heart as he galloped away across the greensward, and trotted fast along the road, home to Castle Richmond. She was compounded of all excellences—so he swore to himself over and over again—and being so compounded, she had consented to bestow all these excellences upon him. Being herself goddess-like, she had promised to take him as the object of her world's worship. So he trotted on fast and faster, as though conscious of the half-continent which he had won by his skill and valour.

She had told him about his cousin Owen. Indeed, the greater number of the soft musical words which she had spoken in that long three hours' colloquy had been spoken on this special point. It had behoved her to tell him all; and she thought that she had done so. Nay, she had done so with absolute truth—to the best of her heart's power.

'You were so young then,' he had argued; 'so very young.'

'Yes, very young. I am not very old now, you know,' and she smiled sweetly on him.

'No, no; but a year makes so much difference. You were all but a child then. You do not love him now, Clara?'

'No; I do not love him now,' she had answered.

And then he exacted a second, a third, a fourth assurance, that she did absolutely, actually, and with her whole heart love him, him Herbert, in lieu of that other him, poor Owen; and with this he, Herbert, was contented. Content; nay, but proud, elated with triumph, and conscious of victory. In this spirit he rode home as fast as his horse could carry him.

He too had to tell his tale to those to whom he owed obedience, and to beg that they would look upon his intended bride with eyes of love and with parental affection. But in this respect he was hardly troubled with more doubt than Clara had felt. How could any one object to his Clara?

There are young men who, from their positions in life, are obliged to abstain from early marriage, or to look for dowries with their wives. But he, luckily, was not fettered in this way.

He could marry as he pleased, so long as she whom he might choose brought with her gentle blood, a good heart, a sweet temper, and such attraction of person and manners as might make the establishment at Castle Richmond proud of his young bride. And of whom could that establishment be more proud than of Lady Clara Desmond? So he rode home without any doubt to clog his happiness.

But he had a source of joy which Clara wanted. She was almost indifferent to her mother's satisfaction; but Herbert looked forward with the liveliest, keenest anticipation to his mother's gratified caresses and unqualified approval—to his father's kind smile and warm assurance of consent. Clara had made herself known at Castle Richmond; and he had no doubt but that all this would be added to his cup of happiness. There was therefore no alloy to debase his virgin gold as he trotted quickly into the stable-yard.

But he resolved that he would say nothing about the matter that night. He could not well tell them all in full conclave together. Early after breakfast he would go to his father's room; and after that, he would find his mother. There would then be no doubt that the news would duly leak out among his sisters and Aunt Letty.

'Again only just barely in time, Herbert,' said Mary, as they clustered round the fire before dinner.

'You can't say I ever keep you waiting; and I really think that's some praise for a man who has got a good many things on his hand.'

'So it is, Herbert,' said Emmeline. 'But we have done something too. We have been over to Berryhill; and the people have already begun there: they were at work with their pick-axes among the rocks by the river-side.'

'So much the better. Was Mr. Somers there?'

'We did not see him; but he had been there,' said Aunt Letty. 'But Mrs. Townsend found us. And who do you think came up to us in the most courteous, affable, condescending way?'

'Who? I don't know. Brady, the builder, I suppose.'

'No, indeed: Brady was not half so civil, for he kept himself to his own work. It was the Rev. Mr. M'Carthy, if you please.'

'I only hope you were civil to him,' said Herbert, with some slight suffusion of colour over his face; for he rather doubted the conduct of his aunt to the priest, especially as her great Protestant ally, Mrs. Townsend, was of the party.

'Civil! I don't know what you would have, unless you wanted me to embrace him. He shook hands with us all round.

I really thought Mrs. Townsend would have looked him into the river when he came to her.'

' She always was the quintessence of absurdity and prejudice,' said he.

' Oh, Herbert!' exclaimed Aunt Letty.

' Well ; and what of " Oh, Herbert ?" I say she is so. If you and Mary and Emmeline did not look him into the river when he shook hands with you, why should she do so ? He is an ordained priest even according to her own tenets,—only she knows nothing of what her own tenets are.'

' I'll tell you what they are. They are the substantial, true, and holy doctrines of the Protestant religion, founded on the gospel. Mrs. Townsend is a thoroughly Protestant woman ; one who cannot abide the sorceries of popery.'

' Hates them as a mad dog hates water ; and with the same amount of judgment. We none of us wish to be drowned ; but nevertheless there are some good qualities in water.'

' But there are no good qualities in popery,' said Aunt Letty, with her most extreme energy.

' Are there not ?' said Herbert. ' I should have thought that belief in Christ, belief in the Bible, belief in the doctrine of a Saviour's atonement, were good qualities. Even the Mahommedan's religion has some qualities that are good.'

' I would sooner be a Mahommedan than a Papist,' said Aunt Letty, somewhat thoughtlessly, but very stoutly.

' You would alter your opinion after the first week in a harem,' said Herbert. And then there was a burst of laughter, in which Aunt Letty herself joined. ' I would sooner go there than go to confession,' she whispered to Mary as they all walked off to dinner.

' And how is the Lady Clara's arm ?' asked Mary, as soon as they were again once more round the fire.

' The Lady Clara's arm is still very blue,' said Herbert.

' And I suppose it took you half an hour to weep over it ?' continued his sister.

' Exactly, by Shrewsbury clock.'

' And while you were weeping over the arm, what happened to the hand ? She did not surrender it, did she, in return for so much tenderness on your part ?'

Emmeline thought that Mary was very pertinacious in her badinage, and was going to bid her hold her tongue ; but she observed that Herbert blushed, and walked away without further answer. He went to the further end of the long room, and there threw himself on to a sofa. ' Could it be that it was all settled ?' thought Emmeline to herself.

She followed him to the sofa, and sitting beside him, took hold of his arm. ' Oh, Herbert! if there is anything to tell, do tell me.'

' Anything to tell !' said he. ' What do you mean ?'

' Oh ! you know. I do love her so dearly. I shall never be contented to love any one else as your wife—not to love her really, really with all my heart.'

' What geese you girls are ! you are always thinking of love, and weddings, and orange-blossoms.'

' It is only for you I think about them,' said Emmeline. ' I know there is something to tell. Dear Herbert, do tell me.'

' There is a young bachelor duke coming here to-morrow. He has a million a year, and three counties all his own : he has blue eyes, and is the handsomest man that ever was seen. Is that news enough ?'

' Very well, Herbert. I would tell you anything.'

' Well ; tell me anything.'

' I'll tell you this. I know you're in love with Clara Desmond, and I'm sure she's in love with you ; and I believe you are both engaged, and you're not nice at all to have a secret from me. I never tease you, as Mary does, and it would make me so happy to know it.'

Upon this he put his arm round her waist and whispered one word into her ear. She gave an exclamation of delight ; and as the tears came into her eyes congratulated him with a kiss. ' Oh dear, oh dear ! I am so happy !' she exclaimed.

' Hush—sh,' he whispered. ' I knew how it would be if I told you.'

' But they will all know to-morrow, will they not ?'

' Leave that to me. You have coaxed me out of my secret, and you are bound to keep it.' And then he went away well pleased. This description of delight on his sister's part was the first instalment of that joy which he had promised himself from the satisfaction of his family.

Lady Fitzgerald had watched all that had passed, and had already learned her mistake—her mistake in that she had prophesied that no immediate proposal was likely to be made by her son. She now knew well enough that he had made such a proposal, and that he had been accepted.

And this greatly grieved her. She had felt certain from the few slight words which Sir Thomas had spoken that there were valid reasons why her son should not marry a penniless girl. That conversation, joined to other things, to the man's visit, and her husband's deep dejection, had convinced her that all was not right. Some misfortune was impending over them, and there had been that in her own early history which filled her with dismay as she thought of this.

She had ardently desired to caution her son in this respect,— to guard him, if possible, against future disappointment and future sorrow. But she could not do so without obtaining in some sort her husband's assent to her doing so. She resolved that she would talk it over with Sir Thomas. But the subject was one so full of pain, and he was so ill, and therefore she had put it off.

And now she saw that the injury was done. Nevertheless, she said nothing either to Emmeline or to Herbert. If the injury were done, what good could now result from talking? She doubtless would hear it all soon enough. So she sat still, watching them.

On the following morning Sir Thomas did not come out to breakfast. Herbert went into his room quite early, as was always his custom; and as he left it for the breakfast-parlour he said, 'Father, I should like to speak to you just now about something of importance.'

'Something of importance, Herbert; what is it? Anything wrong?' For Sir Thomas was nervous, and easily frightened.

'Oh dear, no; nothing is wrong. It is nothing that will annoy you; at least I think not. But it will keep till after breakfast. I will come in again the moment breakfast is over.' And so saying he left the room with a light step.

In the breakfast-parlour it seemed to him as though everybody was conscious of some important fact. His mother's kiss was peculiarly solemn and full of solicitude; Aunt Letty smirked as though she was aware of something—something over and above the great Protestant tenets which usually supported her; and Mary had no joke to fling at him.

'Emmeline,' he whispered, 'you have told.'

'No, indeed,' she replied. But what mattered it? Everybody would know now in a few minutes. So he ate his breakfast, and then returned to Sir Thomas.

'Father,' said he, as soon as he had got into the arm-chair, in which it was his custom to sit when talking with Sir Thomas, 'I hope what I am going to tell you will give you pleasure. I have proposed to a young lady, and she has—accepted me.'

'You have proposed, and have been accepted!'

'Yes, father.'

'And the young lady——?'

'Is Lady Clara Desmond. I hope you will say that you approve of it. She has no fortune, as we all know, but that will hardly matter to me; and I think you will allow that in every other respect she is——'

Perfect, Herbert would have said, had he dared to express his true meaning. But he paused for a moment to look for a less triumphant word ; and then paused again, and left his sentence incomplete, when he saw the expression of his father's face.

'Oh, father ! you do not mean to say that you do not like her ?'

But it was not dislike that was expressed in his father's face, as Herbert felt the moment after he had spoken. There was pain there, and solicitude, and disappoinment; a look of sorrow at the tidings thus conveyed to him; but nothing that seemed to betoken dislike of any person.

'What is it, sir ? Why do you not speak to me ? Can it be that you disapprove of my marrying ?'

Sir Thomas certainly did disapprove of his son's marrying, but he lacked the courage to say so. Much misery that had hither-to come upon him, and that was about to come on all those whom he loved so well, arose from this lack of courage. He did not dare to tell his son that he advised him for the present to put aside all such hopes. It would have been terrible for him to do so ; but he knew that in not doing so he was occasioning sorrow that would be more terrible.

And yet he did not do it. Herbert saw clearly that the project was distasteful to his father,—that project which he had hoped to have seen received with so much delight; but nothing was said to him which tended to make him alter his purpose.

'Do you not like her ?' he asked his father, almost piteously.

'Yes, yes; I do like her, we all like her, very much indeed, Herbert.'

'Then why——'

'You are so young, my boy, and she is so very young, and——'

'And what ?'

'Why, Herbert, it is not always practicable for the son even of a man of property to marry so early in life as this. She has nothing, you know.'

'No,' said the young man, proudly ; 'I never thought of looking for money.'

'But in your position it is so essential if a young man wishes to marry.'

Herbert had always regarded his father as the most liberal man breathing,—as open-hearted and open-handed almost to a fault. To him, his only son, he had ever been so, refusing him nothing, and latterly allowing him to do almost as he would with the management of the estate. He could not understand that this liberality should be turned to parsimony on such an occasion as that of his son's marriage.

'You think then, sir, that I ought not to marry Lady Clara?' said Herbert, very bitterly.

'I like her excessively,' said Sir Thomas. 'I think she is a sweet girl, a very sweet girl, all that I or your mother could desire to see in your wife; but——'

'But she is not rich.'

'Do not speak to me in that tone, my boy,' said Sir Thomas, with an expression that would have moved his enemy to pity, let alone his son. His son did pity him, and ceased to wear the angry expression of face which had so wounded his father.

'But, father, I do not understand you,' he said. 'Is there any real objection why I should not marry? I am more than twenty-two, and you, I think, married earlier than that.'

In answer to this Sir Thomas only sighed meekly and piteously.

'If you mean to say,' continued the son, 'that it will be inconvenient to you to make me any allowance——'

'No, no, no; you are of course entitled to what you want, and as long as I can give it, you shall have it.'

'As long as you can give it, father!'

'As long as it is in my power, I mean. What can I want of anything but for you—for you and them?'

After this Herbert sat silent for a while, leaning on his arm. He knew that there existed some mischief, but he could not fathom it. Had he been prudent, he would have felt that there was some impediment to his love; some evil which it behoved him to fathom before he allowed his love to share it; but when was a lover prudent?

'We should live here, should we not, father? No second establishment would be necessary.'

'Of course you would live here,' said Sir Thomas, glad to be able to look at the subject on any side that was not painful. 'Of course you would live here. For the matter of that, Herbert, the house should be considered as your own if you so wished it.'

Against this the son put in his most violent protest. Nothing on earth should make him consider himself master of Castle Richmond as long as his father lived. Nor would Clara,—his Clara, wish it. He knew her well, he boasted. It would amply suffice to her to live there with them all. Was not the house large enough? And, indeed, where else could he live, seeing that all his interests were naturally centred upon the property?

And then Sir Thomas did give his consent. It would be wrong to say that it was wrung from him. He gave it willingly enough, as far as the present moment was concerned. When it was once settled, he assured his son that he would love Clara as his daughter. But nevertheless——

The father knew that he had done wrong; and Herbert knew
that he also, he himself, had done wrongly. He was aware that
there was something which he did not understand. But he had
promised to see Clara either that day or the next, and he could
not bring himself to unsay all that he had said to her. He left
his father's room sorrowful at heart, and discontented. He had
expected that his tidings would have been received in so far
other a manner; that he would have been able to go from his
father's study up stairs to his mother's room with so exulting a
step; that his news, when once the matter was ratified by his
father's approval, would have flown about the house with so loud
a note of triumph. And now it was so different! His father
had consented; but it was too plain that there was no room for
any triumph.

'Well, Herbert!' said Emmeline, jumping up to meet him as
he returned to a small back drawing-room, through which he
had gone to his father's dressing-room. She had calculated that
he would come there, and that she might thus get the first word
from him after the interview was over.

But there was a frown upon his brow, and displeasure in his
eyes. There was none of that bright smile of gratified pride
with which she had expected that her greeting would have been
met. 'Is there anything wrong?' she said. 'He does not disapprove, does he?'

'Never mind; and do leave me now. I never can make you
understand that one is not always in a humour for joking.' And
so saying, he put her aside, and passed on.

Joking! That was indeed hard upon poor Emmeline, seeing
that her thoughts were so full of him, that her heart beat so
warmly for his promised bride. But she said nothing, shrinking
back abashed, and vanishing out of the way. Could it be
possible that her father should have refused to receive Lady
Clara Desmond as his daughter-in-law?

He then betook himself to a private territory of his own, where
he might be sure that he would remain undisturbed for some
half-hour or so. He would go to his mother, of course, but not
quite immediately. He would think over the matter, endeavouring to ascertain what it was that had made his father's manner
and words so painful to him.

But he could not get his thoughts to work rightly;—which
getting of the thoughts to work rightly is, by-the-by, as I take it,
the hardest work which a man is called upon to do. Not that
the subject to be thought about need in itself be difficult.
Were one to say that thoughts about hydrostatics and pneumatics
are difficult to the multitude, or that mental efforts in regions of

political economy or ethical philosophy are beyond ordinary reach, one would only pronounce an evident truism, an absurd platitude. But let any man take any subject fully within his own mind's scope, and strive to think about it steadily, with some attempt at calculation as to results. The chances are his mind will fly off, will-he-nill-he, to some utterly different matter. When he wishes to debate within himself that question of his wife's temper, he will find himself considering whether he may not judiciously give away half a dozen pairs of those old boots; or when it behoves him to decide whether it shall be manure and a green crop, or a fallow season and then grass seeds, he cannot keep himself from inward inquiry as to the meaning of that peculiar smile on Mrs. Walker's face when he shook hands with her last night.

Lord Brougham and Professor Faraday can, no doubt, command their thoughts. If many men could do so, there would be many Lord Broughams and many Professor Faradays.

At the present moment Herbert Fitzgerald had no right to consider himself as following in the steps of either one or other of these great men. He wished to think about his father's circumstances, but his mind would fly off to Clara Desmond and her perfections. And thus, though he remained there for half an hour, with his back to the fire and his hands in his pockets, his deliberations had done him no good whatever,—had rather done him harm, seeing that he had only warmed himself into a firmer determination to go on with what he was doing. And then he went to his mother.

She kissed him, and spoke very tenderly, nay affectionately, about Clara; but even she, even his mother, did not speak joyously; and she also said something about the difficulty of providing a maintenance for a married son. Then to her he burst forth, and spoke somewhat loudly.

' I cannot understand all this, mother. If either you or my father know any reason why I should be treated differently from other sons, you ought to tell me; not leave me to grope about in the dark.'

' But, my boy, we both think that no son was ever entitled to more consideration, or to kinder or more liberal treatment.'

' Why do I hear all this, then, about the difficulty of my marrying? Or if I hear so much, why do I not hear more? I know pretty well, I believe, what is my father's income.'

' If you do not, he would tell you for the asking.'

' And I know that I must be the heir to it, whatever it is,— not that that feeling would make any difference in my dealings with him, not the least. And, under these circumstances, I

cannot conceive why he and you should look coldly upon my
marriage.'

'I look coldly on it, Herbert!'

'Do you not? Do you not tell me that there will be no income
for me? If that is to be so; if that really is the case; if the
property has so dwindled away, or become embarrassed——'

'Oh, Herbert! there never was a man less likely to injure his
son's property than your father.'

'I do not mean that, mother. Let him do what he likes with
it, I should not upbraid him, even in my thoughts. But if it be
embarrassed; if it has dwindled away; if there be any reason
why I should not regard myself as altogether untrammelled with
regard to money, he ought to tell me. I cannot accuse myself of
expensive tastes.'

'Dearest Herbert, nobody accuses you of anything.'

'But I do desire to marry; and now I have engaged myself,
and will not break from my engagement, unless it be shown to
me that I am bound in honour to do so. Then, indeed——'

'Oh, Herbert! I do not know what you mean.'

'I mean this: that I expect that Clara shall be received as my
wife with open arms——'

'And so she shall be if she comes.'

'Or else that some reason should be given me why she should
not come. As to income, something must be done, I suppose.
If the means at our disposal are less than I have been taught to
believe, I at any rate will not complain. But they cannot, I
think, be so small as to afford any just reason why I should not
marry.'

'Your father, you see, is ill, and one can hardly talk to him
fully upon such matters at present.'

'Then I will speak to Somers. He, at any rate, must know
how the property is circumstanced, and I suppose he will not
hesitate to tell me.'

'I don't think Somers can tell you anything.'

'Then what is it? As for the London estate, mother, that is
all moonshine. What if it were gone altogether? It may be
that it is that which vexes my father; but if so, it is a mono-
mania.'

'Oh, my boy, do not use such a word!'

'You know what I mean. If any doubt as to that is creating
this despondency, it only shows that though we are bound to
respect and relieve my father's state of mind, we are not at all
bound to share it. What would it really matter, mother, if that
place in London were washed away by the Thames? There is
more than enough left for us all, unless——'

' Ah, Herbert, that is it.'

' Then I will go to Somers, and he shall tell me. My father's interest in this property cannot have been involved without his knowledge; and circumstanced as we and my father are, he is bound to tell me.'

' If there be anything within his knowledge to tell, he will tell it.'

' And if there be nothing within his knowledge, then I can only look upon all this as a disease on my poor father's part. I will do all I can to comfort him in it; but it would be madness to destroy my whole happiness because he labours under delusions.'

Lady Fitzgerald did not know what further to say. She half believed that Sir Thomas did labour under some delusion; but then she half believed also that he had upon his mind a sorrow, terribly real, which was in no sort delusive. Under such circumstances, how could she advise her son? Instead of advising him, she caressed him.

' But I may claim this from you, mother, that if Somers tells me nothing which ought to make me break my word to Clara, you will receive her as your daughter. You will promise me that, will you not?'

Lady Fitzgerald did promise, warmly; assuring him that she already dearly loved Clara Desmond, that she would delight in having such a daughter-in-law, and that she would go to her to welcome her as such as soon as ever he should bid her do so. With this Herbert was somewhat comforted, and immediately started on his search after Mr. Somers.

I do not think that any person is to be found, as a rule, attached to English estates whose position is analogous to that of an Irish agent. And there is a wide misunderstanding in England as to these Irish functionaries. I have attempted, some pages back, to describe the national delinquencies of a middleman, or profit-renter. In England we are apt to think that the agents on Irish properties are to be charged with similar shortcomings. This I can assert to be a great mistake; and I believe that, as a class, the agents on Irish properties do their duty in a manner beneficial to the people.

That there are, or were, many agents who were also middlemen, or profit-renters, and that in this second position they were a nuisance to the country, is no doubt true. But they were no nuisance in their working capacity as agents. That there are some bad agents there can be no doubt, as there are also some bad shoemakers.

The duties towards an estate which an agent performs in

Ireland are, I believe, generally shared in England between three or four different persons. The family lawyer performs part, the estate steward performs part, and the landlord himself performs part;—as to small estates, by far the greater part.

In Ireland, let the estate be ever so small—eight hundred a year we will say—all the working of the property is managed by the agent. It is he who knows the tenants, and the limits of their holdings; it is he who arranges leases, and allows—or much more generally does not allow—for improvements. He takes the rent, and gives the order for the ejection of tenants if he cannot get it.

I am far from saying that it would not be well that much of this should be done by the landlord himself;—that all of it should be so done on a small property. But it is done by agents; and, as a rule is, I think, done honestly.

Mr. Somers was agent to the Castle Richmond property, and as he took to himself as such five per cent. on all rents paid, and as he was agent also to sundry other small properties in the neighbourhood, he succeeded in making a very snug income. He had also an excellent house on the estate, and was altogether very much thought of; on the whole, perhaps, more than was Sir Thomas. But in this respect it was probable that Herbert might soon take the lead.

He was a large, heavy, consequential man, always very busy, as though aware of being one of the most important wheels that kept the Irish clock agoing; but he was honest, kind-hearted in the main, true as steel to his employers, and good-humoured—as long as he was allowed to have his own way. In these latter days he had been a little soured by Herbert's interference, and had even gone so far as to say that, ' in his humble judgment, Mr. Fitzgerald was wrong in doing '—so and so. But he generally called him Herbert, was always kind to him, and in his heart of hearts loved him dearly. But that was a matter of course, for had he not been agent to the estate before Herbert was born?

Immediately after his interview with his mother, Mr. Herbert rode over to Mr. Somers's house, and there found him sitting alone in his office. He dashed immediately into the subject that had brought him there. ' I have come, Mr. Somers,' said he, ' to ask you a question about the property.'

' About the Castle Richmond property?' said Mr. Somers, rather surprised by his visitor's manner.

' Yes; you know in what a state my poor father now is.'

' I know that Sir Thomas is not very well. I am sorry to say that it is long since he has been quite himself.'

' There is something that is preying upon his spirits.'

'I am afraid so, Herbert.'

'Then tell me fairly, Mr. Somers, do you know what it is?'

'Not—in—the least. I have no conception whatever, and never have had any. I know no cause for trouble that should disquiet him.'

'There is nothing wrong about the property?'

'Not to my knowledge.'

'Who has the title-deeds?'

'They are at Coutts's.'

'You are sure of that?'

'Well; as sure as a man can be of a thing that he does not see. I have never seen them there; indeed, have never seen them at all; but I feel no doubt in my own mind as to their being at the bankers.'

'Is there much due on the estate?'

'Very little. No estate in county Cork has less on it. Miss Letty has her income, and when Poulnasherry was bought—that townland lying just under Berryhill, where the gorze cover is—part of the purchase money was left on mortgage. That is still due; but the interest is less than a hundred a year.'

'And that is all?'

'All that I know of.'

'Could there be encumbrances without your knowing it?'

'I think not. I think it is impossible. Of all men your father is the last to encumber his estates in a manner unknown to his agent, and to pay off the interest in secret.'

'What is it then, Mr. Somers?'

'I do not know.' And then Mr. Somers paused. 'Of course you have heard of a visit he received the other day from a stranger?'

'Yes; I heard of it.'

'People about here are talking of it. And he—that man, with a younger man—they are still living in Cork, at a little drinking-house in South Main Street. The younger man has been seen down here twice.'

'But what can that mean?'

'I do not know. I tell you everything that I do know.'

Herbert exacted a promise from him that he would continue to tell him everything which he might learn, and then rode back to Castle Richmond.

'The whole thing must be a delusion,' he said to himself; and resolved that there was no valid reason why he should make Clara unhappy by any reference to the circumstance.

CHAPTER XIII.

MR. MOLLETT RETURNS TO SOUTH MAIN STREET.

I MUST now take my readers back to that very unsavoury public-house in South Main Street, Cork, in which, for the present, lived Mr. Matthew Mollett and his son Abraham.

I need hardly explain to a discerning public that Mr. Matthew Mollett was the gentleman who made that momentous call at Castle Richmond, and flurried all that household.

'Drat it!' said Mrs. Jones to herself on that day, as soon as she had regained the solitude of her own private apartment, after having taken a long look at Mr. Mollett in the hall. On that occasion she sat down on a low chair in the middle of the room, put her two hands down substantially on her two knees, gave a long sigh, and then made the above exclamation,—'Drat it!'

Mrs. Jones was still thoroughly a Saxon, although she had lived for so many years among the Celts. But it was only when she was quite alone that she allowed herself the indulgence of so peculiarly Saxon a mode of expressing either her surprise or indignation.

'It's the same man,' she said to herself, 'as come that day, as sure as eggs;' and then for five minutes she maintained her position, cogitating. 'And he's like the other fellow too,' she continued. 'Only, somehow he's not like him.' And then another pause. 'And yet he is; only it can't be; and he ain't just so tall, and he's older like.' And then, still meditating, Mrs. Jones kept her position for full ten minutes longer; at the end of which time she got up and shook herself. She deserved to be bracketed with Lord Brougham and Professor Faraday, for she had kept her mind intent on her subject, and had come to a resolution. 'I won't say nothing to nobody, noways,' was the expression of her mind's purpose. 'Only I'll tell missus as how he was the man as come to Wales.' And she did tell so much to her mistress—as we have before learned.

Mr. Mollett had gone down from Cork to Castle Richmond in one of those delightful Irish vehicles called a covered car. An inside-covered car is an equipage much given to shaking, seeing that it has a heavy top like a London cab, and that it runs on a pair of wheels. It is entered from behind, and slopes backwards. The sitter sits sideways, between a cracked window on one side and a cracked doorway on the other; and as a draught is always going in at the ear next the window, and out at the ear next the door, it is about as cold and comfortless a vehicle for winter as may be well imagined.   Now the journey from Castle Richmond to Cork has to be made right across the Boggeragh Mountains. It is over twenty miles Irish; and the road is never very good. Mr. Mollett, therefore, was five hours in the covered car on his return journey; and as he had stopped for lunch at Kanturk, and had not hurried himself at that meal, it was very dark and very cold when he reached the house in South Main Street.

I think I have explained that Mr. Mollett senior was not absolutely a drunkard; but nevertheless, he was not averse to spirits in cold weather, and on this journey had warmed himself with whisky once or twice on the road. He had found a shebeen house when he crossed the Nad river, and another on the mountain-top, and a third at the point where the road passes near the village of Blarney, and at all these convenient resting-spots Mr. Mollett had endeavoured to warm himself.

There are men who do not become absolutely drunk, but who do become absolutely cross when they drink more than is good for them; and of such men Mr. Mollett was one.   What with the cold air, and what with the whisky, and what with the jolting, Mr. Mollett was very cross when he reached the Kanturk Hotel, so that he only cursed the driver instead of giving him the expected gratuity.

'I'll come to yer honour in the morning,' said the driver.

'You may go to the devil in the morning,' answered Mr. Mollett; and this was the first intimation of his return which reached the ears of his expectant son.

'There's the governor,' said Aby, who was then flirting with Miss O'Dwyer in the bar.   'Somebody's been stroking him the wrong way of the 'air.'

The charms of Miss O'Dwyer in these idle days had been too much for the prudence of Mr. Abraham Mollett; by far too much considering that in his sterner moments his ambition led him to contemplate a match with a young lady of much higher rank in life.   But wine, which inspires us and fires us

'With courage, love, and joy,'

had inspired him with courage to forget his prudence, and with love for the lovely Fanny.

'Now, nonsense, Mr. Aby,' she had said to him a few minutes before the wheels of the covered car were heard in South Main Street.   'You know you main nothing of the sort.'

'By 'eavens, Fanny, I mean every word of it; may this drop be

my poison if I don't.   This piece of business here keeps me and
the governor hon and hoff like, and will do for some weeks
perhaps; but when that's done, honly say the word, and I'll
make you Mrs. M.   Isn't that fair now?'

'But, Mr. Aby——'

'Never mind the mister, Fan, between friends.'

'La! I couldn't call you Aby without it; could I?'

'Try, my darling.'

'Well—Aby—there now.   It does sound so uppish, don't it?
But tell me this now; what is the business that you and the old
gentleman is about down at Kanturk?'

Abraham Mollett hereupon had put one finger to his nose, and
then winked his eye.

'If you care about me, as you say you do, you wouldn't be shy
of just telling me as much as that.'

'That's business, Fan; and business and love don't hamalga-
mate like whisky and sugar.'

'Then I'll tell you what it is, Mr. Aby; I don't want to have
anything to do with a man who won't show his rispect by telling
me his sacrets.'

'That's it, is it, Fan?'

'I suppose you think I can't keep a sacret.   You think I'd be
telling father, I suppose.'

'Well, it's about some money that's due to him down there.'

'Who from?'

'He expects to get it from some of those Fitzgerald people.'

In saying so much Mr. Mollett the younger had not utterly
abandoned all prudence.   He knew very well that the car-driver
and others would be aware that his father had been to Castle
Richmond; and that it was more than probable that either he or
his father would have to make further visits there.   Indeed, he
had almost determined that he would go down to the baronet
himself.   Under these circumstances it might be well that some
pretext for these visits should be given.

'Which Fitzgerald, Mr. Aby?   Is it the Hap House young
man?'

'Hap House.   I never heard of such a place.   These people
live at Castle Richmond.'

'Oh—h—h!   If Mr. Mollett have money due there, sure he
have a good mark to go upon.   Why, Sir Thomas is about the
richest man in these parts.'

'And who is this other man; at 'Appy—what is it you call
his place?'

'Hap House.   Oh, it's he is the thorough-going young gentleman.   Only they say he's a leetle too fast.   To my mind, Mr.

Owen is the finest-looking man to be seen anywhere's in the county Cork.'

'He's a flame of yours, is he, Fan?'

'I don't know what you main by a flame. But there's not a girl in Cork but what likes the glance of his eye. They do say that he'd have Lady Clara Desmond; only there ain't no money.'

'And what's he to these other people?'

'Cousin, I believe; or hardly so much as that, I'm thinking. But all the same if anything was to happen to young Mr. Herbert, it would all go to him.'

'It would, would it?'

'So people say.'

'Mr. 'Erbert is the son of the old cock at Castle Richmond, isn't he?'

'Just so. He's the young cock; he, he, he!'

'And if he was to be—nowhere like; not his father's son at all, for instance, it would all go to this 'andsome 'Appy 'Ouse man; would it?'

'Every shilling, they say; house, title, and all.'

'Hum,' said Mr. Abraham Mollett; and he began again to calculate his family chances. Perhaps, after all, this handsome young man who was at present too poor to marry his noble lady love might be the more liberal man to deal with. But then any dealings with him would kill the golden goose at once. All would depend on the size of the one egg which might be extracted.

He certainly felt, however, that this Fitzgerald family arrangement was one which it was beneficial that he should know; but he felt also that it would be by no means necessary at present to communicate the information to his father. He put it by in his mind, regarding it as a fund on which he might draw if occasion should require. It might perhaps be pleasant for him to make the acquaintance of this 'andsome young Fitzgerald of 'Appy 'Ouse.

'And now, Fan, my darling, give us a kiss,' said he, getting up from his seat.

''Deed and I won't,' said Fan, withdrawing herself among the bottles and glasses.

''Deed and you shall, my love,' said Aby, pertinaciously, as he prepared to follow her through the brittle ware.

'Hu—sh! be aisy now. There's Tom. He's ears for everything, and eyes like a cat.'

'What do I care for Tom?'

'And father 'll be coming in. Be aisy, I tell you. I won't now, Mr. Aby; and that's enough. You'll break the bottle.'

' D—— the bottle. That's smashed hany way. Come, Fan, what's a kiss among friends?'

' Cock you up with kisses, indeed! how bad you are for dainties! There; do you hear that? That's the old gentleman;' and then, as the voice of Mr. Mollett senior was heard abusing the car-driver, Miss O'Dwyer smoothed her apron, put her hands to her side hair, and removed the débris of the broken bottle.

' Well, governor,' said Aby, ' how goes it?'

' How goes it, indeed! It goes pretty well, I dare say, in here, where you can sit drinking toddy all the evening, and doing nothing.'

' Why, what on hearth would you have me be doing? Better here than paddling about in the streets, isn't it?'

' If you could do a stroke of work now and then to earn your bread, it might be better.' Now Aby knew from experience that whenever his father talked to him about earning his bread, he was half drunk and whole cross. So he made no immediate reply on that point.

' You are cold I suppose, governor, and had better get a bit of something to eat, and a little tea.'

' And put my feet in hot water, and tallow my nose, and go to bed, hadn't I? Miss O'Dwyer, I'll trouble you to mix me a glass of brandy-punch. Of all the roads I ever travelled, that's the longest and hardest to get over. Dashed, if I didn't begin to think I'd never be here.' And so saying he flung himself into a chair, and put up his feet on the two hobs.

There was a kettle on one of them, which the young lady pushed a little nearer to the hot coals, in order to show that the water should be boiling; and as she did so Aby gave her a wink over his father's shoulder, by way of conveying to her an intimation that ' the governor was a little cut,' or in other language tipsy, and that the brandy-punch should be brewed with a discreet view to past events of the same description. All which Miss O'Dwyer perfectly understood.

It may easily be conceived that Aby was especially anxious to receive tidings of what had been done this day down in the Kanturk neighbourhood. He had given his views to his father, as will be remembered; and though Mr. Mollett senior had not professed himself as absolutely agreeing with them, he had nevertheless owned that he was imbued with the necessity of taking some great step. He had gone down to take this great step, and Aby was very anxious to know how it had been taken.

When the father and son were both sober, or when the son was tipsy, or when the father was absolutely drunk—an accident which would occur occasionally, the spirit and pluck of the son

was in the ascendant. He at such times was the more masterful
of the two, and generally contrived, either by persuasion or
bullying, to govern his governor. But when it did happen that
Mollett père was half drunk and cross with drink, then, at such
moments, Mollett fils had to acknowledge to himself that his
governor was not to be governed.

And, indeed, at such moments his governor could be very
disagreeable—could say nasty, bitter things, showing very little
parental affection, and make himself altogether bad society, not
only to his son but to his son's companions also. Now it appeared
to Aby that his father was at present in this condition.

He had only to egg him on to further drinking, and the
respectable gentleman would become stupid, noisy, soft, and
affectionate. But then, when in that state, he would blab
terribly. It was much with the view of keeping him from that
state, that under the present circumstances the son remained
with the father. To do the father justice, it may be asserted
that he knew his own weakness, and that, knowing it, he had
abstained from heavy drinking since he had taken in hand this
great piece of diplomacy.

'But you must be hungry, governor; won't you take a bit of
something?'

'Shall we get you a steek, Mr. Mollett?' asked Miss O'Dwyer,
hospitably, 'or jest a bit of bacon with a couple of eggs or so?
It wouldn't be a minute, you know?'

'Your eggs are all addled and bad,' said Mr. Mollett: 'and as
for a beef-steak, it's my belief there isn't such a thing in all
Ireland.' After which civil speech, Miss O'Dwyer winked at
Aby, as much as to say, ' You see what a state he's in.'

'Have a bit of buttered toast and a cup of tea, governor,'
suggested the son.

' I'm d—— if I do,' replied the father. 'You're become uncommon fond of tea of late—that is, for other people. I don't
see you take much of it yourself.'

' A cup of tay is the thing to warm one afther such a journey
as you've had; that's certain, Mr. Mollett,' said Fanny.

' Them's your ideas about warming, are they, my dear?' said
the elderly gentleman. 'Do you come and sit down on my knee
here for a few minutes or so, and that'd warm me better than all
the "tay " in the world.'

Aby showed by his face that he was immeasurably disgusted
by the iniquitous coarseness of this overture. Miss O'Dwyer,
however, looking at the gentleman's age, and his state as regarded
liquor, passed it over as of no moment whatsoever. So that
when, in the later part of the evening, Aby expressed to that

young lady his deep disgust, she merely said, 'Oh, bother; what matters an old man like that?'

And then, when they were at this pass, Mr. O'Dwyer came in. He did not interfere much with his daughter in the bar room, but he would occasionally take a dandy of punch there, and ask how things were going on in doors. He was a fat, thickset man, with a good-humoured face, a flattened nose, and a great aptitude for stable occupations. He was part owner of the Kanturk car, as has been before said, and was the proprietor of sundry other cars, open cars and covered cars, plying for hire in the streets of Cork.

'I hope the mare took your honour well down to Kanturk and back again,' said he, addressing his elder customer with a chuck of his head intended for a bow.

'I don't know what you call well,' said Mr. Mollett. 'She hadn't a leg to stand upon for the last three hours.'

'Not a leg to stand upon! Faix, then, and it's she'd have the four good legs if she travelled every inch of the way from Donagh-a-Dee to Ti-vora,' to which distance Mr. O'Dwyer specially referred as being supposed to be the longest known in Ireland.

'She may be able to do that; but I'm blessed if she's fit to go to Kanturk and back.'

'She's done the work, anyhow,' said Mr. O'Dwyer, who evidently thought that this last argument was conclusive.

'And a precious time she's been about it. Why, my goodness, it would have been better for me to have walked it. As Sir Thomas said to me——'

'What! did you see Sir Thomas Fitzgerald?'

Hereupon Aby gave his father a nudge; but the father either did not appreciate the nudge, or did not choose to obey it.

'Yes; I did see him. Why shouldn't I?'

'Only they do say he's hard to get to speak to now-a-days. He's not over well, you know, these years back.'

'Well or ill he'll see me, I take it, when I go that distance to ask him. There's no doubt about that; is there, Aby?'

'Can't say, I'm sure, not knowing the gentleman,' said Aby.

'We holds land from Sir Thomas, we do; that is, me and my brother Mick, and a better landlord ain't nowhere,' said Mr. O'Dwyer.

'Oh, you're one of the tenants, are you? The rents are paid pretty well, ain't they?'

'To the day,' said Mr. O'Dwyer, proudly.

'What would you think now——' Mr. Mollett was continuing; uAby interrupted him somewhat violently.

'Hold your confounded stupid tongue, will you, you old jolter-head;' and on this occasion he put his hand on his father's shoulder and shook him.

'Who are you calling jolterhead? Who do you dare to speak to in that way? you impudent young cub you. Am I to ask your leave when I want to open my mouth?'

Aby had well known that his father in his present mood would not stand the manner in which the interruption was attempted. Nor did he wish to quarrel before the publican and his daughter But anything was better than allowing his father to continue in the strain in which he was talking.

'You are talking of things which you don't hunderstand, and about people you don't know,' said Aby. 'You've had a drop too much on the road too, and you 'ad better go to bed.'

Old Mollett turned round to strike at his son; but even in his present state he was somewhat quelled by Aby's eye. Aby was keenly alive to the necessity for prudence on his father's part, though he was by no means able to be prudent himself.

'Talking of things which I don't understand, am I?' said the old man. 'That's all you know about it. Give me another glass of that brandy toddy, my dear.'

But Aby's look had quelled, or at any rate silenced him; and though he did advance another stage in tipsiness before they succeeded in getting him off to bed, he said no more about Sir Thomas Fitzgerald or his Castle Richmond secrets.

Nevertheless, he had said enough to cause suspicion. One would not have imagined, on looking at Mr. O'Dwyer, that he was a very crafty person, or one of whose finesse in affairs of the world it would be necessary to stand much in awe. He seemed to be thick, and stolid, and incapable of deep inquiry; but, nevertheless, he was as fond of his neighbours' affairs as another, and knew as much about the affairs of his neighbours at Kanturk as any man in the county Cork.

He himself was a Kanturk man, and his wife had been a Kanturk woman; no less a person, indeed, than the sister of Father Bernard M'Carthy, rest her soul;—for it was now at peace, let us all hope. She had been dead these ten years; but he did not the less keep up his connection with the old town, or with his brother-in-law the priest, or with the affairs of the persons there adjacent; especially, we may say, those of his landlord, Sir Thomas Fitzgerald, under whom he still held a small farm, in conjunction with his brother Mick, the publican at Kanturk.

'What's all that about Sir Thomas?' said he to his daughter in a low voice as soon as the Molletts had left the bar.

'Well, I don't just know,' said Fanny. She was a good daughter, and loved her father, whose indoor affairs she kept tight enough for him. But she had hardly made up her mind as yet whether or no it would suit her to be Mrs. Abraham Mollett. Should such be her destiny, it might be as well for her not to talk about her husband's matters.

'Is it true that the old man did see Sir Thomas to-day?'

'You heard what passed, father; but I suppose it is true.'

'And the young 'un has been down to Kanturk two or three times. What can the like of them have to do with Sir Thomas?'

To this Fanny could only say that she knew nothing about it, which in the main was true. Aby, indeed, had said that his father had gone down to collect money that was due to him; but then Fanny did not believe all that Aby said.

'I don't like that young 'un at all,' continued Mr. O'Dwyer. 'He's a nasty, sneaking fellow, as cares for no one but his own belly. I'm not over fond of the old 'un neither.'

'They is both free enough with their money, father,' said the prudent daughter.

'Oh, they is welcome in the way of business, in course. But look here, Fan; don't you have nothing to say to that Aby; do you hear me?'

'Who? I? ha, ha, ha!'

'It's all very well laughing; but mind what I says, for I won't have it. He is a nasty, sneaking, good-for-nothing fellow, besides being a heretic. What'd your uncle Bernard say?'

'Oh! for the matter of that, if I took a liking to a fellow I shouldn't ask Uncle Bernard what he had to say. If he didn't like it, I suppose he might do the other thing.'

'Well, I won't have it. Do you hear that?'

'Laws, father, what nonsense you do talk. Who's thinking about the man? He comes here for what he wants to ate and dhrink, and I suppose the house is free to him as another. If not we'd betther just shut up the front door.' After which she tossed herself up and began to wipe her glasses in a rather dignified manner.

Mr. O'Dwyer sat smoking his pipe and chewing the cud of his reflections. 'They ain't afther no good; I'm sure of that.' In saying which, however, he referred to the doings of the Molletts down at Kanturk, rather than to any amatory proceedings which might have taken place between the young man and his daughter.

On the following morning Mr. Mollett senior awoke with a racking headache. My belief is, that when men pay this penalty for drinking, they are partly absolved from other penalties. The penalties on drink are various. I mean those which affect the body, exclusive of those which affect the mind. There are great red swollen noses, very disagreeable both to the wearer and his acquaintances; there are morning headaches, awful to be thought of; there are sick stomachs, by which means the offender escapes through a speedy purgatory; there are sallow cheeks, sunken eyes, and shaking shoulders; there are very big bellies, and no bellies at all; and there is delirium tremens. For the most part a man escapes with one of these penalties. If he have a racking headache, his general health does not usually suffer so much as though he had endured no such immediate vengeance from violated nature. Young Aby when he drank had no headaches; but his eye was bloodshot, his cheek bloated, and his hand shook. His father, on the other hand, could not raise his head after a debauch; but when that was gone, all ill results of his imprudence seemed to have vanished.

At about noon on that day Aby was sitting by his father's bedside. Up to that time it had been quite impossible to induce him to speak a word. He could only groan, swallow soda water with 'hairs of the dog that bit him' in it, and lay with his head between his arms. But soon after noon Aby did induce him to say a word or two. The door of the room was closely shut, the little table was strewed with soda-water bottles and last drops of small goes of brandy. Aby himself had a cigar in his mouth, and on the floor near the bed-foot was a plate with a cold, greasy mutton chop, Aby having endeavoured in vain to induce his father to fortify exhausted nature by eating. The appearance of the room and the air within it would not have been pleasant to fastidious people. But then the Molletts were not fastidious.

'You did see Sir Thomas, then?'

'Yes, I did see him. I wish, Aby, you'd let me lie just for another hour or so. I'd be all right then. The jolting of that confounded car has nearly shaken my head to pieces.'

But Aby was by no means inclined to be so merciful. The probability was that he would be able to pump his father more thoroughly in his present weak state than he might do in a later part of the afternoon; so he persevered.

'But, governor, it's so important we should know what we're about. Did you see any one else except himself?'

'I saw them all I believe, except her. I was told she never showed in the morning; but I'm blessed if I don't think I saw the skirt of her dress through an open door. I'll tell you what, Aby, I could not stand that.'

'Perhaps, father, after hall it'll be better I should manage the business down there.'

'I believe there won't be much more to manage. But, Aby,

do leave me now, there's a good fellow; then in another hour or so I'll get up, and we'll have it all out.'

'When you're out in the open air and comfortable, it won't be fair to be bothering you with business. Come, governor, ten minutes will tell the whole of it if you'll only mind your eye. How did you begin with Sir Thomas?' And then Aby went to the door, opened it very gently, and satisfied himself that there was nobody listening on the landing-place.

Mr. Mollett sighed wearily, but he knew that his only hope was to get this job of talking over. 'What was it you were saying, Aby?'

'How did you begin with Sir Thomas?'

'How did I begin with him? Let me see. Oh! I just told him who I was; and then he turned away and looked down under the fire like, and I thought he was going to make a faint of it.'　　　　　　　　　　　　　　　　　　　　　　　　　　　,

'I didn't suppose he would be very glad to see you, governor.

'When I saw how badly he took it, and how wretched he seemed, I almost made up my mind to go away and never trouble him any more.'

'You did, did you?'

'And just to take what he'd choose to give me.'

'Oh, them's your hideas, hare they? Then I tell you what; I shall just take the matter into my own hands hentirely. You have no more 'eart than a chicken.'

'Ah, that's very well, Aby; but you did not see him.'

'Do you think that would make hany difference? When a man's a job of work to do, 'e should do it. Them's my notions. Do you think a man like that is to go and hact in that way, and then not pay for it? Whose wife is she I'd like to know?'

There was a tone of injured justice about Aby which almost roused the father to participate in the son's indignation. 'Well; I did my best, though the old gentleman was in such a taking,' said he.

'And what was your best? Come, out with it at once.'

'I—m-m. I —just told him who I was, you know.'

'I guess he understood that quite well.'

'And then I said things weren't going exactly well with me.'

'You shouldn't have said that at all. What matters that to him? What you hask for you hask for because you're able to demand it. That's the ground for hus to take, and by —— I'll take it too. There shall be no 'alf-measures with me.'

'And then I told him—just what we were agreed, you know.

'That we'd go snacks in the whole concern?'

'I didn't exactly say that.'

'Then what the devil did you say?'

'Why, 1 told him that, looking at what the property was, twelve hundred pounds wasn't much.'

'I should think not either.'

'And that if his son was to be allowed to have it all——'

'A bastard, you know, keeping it away from the proper heir.' It may almost be doubted whether, in so speaking, Aby did not almost think that he himself had a legitimate right to inherit the property at Castle Richmond.

'He must look to pay up handsome.'

'But did you say what 'andsome meant?'

'Well, I didn't—not then.   He fell about upon the table like, and I wasn't quite sure he wouldn't make a die of it; and then heaven knows what might have happened to me.'

'Psha; you 'as no pluck, governor.'

'I'll tell you what it is, Aby, I ain't so sure you'd have such an uncommon deal of pluck yourself.'

'Well, I'll try, at any rate.'

'It isn't such a pleasant thing to see an old gentleman in that state.   And what would happen if he chose to ring the bell and order the police to take me?   Have you ever thought of that?'

'Gammon.'

'But it isn't gammon.   A word from him would put me into quod, and there I should be for the rest of my days.   But what would you care for that?'   And poor Mr. Mollett senior shook under the bedclothes as his attention became turned to this very dreary aspect of his affairs.   'Pluck, indeed!   I'll tell you what it is, Aby, I often wonder at my own pluck.'

'Psha!   Wouldn't a word from you split upon him, and upon her, and upon the young 'un, and ruin 'em?   Or a word from me either, for the matter of that?'

Mr. Mollett senior shook again.   He repented now, as he had already done twenty times, that he had taken that son of his into his confidence.

'And what on hearth did you say to him?' continued Aby.

'Well, not much more then; at least, not very much more. There was a good deal of words, but they didn't seem to lead to much, except this, just to make him understand that he must come down handsome.'

'And there was nothing done about Hemmiline?'

'No,' said the father, rather shortly.

'If that was settled, that would be the clincher.   There would be no further trouble to nobody then.   It would be all smooth sailing for your life, governor, and lots of tin.'

'I tell you what it is, Aby, you may just drop that, for I won't have the young lady bothered about it, nor yet the young lady's father.'

' 'You won't, won't you ?'

' No, I won't; so there's an end of it.'

' I suppose I may pay my distresses to any young lady if I think fitting.'

' And have yourself kicked into the ditch.'

' I know too much for kicking, governor.'

' They shall know as much as you do, and more too, if you go on with that. There's a measure in all things. I won't have it done, so I tell you.' And the father turned his face round to the wall.

This was by no means the end of the conversation, though we need not verbatim go through any more of it. It appeared that old Mollett had told Sir Thomas that his permanent silence could be purchased by nothing short .of a settled ' genteel' income for himself and his son, no absolute sum having been mentioned ; and that Sir Thomas had required a fortnight for his answer, which answer was to be conveyed to Mr. Mollett verbally at the end of that time. It was agreed that Mr. Mollett should repeat his visit to Castle Richmond on that day fortnight.

' In the mean time I'll go down and freshen the old gentleman up a bit,' said Aby, as he left his father's bedroom.

CHAPTER XIV.

THE REJECTED SUITOR.

AFTER the interview between Herbert and his mother, it became an understood thing at Castle Richmond that he was engaged to Lady Clara. Sir Thomas raised no further objection, although it was clear to all the immediate family that he was by no means gratified at his son's engagement. Very little more passed between Sir Thomas and Lady Fitzgerald on the subject. He merely said that he would consider the question of his son's income, and expressed a hope, or perhaps an opinion rather than a hope, that the marriage would not take place quite immediately.

Under these circumstances, Herbert hardly spoke further to his father upon the matter. He certainly did feel sore that he should be so treated—that he should be made to understand that there was a difficulty, but that the difficulty could not be explained to him. No absolute opposition was however made, and he would not therefore complain. As to money, he would say nothing till something should be said to him.

With his mother. however. the matter was different. She had said that she would welcome Clara ; and she did so. Immediately after speaking to Sir Thomas, she drove over to Desmond Court, and said soft, sweet things to Clara in her most winning way ;—said soft things also to the countess, who received them very graciously ; took Clara home to Castle Richmond for that night, somewhat to the surprise and much to the gratification of Herbert, who found her sitting slily with the other girls when he came in before dinner; and arranged for her to make a longer visit after the interval of a week or two. Herbert, therefore, was on thoroughly good terms with his mother, and did enjoy some of the delights which he had promised himself.

With his sisters, also, and especially with Emmeline, he was once more in a good humour. To her he made ample apology for his former crossness, and received ample absolution. ' I was so harassed,' he said, ' by my father's manner that I hardly knew what I was doing. And even now, when I think of his evident dislike to the marriage, it nearly drives me wild.' The truth of all which Emmeline sadly acknowledged. How could any of them talk of their father except in a strain of sadness?

All these things did not happen in the drawing-room at Castle Richmond without also being discussed in the kitchen. It was soon known over the house that Master Herbert was to marry Lady Clara, and, indeed, there was no great pretence of keeping it secret. The girls told the duchess, as they called Mrs. Jones— of course in confidence—but Mrs. Jones knew what such confidence meant, especially as the matter was more than once distinctly alluded to by her ladyship; and thus the story was told, in confidence, to everybody in the establishment, and then repeated by them, in confidence also, to nearly everybody out of it.

Ill news, they say, flies fast; and this news, which, going in that direction, became ill, soon flew to Hap House.

' So young Fitzgerald and the divine Clara are to hit off, are they?' said Captain Donnellan, who had driven over from Buttevant barracks to breakfast at Hap House on a hunting-morning.

There were other men present, more intimate friends of Owen than this captain, who had known of Owen's misfortune in that quarter; and a sign was made to Donnellan to bid him drop the subject; but it was too late.

' Who? my cousin Herbert?' said Owen, sharply. ' Have you heard of this, Barry?'

' Well,' said Barry, ' those sort of things are always being said, you know. I did hear something of it somewhere. But I can't say I thought much about it.' And then the subject was dropped during that morning's breakfast. They all went to the hunt, and in the course of the day Owen contrived to learn that the report was well founded.

That evening, as the countess and her daughter were sitting together over the fire, the gray-headed old butler brought in a letter upon an old silver salver, saying, 'For Lady Clara, if you please, my lady.'

The countess not unnaturally thought that the despatch had come from Castle Richmond, and smiled graciously as Clara put out her hand for the missive. Lady Desmond again let her eyes drop upon the book which she was reading, as though to show that she was by far too confiding a mamma to interfere in any correspondence between her daughter and her daughter's lover. At the moment Lady Clara had been doing nothing. Her work was, indeed, on her lap, and her workbox was at her elbow; but her thoughts had been far away; far away as regards idea, though not so as to absolute locality; for in her mind she was walking beneath those elm-trees, and a man was near her, with a horse following at his heels.

'The messenger is to wait for an answer, my lady,' said the old butler, with a second nod, which on this occasion was addressed to Clara; and then the man withdrew.

Lady Clara blushed ruby red up to the roots of her hair when her eyes fell on the address of the letter, for she knew it to be in the handwriting of Owen Fitzgerald. Perhaps the countess from the corner of her eye may have observed some portion of her daughter's blushes; but if so, she said nothing, attributing them to Clara's natural bashfulness in her present position. 'She will get over it soon,' the countess may probably have said to herself.

Clara was indecisive, disturbed in her mind, and wretched. Owen had sent her other letters; but they had been brought to her surreptitiously, had been tendered to her in secret, and had always been returned by her unopened. She had not told her mother of these; at least, not purposely or at the moment; but she had been at no trouble to conceal the facts: and when the countess had once asked, she freely told her what had happened with an absence of any confusion, which had quite put Lady Desmond at her ease. But this letter was brought to her in the most open manner, and an answer to it openly demanded.

She turned it round slowly in her hand, and then looking up, said, ' Mamma, this is from Owen Fitzgerald; what had I better do with it?'

' From Owen Fitzgerald! Are you sure?'

' Yes, mamma.' And then the countess had also to consider what steps under such circumstances had better be taken. In the mean time Clara held out her hand, tendering the letter to her mother.

'You had better open it, my dear, and read it. No doubt it must be answered.' Lady Desmond felt that now there could be no danger from Owen Fitzgerald. Indeed she thought that there was not a remembrance of him left in her daughter's bosom; that the old love, such baby-love as there had been, had vanished, quite swept out of that little heart by this new love of a brighter sort. But then Lady Desmond knew nothing of her daughter.

So instructed, Clara broke the seal, and read the letter, which ran thus :—

'Hap House, February 184—.

'My promised Love,

'For let what will happen, such you are ; I have this morning heard tidings, which, if true, will go far to drive me to despair. But I will not believe them from any lips save your own. I have heard that you are engaged to marry Herbert Fitzgerald. At once, however, I declare that I do not believe the statement. I have known you too well to think that you can be false.

'But, at any rate, I beg the favour of an interview with you. After what has passed I think that under any circumstances I have a right to demand it. I have pledged myself to you ; and as that pledge has been accepted, I am entitled to some consideration.

'I write this letter to you openly, being quite willing that you should show it to your mother if you think fit. My messenger will wait, and I do implore you to send me an answer. And remember, Lady Clara, that, having accepted my love, you cannot whistle me down the wind as though I were of no account. After what has passed between us, you cannot surely refuse to see me once more.

'Ever your own—if you will have it so,

'OWEN FITZGERALD.'

She read the letter very slowly, ever and anon looking up at her mother's face, and seeing that her mother was—not reading her book, but pretending to read it. When she had finished it, she held it for a moment, and then said, 'Mamma, will you not look at it.'

'Certainly, my dear, if you wish me to do so.' And she took the letter from her daughter's hand, and read it.

'Just what one would expect from him, my dear ; eager, impetuous, and thoughtless. One should not blame him much, for he does not mean to do harm. But if he had any sense, he would know that he was taking trouble for nothing.'

'And what shall I do, mamma?'

'Well, I really think that I should answer him.' It was delightful to see the perfect confidence which the mother had in her daughter. 'And I think I should see him, if he will insist upon it. It is foolish in him to persist in remembering two words which you spoke to him as a child; but perhaps it will be well that you should tell him yourself that you were a child when you spoke those two words.'

And then Clara sent off the following reply, written under her mother's dictation; though the countess strove very hard to convince her daughter that she was wording it out of her own head:—

'Lady Clara Desmond presents her compliments to Mr. Owen Fitzgerald, and will see Mr. Owen Fitzgerald at Desmond Court at two o'clock to-morrow, if Mr. Owen Fitzgerald persists in demanding such an interview. Lady Clara Desmond, however, wishes to express her opinion that it would be better avoided.

'Desmond Court,
    'Thursday evening.'

The countess thought that this note was very cold and formal, and would be altogether conclusive; but, nevertheless, at about eleven o'clock that night there came another messenger from Hap House with another letter, saying that Owen would be at Desmond Court at two o'clock on the following day.

'He is very foolish; that is all I can say,' said the countess.

All that night and all the next morning poor Clara was very wretched. That she had been right to give up a suitor who lived such a life as Owen Fitzgerald lived she could not doubt. But, nevertheless, was she true in giving him up? Had she made any stipulation as to his life when she accepted his love? If he called her false, as doubtless he would call her, how would she defend herself? Had she any defence to offer? It was not only that she had rejected him, a poor lover; but she had accepted a rich lover! What could she say to him when he upbraided her for such sordid conduct?

And then as to her whistling him down the wind. Did she wish to do that? In what state did her heart stand towards him? Might it not be that, let her be ever so much on her guard, she would show him some tenderness,—tenderness which would be treason to her present affianced suitor? Oh, why had her mother desired her to go through such an interview as this!

When two o'clock came Clara was in the drawing-room. She

had said nothing to her mother as to the manner in which this meeting should take place. But then at first she had had an idea that Lady Desmond would be present. But as the time came near Clara was still alone. When her watch told her that it was already two, she was still by herself; and when the old servant, opening the door, announced that Mr. Fitzgerald was there, she was still unsupported by the presence of any companion. It was very surprising that on such an occasion her mother should have kept herself away.

She had not seen Owen Fitzgerald since that day when they had walked together under the elm-trees, and it can hardly be said that she saw him now. She had a feeling that she had injured him—had deceived, and in a manner betrayed him; and that feeling became so powerful with her that she hardly dared to look him in the face.

He, when he entered the room, walked straight up to her, and offered her his hand. He, too, looked round the room to see whether Lady Desmond was there, and not finding her, was surprised. He had hardly hoped that such an opportunity would be allowed to him for declaring the strength of his passion.

She got up, and taking his hand, muttered something; it certainly did not matter what, for it was inaudible; but such as the words were, they were the first spoken between them.

'Lady Clara,' he began; and then stopped himself; and, considering, recommenced—'Clara, a report has reached my ears which I will believe from no lips but your own.'

She now sat down on a sofa, and pointed to a chair for him, but he remained standing, and did so during the whole interview; or rather, walking; for when he became energetic and impetuous, he moved about from place to place in the room, as though incapable of fixing himself in one position.

Clara was ignorant whether or no it behoved her to rebuke him for calling her simply by her Christian name. She thought that she ought to do so, but she did not do it.

'I have been told,' he continued, 'that you have engaged yourself to marry Herbert Fitzgerald; and I have now come to hear a contradiction of this from yourself.'

'But, Mr. Fitzgerald, it is true.'

'It is true that Herbert Fitzgerald is your accepted lover?'

'Yes,' she said, looking down upon the ground, and blushing deeply as she said it.

There was a pause of a few moments, during which she felt that the full fire of his glance was fixed upon her, and then he spoke.

'You may well be ashamed to confess it,' he said; 'you may well feel that you dare not look me in the face as you pronounce the words. I would have believed it, Clara, from no other mouth than your own.'

It appeared to Clara herself now as though she were greatly a culprit. She had not a word to say in her own defence. All those arguments as to Owen's ill course of life were forgotten; and she could only remember that she had acknowledged that she loved him, and that she was now acknowledging that she loved another.

But now Owen had made his accusation; and as it was not answered, he hardly knew how to proceed. He walked about the room, endeavouring to think what he had better say next.

'I know this, Clara; it is your mother's doing, and not your own. You could not bring yourself to be false, unless by her instigation.'

'No,' said she; 'you are wrong there. It is not my mother's doing; what I have done, I have done myself.'

'Is it not true,' he asked, 'that your word was pledged to me? Had you not promised me that you would be my wife?'

'I was very young,' she said, falling back upon the only excuse which occurred to her at the moment as being possible to be used without incriminating him.

'Young! Is not that your mother's teaching? Why, those were her very words when she came to me at my house. I did not know that youth was any excuse for falsehood.'

'But it may be an excuse for folly,' said Clara.

'Folly! what folly? The folly of loving a poor suitor; the folly of being willing to marry a man who has not a large estate! Clara, I did not think that you could have learned so much in so short a time.'

All this was very hard upon her. She felt that it was hard, for she knew that he had done that which entitled her to regard her pledge to him as at an end; but the circumstances were such that she could not excuse herself.

'Am I to understand,' said Owen Fitzgerald, 'that all that has passed between us is to go for nothing? that such promises as we have made to each other are to be of no account? To me they are sacred pledges, from which I would not escape even if I could.'

As he then paused for a reply, she was obliged to say something.

'I hope you have not come here to upbraid me, Mr. Fitzgerald.'

'Clara,' he continued, 'I have passed the last year with perfect reliance upon your faith. I need hardly tell you that it has not been passed happily, for it has been passed without seeing you. But though you have been absent from me, I have never doubted you. I have known that it was necessary that we should wait— wait perhaps till years should make you mistress of your own actions: but nevertheless I was not unhappy, for I was sure of your love.'

Now it was undoubtedly the case that Fitzgerald was treating her unfairly; and though she had not her wits enough about her to ascertain this by process of argument, nevertheless the idea did come home to her. It was true that she had promised her love to this man, as far as such promise could be conveyed by one word of assent; but it was true also that she had been almost a child when she pronounced that word, and that things which had since occurred had entitled her to annul any amount of contract to which she might have been supposed to bind herself by that one word. She bethought herself, therefore, that as she was so hard pressed she was forced to defend herself.·

'I was very young then, Mr. Fitzgerald, and hardly knew what I was saying: afterwards, when mamma spoke to me, I felt that I was bound to obey her.'

'What, to obey her by forgetting me?'

'No; I have never forgotten you, and never shall. I remember too well your kindness to my brother; your kindness to us all.'

'Psha! you know I do not speak of that. Are you bound to obey your mother by forgetting that you have loved me?'

She paused a moment before she answered him, looking now full before her,—hardly yet bold enough to look him in the face. 'No,' she said; 'I have not forgotten that I loved you. I shall never forget it. Child as I was, it shall never be forgotten. But I cannot love you now—not in the manner you would have me?'

'And why not, Lady Clara? Why is love to cease on your part—to be thrown aside so easily by you, while with me it remains so stern a fact, and so deep a necessity? Is that just? When the bargain has once been made, should it not be equally binding on us both?'

'I do not think you are fair to me, Mr. Fitzgerald,' she said; and some spirit was now rising in her bosom.

'Not fair to you? Do you say that I am unfair to you? Speak but one word to say that the troth which you pledged me a year since shall still remain unbroken, and I will at once leave you till you yourself shall name the time when my suit may be renewed.'

'You know that I cannot do that.'

'And why not? I know that you ought to do it.'

'No, Mr. Fitzgerald, I ought not. I am now engaged to your cousin, with the consent of mamma and of his friends. I can say nothing to you now which I cannot repeat to him; nor can I say anything which shall oppose his wishes.'

'He is then so much more to you now than I am ?'

'He is everything to me now.'

'That is all the reply I am to get then! You acknowledge your falseness, and throw me off without vouchsafing me any answer beyond this.'

'What would you have me say? I did do that which was wrong and foolish, when—when we were walking there on the avenue. I did give a promise which I cannot now keep. It was all so hurried that I hardly remember what I said. But of this I am sure, that if I have caused you unhappiness, I am very sorry to have done so. I cannot alter it all now; I cannot unsay what I said then; nor can I offer you that which I have now absolutely given to another.'

And then, as she finished speaking, she did pluck up courage to look him in the face. She was now standing as well as he; but she was so standing that the table, which was placed near the sofa, was still between him and her. As she finished speaking the door opened, and the Countess of Desmond walked slowly into the room.

Owen Fitzgerald, when he saw her, bowed low before her, and then frankly offered her his hand. There was something in his manner to ladies devoid of all bashfulness, and yet never too bold. He seemed to be aware that in speaking to any lady, be she who she might, he was only exercising his undoubted privilege as a man. He never hummed and hawed and shook in his shoes as though the majesty of womanhood were too great for his encounter. There are such men, and many of them, who carry this dread to the last day of their long lives. I have often wondered what women think of men who regard women as too awful for the free exercise of open speech.

'Mr. Fitzgerald,' she said, accepting the hand which he offered to her, but resuming her own very quickly, and then standing before him in all the dignity which she was able to assume, 'I quite concurred with my daughter that it was right that she should see you, as you insisted on such an interview; but you must excuse me if I interrupt it. I must protect her from the embarrassment which your—your vehemence may occasion her.'

'Lady Desmond,' he replied, 'you are quite at liberty, as far as I am concerned, to hear all that passes between us. Your daughter is betrothed to me, and I have come to claim from her the fulfilment of her promise.'

'For shame, Mr. Fitzgerald, for shame! When she was a child you extracted from her one word of folly; and now you would take advantage of that foolish word; now, when you know that she is engaged to a man she loves with the full consent of all her friends. I thought I knew you well enough to feel sure that you were not so ungenerous.'

'Ungenerous! no; I have not that generosity which would enable me to give up my very heart's blood, the only joy of my soul, to such a one as my cousin Herbert.'

'You have nothing to give up, Mr. Fitzgerald: you must have known from the very first that my daughter could not marry you——'

'Not marry me! And why not, Lady Desmond? Is not my blood as good as his?—unless, indeed, you are prepared to sell your child to the highest bidder!'

'Clara, my dear, I think you had better leave the room,' said the countess; 'no doubt you have assured Mr. Fitzgerald that you are engaged to his cousin Herbert.'

'Yes, mamma.'

'Then he can have no further claim on your attendance, and his vehemence will terrify you.'

'Vehement! how can I help being vehement when, like a ruined gambler, I am throwing my last chance for such a stake?'

And then he intercepted Clara as she stepped towards the drawing-room door. She stopped in her course, and stood still, looking down upon the ground.

'Mr. Fitzgerald,' said the countess, 'I will thank you to let Lady Clara leave the room. She has given you the answer for which you have asked, and it would not be right in me to permit her to be subjected to further embarrassment.'

'I will only ask her to listen to one word. Clara——'

'Mr. Fitzgerald, you have no right to address my daughter with that freedom,' said the countess; but Owen hardly seemed to hear her.

'I here, in your hearing, protest against your marriage with Herbert Fitzgerald. I claim your love as my own. I bid you think of the promise which you gave me; and I tell you that as I loved you then with all my heart, so do I love you at this moment; so shall I love you always. Now I will not hinder you any longer.'

And then he opened the door for her, and she passed on, bowing to him, and muttering some word of farewell that was inaudible.

He stood for a moment with the door in his hand, meditating whether he might not say good morning to the countess without returning into the room; but as he so stood she called him. 'Mr. Fitzgerald,' she said; and so he therefore came back, and once more closed the door.

And then he saw that the countenance of Lady Desmond was much changed. Hitherto she had been every inch the countess, stern and cold and haughty; but now she looked at him as she used to look in those old winter evenings when they were accustomed to talk together over the evening fire in close frendliness, while she, Lady Desmond, would speak to him in the intimacy of her heart of her children, Patrick and Clara.

'Mr. Fitzgerald,' she said, and the tone of her voice also was changed. 'You are hardly fair to us; are you?'

'Not fair, Lady Desmond?'

'No, not fair. Sit down now, and listen to me for a moment. If you had a child, a penniless girl like Clara, would you be glad to see her married to such a one as you are yourself?'

'In what way do you mean? Speak out, Lady Desmond.'

'No; I will not speak out, for I would not hurt you. I myself am too fond of you—as an old friend, to wish to do so. That you may marry and live happily, live near us here, so that we may know you, I most heartily desire. But you cannot marry that child.'

'And why not, if she loves me?'

'Nay, not even if she did. Wealth and position are necessary to the station in which she has been born. She is an earl's daughter, penniless as she is. I will have no secrets from you. As a mother, I could not give her to one whose career is such as yours. As the widow of an earl, I could not give her to one whose means of maintaining her are so small. If you will think of this, you will hardly be angry with me.'

'Love is nothing then?'

'Is all to be sacrificed to your love? Think of it, Mr. Fitzgerald, and let me have the happiness of knowing that you consent to this match.'

'Never!' said he. 'Never!' And so he left the room, without wishing her further farewell.

CHAPTER XV.

DIPLOMACY.

ABOUT a week after the last convérsation that has been related as having taken place at the Kanturk Hotel, Mr. Mollett junior was on his way to Castle Richmond. He had on that occasion stated his intention of making such a journey with the view of 'freshening the old gentleman up a bit;' and although his father did all in his power to prevent the journey, going so far on one occasion as to swear that if it was made he would throw over the game altogether, nevertheless Aby persevered.

'You may leave the boards whenever you like, governor,' said Aby. 'I know quite enough of the part to carry on the play.'

'You think you do,' said the father in his anger; 'but you'll find yourself in the dark yet before you've done.'

And then again he expostulated in a different tone. 'You'll ruin it all, Aby; you will indeed; you don't know all the circumstances; indeed you don't.'

'Don't I?' said Aby. 'Then I'll not be long learning them.'

The father did what he could; but he had no means of keeping his son at home, and so Aby went. Aby doubtless entertained an idea that his father was deficient in pluck for the management of so difficult a matter, and that he could supply what his father wanted. So he dressed himself in his best, and having hired a gig and a man who he flattered himself would look like a private servant, he started from Cork, and drove himself to Castle Richmond.

He had on different occasions been down in the neighbourhood, prowling about like a thief in the night, picking up information as he called it, and seeing how the land lay; but he had never yet presented himself to any one within the precincts of the Castle Richmond demesne. His present intention was to drive up to the front door, and ask at once for Sir Thomas Fitzgerald, sending in his card if need be, on which were printed the words :—

MR. ABRAHAM MOLLETT, Junior.

With the additional words, 'Piccadilly, London,' written in the left-hand lower corner.

'I'll take the bull by the horns,' said he to himself. 'It's better to make the spoon at once, even if we do run some small chance of spoiling the horn.' And that he might be well enabled to carry out his purpose with reference to this bull, he lifted his flask to his mouth as soon as he had passed through the great demesne gate, and took a long pull at it. 'There's nothing like a little jumping powder,' he said, speaking to himself again; and then he drove boldly up the avenue.

He had not yet come in sight of the house when he met two gentlemen walking on the road. They, as he approached, stood a little on one side, not only so as to allow him to pass, but to watch him as he did so. They were Mr. Somers and Herbert Fitzgerald.

'It is the younger of those two men. I'm nearly certain of it,' said Somers as the gig approached. 'I saw him as he walked by me in Kanturk Street, and I don't think I can mistake the horrid impudence of his face. I beg your pardon, sir,'—and now he addressed Mollett in the gig—'but are you going up to the house?'

'Yes, sir; that's my notion just at present. Any commands that way?'

'This is Mr. Fitzgerald—Mr. Herbert Fitzgerald; and I am Mr. Somers, the agent. Can we do anything for you?'

Aby Mollett raised his hat, and the two gentlemen touched theirs. 'Thank'ee, sir,' said Aby; 'but I believe my business must be with the worthy baro-nett himself; more particularly as I 'appen to know that he's at home.'

'My father is not very well,' said Herbert, 'and I do not think that he will be able to see you.'

'I'll take the liberty of hasking and of sending in my card,' said Aby; and he gave his horse a flick as intending thus to cut short the conversation. But Mr. Somers had put his hand upon the bridle, and the beast was contented to stand still.

'If you'll have the kindness to wait a moment,' said Mr. Somers; and he put on a look of severity, which he well knew how to assume, and which somewhat cowed poor Aby. 'You have been down here before, I think,' continued Mr. Somers.

'What, at Castle Richmond? No, I haven't. And if I had, what's that to you if Sir Thomas chooses to see me? I hain't hintruding, I suppose.'

'You 've been down at Kanturk before—once or twice; for I have seen you.'

'And supposing I've been there ten or twelve times,—what is there in that?' said Aby.

Mr. Somers still held the horse's head, and stood a moment considering.

'I'll thank you to let go my 'oss,' said Aby raising his whip and shaking the reins.

'What do you say your name is?' asked Mr. Somers.

'I didn't say my name was anything yet. I hain't ashamed of it. however, nor hasn't hany cause to be. That's my name, and if you'll send my card into Sir Thomas, with my compliments, and say that hi've three words to say to him very particular; why hi'll be obliged to you.' And then Mr. Mollett handed Mr. Somers his card.

'Mollett!' said Mr. Somers, very unceremoniously. 'Mollett, Mollett. Do you know the name, Herbert?'

Herbert said that he did not.

'It's about business I suppose?' asked Mr. Somers.

'Yes,' said Aby; 'private business; very particular.'

'The same that brought your father here;' and Mr. Somers again looked into his face with a close scrutiny.

Aby was abashed, and for a moment or two he did not answer. Well, then; it is the same business,' he said at last. 'And I'll thank you to let me go on. I'm not used to be stopped in this way.'

'You can follow us up to the house,' said Mr. Somers to him. 'Come here, Herbert.' And then they walked along the road in such a way that Aby was forced to allow his horse to walk after them.

'These are the men who are doing it,' said Mr. Somers in a whisper to his companion. 'Whatever is in the wind, whatever may be the cause of your father's trouble, they are concerned in it. They are probably getting money from him in some way.'

'Do you think so?'

'I do. We must not force ourselves upon your father's confidence, but we must endeavour to save him from this misery. Do you go into him with this card. Do not show it to him too suddenly; and then find out whether he really wishes to see the man. I will stay about the place; for it may be possible that a magistrate will be wanted, and in such a matter you had better not act.'

They were now at the hall-door, and Somers, turning to Mollett, told him that Mr. Herbert Fitzgerald would carry the card to his father. And then he added, seeing that Mollett was going to come down, 'You had better stay in the gig till Mr. Fitzgerald comes back; just sit where you are; you'll get an answer all in good time.'

Sir Thomas was crouching over the fire in his study when his son entered, with his eyes fixed upon a letter which he held in his hand, and which, when he saw Herbert, he closed up and put away.

'Father,' said Herbert, in a cheerful every-day voice, as though
he had nothing special to communicate, 'there is a man in a gig
out there. He says he wants to see you.'

'A man in a gig!' and Herbert could see that his father had
already begun to tremble. But every sound made him tremble
now.

'Yes; a man in a gig. What is it he says his name is? I
have his card here. A young man.'

'Oh, a young man?' said Sir Thomas.

'Yes, here it is. Abraham Mollett. I can't say that your
friend seems to be very respectable, in spite of his gig,' and
Herbert handed the card to his father.

The son purposely looked away as he mentioned the name, as
his great anxiety was not to occasion distress. But he felt that
the sound of the word had been terrible in his father's ears.
Sir Thomas had risen from his chair; but he now sat down again,
or rather fell into it. But nevertheless he took the card, and
said that he would see the man.

'A young man do you say, Herbert?'

'Yes, father, a young man. And, father, if you are not well,
tell me what the business is, and let me see him.'

But Sir Thomas persisted, shaking his head, and saying that
he would see the man himself.

'Somers is out there. Will you let him do it?'

'No. I wonder, Herbert, that you can tease me so. Let the
man be sent in here. But, oh, Herbert—Herbert——!'

The young man rushed round and kneeled at his father's knee.

'What is it, father? Why will you not tell me? I know you
have some grief, and cannot you trust me? Do you not know
that you can trust me?'

'My poor boy, my poor boy!'

'What is it, father? If this man here is concerned in it, let
me see him.'

'No, no, no.'

'Or at any rate let me be with you when he is here. Let me
share your trouble if I can do nothing to cure it.'

'Herbert, my darling, leave me and send him in. If it be
necessary that you should bear this calamity, it will come upon
you soon enough.'

'But I am afraid of this man—for your sake, father.'

'He will do me no harm; let him come to me. But, Herbert,
say nothing to Somers about this. Somers has not seen the man;
has he?'

'Yes; we both spoke to him together as he drove up the
avenue.'

'And what did he say? Did he say anything?'

'Nothing but that he wanted to see you, and then he gave his card to Mr. Somers. Mr. Somers wished to save you from the annoyance.'

'Why should it annoy me to see any man? Let Mr. Somers mind his own business. Surely I can have business of my own without his interference.' With this Herbert left his father, and returned to the hall-door to usher in Mr. Mollett junior.

'Well?' said Mr. Somers, who was standing by the hall fire, and who joined Herbert at the front door.

'My father will see the man.'

'And have you learned who he is?'

'I have learned nothing but this—that Sir Thomas does not wish that we should inquire. Now, Mr. Mollett, Sir Thomas will see you; so you can come down. Make haste now, and remember that you are not to stay long, for my father is ill.' And then leading Aby through the hall and along a passage, he introduced him into Sir Thomas's room.

'And Herbert—' said the father; whereupon Herbert again turned round. His father was endeavouring to stand, but supporting himself by the back of his chair. 'Do not disturb me for half an hour; but come to me then, and knock at the door. This gentleman will have done by that time.'

'If we do not put a stop to this, your father will be in a mad-house or on his death-bed before long.' So spoke Mr. Somers in a low, solemn whisper when Herbert again joined him at the hall-door.

'Sit down, sir; sit down,' said Sir Thomas, endeavouring to be civil and to seem at his ease at the same time. Aby was himself so much bewildered for the moment, that he hardly perceived the embarrassment under which the baronet was labouring.

Aby sat down, in the way usual to such men in such places, on the corner of his chair, and put his hat on the ground between his feet. Then he took out his handkerchief and blew his nose, and after that he expressed an opinion that he was in the presence of Sir Thomas Fitzgerald.

'And you are Mr. Abraham Mollett,' said Sir Thomas.

'Yes, Sir Thomas, that's my name. I believe, Sir Thomas, that you have the pleasure of some slight acquaintance with my father, Mr. Matthew Mollett?'

What a pleasure under such circumstances! Sir Thomas, however, nodded his head, and Aby went on.

'Well, now, Sir Thomas, business is business; and my father, 'e ain't a good man of business. A gen'leman like you, Sir Thomas, has seen that with 'alf an eye, I know.' And then he waited a moment for an answer; but as he got none he proceeded.

'My governor's one of the best of fellows going, but 'e ain't sharp and decisive. Sharp's the word now-a-days, Sir Thomas; ain't it?' and he spoke this in a manner so suited to the doctrine which he intended to inculcate, that the poor old gentleman almost jumped up in his chair.

And Aby, seeing this, seated himself more comfortably in his own. The awe which the gilt bindings of the books and the thorough comfort of the room had at first inspired was already beginning to fade away. He had come there to bully, and though his courage had failed him for a moment under the stern eye of Mr. Somers, it quickly returned to him now that he was able to see how weak was his actual victim.

'Sharp's the word, Sir Thomas; and my governor, 'e ain't sharp—not sharp as he ought to be in such a matter as this. This is what I calls a real bit of cheese. Now it's no good going on piddling and peddling in such a case as this; is it now, Sir Thomas?'

Sir Thomas muttered something, but it was no more than a groan.

'Not the least use,' continued Aby. 'Now the question, as I takes it, is this. There's your son there as fetched me in 'ere; a fine young gen'leman 'e is, as ever I saw; I will say that. Well, now; who's to have this 'ere property when you walk the plank—as walk it you must some day, in course? Is it to be this son of yours, or is it to be this other Fitzgerald of 'Appy 'Ouse? Now, if you ask me, I'm all for your son, though maybe he mayn't be all right as regards the dam.'

There was certainly some truth in what Aby had said with reference to his father. Mr. Mollett senior had never debated the matter in terms sharp and decisive as these were. Think who they were of whom this brute was talking to that wretched gentleman; the wife of his bosom, than whom no wife was ever more dearly prized; the son of his love, the centre of all his hopes, the heir of his wealth—if that might still be so. And yet he listened to such words as these, and did not call in his servants to turn the speaker of them out of his doors.

'I've no wish for that 'Appy 'Ouse man, Sir Thomas; not the least. And as for your good lady, she's nothing to me one way or the other—whatever she may be to my governor——' and here there fell a spasm upon the poor man's heart, which nearly brought him from the chair to the ground; but, nevertheless, he still contained himself—'my governor's former lady, my own mother,' continued Aby, 'whom I never see'd, she'd gone to kingdom come, you know, before that time, Sir Thomas. There hain't no doubt about that. So you see—— ' and hereupon he dropped his voice from the tone which he had hitherto been using to an absolute whisper, and drawing his chair close to that of the baronet, and putting his hands upon his knees, brought his mouth close to his companion's ear—'So you see,' he said, 'when that youngster was born, Lady F. was Mrs. M.—wasn't she? and for the matter of that, Lady F. is Mrs. M. to this very hour. That's the real chat; ain't it, Sir Thomas? My stepmother, you know. The governor could take her away with him to-morrow if he chose, according to the law of the land—couldn't he now?'

There was no piddling or peddling about this at any rate. Old Mollett in discussing the matter with his victim had done so by hints and inuendos, through long windings, by signs and the dropping of a few dark words. He had never once mentioned in full terms the name of Lady Fitzgerald; had never absolutely stated that he did possess or ever had possessed a wife. It had been sufficient for him to imbue Sir Thomas with the knowledge that his son Herbert was in great danger as to his heritage. Doubtless the two had understood each other; but the absolute naked horror of the surmised facts had been kept delicately out of sight. But such delicacy was not to Aby's taste. Sharp, short, and decisive; that was his motto. No ' longæ ambages' for him. The whip was in his hand, as he thought, and he could best master the team by using it.

And yet Sir Thomas lived and bore it. As he sat there half stupefied, numbed as it were by the intensity of his grief, he wondered at his own power of endurance. 'She is Mrs. M., you know; ain't she now?' He could sit there and hear that, and yet live through it. So much he could do, and did do; but as for speaking, that was beyond him.

Young Mollett thought that this 'freshening up of the old gentleman' seemed to answer; so he continued. 'Yes, Sir Thomas, your son's my favourite, I tell you fairly. But then, you know, if I backs the favourite, in course I likes to win upon him. How is it to be, now?' and then he paused for an answer, which, however, was not forthcoming.

'You see you haven't been dealing quite on the square with the governor. You two is, has it were, in a boat together. We'll call that boat the Lady F., or the Mrs. M., whichever you like;'—and then Aby laughed, for the conceit pleased him—'but the hearnings of that boat should be divided hequally. Ain't that about the ticket? heh, Sir Thomas? Come, don't be down on your luck. A little quiet talkee-talkee between you and me'll soon put this small matter on a right footing.'

'What is it you want? tell me at once,' at last groaned the poor man.

'Well, now, that's something like; and I'll tell you what we want. There are only two of us, you know, the governor and I; and very lonely we are, for it's a sad thing for a man to have the wife of his bosom taken from him.'

Then there was a groan which struck even Aby's ear; but Sir Thomas was still alive and listening, and so he went on.

'This property here, Sir Thomas, is a good twelve thousand a year. I know hall about it as though I'd been 'andling it myself for the last ten years. And a great deal of cutting there is in twelve thousand a year. You've 'ad your whack out of it, and now we wants to have hourn. That's Henglish, hain't it?

'Did your father send you here, Mr. Mollett?'

'Never you mind who sent me, Sir Thomas. Perhaps he did, and perhaps he didn't. Perhaps I came without hany sending. Perhaps I'm more hup to this sort of work than he is. At any rate, I've got the part pretty well by 'eart—you see that, don't you? Well, hour hultimatum about the business is this. Forty thousand pounds paid down on the nail, half to the governor, and half to your 'umble servant, before the end of this year; a couple of thousand more in hand for the year's hexpenses—and —and—a couple of hundred or so now at once before I leave you; for to tell the truth we're run huncommonly dry just at the present moment.' And then Aby drew his breath and paused for an answer.

Poor Sir Thomas was now almost broken down. His head swam round and round, and he felt that he was in a whirlpool from which there was no escape. He had heard the sum named, and knew that he had no power of raising it. His interest in the estate was but for his life, and that life was now all but run out. He had already begun to feel that his son must be sacrificed, but he had struggled and endured in order that he might save his wife. But what could he do now? What further struggle could he make? His present most eager desire was that that horrid man should be removed from his hearing and his eyesight.

But Aby had not yet done: he had hitherto omitted to mention one not inconsiderable portion of the amicable arrangement which, according to him, would have the effect of once more placing the two families comfortably on their feet. 'There's one other pint, Sir Thomas,' he continued, 'and hif I can bring you and your good lady to my way of thinking on that, why, we may all be comfortable for all that is come and gone. You've a daughter Hemmeline.'

'What!' said Sir Thomas, turning upon him; for there was still so much of life left in him that he could turn upon his foe when he heard his daughter's name thus polluted.

'Has lovely a gal, to my way of thinking, as my heyes ever rested on; and I'm not haccounted a bad judge of such cattle, I can tell you, Sir Thomas.'

'That will do, that will do,' said Sir Thomas, attempting to rise, but still holding on by the back of his chair. 'You can go now, sir; I cannot hear more from you.'

'Go!'

'Yes, sir; go.'

'I know a trick worth two of that, Sir Thomas. If you like to give me your daughter Hemmeline for my wife, whatever her fortin's to be, I'll take it as part of my half of the forty thousand pounds. There now.' And then Aby again waited for a reply.

But now there came a knock at the door, and following quick upon the knock Herbert entered the room. 'Well, father,' said the son.

'Herbert!'

'Yes, father;' and he went round and supported his father on his arm.

'Herbert, will you tell that man to go?'

'Come, sir, you have disturbed my father enough; will you have the kindness to leave him now?'

'I may chance to disturb him more, and you too, sir, if you treat me in that way. Let go my arm, sir. Am I to have any answer from you, Sir Thomas?'

But Sir Thomas could make no further attempt at speaking. He was now once more seated in his chair, holding his son's hand, and when he again heard Mollett's voice he merely made a sign for him to go.

'You see the state my father is in, Mr. Mollett,' said Herbert; 'I do not know what is the nature of your business, but whatever it may be, you must leave him now.' And he made a slight attempt to push the visitor towards the door.

'You'd better take care what you're doing, Mr. Fitzgerald,' said Mollett. 'By —— you had! If you anger me, I might say a word that I couldn't unsay again, which would put you into queer street, I can tell you.'

'Don't quarrel with him, my boy; pray don't quarrel with him, but let him leave me,' said Sir Thomas.

'Mr. Mollett, you see my father's state; you must be aware that it is imperative that he should be left alone.'

'I don't know nothing about that, young gen'leman; business is business, and I hain't got hany answer to my proposals. Sir Thomas, do you say "Yes" to them proposals?' But Sir Thomas was still dumb. 'To all but the last? Come,' continued Aby, 'that was put in quite as much for your good as it was for mine.' But not a word came from the baronet.

'Then I shan't stir,' said Aby, again seating himself.

'Then I shall have the servants in,' said Herbert, 'and a magistrate who is in the hall;' and he put his hand towards the handle of the bell.

'Well, as the old gen'leman's hill, I'll go now and come again. But look you here, Sir Thomas, you have got my proposals, and if I don't get an answer to them in three days' time,—why you'll hear from me in another way, that's all. And so will her ladyship.' And with this threat Mr. Abraham Mollett allowed himself to be conducted through the passage into the hall, and from thence to his gig.

'See that he drives away; see that he goes,' said Herbert to Mr. Somers, who was still staying about the place.

'Oh, I'll drive away fast enough,' said Aby, as he stepped into the gig, 'and come back fast enough too,' he muttered to himself. In the mean time Herbert had run back to his father's room.

'Has he gone?' murmured Sir Thomas.

'Yes, he has gone. There; you can hear the wheels of his gig on the gravel.'

'Oh, my boy, my poor boy!'

'What is it, father? Why do you not tell me? Why do you allow such men as that to come and harass you, when a word would keep them from you? Father, good cannot come of it.'

'No, Herbert, no; good will not come of it. There is no good to come at all.'

'Then why will you not tell us?'

'You will know it all soon enough. But Herbert, do not say a word to your mother. Not a word as you value my love. Let us save her while we can. You promise me that.'

Herbert gave him the required promise.

'Look here,' and he took up the letter which he had before crumpled in his hand. 'Mr. Prendergast will be here next week. I shall tell everything to him.'

Soon afterwards Sir Thomas went to his bed, and there by his bedside his wife sat for the rest of the evening. But he said no word to her of his sorrow.

'Mr. Prendergast is coming here,' said Herbert to Mr. Somers.

'I am glad of it, though I do not know him,' said Mr. Somers. 'For, my dear boy, it is necessary that there should be some one here.'

CHAPTER XVI.

THE PATH BENEATH THE ELMS.

It will be remembered that in the last chapter but one Owen Fitzgerald left Lady Desmond in the drawing-room at Desmond Court somewhat abruptly, having absolutely refused to make peace with the Desmond faction by giving his consent to the marriage between Clara and his cousin Herbert. And it will perhaps be remembered, also, that Lady Desmond had asked for this consent in a manner that was almost humble. She had shown herself most anxious to keep on friendly terms with the rake of Hap House,—rake and roué, gambler and spendthrift, as he was reputed to be,—if only he would abandon his insane claim to the hand of Clara Desmond. But this feeling she had shown when they two were alone together, after Clara had left them. As long as her daughter had been present, Lady Desmond had maintained her tone of indignation and defiance; but, when the door was closed and they two were alone, she had become kind in her language and almost tender.

My readers will probably conceive that she had so acted, overcome by her affection for Owen Fitzgerald and with a fixed resolve to win him for herself. Men and women when they are written about are always supposed to have fixed resolves, though in life they are so seldom found to be thus armed. To speak the truth, the countess had had no fixed resolve in the matter, either when she had thought about Owen's coming, or when, subsequently, she had found herself alone with him in her drawing-room. That Clara should not marry him,—on so much she had resolved long ago. But all danger on that head was, it may be said, over. Clara, like a good child, had behaved in the best possible manner; had abandoned her first lover, a lover that was poor and unfitted for her, as soon as told to do so; and had found for herself a second lover, who was rich, and proper, and in every way desirable. As regards Clara, the countess felt herself to be safe; and, to give her her due, she had been satisfied that the matter should so rest. She had not sought any further interview with Fitzgerald. He had come there against her advice, and she had gone to meet him prompted by the necessity of supporting her daughter, and without any other views of her own.

But when she found herself alone with him; when she looked

into his face, and saw how handsome, how noble, how good it was—good in its inherent manliness and bravery—she could not but long that this feud should be over, and that she might be able once more to welcome him as her friend. If only he would give up this frantic passion, this futile, wicked, senseless attempt to make them all wretched by an insane marriage, would it not be sweet again to make some effort to rescue him from the evil ways into which he had fallen?

But Owen himself would make no response to this feeling. Clara Desmond was his love, and he would, of his own consent, yield her to no one. In truth, he was, in a certain degree, mad on this subject. He did think that because the young girl had given him a promise—had said to him a word or two which he called a promise—she was now of right his bride; that there belonged to him an indefeasible property in her heart, in her loveliness, in the inexpressible tenderness of her young springing beauty, of which no subsequent renouncing on her part could fairly and honestly deprive him. That others should oppose the match was intelligible to him; but it was hardly intelligible that she should betray him. And, as yet, he did not believe that she herself was the mainspring of this renouncing. Others, the countess and the Castle Richmond people, had frightened her into falseness; and therefore it became him to maintain his right by any means—almost by any means, within his power. Give her up of his own free will and voice! Say that Herbert Fitzgerald should take her with his consent! that she should go as a bride to Castle Richmond, while he stood by and smiled, and wished them joy! Never! And so he rode away with a stern heart, leaving her standing there with something of sternness about her heart also.

In the mean time, Clara, when she was sure that her rejected suitor was well away from the place, put on her bonnet and walked out. It was her wont at this time to do so; and she was becoming almost a creature of habit, shut up as she was in that old dreary barrack. Her mother very rarely went with her; and she habitually performed the same journey over the same ground, at the same hour, day after day. So it had been, and so it was still,—unless Herbert Fitzgerald were with her.

On the present occasion she saw no more of her mother before she left the house. She passed the drawing-room door, and seeing that it was ajar, knew that the countess was there; but she had nothing to say to her mother as to the late interview, unless her mother had aught to say to her. So she passed on. In truth her mother had nothing to say to her. She was sitting there alone, with her head resting on her hand, with that sternness at her heart and a cloud upon her brow, but she was not thinking of her daughter. Had she not, with her skill and motherly care, provided well for Clara? Had she not saved her daughter from all the perils which beset the path of a young girl? Had she not so brought her child up and put her forth into the world, that, portionless as that child was, all the best things of the world had been showered into her lap. Why should the countess think more of her daughter? It was of herself she was thinking; and of what her life would be all alone, absolutely alone, in that huge frightful home of hers, without a friend, almost without an acquaintance, without one soul near her whom she could love or who would love her. She had put out her hand to Owen Fitzgerald, and he had rejected it. Her he had regarded merely as the mother of the woman he loved. And then the Countess of Desmond began to ask herself if she were old and wrinkled and ugly, only fit to be a dowager in mind, body, and in name!

Over the same ground! Yes, always over the same ground. Lady Clara never varied her walk. It went from the front entrance of the court, with one great curve, down to the old ruined lodge which opened on to the road running from Kanturk to Cork. It was here that the row of elm trees stood, and it was here that she had once walked with a hot, eager lover beside her, while a docile horse followed behind their feet. It was here that she walked daily; and was it possible that she should walk here without thinking of him?

It was always on the little well-worn path by the road-side, not on the road itself, that she took her measured exercise; and now, as she went along, she saw on the moist earth the fresh prints of a horse's hoofs. He also had ridden down the same way, choosing to pass over the absolute spot in which those words had been uttered, thinking of that moment, as she also was thinking of it. She felt sure that such had been the case. She knew that it was this that had brought him there—there on to the foot-traces which they had made together.

And did he then love her so truly,—with a love so hot, so eager, so deeply planted in his very soul? Was it really true that a passion for her had so filled his heart, that his whole life must by that be made or marred? Had she done this thing to him? Had she so impressed her image on his mind that he must be wretched without her? Was she so much to him, so completely all in all as regarded his future worldly happiness? Those words of his, asserting that love—her love—was to him a stern fact, a deep necessity—recurred over and over again to her mind. Could it really be that in doing as she had done, in giving herself to another after she had promised herself to him, she had committed an injustice which would constantly be brought up against her by him and by her own conscience? Had she in truth deceived and betrayed him,—deserted him because he was poor, and given herself over to a rich lover because of his riches?

As she thought of this she forgot again that fact—which, indeed, she had never more than half realized in her mind—that he had justified her in separating herself from him by his reckless course of living; that his conduct must be held to have so justified her, let the pledge between them have been of what nature it might. Now, as she walked up and down that path, she thought nothing of his wickedness and his sins; she thought only of the vows to which she had once listened, and the renewal of those vows to which it was now so necessary that her ear should be deaf.

But was her heart deaf to them? She swore to herself, over and over again, scores and scores of oaths, that it was so; but each time that she swore, some lowest corner in the depth of her conscience seemed to charge her with a falsehood. Why was it that in all her hours of thinking she so much oftener saw his face, Owen's, than she did that other face of which in duty she was bound to think and dream? It was in vain that she told herself that she was afraid of Owen, and therefore thought of him. The tone of his voice that rang in her ears the oftenest was not that of his anger and sternness, but the tone of his first assurance of love —that tone which had been so inexpressibly sweet to her—that to which she had listened on this very spot where she now walked slowly, thinking of him. The look of his which was ever present to her eyes was not that on which she had almost feared to gaze but an hour ago; but the form and spirit which his countenance had worn when they were together on that well-remembered day.

And then she would think, or try to think, of Herbert, and of all his virtues and of all his goodness. He too loved her well. She never doubted that. He had come to her with soft words, and pleasant smiles, and sweet honeyed compliments—compliments which had been sweet to her as they are to all girls; but his soft words, and pleasant smiles, and honeyed love-making had never given her so strong a thrill of strange delight as had those few words from Owen. Her very heart's core had been affected by the vigour of his affection. There had been in it a mysterious grandeur which had half charmed and half frightened her. It had made her feel that he, were it fated that she should belong to him, would indeed be her lord and ruler; that his was a spirit

before which hers would bend and feel itself subdued.   With him
she could realize all that she had dreamed of woman's love; and
that dream which is so sweet to some women—of woman's subju-
gation.   But could it be the same with him to whom she was
now positively affianced, with him to whom she knew that she
did now owe all her duty?   She feared that it was not the same.

And then again she swore that she loved him.   She thought
over all his excellences; how good he was as a son—how fondly
his sisters loved him—how inimitable was his conduct in these
hard, trying times.   And she remembered also that it was right
in every way that she should love him.   Her mother and brother
approved of it.   Those who were to be her new relatives
approved of it.   It was in every way fitting.   Pecuniary considerations were so favourable!   But when she thought of that
her heart sank low within her breast.   Was it true that she had
sold herself at her mother's bidding?   Should not the remembrance of Owen's poverty have made her true to him had nothing
else done so?

But be all that as it might, one thing, at any rate, was clear
to her, that it was now her fate, her duty—and, as she repeated
again and again, her wish to marry Herbert.   No thought of
rebellion against him and her mother ever occurred to her as
desirable or possible.   She would be to him a true and loving
wife, a wife in very heart and soul.   But, nevertheless, walking
thus beneath those trees, she could not but think of Owen
Fitzgerald.

In this mood she had gone twice down from the house to the
lodge and back again; and now again she had reached the lodge
the third time, making thus her last journey: for in these solitary walks her work was measured.   The exercise was needful,
but there was little in the task to make her prolong it beyond
what was necessary.   But now, as she was turning for the last
time, she heard the sound of a horse's hoof coming fast along the
road; and looking from the gate, she saw that Herbert was
coming to her.   She had not expected him, but now she waited
at the gate to meet him.

It had been arranged that she was to go over in a few days to
Castle Richmond, and stay there for a fortnight.   This had been
settled shortly before the visit made by Mr. Mollett junior, at
that place, and had not as yet been unsettled.   But as soon as it
was known that Sir Thomas had summoned Mr. Prendergast from
London, it was felt by them all that it would be as well that
Clara's visit should be postponed.   Herbert had been especially
cautioned by his father, at the time of Mollett's visit, not to tell
his mother anything of what had occurred, and to a certain ex-

tent he hha kept his promise. But it was of course necessary that Lady Fitzgerald should know that Mr. Prendergast was coming to the house, and it was of course impossible to keep from her the fact that his visit was connected with the lamentable state of her husband's health and spirits. Indeed, she knew as much as that without any telling. It was not probable that Mr. Prendergast should come there now on a visit of pleasure.

'Whatever this may be that weighs upon his mind,' Herbert had said, 'he will be better for talking it over with a man whom he trusts.'

'And why not with Somers?' said Lady Fitzgerald.

'Somers is too often with him, too near to him in all the affairs of his life. I really think he is wise to send for Mr. Prendergast. We do not know him, but I believe him to be a good man.'

Then Lady Fitzgerald had expressed herself as satisfied—as satisfied as she could be, seeing that her husband would not take her into his confidence; and after this it was settled that Herbert should at once ride over to Desmond Court, and explain that Clara's visit had better be postponed.

Herbert got off his horse at the gate, and gave it to one of the children at the lodge to lead after him. His horse would not follow him, Clara said to herself as they walked back together towards the house. She could not prevent her mind running off in that direction. She would fain not have thought of Owen as she thus hung upon Herbert's arm, but as yet she had not learned to control her thoughts. His horse had followed him lovingly—the dogs about the place had always loved him—the men and women of the whole country round, old and young, all spoke of him with a sort of love: everybody admired him. As all this passed through her brain, she was hanging on her accepted lover's arm, and listening to his soft sweet words.

'Oh, yes! it will be much better,' she said, answering his proposal that she should put off her visit to Castle Richmond. 'But I am so sorry that Sir Thomas should be ill. Mr. Prendergast is not a doctor, is he?'

And then Herbert explained that Mr. Prendergast was not a doctor, that he was a physician for the mind rather than for the body. Regarding Clara as already one of his own family, he told her as much as he had told his mother. He explained that there was some deep sorrow weighing on his father's heart of which they none of them knew anything save its existence; that there might be some misfortune coming on Sir Thomas of which he, Herbert, could not even guess the nature; but that everything would be told to this Mr. Prendergast.

'It is very sad,' said Herbert.

'Very sad; very sad,' said Clara, with tears in her eyes. 'Poor gentleman! I wish that we could comfort him.'

'And I do hope that we may,' said Herbert. 'Somers seems to think that his mind is partly affected, and that this misfortune, whatever it be, may not improbably be less serious than we anticipate;—that it weighs heavier on him than it would do, were he altogether well.'

'And your mother, Herbert?'

'Oh, yes; she also is to be pitied. Sometimes, for moments, she seems to dread some terrible misfortune; but I believe that in her calm judgment she thinks that our worst calamity is the state of my father's health.'

Neither in discussing the matter with his mother or Clara, nor in thinking it over when alone, did it ever occur to Herbert that he himself might be individually subject to the misfortune over which his father brooded. Sir Thomas had spoken piteously to him, and called him poor, and had seemed to grieve over what might happen to him; but this had been taken by the son as a part of his father's malady.

Everything around him was now melancholy, and therefore these terms had not seemed to have any special force of their own. He did not think it necessary to warn Clara that bad days might be in store for both of them, or to caution her that their path of love might yet be made rough.

'And whom do you think I met, just now, on horseback?' he asked, as soon as this question of her visit had been decided.

'Mr. Owen Fitzgerald, probably,' said Clara. 'He went from hence about an hour since.'

'Owen Fitzgerald here!' he repeated, as though the tidings of such a visit having been made were not exactly pleasant to him. 'I thought that Lady Desmond did not even see him now.'

'His visit was to me, Herbert, and I will explain it to you. I was just going to tell you when you first came in, only you began about Castle Richmond.'

'And have you seen him?'

'Oh yes, I saw him. Mamma thought it best. Yesterday he wrote a note to me which I will show you.' And then she gave him such an account of the interview as was possible to her, making it, at any rate, intelligible to him that Owen had come thither to claim her for himself, having heard the rumour of her engagement to his cousin.

'It was inexcusable on his part—unpardonable!' said Herbert, speaking with an angry spot on his face, and with more energy than was usual with him.

'Was it? why?' said Clara, innocently. She felt uncon-sciously that it was painful to her to hear Owen ill spoken of by her lover, and that she would fain excuse him if she could.

'Why, dearest? Think what motives he could have had; what other object than to place you in a painful position, and to cause trouble and vexation to us all. Did he not know that we were engaged?'

'Oh yes; he knew that;—at least, no; I am not quite sure—I think he said that he had heard it but did not——'

'Did not what, love?'

'I think he said he did not quite believe it;' and then she was forced, much against her will, to describe to her betrothed how Owen had boldly claimed her as his own.

'His conduct has been unpardonable,' said Herbert, again. 'Nay, it has been ungentlemanlike. He has intruded himself where he well knew that he was not wanted; and he has done so taking advantage of a few words which, under the present circumstances, he should force himself to forget.'

'But, Herbert, it is I that have been to blame.'

'No; you have not been in the least to blame. I tell you honestly that I can lay no blame at your door. At the age you were then, it was impossible that you should know your own mind. And even had your promise to him been of a much more binding nature, his subsequent conduct, and your mother's remonstrance, as well as your own age, would have released you from it without any taint of falsehood. He knew all this as well as I do; and I am surprised that he should have forced his way into your mother's house with the mere object of causing you embarrassment.'

It was marvellous how well Herbert Fitzgerald could lay down the law on the subject of Clara's conduct, and on all that was due to her, and all that was not due to Owen. He was the victor; he had gained the prize; and therefore it was so easy for him to acquit his promised bride, and heap reproaches on the head of his rejected rival. Owen had been told that he was not wanted, and of course should have been satisfied with his answer. Why should he intrude himself among happy people with his absurd aspirations? For were they not absurd? Was it not monstrous on his part to suppose that he could marry Clara Desmond?

It was in this way that Herbert regarded the matter. But it was not exactly in that way that Clara looked at it. 'He did not force his way in,' she said. 'He wrote to ask if we would see him; and mamma said that she thought it better.'

'That is forcing his way in the sense that I meant it; and if I find that he gives further annoyance I shall tell him what I think about it. I will not have you persecuted.'

'Herbert, if you quarrel with him you will make me wretched. I think it would kill me.'

'I shall not do it if I can help it, Clara. But it is my duty to protect you, and if it becomes necessary I must do so; you have no father, and no brother of an age to speak to him, and that consideration alone should have saved you from such an attack.'

Clara said nothing more, for she knew that she could not speak out to him the feelings of her heart. She could not plead to him that she had injured Owen, that she had loved him and then given him up; that she had been false to him: she could not confess that, after all, the tribute of such a man's love could not be regarded by her as an offence. So she said nothing further, but walked on in silence, leaning on his arm.

They were now close to the house, and as they drew near to it Lady Desmond met them on the door-step. 'I dare say you have heard that we had a visitor here this morning,' she said, taking Herbert's hand in an affectionate, motherly way, and smiling on him with all her sweetness.

Herbert said that he had heard it, and expressed an opinion that Mr. Owen Fitzgerald would have been acting far more wisely to have remained at home at Hap House.

'Yes, perhaps so; certainly so,' said Lady Desmond, putting her arm within that of her future son, and walking back with him through the great hall. 'He would have been wiser; he would have saved dear Clara from a painful half-hour, and he would have saved himself from perhaps years of sorrow. He has been very foolish to remember Clara's childhood as he does remember it. But, my dear Herbert, what can we do? You lords of creation sometimes will be foolish even about such trifling things as women's hearts.'

And then, when Herbert still persisted that Owen's conduct had been inexcusable and ungentlemanlike, she softly flattered him into quiescence. 'You must not forget,' she said, 'that he perhaps has loved Clara almost as truly as you do. And then what harm can he do? It is not very probable that he should succeed in winning Clara away from you.'

'Oh no, it is not that I mean. It is for Clara's sake.'

'And she, probably, will never see him again till she is your wife. That event will, I suppose, take place at no very remote period.'

'As soon as ever my father's health will admit; that is, if I can persuade Clara to be so merciful.'

'To tell the truth, Herbert, I think you could persuade her to anything. Of course we must not hurry her too much. As for me, my losing her will be very sad; you can understand that; but I would not allow any feeling of my own to stand in her way for half an hour.'

'She will be very near you, you know.'

'Yes, she will; and therefore, as I was saying, it would be absurd for you to quarrel with Mr. Owen Fitzgerald. For myself, I am sorry for him—very sorry or him. You know the whole story of what occurred between him and Clara, and of course you will understand that my duty at that time was plain. Clara behaved admirably, and if only he would not be so foolish, the whole matter might be forgotten. As far as you and I are concerned I think it may be forgotten.'

'But then his coming here?'

'That will not be repeated. I thought it better to show him that we were not afraid of him, and therefore I permitted it. Had I conceived that you would have objected——'

'Oh, no!' said Herbert.

'Well, there was not much for you to be afraid of, certainly,' said the countess. And so he was appeased, and left the house, promising that he, at any rate, would do nothing that might lead to a quarrel with his cousin Owen.

Clara, who had still kept on her bonnet, again walked down with him to the lodge, and encountered his first earnest supplication that an early day should be named for their marriage. She had many reasons, excellent good reasons, to allege why this should not be the case. When was a girl of seventeen without such reasons? And it is so reasonable that she should have such reasons. That period of having love made to her must be by far the brightest in her life. Is it not always a pity that it should be abridged?

'But your father's illness, Herbert, you know.'

Herbert acknowledged that, to a certain extent, his father's illness was a reason—only to a certain extent. It would be worse than useless to think of waiting till his father's health should be altogether strong. Just for the present, till Mr. Prendergast should have gone, and perhaps for a fortnight longer, it might be well to wait. But after that——and then he pressed very closely the hand which rested on his arm. And so the matter was discussed between them with language and arguments which were by no means original.

At the gate, just as Herbert was about to remount his horse, they were encountered by a sight which for years past had not been uncommon in the south of Ireland, but which had become frightfully common during the last two or three months. A woman was standing there, of whom you could hardly say that she was clothed, though she was involved in a mass of rags which covered her nakedness. Her head was all uncovered, and her wild black hair was streaming round her face. Behind her back hung two children enveloped among the rags in some mysterious way; and round about her on the road stood three others, of whom the two younger were almost absolutely naked. The eldest of the five was not above seven. They all had the same wild black eyes, and wild elfish straggling locks; but neither the mother nor the children were comely. She was short and broad in the shoulders, though wretchedly thin; her bare legs seemed to be of nearly the same thickness up to the knee, and the naked limbs of the children were like yellow sticks. It is strange how various are the kinds of physical development among the Celtic peasantry in Ireland. In many places they are singularly beautiful, especially as children; and even after labour and sickness shall have told on them as labour and sickness will tell, they still retain a certain softness and grace which is very nearly akin to beauty. But then again in a neighbouring district they will be found to be squat, uncouth, and in no way attractive to the eye. The tint of the complexion, the nature of the hair, the colour of the eyes, shall be the same. But in one place it will seem as though noble blood had produced delicate limbs and elegant stature, whereas in the other a want of noble blood had produced the reverse. The peasants of Clare, Limerick, and Tipperary are, in this way, much more comely than those of Cork and Kerry.

When Herbert and Clara reached the gate they found this mother with her five children crouching at the ditch-side, although it was still mid-winter. They had seen him enter the demesne, and were now waiting with the patience of poverty for his return.

'An' the holy Virgin guide an' save you, my lady,' said the woman, almost frightening Clara by the sudden way in which she came forward, 'an' you too, Misther Herbert; and for the love of heaven do something for a poor crathur whose five starving childher have not had wholesome food within their lips for the last week past.'

Clara looked at them piteously and put her hand towards her pocket. Her purse was never well furnished, and now in these bad days was usually empty. At the present moment it was wholly so. 'I have nothing to give her; not a penny,' she said, whispering to her lover.

But Herbert had learned deep lessons of political economy, and was by no means disposed to give promiscuous charity on the road-side. 'What is your name,' said he; 'and from where do you come?'

'Shure, an' it's yer hònor knows me well enough; and her ladyship too; may the heavens be her bed! And don't I come from Clady; that is two long miles the fur side of it? And my name is Bridget Sheehy. Shure, an' yer ladyship remembers me at Clady the first day ye war over there about the biler.'

Clara looked at her, and thought that she did remember her, but she said nothing. 'And who is your husband?' said Herbert.

'Murty Brien, plaze yer honor;' and the woman ducked a curtsey with the heavy load of two children on her back. It must be understood that among the poorer classes in the south and west of Ireland it is almost rare for a married woman to call herself or to be called by her husband's name.

' And is he not at work?'

' Shure, an' he is, yer honor—down beyant Kinsale by the say. But what's four shilling a week for a man's diet, let alone a woman and five bairns?'

' And so he has deserted you?'

'No, yer honor; he's not dasarted me thin. He's a good man and a kind, av' he had the mains. But we've a cabin up here, on her ladyship's ground that is; and he has sent me up among my own people, hoping that times would come round; but faix, yer honor, I'm thinking that they'll never come round, no more.'

' And what do you want now, Bridget?'

' What is it I'm wanting? just a thrifle of money then to get a sup of milk for thim five childher as is starving and dying for the want of it.' And she pointed to the wretched, naked brood around her with a gesture which in spite of her ugliness had in it something of tragic grandeur.

' But you know that we will not give money. They will take you in at the poorhouse at Kanturk.'

' Is it the poorhouse, yer honor?'

' Or, if you get a ticket from your priest they will give you meal twice a week at Clady. You know that. Why do you not go to Father Connellan?'

' Is it the mail? An' shure an' haven't I had it, the last month past; nothin' else; not a taste of a praty or a dhrop of milk for nigh a month, and now look at the childher. Look at them, my lady. They are dyin' by the very road-side. And she undid the bundle at her back, and laying the two babes down on the road showed that the elder of them was in truth in a fearful state. It was a child nearly two years of age, but its little legs seemed to have withered away; its cheeks were wan, and yellow and sunken, and the two teeth which it had already cut were seen with terrible plainness through its emaciated lips. Its head and forehead were covered with sores; and then the mother, moving aside the rags, showed that its back and legs were in the same state. 'Look to that,' she said, almost with scorn. 'That's what the mail has done—my black curses be upon it, and the day that it first come nigh the counthry.' And then again she covered the child and began to resume her load.

'Do give her something, Herbert, pray do,' said Clara, with her whole face suffused with tears.

'You know that we cannot give away money,' said Herbert, arguing with Bridget Sheehy, and not answering Clara at the moment. 'You understand enough of what is being done to know that. Why do you not go into the Union?'

'Shure thin an' I'll jist tramp on as fur as Hap House, I and my childher; that is av' they do not die by the road-side. Come on, bairns. Mr. Owen won't be afther sending me to the Kanturk union when I tell him that I've travelled all thim miles to get a dhrink of milk for a sick babe; more by token when I tells him also that I'm one of the Desmond tinantry. It's he that loves the Desmonds, Lady Clara,—loves them as his own heart's blood. And it's I that wish him good luck with his love, in spite of all that's come and gone yet. Come on, bairns, come along; we have seven weary miles to walk.' And then, having rearranged her burden on her back, she prepared again to start.

Herbert Fitzgerald, from the first moment of his interrogating the woman, had of course known that he would give her somewhat. In spite of all his political economy, there were but few days in which he did not empty his pocket of his loose silver, with these culpable deviations from his theoretical philosophy. But yet he felt that it was his duty to insist on his rules, as far as his heart would allow him to do so. It was a settled thing at their relief committee that there should be no giving away of money to chance applicants for alms. What money each had to bestow would go twice further by being brought to the general fund—by being expended with forethought and discrimination. This was the system which all attempted, which all resolved to adopt who were then living in the south of Ireland. But the system was impracticable, for it required frames of iron and hearts of adamant. It was impossible not to waste money in almsgiving.

'Oh, Herbert!' said Clara, imploringly, as the woman prepared to start.

'Bridget, come here,' said Herbert, and he spoke very seriously, for the woman's allusion to Owen Fitzgerald had driven a cloud across his brow. 'Your child is very ill, and therefore I will give you something to help you,' and he gave her a shilling and two sixpences.

'May the God in heaven bless you thin, and make you happy, whoever wins the bright darling by your side; and may the good days come back to yer house and all that belongs to it. May yer wife clave to you all her days, and be a good mother to your childher.' And she would have gone on further with her blessing had not he interrupted her.

'Go on now, my good woman,' said he, 'and take your children where they may be warm. If you will be advised by me, you will go to the Union at Kanturk.' And so the woman passed on still blessing them. Very shortly after this none of them required pressing to go to the workhouse. Every building that could be arranged for the purpose was filled to overflowing as soon as it was ready. But the worst of the famine had not come upon them as yet. And then Herbert rode back to Castle Richmond.

CHAPTER XVII.

FATHER BARNEY.

MICK O'DWYER's public-house at Kanturk was by no means so pretentious an establishment as that kept by his brother in South Main Street, Cork, but it was on the whole much less nasty. It was a drinking-shop and a public car office, and such places in Ireland are seldom very nice; but there was no attempt at hotel grandeur, and the little room in which the family lived behind the bar was never invaded by customers.

On one evening just at this time—at the time, that is, with which we have been lately concerned—three persons were sitting in this room over a cup of tea. There was a gentleman, middle-aged, but none the worse on that account, who has already been introduced in these pages as Father Bernard M'Carthy. He was the parish priest of Drumbarrow; and as his parish comprised a portion of the town of Kanturk, he lived, not exactly in the town, but within a mile of it. His sister had married Mr. O'Dwyer of South Main Street, and therefore he was quite at home in the little back parlour of Mick O'Dwyer's house in Kanturk. Indeed Father Bernard was a man who made himself at home in the houses of most of his parishioners,—and of some who were not his parishioners.

His companions on the present occasion were two ladies who seemed to be emulous in supplying his wants. The younger and more attractive of the two was also an old friend of ours, being no other than Fanny O'Dwyer from South Main Street. Actuated, doubtless, by some important motive, she had left her bar at home for one night, having come down to Kanturk by her father's car, with the intention of returning by it in the morning. She was seated as a guest here on the corner of the sofa near the fire, but nevertheless she was neither too proud nor too strange in her position to administer as best she might to the comfort of her uncle.

The other lady was Mistress O'Dwyer, the lady of the mansion. She was fat, very; by no means fair, and perhaps something over forty. But nevertheless there were those who thought that she had her charms. A better hand at curing a side of bacon there was not in the county Cork, nor a woman who was more knowing in keeping a house straight and snug over her husband's head. That she had been worth more than a fortune to Mick O'Dwyer was admitted by all in Kanturk; for it was known to all that Mick O'Dwyer was not himself a good man at keeping a house straight and snug.

'Another cup of tay, Father Bernard,' said this lady. 'It'll be more to your liking now than the first, you'll find.' Father Barney, perfectly reliant on her word, handed in his cup.

'And the muffin is quite hot,' said Fanny, stooping down to a tray which stood before the peat fire, holding the muffin dish. 'But perhaps you'd like a morsel of buttered toast; say the word, uncle, and I'll make it in a brace of seconds.'

'In course she will,' said Mrs. O'Dwyer: 'and happy too, av you'll only say that you have a fancy, Father Bernard.'

But Father Bernard would not own to any such fancy. The muffin, he said, was quite to his liking, and so was the tea; and from the manner in which he disposed of these delicacies, even Mrs. Townsend might have admitted that this assertion was true, though she was wont to express her belief that nothing but lies could, by any possibility, fall from his mouth.

'And they have been staying with you now for some weeks, haven't they?' said Father Barney.

'Off and on,' said Fanny.

'But there's one of them mostly there, isn't he?' added the priest.

'The two of them is mostly there, just now. Sometimes one goes away for a day or two, and sometimes the other.'

'And they have no business which keeps them in Cork?' continued the priest, who seemed to be very curious on the matter.

'Well, they do have business, I suppose,' said Fanny, 'but av so I never sees it.' Fanny O'Dwyer had a great respect for her uncle, seeing that he filled an exalted position, and was a connection of whom she could be justly proud; but, though she had now come down to Kanturk with the view of having a good talk with her aunt and uncle about the Molletts, she would only tell as much as she liked to tell, even to the parish priest of Drumbarrow. And we may as well explain here that Fanny had now permanently made up her mind to reject the suit of Mr. Abraham Mollett. As she had allowed herself to see more and more of the little domestic ways of that gentleman, and to become intimate with him as a girl should become with the man she intends to marry, she had gradually learned to think that he hardly came up to her beau ideal of a lover. That he was crafty and false did not perhaps offend her as it should have done. Dear Fanny, excellent and gracious as she was, could herself be crafty on occasions. He drank too, but that came in the way of her profession. It is hard, perhaps, for a barmaid to feel much severity against that offence. But in addition to this Aby was selfish and cruel and insolent, and seldom altogether good tempered. He was bad to his father, and bad to those below him whom he employed. Old Mollett would give away his six-pences with a fairly liberal hand, unless when he was exasperated by drink and fatigue. But Aby seldom gave away a penny. Fanny had sharp eyes, and soon felt that her English lover was not a man to be loved, though he had two rings, a gold chain, and half a dozen fine waistcoats.

And then another offence had come to light in which the Molletts were both concerned. Since their arrival in South Main Street they had been excellent customers—indeed quite a godsend, in this light, to Fanny, who had her own peculiar profit out of such house-customers as they were. They had paid their money like true Britons,—not regularly indeed, for regularity had not been desired, but by a five pound now, and another in a day or two, just as they were wanted. Nothing indeed could be better than this, for bills so paid are seldom rigidly scrutinized. But of late, within the last week, Fanny's requests for funds had not been so promptly met, and only on the day before her visit to Kanturk she had been forced to get her father to take a bill from Mr. Mollett senior for 20l. at two months' date. This was a great come-down, as both Fanny and her father felt, and they had begun to think that it might be well to bring their connection with the Molletts to a close. What if an end had come to the money of these people, and their bills should be dishonoured when due? It was all very well for a man to have claims against Sir Thomas Fitzgerald, but Fanny O'Dwyer had already learnt that nothing goes so far in this world as ready cash.

'They do have business, I suppose,' said Fanny.

'It won't be worth much, I'm thinking,' said Mrs. O'Dwyer, 'when they can't pay their weekly bills at a house of public entertainment, without flying their names at two months' date.'

Mrs. O'Dwyer hated any such payments herself, and looked on them as certain signs of immorality. That every man should take his drop of drink, consume it noiselessly, and pay for it immediately—that was her idea of propriety in its highest form.

'And they've been down here three or four times, each of them,' said Father Barney, thinking deeply on the subject.

'I believe they have,' said Fanny. 'But of course I don't know much of where they've been to.'

Father Barney knew very well that his dear niece had been on much more intimate terms with her guest than she pretended. The rumours had reached his ears some time since that the younger of the two strangers in South Main Street was making himself agreeable to the heiress of the hotel, and he had intended to come down upon her with all the might of an uncle, and, if necessary, with all the authority of the Church. But now that Fanny had discarded her lover, he wisely felt that it would be well for him to know nothing about it. Both uncles and priests may know too much—very foolishly.

'I have seen them here myself,' said he, 'and they have both been up at Castle Richmond.'

'They do say as poor Sir Thomas is in a bad way,' said Mrs. O'Dwyer, shaking her head piteously.

'And yet he sees those men,' said Father Barney. 'I know that for certain. He has seen them, though he will rarely see anybody now-a-days.'

'Young Mr. Herbert is a-doing most of the business up about the place,' said Mrs. O'Dwyer. 'And people do say as how he is going to make a match of it with Lady Clara Desmond. And it's the lucky girl she'll be, for he's a nice young fellow entirely.'

'Not half equal to her other Joe, Mr. Owen that is,' said Fanny.

'Well, I don't know that, my dear. Such a house and property as Castle Richmond is not likely to go a-begging among the young women. And then Mr. Herbert is not so rampageous like as him of Hap House, by all accounts.'

But Father Barney still kept to his subject. 'And they are both at your place at the present moment, eh, Fanny?'

'They was to dine there, after I left.'

'And the old man said he'd be down here again next Thursday,' continued the priest. 'I heard that for certain. I'll tell you what it is, they're not after any good here. They are Protestants, ain't they?'

'Oh, black Protestants,' said Mrs. O'Dwyer. 'But you are not taking your tay, Father Bernard,' and she again filled his cup for him.

'If you'll take my advice, Fanny, you'll give them nothing more without seeing their money. They'll come to no good here, I'm sure of that. They're afther some mischief with that poor old gentleman at Castle Richmond, and it's my belief the police will have them before they've done.'

'Like enough,' said Mrs. O'Dwyer.

'They may have them to-morrow, for what I care,' said Fanny, who could not help feeling that Aby Mollett had at one time been not altogether left without hope as her suitor.

'But you wouldn't like anything like that to happen in your father's house,' said Father Barney.

'Bringing throuble and disgrace on an honest name,' said Mrs. O'Dwyer.

'There'd be no disgrace as I knows of,' said Fanny, stoutly. 'Father makes his money by the public, and in course he takes in any that comes the way with money in their pockets to pay the shot.'

'But these Molletts ain't got the money to pay the shot,' said Mrs. O'Dwyer, causticly. 'You've about sucked 'em dhry, I'm thinking, and they owes you more now than you're like to get from 'em.'

'I suppose father 'll have to take that bill up,' said Fanny, assenting. And so it was settled down there among them that the Molletts were to have the cold shoulder, and that they should in fact be turned out of the Kanturk Hotel as quickly as this could be done. 'Better a small loss at first, than a big one at last,' said Mrs. O'Dwyer, with much wisdom. 'They'll come to mischief down here, as sure as my name's M'Carthy,' said the priest. 'And I'd be sorry your father should be mixed up in it.'

And then by degrees the conversation was changed, but not till the tea-things had been taken away, and a square small bottle of very particular whisky put on the table in its place. And the sugar also was brought, and boiling water in an immense jug, as though Father Barney were going to make a deep potation indeed, and a lemon in a wine glass; and then the priest was invited, with much hospitality, to make himself comfortable. Nor did the luxuries prepared for him end here; but Fanny, the pretty Fan herself, filled a pipe for him, and pre-

tended that she would light it, for such priests are merry enough
sometimes, and can joke as well as other men with their pretty
nieces.

'But you're not mixing your punch, Father Bernard,' said
Mrs. O'Dwyer, with a plaintive melancholy voice, 'and the
wather getting cowld and all! Faix then, Father Bernard, I'll
mix it for ye, so I will.' And so she did, and well she knew
how. And then she made another for herself and her niece,
urging that 'a thimbleful would do Fanny all the good in life
afther her ride acrass them cowld mountains,' and the priest
looked on assenting, blowing the comfortable streams of smoke
from his nostrils.

'And so, Father Bernard, you and Parson Townsend is to
meet again to-morrow at Gortnaclough.' Whereupon Father
Bernard owned that such was the case, with a nod, not caring to
disturb the pipe which lay comfortably on his lower lip.

'Well, well; only to think on it,' continued Mrs. O'Dwyer.
'That the same room should hold the two of ye.' And she
lifted up her hands and shook her head.

'It houlds us both very comfortable, I can assure you, Mrs.
O'Dwyer.'

'And he ain't rampageous and highty-tighty? He don't give
hisself no airs?'

'Well, no; nothing in particular. Why should the man be
such a fool as that?'

'Why, in course? But they are such fools, Father Bernard.
They does think theyselves such grand folks. Now don't they?
I'd give a dandy of punch all round to the company just to hear
you put him down once; I would. But he isn't upsetting at all,
then?'

'Not the last time we met, he wasn't; and I don't think he
intends it. Things have come to that now that the parsons
know where they are and what they have to look to. They're
getting a lesson they'll not forget in a hurry. Where are their
rent charges to come from—can you tell me that, Mrs.
O'Dwyer?'

Mrs. O'Dwyer could not, but she remarked that pride would
always have a fall. 'And there's no pride like Protesthant
pride,' said Fanny. 'It is so upsetting, I can't abide it.' All
which tended to show that she had quite given up her Protestant lover.

'And is it getthing worse than iver with the poor crathurs?'
said Mrs. O'Dwyer, referring, not to the Protestants, but to the
victims of the famine.

'Indeed it's getting no betther,' said the priest, 'and I'm

fearing it will be worse before it is over.   I haven't married one
couple in Drumbarrow since November last.'

'And that's a heavy sign, Father Bernard.'

'The surest sign in the world that they have no money among
them at all, at all.   And it is bad with thim, Mrs. O'Dwyer,—
very bad, very bad indeed.'

'Glory be to God, the poor cratures!' said the soft-hearted
lady.   'It isn't much the like of us have to give away, Father
Bernard; I needn't be telling you that.   But we'll help, you
know,—we'll help.'

'And so will father, uncle Bernard.   If you're so bad off
about here I know he'll give you a thrifle for the asking.'   In a
short time, however, it came to pass that those in the cities
could spare no aid to the country.   Indeed it may be a question
whether the city poverty was not the harder of the two.

'God bless you both—you've soft hearts, I know.'   And
Father Barney put his punch to his lips.   'Whatever you can
do for me shall not be thrown away.   And I'll tell you what,
Mrs. O'Dwyer, it does behove us all to put our best foot out now.
We will not let them say that the Papists would do nothing for
their own poor.'

'Deed then an' they'll say anything of us, Father Bernard.
There's nothing too hot or too heavy for them.'

'At any rate let us not deserve it, Mrs. O'Dwyer.   There will
be a lot of them at Gortnaclough to-morrow, and I shall tell
them that we, on our side, won't be wanting.   To give them
their due, I must say that they are working well.   That young
Herbert Fitzgerald's a trump, whether he's Protestant or
Catholic.'

'An' they do say he's a strong bearing towards the ould religion,'
said Mrs. O'Dwyer.   'God bless his sweet young face av' he'd
come back to us.   That's what I say.'

'God bless his face any way, say I,' said Father Barney, with
a wider philanthropy.   'He is doing his best for the people, and
the time has come now when we must hang together, if it be
any way possible.'   And with this the priest finished his pipe,
and wishing the ladies good night, walked away to his own
house.

CHAPTER XVIII.

THE RELIEF COMMITTEE.

AT this time the famine was beginning to be systematised. The sternest among landlords and masters were driven to acknowledge that the people had not got food or the means of earning it. The people themselves were learning that a great national calamity had happened, and that the work was God's work; and the Government had fully recognised the necessity of taking the whole matter into its own hands. They were responsible for the preservation of the people, and they acknowledged their responsibility.

And then two great rules seemed to get themselves laid down —not by general consent, for there were many who greatly contested their wisdom—but by some force strong enough to make itself dominant. The first was, that the food to be provided should be earned and not given away. And the second was, that the providing of that food should be left to private competition, and not in any way be undertaken by the Government. I make bold to say that both these rules were wise and good.

But how should the people work? That Government should supply the wages was of course an understood necessity; and it was also necessary that on all such work the amount of wages should be regulated by the price at which provisions might fix themselves. These points produced questions which were hotly debated by the Relief Committees of the different districts; but at last it got itself decided, again by the hands of Government, that all hills along the country road should be cut away, and that the people should be employed on this work. They were so employed,—very little to the advantage of the roads for that or some following years.

'So you have begun, my men,' said Herbert to a gang of labourers whom he found collected at a certain point on Bally-dahan Hill, which lay on his road from Castle Richmond to Gortnaclough. In saying this he had certainly paid them an unmerited compliment, for they had hitherto begun nothing. Some thirty or forty wretched-looking men were clustered together in the dirt and slop and mud, on the brow of the hill, armed with such various tools as each was able to find—with tools, for the most part, which would go but a little way in making Ballydahan Hill level or accessible. This question of tools also came to a sort of understood settlement before long; and within three months of the time of which I am writing legions of wheelbarrows were to be seen lying near every hill; wheelbarrows in hundreds and thousands. The fate of those myriads of wheelbarrows has always been a mystery to me.

'So you have begun, my men,' said Herbert, addressing them in a kindly voice. There was a couple of gangsmen with them, men a little above the others in appearance, but apparently incapable of commencing the work in hand, for they also were standing idle, leaning against a bit of wooden paling. It had, however, been decided that the works at Ballydahan Hill should begin on this day, and there were the men assembled. One fact admitted of no doubt, namely, this, that the wages would begin from this day.

And then the men came and clustered round Herbert's horse. They were wretched-looking creatures, half-clad, discontented, with hungry eyes, each having at his heart's core a deep sense of injustice done personally upon him. They hated this work of cutting hills from the commencement to the end,—hated it, though it was to bring them wages and save them and theirs from actual famine and death. They had not been accustomed to the discomfort of being taken far from their homes to their daily work. Very many of them had never worked regularly for wages, day after day, and week after week. Up to this time such was not the habit of Irish cottiers. They held their own land, and laboured there for a spell; and then they would work for a spell, as men do in England, taking wages; and then they would be idle for a spell. It was not exactly a profitable mode of life, but it had its comforts; and now these unfortunates who felt themselves to be driven forth like cattle in droves for the first time, suffered the full wretchedness of their position. They were not rough and unruly, or inclined to be troublesome and perhaps violent, as men similarly circumstanced so often are in England;—as Irishmen are when collected in gangs out of Ireland. They had no aptitudes for such roughness, and no spirits for such violence. But they were melancholy, given to complaint, apathetic, and utterly without interest in that they were doing.

'Yz, yer honer,' said one man who was standing, shaking himself, with his hands enveloped in the rags of his pockets. He had on no coat, and the keen north wind seemed to be blowing through his bones; cold, however, as he was, he would do nothing towards warming himself, unless that occasional shake can be considered as a doing of something. 'Yz, yer honer; we've begun thin since before daylight this blessed morning.'

It was now eleven o'clock, and a pick-axe had not been put into the ground, nor the work marked.

'Been here before daylight!' said Herbert. 'And has there been nobody to set you to work?'

'Divil a sowl, yer honer,' said another, who was sitting on a hedge-bank leaning with both his hands on a hoe, which he held between his legs, 'barring Thady Molloy and Shawn Brady; they two do be over us, but they knows nothin' o' such jobs as this.'

Thady Molloy and Shawn Brady had with the others moved up so as to be close to Herbert's horse, but they said not a word towards vindicating their own fitness for command.

'And it's mortial cowld standing here thin,' said another, 'without a bit to ate or a sup to dhrink since last night, and then only a lump of the yally mail.' And the speaker moved about on his toes and heels, desirous of keeping his blood in circulation with the smallest possible amount of trouble.

'I'm telling the boys it's home we'd betther be going,' said a fourth.

'And lose the tizzy they've promised us,' said he of the hoe.

'Sorrow a tizzy they'll pay any of yez for standing here all day,' said an ill-looking little wretch of a fellow, with a black muzzle and a squinting eye; 'ye may all die in the road first.' And the man turned away among the crowd, as an Irishman does who has made his speech and does not want to be answered.

'You need have no fear about that, my men,' said Herbert. 'Whether you be put to work or no you'll receive your wages; you may take my word for that.'

'I've been telling 'em that for the last half-hour,' said the man with the hoe, now rising to his feet. ' "Shure an' didn't Mr. Somers be telling us that we'd have saxpence each day as long we war here afore daylight?" said I, yer honer; "an' shure an' wasn't it black night when we war here this blessed morning, and devil a fear of the tizzy?" said I. But it's mortial cowld, an it'd be asier for uz to be doing a spell of work than crouching about on our hunkers down on the wet ground.'

All this was true. It had been specially enjoined upon them to be early at their work. An Irishman as a rule will not come regularly to his task. It is a very difficult thing to secure his services every morning at six o'clock; but make a special point, —tell him that you want him very early, and he will come to you in the middle of the night. Breakfast every morning punctually at eight o'clock is almost impossible in Ireland; but if you want one special breakfast, so that you may start by a train at 4 A.M., you are sure to be served. No irregular effort is distasteful to an Irishman of the lower classes, not if it entails on him the loss of a day's food and the loss of a night's rest; the actual pleasure of the irregularity repays him for all this, and he never tells you that this or that is not his work. He prefers work that is not his own. Your coachman will have no objection to turn the mangle, but heaven and earth put together won't persuade him to take the horses out to exercise every morning at the same hour. These men had been told to come early, and they had been there on the road-side since five o'clock. It was not surprising that they were cold and hungry, listless and unhappy.

And then, as young Fitzgerald was questioning the so-named gangmen as to the instructions they had received, a jaunting car came up to the foot of the hill. 'We war to wait for the ongineer,' Shawn Brady had said, 'an' shure an' we have waited.' 'An' here's one of Misther Carroll's cars from Mallow,' said Thady Molloy, 'and that's the ongineer hisself.' Thady Molloy was right; this was the engineer himself, who had now arrived from Mallow. From this time forth, and for the next twelve months, the country was full of engineers, or of men who were so called. I do not say this in disparagement; but the engineers were like the yellow meal. When there is an immense demand, and that a suddenly immense demand, for any article, it is seldom easy to get it very good. In those days men became engineers with a short amount of apprenticeship, but, as a rule, they did not do their work badly. In such days as those, men, if they be men at all, will put their shoulders to the wheel.

The engineer was driven up to where they were standing, and he jumped off the car among the men who were to work under him with rather a pretentious air. He had not observed, or probably had not known, Herbert Fitzgerald. He was a very young fellow, still under one-and-twenty, beardless, light-haired, blue-eyed, and fresh from England. 'And what hill is this?' said he to the driver.

'Ballydahan, shure, yer honer. That last war Connick-a-coppul, and that other, the big un intirely, where the crass road takes away to Buttevant, that was Glounthauneroughtymore. Faix and that's been the murthering hill for cattle since first I knew it. Bedad yer honer'll make smooth as a bowling-green.'

'Ballydahan,' said the young man, taking a paper out of his pocket and looking up the names in his list, 'I've got it. There should be thirty-seven of them here.'

'Shure an' here we are these siven hours,' said our friend of the hoe, 'and mighty cowld we are.'

'Thady Molloy and Shawn Brady,' called out the engineer, managing thoroughly to Anglicise the pronunciation of the names, though they were not Celtically composite to any great degree.

'Yez, we's here,' said Thady, coming forward. And then Herbert came up and introduced himself, and the young engineer took off his hat. 'I came away from Mallow before eight,' said he apologetically; 'but I have four of these places to look after, and when one gets to one of them it is impossible to get away again. There was one place where I was kept two hours before I could get one of the men to understand what they were to do. What is it you call that big hill?'

'Glounthauneroughtymore, yer honer,' said the driver, to whom the name was as easy and familiar as his own.

'And you are going to set these men to work now?' said Herbert.

'Well, I don't suppose they'll do much to-day, Mr. Fitzgerald. But I must try and explain to the head men how they are to begin. They have none of them any tools, you see.' And then he called out again, 'Thady Molloy and Shawn Brady.'

'We's here,' said Thady again; 'we did not exactly know whether yer honer'd be afther beginning at the top or the botthom. That's all that war staying us.'

'Never fear,' said Shawn, 'but we'll have ould Ballydahan level in less than no time. We're the boys that can do it, fair and aisy.'

It appeared to Herbert that the young engineer seemed to be rather bewildered by the job of work before him, and therefore he rode on, not stopping to embarrass him by any inspection of his work. In process of time no doubt so much of the top of Ballydahan Hill was carried to the bottom as made the whole road altogether impassable for many months. But the great object was gained; the men were fed, and were not fed by charity. What did it matter, that the springs of every conveyance in the county Cork were shattered by the process, and that the works resulted in myraids of wheelbarrows.

And then, as he rode on towards Gortnaclough, Herbert was overtaken by his friend the parson, who was also going to the meeting of the relief committee. 'You have not seen the men at Ballydahan Hill, have you?' said Herbert.

Mr. Townsend explained that he had not seen them. His road had struck on to that on which they now were not far from the top of the hill. 'But I knew they were to be there this morning,' said Mr. Townsend.

'They have sent quite a lad of a fellow to show them how to work,' said Herbert. 'I fear we shall all come to grief with these road-cuttings.'

'For heaven's sake don't say that at the meeting,' said Mr. Townsend, 'or you'll be playing the priests' game out and out. Father Barney has done all in his power to prevent the works.'

'But what if Father Barney be right?' said Herbert.

'But he's not right,' said the parson, energetically. 'He's altogether wrong. I never knew one of them right in my life yet in anything. How can they be right?'

'But I think you are mixing up road-making and Church doctrine, Mr. Townsend.'

'I hope I may never be in danger of mixing up God and the devil. You cannot touch pitch and not be defiled. Remember that, Herbert Fitzgerald.'

'I will remember nothing of the kind,' said Herbert. 'Am I to set myself up as a judge and say that this is pitch and that is pitch? Do you remember St. Peter on the housetop? Was not he afraid of what was unclean?'

'The meaning of that was that he was to convert the Gentiles, and not give way to their errors. He was to contend with them and not give way an inch till he had driven them from their idolatry.' Mr. Townsend had been specially primed by his wife that morning with vigorous hostility against Father Barney, and was grieved to his heart at finding that his young friend was prepared to take the priest's part in anything. In this matter of the roads Mr. Townsend was doubtless right, but hardly on the score of the arguments assigned by him.

'I don't mean to say that there should be no road-making,' said Herbert, after a pause. 'The general opinion seems to be that we can't do better. I only say that we shall come to grief about it. Those poor fellows there have as much idea of cutting down a hill as I have; and it seems to me that the young lad whom I left with them has not much more.'

'They'll learn all in good time.'

'Let us hope it will be in good time.'

'If we once let them have the idea that we are to feed them in idleness,' said Mr. Townsend, 'they will want to go on for ever in the same way. And then, when they receive such immense sums in money wages, the priests will be sure to get their share. If the matter had been left to me, I would have paid the men in meal. I would never have given them money. They should have worked and got their food. The priest will get a penny out of every shilling; you'll see else.' And so the matter was discussed between them as they went along to Gortnaclough.

When they reached the room in which the committee was held they found Mr. Somers already in the chair. Priest McCarthy was there also, with his coadjutor, the Rev. Columb Creagh—Father Columb as he was always called : and there was a Mr. O'Leary from Boherbuy, one of the middlemen as they were formerly named,—though by the way I never knew that word to be current in Ireland; it is familiar to all, and was I suppose common some few years since, but I never heard the peasants calling such persons by that title. He was one of those with whom the present times were likely to go very hard. He was not a bad man, unless in so far as this, that he had no idea of owing any duty to others beyond himself and his family. His doctrine at present amounted to this, that if you left the people alone and gave them no false hopes, they would contrive to live somehow. He believed in a good deal, but he had no belief whatever in starvation,—none as yet. It was probable enough that some belief in this might come to him now before long. There were also one or two others ; men who had some stake in the country, but men who hadn't a tithe of the interest possessed by Sir Thomas Fitzgerald.

Mr. Townsend again went through the ceremony of shaking hands with his reverend brethren, and, on this occasion, did not seem to be much the worse for it. Indeed, in looking at the two men cursorily a stranger might have said that the condescension was all on the other side. Mr. M'Carthy was dressed quite smartly. His black clothes were spruce and glossy ; his gloves, of which he still kept on one and showed the other, were quite new ; he was clean shaven, and altogether he had a shiny, bright, ebon appearance about him that quite did a credit to his side of the church. But our friend the parson was discreditably shabby. His clothes were all brown, his white neck-tie could hardly have been clean during the last forty-eight hours, and was tied in a knot, which had worked itself nearly round to his ear as he had sat sideways on the car ; his boots were ugly and badly brushed, and his hat was very little better than some of those worn by the workmen—so called—at Ballydahan Hill. But, nevertheless, on looking accurately into the faces of both, one might see which man was the better nurtured and the better born. That operation with the sow's ear is, one may say, seldom successful with the first generation.

'A beautiful morning this,' said the coadjutor, addressing Herbert Fitzgerald, with a very mild voice and an unutterable look of friendship; as though he might have said, ' Here we are in a boat together, and of course we are all very fond of each other.' To tell the truth, Father Columb was not a nice-looking

young man.   He was red-haired, slightly marked with the small
pox, and had a low forehead and cunning eyes.

'Yes, it is, a nice morning,' said Herbert.   'We don't expect
anybody else here, do we, Somers?'

'At any rate we won't wait,' said Somers.   So he sat down in
the arm-chair, and they all went to work.

'I am afraid, Mr. Somers,' said Mr. M'Carthy from the other
end of the table, where he had constituted himself a sort of
deputy chairman, 'I am afraid we are going on a wrong tack.'
The priest had shuffled away his chair as he began to speak, and
was now standing with his hands upon the table.   It is singular
how strong a propensity some men have to get upon their legs
in this way.

'How so, Mr. M'Carthy?' said Somers.   'But sha'n't we be
all more comfortable if we keep our chairs?   There'll be less
ceremony, won't there, Mr. Townsend?'

'Oh! certainly,' said Townsend.

'Less liable to interruption, perhaps, on our legs,' said Father
Columb, smiling blandly.

But Mr. M'Carthy was far too wise to fight the question, so he
sat down.   'Just as you like,' said he; 'I can talk any way,
sitting or standing, walking or riding; it's all one to me.   But
I'll tell you how we are on the wrong tack.   We shall never get
these men to work in gangs on the road.   Never.   They have
not been accustomed to be driven like droves of sheep.'

'But droves of sheep don't work on the road,' said Mr. Townsend.

'I know that, Mr. Townsend,' continued Mr. M'Carthy.   'I
am quite well aware of that.   But droves of sheep are driven,
and these men won't bear it.'

'Deed an' they won't,' said Father Columb, having altogether
laid aside his bland smile now that the time had come, as he
thought, to speak up for the people.   'They may bear it in
England, but they won't here.'   And the sternness of his eye
was almost invincible.

'If they are so foolish, they must be taught better manners,'
said Mr. Townsend.   'But you'll find they'll work just as other
men do—look at the navvies.'

'And look at the navvies' wages,' said Father Columb.

'Besides the navvies only go if they like it,' said the parish
priest.

'And these men need not go unless they like it,' said Mr.
Somers.   'Only with this proviso, that if they cannot manage
for themselves they must fall into our w y of managing for
them.'

'What I say, is this,' said Mr. O'Leary. 'Let 'em manage for 'emselves. God bless my sowl! Why we shall be skinned alive if we have to pay all this money back to Government. If Government chooses to squander thousands in this way, Government should bear the brunt. That's what I say.' Eventually, Government, that is the whole nation, did bear the brunt. But it would not have been very wise to promise this at the time.

'But we need hardly debate all that at the present moment,' said Mr. Somers. 'That matter of the roads has already been decided for us, and we can't alter it if we would.'

'Then we may as well shut up shop,' said Mr. O'Leary.

'It's all very aisy to talk in that way,' said Father Columb; 'but the Government, as you call it, can't make men work. It can't force eight millions of the finest pisantry on God's earth ——,' and Father Columb was, by degrees, pushing away the seat from under him, when he was cruelly and ruthlessly stopped by his own parish priest.

'I beg your pardon for a moment, Creagh,' said he; 'but perhaps we are getting a little out of the track. What Mr. Somers says is very true. If these men won't work on the road —and I don't think they will—the responsibility is not on us. That matter has been decided for us.'

'Men will sooner work anywhere than starve,' said Mr. Townsend.

'Some men will,' said Father Columb, with a great deal of meaning in his tone. What he intended to convey was this— that Protestants, no doubt, would do so, under the dominion of the flesh; but that Roman Catholics, being under the dominion of the Spirit, would perish first.

'At any rate we must try,' said Father M'Carthy.

'Exactly,' said Mr. Somers; 'and what we have now to do is to see how we may best enable these workers to live on their wages, and how those others are to live, who, when all is done, will get no wages.'

'I think we had better turn shopkeepers ourselves, and open stores for them everywhere,' said Herbert. 'That is what we are doing already at Berryhill.'

'And import our own corn,' said the parson.

'And where are we to get the money?' said the priest.

'And why are we to ruin the merchants?' said O'Leary, whose brother was in the flour-trade, in Cork.

'And shut up all the small shopkeepers,' said Father Columb, whose mother was established in that line in the neighbourhood of Castleisland.

'We could not do it,' said Somers. 'The demand upon us

would be so great, that we should certainly break down. And then where would we be?'

'But for a time, Somers,' pleaded Herbert.

'For a time we may do something in that way, till other means present themselves. But we must refuse all out-door relief. They who cannot or do not bring money must go into the workhouses.'

'You will not get houses in county Cork sufficient to hold them,' said Father Bernard. And so the debate went on, not altogether without some sparks of wisdom, with many sparks also of eager benevolence, and some few passing clouds of fuliginous self-interest. And then lists were produced, with the names on them of all who were supposed to be in want—which were about to become, before long, lists of the whole population of the country. And at last it was decided among them, that in their district nothing should be absolutely given away, except to old women and widows,—which kindhearted clause was speedily neutralised by women becoming widows while their husbands were still living; and it was decided also, that as long as their money lasted, the soup-kitchen at Berryhill should be kept open, and mill kept going, and the little shop maintained, so that to some extent a check might be maintained on the prices of the hucksters. And in this way they got through their work, not perhaps with the sagacity of Solomon, but as I have said, with an average amount of wisdom, as will always be the case when men set about their tasks with true hearts and honest minds.

And then, when they parted, the two clergymen of the parish shook hands with each other again, having perhaps less animosity against each other than they had ever felt before. There had been a joke or two over the table, at which both had laughed. The priest had wisely shown some deference to the parson, and the parson had immediately returned it, by referring some question to the priest. How often does it not happen that when we come across those whom we have hated and avoided all our lives, we find that they are not quite so bad as we had thought? That old gentleman of whom we wot is never so black as he has been painted.

The work of the committee took them nearly the whole day, so that they did not separate till it was nearly dark. When they did so, Somers and Herbert Fitzgerald rode home together.

'I always live in mortal fear,' said Herbert, 'that Townsend and the priests will break out into warfare.'

'As they havn't done it yet, they won't do it now,' said Somers. 'M'Carthy is not without sense, and Townsend, queer and intolerant as he is, has good feeling. If he and Father

Columb were left together, I don't know what might happen. Mr. Prendergast is to be with you the day after to-morrow, is he not?'

'So I understood my father to say.'

'Will you let me give you a bit of advice, Herbert?'

'Certainly.'

'Then don't be in the house much on the day after he comes. He'll arrive, probably, to dinner.'

'I suppose he will.'

'If so, leave Castle Richmond after breakfast the next morning, and do not return till near dinner-time. It may be that your father will not wish you to be near him. Whatever this matter may be, you may be sure that you will know it before Mr. Prendergast leaves the country. I am very glad that he is coming.'

Herbert promised that he would take this advice, and he thought himself that among other things he might go over to inspect that Clady boiler, and of course call at Desmond Court on his way. And then, when they got near to Castle Richmond they parted company, Mr. Somers stopping at his own place, and Herbert riding home alone.

CHAPTER XIX.

THE FRIEND OF THE FAMILY.

On the day named by Herbert, and only an hour before dinner, Mr. Prendergast did arrive at Castle Richmond. The Great Southern and Western Railway was not then open as far as Mallow, and the journey from Dublin was long and tedious. 'I'll see him of course,' said Sir Thomas to Lady Fitzgerald; 'but I'll put off this business till to-morrow.' This he said in a tone of distress and agony, which showed too plainly how he dreaded the work which he had before him. 'But you'll come in to dinner,' Lady Fitzgerald had said. 'No,' he answered, 'not to day, love; I have to think about this.' And he put his hand up to his head, as though this thinking about it had already been too much for him.

Mr. Prendergast was a man over sixty years of age, being, in fact, considerably senior to Sir Thomas himself. But no one would have dreamed of calling Mr. Prendergast an old man. He was short of stature, well made, and in good proportion; he was wiry, strong, and almost robust. He walked as though in put-

...is foot to the earth he always wished to proclaim that he ...afraid of no man and no thing. His hair was grizzled, and his whiskers were gray, and round about his mouth his face was wrinkled; but with him even these things hardly seemed to be signs of old age. He was said by many who knew him to be a stern man, and there was that in his face which seemed to warrant such a character. But he had also the reputation of being a very just man; and those who knew him best could tell tales of him which proved that his sternness was at any rate compatible with a wide benevolence. He was a man who himself had known but little mental suffering, and who owned no mental weakness; and it might be, therefore, that he was impatient of such weakness in others. To chance acquaintances his manners were not soft, or perhaps palatable; but to his old friends his very brusqueness was pleasing. He was a bachelor, well off in the world, and, to a certain extent, fond of society. He was a solicitor by profession, having his office somewhere in the purlieus of Lincoln's Inn, and living in an old-fashioned house not far distant from that classic spot. I have said that he owned no mental weakness. When I say further that he was slightly afflicted with personal vanity, and thought a good deal about the set of his hair, the shape of his coat, the fit of his boots, the whiteness of his hands and the external trim of his umbrella, perhaps I may be considered to have contradicted myself. But such was the case. He was a handsome man too, with clear, bright, gray eyes, a well-defined nose, and expressive mouth—of which the lips, however, were somewhat too thin. No man with thin lips ever seems to me to be genially human at all points.

Such was Mr. Prendergast; and my readers will, I trust, feel for Sir Thomas, and pity him, in that he was about to place his wounds in the hands of so ruthless a surgeon. But a surgeon, to be of use, should be ruthless in one sense. He should have the power of cutting and cauterizing, of phlebotomy and bone-handling without effect on his own nerves. This power Mr. Prendergast possessed, and therefore it may be said that Sir Thomas had chosen his surgeon judiciously. None of the Castle Richmond family, except Sir Thomas himself, had ever seen this gentleman, nor had Sir Thomas often come across him of late years. But he was what we in England call an old family friend; and I doubt whether we in England have any more valuable English characteristic than that of having old family friends. Old family feuds are not common with us now-a-days—not so common as with some other people. Sons who now hated their father's enemies would have but a bad chance before a commission of lunacy ; but an old family friend is supposed to stick to one from generation to generation.

On his arrival at Castle Richmond he was taken in to Sir Thomas before dinner. 'You find me but in a poor state,' said Sir Thomas, shaking in his fear of what was before him, as the poor wretch does before an iron-wristed dentist who is about to operate. 'You will be better soon,' Mr. Prendergast had said, as a man always does say under such circumstances. What other remark was possible to him? 'Sir Thomas thinks that he had better not trouble you with business to-night,' said Lady Fitzgerald. To this also Mr. Prendergast agreed willingly. 'We shall both of us be fresher to-morrow, after breakfast,' he remarked, as if any time made any difference to him,—as though he were not always fresh, and ready for any work that might turn up.

That evening was not passed very pleasantly by the family at Castle Richmond. To all of them Mr. Prendergast was absolutely a stranger, and was hardly the man to ingratiate himself with strangers at the first interview. And then, too, they were all somewhat afraid of him. He had come down thither on some business which was to them altogether mysterious, and, as far as they knew, he, and he alone, was to be intrusted with the mystery. He of course said nothing to them on the subject, but he looked in their eyes as though he were conscious of being replete with secret importance ; and on this very account they were afraid of him. And then poor Lady Fitzgerald, though she bore up against the weight of her misery better than did her husband, was herself very wretched. She could not bring herself to believe that all this would end in nothing; that Mr. Prendergast would put everything right, and that after his departure they would go on as happily as ever. This was the doctrine of the younger part of the family, who would not think that anything was radically wrong. But Lady Fitzgerald had always at her heart the memory of her early marriage troubles, and she feared greatly, though she feared she knew not what.

Herbert Fitzgerald and Aunt Letty did endeavour to keep up some conversation with Mr. Prendergast; and the Irish famine was, of course, the subject. But this did not go on pleasantly. Mr. Prendergast was desirous of information ; but the statements which were made to him one moment by young Fitzgerald were contradicted in the next by his aunt. He would declare that the better educated of the Roman Catholics were prepared to do their duty by their country, whereas Aunt Letty would consider herself bound both by party feeling and religious duty, to prove that the Roman Catholics were bad in everything.

'Oh, Herbert, to hear you say so!' she exclaimed at one time, 'it makes me tremble in my shoes. It is dreadful to think that those people should have got such a hold over you.'

'I really think that the Roman Catholic priests are liberal in their ideas and moral in their conduct.' This was the speech which had made Aunt Letty tremble in her shoes, and it may, therefore, be conceived that Mr. Prendergast did not find himself able to form any firm opinion from the statements then made to him. Instead of doing so, he set them both down as 'Wild Irish,' whom it would be insane to trust, and of whom it was absurd to make inquiries. It may, however, be possibly the case that Mr. Prendergast himself had his own prejudices as well as Aunt Letty and Herbert Fitzgerald.

On the following morning they were still more mute at breakfast. The time was coming in which Mr. Prendergast was to go to work, and even he, gifted though he was with iron nerves, began to feel somewhat unpleasantly the nature of the task which he had undertaken. Lady Fitzgerald did not appear at all. Indeed, during the whole of breakfast-time and up to the moment at which Mr. Prendergast was summoned, she was sitting with her husband, holding his hand in hers, and looking tenderly but painfully into his face. She so sat with him for above an hour, but he spoke to her no word of this revelation he was about to make. Herbert and the girls, and even Aunt Letty, sat solemn and silent, as though it was known by them all that something dreadful was to be said and done. At last Herbert, who had left the room, returned to it. 'My father will see you now, Mr. Prendergast, if you will step up to him,' said he; and then he ran to his mother and told her that he should leave the house till dinner-time.

'But if he sends for you, Herbert, should you not be in the way?'

'It is more likely that he should send for you; and, were I to remain here, I should be going into his room when he did not want me.' And then he mounted his horse and rode off.

Mr. Prendergast, with serious air and slow steps, and solemn resolve to do what he had to do at any rate with justice, walked away from the dining-room to the baronet's study. The task of an old friend is not always a pleasant one, and Mr. Prendergast felt that it was not so at the present moment. 'Be gentle with him,' said Aunt Letty, catching hold of his arm as he went through the passage. He merely moved his head twice, in token of assent, and then passed on into the room.

The reader will have learnt by this time, with tolerable accuracy, what was the nature of the revelation which Sir

Thomas was called upon to make, and he will be tolerably certain as to the advice which Mr. Prendergast, as an honest man, would give. In that respect there was no difficulty. The laws of meum and tuum are sufficiently clear if a man will open his eyes to look at them. In this case they were altogether clear. These broad acres of Castle Richmond did belong to Sir Thomas—for his life. But after his death they could not belong to his son Herbert. It was a matter which admitted of no doubt. No question as to whether the Molletts would or would not hold their tongue could bear upon it in the least. Justice in this case must be done, even though the heavens should fall. It was sad and piteous. Stern and hard as was the man who pronounced this doom, nevertheless the salt tear collected in his eyes and blinded him as he looked upon the anguish which his judgment had occasioned.

Yes, Herbert must be told that he in the world was nobody; that he must earn his bread, and set about doing so right soon. Who could say that his father's life was worth a twelvemonth's purchase? He must be told that he was nobody in the world, and instructed also to tell her whom he loved, an earl's daughter, the same tidings; that he was nobody, that he would come to possess no property, and that in the law's eyes did not possess even a name. How would his young heart suffice for the endurance of so terrible a calamity? And those pretty girls, so softly brought up—so tenderly nurtured; it must be explained to them too that they must no longer be proud of their father's lineage and their mother's fame. And that other Fitzgerald must be summoned and told of all this; he on whom they had looked down, whom the young heir had robbed of his love, whom they had cast out from among them as unworthy. Notice must be sent to him that he was the heir to Castle Richmond, that he would reign as the future baronet in those gracious chambers. It was he who could now make a great county lady of the daughter of the countess.

'It will be very soon, very soon,' sobbed forth the poor victim. And indeed, to look at him one might say that it would be soon. There were moments when Mr. Prendergast hardly thought that he would live through that frightful day.

But all of which we have yet spoken hardly operated upon the baronet's mind in creating that stupor of sorrow which now weighed him to the earth. It was none of these things that utterly broke him down and crushed him like a mangled reed. He had hardly mind left to remember his children. It was for the wife of his bosom that he sorrowed.

The wife of his bosom! He persisted in so calling her

through the whole interview, and, even in his weakness, obliged the strong man before him so to name her also. She was his wife before God, and should be his to the end. Ah! for how short a time was that! 'Is she to leave me?' he once said, turning to his friend, with his hands clasped together, praying that some mercy might be shown to his wretchedness. 'Is she to leave me?' he repeated, and then sunk on his knees upon the floor.

And how was Mr. Prendergast to answer this question? How was he to decide whether or no this man and woman might still live together as husband and wife? Oh, my reader, think of it if you can, and put yourself for a moment in the place of that old family friend! 'Tell me, tell me; is she to leave me?' repeated the poor victim of all this misery.

The sternness and justice of the man at last gave way. 'No,' said he, 'that cannot, I should think, be necessary. They cannot demand that.' 'But you won't desert me?' said Sir Thomas, when this crumb of comfort was handed to him. And he remembered as he spoke, the bloodshot eyes of the miscreant who had dared to tell him that the wife of his bosom might be legally torn from him by the hands of another man. 'You won't desert me?' said Sir Thomas; meaning by that, to bind his friend to an obligation that, at any rate, his wife should not be taken from him.

'No,' said Mr. Prendergast, 'I will not desert you; certainly not that; certainly not that.' Just then it was in his heart to promise almost anything that he was asked. Who could have refused such solace as this to a man so terribly overburthened?

But there was another point of view at which Mr. Prendergast had looked from the commencement, but at which he could not get Sir Thomas to look at all. It certainly was necessary that the whole truth in this matter should be made known and declared openly. This fair inheritance must go to the right owner and not to the wrong. Though the affliction on Sir Thomas was very heavy, and would be equally so on all the family, he would not on that account, for the sake of saving him and them from that affliction, be justified in robbing another person of what was legally and actually that other person's property. It was a matter of astonishment to Mr. Prendergast that a conscientious man, as Sir Thomas certainly was, should have been able to look at the matter in any other light; that he should ever have brought himself to have dealings in the matter with Mr. Mollett. Justice in the case was clear, and the truth must be declared. But then they must take good care to find out absolutely what the truth was. Having heard all that Sir

Thomas had to say, and having sifted all that he did hear, Mr. Prendergast thoroughly believed, in his heart of hearts, that that wretched miscreant was the actual and true husband of the poor lady whom he would have to see. But it was necessary that this should be proved. Castle Richmond for the family, and all earthly peace of mind for that unfortunate lady and gentleman were not to be given up on the bare word of a scheming scoundrel, for whom no crime would be too black, and no cruelty too monstrous. The proofs must be looked into before anything was done, and they must be looked into before anything was said—to Lady Fitzgerald. We surely may give her that name as yet.

But then, how were they to get at the proofs—at the proofs one way or the other? That Mollett himself had his marriage certificate Sir Thomas declared. That evidence had been brought home to his own mind of the identity of the man—though what was the nature of that evidence he could not now describe—as to that he was quite explicit. Indeed, as I have said above, he almost refused to consider the question as admitting of a doubt. That Mollett was the man to whom his wife had been married he thoroughly believed; and, to tell the truth, Mr. Prendergast was afraid to urge him to look for much comfort in this direction. The whole manner of the man, Mollett, had been such as to show that he himself was sure of his ground. Mr. Prendergast could hardly doubt that he was the man, although he felt himself bound to remark that nothing should be said to Lady Fitzgerald till inquiry had been made. Mr. Mollett himself would be at Castle Richmond on the next day but one, in accordance with the appointment made by himself; and, if necessary, he could be kept in custody till he had been identified as being the man, or as not being the man, who had married Miss Wainwright.

'There is nobody living with you now who knew Lady Fitzgerald at ——?' asked Mr. Prendergast.

'Yes,' said Sir Thomas, 'there is one maid servant.' And then he explained how Mrs. Jones had lived with his wife before her first marriage, during those few months in which she had been called Mrs. Talbot, and from that day even up to the present hour.

'Then she must have known this man,' said Mr. Prendergast.

But Sir Thomas was not in a frame of mind at all suited to the sifting of evidence. He did not care to say anything about Mrs. Jones; he got no crumb of comfort out of that view of the matter. Things had come out, unwittingly for the most part, in his conversations with Mollett, which made him quite certain

as to the truth of the main part of the story. All those Dorsetshire localities were well known to the man, the bearings of the
house, the circumstances of Mr. Wainwright's parsonage, the
whole history of those months; so that on this subject Sir
Thomas had no doubt; and we may as well know at once that
there was no room for doubt. Our friend of the Kanturk Hotel,
South Main Street, Cork, was the man who, thirty years before,
had married the child-daughter of the Dorsetshire parson.

Mr. Prendergast, however, stood awhile before the fire balancing the evidence. 'The woman must have known him,' he said
to himself, 'and surely she could tell us whether he be like the
man. And Lady Fitzgerald herself would know; but then who
would have the hardness of heart to ask Lady Fitzgerald to con-
front that man?'

He remained with Sir Thomas that day for hours. The long
winter evening had begun to make itself felt by its increasing
gloom before he left him. Wine and biscuits were sent in to
them, but neither of them even noticed the man who brought
them. Twice in the day, however, Mr. Prendergast gave the
baronet a glass of sherry, which the latter swallowed unconsciously; and then, at about four, the lawyer prepared to take
his leave. 'I will see you early to-morrow,' said he, 'immediately after breakfast.'

'You are going then'? said Sir Thomas, who greatly dreaded
being left alone.

'Not away, you know,' said Mr. Prendergast. 'I am not
going to leave the house.'

'No,' said Sir Thomas; 'no, of course not, but—' and then he
paused.

'Eh!' said Mr. Prendergast, 'you were saying something.'

'They will be coming into me now,' said Sir Thomas, wailing
like a child; 'now, when you are gone; and what am I to say
to them?'

'I would say nothing at present; nothing to-day.'

'And my wife?' he asked, again. Through this interview he
studiously called her his wife. 'Is—is she to know it?'

'When we are assured that this man's story is true, Sir
Thomas, she must know it. That will probably be very soon,—
in a day or two. Till then I think you had better tell her
nothing.'

'And what shall I say to her?'

'Say nothing. I think it probable that she will not ask any
questions. If she does, tell her that the business between you
and me is not yet over. I will tell your son that at present he
had better not speak to you on the subject of my visit here.

And then he again took the hand of the unfortunate gentleman, and having pressed it with more tenderness than seemed to belong to him, he left the room.

He left the room, and hurried into the hall and out of the house; but as he did so he could see that he was watched by Lady Fitzgerald. She was on the alert to go to her husband as soon as she should know that he was alone. Of what then took place between those two we need say nothing, but will wander forth for a while with Mr. Prendergast into the wide-spreading park.

Mr. Prendergast had been used to hard work all his life, but he had never undergone a day of severer toil than that through which he had just past. Nor was it yet over. He had laid it down in a broad way as his opinion that the whole truth in this matter should be declared to the world, let the consequences be what they might; and to this opinion Sir Thomas had acceded without a word of expostulation. But in this was by no means included all that portion of the burden which now fell upon Mr. Prendergast's shoulders. It would be for him to look into the evidence, and then it would be for him also—heavy and worst task of all—to break the matter to Lady Fitzgerald.

As he sauntered out into the park, to wander about for half an hour in the dusk of the evening, his head was throbbing with pain. The family friend in this instance had certainly been severely taxed in the exercise of his friendship. And what was he to do next? How was he to conduct himself that evening in the family circle, knowing, as he so well did, that his coming there was to bring destruction upon them all? 'Be tender to him,' Aunt Letty had said, little knowing how great a call there would be on his tenderness of heart, and how little scope for any tenderness of purpose.

And was it absolutely necessary that that blow should fall in all its severity? He asked himself this question over and over again, and always had to acknowledge that it was necessary. There could be no possible mitigation. The son must be told that he was no son—no son in the eye of the law; the wife must be told that she was no wife, and the distant relative must be made acquainted with his golden prospects. The position of Herbert and Clara, and of their promised marriage, had been explained to him,—and all that too must be shivered into fragments. How was it possible that the penniless daughter of an earl should give herself in marriage to a youth, who was not only penniless also, but illegitimate and without a profession? Look at it in which way he would, it was all misery and ruin, and it had fallen upon him to pronounce the doom!

He could not himself believe that there was any doubt as to the general truth of Mollett's statement. He would of course inquire. He would hear what the man had to say and see what he had to adduce. He would also examine that old servant, and, if necessary—and if possible also—he would induce Lady Fitzgerald to see the man. But he did feel convinced that on this point there was no doubt. And then he lifted up his hands in astonishment at the folly which had been committed by a marriage under such circumstances—as wise men will do in the decline of years, when young people in the heyday of youth have not been wise. 'If they had waited for a term of years,' he said, 'and if he then had not presented himself!' A term of years, such as Jacob served for Rachel, seems so light an affair to old bachelors looking back at the loves of their young friends.

And so he walked about in the dusk by no means a happy man, nor in any way satisfied with the work which was still before him. How was he to face Lady Fitzgerald, or tell her of her fate? In what words must he describe to Herbert Fitzgerald the position which in future he must fill? The past had been dreadful to him, and the future would be no less so, in spite of his character as a hard, stern man.

When he returned to the house he met young Fitzgerald in the hall. 'Have you been to your father?' he asked immediately. Herbert, in a low voice, and with a saddened face, said that he had just come from his father's room; but Mr. Prendergast at once knew that nothing of the truth had been told to him. 'You found him very weak,' said Mr. Prendergast. 'Oh, very weak,' said Herbert. 'More than weak; utterly prostrate. He was lying on the sofa almost unable to speak. My mother was with him and is still there.'

'And she?' He was painfully anxious to know whether Sir Thomas had been weak enough—or strong enough—to tell his wife any of the story which that morning had been told to him.

'She is doing what she can to comfort him,' said Herbert; 'but it is very hard for her to be left so utterly in the dark.'

Mr. Prendergast was passing on to his room, but at the foot of the stairs Herbert stopped him again, going up the stairs with him, and almost whispering into his ear—

'I trust, Mr. Prendergast,' said he, 'that things are not to go on in this way.'

'No, no,' said Mr. Prendergast.

'Because it is unbearable—unbearable for my mother and for me, and for us all. My mother thinks that some terrible thing has happened to the property; but if so, why should I not be told?'

'Of anything that really has happened, or does happen, you will be told.'

'I don't know whether you are aware of it, Mr. Prendergast, but I am engaged to be married. And I have been given to understand—that is, I thought that this might take place very soon. My mother seems to think that your coming here may—may defer it. If so, I think I have a right to expect that something shall be told to me.'

'Certainly you have a right, my dear young friend. But Mr. Fitzgerald, for your own sake, for all our sakes, wait patiently for a few hours.'

'I have waited patiently.'

'Yes, I know it. You have behaved admirably. But I cannot speak to you now. This time the day after to-morrow, I will tell you everything that I know. But do not speak of this to your mother. I make this promise only to you.' And then he passed on into his bedroom.

With this Herbert was obliged to be content. That evening he again saw his father and mother, but he told them nothing of what had passed between him and Mr. Prendergast. Lady Fitzgerald remained in the study with Sir Thomas the whole evening, nay, almost the whole night, and the slow hours as they passed there were very dreadful. No one came to table but Aunt Letty, Mr. Prendergast, and Herbert, and between them hardly a word was spoken. The poor girls had found themselves utterly unable to appear. They were dissolved in tears, and crouching over the fire in their own room. And the moment that Aunt Letty left the table Mr. Prendergast arose also. He was suffering, he said, cruelly from headache, and would ask permission to go to his chamber. It would have been impossible for him to have sat there pretending to sip his wine with Herbert Fitzgerald.

After this Herbert again went to his father, and then, in the gloom of the evening, he found Mr. Somers in the office, a little magistrate's room, that was used both by him and by Sir Thomas. But nothing passed between them. Herbert had nothing to tell. And then at about nine he also went up to his bedroom. A more melancholy day than that had never shed its gloom upon Castle Richmond.

CHAPTER XX.

TWO WITNESSES.

MR. PRENDERGAST had given himself two days to do all that was to be done, before he told Herbert Fitzgerald the whole of the family history. He had promised that he would then let him know all that there was to be known; and he had done so advisedly, considering that it would be manifestly unjust to leave him in the dark an hour longer than was absolutely necessary. To expect that Sir Thomas himself should, with his own breath and his own words, make the revelation either to his son or to his wife, was to expect a manifest impossibility. He would, altogether, have sunk under such an effort, as he had already sunk under the effort of telling it to Mr. Prendergast; nor could it be left to the judgment of Sir Thomas to say when the story should be told. He had now absolutely abandoned all judgment in the matter. He had placed himself in the hands of a friend, and he now expected that that friend should do all that there was to be done. Mr. Prendergast had therefore felt himself justified in making this promise.

But how was he to set about the necessary intervening work, and how pass the intervening hours? It had already been decided that Mr. Abraham Mollett, when he called, should be shown, as usual, into the study, but that he should there find himself confronted, not with Sir Thomas, but with Mr. Prendergast. But there was some doubt whether or no Mr. Mollett would come. It might be that he had means of ascertaining what strangers arrived at Castle Richmond; and it might be, that he would, under the present circumstances, think it expedient to stay away. This visit, however, was not to take place till the second day after that on which Mr. Prendergast had heard the story; and, in the meantime, he had that examination of Mrs. Jones to arrange and conduct.

The breakfast was again very sad. The girls suggested to their brother that he and Mr. Prendergast should sit together by themselves in a small breakfast-parlour, but to this he would not assent. Nothing could be more difficult or embarrassing than a conversation between himself and that gentleman, and he moreover was unwilling to let it be thought in the household that affairs were going utterly wrong in the family. On this matter he need hardly have disturbed himself, for the household was fully convinced that things were going very wrong. Maid-servants and men-servants can read the meaning of heavy brows and sad faces, of long meetings and whispered consultations, as well as their betters. The two girls, therefore, and Aunt Letty, appeared at the breakfast-table, but it was as though so many ghosts had assembled round the urn.

Immediately after breakfast, Mr. Prendergast applied to Aunt Letty. 'Miss Fitzgerald,' said he, 'I think you have an old servant of the name of Jones living here.'

'Yes, sure,' said Aunt Letty. 'She was living with my sister-in-law before her marriage.'

'Exactly,—and ever since too, I believe,' said Mr. Prendergast, with a lawyer's instinctive desire to divert suspicion from the true point.

'Oh yes, always; Mrs. Jones is quite one of ourselves.'

'Then would you do me the favour to beg Mrs. Jones to oblige me with her company for half an hour or so. There is an excellent fire in my room, and perhaps Mrs. Jones would not object to step there.'

Aunt Letty promised that Mrs. Jones should be sent, merely suggesting the breakfast-parlour, instead of the bedroom; and to the breakfast-parlour Mr. Prendergast at once betook himself.

'What can she know about the London property, or about the Irish property?' thought Aunt Letty, to herself; and then it occurred to her that, perhaps, all these troubles arose from some source altogether distinct from the property.

In about a quarter of an hour, a knock came to the breakfast-parlour door, and Mrs. Jones, having been duly summoned, entered the room with a very clean cap and apron, and with a very low curtsey. 'Good morning, Mrs. Jones,' said Mr. Prendergast; 'pray take a seat;' and he pointed to an arm-chair that was comfortably placed near the fire, on the further side of the hearth-rug. Mrs. Jones sat herself down, crossed her hands on her lap, and looked the very personification of meek obedience.

And yet there was something about her which seemed to justify the soubriquet of duchess, which the girls had given to her. She had a certain grandeur about her cap, and a majestical set about the skirt of her dress, and a rigour in the lines of her mouth, which indicated a habit of command, and a confidence in her own dignity, which might be supposed to be the very clearest attribute of duchessdom.

'You have been in this family a long time, I am told, Mrs. Jones,' said Mr. Prendergast, using his pleasantest voice.

'A very long time indeed,' said Mrs. Jones.

'And in a very confidential situation, too. I am told by Sir Thomas that pretty nearly the whole management of the house is left in your hands.'

'Sir Thomas is very kind, sir; Sir Thomas always was very kind,—poor gentleman!'

'Poor gentleman indeed! you may well say that, Mrs. Jones. This family is in great affliction; you are no doubt aware of that.' And Mr. Prendergast as he spoke got up, went to the door, and saw that it was firmly closed.

Mrs. Jones acknowledged that she was aware of it. 'It was impossible,' she said, 'for servants to shut their eyes to things, if they tried ever so.'

'Of course, of course,' said Mr. Prendergast; 'and particularly for a person so attached to them all as you are.'

'Well, Mr. Pendrergrass, I am attached to them, certainly. I have seed 'em all born, sir—that is, the young ladies and Mr. Herbert. And as for her ladyship, I didn't see her born, in course, for we're both of an age. But it comes much to the same thing, like.'

'Exactly, exactly; you are quite one of themselves, as Sir Thomas's sister said to me just now. "Mrs Jones is quite one of ourselves." Those were her very words.'

'I'm sure I'm much obliged to Miss Letty.'

'Well, as I was saying, a great sorrow has come upon them all, Mrs. Jones. Now will you tell me this—do you know what it is? Can you guess at all? Do the servants know, down stairs?'

'I'd rather not be guessing on any such matters, Mr. Pendrergrass. And as for them, if they were impudent enough for the like, they'd never dare to tell me. Them Irish servants is very impudent betimes, only they're good at the heart too, and there isn't one 'd hurt a dog belonging to the family.'

'I am sure they would not,' said Mr. Prendergast. 'But you yourself, you don't know what this trouble is?'

'Not a know,' said Mrs. Jones, looking down and smoothing her apron.

'Well, now. Of course you understand, Mrs. Jones—and I must explain this to you to account for my questions. Of course you understand that I am here as Sir Thomas's friend, to set certain matters right for him if I can.'

'I supposed as much as that, if you please, sir.'

'And any questions that I may ask you, I ask altogether on his behalf—on his behalf and on that of his wife, Lady Fitzgerald. I tell you, that you may have no scruples as to answering me.'

'Oh, sir, I have no scruples as to that. But of course, sir, in anything I say I must be guided by—by—'

'By your own judgment you were going to say.'

'Yes, sir; begging pardon for mentioning such a thing to the likes of you, sir.'

'Quite right; quite right. Everybody should use their own judgment in everything they do or say, more or less. But now, Mrs. Jones, I want to know this : you remember her ladyship's first marriage, I dare say.'

'Yes, sir, I remember it,' said Mrs. Jones, shaking her head.

'It was a sad affair, wasn't it? I remember it well, though I was very young then. So were you too, Mrs. Jones.'

'Young enough, surely, sir; and foolish enough too. We were the most of us that, then, sir.'

'True, true; so we were. But you remember the man, don't you—her ladyship's husband? Mr. Talbot, he called himself.' And Mr. Prendergast took some trouble to look as though he did not at all wish to frighten her.

'Yes, I do remember him.' This she said after a considerable pause. 'But it is a very long time ago, you know, Mr. Pendrergrass.'

'A very long time. But I am sure you do remember. You lived in the house, you know, for some months.'

'Yes, I did. He was my master for three months, or thereabouts; and to tell the truth, I never got my wages for those three months yet. But that's neither here nor there.'

'Do you believe now, Mrs. Jones, that that Mr. Talbot is still alive?' He asked the question in a very soft voice, and endeavoured not to startle her by his look as he did so. But it was necessary to his purpose that he should keep his eye upon her. Half the answer to his question was to be conveyed by the effect on the muscles of her face which that question would produce. She might perhaps command her voice to tell a falsehood, but be unable to command her face to support it.

'Believe what, sir?' said she, and the lawyer could immediately perceive that she did believe and probably knew that that man who had called himself Talbot was still alive.

'Do you believe, Mrs. Jones, that he is alive—her ladyship's former husband, you know?'

The question was so terrible in its nature, that Mrs. Jones absolutely shook under it. Did she think that that man was still alive? Why, if she thought that what was she to think of her ladyship? It was in that manner that she would have answered the question, had she known how; but she did not know; she had therefore to look about her for some other words which might be equally evasive. Those which she selected served her turn just as well. 'Lord bless you, sir!' she said.

It was not that the words were expressive, but the tone was decidedly so. It was as though she said, 'How can that man be alive, who has been dead these twenty years and more ?' But nevertheless, she was giving evidence all the time against the cause of her poor mistress.

'You think, then, that he is dead?'

'Dead, sir! Oh, laws! why shouldn't he be dead?' And then there was a pause between them for a couple of minutes.

'Mrs. Jones,' said Mr. Prendergast, when he had well considered the matter, 'my belief is that your only object and wish is to do good to your master and mistress.'

'Surely, sir, surely ; it would be my bounden duty to do them good, if I knew how.'

'I will tell you how. Speak out to me the whole truth openly and freely. I am here as the friend of Sir Thomas and of her ladyship. He has sent to me that I may advise him what to do in a great trouble that has befallen him, and I cannot give him good advice till I know the truth.'

'What good could it do him, poor gentleman, to know that that man is alive ?'

'It will do him good to know the truth ; to know whether he be alive or no. Until he knows that he cannot act properly.'

'Poor gentleman! poor gentleman!' said Mrs. Jones, putting her handkerchief up to her eyes.

'If you have any information in this matter—and I think you have, Mrs. Jones—or even any suspicion, it is your duty to tell me.'

'Well, sir, I'm sure I don't say against that. You are Sir Thomas's friend to be sure, and no doubt you know best. And I'm a poor ignorant woman. But to speak candidly, sir, I don't feel myself free to talk on this matter. I haven't never made nor marred since I've been in this family, not in such matters as them. What I've seed, I've kep' to myself, and when I've had my suspecs, as a woman can't but have 'em, I've kep' them to myself also. And saving your presence, sir, and meaning no offence to a gentleman like you,' and here she got up from her chair and made another curtsey, 'I think I'd liefer hold my tongue than say anything more on this matter.' And then she remained standing as though she expected permission to retire.

But there was still another pause, and Mr. Prendergast sat looking at the fire. 'Don't you know, ma'am,' at last he said, with almost an angry voice, 'that the man was here, in this house, last week?' And now he turned round at her and looked her full in the face. He did not, however, know Mrs. Jones.

It might be difficult to coax her into free communication, but it was altogether out of his power to frighten her into it.

'What I knows, sir, I knows,' said she, 'and what I don't know, I don't know. And if you please, sir, Lady Fitzgerald—she's my missus; and if I'm to be said anything more to about this here matter, why, I'd choose that her ladyship should be by.' And then she made a little motion as though to walk towards the door, but Mr. Prendergast managed to stop her.

'But we want to spare Lady Fitzgerald, if we can—at any rate for a while,' said he. 'You would not wish to bring more sorrow upon her, would you?'

'God forbid, Mr. Pendrergrass; and if I could take the sorrow from her heart, I would willingly, and bear it myself to the grave; for her ladyship has been a good lady to me. But no good never did come, and never will, of servants talking of their missusses. And so if you please, sir, I'll make bold to'—and again she made an attempt to reach the door.

But Mr. Prendergast was not yet persuaded that he could not get from the good old woman the information that he wanted, and he was persuaded that she had the information if only she could be prevailed upon to impart it. So he again stopped her, though on this occasion she made some slight attempt to pass him by as she did so. 'I don't think,' said she, 'that there will be much use in my staying here longer.'

'Wait half a minute, Mrs. Jones, just half a minute. If I could only make you understand how we are all circumstanced here. And I tell you what; though you will trust me with nothing, I will trust you with everything.'

'I don't want no trust, sir; not about all this'

'But listen to me. Sir Thomas has reason to believe—nay, he feels quite sure—that this man is alive.'

'Poor gentleman! poor gentleman!'

'And has been here in this house two or three times within the last month. Sir Thomas is full sure of this. Now can you tell me whether the man who did come was this Talbot, or was not? If you can answer that positively, either one way or the other, you will do a service to the whole family,—which shall not go unrewarded.'

'I don't want no reward, sir. Ask me to tattle of them for rewards, after thirty years!' And she put her apron up to her eyes.

'Well, then, for the good of the family. Can you say positively that the man who came here to your master was Talbot, or that he was not?'

'Indeed then, sir, I can't say anything positively, nor for that

matter, not impositively either.' And then she shut herself up
doggedly, and sat with compressed lips, determined to resist all
the lawyer's arts.

Mr. Prendergast did not immediately give up the game, but
he failed in learning from her any more than what she had already told him. He felt confident that she did know the secret
of this man's existence and presence in the south of Ireland, but
he was forced to satisfy himself with that conviction. So he let
her go, giving her his hand as she went in token of respect, and
receiving her demure curtsey with his kindest smile. 'It may
be,' thought he to himself, 'that I have not done with her yet.'

And then he passed another tedious day,—a day that was
terribly tedious to them all. He paid a visit to Sir Thomas; but
as that arrangement about Mollett's visit had been made between
them, it was not necessary that anything should be done or said
about the business on hand. It was understood that further
action was to be stayed till that visit was over, and therefore for
the present he had nothing to say to Sir Thomas. He did not
see Lady Fitzgerald throughout the whole day, and it appeared
to him, not unnaturally, that she purposely kept out of his way,
anticipating evil from his coming. He took a walk with Herbert
and Mr. Somers, and was driven as far as the soup-kitchen and
mill at Berry Hill, inquiring into the state of the poor, or rather
pretending to inquire. It was a pretence with them all, for at
the present moment their minds were intent on other things.
And then there was that terrible dinner, that mockery of a meal,
at which the three ladies were constrained to appear, but at which
they found it impossible to eat or to speak. Mr. Somers had been
asked to join the party, so that the scene after dinner might be
less painful; but even he felt that he could not talk as was his
ordinary wont. Horrible suspicions of the truth had gradually
come upon him; and with a suspicion of such a truth—of such a
tragedy in the very household—how could he, or how could any
one hold a conversation? and then at about half-past nine,
Mr. Prendergast was again in his bedroom.

On the next morning he was early with Sir Thomas, persuading him to relinquish altogether the use of his study for that day.
On that evening they were to have another interview there, in
which Mr. Prendergast was to tell his friend the result of what
had been done. And then he had to arrange certain manœuvring
with the servants in which he was forced to obtain the assistance
of Herbert. Mollett was to be introduced into the study immediately on his arrival, and this was to be done in such a manner
that Mrs. Jones might assuredly be ignorant of his arrival. On
this duty our old friend Richard was employed, and it was con-

trived that Mrs. Jones should be kept up stairs with her mistress. All this was difficult enough, but he could not explain even to Herbert the reason why such scheming was necessary. Herbert, however, obeyed in silence, knowing that something dreadful was about to fall on them.

Immediately after breakfast Mr. Prendergast betook himself to the study, and there remained with his London newspaper in his hand. A dozen times he began a leading article, in which the law was laid down with great perspicuity and certainty as to the present state of Ireland; but had the writer been treating of the Sandwich Islands he could not have attracted less of his attention. He found it impossible to read. On that evening he would have to reveal to Herbert Fitzgerald what was to be his fate!

Matthew Mollett at his last interview with Sir Thomas had promised to call on this day, and had been counting the days till that one should arrive on which he might keep his promise. He was terribly in want of cash, and as we all know Aby had entirely failed in raising the wind—any immediate fund of wind—on the occasion of his visit to the baronet; and now, when this morning came, old Mollett was early on the road. Aby had talked of going with him, but Aby had failed so signally on the occasion of the visit which he did make to Castle Richmond, that he had been without the moral strength to persist in his purpose.

'Then I shall write to the baronet and go alone to London,' said Mollett, père.

'Bother!' replied Mollett, fils. 'You hain't got the cash, governor.'

'I've got what 'll take me there, my boy, whether you know it or not. And Sir Thomas 'll be ready enough to send me a remittance when I'm once out of this country.'

And so Aby had given way,—partly perhaps in terror of Mr. Somers' countenance; and Matthew Mollett started again in a covered car on that cold journey over the Boggeragh mountains. It was still mid-winter, being now about the end of February, and the country was colder, and wetter, and more wretched, and the people in that desolate district more ragged and more starved than when he had last crossed it. But what were their rags and starvation to him? He was worse off than they were. They were merely dying, as all men must do. But he was inhabiting a hell on earth, which no man need do. They came out to him in shoals begging; but they came in vain, getting nothing from him but a curse through his chattering teeth. What right had they to torment with their misery one so much more wretched than themselves?

At a little before twelve the covered car was at the front door of Castle Richmond house, and there was Richard under the porch. On former occasions Mr. Mollett had experienced some little delay in making his way into the baronet's presence. The servants had looked cold upon him, and he had felt as though there might be hot ploughshares under his feet at any step which he took. But now everything seemed to be made easy. Richard took him in tow without a moment's delay, told him confidentially that Sir Thomas was waiting for him, bade the covered car to be driven round into the yard with a voice that was uncommonly civil, seeing that it was addressed to a Cork carman, and then ushered Mr. Mollett through the hall and down the passage without one moment's delay. Wretched as he had been during his journey—wretched as an infernal spirit—his hopes were now again elated, and he dreamed of a golden paradise. There was something pleasant in feeling his mastery over that poor old shattered baronet.

'The gentleman to wait upon Sir Thomas,' said Richard, opening the study door; and then Mr. Mollett senior found himself in the presence of Mr. Prendergast.

Mr. Prendergast was sitting in a high-backed easy chair, facing the fire, when the announcement was made, and therefore Mollett still fancied that he was in the presence of Sir Thomas until he was well into the room and the door was closed upon him; otherwise he might probably have turned on his heels and bolted. He had had three or four interviews with Mr. Prendergast, having received different sums of money from that gentleman's hands, and had felt on all such occasions that he was being looked through and through. Mr. Prendergast had asked but few questions, never going into the matter of his, Mollett's, pecuniary connexion with Sir Thomas; but there had always been that in the lawyer's eye which had frightened the miscreant, which had quelled his bluster as soon as it was assumed, and had told him that he was known for a blackguard and a scoundrel. And now when this man, with a terrible gray eye, got up from Sir Thomas's chair, and wheeling round confronted him, looking him full in the face, and frowning on him as an honest man does frown on an unconvicted rascal—when, I say, this happened to Mr. Mollett senior, he thoroughly at that moment wished himself back in London. He turned his eye round to the door, but that was closed behind him. He looked round to see whether Sir Thomas was there, but no one was in the room with him but Mr. Prendergast. Then he stood still, and as that gentleman did not address him, he was obliged to speak; the silence was too awful for him—'Oh, Mr. Prendergast!' said he. 'Is that you?'

'Yes, Mr. Mollett, it is I.'

'Oh, ah—I suppose you are here about business of your own. I was wishing to see Sir Thomas about a little business of my own; maybe he's not in the way.'

'No, he is not; not exactly. But perhaps, Mr. Mollett, I can do as well. You have known me before, you know, and you may say to me openly anything you have to say to Sir Thomas.'

'Well; I don't know about that, sir; my business is with the baronet—particular.' Mr. Mollett, as he spoke, strained every nerve to do so without appearance of dismay; but his efforts were altogether ineffectual. He could not bring himself to look Mr. Prendergast in the face for a moment, or avoid feeling like a dog that dreads being kicked. All manner of fears came upon him, and he would at the moment have given up all his hopes of money from the Castle Richmond people to have been free from Mr. Prendergast and his influence. And yet Mollett was not a coward in the ordinary sense of the word. Indeed he had been very daring in the whole management of this affair. But then a course of crime makes such violent demands on a man's courage. Let any one think of the difference of attacking a thief, and being attacked as a thief! We are apt to call bad men cowards without much consideration. Mr. Mollett was not without pluck, but his pluck was now quelled. The circumstances were too strong against him.

'Listen to me, Mr. Mollett——; and, look here, sir; never mind turning to the door; you can't go now till you and I have had some conversation. You may make up your mind to this; you will never see Sir Thomas Fitzgerald again—unless indeed he should be in the witness-box when you are standing in the dock.'

'Mr. Prendergast; sir!'

'Well. Have you any reason to give why you should not be put in the dock? How much money have you got from Sir Thomas during the last two years by means of those threats which you have been using? You were well aware when you set about this business that you were committing felony; and have probably felt tolerably sure at times that you would some day be brought up short. That day has come.'

Mr. Prendergast had made up his mind that nothing could be gained by soft usage with Mr. Mollett. Indeed nothing could be gained in any way, by any usage, unless it could be shown that Mollett and Talbot were not the same person. He could afford therefore to tell the scoundrel that he was a scoundrel, and to declare against him—war to the knife. The more that Mollett trembled, the more abject he became, the easier would be the task Mr. Prendergast now had in hand. 'Well, sir,' he continued, 'are you going to tell me what business has brought you here to-day?'

But Mr. Mollett, though he did shake in his shoes, did not look at the matter exactly in the same light. He could not believe that Sir Thomas would himself throw up the game on any consideration, or that Mr. Prendergast as his friend would throw it up on his behalf. He, Mollett, had a strong feeling that he could have continued to deal easily with Sir Thomas, and that it might be very hard to deal at all with Mr. Prendergast; but nevertheless the game was still open. Mr. Prendergast would probably distrust the fact of his being the lady's husband, and it would be for him therefore to use the indubitable proofs of the facts that were in his possession.

'Sir Thomas knows very well what I've come about,' he began, slowly; 'and if he's told you, why you know too; and in that case——.'

But what might or might not happen in that case Mr. Mollett had not now an opportunity of explaining, for the door opened and Mrs. Jones entered the room.

'When that man comes this morning,' Mr. Prendergast had said to Herbert, 'I must get you to induce Mrs. Jones to come to us in the study as soon as may be.' He had not at all explained to Herbert why this was necessary, nor had he been at any pains to prevent the young heir from thinking and feeling that some terrible mystery hung over the house. There was a terrible mystery—which indeed would be more terrible still when it ceased to be mysterious. He therefore quietly explained to Herbert what he desired to have done, and Herbert, awaiting the promised communication of that evening, quietly did as he was bid.

'You must go down to him, Jones,' he had said.

'But I'd rather not, sir. I was with him yesterday for two mortal hours; and, oh, Mr. Herbert! it ain't for no good.'

But Herbert was inexorable; and Mrs. Jones, feeling herself overcome by the weight of the misfortune that was oppressing them all, obeyed, and descending to her master's study, knocked at the door. She knew that Mr. Prendergast was there, and she knew that Sir Thomas was not; but she did not know that any stranger was in the room with Mr. Prendergast. Mr. Mollett had not heard the knock, nor, indeed, had Mr. Prendergast; but Mrs. Jones having gone through this ceremony, opened the door and entered.

'Sir Thomas knows; does he?' said Mr. Prendergast, when Mollett ceased to speak on the woman's entrance. ' 'Oh, Mrs. Jones, good morning. Here is your old master, Mr. Talbot.'

Mollett of course turned round, and found himself confronted
with the woman, They stared at each other for some moments,
and then Mollett said, in a low dull voice, 'Yes, she knows me;
it was she that lived with her at Tallyho Lodge.'

'You remember him now, Mrs. Jones; don't you?' said Mr.
Prendergast.

For another moment or two Mrs. Jones stood silent; and then
she acknowledged herself overcome, and felt that the world
around her had become too much for her. 'Yes,' said she,
slowly; 'I remembers him,' and then sinking into a chair near
the door, she put her apron up to her eyes, and burst into tears.

'No doubt about that; she remembers me well enough,' said
Mollett, thinking that this was so'much gained on his side. 'But
there ain't a doubt about the matter at all, Mr. Prendergast.
You look here, and you'll see it all as plain as black and white.'
And Mr. Mollett dragged a large pocket-book from his coat, and
took out of it certain documents, which he held before Mr. Prendergast's eyes, still keeping them in his own hand. 'Oh, I'm all
right; I am,' said Mollett.

'Oh, you are, are you?' said the lawyer, just glancing at the
paper, which he would not appear to heed. 'I am glad you
think so.'

'If there were any doubt about it, she'd know,' said he, pointing away up towards the body of the house. Both Mr. Prendergast and Mrs. Jones understood well who was that she to whom
he alluded.

'You are satisfied at any rate, Mrs. Jones,' said the lawyer.
But Mrs. Jones had hidden her face in her apron, and would not
look up. She could not understand why this friend of the family
should push the matter so dreadfully against them. If he would
rise from his chair and destroy that wretch who stood before
them, then indeed he might be called a friend!

Mr. Prendergast had now betaken himself to the door, and
was standing with his back to it, and with his hands in his
trousers-pockets, close to the chair on which Mrs. Jones was
sitting. He had resolved that he would get that woman's spoken
evidence out of her; and he had gotten it. But now, what was
he to do with her next?—with her or with the late Mr. Talbot
of Tallyho Lodge? And having satisfied himself of that fact,
which from the commencement he had never doubted, what could
he best do to spare the poor lady who was so terribly implicated
in this man's presence?

'Mrs. Jones,' said he, standing over her, and gently touching
her shoulder, 'I am sorry to have pained you in this way; but
it was necessary that we should know, without a doubt, who

this man is,—and who he was. Truth is always the best, you know. So good a woman as you cannot but understand that.'

'I suppose it is, sir,—I suppose it is,' said Mrs. Jones, through her tears, now thoroughly humbled. The world was pretty nearly at an end, as far as she was concerned. Here, in this very house of Castle Richmond, in Sir Thomas's own room, was her ladyship's former husband, acknowledged as such! What further fall of the planet into broken fragments could terrify, or drive her from her course more thoroughly than this? Truth! yes, truth in the abstract might be very good. But such a truth as this! how could any one ever say that that was good? Such was the working of her mind; but she took no trouble to express her thoughts.

'Yes,' continued Mr. Prendergast, speaking still in a low voice, with a tone that was almost tender, 'truth is always best. Look at this wretched man here! He would have killed the whole family—destroyed them one by one—had they consented to assist him in concealing the fact of his existence. The whole truth will now be known; and it is very dreadful; but it will not be so dreadful as the want of truth.'

'My poor lady! my poor lady!' almost screamed Mrs. Jones from under her apron, wagging her head and becoming almost convulsive in her grief.

'Yes, it is very sad. But you will live to acknowledge that even this is better than living in that man's power.'

'I don't know that,' said Mollett. 'I am not so bad as you'd make me. I don't want to distress the lady.'

'No, not if you are allowed to rob the gentleman till there's not a guinea left for you to suck at. I know pretty well the extent of the evil that's in you. If we were to kick you from here to Cork, you'd forgive all that, so that we still allowed you to go on with your trade. I wonder how much money you've had from him altogether?'

'What does the money signify? What does the money signify?' said Mrs. Jones, still wagging her head beneath her apron. 'Why didn't Sir Thomas go on paying it, and then my lady need know nothing about it?'

It was clear that Mrs. Jones would not look at the matter in a proper light. As far as she could see, there was no reason why a fair bargain should not have been made between Mollett and Sir Thomas,—made and kept on both sides, with mutual convenience. That doing of justice at the cost of falling heavens was not intelligible to her limited philosophy. Nor did she bethink herself, that a leech will not give over sucking until it be gorged with blood. Mr. Prendergast knew that such leeches as Mr. Mollett never leave the skin as long as there is a drop of blood left within the veins.

Mr. Prendergast was still standing against the door, where he had placed himself to prevent the unauthorized departure of either Mrs. Jones or Mr. Mollett; but now he was bethinking himself that he might as well bring this interview to an end. 'Mr. Mollett,' said he, 'you are probably beginning to understand that you will not get much more money from the Castle Richmond family?'

'I don't want to do any harm to any of them,' said Mollett, humbly; 'and if I don't make myself troublesome, I hope Sir Thomas will consider me.'

'It is out of your power, sir, to do any further harm to any of them. You don't pretend to think that after what has passed, you can have any personal authority over that unfortunate lady?'

'My poor mistress! my poor mistress!' sobbed Mrs. Jones.

'You cannot do more injury than you at present have done. No one is now afraid of you; no one here will ever give you another shilling. When and in what form you will be prosecuted for inducing Sir Thomas to give you money, I cannot yet tell. Now, you may go; and I strongly advise you never to show your face here again. If the people about here knew who you are, and what you are, they would not let you off the property with a whole bone in your skin. Now go, sir. Do you hear me?'

'Upon my word, Mr. Prendergast, I have not intended any harm!'

'Go, sir!'

'And even now, Mr. Prendergast, it can all be made straight, and I will leave the country altogether, if you wish it—'

'Go, sir!' shouted Mr. Prendergast. 'If you do not move at once, I will ring the bell for the servants!'

'Then, if misfortune comes upon them, it is your doing, and not mine,' said Mollett.

'Oh, Mr. Prendrergrass, if it can be hushed up—' said Mrs. Jones, rising from her chair and coming up to him with her hands clasped together. 'Don't send him away in your anger; dont'ee now, sir. Think of her ladyship. Do, do, do;' and the woman took hold of his arm, and looked up into his face with her eyes swimming with tears. Then going to the door she closed it, and returning again, touched his arm, and again appealed to him. 'Think of Mr. Herbert, sir, and the young ladies! What are they to be called, sir, if this man is to be my lady's husband? Oh, Mr. Pendrergrass, let him go away, out of the kingdom; do let him go away.'

'I'll be off to Australia by the next boat, if you'll only say the

word,' said Mollett. To give him his due, he was not at that
moment thinking altogether of himself and of what he might get.
The idea of the misery which he had brought on these people
did, to a certain measure, come home to him. And it certainly
did come home to him also, that his own position was very perilous.

'Mrs. Jones,' said the lawyer, seeming to pay no attention
whatever to Mollett's words, ' you know nothing of such men as
that. If I were to take him at his word now, he would turn
upon Sir Thomas again before three weeks were over.'

' By ——, I would not! By all that is holy, I would not.
Mr. Prendergast, do—.'

' Mr. Mollett, I will trouble you to walk out of this house. I
have nothing further to say to you.'

' Oh, very well, sir.' And then slowly Mollett took his
departure, and finding his covered car at the door, got into it
without saying another word to any of the Castle Richmond
family.

'Mrs. Jones,' said Mr. Prendergast, as soon as Mollett was
gone, ' I believe I need not trouble you any further. Your
conduct has done you great honour, and I respect you greatly as
an honest woman and an affectionate friend.'

Mrs. Jones could only acknowledge this by loud sobs.

' For the present, if you will take my advice, you will say
nothing of this to your mistress.'

' No, sir, no; I shall say nothing. Oh, dear! oh dear!'

' The whole matter will be known soon, but in the mean time,
we may as well remain silent. Good day to you.' And then
Mrs. Jones also left the room, and Mr. Prendergast was alone.

CHAPTER XXI.

FAIR ARGUMENTS.

As Mollett left the house he saw two men walking down the
road away from the sweep before the hall-door, and as he passed
them he recognised one as the young gentleman of the house.
He also saw that a horse followed behind them, on the grass by
the roadside, not led by the hand, but following with the reins
laid loose upon his neck. They took no notice of him or his car,
but allowed him to pass as though he had no concern whatever
with the destinies of either of them. They were Herbert and
Owen Fitzgerald.

The reader will perhaps remember the way in which Owen

left Desmond Court on the occasion of his last visit there. It cannot be said that what he had heard had in any way humbled him, nor indeed had it taught him to think that Clara Desmond looked at him altogether with indifference. Greatly as she had injured him, he could not bring himself to look upon her as the chief sinner. It was Lady Desmond who had done it all. It was she who had turned against him because of his poverty, who had sold her daughter to his rich cousin, and robbed him of the love which he had won for himself. Or perhaps not of the love —it might be that this was yet his; and if so, was it not possible that he might beat the countess at her own weapons? Thinking over this, he felt that it was necessary for him to do something, to take some step; and therefore he resolved to go boldly to his cousin, and tell him that he regarded Lady Clara Desmond as still his own.

On this morning, therefore, he had ridden up to the Castle Richmond door. It was now many months since he had been there, and he was no longer entitled to enter the house on the acknowledged intimate footing of a cousin. He rode up, and asked the servant with grave ceremony whether Mr. Herbert Fitzgerald were at home. He would not go in, he said, but if Mr. Herbert were there he would wait for him at the porch. Herbert at the time was standing in the dining-room, all alone, gloomily leaning against the mantelpiece. There was nothing for him to do during the whole of that day but wait for the evening, when the promised revelation would be made to him. He knew that Mollett and Mrs. Jones were with Mr. Prendergast in the study, but what was the matter now being investigated between them—that he did not know. And till he knew that, closely as he was himself concerned, he could meddle with nothing. But it was already past noon and the evening would soon be there.

In this mood he was interrupted by being told that his cousin Owen was at the door. 'He won't come in at all, Mr. Herbert,' Richard had said; for Richard, according to order, was still waiting about the porch; 'but he says that you are to go to him there.' And then Herbert, after considering the matter for a moment, joined his cousin at the front entrance.

'I want to speak to you a few words,' said Owen; 'but as I hear that Sir Thomas is not well, I will not go into the house; perhaps you will walk with me as far as the lodge. Never mind the mare, she will not go astray.' And so Herbert got his hat and accompanied him. For the first hundred yards neither of them said anything. Owen would not speak of Clara till he was well out of hearing from the house, and at the present moment

Herbert had not much inclination to commence a conversation on any subject.

Owen was the first to speak. 'Herbert,' said he, 'I have been told that you are engaged to marry Lady Clara Desmond.'

'And so I am,' said Herbert, feeling very little inclined to admit of any question as to his privilege in that respect. Things were happening around him which might have—Heaven only knows what consequence. He did fear—fear with a terrible dread that something might occur which would shatter the cup of his happiness, and rob him of the fruition of his hopes. But nothing had occurred as yet. 'And so I am,' he said; 'it is no wonder that you should have heard it, for it has been kept no secret. And I also have heard of your visit to Desmond Court. It might have been as well, I think, if you had stayed away.'

'I thought differently,' said Owen, frowning blackly. 'I thought that the most straightforward thing for me was to go there openly, having announced my intention, and tell them both, mother and daughter, that I hold myself as engaged to Lady Clara, and that I hold her as engaged to me.'

'That is absurd nonsense. She cannot be engaged to two persons.'

'Anything that interferes with you, you will of course think absurd. I think otherwise. It is hardly more than twelve months since she and I were walking there together, and then she promised me her love. I had known her long and well, when you had hardly seen her. I knew her and loved her; and what is more, she loved me. Remember, it is not I only that say so. She said it herself, and swore that nothing should change her. I do not believe that anything has changed her.'

'Do you mean to say that at present she cares nothing for me? Owen, you must be mad on this matter.'

'Mad; yes, of course; if I think that any girl can care for me while you are in the way. Strange as it may appear, I am as mad even as that. There are people who will not sell themselves even for money and titles. I say again, that I do not believe her to be changed. She has been weak, and her mother has persuaded her. To her mother, rank and money, titles and property, are everything. She has sold her daughter, and I have come to ask you, whether, under such circumstances, you intend to accept the purchase.'

In his ordinary mood Herbert Fitzgerald was by no means a quarrelsome man. Indeed we may go further than that, and say that he was very much the reverse. His mind was argumentative rather than impulsive, and in all matters he was readier to persuadeth an overcome. But his ordinary nature had been changed. It was quite new with him to be nervous and fretful, but he was so at the present moment. He was deeply concerned in the circumstances around him, but yet had been allowed no voice in them. In this affair that was so peculiarly his own,— this of his promised bride,—he was determined that no voice should be heard but his own; and now, contrary to his wont, he was ready enough to quarrel with his cousin.

Of Owen we may say, that he was a man prone to fighting of all sorts, and on all occasions. By fighting I do not mean the old-fashioned resource of putting an end to fighting by the aid of two pistols, which were harmless in nineteen cases out of twenty. In saying that Owen Fitzgerald was prone to fight, I do not allude to fighting of that sort; I mean that he was impulsive, and ever anxious to contend and conquer. To yield was to him ignoble, even though he might know that he was yielding to the right. To strive for mastery was to him noble, even though he strove against those who had a right to rule, and strove on behalf of the wrong. Such was the nature of his mind and spirit; and this nature had impelled him to his present enterprise at Castle Richmond. But he had gone thither with an unwonted resolve not to be passionate. He had, he had said to himself, right on his side, and he had purposed to argue it out fairly with his more cold-blooded cousin. The reader may probably guess the result of these fair arguments on such a subject. 'And I have come to ask you,' he said, ' whether under such circumstances you intend to accept the purchase?'

'I will not allow you to speak of Lady Desmond in such language; nor of her daughter,' said Herbert, angrily.

'Ah! but, Herbert, you must allow me; I have been ill used in this matter, and I have a right to make myself heard.'

'Is it I that have ill used you? I did not know before that gentlemen made loud complaints of such ill usage from the hands of ladies.'

'If the ill usage, as you please to call it—'

'It is your own word.'

'Very well. If this ill usage came from Clara Desmond her-self, I should be the last person to complain of it; and you would be the last person to whom I should make complaint. But I feel sure that it is not so. She is acting under the influence of her mother, who has frightened her into this thing which she is doing. I do not believe that she is false herself.'

'I am sure that she is not false. We are quite agreed there, but it is not likely that we should agree further. To tell you the truth frankly I think you are ill-judged to speak to me on such a topic.'

'Perhaps in that respect you will allow me to think for myself. But I have not yet said that which I came to say. My belief is that unfair and improper restraint is put upon Clara Desmond, that she has been induced by her mother to accept your offer in opposition to her own wishes, and that therefore it is my duty to look upon her as still betrothed to me. I do so regard her, and shall act under such conviction. The first thing that I do therefore is to call upon you to relinquish your claim.'

'What, to give her up?'

'Yes, to give her up;—to acknowledge that you cannot honestly call upon her to fulfil her pledge to you.'

'The man must be raving,' Herbert said.

'Very probably; but remember this, it may be that he will rave to some purpose, when such insolence will be but of little avail to you. Raving! Yes, I suppose that a man poor as I am must be mad indeed to set his heart upon anything that you may choose to fancy.'

'All that is nonsense, Owen; I ask for nothing but my own. I won her love fairly, and I mean to keep it firmly.'

'You may possibly have won her hand, but never her heart. You are rich, and it may be that even she will condescend to barter her hand; but I doubt it; I altogether doubt it. It is her mother's doing, as it was plain enough for me to see the other day at Desmond Court; but much as she may fear her mother, I cannot think that she will go to the altar with a lie in her mouth.'

And then they walked on in silence for a few yards. Herbert was anxious to get back to the house, and was by no means desirous of continuing this conversation with his cousin. He at any rate could get nothing by talking about Lady Clara Desmond to Owen Fitzgerald. He stopped therefore on the path, and said, that if Owen had nothing further to say, he, Herbert, would go back to the house.

'Nothing further! Nothing further, if you understand me; but you do not. You are not honest enough in this matter to understand any purpose but your own.'

'I tell you what, Owen; I did not come out here to hear myself abused; and I will not stand it. According to my idea you had no right whatever to speak to me about Lady Clara Desmond. But you are my cousin; and therefore I have borne it. It may be as well that we should both understand that it is once for all. I will not listen to you again on the same subject.'

'Oh, you won't. Upon my word you are a very great man! You will tell me next, I suppose, that this is your demesne, and will warn me off!'

'Even if I did that, I should not be wrong, under such provocation.'

'Very well, sir; then I will go off. But remember this, Herbert Fitzgerald, you shall live to rue the day when you treated me with such insolence. And remember this also, Clara Desmond is not your wife as yet. Everything now seems happy with you, and fortunate; you have wealth and a fine house, and a family round you, while I am there all alone, left like a dog, as far as my own relatives are concerned. But yet it may come to pass that the Earl of Desmond's daughter will prefer my hand to yours, and my house to your house. They who mount high may chance to get a fall.' And then, having uttered this caution, he turned to his mare, and putting his hand upon the saddle, jumped into his seat, and pressing her into a gallop, darted off across the grass.

He had not meant anything specially by his threat; but his heart was sore within him. During some weeks past, he had become sick of the life that he was leading. He had begun to hate his own solitary house—his house that was either solitary, or filled with riot and noise. He sighed for the quiet hours that were once his at Desmond Court, and the privilege of constant entrance there, which was now denied him. His cousin Herbert had everything at his command—wealth, station, family ties, society, and all the consideration of high place. Every blessing was at the feet of the young heir; but every blessing was not enough, unless Clara Desmond was also added. All this seemed so cruel to him, as he sat alone in his parlour at Hap House, meditating on his future course of life! And then he would think of Clara's promise, of her assurance that nothing should frighten her from her pledge. He thought of this as though the words had been spoken to him only yesterday. He pondered over these things till he hated his cousin Herbert; and hating him, he vowed that Clara Desmond should not be his wife. 'Is he to have everything?' he would say to himself. 'No, by heavens! not everything. He has enough, and may be contented; but he shall not have all.' And now, with similar thoughts running through his mind, he rode back to Hap House.

And Herbert turned back to Castle Richmond. As he approached the front door, he met Mr. Prendergast, who was leaving the house; but they had no conversation with each other. Herbert was in hopes that he might now, at once, be put out of suspense. Mollett was gone; and would it not be better that the tale should be told? But it was clear that Mr. Prendergast had no intention of lessening by an hour the interval he had given himself. He merely muttered a few words passing on, and Herbert went into the house.

And then there was another long, tedious, dull afternoon. Herbert sat with his sisters, but they had not the heart to talk to each other. At about four a note was brought to him. It was from Mr. Prendergast, begging Herbert to meet him in Sir Thomas's study at eight. Sir Thomas had not been there during the day; and now did not intend to leave his own room. They dined at half-past six; and the appointment was therefore to take place almost immediately after dinner.

'Tell Mr. Prendergast that I will be there,' he said to the servant. And so that afternoon passed away, and the dinner also, very slowly and very sadly.

CHAPTER XXII.

THE TELLING OF THE TALE.

THE dinner passed away as the former dinners had done; and as soon as Aunt Letty got up Mr. Prendergast also rose, and touching Herbert on his shoulder, whispered into his ear, 'You'll come to me at eight then.' Herbert nodded his head; and when he was alone he looked at his watch. These slow dinners were not actually very long, and there still remained to him some three-quarters of an hour for anticipation.

What was to be the nature of this history? That it would affect himself personally in the closest manner he could not but know. There seemed to be no doubt on the minds of any of them that the affair was one of money, and his father's money questions were his money questions. Mr. Prendergast would not have been sent for with reference to any trifle; nor would any pecuniary difficulty that was not very serious have thrown his father into such a state of misery. Could it be that the fair inheritance was absolutely in danger?

Herbert Fitzgerald was by no means a selfish man. As regarded himself, he could have met ruin in the face with more equanimity than most young men so circumstanced. The gilt of the world had not eaten into his soul; his heart was not as yet wedded to the splendour of pinchbeck. This is saying much for him; for how seldom is it that the hearts and souls of the young are able to withstand pinchbeck and gilding! He was free from this pusillanimity; free as yet as regarded himself; but he was hardly free as regarded his betrothed. He had promised her, not in spoken words but in his thoughts, rank, wealth, and all the luxuries of his promised high position; and now on her behalf, it nearly broke his heart to think that they might be endangered.

Of his mother's history, he can hardly be said to have known anything. That there had been something tragic in her early life; that something had occurred before his father's marriage; and that his mother had been married twice, he had learned,— he hardly knew when or from whom. But on such matters there had never been conversation between him and any of his own family; and it never occurred to him that all this sorrow arose in any way from this subject. That his father had taken some fatal step with regard to the property—had done some foolish thing for which he could not forgive himself, that was the idea with which his mind was filled.

He waited, with his watch in his hand, till the dial showed him that it was exactly eight; and then, with a sinking heart, he walked slowly out of the dining-room along the passage, and into his father's study. For an instant he stood with the handle in his hand. He had been terribly anxious for the arrival of this moment, but now that it had come, he would almost fain have had it again postponed. His heart sank very low as he turned the lock, and entering, found himself in the presence of Mr. Prendergast.

Mr. Prendergast was standing with his back to the fire. For him, too, the last hour had been full of bitterness; his heart also had sunk low within him; his blood had run cold within his veins: he too, had it been possible, would have put off this wretched hour.

Mr. Prendergast, it may be, was not much given to poetry; but the feeling, if not the words, were there within him. The work which a friend has to perform for a friend is so much heavier than that which comes in the way of any profession!

When Herbert entered the room, Mr. Prendergast came forward from where he was standing, and took him by the hand. 'This is a very sad affair,' he said; 'very sad.'

'At present I know nothing about it,' said Herbert. 'As I see people about me so unhappy, I suppose it is sad. If there be anything that I hate, it is a mystery.'

'Sit down, Mr. Fitzgerald,' said the other; 'sit down.' And Mr. Prendergast himself sat down in the chair that was ordinarily occupied by Sir Thomas. Although he had been thinking about it all the day, he had not even yet made up his mind how he was to begin his story. Even now he could not help thinking whether it might be possible for him to leave it untold. But it was not possible.

'Mr. Fitzgerald,' said he, 'you must prepare yourself for tidings which are very grievous indeed—very grievous.'

'Whatever it is I must bear it,' said he.

'I hope you have that moral strength which enables a man to bear misfortune. I have not known you in happy days, and therefore perhaps can hardly judge; but it seems to me that you do possess such courage. Did I not think so, I could hardly go through the task that is before me.'

Here he paused as though he expected some reply, some assurance that his young friend did possess this strength of which he spoke; but Herbert said nothing—nothing out loud. 'If it were only for myself! if it were only for myself!' It was thus that he spoke to his own heart.

'Mr. Fitzgerald,' continued the lawyer, 'I do not know how far you may be acquainted with the history of your mother's first marriage.'

Herbert said that he was hardly acquainted with it in any degree; and explained that he merely knew the fact that his mother had been married before she met Sir Thomas.

'I do not know that I need recount all the circumstances to you now, though doubtless you will learn them. Your mother's conduct throughout was, I believe, admirable.'

'I am quite sure of that. No amount of evidence could make me believe the contrary.'

'And there is no tittle of evidence to make any one think so. But in her early youth, when she was quite a child, she was given in marriage to a man—to a man of whom it is impossible to speak in terms too black, or in language too strong. And now, this day—'

But here he paused. It had been his intention to say that that very man, the first husband of this loved mother now looked upon as dead for so many years, this miscreant of whom he had spoken—that this man had been in that room that very day. But he hardly knew how to frame the words.

'Well,' said Herbert, 'well;' and he spoke in a hoarse voice that was scarcely audible.

Mr. Prendergast was afraid to bring out the very pith of his story in so abrupt a manner. He wished to have the work over, to feel, that as regarded Herbert it was done,—but his heart failed him when he came to it.

'Yes,' he said going back as it were to his former thoughts. 'A heartless, cruel, debauched, unscrupulous man; one in whose bosom no good thing seemed to have been implanted. Your father, when he first knew your mother, had every reason to believe that this man was dead.'

'And he was not dead?' Mr. Prendergast could see that the young man's face became perfectly pale as he uttered these words. He became pale, and clutched hold of the table with his hand, and there sat with mouth open and staring eyes.

'I am afraid not,' said Mr. Prendergast; 'I am afraid not.'

'And—'

'I must go further than that, and tell you that he is still living.'

'Mr. Prendergast, Mr. Prendergast!' exclaimed the poor fellow, rising up from his chair and shouting out as though for mercy. Mr. Prendergast also rose from his seat, and coming up to him took him by the arm. 'My dear boy, my dear boy, I am obliged to tell you. It is necessary that you should know it. The fact is as I say, and it is now for you to show that you are a man.'

Who was ever called upon for a stronger proof of manhood than this? In nine cases out of ten it is not for oneself that one has to be brave. A man, we may almost say, is no man, whose own individual sufferings call for the exercise of much courage. But we are all so mixed up and conjoined with others—with others who are weaker and dearer than ourselves, that great sorrows do require great powers of endurance.

By degrees, as he stood there in silence, the whole truth made its way into his mind,—as he stood there with his arm still tenderly pressed by that old man. No one now would have called the lawyer stern in looking at him, for the tears were coursing down his cheeks. But no tears came to the relief of young Fitzgerald as the truth slowly came upon him, fold by fold, black cloud upon cloud, till the whole horizon of his life's prospect was dark as death. He stood there silent for some few minutes, hardly conscious that he was not alone, as he saw all his joys disappearing from before his mind's eye, one by one; his family pride, the pleasant high-toned duties of his station, his promised seat in Parliament and prosperous ambition, the full respect of all the world around him, his wealth and pride of place—for let no man be credited who boasts that he can part with these without regret. All these were gone. But there were losses more bitter than these. How could he think of his affianced bride? and how could he think of his mother?

No tears came to his relief while the truth, with all its bearings, burnt itself into his very soul, but his face expressed such agony that it was terrible to be seen. Mr. Prendergast could stand that silence no longer, so at last he spoke. He spoke,—for the sake of words; for all his tale had been told.

'You saw the man that was here yesterday? That was he, who then called himself Talbot.'

'What! the man that went away in the car? Mollett?'

'Yes; that was the man.'

Herbert had said that no evidence could be sufficient to make him believe that his mother had been in any way culpable : and such probably was the case. He had that reliance on his mother —that assurance in his mind that everything coming from her must be good—that he could not believe her capable of ill. But, nevertheless, he could not prevent himself from asking within his own breast, how it had been possible that his mother should ever have been concerned with such a wretch as that. It was a question which could not fail to make itself audible. What being on earth was sweeter than his mother, more excellent, more noble, more fitted for the world's high places, more absolutely entitled to that universal respect which seemed to be given to her as her own by right? And what being could be more loathsome, more contemptible than he, who was, as he was now told, his mother's husband? There was in it a want of verisimilitude which almost gave him comfort,—which almost taught him to think that he might disbelieve the story that was told to him. Poor fellow! he had yet to learn the difference that years may make in men and women—for better as well as for worse. Circumstances had given to the poor half-educated village girl the simple dignity of high station ; as circumstances had also brought to the lowest dregs of human existence the man, whose personal bearing, and apparent worldly standing had been held sufficient to give warrant that he was of gentle breeding and of honest standing ; nay, her good fortune in such a marriage had once been almost begrudged her by all her maiden neighbours.

But Herbert, as he thought of this, was almost encouraged to disbelieve the story. To him, with his knowledge of what his mother was, and such knowledge as he also had of that man, it did not seem possible. 'But how is all this known?' he muttered forth at last.

'I fear there is no doubt of its truth,' said Mr. Prendergast. 'Your father has no doubt whatever; has had none—I must tell you this plainly—for some months.'

'For some months ! And why have I not been told?'

'Do not be hard upon your father.'

'Hard ! no; of course I would not be hard upon him.'

'The burden he has had to bear has been very terrible. He has thought that by payments of money to this man the whole thing might be concealed. As is always the case when such payments are made, the insatiable love of money grew by what it fed on. He would have poured out every shilling into that man's hands, and would have died, himself a beggar—have died speedily too under such torments—and yet no good would have been done. The harpy would have come upon you; and you—after you had innocently assumed a title that was not your own and taken a property to which you have no right, you then would have had to own—that which your father must own now.'

'If it be so,' said Herbert, slowly, 'it must be acknowledged.'

'Just so, Mr. Fitzgerald; just so. I know you will feel that—in such matters we can only sail safely by the truth. There is no other compass worth a man's while to look at.'

'Of course not,' said Herbert, with hoarse voice. 'One does not wish to be a robber and a thief. My cousin shall have what is his own.' And then he involuntarily thought of the interview they had had on that very day. 'But why did he not tell me when I spoke to him of her?' he said, with something approaching to bitterness in his voice and a slight struggle in his throat that was almost premonitory of a sob.

'Ah! it is there that I fear for you. I know what your feelings are; but think of his sorrows, and do not be hard on him.'

'Ah me, ah me!' exclaimed Herbert.

'I fear that he will not be with you long. He has already endured till he is now almost past the power of suffering more. And yet there is so much more that he must suffer!'

'My poor father!'

'Think what such as he must have gone through in bringing himself into contact with that man; and all this has been done that he might spare you and your mother. Think of the wound to his conscience before he would have lowered himself to an unworthy bargain with a swindler. But this has been done that you might have that which you have been taught to look on as your own. He has been wrong. No other verdict can be given. But you, at any rate, can be tender to such a fault; you and your mother.'

'I will—I will,' said Herbert. 'But if it had happened a month since I could have borne it.' And then he thought of his mother, and hated himself for what he had said. How could he have borne that with patience? 'And there is no doubt, you say?'

'I think none. The man carries his proofs with him. An old servant here in the house, too, knows him.'

'What, Mrs. Jones?'

'Yes; Mrs. Jones. And the burden of further proof must now, of course, be thrown on us,—not on him. Directly that

we believe the statement, it is for us to ascertain its truth. You
and your father must not be seen to hold a false position before
the world.'

' And what are we to do now ?'

' I fear that your mother must be told, and Mr. Owen Fitzgerald; and then we must together openly prove the facts,
either in one way or in the other. It will be better that we
should do this together;—that is, you and your cousin Owen
conjointly. Do it openly, before the world,—so that the world
may know that each of you desires only what is honestly his
own. For myself I tell you fairly that I have no doubt of the
truth of what I have told you; but further proof is certainly
needed. Had I any doubt I would not propose to tell your
mother. As it is I think it will be wrong to keep her longer in
the dark.'

' Does she suspect nothing ?'

' I do not know. She has more power of self-control than your
father. She has not spoken to me ten words since I have been
in the house, and in not doing so I have thought that she was
right.'

' My own mother; my own dear mother !'

' If you ask me my opinion, I think that she does suspect the
truth,—very vaguely, with an indefinite feeling that the calamity
which weighs so heavily on your father, has come from this
source. She, dear lady, is greatly to be pitied. But God has
made her of firmer material than your father, and I think that
she will bear her sorrow with a higher courage.'

' And she is to be told also?'

' Yes, I think so. I do not see how we can avoid it. If we
do not tell her we must attempt to conceal it, and that attempt
must needs be futile when we are engaged in making open
inquiry on the subject. Your cousin, when he hears of this,
will of course be anxious to know what his real prospects are.'

' Yes, yes. He will be anxious, and determined too.'

' And then, when all the world will know it, how is your
mother to be kept in the dark? And that which she fears and
anticipates is as bad, probably, as the actual truth. If my
advice be followed nothing will be kept from her.'

' We are in your hands, I suppose, Mr. Prendergast.'

' I can only act as my judgment directs me.'

' And who is to tell her ?' This he asked with a shudder, and
almost in a whisper. The very idea of undertaking such a duty
seemed almost too much for him. And yet he must undertake a
duty almost as terrible; he himself—no one but him—must
endure the anguish of repeating this story to Clara Desmond and

to the countess. But now the question had reference to his own mother. ' And who is to tell her?' he asked.

For a moment or two Mr. Prendergast stood silent. He had not hitherto, in so many words, undertaken this task—this that would be the most dreadful of all. But if he did not undertake it, who would? 'I suppose that I must do it,' at last he said, very gently.

'And when?'

' As soon as I have told your cousin. I will go down to him to-morrow after breakfast. Is it probable that I shall find him at home?'

'Yes, if you are there before ten. The hounds meet to-morrow at Cecilstown, within three miles of him, and he will not leave home till near eleven. But it is possible that he may have a house full of men with him.'

' At any rate I will try. On such an occasion as this he may surely let his friends go to the hunt without him.'

And then between nine and ten this interview came to an end. 'Mr. Fitzgerald,' said Mr. Prendergast, as he pressed Herbert's hand, 'you have borne all this as a man should do. No loss of fortune can ruin one who is so well able to endure misfortune.' But in this Mr. Prendergast was perhaps mistaken. His' knowledge of human nature had not carried him sufficiently far. A man's courage under calamity is only tested when he is left in solitude. The meanest among us can bear up while strange eyes are looking at us. And then Mr. Prendergast went away, and he was alone.

It had been his habit during the whole of this period of his father's illness to go to Sir Thomas at or before bedtime. Those visits had usually been made to the study, the room in which he was now standing; but when his father had gone to his bedroom at an earlier hour, Herbert had always seen him there. Was he to go to him now—now that he had heard all this? And if so, how was he to bear himself there, in his father's presence? He stood still, thinking of this, till the hand of the clock showed him that it was past ten, and then it struck him that his father might be waiting for him. It would not do for him now, at such a moment, to appear wanting in that attention which he had always shown. He was still his father's son, though he had lost the right to bear his father's name. He was nameless now, a man utterly without respect or standing-place in the world, a being whom the law ignored except as the possessor of a mere life ; such was he now, instead of one whose rights and privileges, whose property and rank all the statutes of the realm and customs of his country delighted to honour and protect. This he repeated

to himself over and over again. It was to such a pass as this, to
this bitter disappointment that his father had brought him. But
yet it should not be said of him that he had begun to neglect his
father as soon as he had heard the story.

So with a weary step he walked up stairs, and found Sir
Thomas in bed, with his mother sitting by the bedside. His
mother held out her hand to him, and he took it, leaning against
the bedside. 'Has Mr. Prendergast left you?' she asked.

He told her that Mr. Prendergast had left him, and gone to
his own room for the night. 'And have you been with him all
the evening?' she asked. She had no special motive in so asking,
but both the father and the son shuddered at the question. 'Yes,'
said Herbert; 'I have been with him, and now I have come to
wish my father good night; and you too, mother, if you intend
to remain here.' But Lady Fitzgerald got up, telling Herbert
that she would leave him with Sir Thomas; and before either of
them could hinder her from departing, the father and the son
were alone together.

Sir Thomas, when the door closed, looked furtively up into
his son's face. Might it be that he could read there how much
had been already told, or how much still remained to be disclosed?
That Herbert was to learn it all that evening, he knew; but it
might be that Mr. Prendergast had failed to perform his task.
Sir Thomas in his heart trusted that he had failed. He looked
up furtively into Herbert's face, but at the moment there was
nothing there that he could read. There was nothing there but
black misery; and every face round him for many days past had
worn that aspect.

For a minute or two Herbert said nothing, for he had not made
up his mind whether or no he would that night disturb his
father's rest. But he could not speak in his ordinary voice, or
bid his father good-night as though nothing special to him had
happened. 'Father,' said he, after a short pause, 'father, I know
it all now.'

'My boy, my poor boy, my unfortunate boy!'

'Father,' said Herbert, 'do not be unhappy about me, I can
bear it.' And then he thought again of his bride—his bride as
she was to have been; but nevertheless he repeated his last
words, 'I can bear it, father!'

'I have meant it for the best, Herbert,' said the poor man,
pleading to his child.

'I know that; all of us well know that. But what Mr.
Prendergast says is true; it is better that it should be known.
That man would have killed you had you kept it longer to your-
self.'

Sir Thomas hid his face upon the pillow as the remembrance of what he had endured in those meetings came upon him. The blow that had told heaviest was that visit from the son, and the threats which the man had made still rung in his ears—'When that youngster was born Lady F. was Mrs. M., wasn't she? . . . . My governor could take her away to-morrow, according to the law of the land, couldn't he now?' These words, and more such as these, had nearly killed him at the time, and now, as they recurred to him, he burst out into childish tears. Poor man! the days of his manhood had gone, and nothing but the tears of a second bitter childhood remained to him. The hot iron had entered into his soul, and shrivelled up the very muscles of his mind's strength.

Herbert, without much thought of what he was doing, knelt down by the bedside and put his hand upon that of his father, which lay out upon the sheet. There he knelt for one or two minutes, watching and listening to his father's sobs. 'You will be better now, father,' he said, 'for the great weight of this terrible secret will be off your mind.' But Sir Thomas did not answer him. With him there could never be any better. All things belonging to him had gone to ruin. All those around him whom he had loved—and he had loved those around him very dearly—were brought to poverty, and sorrow, and disgrace. The power of feeling this was left to him, but the power of enduring this with manhood was gone. The blow had come upon him too late in life.

And Herbert himself, as he knelt there, could hardly forbear from tears. Now, at such a moment as this, he could think of no one but his father, the author of his being, who lay there so grievously afflicted by sorrows which were in nowise selfish. 'Father,' he said at last, 'will you pray with me?' And then when the poor sufferer had turned his face towards him, he poured forth his prayer to his Saviour that they all in that family might be enabled to bear the heavy sorrows which God in his mercy and wisdom had now thought fit to lay upon them. I will not make his words profane by repeating them here, but one may say confidently that they were not uttered in vain.

'And now, dearest father, good night,' he said as he rose from his knees; and stretching over the bed, he kissed his father's forehead.

CHAPTER XXIII.

IT may be imagined that Mr. Mollett's drive back to Cork after his last visit to Castle Richmond had not been very pleasant; and indeed it may be said that his present circumstances altogether were as unpleasant as his worst enemies could desire. I have endeavoured to excite the sympathy of those who are going with me through this story for the sufferings of that family of the Fitzgeralds; but how shall I succeed in exciting their sympathy for this other family of the Molletts? And yet why not? If we are to sympathize only with the good, or worse still, only with the graceful, how little will there be in our character that is better than terrestrial? Those Molletts also were human, and had strings to their hearts, at which the world would now probably pull with sufficient vigour. For myself I can truly say that my strongest feeling is for their wretchedness.

The father and son had more than once boasted among them-selves that the game they were now playing was a high one; that they were, in fact, gambling for mighty stakes. And in truth, as long as the money came in to them—flowing in as the result of their own craft in this game—the excitement had about it something that was very pleasurable. There was danger, which makes all games pleasant; there was money in handfuls for daily expenses—those daily wants of the appetite, which are to such men more important by far than the distant necessities of life; there was a possibility of future grandeur, an opening out of magnificent ideas of fortune, which charmed them greatly as they thought about it. What might they not do with forty thousand pounds divided between them, or even with a thousand a year each, settled on them for life? and surely their secret was worth that money! Nay, was it not palpable to the meanest calculation that it was worth much more? Had they not the selling of twelve thousand a year for ever and ever to this family of Fitzgerald?

But for the last fortnight things had begun to go astray with them. Money easily come by goes easily, and money badly come by goes badly. Theirs had come easily and badly, and had so gone. What necessity could there be for economy with such a milch-cow as that close to their elbows? So both of them had thought, if not argued; and there had been no economy—no economy in the use of that very costly amusement, the dice-box; and now, at the present moment, ready money having failed to be the result of either of the two last visits to Castle Richmond, the family funds were running low.

It may be said that ready money for the moment was the one desire nearest to the heart of Mollett père, when he took that last journey over the Boggeragh mountains—ready money where-with to satisfy the pressing claims of Miss O'Dwyer, and bring back civility, or rather servility, to the face and manner of Tom the waiter at the Kanturk Hotel. Very little of that servility can be enjoyed by persons of the Mollett class when money ceases to be ready in their hands and pockets, and there is, perhaps, nothing that they enjoy so keenly as servility. Mollett père had gone down determined that that comfort should at any rate be forthcoming to him, whatever answer might be given to those other grander demands, and we know what success had attended his mission. He had looked to find his tame milch-cow trembling in her accustomed stall, and he had found a resolute bull there in her place—a bull whom he could by no means take by the horns. He had got no money, and before he had reached Cork he had begun to comprehend that it was not probable that he should get more from that source.

During a part of the interview between him and Mr. Prender-gast, some spark of mercy towards his victims had glimmered into his heart. When it was explained to him that the game was to be given up, that the family at Castle Richmond was prepared to acknowledge the truth, and that the effort made was with the view of proving that the poor lady up-stairs was not entitled to the name she bore rather than that she was so entitled, then some slight promptings of a better spirit did for a while tempt him to be merciful. ' Oh, what are you about to do?' he would have said had Mr. Prendergast admitted of speech from him. ' Why make this terrible sacrifice? Matters have not come to that. There is no need for you to drag to the light this terrible fact. I will not divulge it—no, not although you are hard upon me in regard to these terms of mine. I will still keep it to my-self, and trust to you,—to you who are all so rich and able to pay, for what consideration you may please to give me.' This was the state of his mind when Mrs. Jones's evidence was being slowly evoked from her ; but it had undergone a considerable change before he reached Cork. By that time he had taught himself to understand that there was no longer a chance to him of any consideration whatever. Slowly he had brought it home to himself that these people had resolutely determined to blow

up the ground on which they themselves stood. This he perceived was their honesty. He did not understand the nature of
a feeling which could induce so fatal a suicide, but he did understand that the feeling was there, and that the suicide would be
completed.

And now what was he to do next in the way of earning his
bread? Various thoughts ran through his brain, and different
resolves—half-formed but still, perhaps, capable of shape—presented themselves to him for the future. It was still on the
cards—on the cards, but barely so—that he might make money
out of these people; but he must wait perhaps for weeks before
he again commenced such an attempt. He might perhaps make
money out of them, and be merciful to them at the same time;—
not money by thousands and tens of thousands; that golden
dream was gone for ever; but still money that might be comfortably luxurious as long as it could be made to last. But then
on one special point he made a firm and final resolution,—whatever new scheme he might hatch he alone would manage.
Never again would he call into his councils that son of his loins
whose rapacious greed had, as he felt sure, brought upon him all
this ruin. Had Aby not gone to Castle Richmond, with his
cruelty and his greed, frightening to the very death the soul of
that poor baronet by the enormity of his demands, Mr. Prendergast would not have been there. Of what further chance of
Castle Richmond pickings there might be Aby should know
nothing. He and his son would no longer hunt in couples. He
would shake him off in that escape which they must both now
make from Cork, and he would not care how long it might be
before he again saw his countenance.

But then that question of ready money; and that other question, perhaps as interesting, touching a criminal prosecution!
How was he to escape if he could not raise the wind? And how
could he raise the wind now that his milch-cow had run so dry?
He had promised the O'Dwyers money that evening, and had
struggled hard to make that promise with an easy face. He now
had none to give them. His orders at the inn were treated
almost with contempt. For the last three days they had given
him what he wanted to eat and drink, but would hardly give him
all that he wanted. When he called for brandy they brought
him whisky, and it had only been by hard begging, and by oaths
as to the promised money, that he had induced them to supply
him with the car which had taken him on his fruitless journey
to Castle Richmond. As he was driven up to the door in South
Main Street, his heart was very sad on all these subjects.

Aby was again sitting within the bar, but was no longer basking in the sunshine of Fanny's smiles. He was sitting there because Fanny had not yet mustered courage to turn him out. He was half-drunk, for it had been found impossible to keep spirits from him. And there had been hot words between him and Fanny, in which she had twitted him with his unpaid bill, and he had twitted her with her former love. And things had gone from bad to worse, and she had all but called in Tom for aid in getting quit of him ; she had, however, refrained, thinking of the money that might be coming, and waiting also till her father should arrive. Fanny's love for Mr. Abraham Mollett had not been long lived.

I will not describe another scene such as those which had of late been frequent in the Kanturk Hotel. The father and the son soon found themselves together in the small room in which they now both slept, at the top of the house ; and Aby, tipsy as he was, understood the whole of what had happened at Castle Richmond. When he heard that Mr. Prendergast was seen in that room in lieu of Sir Thomas, he knew at once that the game had been abandoned. 'But something may yet be done at 'Appy 'ouse,' Aby said to himself, 'only one must be deuced quick.'

The father and the son of course quarrelled frightfully, like dogs over the memory of a bone which had been arrested from the jaws of both of them. Aby said that his father had lost everything by his pusillanimity, and old Mollett declared that his son had destroyed all by his rashness. But we need not repeat their quarrels, nor all that passed between them and Tom before food was forthcoming to satisfy the old man's wants. As he ate he calculated how much he might probably raise upon his watch towards taking him to London, and how best he might get off from Cork without leaving any scent in the nostrils of his son. His clothes he must leave behind him at the inn, at least all that he could not pack upon his person. Lately he had made himself comfortable in this respect, and he sorrowed over the fine linen which he had worn but once or twice since it had been bought with the last instalment from Sir Thomas. Nevertheless in this way he did make up his mind for the morrow's campaign.

And Aby also made up his mind. Something at any rate he had learned from Fanny O'Dwyer in return for his honeyed words. When Herbert Fitzgerald should cease to be the heir to Castle Richmond, Owen Fitzgerald of Hap House would be the happy man. That knowledge was his own in absolute independence of his father, and there might still be time for him to use it. He knew well the locality of Hap House, and he would be there early on the following morning. These tidings had probably not as yet reached the owner of that blessed abode, and if he could be the first to tell him——! The game there too might be pretty enough, if it were played well, by such a master-hand as his own. Yes; he would be at Hap House early in the morning; —but then, how to get there?

He left his father preparing for bed, and going down into the bar found Mr. O'Dwyer and his daughter there in close consultation. They were endeavouring to arrive, by their joint wisdom, at some conclusion as to what they should do with their two guests. Fanny was for turning them out at once. 'The first loss is the least,' said she. 'And they is so disrispectable. I niver know what they're afther, and always is expecting the p'lice will be down on them.' But the father shook his head. He had done nothing wrong; the police could not hurt him; and thirty pounds, as he told his daughter, with much emphasis, was 'a deuced sight of money.' 'The first loss is the least,' said Fanny, perseveringly; and then Aby entered to them.

'My father has made a mull of this matter again,' said he, going at once into the middle of the subject. ''E 'as come back without a shiner.'

'I'll be bound he has,' said Mr. O'Dwyer, sarcastically.

'And that when e'd only got to go two or three miles further, and hall his troubles would have been over.'

'Troubles over, would they?' said Fanny. 'I wish he'd have the goodness to get over his little troubles in this house, by paying us our bill. You'll have to walk if it's not done, and that to-morrow, Mr. Mollett; and so I tell you; and take nothing with you, I can tell you. Father 'll have the police to see to that.'

'Don't you be so cruel now, Miss Fanny,' said Aby, with a leering look. 'I tell you what it is, Mr. O'Dwyer, I must go down again to them diggings very early to-morrow, starting, say, at four o'clock.'

'You'll not have a foot out of my stables,' said Mr. O'Dwyer. 'That's all.'

'Look here, Mr. O'Dwyer; there's been a sight of money due to us from those Fitzgerald people down there. You know 'em; and whether they're hable to pay or not. I won't deny but what father's 'ad the best of it,—'ad the best of it, and sent it trolling, bad luck to him. But there's no good looking hafter spilt milk; is there?'

'If so be that Sir Thomas owed the likes of you money, he would have paid it without your tramping down there time after time to look for it. He's not one of that sort.'

'No, indeed,' said Fanny; 'and I don't believe anything about your seeing Sir Thomas.'

'Oh, we've seed him hoften enough. There's no mistake about that. But now——' and then, with a mysterious air and low voice, he explained to them, that this considerable balance of money still due to them was to be paid by the cousin, 'Mr. Owen of Appy 'ouse.' And to substantiate all his story, he exhibited a letter from Mr. Prendergast to his father, which some months since had intimated that a sum of money would be paid on behalf of Sir Thomas Fitzgerald, if Mr. Mollett would call at Mr. Prendergast's office at a certain hour. The ultimate effect of all this was, that the car was granted for the morning, with certain dire threats as to any further breach of engagement.

Very early on the following morning Aby was astir, hoping that he might manage to complete his not elaborate toilet without disturbing his father's slumbers. For, it must be known, he had been very urgent with the O'Dwyers as to the necessity of keeping this journey of his a secret from his 'governor.' But the governor was wide awake, looking at him out of the corner of his closed eye whenever his back was turned, and not caring much what he was about to do with himself. Mollett père wished to be left alone for that morning, that he also might play his little game in his own solitary fashion, and was not at all disposed to question the movements of his son.

At about five Aby started for Hap House. His toilet; I have said, was not elaborate ; but in this I have perhaps wronged him. Up there in the bed-room he did not waste much time over his soap and water; but he was aware that first impressions are everything, and that one young man should appear smart and clever before another if he wished to carry any effect with him ; so he took his brush and comb in his pocket, and a pot of grease with which he was wont to polish his long side-locks, and he hurriedly grasped up his pins, and his rings, and the satin stock which Fanny in her kinder mood had folded for him ; and then, during his long journey to Hap House, he did perform a toilet which may, perhaps, be fairly called elaborate.

There was a long, tortuous, narrow avenue, going from the Mallow and Kanturk road down to Hap House, which impressed Aby with the idea that the man on whom he was now about to call was also a big gentleman, and made him more uneasy than he would have been had he entered a place with less pretence. There is a story current, that in the west of England the grandeur of middle-aged maiden ladies is measured by the length of the tail of their cats; and Aby had a perhaps equally correct idea, that the length of the private drive up to a gentleman's house, was a fair criterion of the splendour of his position. If this man had about him as much grandeur as Sir Thomas himself, would he be so anxious as Aby had hoped to obtain the additional grandeur of Sir Thomas? It was in that direction that his mind was operating when he got down from the car and rang at the door-bell.

Mr. Owen, as everybody called him, was at home, but not down; and so Aby was shown into the dining-room. It was now considerably past nine; and the servant told him that his master must be there soon, as he had to eat his breakfast and be at the hunt by eleven. The servant at Hap House was more unsophisticated than those at Castle Richmond, and Aby's personal adornments had had their effect. He found himself sitting in the room with the cups and saucers,—aye, and with the silver tea-spoons; and began again to trust that his mission might be successful.

And then the door opened, and a man appeared, clad from top to toe in hunting costume. This was not Owen Fitzgerald, but his friend Captain Donnellan. As it had happened, Captain Donnellan was the only guest who had graced the festivities of Hap House on the previous evening; and now he appeared at the breakfast-table before his host. Aby got up from his chair when the gentleman entered, and was proceeding to business; but the Captain gave him to understand that the master of the house was not yet in presence, and so Aby sat down again. What was he to do when the master did arrive? His story was not one which would well bear telling before a third person.

And then, while Captain Donnellan was scanning this visitor to his friend Owen, and bethinking himself whether he might not be a sheriff's officer, and whether if so some notice ought not to be conveyed up stairs to the master of the house, another car was driven up to the front door. In this case the arrival was from Castle Richmond, and the two servants knew each other well. 'Thady,' said Richard, with much authority in his voice, 'this gentl'man is Mr. Prendergast from our place, and he must see the masther before he goes to the hunt.' 'Faix and the masther 'll have something to do this blessed morning,' said Thady, as he showed Mr. Prendergast also into the dining-room, and went up stairs to inform his master that there was yet another gentleman come on business. 'The Captain has got 'em both to hisself,' said Thady, as he closed the door.

The name of Mr. 'Pendhrergrast,' as the Irish servants generally called him, was quite unknown to the owner of Hap House, as was also that of Mr. Mollett, which had been brought up to him the first of the two; but Owen began to think that there must be something very unusual in a day so singularly ushered in to him. Callers at Hap House on business were very few,

unless when tradesmen in want of money occasionally dropped in
upon him.   But now that he was so summoned Owen began to
bestir himself with his boots and breeches.   A gentleman's
costume for a hunting morning is always a slow one—sometimes
so slow and tedious as to make him think of forswearing such
articles of dress for all future ages.   But now he did bestir himself,—in a moody melancholy sort of manner; for his manner in
all things latterly had become moody and melancholy.

In the mean time Captain Donnellan and the two strangers
sat almost in silence in the dining-room.   The Captain, though
he did not perhaps know much of things noticeable in this
world, did know something of a gentleman, and was therefore
not led away, as poor Thady had been, by Aby's hat and rings.
He had stared Aby full in the face when he entered the
room, and having explained that he was not the master of the
house, had not vouchsafed another word.   But then he had also
seen that Mr. Prendergast was of a different class, and had said
a civil word or two, asking him to come near the fire, and suggesting that Owen would be down in less than five minutes.
'But the old cock wouldn't crow,' as he afterwards remarked to
his friend, and so they all three sat in silence, the Captain being
very busy about his knees, as hunting gentlemen sometimes are
when they come down to bachelor breakfasts.

And then at last Owen Fitzgerald entered the room.   He has
been described as a handsome man, but in no dress did he look
so well as when equipped for a day's sport.   And what dress
that Englishmen ever wear is so handsome as this?   Or we may
perhaps say what other dress does English custom allow them
that is in any respect not the reverse of handsome.   We have
come to be so dingy,—in our taste I was going to say, but it is
rather in our want of taste,—so careless of any of the laws of
beauty in the folds and lines and hues of our dress, so opposed to
grace in the arrangement of our persons, that it is not permitted
to the ordinary English gentleman to be anything else but ugly.
Chimney-pot hats, swallow-tailed coats, and pantaloons that fit
nothing, came creeping in upon us, one after the other, while
the Georges reigned—creeping in upon us with such pictures as
we painted under the reign of West, and such houses as we
built under the reign of Nash, till the English eye required to
rest on that which was constrained, dull, and graceless.   For
the last two score of years it has come to this, that if a man go
in handsome attire he is a popinjay and a vain fool; and as it is
better to be ugly than to be accounted vain I would not counsel
a young friend to leave the beaten track on the strength of his
own judgment.   But not the less is the beaten track to be con-

demned, and abandoned, and abolished, if such be in any way possible. Beauty is good in all things; and I cannot but think that those old Venetian senators, and Florentine men of Council, owed somewhat of their country's pride and power to the manner in which they clipped their beards and wore their flowing garments.

But an Englishman may still make himself brave when he goes forth into the hunting field. Custom there allows him colour, and garments that fit his limbs. Strength is the outward characteristic of manhood, and at the covert-side he may appear strong. Look at men as they walk along Fleet-street, and ask yourself whether any outward sign of manhood or strength can be seen there. And of gentle manhood outward dignity should be the trade mark. I will not say that such outward dignity is incompatible with a black hat and plaid trousers, for the eye instructed by habit will search out dignity for itself wherever it may truly exist, let it be hidden by what vile covering it may. But any man who can look well at his club, will look better as he clusters round the hounds; while many a one who is comely there, is mean enough as he stands on the hearth-rug before his club fire. In my mind men, like churches and books, and women too, should be brave, not mean, in their outward garniture.

And Owen, as I have said, was brave as he walked into his dining-room. The sorrow which weighed on his heart had not wrinkled his brow, but had given him a set dignity of purpose. His tall figure, which his present dress allowed to be seen, was perfect in its symmetry of strength. His bright chestnut hair clustered round his forehead, and his eye shone like that of a hawk. They must have been wrong who said that he commonly spent his nights over the wine-cup. That pleasure always leaves its disgusting traces round the lips; and Owen Fitzgerald's lips were as full and lusty as Apollo's. Mollett, as he saw him, was stricken with envy. 'If I could only get enough money out of this affair to look like that,' was his first thought, as his eye fell on the future heir; not understanding, poor wretch that he was, that all the gold of California could not bring him one inch nearer to the goal he aimed at. I think I have said before, that your silk purse will not get itself made out of that coarse material with which there are so many attempts to manufacture that article. And Mr. Prendergast rose from his chair when he saw him, with a respect that was almost involuntary. He had not heard men speak well of Owen Fitzgerald;—not that ill-natured things had been said by the family at Castle Richmond, but circumstances had prevented the possibility of their praising him. If a relative or friend be spoken of without praise, he is, in fact, censured. From what he had

heard he had certainly not expected a man who would look so
noble as did the owner of Hap House, who now came forward to
ask him his business.

Both Mr. Prendergast and Aby Mollett rose at the same time.
Since the arrival of the latter gentleman, Aby had been wondering who he might be, but no idea that he was that lawyer from
Castle Richmond had entered his head. That he was a stranger
like himself, Aby saw; but he did not connect him with his own
business. Indeed he had not yet realized the belief, though his
father had done so, that the truth would be revealed by those at
Castle Richmond to him at Hap House. His object now was
that the old gentleman should say his say and be gone, leaving
him to dispose of the other young man in the top-boots as best
he might. But then, as it happened, that was also Mr. Prendergast's line of action.

'Gentlemen,' said Owen, 'I beg your pardon for keeping you
waiting; but the fact is that I am so seldom honoured in this
way in a morning, that I was hardly ready. Donnellan, there's
the tea; don't mind waiting. These gentlemen will perhaps
join us.' And then he looked hard at Aby, as though he trusted
in Providence that no such profanation would be done to his
table-cloth.

'Thank you, I have breakfasted,' said Mr. Prendergast.

'And so 'ave I,' said Aby, who had eaten a penny loaf in the
car, and would have been delighted to sit down at that rich table.
But he was a little beside himself, and not able to pluck up
courage for such an effort.

'I don't know whether you two gentlemen have come about
the same business,' said Owen, looking from one to the other.

'No,' said Mr. Prendergast, very confidently, but not very
correctly. 'I wish to speak to you, Mr. Fitzgerald, for a few
minutes: but my business with you is quite private.'

'So is mine,' said Aby, 'very private; very private indeed.'

'Well, gentlemen, I have just half an hour in which to eat
my breakfast, attend to business, get on my horse and leave the
house. Out of that twenty-five minutes are very much at your
service. Donnellan, I beg your pardon. Do pitch into the
broiled bones while they are hot; never mind me. And now,
gentlemen, if you will walk with me into the other room. First
come first served: that I suppose should be the order.' And he
opened the door and stood with it ajar in his hand.

'I will wait, Mr. Fitzgerald, if you please,' said Mr. Prendergast; and as he spoke he motioned Mollett with his hand to go to
the door.

'Oh! I can wait, sir; I'd rather wait, sir. I would indeed

said Aby. 'My business is a little particular; and if you'll go on, sir, I'll take up with the gen'leman as soon as you've done, sir.'

But Mr. Prendergast was accustomed to have his own way. 'I should prefer that you should go first, sir. And to tell the truth, Mr. Fitzgerald, what I have to say to you will take some time. It is of much importance, to yourself and to others; and I fear that you will probably find that it will detain you from your amusement to-day.'

Owen looked black as he heard this. The hounds were going to draw a covert of his own; and he was not in the habit of remaining away from the drawing of any coverts, belonging to himself or others, on any provocation whatever. 'That will be rather hard,' said he, 'considering that I do not know any more than the man in the moon what you've come about.'

'You shall be the sole judge yourself, sir, of the importance of my business with you,' said Mr. Prendergast.

'Well, Mr. ——; I forget your name,' said Owen.

'My name's Mollett,' said Aby. Whereupon Mr. Prendergast looked up at him very sharply, but he said nothing.—He said nothing, but he looked very sharply indeed. He now knew well who this man was, and guessed with tolerable accuracy the cause of his visit. But, nevertheless, at the moment he said nothing.

'Come along, then, Mr. Mollett. I hope your affair is not likely to be a very long one also. Perhaps you'll excuse my having a cup of tea sent into me as you talk to me. There is nothing like saving time when such very important business is on the tapis. Donnellan, send Thady in with a cup of tea, like a good fellow. Now, Mr. Mollett.'

Mr. Mollett rose slowly from his chair, and followed his host. He would have given all he possessed in the world, and that was very little, to have had the coast clear. But in such an emergency, what was he to do? By the time he had reached the door of the drawing-room, he had all but made up his mind to tell Fitzgerald that, seeing there was so much other business on hand this morning at Hap House, this special piece of business of his must stand over. But then, how could he go back to Cork empty-handed? So he followed Owen into the room, and there opened his budget with what courage he had left to him.

Captain Donnellan, as he employed himself on the broiled bones, twice invited Mr. Prendergast to assist him; but in vain. Donnellan remained there, waiting for Owen, till eleven; and then got on his horse. 'You'll tell Fitzgerald, will you, that I've started? He'll see nothing of to-day's hunt; that's clear.'

'I don't think he will,' said Mr. Prendergast.

CHAPTER XXIV.

AFTER BREAKFAST AT HAP HOUSE.

' I don't think he will,' said Mr. Prendergast; and as he spoke, Captain Donnellan's ear could detect that there was something approaching to sarcasm in the tone of the old man's voice. The Captain was quite sure that his friend would not be even at the heel of the hunt that day; and without further compunction proceeded to fasten his buckskin gloves round his wrists. The meet was so near to them, that they had both intended to ride their own hunters from the door; and the two nags were now being led up and down upon the gravel.

But at this moment a terrible noise was heard to take place in the hall. There was a rush and crushing there which made even Mr. Prendergast to jump from his chair, and drove Captain Donnellan to forget his gloves and run to the door.

It was as though all the winds of heaven were being driven down the passage, and as though each separate wind was shod with heavy-heeled boots. Captain Donnellan ran to the door, and Mr. Prendergast with slower steps followed him. When it was opened, Owen was to be seen in the hall, apparently in a state of great excitement; and the gentleman whom he had lately asked to breakfast,—he was to be seen also, in a position of unmistakeable discomfort. He was at that moment proceeding, with the utmost violence, into a large round bed of bushes, which stood in the middle of the great sweep before the door of the house, his feet just touching the ground as he went; and then, having reached his bourne, he penetrated face foremost into the thicket, and in an instant disappeared. He had been kicked out of the house. Owen Fitzgerald had taken him by the shoulders, with a run along the passage and hall, and having reached the door, had applied the flat of his foot violently to poor Aby's back, and sent him flying down the stone steps. And now, as Captain Donnellan and Mr. Prendergast stood looking on, Mr. Mollett junior buried himself altogether out of sight among the shrubs.

' You have done for that fellow, at any rate, Owen,' said Captain Donnellan, glancing for a moment at Mr. Prendergast. ' I should say that he will never get out of that alive.'

'Not if he wait till I pick him out,' said Owen, breathing very hard after his exertion. 'An infernal scoundrel! And now, Mr. Prendergast, if you are ready, sir, I am.' It was as much as he could do to finish these few words with that sang froid which he desired to assume, so violent was his attempt at breathing after his late exercise.

It was impossible not to conceive the idea that, as one disagreeable visitor had been disposed of in a somewhat summary fashion, so might be the other also. Mr. Prendergast did not look like a man who was in the habit of leaving gentlemen's houses in the manner just now adopted by Mr. Mollett; but nevertheless, as they had come together, both unwished for and unwelcome, Captain Donnellan did for a moment bethink himself whether there might not be more of such fun, if he remained there on the spot. At any rate, it would not do for him to go to the hunt while such deeds as these were being done. It might be that his assistance would be wanted.

Mr. Prendergast smiled, with a saturnine and somewhat bitter smile—the nearest approach to a laugh in which he was known to indulge,—for the same notion came also into his head. 'He has disposed of him, and now he is thinking how he will dispose of me.' Such was Mr. Prendergast's thought about the matter; and that made him smile. And then, too, he was pleased at what he had seen. That this Mollett was the son of that other Mollett, with whom he had been closeted at Castle Richmond, was plain enough; it was plain enough also to him, used as he was to trace out in his mind the courses of action which men would follow, that Mollett junior, having heard of his father's calamitous failure at Castle Richmond, had come down to Hap House to see what he could make out of the hitherto unconscious heir. It had been matter of great doubt with Mr. Prendergast, when he first heard young Mollett's name mentioned, whether or no he would allow him to make his attempt. He, Mr. Prendergast, could by a word have spoilt the game; but acting, as he was forced to act, on the spur of the moment, he resolved to permit Mr. Mollett junior to play out his play. He would be yet in time to prevent any ill result to Mr. Fitzgerald, should that gentleman be weak enough to succumb to any such ill results. As things had now turned out Mr. Prendergast rejoiced that Mr. Mollett junior had been permitted to play out his play. 'And now, Mr. Prendergast, if you are ready, I am,' said Owen.

'Perhaps we had better first pick up the gentleman among the trees,' said Mr. Prendergast. And he and Captain Donnellan went down into the bushes.

'Do as you please about that,' said Owen. 'I have touched

him once and shall not touch him again.' And he walked back
into the dining-room.

One of the grooms who were leading the horses had now gone
to the assistance of the fallen hero; and as Captain Donnellan
also had already penetrated as far as Aby's shoulders, Mr. Prendergast, thinking that he was not needed, returned also to the
house. 'I hope he is not seriously hurt,' he said.

'Not he,' said Owen. 'Those sort of men are as used to be
kicked, as girls are to be kissed; and it comes as naturally to
them. But anything short of having his bones broken will be
less than he deserves.'

'May I ask what was the nature of his offence?'

Owen remained silent for a moment, looking his guest full in
the face. 'Well; not exactly,' said he. 'He has been talking
of people of whom he knows nothing, but it would not be well
for me to repeat what he has said to a perfect stranger.'

'Quite right, Mr. Fitzgerald; it would not be well. But there
can be no harm in my repeating it to you. He came here to get
money from you for certain tidings which he brought; tidings
which if true would be of great importance to you. As I take it,
however, he has altogether failed in his object.'

'And how do you come to know all this, sir?'

'Merely from having heard that man mention his own name.
I also have come with the same tidings; and as I ask for no
money for communicating them, you may believe them to be
true on my telling.'

'What tidings?' asked Owen, with a frown, and an angry jerk
in his voice. No remotest notion had yet come in upon his mind
that there was any truth in the story that had been told him.
He had looked upon it all as a lie, and had regarded Mollett as a
sorry knave who had come to him with a poor and low attempt
at raising a few pounds. And even now he did not believe.
Mr. Prendergast's words had been too sudden to produce belief
of so great a fact, and his first thought was that an endeavour
was being made to fool him.

'Those tidings which that man has told you,' said Mr. Prendergast, solemnly. 'That you should not have believed them
from him shows only your discretion. But from me you may
believe them. I have come from Castle Richmond, and am here
as a messenger from Sir Thomas,—from Sir Thomas and from
his son. When the matter became clear to them both, then it
was felt that you also should be made acquainted with it.'

Owen Fitzgerald now sat down, and looked up into the lawyer's
face, staring at him. I may say that the power of saying much
was for the moment taken away from him by the words that he

heard. What! was it really possible that that title, that property, that place of honour in the country was to be his when one frail old man should drop away? And then, again, was it really true that all this immeasurable misery was to fall—had fallen—upon that family whom he had once known so well? It was but yesterday that he had been threatening all manner of evil to his cousin Herbert; and had his threats been proved true so quickly? But there was no shadow of triumph in his feelings. Owen Fitzgerald was a man of many faults. He was reckless, passionate, prone to depreciate the opinion of others, extravagant in his thoughts and habits, ever ready to fight, both morally and physically, those who did not at a moment's notice agree with him. He was a man who would at once make up his mind that the world was wrong when the world condemned him, and who would not in compliance with any argument allow himself to be so. But he was not avaricious, nor cruel, nor self-seeking, nor vindictive. In his anger he could pronounce all manner of ill things against his enemy, as he had pronounced some ill things against Herbert; but it was not in him to keep up a sustained wish that those ill things should really come to pass. This news which he now heard, and which he did not yet fully credit, struck him with awe, but created no triumph in his bosom. He realized the catastrophe as it affected his cousins of Castle Richmond rather than as it affected himself.

'Do you mean to say that Lady Fitzgerald—' and then he stopped himself. He had not the courage to ask the question which was in his mind. Could it really be the case that Lady Fitzgerald,—that she whom all the world had so long honoured under that name, was in truth the wife of that man's father,—of the father of that wretch whom he had just spurned from his house? The tragedy was so deep that he could not believe in it.

'We fear that it is so, Mr. Fitzgerald,' said Mr. Prendergast. 'That it certainly is so I cannot say. And therefore, if I may take the liberty to give you counsel, I would advise you not to make too certain of this change in your prospects.'

'Too certain!' said he, with a bitter laugh. 'Do you suppose then that I would wish to see all this ruin accomplished? Heavens and earth! Lady Fitzgerald—! I cannot believe it.'

And then Captain Donnellan also returned to the room. 'Fitzgerald,' said he, 'what the mischief are we to do with this fellow? He says that he can't walk, and he bleeds from his face like a pig.'

'What fellow? Oh, do what you like with him. Here: give him a pound note, and let him go to the d——. And Donnellan, for heaven's sake go to Cecilstown at once. Do not wait for me. I have business that will keep me here all day.'

'But I do not know what to do with this fellow that's bleeding,' said the captain, piteously, as he took the proffered note. 'If he puts up with a pound note for what you've done to him, he's softer than what I take him for.'

'He will be very glad to be allowed to escape without being given up to the police,' said Mr. Prendergast.

'But I don't know what to do with him,' said Captain Donnellan. 'He says that he can't stand.'

'Then lay him down on the dunghill,' said Owen Fitzgerald; 'but for heaven's sake do not let him interrupt me. And, Donnellan, you will altogether lose the day if you stay any longer.' Whereupon the captain, seeing that in very truth he was not wanted, did take himself off, casting as he went one farewell look on Aby as he lay groaning on the turf on the far side of the tuft of bushes.

'He's kilt intirely, I'm thinking, yer honor,' said Thady, who was standing over him on the other side.

'He'll come to life again before dinner-time,' said the captain.

'Oh, in course he'll do that, yer honor,' said Thady; and then added, sotto voce to himself, as the captain rode down the avenue, 'Faix, an' I don't know about that. Shure an' it's the masther has a heavy hand.' And then Thady stood for a while perplexed, endeavouring to reanimate Aby by a sight of the pound note which he held out visibly between his thumb and fingers.

And now Mr. Prendergast and Owen were again alone. 'And what am I to do?' said Owen, after a pause of a minute or two; and he asked the question with a serious solemn voice.

'Just for the present—for the next day or two—I think that you should do nothing. As soon as the first agony of this time is over at Castle Richmond, I think that Herbert should see you. It would be very desirable that he and you should take in concert such proceedings as will certainly become necessary. The absolute proof of the truth of this story must be obtained. You understand, I hope, Mr. Fitzgerald, that the case still admits of doubt.'

Owen nodded his head impatiently, as though it were needless on the part of Mr. Prendergast to insist upon this. He did not wish to take it for true a moment sooner than was necessary.

'It is my duty to give you this caution. Many lawyers—I presume you know that I am a lawyer—'

'I did not know it,' said Owen; 'but it makes no difference.'

'Thank you; that's very kind,' said Mr. Prendergast; but the sarcasm was altogether lost upon his hearer. 'Some lawyers, as I was saying, would in such a case have advised their clients to keep all their suspicions, nay all their knowledge, to themselves. Why play the game of an adversary? they would ask. But I have thought it better that we should have no adversary.'

'And you will have none,' said Owen; 'none in me at least.'

'I am much gratified in so perceiving, and in having such evidence that my advice has not been indiscreet. It occurred to me that if you received the first intimation of these circumstances from other sources, you would be bound on your own behalf to employ an agent to look after your own interests.'

'I should have done nothing of the kind,' said Owen.

'Ah, but, my dear young friend, in such a case it would have been your duty to do so.'

'Then I should have neglected my duty. And do you tell Herbert this from me, that let the truth be what it may, I shall never interrupt him in his title or his property. It is not there that I shall look either for justice or revenge. He will understand what I mean.'

But Mr. Prendergast did not, by any means; nor did he enter into the tone of Owen Fitzgerald's mind. They were both just men, but just in an essentially different manner. The justice of Mr. Prendergast had come of thought and education. As a young man, when entering on his profession, he was probably less just than he was now. He had thought about matters of law and equity, till thought had shown to him the beauty of equity as it should be practised,—often by the aid of law, and not unfrequently in spite of law. Such was the justice of Mr. Prendergast. That of Owen Fitzgerald had come of impulse and nature, and was the justice of a very young man rather than of a very wise one. That title and property did not, as he felt, of justice belong to him, but to his cousin. What difference could it make, in the true justice of things, whether or no that wretched man was still alive whom all the world had regarded as dead? In justice he ought to be dead. Now that this calamity of the man's life had fallen upon Sir Thomas and Lady Fitzgerald and his cousin Herbert, it would not be for him to aggravate it by seizing upon a heritage which might possibly accrue to him under the letter of the world's law, but which could not accrue to him under heaven's law. Such was the justice of Owen Fitzgerald; and we may say this of it in its dispraise, as comparing it with that other justice, that whereas that of Mr. Prendergast would wear for ever, through ages and ages, that other justice of Owen's would hardly have stood the pull of a ten years' struggle. When children came to him, would he not have thought of what might have been theirs by right; and then have thought of what ought to be theirs by right; and so on?

But in speaking of justice, he had also spoken of revenge, and Mr. Prendergast was altogether in the dark. What revenge? He did not know that poor Owen had lost a love, and that Herbert had found it. In the midst of all the confused thoughts which this astounding intelligence had brought upon him, Owen still thought of his love. There Herbert had robbed him— robbed him by means of his wealth; and in that matter he desired justice—justice or revenge. He wanted back his love. Let him have that and Herbert might yet be welcome to his title and estates.

Mr. Prendergast remained there for some half-hour longer, explaining what ought to be done, and how it ought to be done. Of course he combated that idea of Owen's, that the property might be allowed to remain in the hands of the wrong heir. Had that been consonant with his ideas of justice he would not have made his visit to Hap House this morning. Right must have its way, and if it should be that Lady Fitzgerald's marriage with Sir Thomas had not been legal, Owen, on Sir Thomas's death, must become Sir Owen, and Herbert could not become Sir Herbert. So much to the mind of Mr. Prendergast was as clear as crystal. Let justice be done, even though these Castle Richmond heavens should fall in ruins.

And then he took his departure, leaving Owen to his solitude, much perplexed. 'And where is that man?' Mr. Prendergast asked, as he got on to his car.

'Bedad thin, yer honer, he's very bad intirely. He's jist sitthing over the kitchen fire, moaning and croning this way and that, but sorrow a word he's spoke since the masther hoisted him out o' the big hall door. And thin for blood—why, saving yer honer's presence, he's one mash of gore.'

'You'd better wash his face for him, and give him a little tea,' said Mr. Prendergast, and then he drove away.

And strange ideas floated across Owen Fitzgerald's brain as he sat there alone, in his hunting gear, leaning on the still covered breakfast-table. They floated across his brain backwards and forwards, and at last remained there, taking almost the form of a definite purpose. He would make a bargain with Herbert; let each of them keep that which was fairly his own; let Herbert have all the broad lands of Castle Richmond; let him have the title, the seat in parliament, and the county honour; but for him, Owen—let him have Clara Desmond. He desired nothing that was not fairly his own; but as his own he did regard her, and without her he did not know how to face the future of his life.

And in suggesting this arrangement to himself, he did not altogether throw over her feelings; he did take into account her heart, though he did not take into account her worldly prospects. She had loved him—him—Owen; and he would not teach himself to believe that she did not love him still. Her mother had been too powerful for her, and she had weakly yielded; but as to her heart—Owen could not bring himself to believe that that was gone from him.

They two would make a bargain,—he and his cousin. Honour and renown, and the money and the title would be everything to his cousin. Herbert had been brought up to expect these things, and all the world around him had expected them for him. It would be terrible to him to find himself robbed of them. But the loss of Clara Desmond was equally terrible to Owen Fitzgerald. He allowed his heart to fill itself with a romantic sense of honour, teaching him that it behoved him as a man not to give up his love. Without her he would live disgraced in his own estimation; but who would not think the better of him for refraining from the possession of those Castle Richmond acres? Yes; he would make a bargain with Herbert. Who was there in the world to deny his right to do so?

As he sat revolving these things in his mind, he suddenly heard a rushing sound, as of many horsemen down the avenue, and going to the window, he saw two or three leading men of the hunt, accompanied by the gray-haired old huntsman; and through and about and under the horsemen were the dogs, running in and out of the laurels which skirted the road, with their noses down, giving every now and then short yelps as they caught up the uncertain scent from the leaves on the ground, and hurried on upon the trail of their game.

'Yo ho! to him, Messenger! bark to him, Maybird; good bitch, Merrylass. He's down here, gen'lemen, and he'll never get away alive. He came to a bad place when he looked out for going to ground anywhere near Mr. Owen.'

And then there came, fast trotting down through the other horsemen, making his way eagerly to the front, a stout heavy man, with a florid handsome face and eager eye. He might be some fifty years of age, but no lad there of three-and-twenty was so anxious and impetuous as he. He was riding a large-boned, fast-trotting bay horse, that pressed on as eagerly as his rider. As he hurried forward all made way for him, till he was close to the shrubs in the front of the house.

'Bless my soul, gentlemen,' he said, in an angry voice, 'how, in the name of all that's good, are hounds to hunt if you press them down the road in that way? By heavens, Barry, you are

enough to drive a man wild. Yoicks, Merrylass! there it is,
Pat;'—Pat was the huntsman—' outside the low wall there, down
towards the river.' This was Sam O'Grady, the master of the
Duhallow hounds, the god of Owen's idolatry. No better fellow
ever lived, and no master of hounds, so good; such at least was
the opinion common among Duhallow sportsmen.

Yes, yer honer,—he did skirt round there, I knows that; but
he's been among them laurels at the bottom, and he'll be about
the place and out-houses somewhere. There's a drain here that
I knows on, and he knows on. But Mr. Owen, he knows on it
too; and there aint a chance for him.' So argued Pat, the
Duhallow huntsman, the experienced craft of whose aged mind
enabled him to run counter to the cutest dodges of the cutest fox
in that and any of the three neighbouring baronies.

And now the sweep before the door was crowded with red-
coats; and Owen, looking from his dining-room window, felt
that he must take some step. As an ordinary rule, had the hunt
thus drifted near his homestead, he would have been off his horse
and down among his bottles, sending up sherry and cherry-
brandy; and there would have been comfortable drink in plenty,
and cold meat, perhaps, not in plenty; and every one would
have been welcome in and out of the house. But now there was
that at his heart which forbade him to mix with the men who
knew him so well, and among whom he was customarily so loudly
joyous. Dressed as he was, he could not go among them without explaining why he had remained at home; and as to that, he
felt that he was not able to give any explanation at the present
moment.

'What's the matter with Owen?' said one fellow to Captain
Donnellan.

'Upon my word I hardly know. Two chaps came to him
this morning, before he was up; about business, they said. He
nearly murdered one of them out of hand; and I believe that
he's locked up somewhere with the other this minute.'

But in the meantime a servant came up to Mr. O'Grady, and,
touching his hat, asked the master of the hunt to go into the
house for a moment; and then Mr. O'Grady, dismounting,
entered in through the front door. He was only there two
minutes, for his mind was still outside, among the laurels, with
the fox; but as he put his foot again into the stirrup, he said to
those around him that they must hurry away, and not disturb
Owen Fitzgerald that day. It may, therefore, easily be imagined
that the mystery would spread quickly through that portion of
the county of Cork.

They must hurry away;—but not before they could give an

account of their fox. Neither for gods nor men must he be left, as long as his skin was whole above ground. There is an importance attaching to the pursuit of a fox, which gives it a character quite distinct from that of any other amusement which men follow in these realms. It justifies almost anything that men can do, and that at any place and in any season. There is about it a sanctity which forbids interruption, and makes its votaries safe under any circumstances of trespass or intrusion. A man in a hunting county who opposes the county hunt must be a misanthrope, willing to live in seclusion, fond of being in Coventry, and in love with the enmity of his fellow-creatures. There are such men, but they are regarded as lepers by those around them. All this adds to the nobleness of the noble sport, and makes it worthy of a man's energies.

And then the crowd of huntsmen hurried round from the front of the house to a paddock at the back, and then again through the stable yard to the front. The hounds were about—here, there, and everywhere, as any one ignorant of the craft would have said, but still always on the scent of that doomed beast. From one thicket to another he tried to hide himself, but the moist leaves of the underwood told quickly of his whereabouts. He tried every hole and cranny about the house, but every hole and corner had been stopped by Owen's jealous care. He would have lived disgraced for ever in his own estimation, had a fox gone to ground anywhere about his domicile. At last a loud whoop was heard just in front of the hall door. The poor fox, with his last gasp of strength, had betaken himself to the thicket before the door, and there the dogs had killed him, at the very spot on which Aby Mollett had fallen.

Standing well back from the window, still thinking of Clara Desmond, Owen Fitzgerald saw the fate of the hunted animal; he saw the head and tail severed from the carcase by old Pat, and the body thrown to the hounds,—a ceremony over which he had presided so many scores of times; and then, when the dogs had ceased to growl over the bloody fragments, he saw the hunt move away, back along the avenue to the high road. All this he saw, but still he was thinking of Clara Desmond.

CHAPTER XXV.

A MUDDY WALK ON A WET MORNING.

ALL that day of the hunt was passed very quietly at Castle Richmond. Herbert did not once leave the house, having begged Mr. Somers to make his excuse at a Relief Committee which it would have been his business to attend. A great portion of the day he spent with his father, who lay all but motionless, in a state that was apparently half comatose. During all those long hours very little was said between them about this tragedy of their family. Why should more be said now; now that the worst had befallen them—all that worst, to hide which Sir Thomas had endured such superhuman agony? And then four or five times during the day he went to his mother, but with her he did not stay long. To her he could hardly speak upon any subject, for to her as yet the story had not been told.

And she, when he thus came to her from time to time, with a soft word or two, or a softer kiss, would ask him no question. She knew that he had learned the whole, and knew also from the solemn cloud on his brow that that whole must be very dreadful. Indeed we may surmise that her woman's heart had by this time guessed somewhat of the truth. But she would inquire of no one. Jones, she was sure, knew it all; but she did not ask a single question of her servant. It would be told to her when it was fitting. Why should she move in the matter?

Whenever Herbert entered her room she tried to receive him with something of a smile. It was clear enough that she was always glad of his coming, and that she made some little show of welcoming him. A book was always put away, very softly and by the slightest motion; but Herbert well knew what that book was, and whence his mother sought that strength which enabled her to live through such an ordeal as this.

And his sisters were to be seen, moving slowly about the house like the very ghosts of their former selves. Their voices were hardly heard; no ring of customary laughter ever came from the room in which they sat; when they passed their brother in the house they hardly dared to whisper to him. As to sitting down at table now with Mr. Prendergast, that effort was wholly abandoned; they kept themselves even from the sound of his footsteps.

Aunt Letty perhaps spoke more than the others, but what could she speak to the purpose? 'Herbert,' she once said, as she caught him close by the door of the library and almost pulled him into the room,—'Herbert, I charge you to tell me what all this is!'

'I can tell you nothing, dear aunt, nothing;—nothing as yet.'

'But, Herbert, tell me this; is it about my sister?' For very many years past Aunt Letty had always called Lady Fitzgerald her sister.

'I can tell you nothing;—nothing to-day,'

'Then, to-morrow.'

'I do not know—we must let Mr. Prendergast manage this matter as he will. I have taken nothing on myself, Aunt Letty —nothing.'

'Then I tell you what, Herbert; it will kill me. It will kill us all, as it is killing your father and your darling mother. I tell you that it is killing her fast. Human nature cannot bear it. For myself I could endure anything if I were trusted.' And sitting down in one of the high-backed library chairs she burst into a flood of tears; a sight which, as regarded Aunt Letty, Herbert had never seen before.

What if they all died? thought Herbert to himself in the bitterness of the moment. There was that in store for some of them which was worse than death. What business had Aunt Letty to talk of her misery? Of course she was wretched, as they all were; but how could she appreciate the burden that was on his back? What was Clara Desmond to her?

Shortly after noon Mr. Prendergast was back at the house; but he slank up to his room, and no one saw anything of him. At half-past six he came down, and Herbert constrained himself to sit at the table while dinner was served; and so the day passed away. One more day only Mr. Prendergast was to stay at Castle Richmond; and then, if, as he expected, certain letters should reach him on that morning, he was to start for London late on the following day. It may well be imagined that he was not desirous of prolonging his visit.

Early on the following morning Herbert started for a long solitary walk. On that day Mr. Prendergast was to tell everything to his mother, and it was determined between them that her son should not be in the house during the telling. In the evening, when he came home, he was to see her. So he started on his walk, resolving some other things also in his mind before he went. He would reach Desmond Court before he returned home that day, and let the two ladies there know the fate that was before them. Then, after that, they might let him know what was to be his fate;—but on this head he would not hurry them.

So he started on his walk, resolving to go round by Gortna-clough on his way to Desmond Court, and then to return home from that place. The road would be more than twenty long Irish miles; but he felt that the hard work would be of service. It was instinct rather than thought which taught him that it would be good for him to put some strain on the muscles of his body, and thus relieve the muscles of his mind. If his limbs could become thoroughly tired,—thoroughly tired so that he might wish to rest,—then he might hope that for a moment he might cease to think of all this sorrow which encompassed him.

So he started on his walk, taking with him a thick cudgel and his own thoughts. He went away across the demesne and down into the road that led away by Gortnaclough and Boherbue towards Castleisland and the wilds of county Kerry. As he went, the men about the place refrained from speaking to him, for they all knew that bad news had come to the big house. They looked at him with lowered eyes and with tenderness in their hearts, for they loved the very name of Fitzgerald. The love which a poor Irishman feels for the gentleman whom he regards as his master—'his masther,' though he has probably never received from him, in money, wages for a day's work, and in all his intercourse has been the man who has paid money and not the man who received it—the love which he nevertheless feels, if he has been occasionally looked on with a smiling face and accosted with a kindly word, is astonishing to an English-man. I will not say that the feeling is altogether good. Love should come of love. Where personal love exists on one side, and not even personal regard on the other, there must be some mixture of servility. That unbounded respect for human grandeur cannot be altogether good; for human greatness, if the greatness be properly sifted, it may be so.

He got down into the road, and went forth upon his journey at a rapid pace. The mud was deep upon the way, but he went through the thickest without a thought of it. He had not been out long before there came on a cold, light, drizzling rain, such a rain as gradually but surely makes its way into the innermost rag of a man's clothing, running up the inside of his waterproof coat, and penetrating by its perseverance the very folds of his necktie. Such cold, drizzling rain is the commonest phase of hard weather during Irish winters, and those who are out and about get used to it and treat it tenderly. They are euphemis-tical as to the weather, calling it hazy and soft, and never allowing themselves to carry bad language on such a subject

beyond the word dull. And yet at such a time one breathes the
rain and again exhales it, and become as it were oneself a water
spirit, assuming an aqueous fishlike nature into one's inner
fibres. It must be acknowledged that a man does sometimes get
wet in Ireland; but then a wetting there brings no cold in the
head, no husky voice, no need for multitudinous pocket-handker-
chiefs, as it does here in this land of catarrhs. It is the east
wind and not the rain that kills; and of east wind in the south
of Ireland they know nothing.

But Herbert walked on quite unmindful of the mist, swinging
his thick stick in his hand, and ever increasing his pace as he
went. He was usually a man careful of such things, but it was
nothing to him now whether he were wet or dry. His mind was
so full of the immediate circumstances of his destiny that he
could not think of small external accidents. What was to be his
future life in this world, and how was he to fight the battle that
was now before him? That was the question which he continually asked himself, and yet never succeeded in answering.
How was he to come down from the throne on which early
circumstances had placed him, and hustle and struggle among
the crowd for such approach to other thrones as his sinews and
shoulders might procure for him? If he had been only born to
the struggle, he said to himself, how easy and pleasant it would
have been to him! But to find himself thus cast out from his
place by an accident—cast out with the eyes of all the world
upon him; to be talked of, and pointed at, and pitied; to have
little aids offered him by men whom he regarded as beneath
him—all this was terribly sore, and the burden was almost too
much for his strength. 'I do not care for the money,' he said
to himself a dozen times; and in saying so he spoke in one sense
truly. But he did care for things which money buys; for
outward respect, permission to speak with authority among his
fellow-men, for power and place, and the feeling that he was
prominent in his walk of life. To be in advance of other men,
that is the desire which is strongest in the hearts of all strong
men; and in that desire how terrible a fall had he not received
from this catastrophe!

And what were they all to do, he and his mother and his
sisters? How were they to act—now, at once? In what way
were they to carry themselves when this man of law and judgment should have gone from them? For himself, his course of
action must depend much upon the word which might be spoken
to him to-day at Desmond Court. There would still be a drop
of comfort left at the bottom of his cup if he might be allowed to
hope there. But in truth he feared greatly. What the countess

would say to him he thought he could foretell; what it would
behove him to say himself—in matter, though not in words—
that he knew well. Would not the two sayings tally well
together? and could it be right for him even to hope that the
love of a girl of seventeen should stand firm against her mother's
will, when her lover himself could not dare to press his suit?
And then another reflection pressed on his mind sorely. Clara
had already given up one poor lover at her mother's instance;
might she not resume that lover, also at her mother's instance,
now that he was no longer poor? What if Owen Fitzgerald
should take from him everything!

And so he walked on through the mud and rain, always
swinging his big stick. Perhaps, after all, the worst of it was
over with him, when he could argue with himself in this way.
It is the first plunge into the cold water that gives the shock.
We may almost say that every human misery will cease to be
miserable if it be duly faced; and something is done towards
conquering our miseries, when we face them in any degree, even
if not with due courage. Herbert had taken his plunge into the
deep, dark, cold, comfortless pool of misfortune; and he felt
that the waters around him were very cold. But the plunge had
been taken, and the worst, perhaps, was gone by.

As he approached near to Gortnaclough, he came upon one of
those gangs of road-destroyers who were now at work everywhere, earning their pittance of 'yellow meal' with a pickaxe
and a wheelbarrow. In some sort or other the labourers had
been got to their work. Gangsmen there were with lists, who
did see, more or less accurately, that the men, before they
received their sixpence or eightpence for their day's work, did
at any rate pass their day with some sort of tool in their hands.
And consequently the surface of the hill began to disappear, and
there were chasms in the road, which caused those who travelled
on wheels to sit still, staring across with angry eyes, and sometimes to apostrophize the doer of these deeds with very naughty
words. The doer was the Board of Works, or the 'Board' as it
was familiarly termed; and were it not that those ill words
must have returned to the bosoms which vented them, and have
flown no further, no Board could ever have been so terribly
curse-laden. To find oneself at last utterly stopped, after proceeding with great strain to one's horse for half a mile through
an artificial quagmire of slush up to the wheelbox, is harassing
to the customary traveller; and men at that crisis did not
bethink themselves quite so frequently as they should have done,
that a people perishing from famine is more harassing.

But Herbert was not on wheels, and was proceeding through

the slush and across the chasm, regardless of it all, when he was
stopped by some of the men. All the land thereabouts was
Castle Richmond property; and it was not probable that the
young master of it all would be allowed to pass through some
two score of his own tenantry without greetings, and petitions,
and blessings, and complaints.

'Faix, yer honer, thin, Mr. Herbert,' said one man, standing
at the bottom of the hill, with the half-filled wheelbarrow still
hanging in his hands—an Englishman would have put down the
barrow while he was speaking, making some inner calculation
about the waste of his muscles; but an Irishman would despise
himself for such low economy—'Faix, thin, yer honer, Mr.
Herbert; an' it's yourself is a sight good for sore eyes. May
the heavens be your bed, for it's you is the frind to a poor man.'

'How are you, Pat?' said Herbert, without intending to stop.
'How are you, Mooney? I hope the work suits you all.' And
then he would at once have passed on, with his hat pressed down
low over his brow.

But this could be by no means allowed. In the first place,
the excitement arising from the young master's presence was too
valuable to be lost so suddenly; and then, when might again
occur so excellent a time for some mention of their heavy griev-
ances? Men whose whole amount of worldly good consists in a
bare allowance of nauseous food, just sufficient to keep body and
soul together, must be excused if they wish to utter their complaints to ears that can hear them.

'Arrah, yer honer, thin, we're none on us very well; and
how could we, with the male at a penny a pound?' said Pat.

'Sorrow to it for male,' said Mooney. 'It's the worst vittles
iver a man tooked into the inside of him. Saving yer honer's
presence it's as much as I can do to raise the bare arm of me
since the day I first began with the yally male.'

'It's as wake as cats we all is,' said another, who from the
weary way in which he dragged his limbs about certainly did
not himself seem to be gifted with much animal strength.

'And the childer is worse, yer honer,' said a fourth. 'The
male is bad for them intirely. Saving yer honer's presence,
their bellies is gone away most to nothing.'

'And there's six of us in family, yer honer,' said Pat. 'Six
mouths to feed; and what's eight pennorth of yally male among
such a lot as that; let alone the Sundays, when there's nothing?'

'An' shure, Mr. Herbert,' said another, a small man with a
squeaking voice, whose rags of clothes hardly hung on to his
body, 'warn't I here with the other boys the last Friday as iver
was? Ax Pat Condon else, yer honer; and yet when they

comed to give out the wages, they sconced me of ——.' And so on. There were as many complaints to be made as there were men, if only he could bring himself to listen to them.

On ordinary occasions Herbert would listen to them, and answer them, and give them, at any rate, the satisfaction which they derived from discoursing with him, if he could give them no other satisfaction. But now, on this day, with his own burden so heavy at his heart, he could not even do this. He could not think of their sorrows; his own sorrow seemed to him to be so much the heavier. So he passed on, running the gauntlet through them as best he might, and shaking them off from him, as they attempted to cling round his steps. Nothing is so powerful in making a man selfish as misfortune.

And then he went on to Gortnaclough. He had not chosen his walk to this place with any fixed object, except this perhaps, that it enabled him to return home round by Desmond Court. It was one of the places at which a Relief Committee sat every fortnight, and there was a soup-kitchen here, which, however, had not been so successful as the one at Berryhill; and it was the place of residence selected by Father Barney's coadjutor. But in spite of all this, when Herbert found himself in the wretched, dirty, straggling, damp street of the village, he did not know what to do or where to betake himself. That every eye in Gortnaclough would be upon him was a matter of course. He could hardly turn round on his heel and retrace his steps through the village, as he would have to do in going to Desmond Court, without showing some pretext for his coming there; so he walked into the little shop which was attached to the soup-kitchen, and there he found the Rev. Mr. Columb Creagh, giving his orders to the little girl behind the counter.

Herbert Fitzgerald was customarily very civil to the Roman Catholic priests around him,—somewhat more so, indeed, than seemed good to those very excellent ladies, Mrs. Townsend and Aunt Letty; but it always went against the grain with him to be civil to the Rev. Columb Creagh; and on this special day it would have gone against the grain with him to be civil to anybody. But the coadjutor knew his character, and was delighted to have an opportunity of talking to him, when he could do so without being snubbed either by Mr. Somers, the chairman, or by his own parish priest. Mr. Creagh had rejoiced much at the idea of forming one at the same council board with county magistrates and Protestant parsons; but the fruition of his promised delights had never quite reached his lips. He had been like Sancho Panza in his government; he had sat down to the grand table day after day, but had never yet been allowed to

enjoy the rich dish of his own oratory. Whenever he had proposed to help himself, Mr. Somers or Father Barney had stopped
his mouth. Now probably he might be able to say a word or
two; and though the glory would not be equal to that of making
a speech at the Committee, still it would be something to be
seen talking on equal terms, and on affairs of state, to the young
heir of Castle Richmond.

'Mr. Fitzgerald! well, I declare! And how are you, sir?'
And he took off his hat and bowed, and got hold of Herbert's
hand, shaking it ruthlessly; and altogether he made him very
disagreeable.

Herbert, though his mind was not really intent on the subject,
asked some question of the girl as to the amount of meal that
had been sold, and desired to see the little passbook that they
kept at the shop.

'We are doing pretty well, Mr. Fitzgerald,' said the coadjutor;
'pretty well. I always keep my eye on, for fear things should
go wrong, you know.'

'I don't think they'll do that,' said Herbert.

'No; I hope not. But it's always good to be on the safe side,
you know. And to tell you the truth, I don't think we're
altogether on the right tack about them shops. It's very hard
on a poor woman—'

Now the fact was, though the Relief Committee at Gortnaclough
was attended by magistrates, priests, and parsons, the shop there
was Herbert Fitzgerald's own affair. It had been stocked with
his or his father's money; the flour was sold without profit at
his risk, and the rent of the house and wages of the woman who
kept it came out of his own pocket-money. Under these circumstances he did not see cause why Mr. Creagh should interfere,
and at the present moment was not well inclined to put up with
such interference.

'We do the best we can, Mr. Creagh,' said he, interrupting the
priest. 'And no good will be done at such a time as this by
unnecessary difficulties.'

'No, no, certainly not. But still I do think—' And Mr. Creagh
was girding up his loins for eloquence, when he was again
interrupted.

'I am rather in a hurry to-day,' said Herbert, 'and therefore,
if you please, we won't make any change now. Never mind the
book to-day, Sally. Good day, Mr. Creagh.' And so saying, he
left the shop and walked rapidly back out of the village.

The poor coadjutor was left alone at the shop-door, anathema-
tizing in his heart the pride of all Protestants. He had been
told that this Mr. Fitzgerald was different from others, that he

was a man fond of priests and addicted to the 'ould religion;' and so hearing, he had resolved to make the most of such an excellent disposition. But he was forced to confess to himself that they were all alike. Mr. Somers could not have been more imperious, nor Mr. Townsend more insolent.

And then, through the still drizzling rain, Herbert walked on to Desmond Court. By the time that he reached the desolate-looking lodge at the demesne gate, he was nearly wet through, and was besmeared with mud up to his knees. But he had thought nothing of this as he walked along. His mind had been intent on the scene that was before him. In what words was he to break the news to Clara Desmond and her mother? and with what words would they receive the tidings? The former question he had by no means answered to his own satisfaction, when, all muddy and wet, he passed up to the house through that desolate gate.

'Is Lady Desmond at home?' he asked of the butler. 'Her ladyship is at home,' said the gray-haired old man, with his blandest smile, 'and so is Lady Clara.' He had already learned to look on the heir of Castle Richmond as the coming saviour of the impoverished Desmond family.

CHAPTER XXVI.

COMFORTLESS.

'But, Mr. Herbert, yer honor, you're wet through and through—surely,' said the butler, as soon as Fitzgerald was well inside the hall. Herbert muttered something about his being only damp, and that it did not signify. But it did signify,—very much,—in the butler's estimation. Whose being wet through could signify more, for was not Mr. Herbert to be a baronet, and to have the spending of twelve thousand a year; and would he not be the future husband of Lady Clara? not signify indeed!

'An' shure, Mr. Herbert, you haven't walked to Desmond Court this blessed morning. Tare an' ages! Well; there's no knowing what you young gentlemen won't do. But I'll see and get a pair of trousers of my Lord's ready for you in two minutes. Faix, and he's nearly as big as yourself now, Mr. Herbert.'

But Herbert would hardly speak to him, and gave no assent whatever as to his proposition for borrowing the earl's clothes. 'I'll go in as I am,' said he. And the old man looking into his face saw that there was something wrong. 'Shure an' he ain't ing to sthrike off now,' said this Irish Caleb Balderstone to himself. He also as well as some others about Desmond Court had feared greatly that Lady Clara would throw herself away upon a poor lover.

It was now past noon, and Fitzgerald pressed forward into the room in which Lady Clara usually sat. It was the same in which she had received Owen's visit, and here of a morning she was usually to be found alone; but on this occasion when he opened the door he found that her mother was with her. Since the day on which Clara had disposed of herself so excellently, the mother had spent more of her time with her daughter. Looking at Clara now through Herbert Fitzgerald's eyes, the countess had begun to confess to herself that her child did possess beauty and charms.

She got up to greet her future son-in-law with a sweet smile and that charming quiet welcome with which a woman so well knows how to make her house pleasant to a man that is welcome to it. And Clara, not rising, but turning her head round and looking at him, greeted him also. He came forward and took both their hands, and it was not till he had held Clara's for half a minute in his own that they both saw that he was more than ordinarily serious. 'I hope Sir Thomas is not worse,' said Lady Desmond, with that voice of feigned interest which is so common. 'After all, if anything should happen to the poor old weak gentleman, might it not be as well?'

'My father has not been very well these last two days,' he said.

'I am so sorry,' said Clara. 'And your mother, Herbert?'

'But Herbert, how wet you are. You must have walked,' said the countess.

Herbert, in a few dull words said that he had walked. He had thought that the walk would be good for him, and he had not expected that it would be so wet. And then Lady Desmond, looking carefully into his face, saw that in truth he was very serious;—so much so that she knew that he had come there on account of his seriousness. But still his sorrow did not in any degree go to her heart. He was grieving doubtless for his father,—or his mother. The house at Castle Richmond was probably sad, because sickness and fear of death were there;— nay, perhaps death itself now hanging over some loved head. But what was this to her? She had had her own sorrows;— enough of them perhaps to account for her being selfish. So with a solemn face, but with nothing amiss about her heart, she again asked for tidings from Castle Richmond.

'Do tell us,' said Clara, getting up. 'I am afraid Sir Thomas is very ill.' The old baronet had been kind to her, and she did regard him. To her it was a sorrow to think that there should be any sorrow at Castle Richmond.

'Yes; he is ill,' said Herbert. 'We have had a gentleman from London with us for the last few days—a friend of my father's. His name is Mr. Prendergast.'

'Is he a doctor?' asked the countess.

'No, not a doctor,' said Herbert. 'He is a lawyer.'

It was very hard for him to begin his story; and perhaps the more so in that he was wet through and covered with mud. He now felt cold and clammy, and began to have an idea that he should not be seated there in that room in such a guise. Clara, too, had instinctively learned from his face, and tone, and general bearing that something truly was the matter. At other times when he had been there, since that day on which he had been accepted, he had been completely master of himself. Perhaps it had almost been deemed a fault in him that he had had none of the timidity or hesitation of a lover. He had seemed to feel, no doubt, that he, with his fortune and position at his back, need feel no scruple in accepting as his own the fair hand for which he had asked. But now—nothing could be more different from this than his manner was now.

Lady Desmond was now surprised, though probably not as yet frightened. Why should a lawyer have come from London to visit Sir Thomas at a period of such illness? and why should Herbert have walked over to Desmond Court to tell them of this illness? There must be something in this lawyer's coming which was intended to bear in some way on her daughter's marriage. 'But, Herbert,' she said, 'you are quite wet. Will you not put on some of Patrick's things?'

'No, thank you,' said he; 'I shall not stay long. I shall soon have said what I have got to say.'

'But do, Herbert,' said Clara. 'I cannot bear to see you so uncomfortable. And then you will not be in such a hurry to go back.'

'Ill as my father is,' said he, 'I cannot stay long; but I have thought it my duty to come over and tell you—tell you what has happened at Castle Richmond.'

And now the countess was frightened. There was that in Herbert's tone of voice and the form of his countenance which was enough to frighten any woman. What had happened at Castle Richmond? what could have happened there to make necessary the presence of a lawyer, and at the same time thus to sadden her future son-in-law? And Clara also was frightened, though she knew not why. His manner was so different from that which was usual; he was so cold, and serious, and awe-struck, that she could not but be unhappy.

'And what is it?' said the countess.

Herbert then sat for a few minutes silent, thinking how best he should tell them his story. He had been all the morning resolving to tell it, but he had in nowise as yet fixed upon any method. It was all so terribly tragic, so frightful in the extent of its reality, that he hardly knew how it would be possible for him to get through his task.

'I hope that no misfortune has come upon any of the family,' said Lady Desmond, now beginning to think that there might be misfortunes which would affect her own daughter more nearly than the illness either of the baronet or of his wife.

'Oh, I hope not!' said Clara, getting up and clasping her hands. 'What is it, Herbert? why don't you speak?' And coming round to him, she took hold of his arm.

'Dearest Clara,' he said, looking at her with more tenderness than had ever been usual with him, 'I think that you had better leave us. I could tell it better to your mother alone.'

'Do, Clara, love. Go, dearest, and we will call you by-and-by.'

Clara moved away very slowly towards the door, and then she turned round. 'If it is anything that makes you unhappy, Herbert,' she said, 'I must know it before you leave me.'

'Yes, yes; either I or your mother—. You shall be told, certainly.'

'Yes, yes, you shall be told,' said the countess. 'And now go, my darling.' Thus dismissed, Clara did go, and betook herself to her own chamber. Had Owen had sorrows to tell her, he would have told them to herself; of that she was quite sure. 'And now, Herbert, for heaven's sake what is it?' said the countess, pale with terror. She was fully certain now that something was to be spoken which would be calculated to inter-fere with her daughter's prospects.

We all know the story which Herbert had to tell, and we need not therefore again be present at the telling of it. Sitting there, wet through, in Lady Desmond's drawing-room, he did contrive to utter it all—the whole of it from the beginning to the end, making it clearly to be understood that he was no longer Fitzgerald of Castle Richmond, but a nameless, penniless outcast, without the hope of portion or position, doomed from henceforth to earn his bread in the sweat of his brow—if only he could be fortunate enough to find the means of earning it.

Nor did Lady Desmond once interrupt him in his story. She sat perfectly still, listening to him almost with unmoved face.

She was too wise to let him know what the instant working of her mind might be before she had made her own fixed resolve; and she had conceived the truth much before he had completed the telling of it. We generally use three times the number of words which are necessary for the purpose which we have in hand; but had he used six times the number, she would not have interrupted him. It was good in him to give her this time to determine in what tone and with what words she would speak, when speaking on her part should become absolutely necessary. 'And now,' he concluded by saying—and at this time he was standing up on the rug—'you know it all, Lady Desmond. It will perhaps be best that Clara should learn it from you.'

He had said not a word of giving up his pretensions to Lady Clara's hand; but then neither had he in any way hinted that the match should, in his opinion, be regarded as unbroken. He had not spoken of his sorrow at bringing down all this poverty on his wife; and surely he would have so spoken had he thought their engagement was still valid; but then he had not himself pointed out that the engagement must necessarily be broken, as, in Lady Desmond's opinion, he certainly should have done.

'Yes,' said she, in a cold, low, meaningless voice—in a voice that told nothing by its tones—'Lady Clara had better hear it from me.' But in the title which she gave her daughter, Herbert instantly read his doom. He, however, remained silent. It was for the countess now to speak.

'But it is possible it may not be true,' she said, speaking almost in a whisper, looking, not into his face, but by him, at the fire.

'It is possible; but so barely possible, that I did not think it right to keep the matter from you any longer.'

'It would have been very wrong—very wicked, I may say,' said the countess.

'It is only two days since I knew anything of it myself,' said he, vindicating himself.

'You were of course bound to let me know immediately,' she said, harshly.

'And I have let you know immediately, Lady Desmond.' And then they were both again silent for a while.

'And Mr. Prendergast thinks there is no doubt?' she asked.

'None,' said Herbert, very decidedly.

'And he has told your cousin Owen?'

'He did so yesterday; and by this time my poor mother knows it also.' And then there was another period of silence.

During the whole time Lady Desmond had uttered no one word of condolence—not a syllable of commiseration for all the sufferings that had come upon Herbert and his family ; and he was beginning to hate her for her harshness. The tenor of her countenance had become hard ; and she received all his words as a judge might have taken them, merely wanting evidence before he pronounced his verdict. The evidence she was beginning to think sufficient, and there could be no doubt as to her verdict. After what she had heard, a match between Herbert Fitzgerald and her daughter would be out of the question. 'It is very dreadful,' she said, thinking only of her own child, and absolutely shivering at the danger which had been incurred.

'It is very dreadful,' said Herbert, shivering also. It was almost incredible to him that his great sorrow should be received in such a way by one who had professed to be so dear a friend to him.

'And what do you propose to do, Mr. Fitzgerald?' said the countess.

'What do I propose?' he said, repeating her words. 'Hitherto I have had neither time nor heart to propose anything. Such a misfortune as that which I have told you does not break upon a man without disturbing for a while his power of resolving. I have thought so much of my mother, and of Clara, since Mr. Prendergast told me all this, that—that—that—' And then a slight gurgling struggle fell upon his throat and hindered him from speaking. He did not quite sob out, and he determined that he would not do so. If she could be so harsh and strong, he would be harsh and strong also.

And again Lady Desmond sat silent, still thinking how she had better speak and act. After all she was not so cruel nor so bad as Herbert Fitzgerald thought her. What had the Fitzgeralds done for her that she should sorrow for their sorrows ? She had lived there, in that old ugly barrack, long desolate, full of dreary wretchedness and poverty, and Lady Fitzgerlad in her prosperity had never come to her to soften the hardness of her life. She had come over to Ireland a countess, and a countess she had been, proud enough at first in her little glory—too proud, no doubt ; and proud enough afterwards in her loneliness and poverty ; and there she had lived—alone. Whether the fault had been her own or no, she owed little to the kindness of any one ; for no one had done aught to relieve her bitterness. And then her weak puny child had grown up in the same shade, and was now a lovely woman, gifted with high birth, and that special priceless beauty which high blood so often gives. There was a prize now within the walls of that old barrack—something to be won—something for which a man would strive, and a mother smile that her son might win it. And now Lady Fitzgerald had come to her. She had never complained of this, she said to herself. The bargain between Clara Desmond and Herbert Fitzgerald had been good for both of them, and let it be made and settled as a bargain. Young Herbert Fitzgerald had money and position; her daughter had beauty and high blood. Let it be a bargain. But in all this there was nothing to make her love that rich prosperous family at Castle Richmond. There are those whose nature it is to love new-found friends at a few hours' warning, but the Countess of Desmond was not one of them. The bargain had been made, and her daughter would have been able to perform her part of it. She was still able to give that which she had stipulated to give. But Herbert Fitzgerald was now a bankrupt, and could give nothing! Would it not have been madness to suppose that the bargain should still hold good?

One person and one only had come to her at Desmond Court, whose coming had been a solace to her weariness. Of all those among whom she had lived in cold desolateness for so many years, one only had got near her heart. There had been but one Irish voice that she had cared to hear; and the owner of that voice had loved her child instead of loving her.

And she had borne that wretchedness too, if not well, at least bravely. True she had separated that lover from her daughter; but the circumstances of both had made it right for her, as a mother, to do so. What mother, circumstanced as she had been, would have given her girl to Owen Fitzgerald? So she had banished from the house the only voice that sounded sweetly in her ears, and again she had been alone.

And then, perhaps, thoughts had come to her, when Herbert Fitzgerald was frequent about the place, a rich and thriving wooer, that Owen might come again to Desmond Court, when Clara had gone to Castle Richmond. Years were stealing over her. Ah, yes. She knew that full well. All her youth and the pride of her days she had given up for that countess-ship which she now wore so gloomily—given up for pieces of gold which had turned to stone and slate and dirt within her grasp. Years, alas, were fast stealing over her! But nevertheless she had something to give. Her woman's beauty was not all faded; and she had a heart which was as yet virgin—which had hitherto loved no other man. Might not that suffice to cover a few years, seeing that in return she wanted nothing but love? And so she had thought, lingering over her hopes, while Herbert was there at his wooing.

It may be imagined with what feelings at her heart she had seen and listened to the frantic attempt made by Owen to get back his childish love. But that too she had borne, bravely, if not well. It had not angered her that her child was loved by the only man she had ever loved herself. She had stroked her daughter's hair that day, and kissed her cheek, and bade her be happy with her better, richer lover. And had she not been right in this? Nor had she been angry even with Owen. She could forgive him all, because she loved him. But might there not even yet be a chance for her when Clara should in very truth have gone to Castle Richmond?

But now! How was she to think about all this now? And thinking of these things, how was it possible that she should have heart left to feel for the miseries of Lady Fitzgerald? With all her miseries would not Lady Fitzgerald still be more fortunate than she? Let come what might, Lady Fitzgerald had had a life of prosperity and love. No; she could not think of Lady Fitzgerald, nor of Herbert: she could only think of Owen Fitzgerald, of her daughter, and of herself.

He, Owen, was now the heir to Castle Richmond, and would, as far as she could learn, soon become the actual possessor. He, who had been cast forth from Desmond Court as too poor and contemptible in the world's eye to be her daughter's suitor, would become the rich inheritor of all those broad acres, and that old coveted family honour. And this Owen still loved her daughter—loved her not as Herbert did, with a quiet, gentleman-like, every-day attachment, but with the old, true, passionate love of which she had read in books, and dreamed herself, before she had sold herself to be a countess. That Owen did so love her daughter, she was very sure. And then, as to her daughter; that she did not still love this new heir in her heart of hearts—of that the mother was by no means sure. That her child had chosen the better part in choosing money and a title, she had not doubted; and that having so chosen Clara would be happy,—of that also she did not doubt. Clara was young, she would say, and her heart in a few months would follow her hand.

But now! How was she to decide, sitting there with Herbert Fitzgerald before her, gloomy as death, cold, shivering, and muddy, telling of his own disasters with no more courage than a whipped dog? As she looked at him she declared to herself twenty times in half a second that he had not about him a tithe of the manhood of his cousin Owen. Women love a bold front, and a voice that will never own its master to have been beaten in the world's fight. Had Owen came there with such a story, he would have claimed his right boldly to the lady's hand, in spite of all that the world had done to him.

'Let her have him,' said Lady Desmond to herself; and the struggle within her bosom was made and over. No wonder that Herbert, looking into her face for pity, should find that she was harsh and cruel. She had been sacrificing herself, and had completed the sacrifice. Owen Fitzgerald, the heir to Castle Richmond, Sir Owen as he would soon be, should have her daughter. They two, at any rate, should be happy. And she—she would live there at Desmond Court, lonely as she had ever lived. While all this was passing through her mind, she hardly thought of Herbert and his sorrows. That he must be given up and abandoned, and left to make what best fight he could by himself; as to that how was it possible that she as a mother should have any doubt?

And yet it was a pity—a thousand pities. Herbert Fitzgerald, with his domestic virtues, his industry and thorough respectability, would so exactly have suited Clara's taste and mode of life—had he only continued to be the heir of Castle Richmond. She and Owen would not enter upon the world together with nearly the same fair chance of happiness. Who could prophesy to what Owen might be led with his passionate impulses, his strong will, his unbridled temper, and his love of pleasure? That he was noble-hearted, affectionate, brave, and tender in his inmost spirit, Lady Desmond was very sure; but were such the qualities which would make her daughter happy? When Clara should come to know her future lord as Clara's mother knew him, would Clara love him and worship him as her mother did? The mother believed that Clara had not in her bosom heart enough for such a love. But then, as I have said before, the mother did not know the daughter.

'You say that you will break all this to Clara,' said Herbert, having during this silence turned over some of his thoughts also in his mind. 'If so I may as well leave you now. You can imagine that I am anxious to get back to my mother.'

'Yes, it will be better that I should tell her. It is very sad, very sad, very sad indeed.'

'Yes; it is a hard load for a man to bear,' he answered, speaking very, very slowly. 'But for myself I think I can bear it, if—'

'If what?' asked the countess.

'If Clara can bear it.'

And now it was necessary that Lady Desmond should speak out. She did not mean to be unnecessarily harsh; but she did mean to be decided, and as she spoke her face became stern and ill-favoured. 'That Clara will be terribly distressed,' she said, 'terribly, terribly distressed,' repeating her words with great emphasis, 'of that I am quite sure. She is very young, and will, I hope, in time get over it. And then too I think she is one whose feelings, young as she is, have never conquered her judgment. Therefore I do believe that, with God's mercy, she will be able to bear it. But, Mr. Fitzgerald—'

'Well?'

'Of course you feel with me—and I am sure that with your excellent judgment it is a thing of course—that everything must be over between you and Lady Clara.' And then she came to a full stop as though all had been said that could be considered necessary.

Herbert did not answer at once, but stood there shivering and shaking in his misery. He was all but overcome by the chill of his wet garments; and though he struggled to throw off the dead feeling of utter cold which struck him to the heart, he was quite unable to master it. He could hardly forgive himself that on such an occasion he should have been so conquered by his own outer feelings, but now he could not help himself. He was weak with hunger too—though he did not know it, for he had hardly eaten food that day, and was nearly exhausted with the unaccustomed amount of hard exercise which he had taken. He was moreover thoroughly wet through, and heavy laden with the mud of the road. It was no wonder that Lady Desmond had said to herself that he looked like a whipped dog.

'That must be as Lady Clara shall decide,' he said at last, barely uttering the words through his chattering teeth.

'It must be as I say,' said the countess, firmly; 'whether by her decision or by yours—or if necessary by mine. But if your feelings are, as I take them to be, those of a man of honour, you will not leave it to me or to her. What! now that you have the world to struggle with, would you seek to drag her down into the struggle?'

'Our union was to be for better or worse. I would have given her all the better, and—'

'Yes; and had there been a union she would have bravely borne her part in sharing the worst. But who ought to be so thankful as you that this truth has broken upon you before you had clogged yourself with a wife of high birth but without fortune? Alone, a man educated as you are, with your talents, may face the world without fearing anything. But how could you make your way now if my daughter were your wife? When you think of it, Mr. Fitzgerald, you will cease to wish for it.'

'Never; I have given my heart to your daughter and I cannot take back the gift. She has accepted it, and she cannot return it.'

'And what would you have her do?' Lady Desmond asked, with anger and almost passion in her voice.

'Wait—as I must wait,' said Herbert. 'That will be her duty, as I believe it will also be her wish.'

'Yes, and wear out her young heart here in solitude for the next ten years, and then learn, when her beauty and her youth are gone—. But no, Mr. Fitzgerald; I will not allow myself to contemplate such a prospect either for her or for you. Under the lamentable circumstances which you have now told me it is imperative that this match should be broken off. Ask your own mother and hear what she will say. And if you are a man you will not throw upon my poor child the hard task of declaring that it must be so. You, by your calamity, are unable to perform your contract with her; and it is for you to announce that that contract is therefore over.'

Herbert in his present state was unable to argue with Lady Desmond. He had in his brain, and mind, and heart, and soul —at least so he said to himself afterwards, having perhaps but a loose idea of the different functions of these four different properties—a thorough conviction that as he and Clara had sworn to each other that for life they would live together and love each other, no misfortune to either of them could justify the other in breaking that oath;—could even justify him in breaking it, though he was the one on whom misfortune had fallen. He, no doubt, had first loved Clara for her beauty; but would he have ceased to love her, or have cast her from him, if, by God's will, her beauty had perished and gone from her? Would he not have held her closer to his heart, and told her, with strong comforting vows, that his love had now gone deeper than that ; that they were already of the same bone, of the same flesh, of the same family and hearthstone? He knew himself in this, and knew that he would have been proud so to do, and so to feel,— that he would have cast from him with utter indignation any who would have counselled him to do or to feel differently. And why should Clara's heart be different from his?

All this, I say, was his strong conviction. But, nevertheless, her heart might be different. She might look on that engagement of theirs with altogether other thoughts and other ideas ; and if so his voice should never reproach her ;—not his voice, however his heart might do so. Such might be the case with her, but he did not think it ; and therefore he would not pronounce that decision which Clara's mother expected from him.

'When you have told her of this, I suppose I may be allowed to see her,' he said, avoiding the direct proposition which Lady Desmond had made to him.

'Allowed to see her?' said Lady Desmond, now also in her turn speaking very slowly. 'I cannot answer that question as yet; not quite immediately, I should say. But if you will leave the matter in my hands, I will write to you, if not to-morrow, then the next day.'

'I would sooner that she should write.'

'I cannot promise that—I do not know how far her good sense and strength may support her under this affliction. That she will suffer terribly, on your account as well as on her own, you may be quite sure.' And then, again, there was a pause of some moments.

'I at any rate shall write to her,' he then said, 'and shall tell her that I expect her to see me. Her will in this matter shall be my will. If she thinks that her misery will be greater in being engaged to a poor man, than,—than in relinquishing her love, she shall hear no word from me to overpersuade her. But, Lady Desmond, I will say nothing that shall authorize her to think that she is given up by me, till I have in some way learned from herself what her own feelings are. And now I will say good-bye to you.'

'Good-bye,' said the countess, thinking that it might be as well that the interview should be ended. 'But, Mr. Fitzgerald, you are very wet; and I fear that you are very cold. You had better take something before you go.' Countess as she was she had no carriage in which she could send him home; no horse even on which he could ride. 'Nothing, thank you, Lady Desmond,' he said; and so, without offering her the courtesy of his hand, he walked out of the room.

He was very angry with her, as he tried to make the blood run quicker in his veins by hurrying down the avenue into the road at his quickest pace. So angry with her, that for a while, in his indignation, he almost forgot his father and his mother and his own family tragedy. That she should have wished to save her daughter from such a marriage might have been natural; but that she should have treated him so coldly, so harshly—without one spark of love or pity,—him, who to her had been so loyal during his courtship of her daughter! It was almost incredible to him. Was not his story one that would have melted the heart of a stranger—at which men would weep? He himself had seen tears in the eyes of that dry time-worn world-used London lawyer, as the full depth of the calamity had forced itself upon his heart. Yes, Mr. Prendergast had not been able to repress his tears when he told the tale ; but Lady Desmond had shed no tears when the tale had been told to her. No soft woman's message had been sent to the afflicted mother on whom it had pleased God to allow so heavy a hand to fall. No word of tenderness had been uttered for the sinking father. There had been no feeling for the household which was to have been so nearly linked with her own. No. Looking round with greedy eyes for wealth for her daughter, Lady Desmond had found a match that suited her. Now that match no longer suited her greed, and she could throw from her without a struggle to her feelings the suitor that was now poor, and the family of the suitor that was now neither grand nor powerful.

And then too he felt angry with Clara, though he knew that as yet, at any rate, he had no cause. In spite of what he had said and felt, he would imagine to himself that she also would be cold and untrue. ' Let her go,' he said to himself. ' Love is worth nothing—nothing if it does not believe itself to be of more worth than everything beside. If she does not love me now in my misery—if she would not choose me now for her husband—her love has never been worthy the name. Love that has no faith in itself, that does not value itself above all worldly things, is nothing. If it be not so with her, let her go back to him.'

It may easily be understood who was the him. And then Herbert walked on so rapidly that at length his strength almost failed him, and in his exhaustion he had more than once to lean against a gate on the road-side. With difficulty at last he got home, and dragged himself up the long avenue to the front door. Even yet he was not warm through to his heart, and he felt as he entered the house that he was quite unfitted for the work which he might yet have to do before he could go to his bed.

CHAPTER XXVII.

COMFORTED.

WHEN Herbert Fitzgerald got back to Castle Richmond it was nearly dark. He opened the hall door without ringing the bell, and walking at once into the dining-room, threw himself into a large leathern chair which always stood near the fire-place. There was a bright fire burning on the hearth, and he drew himself close to it, putting his wet feet up on to the fender, thinking that he would at any rate warm himself before he went in among any of the family. The room, with its deep red curtains and ruby-embossed paper, was almost dark, and he knew that he might remain there unseen and unnoticed for the next half hour. If he could only get a glass of wine! He tried the cellaret, which was as often open as locked, but now unfortunately it was closed. In such a case it was impossible to say whether the butler had the key or Aunt Letty; so he sat himself down without that luxury.

By this time, as he well knew, all would have been told to his mother, and his first duty would be to go to her—to go to her and comfort her, if comfort might be possible, by telling her that he could bear it all; that as far as he was concerned title and wealth and a proud name were as nothing to him in comparison with his mother's love. In whatever guise he may have appeared before Lady Desmond, he would not go to his mother with a fainting heart. She should not hear his teeth chatter, nor see his limbs shake. So he sat himself down there that he might become warm, and in five minutes he was fast asleep.

How long he slept he did not know; not very long, probably; but when he awoke it was quite dark. He gazed at the fire for a moment, bethought himself of where he was and why, shook himself to get rid of his slumber, and then roused himself in his chair. As he did so a soft sweet voice close to his shoulder spoke to him. 'Herbert,' it said, 'are you awake?' And he found that his mother, seated by his side on a low stool, had been watching him in his sleep.

'Mother!' he exclaimed.

'Herbert, my child, my son!' And the mother and son were fast locked in each other's arms.

He had sat down there thinking how he would go to his mother and offer her solace in her sorrow; how he would bid her be of good cheer, and encourage her to bear the world as the world had now fallen to her lot. He had pictured to himself that he would find her sinking in despair, and had promised himself that with his vows, his kisses, and his prayers, he would bring her back to her self-confidence, and induce her to acknowledge that God's mercy was yet good to her. But now, on awakening, he discovered that she had been tending him in his misery, and watching him while he slept, that she might comfort him with her caresses the moment that he awoke to the remembrance of his misfortunes.

'Herbert, Herbert, my son, my son!' she said again, as she pressed him close in her arms.

Mother, has he told you?'

Yes, she had learned it all; but hardly more than she had known before; or, at any rate, not more than she had expected.

As she now told him, for many days past she had felt that this trouble which had fallen upon his father must have come from the circumstances of their marriage. And she would have spoken out, she said, when the idea became clear to her, had she not then been told that Mr. Prendergast had been invited to come thither from London. Then she knew that she had better remain silent, at any rate till his visit had been made.

And Herbert again sat in the chair, and his mother crouched, or almost kneeled, on the cushion at his knee. 'Dearest, dearest, dearest mother,' he said, as he supported her head against his shoulder, 'we must love each other now more than ever we have loved.'

'And you forgive us, Herbert, for all that we have done to you?'

'Mother, if you speak in that way to me you will kill me. My darling, darling mother!'

There was but little more said between them upon the matter —but little more, at least, in words; but there was an infinity of caresses, and deep—deep assurances of undying love and confidence. And then she asked him about his bride, and he told her where he had been, and what had happened. 'You must not claim her, Herbert,' she said to him. 'God is good, and will teach you to bear even that also.'

'Must I not?' he asked, with a sadly plaintive voice.

'No, my child. You invited her to share your prosperity, and would it be just—'

'But, mother, if she wills it?'

'It is for you to give her back her troth, then leave it to time and her own heart.'

'But if she love me, mother, she will not take back her troth. Would I take back hers because she was in sorrow?'

'Men and women, Herbert, are different. The oak cares not whether the creeper which hangs to it be weak or strong. If it be weak the oak can give it strength. But the staff which has to support the creeper must needs have strength of its own.'

He made no further answer to her, but understood that he must do as she bade him. He understood now also, without many arguments within himself, that he had no right to expect from Clara Desmond that adherence to him and his misfortunes which he would have owed to her had she been unfortunate. He understood this now; but still he hoped. 'Two hearts that have once become as one cannot be separated,' he said to himself that night, as he resolved that it was his duty to write to her, unconditionally returning to her her pledges.

'But, Herbert, what a state you are in!' said Lady Fitzgerald,

as the flame of the coal glimmering out, threw a faint light upon
his clothes.

'Yes, mother; I have been walking.'

'And you are wet !'

'I am nearly dry now. I was wet. But, mother, I am tired
and fagged. It would do me good if I could get a glass of wine.'

She rang the bell, and gave her orders calmly—though every
servant in the house now knew the whole truth,—and then lit a
candle herself, and looked at him. 'My child, what have you
done to yourself? Oh, Herbert, you will be ill !' And then,
with his arm round her waist, she took him up to her own room,
and sat by him while he took off his muddy boots and clammy
socks, and made him hot drinks, and tended him as she had done
when he was a child. And yet she had that day heard of her
great ruin! With truth, indeed, had Mr. Prendergast said that
she was made of more enduring material than Sir Thomas.

And she endeavoured to persuade him to go to his bed; but
in this he would not listen to her. He must, he said, see his
father that night. You have been with him, mother, since—
since—.'

'Oh, yes; directly after Mr. Prendergast left me.'

'Well?'

'He cried like a child, Herbert. We both sobbed together
like two children. It was very piteous. But I think I left him
better than he has been. He knows now that those men cannot
come again to harass him.'

Herbert gnashed his teeth, and clenched his fist as he thought
of them; but he could not speak of them, or mention their name
before his mother. What must her thoughts be, as she remembered that elder man and looked back to her early childhood!

'He is very weak,' she went on to say: 'almost helplessly
weak now, and does not seem to think of leaving his bed. I
have begged him to let me send to Dublin for Sir Henry; but he
says that nothing ails him.'

'And who is with him now, mother?'

'The girls are both there.'

'And Mr. Prendergast?'

Lady Fitzgerald then explained to him, that Mr. Prendergast
had returned to Dublin that afternoon, starting twenty-four
hours earlier than he intended,—or, at any rate, than he had said
that he intended. Having done his work there, he had felt that
he would now only be in the way. And, moreover, though his
work was done at Castle Richmond, other work in the same
matter had still to be done in England. Mr. Prendergast had

very little doubt as to the truth of Mollett's story;—indeed we may say he had no doubt; otherwise he would hardly have made it known to all that world round Castle Richmond. But nevertheless it behoved him thoroughly to sift the matter. He felt tolerably sure that he should find Mollett in London; and whether he did or no, he should be able to identify, or not to identify, that scoundrel with the Mr. Talbot who had hired Chevy Chase Lodge, in Dorsetshire, and who had undoubtedly married poor Mary Wainwright.

'He left a kind message for you,' said Lady Fitzgerald.—My readers must excuse me if I still call her Lady Fitzgerald, for I cannot bring my pen to the use of any other name. And it was so also with the dependents and neighbours of Castle Richmond when the time came that the poor lady felt that she was bound publicly to drop her title. It was not in her power to drop it; no effort that she could make would induce those around her to call her by another name.

'He bade me say,' she continued, 'that if your future course of life should take you to London, you are to go to him, and look to him as another father. He has no child of his own,' he said, 'and you shall be to him as a son.'

'I will be no one's son but yours,—yours and my father's,' he said, again embracing her.

And then, when, under his mother's eye, he had eaten and drunk and made himself warm, he did go to his father and found both his sisters sitting there. They came and clustered round him, taking hold of his hands and looking up into his face, loving him, and pitying him, and caressing him with their eyes; but standing there by their father's bed, they said little or nothing. Nor did Sir Thomas say much;—except this, indeed, that, just as Herbert was leaving him, he declared with a faint voice that henceforth his son should be master of that house, and the disposer of that property—'As long as I live!' he exclaimed with his weak voice; 'as long as I live!'

'No, father; not so.'

'Yes, yes! as long as I live. It will be little that you will have, even so—very little. But so it shall be as long as I live.'

Very little indeed, poor man, for, alas! his days were numbered.

And then, when Herbert left the room, Emmeline followed him. She had ever been his dearest sister, and now she longed to be with him that she might tell him how she loved him, and comfort him with her tears. And Clara too—Clara whom she had ever welcomed as a sister!—she must learn now how Clara would behave, for she had already made herself sure that her brother had been at Desmond Court, the herald of his own ruin.

'May I come with you, Herbert?' she asked, closing in round him and getting under his arm. How could he refuse her? So they went together and sat over a fire in a small room that was sacred to her and her sister, and there, with many sobs on her part and much would-be brave contempt of poverty on his, they talked over the altered world as it now showed itself before them.

'And you did not see her?' she asked, when with many efforts she had brought the subject round to Clara Desmond and her brother's walk to Desmond Court.

No; she left the room at my own bidding. I could not have told it myself to her.'

'And you cannot know then what she would say?'

'No, I cannot know what she would say; but I know now what I must say myself. All that is over, Emmeline. I cannot ask her to marry a beggar.'

'Ask her; no! there will be no need of asking her; she has already given you her promise. You do not think that she will desert you? you do not wish it?'

Herein were contained two distinct questions, the latter of which Herbert did not care to answer. 'I shall not call it desertion,' he said; 'indeed the proposal will come from me. I shall write to her, telling her that she need think about me no longer. Only that I am so weary I would do it now.'

'And how will she answer you? If she is the Clara that I take her for she will throw your proposal back into your face. She will tell you that it is not in your power to reject her now. She will swear to you, that let your words be what they may, she will think of you—more now than she has ever thought in better days. She will tell you of her love in words that she could not use before. I know she will. I know that she is good, and true, and honest, and generous. Oh, I should die if I thought she were false! But, Herbert, I am sure that she is true. You can write your letter, and we shall see.'

Herbert, with wise arguments learned from his mother, reasoned with his sister, explaining to her that Clara was now by no means bound to cling to him; but as he spoke them his arm fastened itself closely round his sister's waist, for the words which she uttered with so much energy were comfortable to him.

And then, seated there, before he moved from the room, he made her bring him pens, ink, and paper, and he wrote his letter to Clara Desmond. She would fain have stayed with him while he did so, sitting at his feet, and looking into his face, and trying to encourage his hope as to what Clara's answer might be; but this he would not allow; so she went again to her father's room, having succeeded in obtaining a promise that Clara's answer should be shown to her. And the letter, when it was written, copied, and recopied, ran as follows :—

'Castle Richmond, —— night.

'My dearest Clara,'——It was with great difficulty that he could satisfy himself with that, or indeed with any other mode of commencement. In the short little love-notes which had hitherto gone from him, sent from house to house, he had written to her with appellations of endearment of his own—as all lovers do; and as all lovers seem to think that no lovers have done before themselves—with appellations which are so sweet to those who write, and so musical to those who read, but which sound so ludicrous when barbarously made public in hideous law courts by brazen-browed lawyers with mercenary tongues. In this way only had he written, and each of these sweet silly songs of love had been as full of honey as words could make it. But he had never yet written to her, on a full sheet of paper, a sensible positive letter containing thoughts and facts, as men do write to women and women also to men, when the lollypops and candied sugar-drops of early love have passed away. Now he was to write his first serious letter to her,—and probably his last,—and it was with difficulty that he could get himself over the first three words; but there they were decided on at last.

'My dearest Clara,

'Before you get this your mother will have told you all that which I could not bring myself to speak out yesterday, as long as you were in the room. I am sure you will understand now why I begged you to go away, and will not think the worse of me for doing so. You now know the whole truth, and I am sure that you will feel for us all here.

'Having thought a good deal upon the matter, chiefly during my walk home from Desmond Court, and indeed since I have been at home, I have come to the resolution that everything between us must be over. It would be unmanly in me to wish to ruin you because I myself am ruined. Our engagement was, of course, made on the presumption that I should inherit my father's estate; as it is I shall not do so, and therefore I beg that you will regard that engagement as at an end. Of my own love for you I will say nothing. But I know that you have loved me truly, and that all this, therefore, will cause you great grief. It is better, however, that it should be so, than that I should seek to hold you to a promise which was made under such different circumstances.

'You will, of course, show this letter to your mother. She, at any rate, will approve of what I am now doing; and so will you when you allow yourself to consider it calmly.

'We have not known each other so long that there is much for us to give back to each other. If you do not think it wrong I should like still to keep that lock of your hair, to remind me of my first love—and, as I think, my only one. And you, I hope, will not be afraid to have near you the one little present that I made you.

'And now, dearest Clara, good-bye. Let us always think, each of the other, as of a very dear friend. May God bless you, and preserve you, and make you happy.

'Yours, with sincere affection,

'HERBERT FITZGERALD.'

This, when at last he had succeeded in writing it, he read over and over again; but on each occasion he said to himself that it was cold and passionless, stilted and unmeaning. It by no means pleased him, and seemed as though it could bring but one answer—a cold acquiescence in the proposal which he so coldly made. But yet he knew not how to improve it. And after all it was a true exposition of that which he had determined to say. All the world—her world and his world—would think it better that they should part; and let the struggle cost him what it would, he would teach himself to wish that it might be so—if not for his own sake, then for hers. So he fastened the letter, and taking it with him determined to send it over, so that it should reach Clara quite early on the following morning.

'And then having once more visited his father, and once more kissed his mother, he betook himself to bed. It had been with him one of those days which seem to pass away without reference to usual hours and periods. It had been long dark, and he seemed to have been hanging about the house, doing nothing and aiding nobody, till he was weary of himself. So he went off to bed, almost wondering, as he bethought himself of what had happened to him within the last two days, that he was able to bear the burden of his life so easily as he did. He betook himself to bed; and with the letter close at his hand, so that he might despatch it when he awoke, he was soon asleep. After all, that walk, terrible as it had been, was in the end serviceable to him.

He slept without waking till the light of the February morning was begining to dawn into his room, and then he was roused by a servant knocking at the door. It was grievous enough, that awaking to his sorrow after the pleasant dreams of the night.

'Here is a letter, Mr. Herbert, from Desmond Court,' said Richard. 'The boy as brought it says as how—'

'A letter from Desmond Court,' said Herbert, putting out his hand greedily.

'Yes, Mr. Herbert. The boy's been here this hour and better. I warn't just up and about myself, or I wouldn't have let 'em keep it from you, not half a minute.'

'And where is he? I have a letter to send to Desmond Court. But never mind. Perhaps—'

'It's no good minding, for the gossoon's gone back any ways.' And then Richard, having drawn the blind, and placed a little table by the bed-head, left his young master to read the despatch from Desmond Court. Herbert, till he saw the writing, feared that it was from the countess; but the letter was from Clara. She also had thought good to write before she betook herself to bed, and she had been earlier in despatching her messenger. Here is her letter:

'Dear Herbert, my own Herbert,

'I have heard it all. But remember this; nothing, nothing, *nothing* can make any change between you and me. I will hear of no arguments that are to separate us. I know beforehand what you will say, but I will not regard it—not in the least. I love you ten times the more for all your unhappiness; and as I would have shared your good fortune, I claim my right to share your bad fortune. *Pray believe me*, that nothing shall turn me from this; for I will *not be given up*.

'Give my kindest love to your dear, dear, dearest mother— my mother, as she is and must be; and to my darling girls. I do so wish I could be with them, and with you, my own Herbert. I cannot help writing in confusion, but I will explain all when I see you. I have been so unhappy.

'Your own faithful
'CLARA.'

Having read this, Herbert Fitzgerald, in spite of his affliction, was comforted.

CHAPTER XXVIII.

FOR A' THAT AND A' THAT.

HERBERT as he started from his bed with this letter in his hand felt that he could yet hold up his head against all that the world could do to him. How could he be really unhappy while he possessed such an assurance of love as this, and while his mother

was able to give him so glorious an example of endurance? He
was not really unhappy. The low-spirited broken-hearted
wretchedness of the preceding day seemed to have departed
from him as he hurried on his clothes, and went off to his sister's
room that he might show his letter to Emmeline in accordance
with the promise he had made her.

'May I come in?' he said, knocking at the door. 'I must
come in, for I have something to show you.' But the two girls
were dressing and he could not be admitted. Emmeline, however, promised to come to him, and in about three minutes she
was out in the cold little sitting-room which adjoined their bedroom, with her slippers on, and her dressing-gown wrapped round
her, an object presentable to no male eyes but those of her
brother.

'Emmeline,' said he, 'I have got a letter this morning.'

'Not from Clara?'

'Yes, from Clara. There; you may read it;' and he handed
her the precious epistle.

'But she could not have got your letter,' said Emmeline,
before she looked at the one in her hand.

'Certainly not, for I have it here. I must write another now;
but in truth I do not know what to say. I can be as generous
as she is.'

And then his sister read the letter. 'My own Clara!' she
exclaimed, as she saw what was the tenor of it. 'Did I not tell
you so, Herbert? I knew well what she would do and say.
Love you ten times better!—of course she does. What honest
girl would not? My own beautiful Clara, I knew I could
depend on her. I did not doubt her for one moment.' But in
this particular it must be acknowledged that Miss Emmeline
Fitzgerald hardly confined herself to the strictest veracity, for
she had lain awake half the night perplexed with doubt. What,
oh what, if Clara should be untrue! Such had been the burden
of her doubting midnight thoughts. '"I will not be given up,"'
she continued, quoting the letter. 'No; of course not. And I
tell you what, Herbert, you must not dare to talk of giving her
up. Money and titles may be tossed to and fro, but not hearts.
How beautifully she speaks of dear mamma!' and now the tears
began to run down the young lady's cheeks. 'Oh, I do wish she
could be with us! My darling, darling, darling Clara! Unhappy? Yes: I am sure Lady Desmond will give her no peace.
But never mind. She will be true through it all; and I said so
from the first.' And then she fell to crying, and embracing her
brother, and declaring that nothing now should make her altogether unhappy.

'But, Emmeline, you must not think that I shall take her at her word. It is very generous of her—'

'Nonsense, Herbert!' And then there was another torrent of eloquence, in answering which Herbert found that his arguments were of very little efficacy.

And now we must go back to Desmond Court, and see under what all but overwhelming difficulties poor Clara wrote her affectionate letter. And in the first place it should be pointed out how very wrong Herbert had been in going to Desmond Court on foot, through the mud and rain. A man can hardly bear himself nobly unless his outer aspect be in some degree noble. It may be very sad, this having to admit that the tailor does in great part make the man; but such, I fear, is undoubtedly the fact. Could the Chancellor look dignified on the woolsack, if he had had an accident with his wig, or allowed his robes to be torn or soiled? Does not half the piety of a bishop reside in his lawn sleeves, and all his meekness in his anti-virile apron? Had Herbert understood the world he would have had out the best pair of horses standing in the Castle Richmond stables, when going to Desmond Court on such an errand. He would have brushed his hair, and anointed himself; he would have clothed himself in his rich Spanish cloak; he would have seen that his hat was brushed, and his boots spotless; and then with all due solemnity, but with head erect, he would have told his tale out boldly. The countess would still have wished to be rid of him hearing that he was a pauper; but she would have lacked the courage to turn him from the house as she had done.

But seeing how wobegone he was and wretched, how mean to look at, and low in his outward presence, she had been able to assume the mastery, and had kept it throughout the interview. And having done this her opinion of his prowess naturally became low, and she felt that he would have been unable to press his cause against her.

For some time after he had departed, she sat alone in the room in which she had received him. She expected every minute that Clara would come down to her, still wishing however that she might be left for a while alone. But Clara did not come, and she was able to pursue her thoughts.

How very terrible was this tragedy that had fallen out in her close neighbourhood! That was the first thought that came to her now that Herbert had left her. How terrible, overwhelming, and fatal! What calamity could fall upon a woman so calamitous as this which had now overtaken that poor lady at Castle Richmond? Could she live and support such a burden? Could she bear the eyes of people, when she knew the light in which she must be now regarded? To lose at one blow, her name, her pride of place, her woman's rank and high respect! Could it be possible that she would still live on? It was thus that Lady Desmond thought; and had any one told her that this degraded mother would that very day come down from her room, and sit watchful by her sleeping son, in order that she might comfort and encourage him when he awoke, she would not have found it in her heart to believe such a marvel. But then Lady Desmond knew but one solace in her sorrows—had but one comfort in her sad reflections. She was Countess of Desmond, and that was all. To Lady Fitzgerald had been vouchsafed other solace and other comforts.

And then, on one point the countess made herself fixed as fate, by thinking and re-thinking upon it till no doubt remained upon her mind. The match between Clara and Herbert must be broken off, let the cost be what it might; and—a point on which there was more room for doubt, and more pain in coming to a conclusion—that other match with the more fortunate cousin must be encouraged and carried out. For herself, if her hope was small while Owen was needy and of poor account, what hope could there be now that he would be rich and great? Moreover, Owen loved Clara, and not herself; and Clara's hand would once more be vacant and ready for the winning. For herself, her only chance had been in Clara's coming marriage.

In all this she knew that there would be difficulty. She was sure enough that Clara would at first feel the imprudent gene-rosity of youth and offer to join her poverty to Herbert's poverty. That was a matter of course. She, Lady Desmond herself, would have done this, at Clara's age,—so at least to herself she said, and also to her daughter. But a little time, and a little patience, and a little care would set all this in a proper light. Herbert would go away and would gradually be forgotten. Owen would again come forth from beneath the clouds, with renewed splendour; and then, was it not probable that, in her very heart of hearts, Owen was the man whom Clara had ever loved?

And thus having realized to herself the facts which Herbert had told her, she prepared to make them known to her daughter. She got up from her chair, intending at first to seek her, and then, changing her purpose, rang the bell and sent for her. She was astonished to find how violently she herself was affected; not so much by the circumstances, as by this duty which had fallen to her of telling them to her child. She put one hand upon the other and felt that she herself was in a tremor, and was conscious that the blood was running quick round her heart. Clara came down, and going to her customary seat waited till her mother should speak to her.

'Mr. Fitzgerald has brought very dreadful news,' Lady Desmond said, after a minute's pause.

'Oh mamma!' said Clara. She had expected bad tidings, having thought of all manner of miseries while she had been up stairs alone; but there was that in her mother's voice which seemed to be worse than the worst of her anticipations.

'Dreadful, indeed, my child! It is my duty to tell them to you; but I must caution you, before I do so, to place a guard upon your feelings. That which I have to say must necessarily alter all your future prospects, and, unfortunately, make your marrying Herbert Fitzgerald quite impossible.'

'Mamma!' she exclaimed, with a loud voice, jumping from her chair. 'Not marry him! Why; what can he have done? Is it his wish to break it off?'

Lady Desmond had calculated that she would best effect her object by at once impressing her daughter with the idea that, under the circumstances which were about to be narrated, this marriage would not only be imprudent, but altogether impracticable and out of the question. Clara must be made to understand at once, that the circumstances gave her no option,—that the affair was of such a nature as to make it a thing manifest to everybody, that she could not now marry Herbert Fitzgerald. She must not be left to think whether she could, or whether she could not, exercise her own generosity. And therefore, not without discretion, the countess announced at once to her the conclusion at which it would be necessary to arrive. But Clara was not a girl to adopt such a conclusion on any other judgment than her own, or to be led in such a matter by the feelings of any other person.

'Sit down, my dear, and I will explain it all. But, dearest Clara, grieved as I must be to grieve you, I am bound to tell you again that it must be as I say. For both your sakes it must be so; but especially, perhaps, for his. But when I have told you my story, you will understand that this must be so.'

'Tell me, then, mother.' She said this, for Lady Desmond had again paused.

'Won't you sit down, dearest?'

'Well, yes; it does not matter;' and Clara, at her mother's bidding, sat down, and then the story was told to her.

It was a difficult tale for a mother to tell to so young a child— to a child whom she had regarded as being so very young. There were various little points of law which she thought that she was obliged to explain; how it was necessary that the Castle Richmond property should go to an heir-at-law, and how it was impossible that Herbert should be that heir-at-law, seeing that he had not been born in lawful wedlock. All these things Lady Desmond attempted to explain, or was about to attempt such explanation, but desisted on finding that her daughter understood them as well as she herself did. And then she had to make it also intelligible to Clara that Owen would be called on, when Sir Thomas should die, to fill the position and enjoy the wealth accruing to the heir of Castle Richmond. When Owen Fitzgerald's name was mentioned a slight blush came upon Clara's cheek; it was very slight, but nevertheless her mother saw it, and took advantage of it to say a word in Owen's favour.

'Poor Owen!' she said. 'He will not be the first to triumph in this change of fortune.'

'I am sure he will not,' said Clara. 'He is much too generous for that.' And then the countess began to hope that the task might not be so very difficult. Ignorant woman! Had she been able to read one page in her daughter's heart, she would have known that the task was impossible. After that the story was told out to the end without further interruption ; and then Clara, hiding her face within her hands on the head of the sofa, uttered one long piteous moan.

'It is all very dreadful,' said the countess.

'Oh, Lady Fitzgerald, dear Lady Fitzgerald!' sobbed forth Clara.

'Yes, indeed. Poor Lady Fitzgerald! Her fate is so dreadful that I know not how to think of it.'

'But, mamma—' and as she spoke Clara pushed back from her forehead her hair with both her hands, showing, as she did so, the form of her forehead, and the firmness of purpose that was written there, legible to any eyes that could read. 'But, mamma, you are wrong about my not marrying Herbert Fitzgerald. Why should I not marry him ? Not now, as we, perhaps, might have done but for this; but at some future time when he may think himself able to support a wife. Mamma, I shall not break our engagement; certainly not.'

This was said in a tone of voice so very decided that Lady Desmond had to acknowledge to herself that there would be difficulty in her task. But she still did not doubt that she would have her way, if not by concession on the part of her daughter, then by concession on the part of Herbert Fitzgerald. 'I can understand your generosity of feeling, my dear,' she said ; 'and at your age I should probably have felt the same. And therefore I do not ask you to take any steps towards breaking your engagement. The offer must come from Mr. Fitzgerald, and I have no doubt that it will come. He, as a man of honour, will know that he cannot now offer to marry you; and he will also know, as a man of sense, that it would be ruin for him to think of—of such a marriage under his present circumstances.'

'Why, mamma? Why should it be ruin to him?'

'Why, my dear? Do you think that a wife with a titled name can be of advantage to a young man who has not only got his bread to earn, but even to look out for a way in which he may earn it?'

'If there be nothing to hurt him but the titled name, that difficulty shall be easily conquered.'

'Dearest Clara, you know what I mean. You must be aware that a girl of your rank, and brought up as you have been, cannot be a fitting wife for a man who will now have to struggle with the world at every turn.'

Clara, as this was said to her, and as she prepared to answer, blushed deeply, for she felt herself obliged to speak on a matter which had never yet been subject of speech between her and her mother. 'Mamma,' she said, 'I cannot agree with you there. I may have what the world calls rank; but nevertheless we have been poor, and I have not been brought up with costly habits. Why should I not live with my husband as—as—as poorly as I have lived with my mother? You are not rich, dear mamma, and why should I be?'

Lady Desmond did not answer her daughter at once; but she was not silent because an answer failed her. Her answer would have been ready enough had she dared to speak it out. 'Yes, it is true; we have been poor. I, your mother, did by my imprudence bring down upon my head and on yours absolute, unrelenting, pitiless poverty. And because I did so, I have never known one happy hour. I have spent my days in bitter remorse—in regretting the want of those things which it has been the more terrible to want as they are the customary attributes of people of my rank. I have been driven to hate those around me who have been rich, because I have been poor. I have been utterly friendless because I have been poor. I have been able to do none of those sweet, soft, lovely things, by doing which other women win the smiles of the world, because I have been poor. Poverty and rank together have made me wretched—have left me without employment, without society, and without love. And now would you tell me that because I have been poor you would choose to be poor also?' It would have been thus that she would have answered, had she been accustomed to speak out her thoughts. But she had ever been accustomed to conceal them.

'I was thinking quite as much of him as of you,' at last she said. 'Such an engagement to you would be fraught with much misery, but to him it would be ruinous.'

'I do not think it, mamma.'

'But it is not necessary, Clara, that you should do anything. You will wait, of course, and see what Herbert may say himself.'

'Herbert—'

'Wait half a moment, my love. I shall be very much surprised if we do not find that Mr. Fitzgerald himself will tell you that the match must be abandoned.'

'But that will make no difference, mamma.'

'No difference, my dear! You cannot marry him against his will. You do not mean to say that you would wish to bind him to his engagement, if he himself thought it would be to his disadvantage?'

'Yes; I will bind him to it.'

'Clara!'

'I will make him know that it is not for his disadvantage. I will make him understand that a friend and companion who loves him as I love him—as no one else will ever love him now—for I love him because he was so high-fortuned when he came to me, and because he is now so low-fortuned—that such a wife as I will be, cannot be a burden to him. I will cling to him whether he throws me off or no. A word from him might have broken our engagement before, but a thousand words cannot do it now.'

Lady Desmond stared at her daughter, for Clara, in her excitement, was walking up and down the room. The countess had certainly not expected all this, and she was beginning to think that the subject for the present might as well be left alone. But Clara had not done as yet.

'Mamma,' she said, 'I will not do anything without telling you; but I cannot leave Herbert in all his misery to think that I have no sympathy with him. I shall write to him.'

'Not before he writes to you, Clara! You would not wish to be indelicate?'

'I know but little about delicacy—what people call delicacy; but I will not be ungenerous or unkind. Mamma, you brought us two together. Was it not so? Did you not do so, fearing that I might—might still care for Herbert's cousin? You did it; and half wishing to obey you, half attracted by all his goodness, I did learn to love Herbert Fitzgerald; and I did learn to forget—no; but I learned to cease to love his cousin. You did this and rejoiced at it; and now what you did must remain done.'

'But, dearest Clara, it will not be for his good.'

'It shall be for his good. Mamma, I would not desert him now for all that the world could give me. Neither for mother nor brother could I do that. Without your leave I would not have given him the right to regard me as his own; but now I cannot take that right back again, even at your wish. I must write to him at once, mamma, and tell him this.'

'Clara, at any rate you must not do that; that at least I must forbid.'

'Mother, you cannot forbid it now,' the daughter said, after walking twice the length of the room in silence. 'If I be not allowed to send a letter I shall leave the house and go to him.'

This was all very dreadful. Lady Desmond was astounded at the manner in which her daughter carried herself, and the voice with which she spoke. The form of her face was altered, and the very step with which she trod was unlike her usual gait. What would Lady Desmond do? She was not prepared to confine her daughter as a prisoner, nor could she publicly forbid the people about the place to go upon her message.

'I did not expect that you would have been so undutiful,' she said.

'I hope I am not so,' Clara answered. 'But now my first duty is to him. Did you not sanction our loving each other? People cannot call back their hearts and their pledges.'

'You will at any rate wait till to-morrow, Clara.'

'It is dark now,' said Clara, despondingly, looking out through the window upon the falling night; 'I suppose I cannot send to-night.'

'And you will show me what you write, dearest?'

'No, mamma. If I wrote it for your eyes it could not be the same as if I wrote it only for his.'

Very gloomy, sombre, and silent was the Countess of Desmond all that night. Nothing further was said about the Fitzgeralds between her and her daughter before they went to bed; and then Lady Desmond did speak a few futile words.

'Clara,' she said, 'you had better think over what we have been saying, in bed to-night. You will be more collected to-morrow morning.'

'I shall think of it, of course,' said Clara; 'but thinking can make no difference,' and then just touching her mother's forehead with her lips she went off slowly to her room.

What sort of a letter she wrote when she got there we have already seen; and have seen also that she took effective steps to have her letter carried to Castle Richmond at an hour sufficiently early in the morning. There was no danger that the countess would stop the message, for the letter had been read twenty

times by Emmeline and Mary, and had been carried by Herbert
to his mother's room, before Lady Desmond had left her bed.
'Do not set your heart on it too warmly,' said Herbert's mother
to him.

'But is she not excellent?' said Herbert. 'It is because she
speaks of you in such a way—'

'You would not wish to bring her into misery, because of her
excellence?'

'But, mother, I am still a man,' said Herbert. This was too
much for the suffering woman, the one fault of whose life had
brought her son to such a pass, and throwing her arm round his
neck she wept upon his shoulders.

There were other messengers went and came that day between
Desmond Court and Castle Richmond. Clara and her mother
saw nothing of each other early in the morning; they did not
breakfast together, nor was there a word said between them on
the subject of the Fitzgeralds. But Lady Desmond early in the
morning—early for her that is—sent her note also to Castle
Richmond. It was addressed to Aunt Letty, Miss Letitia Fitzgerald, and went to say that Lady Desmond was very anxious to
see Miss Letty. Under the present circumstances of the family,
as described to Lady Desmond by Mr. Herbert Fitzgerald, she
felt that she could not ask to see ' his mother;'—it was thus that
she overcame the difficulty which presented itself to her as to the
proper title now to be given to Lady Fitzgerald;—but perhaps
Miss Letty would be good enough to see her, if she called at such
and such an hour. Aunt Letty, much perplexed, had nothing
for it, but to say that she would see her. The countess must
now be looked on as closely connected with the family—at any
rate until that match were broken off; and therefore Aunt Letty
had no alternative. And so, precisely at the hour named, the
countess and Aunt Letty were seated together in the little
breakfast-room of which mention has before been made.

No two women were ever closeted together who were more
unlike each other,—except that they had one common strong
love for family rank. But in Aunt Letty it must be acknowledged that this passion was not unwholesome or malevolent in
its course of action. She delighted in being a Fitzgerald, and in
knowing that her branch of the Fitzgeralds had been considerable
people ever since her Norman ancestor had come over to Ireland
with Strongbow. But then she had a useful idea that considerable people should do a considerable deal of good. Her family
pride operated more inwardly than outwardly,—inwardly as
regarded her own family, and not outwardly as regarded the
world. Her brother, and her nephew, and her sister-in-law, and

nieces, were, she thought, among the highest commoners in Ireland; they were gentlefolks of the first water, and walked openly before the world accordingly, proving their claim to gentle blood by gentle deeds and honest conduct. Perhaps she did think too much of the Fitzgeralds of Castle Richmond; but the sin was one of which no recording angel could have made much in his entry. That she was a stupid old woman, prejudiced in the highest degree, and horribly ignorant of all the world beyond her own very narrow circle,—even of that, I do not think that the recording angel could, under the circumstances, have made a great deal.

And now how was her family pride affected by this horrible catastrophe that had been made known to her? Herbert the heir, whom as heir she had almost idolized, was nobody. Her sister-in-law, whom she had learned to love with the whole of her big heart, was no sister-in-law. Her brother was one, who, in lieu of adding glory to the family, would always be regarded as the most unfortunate of the Fitzgerald baronets. But with her, human nature was stronger than family pride, and she loved them all, not better, but more tenderly than ever.

The two ladies were closeted together for about two hours; and then, when the door was opened, Aunt Letty might have been seen with her bonnet much on one side, and her poor old eyes and cheeks red with weeping. The countess, too, held her handkerchief to her eyes as she got back into her pony carriage. She saw no one else there but Aunt Letty; and from her mood when she returned to Desmond Court it might be surmised that from Aunt Letty she had learned little to comfort her.

' They will be beggars!' she said to herself—' beggars!'—when the door of her own room had closed upon her. And there are few people in the world who held such beggary in less esteem than did the Countess of Desmond. It may almost be said that she hated herself on account of her own poverty.

CHAPTER XXIX.

ILL NEWS FLIES FAST.

A DULL, cold, wretched week passed over their heads at Castle Richmond, during which they did nothing but realize the truth of their position; and then came a letter from Mr. Prendergast, addressed to Herbert, in which he stated that such inquiries as he had hitherto made left no doubt on his mind that the man named Mollett, who had lately made repeated visits at Castle

Richmond, was he who had formerly taken the house in Dorset-shire under the name of Talbot. In his packet Mr. Prendergast sent copies of documents and of verbal evidence which he had managed to obtain; but with the actual details of these it is not necessary that I should trouble those who are following me in this story. In this letter Mr. Prendergast also recommended that some intercourse should be had with Owen Fitzgerald. It was expedient, he said, that all the parties concerned should recognise Owen's position as the heir presumptive to the title and estate; and as he, he said, had found Mr. Fitzgerald of Hap House to be forbearing, generous, and high-spirited, he thought that this intercourse might be conducted without enmity or ill blood. And then he suggested that Mr. Somers should see Owen Fitzgerald.

All this Herbert explained to his father gently and without complaint; but it seemed now as though Sir Thomas had ceased to interest himself in the matter. Such battle as it had been in his power to make he had made to save his son's heritage and his wife's name and happiness, even at the expense of his own conscience. That battle had gone altogether against him, and now there was nothing left for him but to turn his face to the wall and die. Absolute ruin, through his fault, had come upon him and all that belonged to him,—ruin that would now be known to the world at large; and it was beyond his power to face that world again. In that the glory was gone from the house of his son, and of his son's mother, the glory was gone from his own house. He made no attempt to leave his bed, though strongly recommended so to do by his own family doctor. And then a physician came down from Dublin, who could only feel, whatever he might say, how impossible it is to administer to a mind diseased. The mind of that poor man was diseased past all curing in this world, and there was nothing left for him but to die.

Herbert, of course, answered Clara's letter, but he did not go over to see her during that week, nor indeed for some little time afterwards. He answered it at considerable length, professing his ready willingness to give back to Clara her troth, and even recommending her, with very strong logic and unanswerable arguments of worldly sense, to regard their union as unwise and even impossible; but nevertheless there protruded through all his sense and all his rhetoric, evidences of love and of a desire for love returned, which were much more unanswerable than his arguments, and much stronger than his logic. Clara read his letter, not as he would have advised her to read it, but certainly in the manner which best pleased his heart, and answered it again, declaring that all that he said was no avail. He might be false to her if he would. If through fickleness of heart and purpose he chose to abandon her, she would never complain—never at least aloud. But she would not be false to him; nor were her inclinations such as to make it likely that she should be fickle, even though her affection might be tried by a delay of years. Love with her had been too serious to be thrown aside. All which was rather strong language on the part of a young lady, but was thought by those other young ladies at Castle Richmond to show the very essence of becoming young-ladyhood. They pronounced Clara to be perfect in feeling and in judgment, and Herbert could not find it in his heart to contradict them.

And of all these doings, writings, and resolves, Clara dutifully told her mother. Poor Lady Desmond was at her wits' end in the matter. She could scold her daughter, but she had no other power of doing anything. Clara had so taken the bit between her teeth that it was no longer possible to check her with any usual rein. In these days young ladies are seldom deprived by force of paper, pen, and ink; and the absolute incarceration of such an offender would be still more unusual. Another countess would have taken her daughter away, either to London and a series of balls, or to the South of Italy, or to the family castle in the North of Scotland; but poor Lady Desmond had not the power of other countesses. Now that it was put to the trial, she found that she had no power, even over her own daughter. 'Mamma, it was your own doing,' Clara would say; and the countess would feel that this alluded not only to her daughter's engagement with Herbert the disinherited, but also to her non-engagement with Owen the heir.

Under these circumstances Lady Desmond sent for her son. The earl was still at Eton, but was now grown to be almost a man—such a man as forward Eton boys are at sixteen—tall, and lathy, and handsome, with soft incipient whiskers, a bold brow and blushing cheeks, with all a boy's love for frolic still strong within him, but some touch of a man's pride to check it. In her difficulty Lady Desmond sent for the young earl, who had now not been home since the previous midsummer, hoping that his young manhood might have some effect in saving his sister from the disgrace of a marriage which would make her so totally bankrupt both in wealth and rank.

Mr. Somers did go once to Hap House, at Herbert's instigation; but very little came of his visit. He had always disliked Owen, regarding him as an unthrift, and close connexion with whom could only bring contamination on the Fitzgerald property; and Owen had returned the feeling tenfold. His pride had been wounded by what he had considered to be the agent's insolence, and he had stigmatised Mr. Somers to his friends as a self-seeking, mercenary prig. Very little, therefore, came of the visit. Mr. Somers, to give him his due, had attempted to do his best; being anxious, for Herbert's sake, to conciliate Owen; perhaps having —and why not?—some eye to the future agency. But Owen was hard, and cold, and uncommunicative,—very unlike what he had before been to Mr. Prendergast. But then Mr. Prendergast had never offended his pride.

'You may tell my cousin Herbert,' he said, with some little special emphasis on the word cousin, 'that I shall be glad to see him, as soon as he feels himself able to meet me. It will be for the good of us both that we should have some conversation together. Will you tell him, Mr. Somers, that I shall be happy to go to him, or to see him here? Perhaps my going to Castle Richmond, during the present illness of Sir Thomas, may be inconvenient.' And this was all that Mr. Somers could get from him.

In a very short time the whole story became known to everybody round the neighbourhood. And what would have been the good of keeping it secret? There are some secrets,—kept as secrets because they cannot well be discussed openly,—which may be allowed to leak out with so much advantage! The day must come, and that apparently at no distant time, when all the world would know the fate of that Fitzgerald family; when Sir Owen must walk into the hall of Castle Richmond, the undoubted owner of the mansion and demesne. Why then keep it secret? Herbert openly declared his wish to Mr. Somers that there should be no secret in the matter. 'There is no disgrace,' he said, thinking of his mother; 'nothing to be ashamed of, let the world say what it will.'

Down in the servants' hall the news came to them gradually, whispered about from one to another. They hardly understood what it meant, or how it had come to pass; but they did know that their master's marriage had been no marriage, and that their master's son was no heir. Mrs. Jones said not a word in the matter to any one. Indeed, since that day on which she had been confronted with Mollett, she had not associated with the servants at all, but had kept herself close to her mistress. She understood what it all meant perfectly; and the depth of the tragedy had so cowed her spirit that she hardly dared to speak of it. Who told the servants;—or who does tell the servants of such matters, it is impossible to say; but before Mr. Prendergast had been three days out of the house they all knew that the Mr. Owen of Hap House was to be the future master of Castle Richmond.

'An' a sore day it'll be; a sore day, a sore day,' said Richard, seated in an arm-chair by the fire, at the end of the servants' hall, shaking his head despondingly.

'Faix, an' you may say that,' said Corney, the footman. 'That Misther Owen will go tatthering away to the divil, when the old place comes into his hans. No fear he'll make it fly.'

'Sorrow seize the ould lawyer for coming down here at all at all,' said the cook.

'I never knew no good come of thim dry ould bachelors,' said Biddy the housemaid; 'specially the Englishers.'

'The two of yez are no better nor simpletons,' said Richard, magisterially. 'Twarn't he that done it. The likes of him couldn't do the likes o' that.'

'And what was it as done it?' said Biddy.

'Ax no questions, and may be you'll be tould no lies,' replied Richard.

'In course we all knows it's along of her ladyship's marriage which warn't no marriage,' said the cook. 'May the heavens be her bed when the Lord takes her! A betther lady nor a kinder-hearted niver stepped the floor of a kitchen.'

''Deed an' that's thrue for you, cook,' said Biddy, with the corner of her apron up to her eyes. 'But tell me, Richard, won't poor Mr. Herbert have nothing?'

'Never you mind about Mr. Herbert,' said Richard, who had seen Biddy grow up from a slip of a girl, and therefore was competent to snub her at every word.

'Ah, but I do mind,' said the girl. 'I minds more about him than ere a one of 'em; and av' that Lady Clara won't have em a cause of this—'

'Not a step she won't, thin,' said Corney. 'She'll go back to Mr. Owen. He was her fust love. You'll see else.' And so the matter was discussed in the servants' hall at the great house.

But perhaps the greatest surprise, the greatest curiosity, and the greatest consternation, were felt at the parsonage. The rumour reached Mr. Townsend at one of the Relief Committees; —and Mrs. Townsend from the mouth of one of her servants, during his absence, on the same day; and when Mr. Townsend returned to the parsonage, they met each other with blank faces.

'Oh, Æneas!' said she, before she could get his greatcoat from off his shoulders, 'have you heard the news?'

'What news?—about Castle Richmond?'

'Yes; about Castle Richmond.' And then she knew that he had heard it.

Some glimmering of Lady Fitzgerald's early history had been known to both of them, as it had been known almost to all in the

country; but in late years this history had been so much forgotten, that men had ceased to talk of it, and this calamity
therefore came with the weight of a new misfortune.

'And, Æneas, who told you of it?' she asked, as they sat
together over the fire, in their dingy, dirty parlour.

'Well, strange to say, I heard it first from Father Barney.'

'Oh, mercy! and is it all about the country in that way?'

'Herbert, you know, has not been at any one of the Committees for the last ten days, and Mr. Somers, for the last week
past has been as silent as death; so much so, that that horrid
creature, Father Columb, would have made a regular set speech
the other day at Gortnaclough, if I hadn't put him down.'

'Dear, dear, dear!' said Mrs. Townsend.

'And I was talking to Father Barney about this, to-day—
about Mr. Somers, that is.'

'Yes, yes, yes!'

'And then he said, "I suppose you know what has happened
at Castle Richmond?"'

'How on earth had he learned?' asked Mrs. Townsend, jealous
that a Roman Catholic priest should have heard such completely
Protestant news before the Protestant parson and his wife.

'Oh, they learn everything—from the servants I suppose.'

'Of course, the mean creatures!' said Mrs. Townsend, forgetting, probably, her own little conversation with her own man
of all work that morning. 'But go on, Æneas.'

"'What has happened," said I, "at Castle Richmond?" "Oh,
you haven't heard," said he. And I was obliged to own that I
had not, though I saw that it gave him a kind of triumph.
"Why," said he, "very bad news has reached them indeed; the
worst of news." And then he told me about Lady Fitzgerald.
To give him his due, I must say that he was very sorry—very
sorry. "The poor young fellow!" he said—"The poor young
fellow!" And I saw that he turned away his face to hide a tear.'

'Crocodile tears!' said Mrs. Townsend.

'No, they were not,' said her reverend lord; 'and Father
Barney is not so bad as I once thought him.'

'I hope you are not going over too, Æneas?' And his consort
almost cried as such a horrid thought entered her head. In her
ideas any feeling short of absolute enmity to a servant of the
Church of Rome was an abandonment of some portion of the
Protestant basis of the Church of England. 'The small end of
the wedge,' she would call it, when people round her would
suggest that the heart of a Roman Catholic priest might possibly
not be altogether black and devilish.

'Well, I hope not, my dear,' said Mr. Townsend, with a slight touch of sarcasm in his voice. 'But, as I was saying, Father Barney told me then that this Mr. Prendergast—'

'Oh, I had known of his being there from the day of his coming.'

'This Mr. Prendergast, it seems, knew the whole affair, from beginning to end.'

'But how did he know it, Æneas?'

'That I can't tell you. He was a friend of Sir Thomas before his marriage; I know that. And he has told them that it is of no use their attempting to keep it secret. He was over at Hap House with Owen Fitzgerald before he went.'

'And has Owen Fitzgerald been told?'

'Yes; he has been told—told that he is to be the next heir; so Father Barney says.'

Mrs. Townsend wished in her heart that the news could have reached her through a purer source; but all this, coming though it did from Father Barney, tallied too completely with what she herself had heard to leave on her mind any doubt of its truth. And then she began to think of Lady Fitzgerald and her condition, of Herbert and of his, and of the condition of them all, till by degrees her mind passed away from Father Barney and all his iniquities.

'It is very dreadful,' she said, in a low voice.

'Very dreadful, very dreadful. I hardly know how to think of it. And I fear that Sir Thomas will not live many months to give them even the benefit of his life interest.'

'And when he dies all will be gone?'

'Everything.'

And then tears stood in her eyes also, and in his also after a while. It is very easy for a clergyman in his pulpit to preach eloquently upon the vileness of worldly wealth, and the futility of worldly station; but where will you ever find one, who, when the time of proof shall come, will give proof that he himself feels what he preaches? Mr. Townsend was customarily loud and eager upon this subject, and yet he was now shedding tears because his young friend Herbert was deprived of his inheritance.

CHAPTER XXX.

PALLIDA MORS.

MR. SOMERS, returning from Hap House, gave Owen's message to Herbert Fitzgerald, but at the same time told him that he did not think any good would come of such a meeting.

'I went over there,' he said, 'because I would not willingly omit anything that Mr. Prendergast had suggested; but I did not expect any good to come of it. You know what I have always thought of Owen Fitzgerald.'

'But Mr. Prendergast said that he behaved so well.'

'He did not know Prendergast, and was cowed for the moment by what he had heard. That was natural enough. You do as you like, however; only do not have him over to Castle Richmond.'

Owen, however, did not trust solely to Mr. Somers, but on the following day wrote to Herbert, suggesting that they had better meet, and begging that the place and time of meeting might be named. He himself again suggested Hap House, and declared that he would be at home on any day and at any hour that his 'cousin' might name, 'only,' as he added, 'the sooner the better.' Herbert wrote back by the same messenger, saying that he would be with him early on the following morning; and on the following morning he drove up to the door of Hap House, while Owen was still sitting with his coffee-pot and knife and fork before him.

Captain Donnellan, whom we saw there on the occasion of our first morning visit, was now gone, and Owen Fitzgerald was all alone in his home. The captain had been an accustomed guest, spending perhaps half his time there during the hunting season; but since Mr. Prendergast had been at Hap House, he had been made to understand that the master would fain be alone. And since that day Owen had never hunted, nor been noticed in his old haunts, nor had been seen talking to his old friends. He had remained at home, sitting over the fire thinking, wandering up and down his own avenue, or standing about the stable, idly, almost unconscious of the grooming of his horses. Once and once only he had been mounted; and then as the dusk of evening was coming on he had trotted over quickly to Desmond Court, as though he had in hand some purport of great moment; but if so he changed his mind when he came to the gate, for he walked on slowly for three or four hundred yards beyond it, and then turning his horse's head, slowly made his way back past the gate, and then trotted quickly home to Hap House. In these moments of his life he must make or mar himself for life; 'twas so that he felt it; and how should he make himself, or how avoid the marriage? That was the question which he now strove to answer.

When Herbert entered the room, he rose from his chair, and walked quickly up to his visitor, with extended hand, and a look of welcome in his face. His manner was very different from that with which he had turned and parted from his cousin, not many days since in the demesne of Castle Richmond. Then he had intended absolutely to defy Herbert Fitzgerald; but there was no spirit of defiance now, either in his hand, or face, or in the tone of his voice.

' I am very glad you have come,' said he. ' I hope you understood that I would have gone to you, only that I thought it might be better for both of us to be here.'

Herbert said something to the effect that he had been quite willing to come over to Hap House. But he was not at the moment so self-possessed as the other, and hardly knew how to begin the subject which was to be discussed between them.

' Of course you know that Mr. Prendergast was here ?' said Owen.

' Oh yes,' said Herbert.

' And Mr. Somers also? I tell you fairly, Herbert, that when Mr. Somers came, I was not willing to say much to him. What has to be said must be said between you and me, and not to any third party. I could not open my heart, nor yet speak my thoughts to Mr. Somers.'

In answer to this, Herbert again said that Owen need have no scruple in speaking to him. ' It is all plain sailing; too plain, I fear,' said he. ' There is no doubt whatever now as to the truth of what Mr. Prendergast has told you.'

And then having said so much, Herbert waited for Owen to speak. He, Herbert himself, had little or nothing to say. Castle Richmond with its title and acres was not to be his, but was to be the property of this man with whom he was now sitting. When that was actually and positively understood between them, there was nothing further to be said; nothing as far as Herbert knew. That other sorrow of his, that other and deeper sorrow which affected his mother's name and station,—as to that he did not find himself called on to speak to Owen Fitzgerald. Nor was it necessary that he should say anything as to his great consolation—the consolation which had reached him from Clara Desmond.

' And is it true, Herbert,' asked Owen at last, ' that my uncle is so very ill?' In the time of their kindly intercourse, Owen had always called Sir Thomas his uncle, though latterly he had ceased to do so.

' He is very ill; very ill indeed,' said Herbert. This was a subject in which Owen had certainly a right to feel interested, seeing that his own investiture would follow immediately on the death of Sir Thomas; but Herbert almost felt that the question might as well have been spared. It had been asked, however, almost solely with the view of gaining some few moments.

'Herbert,' he said at last, standing up from his chair, as he made an effort to begin his speech, 'I don't know how far you will believe me when I tell you that all this news has caused me great sorrow. I grieve for your father and your mother, and for you, from the very bottom of my heart.'

'It is very kind of you,' said Herbert. 'But the blow has fallen, and as for myself, I believe that I can bear it. I do not care so very much about the property.'

'Nor do I;' and now Owen spoke rather louder, and with his own look of strong impulse about his mouth and forehead. 'Nor do I care so much about the property. You were welcome to it; and are so still. I have never coveted it from you, and do not covet it.'

'It will be yours now without coveting,' replied Herbert; and then there was another pause, during which Herbert sat still, while Owen stood leaning with his back against the mantelpiece.

'Herbert,' said he, after they had thus remained silent for two or three minutes, 'I have made up my mind on this matter, and I will tell you truly what I do desire, and what I do not. I do not desire your inheritance, but I do desire that Clara Desmond shall be my wife.'

'Owen,' said the other, also getting up, 'I did not expect when I came here that you would have spoken to me about this.'

'It was that we might speak about this that I asked you to come here. But listen to me. When I say that I want Clara Desmond to be my wife, I mean to say that I want that, and that only. It may be true that I am, or shall be, legally the heir to your father's estate. Herbert, I will relinquish all that, because I do not feel it to be my own. I will relinquish it in any way that may separate myself from it most thoroughly. But in return, do you separate yourself from her who was my own before you had ever known her.'

And thus he did make the proposition as to which he had been making up his mind since the morning on which Mr. Prendergast had come to him.

Herbert for a while was struck dumb with amazement, not so much at the quixotic generosity of the proposal, as at the singular mind of the man in thinking that such a plan could be carried out. Herbert's best quality was no doubt his sturdy common sense, and that was shocked by a suggestion which presumed that all the legalities and ordinary bonds of life could be upset by such an agreement between two young men. He knew that Owen Fitzgerald could not give away his title to an estate of fourteen thousand a year in this off-hand way, and that no one could accept such a gift were it possible to be given. The estate and title must belong to Owen, and could not possibly belong to any one else, merely at his word and fancy. And then again, how could the love of a girl like Clara Fitzgerald be bandied to and fro at the will of any suitor or suitors? That she had once accepted Owen's love, Herbert knew; but since that, in a soberer mood, and with maturer judgment, she had accepted his. How could he give it up to another, or how could that other take possession of it if so abandoned? The bargain was one quite impossible to be carried out; and yet Owen in proposing it had fully intended to be as good as his word.

'That is impossible,' said Herbert, in a low voice.

'Why impossible? May I not do what I like with that which is my own? It is not impossible. I will have nothing to do with that property of yours. In fact, it is not my own, and I will not take it; I will not rob you of that which you have been born to expect. But in return for this——'

'Owen, do not talk of it; would you abandon a girl whom you loved for any wealth, or any property?'

'You cannot love her as I love her. I will talk to you on this matter openly, as I have never yet talked to any one. Since first I saw Clara Desmond, the only wish of my life has been that I might have her for my wife. I have longed for her as a child longs—if you know what I mean by that. When I saw that she was old enough to understand what love meant, I told her what was in my heart, and she accepted my love. She swore to me that she would be mine, let mother or brother say what they would. As sure as you are standing there a living man she loved me with all truth. And that I loved her—— ! Herbert, I have never loved aught but her; nothing else!—neither man nor woman, nor wealth nor title. All I ask is that I may have that which was my own.'

'But, Owen——' and Herbert touched his cousin's arm.

'Well; why do you not speak? I have spoken plainly enough.'

'It is not easy to speak plainly on all subjects. I would not, if I could avoid it, say a word that would hurt your feelings.'

'Never mind my feelings. Speak out, and let us have the truth, in God's name. My feelings have never been much considered yet—either in this matter or in any other.'

'It seems to me,' said Herbert, 'that the giving of Lady Clara's hand cannot depend on your will, or on mine.'

'You mean her mother.'

'No, by no means. Her mother now would be the last to

favour me. I mean herself. If she loves me, as I hope and believe—nay, am sure—'

'She did love me!' shouted Owen.

'But even if so——. I do not now say anything of that; but even if so, surely you would not have her marry you if she does not love you still? You would not wish her to be your wife if her heart belongs to me?'

'It has been given you at her mother's bidding.'

'However given it is now my own and it cannot be returned. Look here, Owen. I will show you her last two letters, if you will allow me; not in pride, I hope, but that you may truly know what are her wishes.' And he took from his breast, where they had been ever since he received them, the two letters which Clara had written to him. Owen read them both twice over before he spoke, first one and then the other, and an indescribable look of pain fell on his brow as he did so. They were so tenderly worded, so sweet, so generous! He would have given all the world to have had those letters addressed by her to himself. But even they did not convince him. His heart had never changed, and he could not believe that there had been any change in hers.

'I might have known,' he said, as he gave them back, 'that she would be too noble to abandon you in your distress. As long as you were rich I might have had some chance of getting her back, despite the machinations of her mother. But now that she thinks you are poor—.' And then he stopped, and hid his face between his hands.

And in what he had last said there was undoubtedly something of truth. Clara's love for Herbert had never been passionate, till passion had been created by his misfortune. And in her thoughts of Owen there had been much of regret. Though she had resolved to withdraw her love, she had not wholly ceased to love him. Judgment had bade her to break her word to him, and she had obeyed her judgment. She had admitted to herself that her mother was right in telling her that she could not join her own bankrupt fortunes to the fortunes of one who was both poor and a spendthrift; and thus she had plucked from her heart the picture of the man she had loved,—or endeavoured so to pluck it. Some love for him, however, had unwittingly lingered there. And then Herbert had come with his suit, a suitor fitted for her in every way. She had not loved him as she had loved Owen. She had never felt that she could worship him, and tremble at the tones of his voice, and watch the glance of his eye, and gaze into his face as though he were half divine. But she acknowledged his worth, and valued him: she knew that it behoved her to choose some suitor as her husband; and now that her dream was gone, where could she choose better than here? And thus Herbert had been accepted. He had been accepted, but the dream was not wholly gone. Owen was in adversity, ill spoken of by those around her, shunned by his own relatives, living darkly, away from all that is soft in life; and for these reasons Clara could not wholly forget her dream. She had, in some sort, unconsciously clung to her old love, till he to whom she had plighted her new troth was in adversity,— and then all was changed. Then her love for Herbert did become a passion; and then, as Owen had become rich, she felt that she could think of him without remorse. He was quite right in perceiving that his chance was gone now that Herbert had ceased to be rich.

'Owen,' said Herbert, and his voice was full of tenderness, for at this moment he felt that he did love and pity his cousin, 'we must each of us bear the weight which fortune has thrown on us. It may be that we are neither of us to be envied. I have lost all that men generally value, and you—'

'I have lost all on earth that is valuable to me. But no; it is not lost,—not lost as yet. As long as her name is Clara Desmond, she is as open for me to win as she is for you. And, Herbert, think of it before you make me your enemy. See what I offer you,—not as a bargain, mind you. I give up all my title to your father's property. I will sign any paper that your lawyers may bring to me, which may serve to give you back your inheritance. As for me, I would scorn to take that which belongs in justice to another. I will not have your property. Come what may, I will not have it. I will give it up to you, either as to my enemy or as to my friend.'

'I sincerely hope that we may be friends, but what you say is impossible.'

'It is not impossible. I hereby pledge myself that I will not take an acre of your father's lands; but I pledge myself also that I will always be your enemy if Clara Desmond becomes your wife and I mean what I say. I have set my heart on one thing, ana one thing only, and if I am ruined in that I am ruined indeed.'

Herbert remained silent, for he had nothing further that he knew how to plead; he felt, as other men would feel, that each of them must keep that which Fate had given him. Fate had decreed that Owen should be the heir to Castle Richmond, and the decree thus gone forth must stand valid; and Fate had also decreed that Owen should be rejected by Clara Desmond, which other decree, as Herbert thought, must be held as valid also. But he had no further inclination to argue upon the subject:

his cousin was becoming hot and angry; and Herbert was beginning to wish that he was on his way home, that he might be once more at his father's bedside, or in his mother's room, comforting her and being comforted.

'Well,' said Owen, after a while in his deep-toned voice; 'what do you say to my offer?'

'I have nothing further to say: we must each take our own course; as for me, I have lost everything but one thing, and it is not likely that I shall throw that away from me.'

'Nor, so help me Heaven in my need! will I let that thing be filched from me. I have offered you kindness and brotherly love, and wealth, and all that friendship could do for a man; give me my way in this, and I will be to you such a comrade and such a brother.'

'Should I be a man, Owen, were I to give up this?'

'Be a man! Yes! It is pride on your part. You do not love her; you have never loved her as I have loved; you have not sat apart long months and months thinking of her, as I have done. From the time she was a child I marked her as my own. As God will help me when I die, she is all that I have coveted in this world;—all! But her I have coveted with such longings of the heart, that I cannot bring myself to live without her; —nor will I.' And then again they both were silent.

'It may be as well that we should part now,' said Herbert at last. 'I do not know that we can gain anything by further talking on this subject.'

'Well, you know that best; but I have one further question to ask you.'

'What is it, Owen?'

'You still think of marrying Clara Desmond?'

'Certainly; of course I think of it.'

'And when? I presume you are not so chicken-hearted as to be afraid of speaking out openly what you intend to do.'

'I cannot say when; I had hoped that it would have been very soon; but all this will of course delay it. It may be years first.'

These last were the only pleasant words that Owen had heard. If there were to be a delay of years, might not his chance still be as good as Herbert's? But then this delay was to be the consequence of his cousin's ruined prospects—and the accomplishment of that ruin Owen had pledged himself to prevent! Was he by his own deed to enable his enemy to take that very step which he was so firmly resolved to prevent?

'You will give me your promise,' said he, 'that you will not marry her for the next three years? Make me that promise, and I will make you the same.'

Herbert felt that there could be no possibility of his now marrying within the time named, but nevertheless he would not bring himself to make such a promise as this. He would make no bargain about Clara Desmond, about his Clara, which could in any way admit a doubt as to his own right. Had Owen asked him to promise that he would not marry her during the next week he would have given no such pledge. ' No,' said he, ' I cannot promise that.'

' She is now only seventeen.'

' It does not matter. I will make no such promise, because on such a subject you have no right to ask for any. When she will consent to run her risk of happiness in coming to me, then I shall marry her.'

Owen was now walking up and down the room with rapid steps. ' You have not the courage to fight me fairly,' said he.

' I do not wish to fight you at all.'

' Ah, but you must fight me! Shall I see the prey taken out of my jaws, and not struggle for it? No, by heavens! you must fight me; and I tell you fairly, that the fight shall be as hard as I can make it. I have offered you that which one living man is seldom able to offer to another,—money, and land, and wealth, and station; all these things I throw away from me, because I feel that they should be yours; and I ask only in return the love of a young girl. I ask that because I feel that it should be mine. If it has gone from me—which I do not believe—it has been filched and stolen by a thief in the night. She did love me, if a girl ever loved a man; but she was separated from me, and I bore that patiently because I trusted her. But she was young and weak, and her mother was strong and crafty. She has accepted you at her mother's instance, and were I base enough to keep from you your father's inheritance, her mother would no more give her to you now than she would to me then. This is true; and if you know it to be true—as you do know, you will be mean, and dastard, and a coward—you will be no Fitzgerald if you keep from me that which I have a right to claim as my own. Not fight! Ay, but you must fight! We cannot both live here in this country if Clara Desmond become your wife. Mark my words, if that take place, you and I cannot live here alongside of each other's houses.' He paused for a moment after this, and then added, ' You can go now if you will, for I have said out my say.'

And Herbert did go,—almost without uttering a word of adieu. What could he say in answer to such threats as these? That his cousin was in every way unreasonable,—as unreasonable in his generosity as he was in his claims, he felt convinced. But

an unreasonable man, though he is one whom one would fain
conquer by arguments were it possible, is the very man on
whom arguments have no avail. A madman is mad because he
is mad. Herbert had a great deal that was very sensible to allege in favour of his views, but what use of alleging anything
of sense to such a mind as that of Owen Fitzgerald? So he
went his way without further speech.

When he was gone, Owen for a time went on walking his
room, and then sank again into his chair. Abominably irrational as his method of arranging all these family difficulties will
no doubt seem to all who may read of it, to him it had appeared
not only an easy but a happy mode of bringing back contentment to everybody. He was quite serious in his intention of
giving up his position as heir to Castle Richmond. Mr. Prendergast had explained to him that the property was entailed as
far as him, but no farther; and had done this, doubtless, with
the view, not then expressed, to some friendly arrangement by
which a small portion of the property might be saved and
restored to the children of Sir Thomas. But Owen had looked
at it quite in another light. He had, in justice, no right to
inquire into all those circumstances of his old cousin's marriage.
Such a union was a marriage in the eye of God, and should be
held as such by him. He would take no advantage of so terrible
an accident.

He would take no advantage. So he said to himself over and
over again; but yet, as he said it, he resolved that he would
take advantage. He would not touch the estate; but surely if
he abstained from touching it, Herbert would be generous
enough to leave to him the solace of his love! And he had no
scruple in allotting to Clara the poorer husband instead of
the richer. He was no poorer now than when she had accepted him. Looking at it in that light, had he not a right to
claim that she should abide by her first acceptance? Could any
one be found to justify the theory that a girl may throw over a
poor lover because a rich lover comes in the way? Owen had
his own ideas of right and wrong—ideas which were not without a basis of strong, rugged justice; and nothing could be more
antagonistic to them than such a doctrine as this. And then he
still believed in his heart that he was dearer to Clara than that
other richer suitor. He heard of her from time to time, and
those who had spoken to him had spoken of her as pining for
love of him. In this there had been much of the flattery of
servants, and something of the subservience of those about him
who wished to stand well in his graces. But he had believed it.
He was not a conceited man, nor even a vain man. He did not

think himself more clever than his cousin; and as for personal appearance, it was a matter to which his thoughts never descended; but he had about him a self-dependence and assurance in his own manhood, which forbade him to doubt the love of one who had told him that she loved him.

And he did not believe in Herbert's love. His cousin was, as he thought, of a calibre too cold for love. That Clara was valued by him, Owen did not doubt—valued for her beauty, for her rank, for her grace and peerless manner; but what had such value as that to do with love? Would Herbert sacrifice everything for Clara Desmond? would he bid Pelion fall on Ossa? would he drink up Esil? All this would Owen do, and more; he would do more than any Laertes had ever dreamed. He would give up for now and for ever all title to those rich lands which made the Fitzgeralds of Castle Richmond the men of greatest mark in all their county.

And thus he fanned himself into a fury as he thought of his cousin's want of generosity. Herbert would be the heir, and because he was the heir he would be the favoured lover. But there might yet be time and opportunity; and at any rate Clara should not marry without knowing what was the whole truth. Herbert was ungenerous, but Clara still might be just. If not,—then, as he had said before, he would fight out the battle to the end as with an enemy.

Herbert, when he got on to his horse to ride home, was forced to acknowledge to himself that no good whatever had come from his visit to Hap House. Words had been spoken which might have been much better left unspoken. An angry man will often cling to his anger because his anger has been spoken; he will do evil because he has threatened evil, and is ashamed to be better than his words. And there was no comfort to be derived from those lavish promises made by Owen with regard to the property. To Herbert's mind they were mere moonshine—very graceful on the part of the maker, but meaning nothing. No one could have Castle Richmond but him who owned it legally. Owen Fitzgerald would become Sir Owen, and would, as a matter of course, be Sir Owen of Castle Richmond. There was no comfort on that score; and then, on that other score, there was so much discomfort. Of giving up his bride Herbert never for a moment thought; but he did think, with increasing annoyance, of the angry threats which had been pronounced against him.

When he rode into the stable-yard as was his wont, he found Richard waiting for him. This was not customary; as in these latter days Richard, though he always drove the car, as a sort of subsidiary coachman to the young ladies to whom the car was supposed to belong in fee, did not act as general groom. He had been promoted beyond this, and was a sort of hanger-on about the house, half indoor servant and half out, doing very much what he liked, and giving advice to everybody, from the cook downwards. He thanked God that he knew his place, he would often say; but nobody else knew it. Nevertheless everybody liked him; even the poor housemaid whom he snubbed.

'Is anything the matter?' asked Herbert, looking at the man's sorrow-laden face.

' 'Deed an' there is, Mr. Herbert; Sir Thomas is—'

'My father is not dead!' exclaimed Herbert.

'Oh no, Mr. Herbert; it's not so bad as that; but he is very failing,—very failing. My lady is with him now.'

Herbert ran into the house, and at the bottom of the chief stairs he met one of his sisters who had heard the steps of his horse. 'Oh, Herbert, I am so glad you have come!' said she. Her eyes and cheeks were red with tears, and her hand, as her brother took it, was cold and numbed.

'What is it, Mary? is he worse?'

'Oh, so much worse. Mamma and Emmeline are there. He has asked for you three or four times, and always says that he is dying. I had better go up and say that you are here.'

'And what does my mother think of it?'

'She has never left him, and therefore I cannot tell; but I know from her face that she thinks that he is—dying. Shall I go up, Herbert?' and so she went, and Herbert, following softly on his toes, stood in the corridor outside the bedroom-door, waiting till his arrival should have been announced. It was but a minute, and then his sister, returning to the door, summoned him to enter.

The room had been nearly darkened, but as there were no curtains to the bed, Herbert could see his mother's face as she knelt on a stool at the bedside. His father was turned away from him, and lay with his hand inside his wife's, and Emmeline was sitting on the foot of the bed, with her face between her hands, striving to stifle her sobs. 'Here is Herbert now, dearest,' said Lady Fitzgerald, with a low, soft voice, almost a whisper, yet clear enough to cause no effort in the hearing. 'I knew that he would not be long.' And Herbert, obeying the signal of his mother's eye, passed round to the other side of the bed.

'Father,' said he, 'are you not so well to-day?'

'My poor boy, my poor ruined boy!' said the dying man, hardly articulating the words as he dropped his wife's hand and took that of his son. Herbert found that it was wet, and clammy, and cold, and almost powerless in its feeble grasp.

'Dearest father, you are wrong if you let that trouble you; all that will never trouble me. Is it not well that a man should earn his own bread? Is it not the lot of all good men?' But still the old man murmured with his broken voice, 'My poor boy, my poor boy!'

The hopes and aspirations of his eldest son are as the breath of his nostrils to an Englishman who has been born to land and fortune. What had not this poor man endured in order that his son might be Sir Herbert Fitzgerald of Castle Richmond? But this was no longer possible; and from the moment that this had been brought home to him, the father had felt that for him there was nothing left but to die. 'My poor boy,' he muttered, 'tell me that you have forgiven me.'

And then they all knelt round the bed and prayed with him; and afterwards they tried to comfort him, telling him how good he had been to them; and his wife whispered in his ear that if there had been fault, the fault was hers, but that her conscience told her that such fault had been forgiven; and while she said this she motioned the children away from him, and strove to make him understand that human misery could never kill the soul, and should never utterly depress the spirit. 'Dearest love,' she said, still whispering to him in her low, sweet voice—so dear to him, but utterly inaudible beyond—'if you would cease to accuse yourself so bitterly, you might yet be better, and remain with us to comfort us.'

But the slender, half-knit man, whose arms are without muscles and whose back is without pith, will strive in vain to lift the weight which the brawny vigour of another tosses from the ground almost without an effort. It is with the mind and the spirit as with the body; only this, that the muscles of the body can be measured, but not so those of the spirit. Lady Fitzgerald was made of other stuff than Sir Thomas; and that which to her had cost an effort, but with an effort had been done surely, was to him as impossible as the labour of Hercules. 'My poor boy, my poor ruined boy!' he still muttered, as she strove to comfort him.

'Mamma has sent for Mr. Townsend,' Emmeline whispered to her brother, as they stood together in the bow of the window.

'And do you really think he is so bad as that?'

'I am sure that mamma does. I believe he had some sort of a fit before you came. At any rate, he did not speak for two hours.'

'And was not Finucane here?' Finucane was the Mallow doctor.

'Yes; but he had left before papa became so much worse. Mamma has sent for him also.'

But I do not know that it boots to dally longer in a dying chamber. It is an axiom of old that the stage curtain should be drawn before the inexorable one enters in upon his final work. Doctor Finucane did come, but his coming was all in vain. Sir Thomas had known that it was in vain, and so also had his patient wife. There was that mind diseased, towards the cure of which no Doctor Finucane could make any possible approach. And Mr. Townsend came also, let us hope not in vain; though the cure which he fain would have perfected can hardly be effected in such moments as those. Let us hope that it had been already effected. The only crying sin which we can lay to the charge of the dying man is that of which we have spoken; he had endeavoured by pensioning falsehood and fraud to preserve for his wife her name, and for his son that son's inheritance. Even over this, deep as it was, the recording angel may have dropped some cleansing tears of pity.

That night the poor man died, and the Fitzgeralds who sat in the chambers of Castle Richmond were no longer the owners of the mansion. There was no speech of Sir Herbert among the servants as there would have been had these tidings not have reached them. Dr. Finucane had remained in the house, and even he, in speaking of the son, had shown that he knew the story. They were strangers there now, as they all knew—intruders, as they would soon be considered in the house of their cousin Owen; or rather not their cousin. In that he was above them by right of his blood, they had no right to claim him as their relation.

It may be said that at such a moment all this should not have been thought of; but those who say so know little, as I imagine, of the true effect of sorrow. No wife and no children ever grieved more heartily for a father; but their grief was blacker and more gloomy in that they knew that they were outcasts in the world.

And during that long night as Herbert and his sisters sat up cowering round the fire, he told them of all that had been said at Hap House. 'And can it not be as he says?' Mary had asked.

'And that Herbert should give up his wife!' said Emmeline.

'No; but that other thing.'

'Do not dream of it,' said Herbert. 'It is all, all impossible. The house that we are now in belongs to Sir Owen Fitzgerald.'

CHAPTER XXXI.

THE FIRST MONTH.

AND now I will beg my readers to suppose a month to have passed by since Sir Thomas Fitzgerald died. It was a busy month in Ireland. It may probably be said that so large a sum of money had never been circulated in the country in any one month since money had been known there; and yet it may also be said that so frightful a mortality had never occurred there from the want of that which money brings. It was well understood by all men now that the customary food of the country had disappeared. There was no longer any difference of opinion between rich and poor, between Protestant and Roman Catholic; as to that, no man dared now to say that the poor, if left to themselves, could feed themselves, or to allege that the sufferings of the country arose from the machinations of money-making speculators. The famine was an established fact, and all men knew that it was God's doing,—all men knew this, though few could recognize as yet with how much mercy God's hand was stretched out over the country.

Or may it not perhaps be truer to say that in such matters there is no such thing as mercy—no special mercies—no other mercy than that fatherly, forbearing, all-seeing, perfect goodness by which the Creator is ever adapting this world to the wants of his creatures, and rectifying the evils arising from their faults and follies? *Sed quo Musa tendis?* Such discourses of the gods as these are not to be fitly handled in such small measures.

At any rate, there was the famine, undoubted now by any one; and death, who in visiting Castle Richmond may be said to have knocked at the towers of a king, was busy enough also among the cabins of the poor. And now the great fault of those who were the most affected was becoming one which would not have been at first expected. One would think that starving men would become violent, taking food by open theft—feeling, and perhaps not without some truth, that the agony of their want robbed such robberies of its sin. But such was by no means the case. I only remember one instance in which the bakers' shops were attacked; and in that instance the work was done by those who were undergoing no real suffering. At Clonmel, in Tipperary, the bread was one morning stripped away from the

bakers' shops; but at that time, and in that place, there was nothing approaching to famine. The fault of the people was
apathy. It was the feeling of the multitude that the world and
all that was good in it was passing away from them; that exertion was useless, and hope hopeless. 'Ah, me! your honour,'
said a man to me, 'there'll never be a bit and a sup again in the
county Cork! The life of the world is fairly gone!'

And it was very hard to repress this feeling. The energy of
a man depends so much on the outward circumstances that encumber him! It is so hard to work when work seems hopeless
—so hard to trust where the basis of our faith is so far removed
from sight! When large tracts of land went out of cultivation,
was it not natural to think that agriculture was receding from
the country, leaving the green hills once more to be brown and
barren, as hills once green have become in other countries?
And when men were falling in the highways, and women would
sit with their babes in their arms, listless till death should come
to them, was it not natural to think that death was making a
huge success—that he, the inexorable one, was now the inexorable indeed?

There were greatly trusting hearts that could withstand the
weight of this terrible pressure, and thinking minds which saw
that good would come out of this great evil; but such hearts and
such minds were not to be looked for among the suffering poor;
and were not, perhaps, often found even among those who were
not poor or suffering. It was very hard to be thus trusting and
thoughtful while everything around was full of awe and agony.

The people, however, were conscious of God's work, and were
becoming dull and apathetic. They clustered about the roads,
working lazily while their strength lasted them; and afterwards,
when strength failed them for this, they clustered more largely
in the poor-houses. And in every town—in every assemblage of houses which in England would be called a village,
there was a poor-house. Any big barrack of a tenement that
could be obtained at a moment's notice, whatever the rent,
became a poor-house in the course of twelve hours;—in twelve,
nay, in two hours. What was necessary but the bare walls, and
a supply of yellow meal? Bad provision this for all a man's
wants,—as was said often enough by irrational philanthropists;
but better provision than no shelter and no yellow meal! It
was bad that men should be locked up at night without any of
the appliances of decency; bad that they should be herded
together for day after day with no resource but the eating twice
a day of enough unsavoury food to keep life and soul together;—
very bad, ye philanthropical irrationalists! But is not a choice

of evils all that is left to us in many a contingency? W
even this better than that life and soul should be allowed t
without any effort at preserving their union?

And thus life and soul were kept together, the government of
the day having wisely seen what, at so short a notice, was possible for them to do, and what was absolutely impossible. It is
in such emergencies as these that the watching and the wisdom
of a government are necessary; and I shall always think—as I did
think then—that the wisdom of its action and the wisdom of its abstinence from action were very good. And now again the fields in
Ireland are green, and the markets are busy, and money is chucked
to and fro like a weathercock which the players do not wish to have
abiding with them; and the tardy speculator going over to look for
a bit of land comes back muttering angrily that fancy prices are
demanded. 'They'll run you up to thirty-three years' purchase,'
says the tardy speculator, thinking, as it seems, that he is
specially ill used. Agricultural wages have been nearly doubled
in Ireland during the last fifteen years. Think of that, Master
Brook. Work for which, at six shillings a week, there would be
a hundred hungry claimants in 1845,—in the good old days
before the famine, when repeal was so immediately expected—
will now fetch ten shillings, the claimants being by no means
numerous. In 1843 and 1844, I knew men to work for four-
pence a day—something over the dole on which we are told,
being mostly incredulous as we hear it, that a Coolie labourer
can feed himself with rice in India;—not one man or two men,
the broken-down incapables of the parish, but the best labour of
the country. One and twopence is now about the cheapest rate
at which a man can be hired for agricultural purposes. While
this is so, and while the prices are progressing, there is no cause
for fear, let Bishops A and B, and Archbishops C and D fret and
fume with never so great vexation touching the clipped honours
of their father the Pope.

But again; Quo Musa tendis? I could write on this subject
for a week were it not that Rhadamanthus awaits me, Rhadamanthus the critic; and Rhadamanthus is, of all things, impatient
of an episode.

Life and soul were kept together in those terrible days;—that
is, the Irish life and soul generally. There were many slips, in
which the union was violently dissolved,—many cases in which
the yellow meal allowed was not sufficient, or in which it did
not reach the sufferer in time to prevent such dissolution,—cases
which when numbered together amounted to thousands. And
then the pestilence came, taking its victims by tens of thousands,
—but that was after the time with which we shall have concern

here; and immigration followed, taking those who were saved by hundreds of thousands. But the millions are still there, a thriving people ; for His mercy endureth for ever.

During this month, the month ensuing upon the death of Sir Thomas Fitzgerald, Herbert could of course pay no outward attention to the wants or relief of the people. He could make no offer of assistance, for nothing belonged to him ; nor could he aid in the councils of the committees, for no one could have defined the position of the speaker. And during that month nothing was defined about Castle Richmond. Lady Fitzgerald was still always called by her title. The people of the country, including the tradesmen of the neighbouring towns, addressed the owner of Hap House as Sir Owen ; and gradually the name was working itself into common use, though he had taken no steps to make himself legally entitled to wear it. But no one spoke of Sir Herbert. The story was so generally known, that none were so ignorant as to suppose him to be his father's heir. The servants about the place still called him Mr. Herbert, orders to that effect having been specially given ; and the peasants of the country, with that tact which graces them, and with that anxiety to abstain from giving pain which always accompanies them unless when angered, carefully called him by no name. They knew that he was not Sir Herbert ; but they would not believe but what, perchance, he might be so yet on some future day. So they took off their old hats to him, and passed him silently in his sorrow ; or if they spoke to him, addressed his honour simply, omitting all mention of that Christian name, which the poor Irishman is generally so fond of using. 'Mister Blake' sounds cold and unkindly in his ears. It is the ' Masther,' or ' His honour,' or if possible ' Misther Thady.' Or if there be any handle, that is used with avidity ; Pat is a happy man when he can address his landlord as ' Sir Patrick.'

But now the ' ould masther's son ' could be called by no name. Men knew not what he was to be, though they knew well that he was not that which he ought to be. And there were some who attempted to worship Owen as the rising sun ; but for such of them as had never worshipped him before that game was rather hopeless. In those days he was not much seen, neither hunting nor entertaining company ; but when seen he was rough enough with those who made any deep attempt to ingratiate themselves with his coming mightiness. And during this month he went over to London, having been specially in-vited so to do by Mr. Prendergast : but very little came of his visit there, except that it was certified to him that he was beyond all doubt the baronet. ' And there shall be no unnecessary delay, Sir Owen,' said Mr. Prendergast, 'in putting you into full possession of all your rights.' In answer to which Owen had replied that he was not anxious to be put in possession of any rights. That as far as any active doing of his own was concerned, the title might lie in abeyance, and that regarding the property he would make known his wish to Mr. Prendergast very quickly after his return to Ireland. But he intimated at the same time that there could be no ground for disturbing Lady Fitzgerald, as he had no intention under any circumstances of living at Castle Richmond.

'Had you not better tell Lady Fitzgerald that yourself?' said Mr. Prendergast, catching at the idea that his friend's widow— my readers will allow me so to call her—might be allowed to live undisturbed at the family mansion, if not for life, at any rate for a few years. If this young man were so generous, why should it not be so? He would not want the big house, at any rate, till he were married.

'It would be better that you should say so,' said Owen. 'I have particular reasons for not wishing to go there.'

'But allow me to say, my dear young friend—and I hope I may call you so, for I greatly admire the way in which you have taken all these tidings—that I would venture to advise you to drop the remembrance of any unpleasantness that may have existed. You should now feel yourself to be the closest friend of that family.'

'So I would if——,' and then Owen stopped short, though Mr. Prendergast gave him plenty of time to finish his sentence were he minded to do so.

'In your present position,' continued the lawyer, 'your influence will be very great.'

'I can't explain it all,' said Owen; 'but I don't think my influence will be great at all. And what is more, I do not want any influence of that sort. I wish Lady Fitzgerald to understand that she is at perfect liberty to stay where she is,—as far. I am concerned. Not as a favour from me, mind; for I do not think that she would take a favour from my hands.'

'But, my dear sir!'

'Therefore you had better write to her about remaining there.'

Mr. Prendergast did write to her, or rather to Herbert: but in doing so he thought it right to say that the permission to live at Castle Richmond should be regarded as a kindness granted them by their relative. 'It is a kindness which, under the circumstances, your mother may, I think, accept without compunction; at any rate, for some time to come,—till she shall have suited herself without hurrying her choice; but, nevertheless, it must be regarded as a generous offer on his part; and I do hope, my dear Herbert, that you and he will be fast friends.'

But Mr. Prendergast did not in the least comprehend the workings of Owen's mind; and Herbert, who knew more of them than any one else, did not understand them altogether. Owen had no idea of granting any favour to his relatives, who, as he thought, had never granted any to him. What Owen wanted,—or what he told himself that he wanted,—was justice. It was his duty as a just man to abstain from taking hold of those acres, and he was prepared to do his duty. But it was equally Herbert's duty as a just man to abstain from taking hold of Clara Desmond, and he was resolved that he would never be Herbert's friend if Herbert did not perform that duty. And then, though he felt himself bound to give up the acres,—though he did regard this as an imperative duty, he nevertheless felt also that something was due to him for his readiness to perform such a duty,—that some reward should be conceded to him; what this reward was to be, or rather what he wished it to be, we all know.

Herbert had utterly refused to engage in any such negotiation; but Owen, nevertheless, would not cease to think that something might yet be done. Who was so generous as Clara, and would not Clara herself speak out if she knew how much her old lover was prepared to do for this newer lover? Half a dozen times Owen made up his mind to explain the whole thing to Mr. Prendergast; but when he found himself in the presence of the lawyer, he could not talk about love. Young men are so apt to think that their seniors in age cannot understand romance, or acknowledge the force of a passion. But here they are wrong, for there would be as much romance after forty as before, I take it, were it not checked by the fear of ridicule. So Owen stayed a week in London, seeing Mr. Prendergast every day; and then he returned to Hap House.

In the mean time life went on at a very sad pace at Desmond Court. There was no concord whatever between the two ladies residing there. The mother was silent, gloomy, and sometimes bitter, seldom saying a word about Herbert Fitzgerald or his prospects, but saying that word with great fixity of purpose when it was spoken. 'No one,' she said, 'should attribute to her the poverty and misery of her child. That marriage should not take place from her house, or with her consent.' And Clara for the most part was silent also. In answer to such words as the above she would say nothing; but when, as did happen once or twice, she was forced to speak, she declared openly enough that no earthly consideration should induce her to give up her engagement.

And then the young earl came home, brought away from his school in order that his authority might have effect on his sister. To speak the truth, he was unwilling enough to interfere, and would have declined to come at all could he have dared to do so. Eton was now more pleasant to him than Desmond Court, which, indeed, had but little of pleasantness to offer to a lad such as he was now. He was sixteen, and manly for his age, but the question in dispute at Desmond Court offered little attraction even to a manly boy of sixteen. In that former question as to Owen he had said a word or two, knowing that Owen could not be looked upon as a fitting husband for his sister; but now he knew not how to counsel her again as to Herbert, seeing that it was but the other day that he had written a long letter, congratulating her on that connexion.

Towards the end of the month, however, he did arrive, making glad his mother's heart as she looked at his strong limbs and his handsome open face. And Clara, too, threw herself so warmly into his arms that he did feel glad that he had come to her. 'Oh, Patrick, it is so sweet to have you here!' she said, before his mother had had time to speak to him.

'Dearest Clara!'

'But, Patrick, you must not be cruel to me. Look here, Patrick; you are my only brother, and I so love you that I would not offend you or turn you against me for worlds. You are the head of our family, too, and nothing should be done that you do not like. But if so much depends on you, you must think well before you decide on anything.'

He opened his young eyes and looked intently into her face, for there was an earnestness in her words that almost frightened him. 'You must think well of it all before you speak, Patrick; and remember this, you and I must be honest and honourable, whether we be poor or no. You remember about Owen Fitzgerald, how I gave way then because I could do so without dishonour. But now—'

'But, Clara, I do not understand it all as yet.'

'No; you cannot,—not as yet—and I will let mamma tell you the story. All I ask is this, that you will think of my honour before you say a word that can favour either her or me.' And then he promised her that he would do so; and his mother, when on the following morning she told him all the history, found him reserved and silent.

'Look at his position,' said the mother, pleading her cause before her son. 'He is illegitimate, and—'

'Yes, but mother—'

'I know all that, my dear; I know what you would say; and

no one can pity Mr. Fitzgerald's position more than I do; but you would not on that account have your sister ruined. It is romance on her part.'

'But what does he say?'

'He is quite willing to give up the match. He has told me so, and said as much to his aunt, whom I have seen three times on the subject.'

'Do you mean that he wishes to give it up?'

'No,—at least I don't know. If he does, he cannot express such a wish, because Clara is so headstrong. Patrick, in my heart I do not believe that she cares for him. I have doubted it for some time.'

'But you wanted her to marry him.'

'So I did. It was an excellent match, and in a certain way she did like him; and then, you know, there was that great danger about poor Owen. It was a great danger then. But now she is so determined about this, because she thinks it would be ungenerous to go back from her word; and in this way she will ruin the very man she wishes to serve. Of course he cannot break off the match if she persists in it. What I want you to perceive is this, that he, utterly penniless as he is, will have to begin the world with a clog round his neck, because she is so obstinate. What could possibly be worse for him than a titled wife without a penny?' And in this way the countess pleaded her side of the question before her son.

It was quite true that she had been three times to Castle Richmond, and had thrice driven Aunt Letty into a state bordering on distraction. If she could only get the Castle Richmond people to take it up as they ought to do! It was thus she argued with herself,—and with Aunt Letty also, endeavouring to persuade her that these two young people would undoubtedly ruin each other, unless those who were really wise and prudent, and who understood the world—such as Aunt Letty, for instance —would interfere to prevent it.

Aunt Letty on the whole did agree with her, though she greatly disliked her. Miss Fitzgerald had strongly planted within her bosom the prudent old-world notion, that young gentlefolks should not love each other unless they have plenty of money; and that if unfortunately such did love each other, it was better that they should suffer all the pangs of hopeless love than marry and trust to God and their wits for bread and cheese. To which opinion of Aunt Letty's, as well as to some others entertained by that lady with much pertinacity, I cannot subscribe myself as an adherent.

Lady Desmond had wit enough to discover that Aunt Letty

did agree with her in the main, and on this account she was
eager in seeking her assistance. Lady Fitzgerald of course
could not be seen, and there was no one else at Castle Richmond
who could be supposed to have any weight with Herbert. And
therefore Lady Desmond was very eloquent with Aunt Letty,
talking much of the future miseries of the two young people, till
the old lady had promised to use her best efforts in enlisting
Lady Fitzgerald on the same side. 'You cannot wonder, Miss
Fitzgerald, that I should wish to put an end to the cruel position
in which my poor girl is placed. You know how much a girl
suffers from that kind of thing.'

Aunt Letty did dislike Lady Desmond very much; but,
nevertheless, she could not deny the truth of all this; and
therefore it may be said that the visits of the countess to Castle
Richmond were on the whole successful.

And the month wore itself away also in that sad household,
and the Fitzgeralds were gradually becoming used to their
position. Family discussions were held among them as to what
they should do, and where they should live in future. Mr.
Prendergast had written, seeing that Owen had persisted in
refusing to make the offer personally himself—saying that there
was no hurry for any removal. 'Sir Owen,' he said,—having
considered deeply whether or no he would call him by the title
or no, and having resolved that it would be best to do so at once
—'Sir Owen was inclined to behave very generously. Lady
Fitzgerald could have the house and demesne at any rate for
twelve months, and by that time the personal property left
by Sir Thomas would be realized, and there would be enough,'
Mr. Prendergast said, ' for the three ladies to live " in decent
quiet comfort."' Mr. Prendergast had taken care before he left
Castle Richmond that a will should be made and duly executed
by Sir Thomas, leaving what money he had to his three children by name,—in trust for their mother's use. Till the girls
should be of age that trust would be vested in Herbert.

'Decent quiet comfort!' said Mary to her brother and sister
as they conned the letter over; 'how comfortless it sounds!'

And so the first month after the death of Sir Thomas passed
by, and the misfortunes of the Fitzgerald family ceased to be the
only subject spoken of by the inhabitants of county Cork.

CHAPTER XXXII.

At the end of the month, Herbert began to prepare himself for facing the world. The first question to be answered, was that one which is so frequently asked in most families, but which had never yet been necessary in this—What profession would he follow? All manners of ways by which an educated man can earn his bread had been turned over in his mind, and in the minds of those who loved him, beginning with the revenues of the Archbishop of Armagh, which was Aunt Letty's idea, and ending with a seat at a government desk, which was his own. Mr. Prendergast had counselled the law; not his own lower branch of the profession, but a barrister's full-blown wig, adding, in his letter to Lady Fitzgerald, that if Herbert would come to London, and settle in chambers, he, Mr. Prendergast, would see that his life was made agreeable to him. But Mr. Somers gave other advice. In those days Assistant Poor-Law Commissioners were being appointed in Ireland, almost by the score, and Mr. Somers declared that Herbert had only to signify his wish for such a position, and he would get it. The interest which he had taken in the welfare of the poor around him was well known, and as his own story was well known also, there could be no doubt that the government would be willing to assist one so circumstanced, and who when assisted would make himself so useful. Such was the advice of Mr. Somers; and he might have been right but for this, that both Herbert and Lady Fitzgerald felt that it would be well for them to move out of that neighbourhood,—out of Ireland altogether, if such could be possible.

Aunt Letty was strong for the Church. A young man who had distinguished himself at the University so signally as her nephew had done, taking his degree at the very first attempt, and that in so high a class of honour as the fourth, would not fail to succeed in the Church. He might not perhaps succeed as to Armagh; that she admitted; but there were some thirty other bishoprics to be had, and it would be odd if, with his talents, he did not get one of them. Think what it would be if he were to return to his own country as Bishop of Cork, Cloyne, and Ross, as to which amalgamation of sees, however, Aunt Letty had her own ideas. He was slightly tainted with the venom of

Puseyism, Aunt Letty said to herself; but nothing would dispel this with so much certainty as the theological studies necessary for ordination. And then Aunt Letty talked it over by the hour together with Mrs. Townsend, and both those ladies were agreed that Herbert should get himself ordained as quickly as possible; —not in England, where there might be danger even in ordination, but in good, wholesome, Protestant Ireland, where a Church of England clergyman was a clergyman of the Church of England, and not a priest, slipping about in the mud half way between England and Rome.

Herbert himself was anxious to get some employment by which he might immediately earn his bread, but not unnaturally wished that London should be the scene of his work. Anywhere in Ireland he would be known as the Fitzgerald who ought to have been Fitzgerald of Castle Richmond. And then too, he, as other young men, had an undefined idea that, as he must earn his bread, London should be his ground. He had at first been not ill inclined to that Church project, and had thus given a sort of ground on which Aunt Letty was able to stand,— had, as it were, given her some authority for carrying on an agitation in furtherance of her own views; but Herbert himself soon gave up this idea. A man, he thought, to be a clergyman should have a very strong predilection in favour of that profession; and so he gradually abandoned that idea,—actuated, as poor Aunt Letty feared, by the agency of the evil one, working through the means of Puseyism.

His mother and sisters were in favour of Mr. Prendergast's views, and as it was gradually found by them all that there would not be any immediate pressure as regarded pecuniary means, that seemed at last to be their decision. Herbert would remain yet for three or four weeks at Castle Richmond, till matters there were somewhat more thoroughly settled, and would then put himself into the hands of Mr. Prendergast in London. Mr. Prendergast would select a legal tutor for him, and proper legal chambers; and then not long afterwards his mother and sisters should follow, and they would live together at some small villa residence near St. John's Wood Road, or perhaps out at Brompton.

It is astonishing how quickly in this world of ours chaos will settle itself into decent and graceful order, when it is properly looked in the face, and handled with a steady hand which is not sparing of the broom. Some three months since, everything at Castle Richmond was ruin; such ruin, indeed, that the very power of living under it seemed to be doubtful. When first Mr. Prendergast arrived there, a feeling came upon them all as though they might hardly dare to live in a world which would look at them as so thoroughly degraded. As regards means, they would be beggars! and as regards position, so much worse than beggars! A broken world was in truth falling about their ears, and it was felt to be impossible that they should endure its convulsions and yet live.

But now the world had fallen, the ruin had come, and they were already strong in future hopes. They had dared to look at their chaos, and found that it still contained the elements of order. There was much still that marred their happiness, and forbade the joyousness of other days. Their poor father had gone from them in their misery, and the house was still a house of mourning; and their mother too, though she bore up so wonderfully against her fate, and for their sakes hoped and planned and listened to their wishes, was a stricken woman. That she would never smile again with any heartfelt joy they were all sure. But, nevertheless, their chaos was conquered, and there was hope that the fields of life would again show themselves green and fruitful.

On one subject their mother never spoke to them, nor had even Herbert dared to speak to her: not a word had been said in that house since Mr. Prendergast left it as to the future whereabouts or future doings of that man to whom she had once given her hand at the altar. But she had ventured to ask by letter a question of Mr. Prendergast. Her question had been this: What must I do that he may not come to me or to my children? In answer to this Mr. Prendergast had told her, after some delay, that he believed she need fear nothing. He had seen the man, and he thought that he might assure her that she would not be troubled in that respect.

'It is possible,' said Mr. Prendergast, 'that he may apply to you by letter for money. If so, give him no answer whatever, but send his letters to me.'

'And are you all going?' asked Mrs. Townsend of Aunt Letty, with a lachrymose voice soon after the fate of the family was decided. They were sitting together with their knees over the fire in Mrs. Townsend's dining-parlour, in which the perilous state of the country had been discussed by them for many a pleasant hour together.

'Well, I think we shall; you see, my sister would never be happy here.'

'No, no; the shock and the change would be too great for her. Poor Lady Fitzgerald! And when is that man coming into the house?'

'What, Owen?'

'Yes! Sir Owen I suppose he is now.'

'Well, I don't know; he does not seem to be in any hurry. I believe that he has said that my sister may continue to live there if she pleases. But of course she cannot do that.'

'They do say about the country,' whispered Mrs. Townsend, 'that he refuses to be the heir at all. He certainly has not had any cards printed with the title on them—I know that as a fact.'

'He is a very singular man, very. You know I never could bear him,' said Aunt Letty.

'No, nor I either. He has not been to our church once these six months. But it's very odd, isn't it? Of course you know the story?'

'What story?' asked Aunt Letty.

'About Lady Clara. Owen Fitzgerald was dreadfully in love with her before your Herbert had ever seen her. And they do say that he has sworn his cousin shall never live if he marries her.'

'They can never marry now, you know. Only think of it. There would be three hundred a year between them.—Not at present, that is,' added Aunt Letty, looking forward to a future period after her own death.

'That is very little, very little indeed,' said Mrs. Townsend, remembering, however, that she herself had married on less. 'But, Miss Fitzgerald, if Herbert does not marry her do you think this Owen will?'

'I don't think she'd have him. I am quite sure she would not.'

'Not when he has all the property, and the title too?'

'No, nor double as much. What would people say of her if she did? But, however, there is no fear, for she declares that nothing shall induce her to give up her engagement with our Herbert.'

And so they discussed it backward and forward in every way, each having her own theory as to that singular rumour which was going about the country, signifying that Owen had declined to accept the title. Aunt Letty, however, would not believe that any good could come from so polluted a source, and declared that he had his own reasons for the delay. 'It's not for any love of us,' she said, 'if he refuses to take either that or the estate.' And in this she was right. But she would have been more surprised still had she learned that Owen's forbearance arose from a strong anxiety to do what was just in the matter.

'And so Herbert won't go into the Church?'

And Letty shook her head sorrowing.

'Æneas would have been so glad to have taken him for a

twelvemonth's reading,' said Mrs. Townsend. 'He could have
come here, you know, when you went away, and been ordained
at Cork, and got a curacy close in the neighbourhood, where he
was known. It would have been so nice ; wouldn't it?'

Aunt Letty would not exactly have advised the scheme
as suggested by Mrs. Townsend. Her ideas as to Herbert's
clerical studies would have been higher than this. Trinity
College, Dublin, was in her estimation the only place left for
good Church of England ecclesiastical teaching. But as Herbert
was obstinately bent on declining sacerdotal life, there was no
use in dispelling Mrs. Townsend's bright vision.

'It's all of no use,' she said ; 'he is determined to go to the
bar.'

'The bar is very respectable,' said Mrs. Townsend, kindly.

'And you mean to go with them, too?' said Mrs. Townsend,
after another pause. ' You'll hardly be happy, I'm thinking, so
far away from your old home.'

'It is sad to change at my time of life,' said Aunt Letty,
plaintively. 'I'm sixty-two now.'

'Nonsense,' said Mrs. Townsend, who, however, knew her
age to a day.

'Sixty-two if I live another week, and I have never yet had
any home but Castle Richmond. There I was born, and till the
other day I had every reason to trust that there I might die.
But what does it matter?'

'No, that's true of course ; what does it matter where we are
while we linger in this vale of tears? But couldn't you get a
little place for yourself somewhere near here? There's Callaghan's cottage, with the two-acre piece for a cow, and as nice a
spot of a garden as there is in the county Cork.'

'I wouldn't separate myself from her now,' said Aunt Letty,
'for all the cottages and all the gardens in Ireland. The Lord has
been pleased to throw us together, and together we will finish our
pilgrimage. Whither she goes, I will go, and where she lodges,
I will lodge ; her people shall be my people, and her God my
God.' And then Mrs. Townsend said nothing further of Callaghan's pretty cottage, or of the two-acre piece.

But one reason for her going Aunt Letty did not give, even to
her friend Mrs. Townsend. Her income, that which belonged
exclusively to herself, was in no way affected by these sad
Castle Richmond revolutions. This was a comfortable,—we
may say a generous provision for an old maiden lady, amounting
to some six hundred a year, settled upon her for life, and this, if
added to what could be saved and scraped together, would
enable them to live comfortably as far as means were concerned,

in that suburban villa to which they were looking forward.
But without Aunt Letty's income that suburban villa must be but
a poor home. Mr. Prendergast had calculated that some fourteen
thousand pounds would represent the remaining property of the
family, with which it would be necessary to purchase government
stock. Such being the case, Aunt Letty's income was very material to them.

' I trust you will be able to find some one there who will
preach the gospel to you,' said Mrs. Townsend, in a tone that
showed how serious were her misgivings on the subject.

' I will search for such a one at any rate,' said Aunt Letty.
' You need not be afraid that I shall be a backslider.'

' But they have crosses now over the communion tables in the
churches of England,' said Mrs. Townsend.

' I know it is very bad,' said Aunt Letty. ' But there will
always be a remnant left. The Lord will not utterly desert us.'
And then she took her departure, leaving Mrs. Townsend with
the conviction that the land to which her friend was going was
one in which the light of the gospel no longer shone in its
purity.

It was not wonderful that they should all be anxious to get
away from Castle Richmond, for the house there was now not a
pleasant one in which to live. Let all those who have houses
and the adjuncts of houses think how considerable a part of their
life's pleasures consists in their interest in the things around
them. When will the sea-kale be fit to cut, and when will the
crocuses come up? will the violets be sweeter than ever? and
the geranium cuttings, are they thriving? we have dug, and
manured, and sown, and we look forward to the reaping, and to
see our garners full. The very furniture which ministers to our
daily uses is loved and petted; and in decorating our rooms we
educate ourselves in design. The place in church which has
been our own for years,—is not that dear to us, and the voice
that has told us of God's tidings—even though the drone become
more evident as it waxes in years, and though it grows feeble
and indolent? And the faces of those who have lived around
us, do we not love them too, the servants who have worked for
us, and the children who have first toddled beneath our eyes and
prattled in our ears, and now run their strong races, screaming
loudly, splashing us as they pass—very unpleasantly? Do we
not love them all? Do they not all contribute to the great sum
of our enjoyment? All men love such things, more or less, even
though they know it not. And women love them even more
than men.

And the Fitzgeralds were about to leave them all. The early

buds of spring were now showing themselves, but how was it possible that they should look to them? One loves the bud because one expects the flower. The sea-kale now was beyond their notice, and though they plucked the crocuses, they did so with tears upon their cheeks. After much consideration the church had been abandoned by all except Aunt Letty and Herbert. That Lady Fitzgerald should go there was impossible, and the girls were only too glad to be allowed to stay with their mother. And the schools in which they had taught since the first day in which teaching had been possible for them, had to be abandoned with such true pangs of heartfelt sorrow.

From the time when their misery first came upon them, from the days when it first began to be understood that the world had gone wrong at Castle Richmond, this separation from the schools had commenced. The work had been dropped for a while, but the dropping had in fact been final, and there was nothing further to be done than the saddest of all leave-taking. The girls had sent word to the children, perhaps imprudently, that they would go down and say a word of adieu to their pupils. The children had of course told their mothers, and when the girls reached the two neat buildings, which stood at the corner of the park, there were there to meet them, not unnaturally, a concourse of women and children.

In former prosperous days the people about Castle Richmond had, as a rule, been better to do than their neighbours. Money wages had been more plentiful, and there had been little or no sub-letting of land; the children had been somewhat more neatly clothed, and the women less haggard in their faces; but this difference was hardly perceptible any longer. To them, the Miss Fitzgeralds, looking at the poverty-stricken assemblage, it almost seemed as though the misfortune of their house had brought down its immediate consequences on all who had lived within their circle; but this was the work of the famine. In those days one could rarely see any member of a peasant's family bearing in his face a look of health. The yellow meal was a useful food—the most useful, doubtless, which could at that time be found; but it was not one that was gratifying either to the eye or palate.

The girls had almost regretted their offer before they had left the house. It would have been better, they said to themselves, to have had the children up in the hall, and there to have spoken their farewells, and made their little presents. The very entering those schoolrooms again would almost be too much for them; but this consideration was now too late, and when they got to the corner of the gate, they found that there was a crowd to receive them. 'Mary, I must go back,' said Emmeline, when she first saw them; but Aunt Letty, who was with them, stepped forward, and they soon found themselves in the schoolroom.

'We have come to say good-bye to you all,' said Aunt Letty, trying to begin a speech.

'May the heavens be yer bed then, the lot of yez, for ye war always good to the poor. May the Blessed Virgin guide and protect ye wherever ye be;'—a blessing against which Aunt Letty at once entered a little inward protest, perturbed though she was in spirit. 'May the heavens rain glory on yer heads, for ye war always the finest family that war over in the county Cork!'

'You know, I dare say, that we are going to leave you,' continued Aunt Letty.

'We knows it, we knows it; sorrow come to them as did it all. Faix, an' there'll niver be any good in the counthry, at all at all, when you're gone, Miss Emmeline; an' what'll we do at all for the want of yez, and when shall we see the likes of yez? Eh, Miss Letty, but there'll be sore eyes weeping for ye; and for her leddyship too; may the Lord Almighty bless her, and presarve her, and carry her sowl to glory when she dies; for av there war iver a good woman on God's 'arth, that woman is Leddy Fitzgerald.'

And then Aunt Letty found that there was no necessity for her to continue her speech, and indeed no possibility of her doing so even if she were so minded. The children began to wail and cry, and the mothers also mixed loud sobbings with their loud prayers; and Emmeline and Mary, dissolved in tears, sat themselves down, drawing to them the youngest bairns and those whom they had loved the best, kissing their sallow, famine-stricken, unwholesome faces, and weeping over them with a love of which hitherto they had been hardly conscious.

There was not much more in the way of speech possible to any of them, for even Aunt Letty was far gone in tender wailing; and it was wonderful to see the liberties that were taken even with that venerable bonnet. The women had first of all taken hold of her hands to kiss them, and had kissed her feet, and her garments, and her shoulders, and then behind her back they had made crosses on her, although they knew how dreadfully she would have raged had she caught them polluting her by such doings; and they grasped her arms and embraced them, till at last, those who were more daring, reached her forehead and her face, and poor old Aunt Letty, who in her emotion could not now utter a syllable, was almost pulled to pieces among them.

Mary and Emmeline had altogether surrendered themselves, and were the centres of clusters of children who hung upon them. And the sobs now were no longer low and tearful, but they had grown into long, protracted groanings, and loud wailings, and clapping of hands, and tearings of the hair. O, my reader, have you ever seen a railway train taking its departure from an Irish station with a freight of Irish emigrants? if so, you know how the hair is torn, and how the hands are clapped, and how the low moanings gradually swell into notes of loud lamentation. It means nothing, I have heard men say,—men and women too. But such men and women are wrong. It means much; it means this: that those who are separated, not only love each other, but are anxious to tell each other that they so love. We have all heard of demonstrative people. A demonstrative person, I take it, is he who is desirous of speaking out what is in his heart. For myself I am inclined to think that such speaking out has its good ends. 'The faculty of silence! is it not of all things the most beautiful?' That is the doctrine preached by a great latter-day philosopher; for myself I think that the faculty of speech is much more beautiful—of speech if it be made but by howlings, and wailings, and loud clappings of the hand. What is in a man, let it come out and be known to those around him; if it be bad it will find correction; if it be good it will spread and be beneficent.

And then one woman made herself audible over the sobs of the crowding children; she was a gaunt, high-boned woman, but she would have been comely, if not handsome, had not the famine come upon her. She held a baby in her arms, and another little toddling thing had been hanging on her dress till Emmeline had seen it, and plucked it away; and it was now sitting in her lap quite composed, and sucking a piece of cake that had been given to it. 'An' it's a bad day for us all,' said the woman, beginning in a low voice, which became louder and louder as she went on; 'it's a bad day for us all that takes away from us the only rale friends that we iver had, and the back of my hand to them that have come in the way, bringin' sorrow an' desolation, an' misery on gentlefolks that have been good to the poor since iver the poor have been in the land; rale gentlefolks, sich as there ain no others to be found now-a-days in any of these parts. O'hone. o'hone! but it's a bad day for us and for the childer; for where shall we find the dhrop to comfort us or the bit to ate when the sickness comes on us, as it's likely to come now, when the Fitzgeralds is out of the counthry. May the Lord bless them, and keep them, and presarve them, and the Holy Virgin have them in her keepin'!'

'Wh—i—s—h—h,' said Aunt Letty, who could not allow such idolatry to pass by unobserved or unrebuked.

'An' shure the blessin' of a poor woman cannot haram you,' continued the mother; 'an' I'll tell you what, neighbours, it'll be a bad day for him that folk call the heir when he puts his foot in that house.'

'Deed an' that's thrue for you, Bridget Magrath,' said another voice from among the crowd of women.

'A bad day intirely,' continued the woman with the baby; 'av the house stans over his head when he does the like o' that, there'll be no justice in the heavens.'

'But, Mrs. Magrath,' said Aunt Letty, trying to interrupt her, 'you must not speak in that way; you are mistaken in supposing that Mr. Owen—'

'We'll all live to see,' said the woman; 'for the time's comin' quick upon us now. But it's a bad law that kills our ould masther over our heads, an' takes away from us our ould misthress. An' as for him they calls Mr. Owen—'

But the ladies found it impossible to listen to her any longer, so with some difficulty they extricated themselves from the crowd by which they were surrounded, and once more shaking hands with those who were nearest to them escaped into the park, and made their way back towards the house.

They had not expected so much demonstration, and were not a little disconcerted at the scene which had taken place. Aunt Letty had never been so handled in her life, and hardly knew how to make her bonnet sit comfortably on her head; and the two girls were speechless till they were half across the park.

'I am glad we have been,' said Emmeline at last, as soon as the remains of her emotion would allow her to articulate her words.

'It would have been dreadful to have gone away without seeing them,' said Mary. 'Poor creatures, poor dear creatures; we shall never again have any more people to be fond of us like that!'

'There is no knowing,' said Aunt Letty; 'the Lord giveth and the Lord taketh away, and blessed is the name of the Lord. You are both young, and may come back again; but for me—'

'Dear Aunt Letty, if we come back you shall come too.'

'If I only thought that my bones could lie here near my brother's. But never mind; what signifies it where our bones lie?' And then they were silent for a while, till Aunt Letty spoke again. 'I mean to be quite happy over in England; I believe I shall be happiest of you all if I can find any clergyman who is not half perverted to idolatry.'

This took place some time before the ladies left Castle Richmond,—perhaps as much as three weeks; it was even before

Herbert's departure, who started for London the day but one after the scene here recorded; he had gone to various places to take his last farewell; to see the Townsends at the parsonage; ta call on Father Barney at Kanturk, and had even shaken hands with the Rev. Mr. Creagh, at Gortnaclough. But one farewell visit had been put off for the last. It was now arranged that he was to go over to Desmond Court and see Clara before he went. There had been some difficulty in this, for Lady Desmond had at first declared that she could not feel justified in asking him into her house; but the earl was now at home, and her ladyship had at last given her consent: he was to see the countess first, and was afterwards to see Clara—alone. He had declared that he would not go there unless he were to be allowed an interview with her in private. The countess, as I have said, at last consented, trusting that her previous eloquence might be efficacious in counteracting the ill effects of her daughter's imprudence. On the day after that interview he was to start for London; 'never to return,' as he said to Emmeline, 'unless he came to seek his wife.'

'But you will come to seek your wife,' said Emmeline, stoutly; 'I shall think you faint-hearted if you doubt it.'

CHAPTER XXXIII.

THE LAST STAGE.

ON the day before his departure for London, Herbert Fitzgerald once more got on his horse—the horse that was to be no longer his after that day—and rode off towards Desmond Court. He had already perceived how foolish he had been in walking thither through the mud and rain when last he went there, and how much he had lost by his sad appearance that day, and by his want of personal comfort. So he dressed himself with some care —dressing not for his love, but for the countess,—and taking his silver-mounted whip in his gloved hand, he got up on his well-groomed nag with more spirit than he had hitherto felt.

Nothing could be better than the manner in which, at this time, the servants about Castle Richmond conducted themselves. Most of them—indeed, all but three—had been told that they must go; and in so telling them, the truth had been explained. It had been 'found,' Aunt Letty said to one of the elder among them, that Mr. Herbert was not the heir to the property, and therefore the family was obliged to go away. Mrs. Jones of course accompanied her mistress. Richard had been told, both by Herbert and by Aunt Letty, that he had better remain and live on a small patch of land that should be provided for him. But in answer to this he stated his intention of removing himself to London. If the London air was fit for 'my leddy and Miss Letty,' it would be for him. It's no good any more talking, Mr. Herbert,' said Richard, 'I main to go.' So there was no more talking, and he did go.

But all the other servants took their month's warning with tears and blessings, and strove one beyond another how they might best serve the ladies of the family to the end. 'I'd lose the little fingers off me to go with you, Miss Emmeline; so I would,' said one poor girl,—all in vain. If they could not keep a retinue of servants in Ireland, it was clear enough that they could not keep them in London.

The groom who held the horse for Herbert to mount, touched his hat respectfully as his young master rode off slowly down the avenue, and then went back to the stables to meditate with awe on the changes which had happened in his time, and to bethink himself whether or no he could bring himself to serve in the stables of Owen the usurper.

Herbert did not take the direct road to Desmond Court, but went round as though he were going to Gortnaclough, and then turning away from the Gortnaclough road, made his way by a cross lane towards Clady and the mountains. He hardly knew himself whether he had any object in this beyond one which he did not express even to himself,—that, namely, of not being seen on the way leading to Desmond Court. But this he did do, thereby riding out of the district with which he was most thoroughly acquainted, and passing by cabins and patches of now deserted land which were strange to him. It was a poor, bleak, damp, undrained country, lying beyond the confines of his father's property, which in good days had never been pleasant to the eye, but which now in these days—days that were so decidedly bad, was anything but pleasant. It was one of those tracts of land which had been divided and subdivided among the cottiers till the fields had dwindled down to parts of acres, each surrounded by rude low banks, which of themselves seemed to occupy a quarter of the surface of the land. The original landmarks, the big earthen banks,—banks so large that a horse might walk on the top of them,—were still visible enough, showing to the practised eye what had once been the fields into which the land had been divided; but these had since been bisected and crossected, and intersected by family arrangements, in which brothers had been jealous of brothers, and fathers of their children, till each little lot contained but a rood or two of available surface.

This had been miserable enough to look at, even when those roods had been cropped with potatoes or oats; but now they were not cropped at all, nor was there preparation being made for cropping them. They had been let out under the con-acre system, at so much a rood, for the potato season, at rents amounting sometimes to ten or twelve pounds an acre; but nobody would take them now. There, in that electoral division, the whole proceeds of such land would hardly have paid the poor rates, and therefore the land was left uncultivated.

The winter was over, for it was now April, and had any tillage been intended, it would have been commenced—even in Ireland. It was the beginning of April, but the weather was still stormy and cold, and the east wind, which, as a rule, strikes Ireland with but a light hand, was blowing sharply. On a sudden a squall of rain came on,—one of those spring squalls which are so piercingly cold, but which are sure to pass by rapidly, if the wayfarer will have patience to wait for them. Herbert, remembering his former discomfiture, resolved that he would have such patience, and dismounting from his horse at a cabin on the roadside, entered it himself, and led his horse in after him. In England no one would think of taking his steed into a poor man's cottage, and would hardly put his beast into a cottager's shed without leave asked and granted; but people are more intimate with each other, and take greater liberties in Ireland. It is no uncommon thing on a wet hunting-day to see a cabin packed with horses, and the children moving about among them, almost as unconcernedly as though the animals were pigs. But then the Irish horses are so well mannered and good-natured.

The cabin was one abutting as it were on the road, not standing back upon the land, as is most customary; and it was built in an angle at a spot where the road made a turn, so that two sides of it stood close out in the wayside. It was small and wretched to look at, without any sort of outside shed, or even a scrap of potato-garden attached to it,—a miserable, low-roofed, damp, ragged tenement, as wretched as any that might be seen even in the county Cork.

But the nakedness of the exterior was as nothing to the nakedness of the interior. When Herbert entered, followed by his horse, his eye glanced round the dark place, and it seemed to be empty of everything. There was no fire on the hearth, though a fire on the hearth is the easiest of all luxuries for an Irishman to acquire and the last which he is willing to lose. There was not an article of furniture in the whole place; neither chairs, nor table, nor bed, nor dresser; there was there neither dish, nor cup, nor plate, nor even the iron pot in which all the cookery of the Irish cottiers' ménage is usually carried on. Beneath his feet was the damp earthen floor, and around him were damp, cracked walls, and over his head was the old lumpy thatch, through which the water was already dropping; but inside was to be seen none of those articles of daily use which are usually to be found in the houses even of the poorest.

But, nevertheless, the place was inhabited. Squatting in the middle of the cabin, seated on her legs crossed under her, with nothing between her and the wet earth, there crouched a woman with a child in her arms. At first, so dark was the place, Herbert hardly thought that the object before him was a human being. She did not move when he entered, or speak to him, or in any way show sign of surprise that he should come there. There was room for him and his horse without pushing her from her place; and, as it seemed, he might have stayed there and taken his departure without any sign having been made by her.

But as his eyes became used to the light he saw her eyes gleaming brightly through the gloom. They were very large and bright as they turned round upon him while he moved— large and bright, but with a dull, unwholesome brightness,—a brightness that had in it none of the light of life.

And then he looked at her more closely. She had on her some rag of clothing which barely sufficed to cover her nakedness, and the baby which she held in her arms was covered in some sort; but he could see, as he came to stand close over her, that these garments were but loose rags which were hardly fastened round her body. Her rough short hair hung down upon her back, clotted with dirt, and the head and face of the child which she held was covered with dirt and sores. On no more wretched object, in its desolate solitude, did the eye of man ever fall.

In those days there was a form of face which came upon the sufferers when their state of misery was far advanced, and which was a sure sign that their last stage of misery was nearly run. The mouth would fall and seem to hang, the lips at the two ends of the mouth would be dragged down, and the lower parts of the cheeks would fall as though they had been dragged and pulled. There were no signs of acute agony when this phasis of countenance was to be seen, none of the horrid symptoms of gnawing hunger by which one generally supposes that famine is accompanied. The look is one of apathy, desolation, and death. When custom had made these signs easily legible, the poor doomed wretch was known with certainty. 'It's no use in life meddling with him; he's gone,' said a lady to me in the far west of the south of Ireland, while the poor boy, whose doom was thus spoken, stood by listening. Her delicacy did not equal her energy in doing good,—for she did much good; but in truth it was difficult to be delicate when the hands were so full. And then she pointed out to me the signs on the lad's face, and I found that her reading was correct.

The famine was not old enough at the time of which we are speaking for Herbert to have learned all this, or he would have known that there was no hope left in this world for the poor creature whom he saw before him. The skin of her cheek had fallen, and her mouth was dragged, and the mark of death was upon her; but the agony of want was past. She sat there listless, indifferent, hardly capable of suffering, even for her child, waiting her doom unconsciously.

As he had entered without eliciting a word from her, so might he have departed without any outward sign of notice; but this would have been impossible on his part. 'I have come in out of the rain for shelter,' said he, looking down on her.

'Out o' the rain, is it?' said she, still fixing on him her glassy bright eyes. 'Yer honour's welcome thin.' But she did not attempt to move, nor show any of those symptoms of reverence which are habitual to the Irish when those of a higher rank enter their cabins.

'You seem to be very poorly off here,' said Herbert, looking round the bare walls of the cabin. 'Have you no chair, and no bed to lie on?'

''Deed no,' said she.

'And no fire?' said he, for the damp and chill of the place struck through his bones.

''Deed no,' she said again; but she made no wail as to her wants, and uttered no complaint as to her misery.

'And are you living here by yourself, without furniture or utensils of any kind?'

'It's jist as yer honour sees it,' answered she.

For a while Herbert stood still, looking round him, for the woman was so motionless and uncommunicative that he hardly knew how to talk to her. That she was in the lowest depth of distress was evident enough, and it behoved him to administer to her immediate wants before he left her; but what could he do for one who seemed to be so indifferent to herself? He stood for a time looking round him till he could see through the gloom that there was a bundle of straw lying in the dark corner beyond the hearth, and that the straw was huddled up, as though there

were something lying under it. Seeing this he left the bridle
of his horse, and stepping across the cabin moved the straw with
the handle of his whip. As he did so he turned his back from
the wall in which the small window-hole had been pierced, so
that a gleam of light fell upon the bundle at his feet, and he
could see that the body of a child was lying there, stripped of
every vestige of clothing.

For a minute or two he said nothing—hardly, indeed, knowing
how to speak, and looking from the corpse-like woman back to
the life-like corpse, and then from the corpse back to the woman,
as though he expected that she would say something unasked.
But she did not say a word, though she so turned her head that
her eyes rested on him.

He then knelt down and put his hand upon the body, and
found that it was not yet stone cold. The child apparently had
been about four years old, while that still living in her arms
might perhaps be half that age.

'Was she your own?' asked Herbert, speaking hardly above
his breath.

''Deed, yes!' said the woman. 'She was my own, own little
Kitty.' But there was no tear in her eye or gurgling sob audible
from her throat.

'And when did she die?' he asked.

''Deed, thin, and I don't jist know—not exactly;' and sinking
lower down upon her haunches, she put up to her forehead the
hand with which she had supported herself on the floor—the
hand which was not occupied with the baby—and pushing back
with it the loose hairs from her face, tried to make an effort at
thinking.

'She was alive in the night, wasn't she?' he said.

'I b'lieve thin she was, yer honour. 'Twas broad day, I'm
thinking, when she guv' over moaning. She warn't that way
when he went away.'

And who's he?'

'Jist Mike, thin.'

'And is Mike your husband?' he asked. She was not very
willing to talk; but it appeared at last that Mike was her
husband, and that having become a cripple through rheumatism,
he had not been able to work on the roads. In this condition
he and his should of course have gone into a poor-house. It was
easy enough to give such advice in such cases when one came
across them, and such advice when given at that time was usually
followed; but there were so many who had no advice, who could
get no aid, who knew not which way to turn themselves! This
wretched man had succeeded in finding some one who would give

him his food—food enough to keep himself alive—for such work as he could do in spite of his rheumatism, and this work to the last he would not abandon. Even this was better to him than the poor-house. But then, as long as a man found work out of the poor-house, his wife and children would not be admitted into it. They would not be admitted if the fact of the working husband was known. The rule in itself was salutary, as without it a man could work, earning such wages as were adjudged to be needful for a family, and at the same time send his wife and children to be supported on the rates. But in some cases, such as this, it pressed very cruelly. Exceptions were of course made in such cases, if they were known: but then it was so hard to know them!

This man Mike, the husband of that woman, and the father of those children, alive and dead, had now gone to his work, leaving his home without one morsel of food within it, and the wife of his bosom and children of his love without the hope of getting any. And then looking closely round him, Herbert could see that a small basin or bowl lay on the floor near her, capable of holding perhaps a pint; and on lifting it he saw that there still clung to it a few grains of uncooked Indian corn-flour—the yellow meal, as it was called. Her husband, she said at last, had brought home with him in his cap a handful of this flour, stolen from the place where he was working—perhaps a quarter of a pound, then worth over a farthing, and she had mixed this with water in a basin; and this was the food which had sustained her, or rather had not sustained her, since yesterday morning—her and her two children, the one that was living and the one that was dead.

Such was her story, told by her in the fewest of words. And then he asked her as to her hopes for the future. But though she cared, as it seemed, but little for the past, for the future she cared less. ' 'Deed, thin, an' I don't jist know.' She would say no more than that, and would not even raise her voice to ask for alms when he pitied her in her misery. But with her the agony of death was already over.

' And the child that you have in your arms,' he said, ' is it not cold?' And he stood close over her, and put out his hand and touched the baby's body. As he did so, she made some motion as though to arrange the clothing closer round the child's limbs, but Herbert could see that she was making an effort to hide her own nakedness. It was the only effort that she made while he stood there beside her.

' Is she not cold?' he said again, when he had turned his face away to relieve her from her embarrassment.

'Cowld,' she muttered, with a vacant face and wondering tone of voice, as though she did not quite understand him. 'I suppose she is cowld. Why wouldn't she be cowld? We're cowld enough, if that's all.' But still she did not stir from the spot on which she sat; and the child, though it gave from time to time a low moan that was almost inaudible, lay still in her arms, with its big eyes staring into vacancy.

He felt that he was stricken with horror as he remained there in the cabin with the dying woman and the naked corpse of the poor dead child. But what was he to do? He could not go and leave them without succour. The woman had made no plaint of her suffering, and had asked for nothing; but he felt that it would be impossible to abandon her without offering her relief; nor was it possible that he should leave the body of the child in that horribly ghastly state. So he took from his pocket his silk handkerchief, and, returning to the corner of the cabin, spread it as a covering over the corpse. At first he did not like to touch the small naked dwindled remains of humanity from which life had fled; but gradually he overcame his disgust, and kneeling down, he straightened the limbs and closed the eyes, and folded the handkerchief round the slender body. The mother looked on him the while, shaking her head slowly, as though asking him with all the voice that was left to her, whether it were not piteous; but of words she still uttered none.

And then he took from his pocket a silver coin or two, and tendered them to her. These she did take, muttering some word of thanks, but they caused her no emotion of joy. 'She was there waiting,' she said, 'till Mike should return,' and there she would stil wait, even though she should die with the silver in her hand.

'I will send some one to you,' he said, as he took his departure; 'some one that shall take the poor child and bury it, and who shall move you and the other one into the workhouse.' She thanked him once more with some low muttered words, but the promise brought her no joy. And when the succour came it was all too late, for the mother and the two children never left the cabin till they left it together, wrapped in their workhouse shrouds.

Herbert, as he remounted his horse and rode quietly on, forgot for a while both himself and Clara Desmond. Whatever might be the extent of his own calamity, how could he think himself unhappy after what he had seen? how could he repine at aught that the world had done for him, having now witnessed to how low a state of misery a fellow human being might be brought? Could he, after that, dare to consider himself unfortunate?

Before he reached Desmond Court he did make some arrangements for the poor woman, and directed that a cart might be sent for her, so that she might be carried to the union workhouse at Kanturk. But his efforts in her service were of little avail. People then did not think much of a dying woman, and were in no special hurry to obey Herbert's behest.

'A woman to be carried to the union, is it? For Mr. Fitzgerald, eh? What Mr. Fitzgerald says must be done, in course. But sure av' it's done before dark, won't that be time enough for the likes of her?'

But had they flown to the spot on the wings of love, it would not have sufficed to prolong her life one day. Her doom had been spoken before Herbert had entered the cabin.

CHAPTER XXXIV.

FAREWELL.

He was two hours later than he had intended as he rode up the avenue to Lady Desmond's gate, and his chief thought at the moment was how he should describe to the countess the scene he had just witnessed. Why describe it at all? That is what we should all say. He had come there to talk about other things—about other things which must be discussed, and which would require all his wits. Let him keep that poor woman on his mind, but not embarrass himself with any mention of her for the present. This, no doubt, would have been wise if only it had been possible; but out of the full heart the mouth speaks.

But Lady Desmond had not witnessed the scene which I have attempted to describe, and her heart, therefore, was not full of it, and was not inclined to be so filled. And so, in answer to Herbert's exclamation, 'Oh, Lady Desmond, I have seen such a sight!' she gave him but little encouragement to describe it, and by her coldness, reserve, and dignity, soon quelled the expression of his feelings.

The earl was present and shook hands very cordially with Herbert when he entered the room; and he, being more susceptible as being younger, and not having yet become habituated to the famine as his mother was, did express some eager sympathy. He would immediately go down, or send Fahy with the car, and have her brought up and saved; but his mother had other work to do and soon put a stop to all this.

'Mr. Fitzgerald,' said she, speaking with a smile upon her

face, and with much high-bred dignity of demeanour, 'as you and Lady Clara both wish to see each other before you leave the country, and as you have known each other so intimately, and considering all the circumstances, I have not thought it well absolutely to forbid an interview. But I do doubt its expediency ; I do, indeed. And Lord Desmond, who feels for your late misfortune as we all do, perfectly agrees with me. He thinks that it would be much wiser for you to have parted without the pain of a meeting, seeing how impossible it is that you should ever be more to each other than you are now.' And then she appealed to her son, who stood by, looking not quite so wise, nor even quite so decided as his mother's words would seem to make him.

'Well, yes ; upon my word I don't see how it's to be,' said the young earl. 'I am deuced sorry for it for one, and I wish I was well off, so that I could give Clara a pot of money, and then I should not care so much about your not being the baronet.'

'I am sure you must see, Mr. Fitzgerald, and I know that you do see it because you have very properly said so, that a marriage between you and Lady Clara is now impossible. For her such an engagement would be very bad—very bad indeed ; but for you it would be utter ruin. Indeed, it would be ruin for you both. Unencumbered as you will be, and with the good connection which you will have, and with your excellent talents, it will be quite within your reach to win for yourself a high position. But with you, as with other gentlemen who have to work their way, marriage must come late in life, unless you marry an heiress. This I think is thoroughly understood by all people in our position ; and I am sure that it is understood by your excellent mother, for whom I always had and still have the most unfeigned respect. As this is so undoubtedly the case, and as I cannot of course consent that Lady Clara should remain hampered by an engagement which would in all human probability hang over the ten best years of her life, I thought it wise that you should not see each other. I have, however, allowed myself to be overruled ; and now I must only trust to your honour, forbearance, and prudence to protect my child from what might possibly be the ill effects of her own affectionate feelings. That she is romantic,—enthusiastic to a fault I should perhaps rather call it—I need not tell you. She thinks that your misfortune demands from her a sacrifice of herself ; but you, I know, will feel that, even were such a sacrifice available to you, it would not become you to accept it. Because you have fallen, you will not wish to drag her down ; more especially as you can rise again—and she could not.'

So spoke the countess, with much worldly wisdom, and with

considerable tact in adjusting her words to the object which she had in view. Herbert, as he stood before her silent during the period of her oration, did feel that it would be well for him to give up his love, and go away in utter solitude of heart to those dingy studies which Mr. Prendergast was preparing for him. His love, or rather the assurance of Clara's love, had been his great consolation. But what right had he, with all the advantages of youth, and health, and friends, and education, to require consolation? And then from moment to moment he thought of the woman whom he had left in the cabin, and confessed that he did not dare to call himself unhappy.

He had listened attentively, although he did thus think of other eloquence besides that of the countess—of the eloquence of that silent, solitary, dying woman; but when she had done he hardly knew what to say for himself. She did make him feel that it would be ungenerous in him to persist in his engagement; but then again, Clara's letters and his sister's arguments had made him feel that it was impossible to abandon it. They pleaded of heart-feelings so well that he could not resist them; and the countess—she pleaded so well as to world's prudence that he could not resist her.

'I would not willingly do anything to injure Lady Clara,' he said.

'That's what we all know,' said the young earl. 'You see, what is a girl to do like her? Love in a cottage is all very well, and all that; and as for riches, I don't care about them. It would be a pity if I did, for I shall be about the poorest nobleman in the three kingdoms, I suppose. But a chap when he marries should have something; shouldn't he now?'

To tell the truth the earl had been very much divided in his opinions since he had come home, veering round a point or two this way or a point or two that, in obedience to the blast of eloquence to which he might be last subjected. But latterly the idea had grown upon him that Clara might possibly marry Owen Fitzgerald. There was about Owen a strange fascination which all felt who had once loved him. To the world he was rough and haughty, imperious in his commands, and exacting even in his fellowship; but to the few whom he absolutely loved, whom he had taken into his heart's core, no man ever was more tender or more gracious. Clara, though she had resolved to banish him from her heart, had found it impossible to do so till Herbert's misfortunes had given him a charm in her eyes which was not all his own. Clara's mother had loved him—had loved him as she never before had loved; and now she loved him still, though she had so strongly determined that her love should be that of a

mother, and not that of a wife. And the young earl, now that
Owen's name was again rife in his ears, remembered all the
pleasantness of former days. He had never again found such a
companion as Owen had been. He had met no other friend to
whom he could talk of sport and a man's outward pleasures when
his mind was that way given, and to whom he could also talk of
soft inward things,—the heart's feelings, and aspirations, and
wants. Owen would be as tender with him as a woman, allowing
the young lad's arm round his body, listening to words which
the outer world would have called bosh—and have derided as
girlish. So at least thought the young earl to himself. And all
boys long to be allowed utterance occasionally for these soft
tender things;—as also do all men, unless the devil's share in
the world has become altogether uppermost with them.

And the young lad's heart hankered after his old friend. He
had listened to his sister, and for a while had taken her part;
but his mother had since whispered to him that Owen would
now be the better suitor, the preferable brother-in-law; and that
in fact Clara loved Owen the best, though she felt herself bound
by honour to his kinsman. And then she reminded her son of
Clara's former love for Owen—a love which he himself had
witnessed; and he thought of the day when with so much regret
he had told his friend that he was unsuited to wed with an earl's
penniless daughter. Of the subsequent pleasantness which had
come with Herbert's arrival, he had seen little or nothing. He
had been told by letter that Herbert Fitzgerald, the prosperous
heir of Castle Richmond, was to be his future brother-in-law,
and he had been satisfied. But now, if Owen could return—how
pleasant it would be!

'But a chap when he marries should have something, shouldn't
he now?' So spoke the young earl, re-echoing his mother's
prudence.

Herbert did not quite like this interference on the boy's part.
Was he to explain to a young lad from Eton what his future
intentions were with reference to his mode of living and period
of marriage? 'Of course,' he said, addressing himself to the
countess, 'I shall not insist on an engagement made under such
different circumstances.'

'Nor will you allow her to do so through a romantic feeling of
generosity,' said the countess.

'You should know your own daughter, Lady Desmond, better
than I do,' he answered; 'but I cannot say what I may do at her
instance till I shall have seen her.'

'Do you mean to say that you will allow a girl of her age to
talk you into a proceeding which you know to be wrong?'

'I will allow no one,' he said, 'to talk me into a proceeding which I know to be wrong; nor will I allow any one to talk me out of a proceeding which I believe to be right.' And then, having uttered these somewhat grandiloquent words, he shut himself up as though there were no longer any need for discussing the subject.

'My poor child!' said the countess, in a low tremulous voice, as though she did not intend him to hear them. 'My poor unfortunate child!' Herbert as he did hear them thought of the woman in the cabin, and of her misfortunes and of her children. 'Come, Patrick,' continued the countess, 'it is perhaps useless for us to say anything further at present. If you will remain here, Mr. Fitzgerald, for a minute or two, I will send Lady Clara to wait upon you;' and then curtsying with great dignity she withdrew, and the young earl scuffled out after her. 'Mamma,' he said, as he went, 'he is determined that he will have her.'

'My poor child!' answered the countess.

'And if I were in his place I should be determined also. You may as well give it up. Not but that I like Owen a thousand times the best.'

Herbert did wait there for some five minutes, and then the door was opened very gently, was gently closed again, and Clara Desmond was in the room. He came towards her respectfully, holding out his hand that he might take hers; but before he had thought of how she would act she was in his arms. Hitherto, of all betrothed maidens, she had been the most retiring. Sometimes he had thought her cold when she had left the seat by his side to go and nestle closely by his sister. She had avoided the touch of his hand and the pressure of his arm, and had gone from him speechless, if not with anger then with dismay, when he had carried the warmth of his love beyond the touch of his hand or the pressure of his arm. But now she rushed into his embrace and hid her face upon his shoulder, as though she were over glad to return to the heart from which those around her had endeavoured to banish her. Was he or was he not to speak of his love? That had been the question which he had asked himself when left alone there for those five minutes, with the eloquence of the countess ringing in his ears. Now that question had in truth been answered for him.

'Herbert,' she said, 'Herbert! I have so sorrowed for you; but I know that you have borne it like a man.'

She was thinking of what he had now half forgotten,—the position which he had lost, those hopes which had all been shipwrecked, his title surrendered to another, and his lost estates. She was thinking of them as the loss affected him; but he, he had reconciled himself to all that,—unless all that were to separate him from his promised bride.

'Dearest Clara,' he said, with his arm close round her waist, while neither anger nor dismay appeared to disturb the sweetness of that position, 'the letter which you wrote me has been my chief comfort.' Now if he had any intention of liberating Clara from the bond of her engagement,—if he really had any feeling that it behoved him not to involve her in the worldly losses which had come upon him,—he was taking a very bad way of carrying out his views in that respect. Instead of confessing the comfort which he had received from that letter, and holding her close to his breast while he did confess it, he should have stood away from her—quite as far apart as he had done from the countess ; and he should have argued with her, showing her how foolish and imprudent her letter had been, explaining that it behoved her now to repress her feelings, and teaching her that peers' daughters as well as housemaids should look out for situations which would suit them, guided by prudence and a view to the wages,—not follow the dictates of impulse and of the heart. This is what he should have done, according, I believe, to the views of most men and women. Instead of that he held her there as close as he could hold her, and left her to do the most of the speaking. I think he was right. According to my ideas woman's love should be regarded as fair prize of war,—as long as the war has been carried on with due adherence to the recognized law of nations. When it has been fairly won, let it be firmly held. I have no opinion of that theory of giving up.

'You knew that I would not abandon you! Did you not know it? say that you knew it?' said Clara, and then she insisted on having an answer.

'I could hardly dare to think that there was so much happiness left for me,' said Herbert.

'Then you were a traitor to your love, sir; a false traitor.' But deep as was the offence for which she arraigned him, it was clear to see that the pardon came as quick as the conviction.

'And was Emmeline so untrue to me also as to believe that?'

'Emmeline said—' and then he told her what Emmeline had said.

'Dearest, dearest Emmeline! give her a whole heart-load of love from me; now mind you do,—and to Mary, too. And remember this, sir; that I love Emmeline ten times better than I do you; twenty times—because she knew me. Oh, if she had mistrusted me—!'

'And do you think that I mistrusted you?'

'Yes, you did; you know you did, sir. You wrote and told

me so;—and now, this very day, you come here to act as though you mistrusted me still. You know you have, only you have not the courage to go on with the acting.'

And then he began to defend himself, showing how ill it would have become him to have kept her bound to her engagements had she feared poverty as most girls in her position would have feared it. But on this point she would not hear much from him, lest the very fact of her hearing it should make it seem that such a line of conduct were possible to her.

'You know nothing about most girls, sir, or about any, I am afraid; not even about one. And if most girls were frightfully heartless, which they are not, what right had you to liken me to most girls? Emmeline knew better, and why could not you take her as a type of most girls? You have behaved very badly, Master Herbert, and you know it; and nothing on earth shall make me forgive you; nothing—but your promise that you will not so misjudge me any more.' And then the tears came to his eyes, and her face was again hidden on his shoulder.

It was not very probable that after such a commencement the interview would terminate in a manner favourable to the wishes of the countess. Clara swore to her lover that she had given him all that she had to give,—her heart, and will, and very self; and swore, also, that she could not and would not take back the gift. She would remain as she was now as long as he thought proper, and would come to him whenever he should tell her that his home was large enough for them both. And so that matter was settled between them.

Then she had much to say about his mother and sisters, and a word too about his poor father. And now that it was settled between them so fixedly, that come what might they were to float together in the same boat down the river of life, she had a question or two also to ask, and her approbation to give or to withhold, as to his future prospects. He was not to think, she told him, of deciding on anything without at any rate telling her. So he had to explain to her all the family plans, making her know why he had decided on the law as his own path to fortune, and asking for and obtaining her consent to all his pro· posed measures.

In this way her view of the matter became more and more firmly adopted as that which should be the view resolutely to be taken by them both. The countess had felt that that interview would be fatal to her; and she had been right. But how could she have prevented it? Twenty times she had resolved that she would prevent it; but twenty times she had been forced to confess that she was powerless to do so. In these days a mother even can only exercise such power over a child as public opinion permits her to use. 'Mother, it was you who brought us together, and you cannot separate us now.' That had always been Clara's argument, leaving the countess helpless, except as far as she could work on Herbert's generosity. That she had tried,—and, as we have seen, been foiled there also. If only she could have taken her daughter away while the Castle Richmond family were still mersed in the bitter depth of their suffering,—at that moment when the blows were falling on them! Then, indeed, she might have done something; but she was not like other titled mothers. In such a step as this she was absolutely without the means.

Thus talking together they remained closeted for a most unconscionable time. Clara had had her purpose to carry out, and to Herbert the moments had been too precious to cause him any regret as they passed. But now at last a knock was heard at the door, and Lady Desmond, without waiting for an answer to it, entered the room. Clara immediately started from her seat, not as though she were either guilty or tremulous, but with a brave resolve to go on with her purposed plan.

'Mamma,' she said, 'it is fixed now; it cannot be altered now.'

'What is fixed, Clara?'

'Herbert and I have renewed our engagement, and nothing must now break it, unless we die.'

'Mr. Fitzgerald, if this be true your conduct to my daughter has been unmanly as well as ungenerous.'

'Lady Desmond, it is true; and I think that my conduct is neither unmanly nor ungenerous.'

'Your own relations are against you, sir.'

'What relations?' asked Clara, sharply.

'I am not speaking to you, Clara; your absurdity and romance are so great that I cannot speak to you.'

'What relations, Herbert?' again asked Clara; for she would not for the world have had Lady Fitzgerald against her.

'Lady Desmond has, I believe, seen my Aunt Letty two or three times lately; I suppose she must mean her.'

'Oh,' said Clara, turning away as though she were now satisfied. And then Herbert, escaping from the house as quickly as he could, rode home with a renewal of that feeling of triumph which he had once enjoyed before when returning from Desmond Court to Castle Richmond.

On the next day Herbert started for London. The parting was sad enough, and the occasion of it was such that it could hardly be otherwise. 'I am quite sure of one thing,' he said to his sister Emmeline; 'I shall never see Castle Richmond again.'

And, indeed, one may say that small as might be his chance of doing so, his wish to do so must be still less. There could be no possible inducement to him to come back to a place which had so nearly been his own, and the possession of which he had lost in so painful a manner. Every tree about the place, every path across the wide park, every hedge and ditch and hidden leafy corner, had had for him a special interest,—for they had all been his own. But all that was now over. They were not only not his own, but they belonged to one who was mounting into his seat of power over his head.

He had spent the long evening before his last dinner in going round the whole demesne alone, so that no eye should witness what he felt. None but those who have known the charms of a country-house early in life can conceive the intimacy to which a man attains with all the various trifling objects round his own locality; how he knows the bark of every tree, and the bend of every bough; how he has marked where the rich grass grows in tufts, and where the poorer soil is always dry and bare; how he watches the nests of the rooks, and the holes of the rabbits, and has learned where the thrushes build, and can show the branch on which the linnet sits. All these things had been dear to Herbert, and they all required at his hand some last farewell. Every dog, too, he had to see, and to lay his hand on the neck of every horse. This making of his final adieu under such circumstances was melancholy enough.

And then, too, later in the evening, after dinner, all the servants were called into the parlour that he might shake hands with them. There was not one of them who had not hoped, as lately as three months since, that he or she would live to call Herbert Fitzgerald master. Indeed, he had already been their master—their young master. All Irish servants especially love to pay respect to the 'young masther;' but Herbert now was to be their master no longer, and the probability was that he would never see one of them again.

He schooled himself to go through the ordeal with a manly gait and with dry eyes, and he did it; but their eyes were not dry, not even those of the men. Mrs. Jones and a favourite girl whom the young ladies patronized were not of the number, for it had been decided that they should follow the fortunes of their mistress; but Richard was there, standing a little apart from the others, as being now on a different footing. He was to go also, but before the scene was over he also had taken to sobbing violently.

'I wish you all well and happy,' said Herbert, making his little speech, ' and regret deeply that the intercourse between us should be thus suddenly severed. You have served me and mine well and truly, and it is hard upon you now, that you should be bid to go and seek another home elsewhere.'

'It isn't that we mind, Mr. Herbert; it ain't that as frets us,' said one of the men.

'It ain't that at all, at all,' said Richard, doing chorus; 'but that yer honour should be robbed of what is yer honour's own.'

'But you all know that we cannot help it,' continued Herbert; 'a misfortune has come upon us which nobody could have foreseen, and therefore we are obliged to part with our old friends and servants.'

At the word friends the maid-servants all sobbed. 'And 'deed we is your frinds, and true frinds, too,' wailed the cook.

'I know you are, and it grieves me to feel that I shall see you no more. But you must not be led to think by what Richard says that anybody is depriving me of that which ought to be my own. I am now leaving Castle Richmond because it is not my own, but justly belongs to another;—to another who, I must in justice tell you, is in no hurry to claim his inheritance. We none of us have any ground for displeasure against the present owner of this place, my cousin, Sir Owen Fitzgerald.'

'We don't know nothing about Sir Owen,' said one voice.

'And don't want,' said another, convulsed with sobs.

'He's a very good sort of young gentleman—of his own kind, no doubt,' said Richard.

'But you can all of you understand,' continued Herbert, 'that as this place is no longer our own, we are obliged to leave it; and as we shall live in a very different way in the home to which we are going, we are obliged to part with you, though we have no reason to find fault with any one among you. I am going to-morrow morning early, and my mother and sisters will follow after me in a few weeks. It will be a sad thing too for them to say good-bye to you all, as it is for me now; but it cannot be helped. God bless you all, and I hope that you will find good masters and kind mistresses, with whom you may live comfortably, as I hope you have done here.'

'We can't find no other mistresses like her leddyship,' sobbed out the senior housemaid.

'There ain't niver such a one in the county Cork,' said the cook; 'in a week of Sundays you wouldn't hear the breath out of her above her own swait nathural voice.'

'I've driv' her since iver—' began Richard: he was going to say since ever she was married, but he remembered that this allusion would be unbecoming, so he turned his face to the door-post, and began to wail bitterly.

And then Herbert shook hands with them all, and it was pretty

to see how the girls wiped their hands in their aprons before
they gave them to him, and how they afterwards left the room
with their aprons up to their faces.   The women walked out
first, and then the men, hanging down their heads, and muttering
as they went, each some little prayer that fortune and prosperity
might return to the house of Fitzgerald.   The property might
go, but according to their views Herbert was always, and always
would be, the head of the house.   And then, last of all, Richard
went.   'There ain't one of 'em, Mr. Herbert, as wouldn't guv
his fist to go wid yer, and think nothing about the wages.'
    He was to start very early, and his packing was all completed
that night.   'I do so wish we were going with you,' said Emmeline sitting in his room on the top of a corded box, which was
to follow him by some slower conveyance.
    'And I do so wish I was staying with you,' said he.
    'What is the good of staying here now?' said she; 'what
pleasure can there be in it?   I hardly dare to go outside the
house door for fear I should be seen.'
    'But why?   We have done nothing that we need be ashamed
of.'
    'No; I know that.   But, Herbert, do you not find that the
pity of the people is hard to bear?   It is written in their eyes,
and meets one at every turn.'
    'We shall get rid of that very soon.   In a few months we
shall be clean forgotten.'
    'I do not know about being forgotten.'
    'You will be as clean forgotten,—as though you had never
existed.   And all these servants who are now so fond of us, in
three months' time will be just as fond of Owen Fitzgerald, if he
will let them stay here; it's the way of the world.'
    That Herbert should have indulged in a little morbid misan-
thropy on such an occasion was not surprising.   But I take leave
to think that he was wrong in his philosophy; we do make new
friends when we lose our old friends, and the heart is capable of
cure as is the body; were it not so, how terrible would be our
fate in this world!   But we are so apt to find fault with God's
goodness to us in this respect, arguing, of others if not of ourselves,
that the heart once widowed should remain a widow through all
time.   I, for one, think that the heart should receive its new
spouses with what alacrity it may, and always with thankfulness.
    'I suppose Lady Desmond will let us see Clara,' said Emme-
line.
    'Of course you must see her.   If you knew how much she
talks about you, you would not think of leaving Ireland without
seeing her.'

'Dear Clara! I am sure she does not love me better than I do her. But suppose that Lady Desmond won't let us see her! and I know that it will be so. That grave old man with the bald head will come out and say that "the Lady Clara is not at home," and then we shall have to leave without seeing her. But it does not matter with her as it might with others, for I know that her heart will be with us.'

'If you write beforehand to say that you are coming, and explain that you are doing so to say good-bye, then I think they will admit you.'

'Yes; and the countess would take care to be there, so that I could not say one word to Clara about you. Oh, Herbert! I would give anything if I could have her here for one day,—only for one day.' But when they talked it over they both of them decided that this would not be practicable. Clara could not stay away from her own house without her mother's leave, and it was not probable that her mother would give her permission to stay at Castle Richmond.

CHAPTER XXXV.

HERBERT FITZGERALD IN LONDON.

On the following morning the whole household was up and dressed very early. Lady Fitzgerald—the poor lady made many futile attempts to drop her title, but hitherto without any shadow of success—Lady Fitzgerald was down in the breakfast parlour at seven, as also were Aunt Lotty, and Mary, and Emmeline. Herbert had begged his mother not to allow herself to be disturbed, alleging that there was no cause, seeing that they all so soon would meet in London; but she was determined that she would superintend his last meal at Castle Richmond. The servants brought in the trays with melancholy silence, and now that the absolute moment of parting had come the girls could not speak lest the tears should come and choke them. It was not that they were about to part with him; that parting would only be for a month. But he was now about to part from all that ought to have been his own. He sat down at the table in his accustomed place, with a forced smile on his face, but without a word, and his sisters put before him his cup of tea, and the slice of ham that had been cut for him, and his portion of bread. That he was making an effort they all saw. He bowed his head down over the tea to sip it and took the knife in his hand, and then he looked up at them, for he knew that their eyes were on him; he looked up at them to show that he could still endure it. But, alas! he could not endure it. The struggle was too much for him; he pushed his plate violently from him into the middle of the table, and dropping his head upon his hands he burst forth into audible lamentations.

Oh, my friends! be not hard on him in that he was thus weeping like a woman. It was not for his lost wealth that he was wailing, nor even for the name or splendour that could be no longer his; nor was it for his father's memory, though he had truly loved his father; nor for his mother's sorrow, or the tragedy of her life's history. For none of these things were his tears flowing and his sobs coming so violently that it nearly choked him to repress them. Nor could he himself have said why he was weeping.

It was the hundred small things from which he was parting for ever that thus disturbed him. The chair on which he sat, the carpet on the floor, the table on which he leaned, the dull old picture of his great-grandfather over the fireplace,—they were all his old familiar friends, they were all part of Castle Richmond,—of that Castle Richmond which he might never be allowed to see again.

His mother and sisters came to him, hanging over him, and they joined their tears together. 'Do not tell her that I was like this,' said he at last.

'She will love you the better for it if she has a true woman's heart within her breast,' said his mother.

'As true a heart as ever breathed,' said Emmeline through her sobs.

And then they pressed him to eat, but it was in vain. He knew that the food would choke him if he attempted it. So he gulped down the cup of tea, and with one kiss to his mother he rushed from them, refusing Aunt Letty's proffered embrace, passing through the line of servants without another word to one of them, and burying himself in the post-chaise which was to carry him the first stage on his melancholy journey.

It was a melancholy journey all through. From the time that he left the door at Castle Richmond that was no longer his own, till he reached the Euston Station in London, he spoke no word to any one more than was absolutely necessary for the purposes of his travelling. Nothing could be more sad than the prospect of his residence in London. Not that he was without friends there, for he belonged to a fashionable club to which he could still adhere if it so pleased him, and had all his old Oxford comrades to fall back upon if that were of any service to him. But how is a man to walk into his club who yesterday was known as his father's eldest son and the heir to a baronetcy and twelve thousand a year, and who to-day is known as nobody's son and the heir to nothing? Men would feel so much for him and pity him so deeply! That was the worst feature of his present position. He could hardly dare to show himself more than was absolutely necessary till the newness of his tragedy was worn off.

Mr. Prendergast had taken lodgings for him, in which he was to remain till he could settle himself in the same house with his mother. And this house, in which they were all to live, had also been taken,—up in that cheerful locality near Harrow-on-the-Hill, called St. John's Wood Road, the cab fares to which from any central part of London are so very ruinous. But that house was not yet ready, and so he went into lodgings in Lincoln's Inn Fields. Mr. Prendergast had chosen this locality because it was near the chambers of that great Chancery barrister, Mr. Die, under whose beneficent wing Herbert Fitzgerald was destined to learn all the mysteries of the Chancery bar. The sanctuary of Mr. Die's wig was in Stone Buildings, immediately close to that milky way of vice-chancellors, whose separate courts cluster about the old chapel of Lincoln's Inn ; and here was Herbert to sit, studious, for the next three years,—to sit there instead of at the various relief committees in the vicinity of Kanturk. And why could he not be as happy at the one as at the other? Would not Mr. Die be as amusing as Mr. Townsend ; and the arguments of Vice-Chancellor Stuart's court quite as instructive as those heard in the committee room at Gortnaclough?

On the morning of his arrival in London he drove to his lodgings, and found a note there from Mr. Prendergast asking him to dinner on that day, and promising to take him to Mr. Die on the following morning. Mr. Prendergast kept a bachelor's house in Bloomsbury Square, not very far from Lincoln's Inn—just across Holborn, as all Londoners know; and there he would expect Herbert at seven o'clock. 'I will not ask any one to meet you,' he said, ' because you will be tired after your journey, and perhaps more inclined to talk to me than to strangers.'

Mr. Prendergast was one of those old-fashioned people who think that a spacious substantial house in Bloomsbury Square, at a rent of a hundred and twenty pounds a year, is better worth having than a narrow, lath and plaster, ill-built tenement at nearly double the price out westward of the parks. A quite new man is necessarily afraid of such a locality as Bloomsbury Square, for he has no chance of getting any one into his house if he do not live westward. Who would dine with Mr. Jones in Woburn Terrace, unless he had known Mr. Jones all his days, or unless Jones were known as a top sawyer in some walk of life? But Mr. Prendergast was well enough known to his old friends to be allowed to live where he pleased, and he was not very anxious to add to their number by any new fashionable allurements.

Herbert sent over to Bloomsbury Square to say that he would be there at seven o'clock, and then sat himself down in his new lodgings. It was but a dingy abode, consisting of a narrow sitting-room looking out into the big square from over a covered archway, and a narrower bedroom looking backwards into a dull, dirty-looking, crooked street. Nothing, he thought, could be more melancholy than such a home. But then what did it signify? His days would be passed in Mr. Die's chambers, and his evenings would be spent over his law books with closed windows and copious burnings of the midnight oil. For Herbert had wisely resolved that hard work, and hard work alone, could mitigate the misery of his present position.

But he had no work for the present day. He could not at once unpack his portmanteau and begin his law studies on the moment. It was about noon when he had completed the former preparation, and eaten such breakfast as his new London landlady had gotten for him. And the breakfast had not of itself been bad, for Mrs. Whereas had been a daughter of Themis all her life, waiting upon scions of the law since first she had been able to run for a penn'orth of milk. She had been laundress on a stairs for ten years, having married a law stationer's apprentice, and now she owned the dingy house over the covered way, and let her own lodgings with her own furniture; nor was she often without friends who would recommend her zeal and honesty, and make excuse for the imperiousness of her ways and the too great fluency of her by no means servile tongue.

'Oh, Mrs. ——,' said Herbert. 'I beg your pardon, but might I ask your name?'

'No offence, sir; none in life. My name's Whereas. Martha Whereas, and 'as been now for five-and-twenty year. There be'ant many of the gen'lemen about the courts here as don't know some'at of me. And I knew some'at of them too, before they carried their wigs so grandly. My husband, that's Whereas, —you'll all'ays find him at the little stationer's shop outside the gate in Carey Street. You'll know him some of these days, I'll go bail, if you're going to Mr. Die; anyways you'll know his handwrite. Tea to your liking, sir? I all'ays gets cream for gentlemen, sir, unless they tells me not. Milk a 'alfpenny, sir; cream tuppence; three 'alfpence difference; hain't it, sir? So now you can do as you pleases, and if you like bacon and heggs to your breakfastesses you've only to say the words. But then the heggs hain't heggs, that's the truth ; and they hain't chickens, but some'at betwixt the two.'

And so she went on during the whole time that he was eating, moving about from place to place, and putting back into the places which she had chosen for them anything which he had chanced to move; now dusting a bit of furniture with her apron, and then leaning on the back of a chair while she asked him some question as to his habits and future mode of living. She also wore a bonnet, apparently as a customary part of her house costume, and Herbert could not help thinking that she looked very like his Aunt Letty.

But when she had gone and taken the breakfast things with her, then began the tedium of the day. It seemed to him as though he had no means of commencing his life in London until he had been with Mr. Prendergast or Mr. Die. And so new did it all feel to him, so strange and wonderful, that he hardly dared to go out of the house by himself and wander about the premises of the Inn. He was not absolutely a stranger in London, for he had been elected at a club before he had left Oxford, and had been up in town twice, staying on each occasion some few weeks. Had he therefore been asked about the metropolis some four months since at Castle Richmond, he would have professed that he knew it well. Starting from Pall Mall he could have gone to any of the central theatres, or to the Parks, or to the houses of Parliament, or to the picture galleries in June. But now in that dingy big square he felt himself to be absolutely a stranger ; and when he did venture out he watched the corners, in order that he might find his way back without asking questions.

And then he roamed round the squares and about the little courts, and found out where were Stone Buildings,—so called because they are so dull and dead and stony-hearted : and as his courage increased he made his way into one of the courts, and stood up for a while on an uncomfortable narrow step, so that he might watch the proceedings as they went on, and it all seemed to him to be dull and deadly. There was no life and amusement such as he had seen at the Assize Court in county Cork, when he was sworn in as one of the Grand Jury. There the gentlemen in wigs—for on the Munster circuit they do wear wigs, or at any rate did then—laughed and winked and talked together joyously ; and when a Roman Catholic fisherman from Berehaven was put into the dock for destroying the boat and nets of a Protestant fisherman from Dingle in county Kerry, who had chanced to come that way, 'not fishing at all, at all, yer honour, but just souping,' as the Papist prisoner averred with great emphasis, the gentiemen of the robe had gone to the fight with all the animation and courage of Matadors and Picadors in a bull-ring. It was delightful to see the way in which Roman Catholic skill combated Protestant fury, with a substratum below of Irish fun which showed to everybody that it was not all quite in earnest;—that the great O'Fagan and the great Fitzberesford could sit down together afterwards with all the pleasure in life over their modicum of claret in the barristers' room at the Imperial hotel. And then the judge had added to the life of the meeting, helping to bamboozle and make miserable a wretch of a witness who had been caught in the act of seeing the boat smashed with a fragment of rock, and was now, in consequence, being impaled alive by his lordship's assistance.

'What do you say your name is?' demanded his lordship, angrily.

'Rowland Houghton,' said the miserable stray Saxon tourist who had so unfortunately strayed that way on the occasion

'What?' repeated the judge, whose ears were sharper to such sounds as O'Shaughnessy, Macgillycuddy, and O'Callaghan.

'Rowland Houghton,' said the offender, in his distress; quicker, louder, and perhaps not more distinctly than before.

'What does the man say?' said the judge, turning his head down towards a satellite who sat on a bench beneath his cushion.

The gentleman appealed to pronounced the name for the judge's hearing with a full rolling Irish brogue, that gave great delight through all the court; 'R-rowland Hough-h-ton, me lor-r-d.'

Whereupon his lordship threw up his hands in dismay. 'Oulan Outan!' said he. 'Oulan Outan! I never heard such a name in my life!' And then, having thoroughly impaled the wicked witness, and added materially to the amusement of the day, the judge wrote down the name in his book; and there it is to this day, no doubt, Oulan Outan. And when one thinks of it, it was monstrous that an English witness should go into an Irish law court with such a name as Rowland Houghton.

But here, in the dark dingy court to which Herbert had pene-trated in Lincoln's Inn, there was no such life as this. Here, whatever skill there might be, was of a dark subterranean nature, quite unintelligible to any minds but those of experts; and as for fury or fun, there was no spark either of one or of the other. The judge sat back in his seat, a tall, handsome, speechless man, not asleep, for his eye from time to time moved slowly from the dingy barrister who was on his legs to another dingy barrister who was sitting with his hands in his pockets, and with his eyes fixed upon the ceiling. The gentleman who was in the act of pleading had a huge open paper in his hand, from which he droned forth certain legal quiddities of the dullest and most uninteresting nature. He was in earnest, for there was a perpetual energy in his drone, as a droning bee might drone who was known to drone louder than other drones. But it was a continuous energy supported by perseverance, and not by impulse; and seemed to come of a fixed determination to continue the reading of that paper till all the world should be asleep. A great part of the world around was asleep; but the judge's eye was still open, and one might say that the barrister was resolved to go on till that eye should have become closed in token of his success.

Herbert remained there for an hour, thinking that he might learn something that would be serviceable to him in his coming legal career; but at the end of the hour the same thing was going on,—the judge's eye was still open, and the lawyer's drone was still sounding; and so he came away, having found himself absolutely dozing in the uncomfortable position in which he was standing.

At last the day wore away, and at seven o'clock he found himself in Mr. Prendergast's hall in Bloomsbury Square; and his hat and umbrella were taken away from him by an old servant looking very much like Mr. Prendergast himself;—having about him the same look of the stiffness of years, and the same look also of excellent preservation and care.

'Mr. Prendergast is in the library, sir, if you please,' said the old servant; and so saying he ushered Herbert into the back down-stairs room. It was a spacious, lofty apartment, well fitted up for a library, and furnished for that purpose with exceeding care;—such a room as one does not find in the flashy new houses in the west, where the dining-room and drawing-room occupy all of the house that is visible. But then, how few of those who live in flashy new houses in the west require to have libraries in London!

As he entered the room Mr. Prendergast came forward to meet him, and seemed heartily glad to see him. There was a cordiality about him which Herbert had never recognized at Castle Richmond, and an appearance of enjoyment which had seemed to be almost foreign to the lawyer's nature. Herbert perhaps had not calculated, as he should have done, that Mr. Prendergast's mission in Ireland had not admitted of much enjoyment. Mr. Prendergast had gone there to do a job of work, and that he had done, very thoroughly; but he certainly had not enjoyed himself.

There was time for only few words before the old man again entered the room, announcing dinner; and those few words had

no reference whatever to the Castle Richmond sorrow. He had
spoken of Herbert's lodging, and of his journey, and a word or
two of Mr. Die, and then they went in to dinner. And at dinner
too the conversation wholly turned upon indifferent matters,
upon reform at Oxford, the state of parties, and of the peculiar
idiosyncrasies of the Irish Low Church clergymen, on all of
which subjects Herbert found that Mr. Prendergast had a
tolerably strong opinion of his own. The dinner was very good,
though by no means showy,—as might have been expected in
a house in Bloomsbury Square — and the wine excellent, as
might have been expected in any house inhabited by Mr. Prendergast.

And then, when the dinner was over, and the old servant had
slowly removed his last tray, when they had each got into an
arm-chair, and were seated at properly comfortable distances
from the fire, Mr. Prendergast began to talk freely; not that he
at once plunged into the middle of the old history, or began with
lugubrious force to recapitulate the horrors that were now partly
over; but gradually he veered round to those points as to which
he thought it good that he should speak before setting Herbert
at work on his new London life.

'You drink claret, I suppose?' said Mr. Prendergast, as he
adjusted a portion of the table for their evening symposium.

'Oh yes,' said Herbert, not caring very much at that moment
what the wine was.

'You'll find that pretty good; a good deal better than what
you'll get in most houses in London now-a-days. But you know
a man always likes his own wine, and especially an old man.'

Herbert said something about it being very good, but did not
give that attention to the matter which Mr. Prendergast thought
that it deserved. Indeed, he was thinking more about Mr. Die
and Stone Buildings than about the wine.

'And how do you find my old friend Mrs. Whereas?' asked
the lawyer.

'She seems to be a very attentive sort of woman.'

'Yes; rather too much so sometimes. People do say that she
never knows how to hold her tongue. But she won't rob you,
nor yet poison you; and in these days that is saying a very great
deal for a woman in London.' And then there was a pause, as
Mr. Prendergast sipped his wine with slow complacency. 'And
we are to go to Mr. Die to-morrow, I suppose?' he said, beginning
again. To which Herbert replied that he would be ready at any
time in the morning that might be suitable.

'The sooner you get into harness the better. It is not only
that you have much to learn, but you have much to forget also.'

'Yes,' said Herbert, 'I have much to forget indeed; more than I can forget, I'm afraid, Mr. Prendergast.'

'There is, I fancy, no sorrow which a man cannot forget; that is, as far as the memory of it is likely to be painful to him. You will not absolutely cease to remember Castle Richmond and all its circumstances; you will still think of the place and all the people whom you knew there; but you will learn to do so without the pain which of course you now suffer. That is what I mean by forgetting.'

'Oh, I don't complain, sir.'

'No, I know you don't; and that is the reason why I am so anxious to see you happy. You have borne the whole matter so well that I am quite sure that you will be able to live happily in this new life. That is what I mean when I say that you will forget Castle Richmond.'

Herbert bethought himself of Clara Desmond, and of the woman whom he had seen in the cabin, and reflected that even at present he had no right to be unhappy.

'I suppose you have no thought of going back to Ireland?' said Mr. Prendergast.

'Oh, none in the least.'

'On the whole I think you are right. No doubt a family connection is a great assistance to a barrister, and there would be reasons which would make attorneys in Ireland throw business into your hands at an early period of your life. Your history would give you an *éclat* there, if you know what I mean.'

'Oh, yes, perfectly; but I don't want that.'

'No. It is a kind of assistance which in my opinion a man should not desire. In the first place, it does not last. A man so buoyed up is apt to trust to such support, instead of his own steady exertions; and the firmest of friends won't stick to a lawyer long if he can get better law for his money elsewhere.'

'There should be no friendship in such matters, I think.'

'Well, I won't say that. But the friendship should come of the service, not the service of the friendship. Good, hard, steady, and enduring work,—work that does not demand immediate acknowledgment and reward, but that can afford to look forward for its results,—it is that, and that only which in my opinion will insure to a man permanent success.'

'It is hard though for a poor man to work so many years without an income,' said Herbert, thinking of Lady Clara Desmond.

'Not hard if you get the price of your work at last. But you can have your choice. A moderate fixed income can now be had by any barrister early in life,—by any barrister of fair parts and sound acquirements. There are more barristers now filling salaried places than practising in the courts.'

'But those places are given by favour.'

'No; not so generally,—or if by favour, by that sort of favour which is as likely to come to you as to another. Such places are not given to incompetent young men because their fathers and mothers ask for them. But won't you fill your glass?'

'I am doing very well, thank you.'

'You'll do better if you'll fill your glass, and let me have the bottle back. But you are thinking of the good old historical days when you talk of barristers having to wait for their incomes. There has been a great change in that respect,—for the better, as you of course will think. Now-a-days a man is taken away from his boat-racing and his skittle-ground to be made a judge. A little law and a great fund of physical strength—that is the extent of the demand.' And Mr. Prendergast plainly showed by the tone of his voice that he did not admire the wisdom of this new policy of which he spoke.

'But I suppose a man must work five years before he can earn anything,' said Herbert, still despondingly; for five years is a long time to an expectant lover.

'Fifteen years of unpaid labour used not to be thought too great a price to pay for ultimate success,' said Mr. Prendergast, almost sighing at the degeneracy of the age. 'But men in those days were ambitious and patient.'

'And now they are ambitious and impatient,' suggested Herbert.

'Covetous and impatient might perhaps be the truer epithets,' said Mr. Prendergast with grim sarcasm.

It is sad for a man to feel, when he knows that he is fast going down the hill of life, that the experience of old age is to be no longer valued nor its wisdom appreciated. The elderly man of this day thinks that he has been robbed of his chance in life. When he was in his full physical vigour he was not old enough for mental success. He was still winning his spurs at forty. But at fifty—so does the world change—he learns that he is past his work. By some unconscious and unlucky leap he has passed from the unripeness of youth to the decay of age, without even knowing what it was to be in his prime. A man should always seize his opportunity; but the changes of the times in which he has lived have never allowed him to have one. There has been no period of flood in his tide which might lead him on to fortune. While he has been waiting patiently for high water the ebb has come upon him. Mr. Prendergast himself had been a successful man, and his regrets, therefore, were philosophical rather than practical. As for Herbert, he did not look upon the question at all in the same light as his elderly friend, and on the whole was rather exhilarated by the tone of Mr. Prendergast's sarcasm. Perhaps Mr. Prendergast had intended that such should be its effect.

The long evening passed away cosily enough, leaving on Herbert's mind an impression that in choosing to be a barrister he had certainly chosen the noblest walk of life in which a man could earn his bread. Mr. Prendergast did not promise him either fame or fortune, nor did he speak by any means in high enthusiastic language; he said much of the necessity of long hours, of tedious work, of Amaryllis left by herself in the shade, and of Neæra's locks unheeded; but nevertheless he spoke in a manner to arouse the ambition and satisfy the longings of the young man who listened to him. There was much wisdom in what he did, and much benevolence also.

And then at about eleven o'clock, Herbert having sat out the second bottle of claret, betook himself to his bed at the lodgings over the covered way.

CHAPTER XXXVI.

HOW THE EARL WAS WON.

It was not quite at first that the countess could explain to her son how she now wished that Owen Fitzgerald might become her son-in-law. She had been so steadfast in her opposition to Owen when the earl had last spoken of the matter, and had said so much of the wickedly dissipated life which Owen was leading, that she feared to shock the boy. But by degrees she brought the matter round, speaking of Owen's great good fortune, pointing out how much better he was suited for riches than for poverty, insisting warmly on all his good qualities and high feelings, and then saying at last, as it were without thought, 'Poor Clara! She has been unfortunate, for at one time she loved Owen Fitzgerald much better than she will ever love his cousin Herbert.'

'Do you think so, mother?'

'I am sure of it. The truth is, Patrick, you do not understand your sister; and indeed it is hard to do so. I have also always had an inward fear that she had now engaged herself to a man whom she did not love. Of course as things were then it was impossible that she should marry Owen; and I was glad to break her off from that feeling. But she never loved Herbert Fitzgerald.'

'Why, she is determined to have him, even now.'

'Ah, yes! That is where you do not understand her. Now, at this special moment, her heart is touched by his misfortune, and she thinks herself bound by her engagement to sacrifice herself with him. But that is not love. She has never loved any one but Owen,—and who can wonder at it? for he is a man made for a woman to love.'

The earl said nothing for a while, but sat balancing himself on the back legs of his chair. And then, as though a new idea had struck him, he exclaimed, 'If I thought that, mother, I would find out what Owen thinks of it himself.'

'Poor Owen!' said the countess. 'There is no doubt as to what he thinks;' and then she left the room, not wishing to carry the conversation any further.

Two days after this, and without any further hint from his mother, he betook himself along the banks of the river to Hap House. In his course thither he never let his horse put a foot upon the road, but kept low down upon the water meadows, leaping over all the fences, as he had so often done with the man whom he was now going to see. It was here, among these banks, that he had received his earliest lessons in horsemanship, and they had all been given by Owen Fitzgerald. It had been a thousand pities, he had thought, that Owen had been so poor as to make it necessary for them all to discourage that love affair with Clara. He would have been so delighted to welcome Owen as his brother-in-law. And as he strode along over the ground, and landed himself knowingly over the crabbed fences, he began to think how much pleasanter the country would be for him if he had a downright good fellow and crack sportsman as his fast friend at Castle Richmond. Sir Owen Fitzgerald of Castle Richmond! He would be the man to whom he would be delighted to give his sister Clara.

And then he hopped in from one of Owen's fields into a small paddock at the back of Owen's house, and seeing one of the stable-boys about the place, asked him if his master was at home.

'Shure an' he's here thin, yer honour;' and Lord Desmond could hear the boy whispering, 'It's the young lord hisself.' In a moment Owen Fitzgerald was standing by his horse's side. It was the first time that Owen had seen one of the family since the news had been spread abroad concerning his right to the inheritance of Castle Richmond.

'Desmond,' said he, taking the lad's hand with one of his, and putting the other on the animal's neck, 'this is very good of you. I am delighted to see you. I had heard that you were in the country.'

'Yes; I have been home for this week past. But things are

all so at sixes and sevens among us all that a fellow can't go and do just what he would like.'

Owen well understood what he meant. ' Indeed they are at sixes and sevens; you may well say that. But get off your horse, old fellow, and come into the house. Why, what a lather of heat the mare's in.'

' Isn't she? it's quite dreadful. That chap of ours has no more idea of condition than I have of—of—of—of an archbishop. I've just trotted along the fields, and put her over a ditch or two, and you see the state she's in. It's a beastly shame.'

' I know of old what your trottings are, Desmond; and what a ditch or two means. You've been at every bank between this and Banteer as though you were going for a steeplechase plate.'

' Upon my honour, Owen—'

' Look here, Patsey. Walk that mare up and down here, between this gate and that post, till the big sweat has all dried on her; and then stick to her with a wisp of straw till she's as soft as silk. Do you hear?'

Patsey said that he did hear; and then Owen, throwing his arm over the earl's shoulder, walked slowly towards the house.

' I can't tell you how glad I am to see you, old boy,' said Owen, pressing his young friend with something almost like an embrace. ' You will hardly believe how long it is since I have seen a face that I cared to look at.'

' Haven't you?' said the young lord, wondering. He knew that Fitzgerald had now become heir to a very large fortune, or rather the possessor of that fortune, and he could not understand why a man who had been so popular while he was poor should be deserted now that he was rich.

' No, indeed, have I not. Things are all at sixes and sevens as you say. Let me see. Donnellan was here when you last saw me ; and I was soon tired of him when things became serious.'

' I don't wonder you were tired of him.'

' But, Desmond, how's your mother?'

' Oh, she's very well. These are bad times for poor people like us, you know.'

' And your sister?'

' She's pretty well too, thank you.' And then there was a pause. ' You have had a great change in your fortune since I saw you, have you not?' said the earl, after a minute or two. And there it occurred to him for the first time, that, having refused his sister to this man when he was poor, he had now come to offer her to him when he was rich. ' Not that that was the reason,' he said to himself. ' But it was impossible then, and now it would be so pleasant.'

'It is a sad history, is it not?' said Owen.

'Very sad,' said the earl, remembering, however, that he had ridden over there with his heart full of joy,—of joy occasioned by that very catastrophe which now, following his friend's words like a parrot, he declared to be so very sad.

And now they were in the dining-room in which Owen usually lived, and were both standing on the rug, as two men always do stand when they first get into a room together. And it was clear to see that neither of them knew how to break at once into the sort of loving, genial talk which each was longing to have with the other. It is so easy to speak when one has little or nothing to say; but often so difficult when there is much that must be said: and the same paradox is equally true of writing.

Then Owen walked away to the window, looking out among the shrubs into which Aby Mollett had been precipitated, as though he could collect his thoughts there; in a moment or two the earl followed him, and looked out also among the shrubs.

'They killed a fox exactly there the other day; didn't they?' asked the earl, indicating the spot by a nod of his head.

'Yes, they did.' And then there was another pause. 'I'll tell you what it is, Desmond,' Owen said at last, going back to the rug and speaking with an effort. 'As the people say, "a sight of you is good for sore eyes." There is a positive joy to me in seeing you. It is like a cup of cold water when a man is thirsty. But I cannot put the drink to my lips till I know on what terms we are to meet. When last we saw each other, we were speaking of your sister; and now that we meet again, we must again speak of her. Desmond, all my thoughts are of her; I dream of her at night, and find myself talking to her spirit when I wake in the morning. I have much else that I ought to think of; but I go about thinking of nothing but of her. I am told that she is engaged to my cousin Herbert. Nay, she has told me so herself, and I know that it is so. But if she becomes his wife—any man's wife but mine—I cannot live in this country.'

He had not said one word of that state of things in his life's history of which the country side was so full. He had spoken of Herbert, but he had not alluded to Herbert's fall. He had spoken of such hope as he still might have with reference to Clara Desmond; but he did not make the slightest reference to that change in his fortunes—in his fortunes, and those of his rival—which might have so strong a bias on those hopes, and which ought so to have in the minds of all worldly, prudent people. It was to speak of this specially that Lord Desmond had come thither; and then, if opportunity should offer, to lead away the subject to that other one; but now Owen had begun at the wrong end. If called upon to speak about his sister at once, what could the brother say, except that she was engaged to Herbert Fitzgerald?

'Tell me this, Desmond; whom does your sister love?' said Owen, speaking almost fiercely in his earnestness. 'I know so much of you, at any rate, that whatever may be your feelings you will not lie to me,'—thereby communicating to the young lord an accusation, which he very well understood, against the truth of the countess, his mother.

'When I have spoken to her about this she declares that she is engaged to Herbert Fitzgerald.'

'Engaged to him! yes, I know that; I do not doubt that. It has been dinned into my ears now for the last six months till it is impossible to doubt it. And she will marry him too, if no one interferes to prevent it. I do not doubt that either. But, Desmond, that is not the question that I have asked. She did love me; and then she was ordered by her mother to abandon that love, and to give her heart to another. That in words she has been obedient, I know well; but what I doubt is this,—that she has in truth been able so to chuck her heart about like a shuttlecock. I can only say that I am not able to do it.'

How was the earl to answer him? The very line of argument which Owen's mind was taking was exactly that which the young lord himself desired to promote. He too was desirous that Clara should go back to her first love. He himself thought strongly that Owen was a man more fitted than Herbert for the worshipful adoration of such a girl as his sister Clara. But then he, Desmond, had opposed the match while Owen was poor, and how was he to frame words by which he might encourage it now that Owen was rich?

'I have been so little with her, that I hardly know,' he said. 'But, Owen—'

'Well?'

'It is so difficult for me to talk to you about all this.'

'Is it?'

'Why, yes. You know that I have always liked you—always. No chap was ever such a friend to me as you have been;' and he squeezed Owen's arm with strong boyish love.

'I know all about it,' said Owen.

'Well; then all that happened about Clara. I was young then, you know,'—he was now sixteen—'and had not thought anything about it. The idea of you and Clara falling in love had never occurred to me. Boys are so blind, you know. But when it did happen—you remember that day, old fellow, when you and I met down at the gate?'

'Remember it!' said Owen. He would remember it, as he thought, when half an eternity should have passed over his head.

'And I told you then what I thought. I don't think I am a particular fellow myself about money and rank and that sort of thing. I am as poor as a church mouse, and so I shall always remain; and for myself I don't care about it. But for one's sister, Owen—you never had a sister, had you?'

'Never,' said Owen, hardly thinking of the question.

'One is obliged to think of such things for her. We should all go to rack and ruin, the whole family of us, box and dice,—as indeed we have pretty well already—if some of us did not begin to look about us. I don't suppose I shall ever marry and have a family. I couldn't afford it, you know. And in that case Clara's son would be Earl of Desmond; or if I died she would be Countess of Desmond in her own right.' And the young lord looked the personification of family prudence.

'I know all that,' said Owen; 'but you do not suppose that I was thinking of it?'

'What; as regards yourself. No; I am sure you never did. But, looking to all that, it would never have done for her to marry a man as poor as you were. It is not a comfortable thing to be a very poor nobleman, I can tell you.'

Owen again remained silent. He wanted to talk the earl over into favouring his views, but he wanted to do so as Owen of Hap House, not as Owen of Castle Richmond. He perceived at once from the tone of the boy's voice, and even from his words, that there was no longer anything to be feared from the brother's opposition; and perceiving this, he thought that the mother's opposition might now perhaps also be removed. But it was quite manifest that this had come from what was supposed to be his altered position. 'A man as poor as you were,' Lord Desmond had said, urging that though now the marriage might be well enough, in those former days it would have been madness. The line of argument was very clear; but as Owen was as poor as ever, and intended to remain so, there was nothing in it to comfort him.

'I cannot say that I, myself, have so much worldly wisdom as you have,' said he at last, with something like a sneer.

'Ah, that is just what I knew you would say. You think that I am coming to you now, and offering to make up matters between you and Clara because you are rich!'

'But can you make up matters between me and Clara?' said Owen, eagerly.

'Well, I do not know. The countess seems to think it might be so.'

And then again Owen was silent, walking about the room with his hands behind his back   Then after all the one thing of this world which his eye regarded as desirable was within his reach. He had then been right in supposing that that face which had once looked up to his so full of love had been a true reflex of the girl's heart,—that it had indicated to him love which was not changeable. It was true that Clara, having accepted a suitor at her mother's order, might now be allowed to come back to him! As he thought of this. he wondered at the endurance and obedience of a woman's heart which could thus give up all that it held as sacred at the instance of another. But even this, though it was but little flattering to Clara, by no means lessened the transport which he felt. He had had that pride in himself, that he had never ceased to believe that she loved him. Full of that thought, of which he had not dared to speak, he had gone about, gloomily miserable since the news of her engagement with Herbert had reached him, and now he learned, as he thought with certainty, that his belief had been well grounded. Through all that had passed Clara Desmond did love him still!

But as to this overture of reconciliation that was now made to him; how was he to accept it or reject it? It was made to him because he was believed to be Sir Owen Fitzgerald of Castle Richmond, a baronet of twelve thousand a year, instead of a poor squire, whose wife would have to look narrowly to the kitchen, in order that food in sufficiency might be forthcoming for the parlour. That he would become Sir Owen he thought probable ; but that he would be Sir Owen of Hap House and not of Castle Richmond he had firmly resolved. He had thought of this for long hours and hours together, and felt that he could never again be happy were he to put his foot into that house as its owner. Every tenant would scorn him, every servant would hate him, every neighbour would condemn him; but this would be as nothing to his hatred of himself, to his own scorn and his own condemnation. And yet how great was the temptation to him now ! If he would consent to call himself master of Castle Richmond, Clara's hand might still be his.

So he thought; but those who know Clara Desmond better than he did will know how false were his hopes. She was hardly the girl to have gone back to a lover when he was rich, whom she had rejected when he was poor.

' Desmond,' said he, ' come here and sit down;' and both sat leaning on the table together, with their arms touching. ' I understand it all now I think; and remember this, my boy, that whomever I may blame, I do not blame you; that you are true and honest I am sure; and, indeed, there is only one person whom I do blame.' He did not say that this one person was the countess, but the earl knew just as well as though he had been told.

'I understand all this now,' he repeated, 'and before we go any further, I must tell you one thing; I shall never be owner of Castle Richmond.'

'Why, I thought it was all settled!' said the earl, looking up with surprise.

'Nothing at all is settled. To every bargain there must be two parties, and I have never yet become a party to the bargain which shall make me owner of Castle Richmond.'

'But is it not yours of right?'

'I do not know what you call right.'

'Right of inheritance,' said the earl, who, having succeeded to his own rank by the strength of the same right enduring through many ages, looked upon it as the one substantial palladium of the country.

'Look here, old fellow, and I'll tell you my views about this. Sir Thomas Fitzgerald, when he married that poor lady who is still staying at Castle Richmond, did so in the face of the world with the full assurance that he made her his legal wife. Whether such a case as this ever occurred before I don't know, but I am sure of this that in the eye of God she is his widow. Herbert Fitzgerald was brought up as the heir to all that estate, and I cannot see that he can fairly be robbed of that right because another man has been a villain. The title he cannot have, I suppose, because the law won't give it him; but the property can be made over to him, and as far as I am concerned it shall be made over. No earthly consideration shall induce me to put my hand upon it, for in doing so I should look upon myself as a thief and a scoundrel.'

'And you mean then that Herbert will have it all, just the same as it was before?'

'Just the same as regards the estate.'

'Then why has he gone away?'

'I cannot answer for him. I can only tell you what I shall do. I dare say it may take months before it is all settled. But now, Desmond, you know how I stand; I am Owen Fitzgerald of Hap House, now as I have ever been, that and nothing more, —for as to the handle to my name it is not worth talking about.'

They were still sitting at the table, and now they both sat silent, not looking at each other, but with their eyes fixed on the wood. Owen had in his hand a pen, which he had taken from the mantelpiece, and unconsciously began to trace signs on the polished surface before him. The earl sat with his forehead leaning on his two hands, thinking what he was to say next. He felt that he himself loved the man better than ever; but when his mother should come to hear all this, what would she say?

'You know it all now, my boy,' said Owen, looking up at last; and as he did so there was an expression about his face to which the young earl thought that he had never seen the like. There was a gleam in his eye which, though not of joy, was so bright; and a smile round his mouth which was so sweet, though full of sadness! 'How can she not love him?' said he to himself, thinking of his sister. 'And now, Desmond, go back to your mother and tell her all. She has sent you here.'

'No, she did not send me,' said the boy, stoutly,—almost angrily; 'she does not even know that I have come.'

'Go back then to your sister.'

'Nor does she know it.'

'Nevertheless, go back to them, and tell them both what I have told you; and tell them this also, that I, Owen Fitzgerald of Hap House, still love her better than all that the world else can give me; indeed, there is nothing else that I do love,— except you, Desmond. But tell them, also, that I am Owen of Hap House still—that and nothing more.'

'Owen,' said the lad, looking up at him; and Fitzgerald as he glanced into the boy's face could see that there was that arising within his breast which almost prevented him from speaking.

'And look, Desmond,' continued Fitzgerald; 'do not think that I shall blame you because you turn from me, or call you mercenary. Do you do what you think right. What you said just now of your sister's ——, well, of the possibility of our marriage, you said under the idea that I was a rich man. You now find that I am a poor man; and you may consider that the words were never spoken.'

'Owen!' said the boy again; and now that which was before rising in his breast had risen to his brow and cheeks, and was telling its tale plainly in his eyes. And then he rose from his chair, turning away his face, and walking towards the window; but before he had gone two steps he turned again, and throwing himself on Fitzgerald's breast, he burst out into a passion of tears.

'Come, old fellow, what is this? This will never do,' said Owen. But his own eyes were full of tears also, and he too was nearly past speaking.

'I know you will think—I am a boy and a—fool,' said the earl, through his sobs, as soon as he could speak; 'but I can't— help it.'

'I think you are the dearest, finest, best fellow that ever lived,' said Fitzgerald, pressing him with his arm.

'And I'll tell you what, Owen, you should have her to-morrow if it were in my power, for, by heaven! there is not another man so worthy of a girl in all the world; and I'll tell her so; and I don't care what the countess says. And, Owen, come what come may, you shall always have my word;' and then he stood apart, and rubbing his eyes with his arm tried to look like a man who was giving his pledge from his judgment, not from his impulse.

'It all depends on this, Desmond; whom does she love? See her alone, Desmond, and talk softly to her, and find out that.' This he said thoughtfully, for in his mind 'love should still be lord of all.'

'By heavens! if I were her, I know whom I should love,' said the brother.

'I would not have her as a gift if she did not love me,' said Owen, proudly; 'but if she do, I have a right to claim her as my own.'

And then they parted, and the earl rode back home with a quieter pace than that which had brought him there, and in a different mood. He had pledged himself now to Owen,—not to Owen of Castle Richmond, but to Owen of Hap House—and he intended to redeem his pledge if it were possible. He had been so conquered by the nobleness of his friend, that he had forgotten his solicitude for his family and his sister.

<hr>

CHAPTER XXXVII.

A TALE OF A TURBOT.

IT would have been Owen Fitzgerald's desire to disclaim the inheritance which chance had put in his way in absolute silence, had such a course been possible to him. And, indeed, not being very well conversant with matters of business, he had thought for a while that this might be done—or at any rate something not far different from this. To those who had hitherto spoken to him upon the subject, to Mr. Prendergast, Mr. Somers, and his cousin, he had disclaimed the inheritance, and that he had thought would have sufficed. That Sir Thomas should die so quickly after the discovery had not of course been expected by anybody; and much, therefore, had not been thought at the moment of these disclaimers;—neither at the moment, nor indeed afterwards, when Sir Thomas did die.

Even Mr. Somers was prepared to admit that as the game had

been given up,—as his branch of the Fitzgeralds, acting under the advice of their friend and lawyer, admitted the property must go from them—even he, much as he contested within his own breast the propriety of Mr. Prendergast's decisions, was fair to admit now that it was Owen's business to walk in upon the property. Any words which he may have spoken on the impulse of the moment were empty words. When a man becomes heir to twelve thousand a year, he does not give it up in a freak of benevolence. And, therefore, when Sir Thomas had been dead some four or five weeks, and when Herbert had gone away from the scene which was no longer one of interest to him, it was necessary that something should be done.

During the last two or three days of his life Sir Thomas had executed a new will, in which he admitted that his son was not the heir to his estates, and so disposed of such moneys as it was in his power to leave as he would have done had Herbert been a younger son. Early in his life he himself had added something to the property, some two or three hundred a year, and this, also, he left of course to his own family. Such having been done, there would have been no opposition made to Owen had he immediately claimed the inheritance ; but as he made no claim, and took no step whatever,—as he appeared neither by himself, nor by letter, nor by lawyer, nor by agent,—as no rumour ever got about as to what he intended to do, Mr. Somers found it necessary to write to him. This he did on the day of Herbert's departure, merely asking him, perhaps with scant courtesy, who was his man of business, in order that he, Mr. Somers, as agent to the late proprietor, might confer with him. With but scant courtesy,—for Mr. Somers had made one visit to Hap House since the news had been known, with some intention of ingratiating himself with the future heir ; but his tenders had not been graciously received. Mr. Somers was a proud man, and though his position in life depended on the income he received from the Castle Richmond estate, he would not make any further overture. So his letter was somewhat of the shortest, and merely contained the request above named.

Owen's reply was sharp, immediate, and equally short, and was carried back by the messenger from Castle Richmond who had brought the letter, to which it was an answer. It was as follows :—

'Hap House, Thursday morning, two o'clock.'

(There was no other date ; and Owen probably was unaware that his letter being written at two P.M. was not written on Thursday morning.)

' Dear Sir,
            ' I have got no lawyer, and no man of business ; nor do
I mean to employ any if I can help it.   I intend to make no claim
to Mr. Herbert Fitzgerald's property of Castle Richmond ; and if
it be necessary that I should sign any legal document making
over to him any claim that I may have, I am prepared to do so
at any moment. As he has got a lawyer, he can get this arranged,
and I suppose Mr. Prendergast had better do it.
                        ' I am, dear sir,
                                ' Your faithful servant,
                        ' OWEN FITZGERALD of Hap House.'
And with those four or five lines he thought it would be
practicable for him to close the whole affair.

   This happened on the day of Herbert's departure, and on the
day preceding Lord Desmond's visit to Hap House ; so that on
the occasion of that visit, Owen looked upon the deed as fully
done.   He had put it quite beyond his own power to recede
now, even had he so wished.   And then came the tidings to him,
—true tidings as he thought,—that Clara was still within his
reach if only he were master of Castle Richmond.   That this view
of his position did for a moment shake him I will not deny ; but
it was only for a moment : and then it was that he had looked up at
Clara's brother, and bade him go back to his mother and sister,
and tell them that Owen of Hap House was Owen of Hap House
still ;—that and nothing more.   Clara Desmond might be bought
at a price which would be too costly even for such a prize as her.
It was well for him that he so resolved, for at no price could she
have been bought.

   Mr. Somers, when he received that letter, was much inclined
to doubt whether or no it might be well to take Owen at his
word.   After all, what just right had he to the estate ?   According
to the eternal and unalterable laws of right and wrong ought it not
to belong to Herbert Fitzgerald ?   Mr. Somers allowed his wish on
this occasion to be father to many thoughts much at variance
from that line of thinking which was customary to him as a man
of business.   In his ordinary moods, law with him was law, and
a legal claim a legal claim.   Had he been all his life agent
to the Hap House property instead of to that of Castle Richmond,
a thought so romantic would never have entered his head.   He
would have scouted a man as nearly a maniac who should suggest
to him that his client ought to surrender an undoubted inheritance of twelve thousand a year on a point of feeling.   He
would have rejected it as a proposed crime, and talked much of
the indefeasible rights of the coming heirs of the new heir.   He
would have been as firm as a rock, and as trenchant as a sword

in defence of his patron's claims. But now, having in his hands that short, pithy letter from Owen Fitzgerald, he could not but look at the matter in a more Christian light. After all was not justice, immutable justice, better than law? And would not the property be enough for both of them? Might not law and justice make a compromise? Let Owen be the baronet, and take a slice of four or five thousand, and add that to Hap House; and then if these things were well arranged, might not Mr. Somers still be agent to them both?

Meditating all this in his newly tuned romantic frame of mind Mr. Somers sat down and wrote a long letter to Mr. Prendergast, enclosing the short letter from Owen, and saying all that he, as a man of business with a new dash of romance, could say on such a subject. This letter, not having slept on the road as Herbert did in Dublin, and having been conveyed with that lightning rapidity for which the British Post-office has ever been remarkable—and especially that portion of it which has reference to the sister island,—was in Mr. Prendergast's pocket when Herbert dined with him. That letter, and another to which we shall have to refer more specially. But so much at variance were Mr. Prendergast's ideas from those entertained by Mr. Somers, that he would not even speak to Herbert on the subject. Perhaps, also, that other more important letter, which, if we live, we shall read at length, might also have had some effect in keeping him silent.

But in truth Mr. Somers' mind, and that of Mr. Prendergast, did not work in harmony on this subject. Judging of the two men together by their usual deeds and ascertained character, we may say that there was much more romance about Mr. Prendergast than there was about Mr. Somers. But then it was a general romance, and not one with an individual object. Or perhaps we may say, without injury to Mr. Somers, that it was a true feeling, and not a false one. Mr. Prendergast, also, was much more anxious for the welfare of Herbert Fitzgerald than that of his cousin; but then he could feel on behalf of the man for whom he was interested that it did not behove him to take a present of an estate from the hands of the true owner.

For more than a week Mr. Somers waited, but got no reply to his letter, and heard nothing from Mr. Prendergast; and during this time he was really puzzled as to what he should do. As regarded himself, he did not know at what moment his income might end, or how long he and his family might be allowed to inhabit the house which he now held: and then he could take no steps as to the tenants; could neither receive money nor pay it away, and was altogether at his wits' ends. Lady Fitzgerald

looked to him for counsel in everything, and he did not know
how to counsel her. Arrangements were to be made for an
auction in the house as soon as she should be able to move; but
would it not be a thousand pities to sell all the furniture if there
was a prospect of the family returning? And so he waited for
Mr. Prendergast's letter with an uneasy heart and vexation of
spirit.

But still he attended the relief committees, and worked at the
soup-kitchens attached to the estate, as though he were still the
agent to Castle Richmond; and still debated warmly with Father
Barney on one side, and Mr. Townsend on the other, on that
vexatious question of out-door relief. And now the famine was
in full swing; and strange to say, men had ceased to be uncomfortable about it;—such men, that is, as Mr. Somers and Mr.
Townsend. The cutting off of maimed limbs, and wrenching out
from their sockets of smashed bones, is by no means shocking to
the skilled practitioner. And dying paupers, with 'the drag' in
their face—that certain sign of coming death of which I have
spoken—no longer struck men to the heart. Like the skilled
surgeon, they worked hard enough at what good they could do,
and worked the better in that they could treat the cases without
express compassion for the individuals that met their eyes. In
administering relief one may rob five unseen sufferers of what
would keep them in life if one is moved to bestow all that is
comfortable on one sufferer that is seen. Was it wise to spend
money in alleviating the last hours of those whose doom was
already spoken, which money, if duly used, might save the lives
of others not yet so far gone in misery? And so in one sense
those who were the best in the county, who worked the hardest
for the poor and spent their time most completely among them,
became the hardest of heart, and most obdurate in their denials. It
was strange to see devoted women neglecting the wants of the dying, so that they might husband their strength and time and means
for the wants of those who might still be kept among the living.

At this time there came over to the parish of Drumbarrow a
young English clergyman who might be said to be in many respects
the very opposite to Mr. Townsend. Two men could hardly be
found in the same profession more opposite in their ideas, lives,
purposes, and pursuits :—with this similarity, however, that each
was a sincere, and on the whole an honest man. The Rev. Mr.
Carter was much the junior, being at that time under thirty.
He had now visited Ireland with the sole object of working
among the poor, and distributing, according to his own judgment, certain funds which had been collected for this purpose in
England.

And indeed there did often exist in England at this time a misapprehension as to Irish wants, which led to some misuses of the funds which England so liberally sent. It came at that time to be the duty of a certain public officer to inquire into a charge made against a seemingly respectable man in the far west of Ireland, purporting that he had appropriated to his own use a sum of twelve pounds sent to him for the relief of the poor of his parish. It had been sent by three English maiden ladies to the relieving officer of the parish of Kilcoutymorrow, and had come to his hands, he then filling that position. He, so the charge said,—and unfortunately said so with only too much truth,—had put the twelve pounds into his own private pocket. The officer's duty in the matter took him to the chairman of the relief committee, a stanch old Roman Catholic gentleman nearly eighty years of age, with a hoary head and white beard, and a Milesian name that had come down to him through centuries of Catholic ancestors;—a man urbane in his manner, of the old school, an Irishman such as one does meet still here and there through the country, but now not often—one who above all things was true to the old religion.

Then the officer of the government told his story to the old Irish gentleman—with many words, for there were all manner of small collateral proofs, to all of which the old Irish gentleman listened with a courtesy and patience which were admirable. And when the officer of the government had done, the old Irish gentleman thus replied :—

' My neighbour Hobbs,'—such was the culprit's name—' has undoubtedly done this thing. He has certainly spent upon his own uses the generous offering made to our poor parish by those noble-minded ladies, the three Miss Walkers. But he has acted with perfect honesty in the matter.'

' What !' said the government officer, ' robbing the poor, and at such a time as this !'

' No robbery at all, dear sir,' said the good old Irish gentleman, with the blandest of all possible smiles; ' the excellent Miss Walkers sent their money for the Protestant poor of the parish of Kilcoutymorrow, and Mr. Hobbs is the only Protestant within it.' And from the twinkle in the old man's eye, it was clear to see that his triumph consisted in this,—that not only he had but one Protestant in the parish, but that that Protestant should have learned so little from his religion.

But this is an episode. And nowadays no episodes are allowed.

And now Mr. Carter had come over to see that if possible certain English funds were distributed according to the wishes of the generous English hearts by whom they had been sent. For as some English, such as the three Miss Walkers, feared on the one hand that the Babylonish woman so rampant in Ireland might swallow up their money for Babylonish purposes ; so, on the other hand, did others dread that the too stanch Protestantism of the church militant in that country might expend the funds collected for undoubted bodily wants in administering to the supposed wants of the soul. No such faults did, in truth, at that time prevail. The indomitable force of the famine had absolutely knocked down all that; but there had been things done in Ireland, before the famine came upon them, which gave reasonable suspicion for such fears.

Mr. Townsend among others had been very active in soliciting aid from England, and hence had arisen a correspondence between him and Mr. Carter; and now Mr. Carter had arrived at Drumbarrow with a respectable sum to his credit at the provincial bank, and an intense desire to make himself useful in this time of sore need. Mr. Carter was a tall, thin, austere-looking man ; one, seemingly, who had macerated himself inwardly and outwardly by hard living. He had a high, narrow forehead, a sparse amount of animal development, thin lips, and a piercing, sharp, gray eye. He was a man, too, of few words, and would have been altogether harsh in his appearance had there not been that in the twinkle of his eye which seemed to say that, in spite of all that his gait said to the contrary, the cockles of his heart might yet be reached by some play of wit—if only the wit were to his taste.

Mr. Carter was a man of personal means, so that he not only was not dependent on his profession, but was able—as he also was willing—to aid that profession by his liberality. In one thing only was he personally expensive. As to his eating and drinking it was, or it might have been for any solicitude of his own, little more than bread and water. As for the comforts of home, he had none, for since his ordination his missions had ever been migrating. But he always dressed with care, and consequently with expense, for careful dressing is ever expensive. He always wore new black gloves, and a very long black coat which never degenerated to rust, black cloth trousers, a high black silk waistcoat, and a new black hat. Everything about him was black except his neck, and that was always scrupulously white.

Mr. Carter was a good man,—one may say a very good man— for he gave up himself and his money to carry out high views of charity and religion, in which he was sincere with the sincerity of his whole heart, and from which he looked for no reward save such as the godly ever seek. But yet there was about him too much of the Pharisee. He was greatly inclined to condemn other men, and to think none righteous who differed from him. And now he had come to Ireland with a certain conviction that the clergy of his own church there were men not to be trusted; that they were mere Irish, and little better in their habits and doctrines than under-bred dissenters. He had been elsewhere in the country before he visited Drumbarrow, and had shown this too plainly; but then Mr. Carter was a very young man, and it is not perhaps fair to expect zeal and discretion also from those who are very young.

Mrs. Townsend had heard of him, and was in dismay when she found that he was to stay with them at Drumbarrow parsonage for three days. If Mr. Carter did not like clerical characters of her stamp neither did she like them of the stamp of Mr. Carter. She had heard of him, of his austerity, of his look, of his habits, and in her heart she believed him to be a Jesuit. Had she possessed full sway herself in the parish of Drumbarrow, no bodies should have been saved at such terrible peril to the souls of the whole parish. But this Mr. Carter came with such recommendation—with such assurances of money given and to be given, of service done and to be done,—that there was no refusing him. And so the husband, more worldly wise than his wife, had invited the Jesuit to his parsonage.

'You'll find, Æneas, he'll have mass in his room in the morning instead of coming to family prayers,' said the wife.

'But what on earth shall we give him for dinner?' said the husband, whose soul at the present moment was among the fleshpots; and indeed Mrs. Townsend had also turned over that question in her prudent mind.

'He'll not eat meat in Lent, you may be sure,' said Mrs. Townsend, remembering that that was the present time of the year.

'And if he would there is none for him to eat,' said Mr. Townsend, calling to mind the way in which the larder had of late been emptied.

Protestant clergymen in Ireland in those days had very frequently other reasons for fasting than those prescribed by ecclesiastical canons. A well-nurtured lady, the wife of a parish rector in the county Cork, showed me her larder one day about that time. It contained two large loaves of bread, and a pan full of stuff which I should have called paste, but which she called porridge. It was all that she had for herself, her husband, her children, and her charity. Her servants had left her before she came to that pass. And she was a well-nurtured, handsome, educated woman, born to such comforts as you and I enjoy every day,—oh, my reader! perhaps without much giving of thanks for them. Poor lady! the struggle was too much for her, and she died under it.

Mr. Townsend was, as I have said, the very opposite to Mr. Carter, but he also was a man who could do without the comforts of life, if the comforts of life did not come readily in his way. He liked his glass of whisky punch dearly, and had an idea that it was good for him. Not caring much about personal debts, he would go in debt for whisky. But if the whisky and credit were at an end, the loss did not make him miserable. He was a man with a large appetite, and who took great advantage of a good dinner when it was before him; nay, he would go a long distance to insure a good dinner; but, nevertheless, he would leave himself without the means of getting a mutton chop, and then not be unhappy. Now Mr. Carter would have been very unhappy had he been left without his superfine long black coat.

In tendering his invitation to Mr. Carter, Mr. Townsend had explained that with him the *res angusta domi*, which was always a prevailing disease, had been heightened by the circumstances of the time; but that of such crust and cup as he had, his brother English clergyman would be made most welcome to partake. In answer to this, Mr. Carter had explained that in these days good men thought but little of crusts and cups, and that as regarded himself, nature had so made him that he had but few concupiscences of that sort. And then, all this having been so far explained and settled, Mr. Carter came.

The first day the two clergymen spent together at Berryhill, and found plenty to employ them. They were now like enough to be in want of funds at that Berryhill soup-kitchen, seeing that the great fount of supplies, the house, namely, of Castle Richmond, would soon have stopped running altogether. And Mr. Carter was ready to provide funds to some moderate extent if all his questions were answered satisfactorily. 'There was to be no making of Protestants,' he said, 'by giving away of soup purchased with his money.' Mr. Townsend thought that this might have been spared him. 'I regret to say,' replied he, with some touch of sarcasm, 'that we have no time for that now.' 'And so better,' said Mr. Carter, with a sarcasm of a blunter sort. 'So better. Let us not clog our alms with impossible conditions which will only create falsehood.' 'Any conditions are out of the question when one has to feed a whole parish,' answered Mr. Townsend.

And then Mr. Carter would teach them how to boil their yellow meal, on which subject he had a theory totally opposite to the practice of the woman employed at the soup-kitchen. 'Av

we war to hocus it that, yer riverence,' said Mrs. Daly, turning
to Mr. Townsend, ' the crathurs couldn't ate a bit of it ; it wouldn't
bile at all, at all, not like that.'

' Try it, woman,' said Mr. Carter, when he he had uttered his
receipt oracularly for the third time.

' 'Deed an' I won't,' said Mrs. Daly, whose presence there was
pretty nearly a labour of love, and who was therefore independent.
' It 'd be a sin an' a shame to spile Christian vittels in them
times, an' I won't do it.'   And then there was some hard work
that day ; and though Mr. Townsend kept his temper with his
visitor, seeing that he had much to get and nothing to give, he
did not on this occasion learn to alter his general opinion of
his brethren of the English high church.

And then, when they got home, very hungry after their
toil, Mr. Townsend made another 'apology for the poorness of
his table.   ' I am almost ashamed,' said he, ' to ask an English
gentleman to sit down to such a dinner as Mrs. Townsend will
put before you.'

' And indeed then it isn't much,' said Mrs. Townsend ; ' just a
bit of fish I found going the road.'

' My dear madam, anything will suffice,' said Mr. Carter,
somewhat pretentiously.   And anything would have sufficed.
Had they put before him a mess of that paste of which I have
spoken he would have ate it and said nothing,—ate enough of it
at least to sustain him till the morrow.

But things had not come to so bad a pass as this at Drumbarrow
parsonage ; and, indeed, that day fortune had been propitious ;—
fortune which ever favours the daring.   Mrs. Townsend, knowing that she had really nothing in the house, had sent Jerry to
waylay the Lent fishmonger, who twice a week was known to
make his way from Kanturk to Mallow with a donkey and
panniers ; and Jerry had returned with a prize.

And now they sat down to dinner, and lo and behold, to the
great surprise of Mr. Carter, and perhaps also to the surprise of
the host, a magnificent turbot smoked upon the board.   The fins
no doubt had been cut off to render possible the insertion of the
animal into the largest of the Drumbarrow parsonage kitchen-
pots,—an injury against which Mr. Townsend immediately exclaimed angrily.   ' My goodness, they have cut off the fins !' said
he, holding up both hands in deep dismay.   According to his philosophy, if he did have a turbot, why should he not have it with
all its perfections about it—fins and all ?

' My dear Æneas !' said Mrs. Townsend, looking at him with
that agony of domestic distress which all wives so well know
how to assume.

Mr. Carter said nothing. He said not a word, but he thought much. This then was their pretended poorness of living! with all their mock humility, these false Irishmen could not resist the opportunity of showing off before the English stranger, and of putting on their table before him a dish which an English dean could afford only on gala days. And then this clergyman, who was so loudly anxious for the poor, could not repress the sorrow of his heart because the rich delicacy was somewhat marred in the cooking. 'It was too bad,' thought Mr. Carter to himself, 'too bad.'

'None, thank you,' said he, drawing himself up with gloomy reprobation of countenance. 'I will not take any fish, I am much obliged to you.'

Then the face of Mrs. Townsend was one on which neither Christian nor heathen could have looked without horror and grief. What, the man whom in her heart she believed to be a Jesuit, and for whom nevertheless, Jesuit though he was, she had condescended to cater with all her woman's wit!—this man, I say, would not eat fish in Lent! And it was horrible to her warm Irish heart to think that after that fish now upon the table there was nothing to come but two or three square inches of cold bacon. Not eat turbot in Lent! Had he been one of her own sort she might have given him credit for true antagonism to popery; but every inch of his coat gave the lie to such a supposition as that.

'Do take a bit,' said Mr. Townsend, hospitably. 'The fins should not have been cut off, otherwise I never saw a finer fish in my life.'

'None, I am very much obliged to you,' said Mr. Carter, with sternest reprobation of feature.

It was too much for Mrs. Townsend. 'Oh, Æneas,' said she, 'what are we to do?' Mr. Townsend merely shrugged his shoulders, while he helped himself. His feelings were less acute, perhaps, than those of his wife, and he, no doubt, was much more hungry. Mr. Carter the while sat by, saying nothing, but looking daggers. He also was hungry, but under such circumstances he would rather starve than eat.

'Don't you ever eat fish, Mr. Carter?' said Mr. Townsend, proceeding to help himself for a second time, and poking about round the edges of the delicate creature before him for some relics of the glutinous morsels which he loved so well. He was not, however, enjoying it as he should have done, for seeing that his guest ate none, and that his wife's appetite was thoroughly marred, he was alone in his occupation. No one but a glutton could have feasted well under such circumstances, and Mr. Townsend was not a glutton.

'Thank you, I will eat none to-day,' said Mr. Carter, sitting bolt upright, and fixing his keen gray eyes on the wall opposite.

'Then you may take away, Biddy; I've done with it. But it's a thousand pities such a fish should have been so wasted.'

The female heart of Mrs. Townsend could stand these wrongs no longer, and with a tear in one corner of her eye, and a gleam of anger in the other, she at length thus spoke out. 'I am sure then I don't know what you will eat, Mr. Carter, and I did think that all you English clergymen always ate fish' in Lent,—and indeed nothing else; for indeed people do say that you are much the same as the papists in that respect.'

'Hush, my dear!' said Mr. Townsend.

'Well, but I can't hush when there's nothing for the gentleman to eat.'

'My dear madam, such a matter does not signify in the least,' said Mr. Carter, not unbending an inch.

'But it does signify; it signifies a great deal; and so you'd know if you were a family man;'—'as you ought to be,' Mrs. Townsend would have been delighted to add. 'And I'm sure I sent Jerry five miles, and he was gone four hours to get that bit of fish from Paddy Magrath, as he stops always at Ballygibblin Gate; and indeed I thought myself so lucky, for I only gave Jerry one and sixpence. But they had an uncommon take of fish yesterday at Skibbereen, and—'

'One and sixpence!' said Mr. Carter, now slightly relaxing his brow for the first time.

'I'd have got it for one and three,' said Mr. Townsend, upon whose mind an inkling of the truth was beginning to dawn.

'Indeed and you wouldn't, Æneas; and Jerry was forced to promise the man a glass of whisky the first time he comes this road, which he does sometimes. That fish weighed over nine pounds, every ounce of it.'

'Nine fiddlesticks,' said Mr. Townsend.

'I weighed it myself, Æneas, with my own hands, and it was nine pounds four ounces before we were obliged to cut it, and as firm as a rock the flesh was.'

'For one and sixpence!' said Mr. Carter, relaxing still a little further, and condescending to look his hostess in the face.

'Yes, for one and six; and now—'

'I'm sure I'd have bought it for one and four, fins and all,' said the parson, determined to interrupt his wife in her pathos.

'I'm sure you would not then,' said his wife, taking his assertion in earnest. 'You could never market against Jerry in your life; I will say that for him.'

'If you'll allow me to change my mind, I think I will have a little bit of it,' said Mr. Carter, almost humbly.

'By all means,' said Mr. Townsend. 'Biddy, bring that fish back. Now I think of it, I have not half dined myself yet.'

And then they all three forgot their ill humours, and enjoyed their dinner thoroughly,—in spite of the acknowledged fault as touching the lost fins of the animal.

CHAPTER XXXVIII.

CONDEMNED.

I HAVE said that Lord Desmond rode home from Hap House that day in a quieter mood and at a slower pace than that which had brought him thither; and in truth it was so. He had things to think of now much more serious than any that had filled his mind as he had cantered along, joyously hoping that after all he might have for his brother the man that he loved, and the owner of Castle Richmond also. This was now impossible; but he felt that he loved Owen better than ever he had done, and he was pledged to fight Owen's battle, let Owen be ever so poor.

'And what does it signify after all?' he said to himself, as he rode along. 'We shall all be poor together, and then we sha'n't mind it so much; and if I don't marry, Hap House itself will be something to add to the property;' and then he made up his mind that he could be happy enough, living at Desmond Court all his life, so long as he could have Owen Fitzgerald near him to make life palatable.

That night he spoke to no one on the subject, at least to no one of his own accord. When they were alone his mother asked him where he had been; and when she learned that he had been at Hap House, she questioned him much as to what had passed between him and Owen; but he would tell her nothing, merely saying that Owen had spoken of Clara with his usual ecstasy of love, but declining to go into the subject at any length. The countess, however, gathered from him that he and Owen were on kindly terms together, and so far she felt satisfied.

On the following morning he made up his mind 'to have it out,' as he called it, with Clara; but when the hour came his courage failed him: it was a difficult task—that which he was now to undertake—of explaining to her his wish that she should go back to her old lover, not because he was no longer poor, but, as it were in spite of his poverty, and as reward to him for consenting to remain poor. As he had thought about it while riding home, it had seemed feasible enough. He would tell her how nobly Owen was going to behave to Herbert, and would put it to her whether, as he intended willingly to abandon the estate, he ought not to be put into possession of the wife. There was a romantic justice about this which he thought would touch Clara's heart. But on the following morning when he came to think what words he would use for making his little proposition, the picture did not seem to him to be so beautiful. If Clara really loved Herbert—and she had declared that she did twenty times over—it would be absurd to expect her to give him up merely because he was not a ruined man. But then, which did she love? His mother declared that she loved Owen. 'That's the real question,' said the earl to himself, as on the second morning he made up his mind that he would 'have it out' with Clara without any further delay. He must be true to Owen; that was his first great duty at the present moment.

'Clara, I want to talk to you,' he said, breaking suddenly into the room where she usually sat alone o' mornings. 'I was at Hap House the day before yesterday with Owen Fitzgerald, and to tell you the truth at once, we were talking about you the whole time we were there. And now what I want is, that something should be settled, so that we may all understand one another.'

These words he spoke to her quite abruptly. When he first said that he wished to speak to her, she had got up from her chair to welcome him, for she dearly loved to have him there. There was nothing she liked better than having him to herself when he was in a soft brotherly humour; and then she would interest herself about his horse, and his dogs, and his gun, and predict his life for him, sending him up as a peer to parliament, and giving him a noble wife, and promising him that he should be such a Desmond as would redeem all the family from their distresses. But now as he rapidly brought out his words, she found that on this day her prophecies must regard herself chiefly.

'Surely, Patrick, it is easy enough to understand me,' she said.

'Well, I don't know; I don't in the least mean to find fault with you.'

'I am glad of that, dearest,' she said, laying her hand upon his arm.

'But my mother says one thing, and you another, and Owen another; and I myself, I hardly know what to say.'

'Look here, Patrick, it is simply this: I became engaged to Herbert with my mother's sanction and yours; and now—'

'Stop a moment,' said the impetuous boy, 'and do not pledge

yourself to anything till you have heard me. I know that you are cut to the heart about Herbert Fitzgerald losing his property.'

'No, indeed; not at all cut to the heart; that is as regards myself.'

'I don't mean as regards yourself; I mean as regards him. I have heard you say over and over again that it is a piteous thing that he should be so treated. Have I not?'

'Yes, I have said that, and I think so.'

'And I think that most of your great—great—great love for him, if you will, comes from that sort of feeling.'

'But, Patrick, it came long before.'

'Dear Clara, do listen to me, will you? You may at any rate do as much as that for me.' And then Clara stood perfectly mute, looking into his handsome face as he continued to rattle out his words at her.

'Now if you please, Clara, you may have the means of giving back to him all his property, every shilling that he ever had, or expected to have. Owen Fitzgerald,—who certainly is the finest fellow that ever I came across in all my life, or ever shall, if I live to five hundred,—says that he will make over every acre of Castle Richmond back to his cousin Herbert if—' Oh, my lord, my lord, what a scheme is this you are concocting to entrap your sister! Owen Fitzgerald inserted no 'if,' as you are well aware! 'If' he continued, with some little qualm of conscience, 'if you will consent to be his wife.'

'Patrick!'

'Listen, now listen. He thinks, and, Clara, by the heavens above me! I think also that you did love him better than you ever loved Herbert Fitzgerald.' Clara as she heard these words blushed ruby red up to her very hair, but she said never a word. 'And I think, and he thinks, that you are bound now to Herbert by his misfortunes—that you feel that you cannot desert him because he has fallen so low. By George, Clara, I am proud of you for sticking to him through thick and thin, now that he is down! But the matter will be very difficult if you have the means of giving back to him all that he has lost, as you have. Owen will be poor, but he is a prince among men. By heaven, Clara, if you will only say that he is your choice, Herbert shall have back all Castle Richmond! and I—I shall never marry, and you may give to the man that I love as my brother all that there is left to us of Desmond.'

There was something grand about the lad's eager tone of voice as he made his wild proposal, and something grand also about his heart. He meant what he said, foolish as he was either to mean or to say it. Clara burst into tears, and threw herself into his arms. ' You don't understand,' she said, through her sobs, ' my own, own brother; you do not understand.'

' But, by Jove! I think I do understand. As sure as you are a living girl he will give back Castle Richmond to Herbert Fitzgerald.'

She recovered herself, and leaving her brother's arms, walked away to the window, and from thence looked down to that path beneath the elms which was the spot in the world which she thought of the oftenest; but as she gazed, there was no lack of loyalty in her heart to the man to whom she was betrothed. It seemed to her as though those childish days had been in another life; as though Owen had been her lover in another world,—a sweet, childish, innocent, happy world which she remembered well, but which was now dissevered from her by an impassable gulf. She thought of his few words of love,—so few that she remembered every word that he had then spoken, and thought of them with a singular mixture of pain and pleasure. And now she heard of his noble self-denial with a thrill which was in no degree enhanced by the fact that she, or even Herbert, was to be the gainer by it. She rejoiced at his nobility, merely because it was a joy to her to know that he was so noble. And yet all through this she was true to Herbert. Another work-a-day world had come upon her in her womanhood, and as that came she had learned to love a man of another stamp, with a love that was quieter, more subdued, and perhaps, as she thought, more enduring. Whatever might be Herbert's lot in life, that lot she would share. Her love for Owen should never be more to her than a dream.

' Did he send you to me?' she said at last, without turning her face away from the window.

' Yes, then, he did; he did send me to you, and he told me to say that as Owen of Hap House he loved you still. And I, I promised to do his bidding; and I promised, moreover, that as far as my good word could go with you, he should have it. And now you know it all; if you care for my pleasure in the matter you will take Owen, and let Herbert have his property. By Jove! if he is treated in that way he cannot complain.'

' Patrick,' said she, returning to him and again laying her hand on him, ' you must now take my message also. You must go to him and bid him come here that I may see him.'

' Who? Owen?'

' Yes, Owen Fitzgerald.'

' Very well, I have no objection in life.' And the earl thought that the difficulty was really about to be overcome. ' And about my mother?'

' I will tell mamma.'

' And what shall I say to Owen?'

' Say nothing to him, but bid him come here. But wait,
Patrick; yes; he must not misunderstand me; I can never,
never, never marry him.'

' Clara!'

' Never, never; it is impossible. Dear Patrick, I am so sorry
to make you unhappy, and I love you so very dearly,—better
than ever, I think, for speaking as you do now. But that can
never be. Let him come here, however, and I myself will tell
him all.' At last, disgusted and unhappy though he was, the
earl did accept the commission, and again on that afternoon rode
across the fields to Hap House.

' I will tell him nothing but that he is to come,' said the earl
to himself as he went thither. And he did tell Owen nothing
else. Fitzgerald questioned him much, but learned but little
from him. ' By heavens, Owen,' he said, ' you must settle the
matter between you, for I don't understand it. She has bid me
ask you to come to her; and now you must fight your own
battle.' Fitzgerald of course said that he would obey, and so
Lord Desmond left him.

In the evening Clara told her mother. ' Owen Fitzgerald is
to be here to-morrow,' she said.

' Owen Fitzgerald; is he?' said the countess. She hardly
knew how to bear herself, or how to interfere so as to assist her
own object; or how not to interfere, lest she should mar it.

' Yes, mamma. Patrick saw him the other day, and I think it
is better that I should see him also.'

' Very well, my dear. But you must be aware, Clara, that
you have been so very—I don't wish to say headstrong exactly—
so very *entêtée* about your own affairs, that I hardly know how to
speak of them. If your brother is in your confidence I shall be
satisfied.'

' He is in my confidence; and so may you be also, mamma, if
you please.'

But the countess thought it better not to have any conversation
forced upon her at that moment; and so she asked her daughter
for no further show of confidence then. It would probably be
as well that Owen should come and plead his own cause.

And Owen did come. All that night and on the next morning
the poor girl remained alone in a state of terrible doubt. She
had sent for her old lover, thinking at the moment that no one
could explain to him in language so clear as her own what was
her fixed resolve. And she had too been so moved by the splendour of his offer, that she longed to tell him what she thought of

it. The grandeur of that offer was enhanced tenfold in her mind by the fact that it had been so framed as to include her in this comparative poverty with which Owen himself was prepared to rest contented. He had known that she was not to be bought by wealth, and had given her credit for a nobility that was akin to his own.

But yet, now that the moment was coming, how was she to talk to him? How was she to speak the words which would rob him of his hope, and tell him that he did not, could not, never could possess that one treasure which he desired more ,than houses and lands, or station and rank? Alas, alas! If it could have been otherwise! If it could have been otherwise! She also was in love with poverty;—but at any rate no one could accuse her now of sacrificing a poor lover for a rich one. Herbert Fitzgerald would be poor enough.

And then he came. They had hitherto met but once since that afternoon, now so long ago—that afternoon to which she looked back as to another former world—and that meeting had been in the very room in which she was now prepared to receive him. But her feelings towards him had been very different then. Then he had almost forced himself upon her, and for months previously she had heard nothing of him but what was evil. He had come complaining loudly, and her heart' had been somewhat hardened against him. Now he was there at her bidding, and her heart and very soul were full of tenderness. She rose rapidly, and sat down again, and then again rose as she heard his footsteps; but when he entered the room she was standing in the middle of it.

' Clara,' he said, taking the hand which she mechanically held out, ' I have come here now at your brother's request.'

Her name sounded so sweet upon his lips. No idea occurred to her that she ought to be angry with him for using it. Angry with him! Could it be possible that she should ever be angry with him—that she ever had been so?

'Yes,' she said. ' Patrick said something to me which made me think that it would be better that we should meet.'

' Well, yes; it is better. If people are honest they had always better say to each other's faces that which they have to say.'

' I mean to be honest, Mr. Fitzgerald.'

' Yes, I am sure you do; and so do I also. And if this is so, why cannot we say each to the other that which we have to say? My tale will be a very short one; but it will be true if it is short.'

' But, Mr. Fitzgerald—'

' Well, Clara?'

'Will you not sit down?' And she herself sat upon the sofa; and he drew a chair for himself near to her; but he was too impetuous to remain seated on it long. During the interview between them he was sometimes standing, and sometimes walking quickly about the room; and then for a moment he would sit down, or lean down over her on the sofa arm.

'But, Mr. Fitzgerald, it is my tale that I wish you to hear.'

'Well; I will listen to it.' But he did not listen; for before she had spoken a dozen words he had interrupted her, and poured out upon her his own wild plans and generous schemes. She, poor girl, had thought to tell him that she loved Herbert, and Herbert only—as a lover. But that if she could love him, him Owen, as a brother and a friend, that love she would so willingly give him. And then she would have gone on to say how impossible it would have been for Herbert, under any circumstances, to have availed himself of such generosity as that which had been offered. But her eloquence was all cut short in the bud. How could she speak with such a storm of impulse raging before her as that which was now strong within Owen Fitzgerald's bosom?

He interrupted her before she had spoken a dozen words, in order that he might exhibit before her eyes the project with which his bosom was filled. This he did, standing for the most part before her, looking down upon her as she sat beneath him, with her eyes fixed upon the floor, while his were riveted on her down-turned face. She knew it all before—all this that he had to say to her, or she would hardly have understood it from his words, they were so rapid and vehement. And yet they were tender, too; spoken in a loving tone, and containing ever and anon assurances of respect, and a resolve to be guided now and for ever by her wishes,—even though those wishes should be utterly subversive of his happiness.

'And now you know it all,' he said, at last. 'And as for my cousin's property, that is safe enough. No earthly consideration would induce me to put a hand upon that, seeing that by all justice it is his.' But in this she hardly yet quite understood him. 'Let him have what luck he may in other respects, he shall still be master of Castle Richmond. If it were that that you wanted—as I know it is not—that I cannot give you. I cannot tell you with what scorn I should regard myself if I were to take advantage of such an accident as this to rob any man of his estate.'

Her brother had been right, so Clara felt, when he declared that Owen Fizgerald was the finest fellow that ever he had come across. She made another such declaration within her own heart, only with words that were more natural to her. He was the noblest gentleman of whom she had ever heard, or read, or thought.

'But,' continued Owen, 'as I will not interfere with him in that which should be his, neither should he interfere with me in that which should be mine. Clara, the only estate that I claim is your heart.'

And that estate she could not give him. On that at any rate she was fixed. She could not barter herself about from one to the other either as a make-weight or a counterpoise. All his pleading was in vain; all his generosity would fail in securing to him this one reward that he desired. And now she had to tell him so.

'Your brother seems to think,' he continued, 'that you still——;' but now it was her turn to interrupt him.

'Patrick is mistaken,' she said, with her eyes still fixed upon the ground.

'What! You will tell me, then, that I am utterly indifferent to you?'

'No, no, no; I did not say so.' And now she got up and took hold of his arm, and looked into his face imploringly. 'I did not say so. But, oh, Mr. Fitzgerald, be kind to me, be forbearing with me, be good to me,' and she almost embraced his arm as she appealed to him, with her eyes all swimming with tears.

'Good to you!' he said. And a strong passion came upon him, urging him to throw his arm round her slender body, and press her to his bosom. Good to her! would he not protect her with his life's blood against all the world if she would only come to him? 'Good to you, Clara! Can you not trust me that I will be good to you if you will let me?'

'But not so, Owen.' It was the first time she had ever called him by his name, and she blushed again as she remembered that it was so. 'Not good, as you mean, for now I must trust to another for that goodness. Herbert must be my husband, Owen; but will you not be our friend?'

'Herbert must be your husband!'

'Yes, yes, yes. It is so. Do not look at me in that way, pray do not; what would you have me do? You would not have me false to my troth, and false to my own heart, because you are generous. Be generous to me—to me also.'

He turned away from her, and walked the whole length of the long room; away and back before he answered her, and even then, when he had returned to her, he stood looking at her before he spoke. And she now looked full into his face, hoping, but yet fearing; hoping that he might yield to her; and fearing his terrible displeasure should he not yield.

'Clara,' he said; and he spoke solemnly, slowly, and in a mood unlike his own,—'I cannot as yet read your heart clearly; nor do I know whether you can quite so read it yourself.'

'I can, I can,' she answered quickly; 'and you shall know it all—all, if you wish.'

'I want to know but one thing. Whom is it that you love? And, Clara—,' and this he said interrupting her as she was about to speak. 'I do not ask you to whom you are engaged. You have engaged yourself both to him and to me.'

'Oh, Mr. Fitzgerald!'

'I do not blame you; not in the least. But is it not so? As to that I will ask no question, and say nothing; only this, that so far we are equal. But now ask of your own heart, and then answer me. Whom is it then you love?'

'Herbert Fitzgerald,' she said. The words hardly formed themselves into a whisper, but nevertheless they were audible enough to him.

'Then I have no further business here,' he said, and turned about as though to leave the room.

But she ran forward and stopped him, standing between him and the door. 'Oh, Mr. Fitzgerald, do not leave me like that. Say one word of kindness to me before you go. Tell me that you forgive me for the injury I have done you.'

'Yes, I forgive you.'

'And is that all? Oh, I will love you so, if you will let me;— as your friend, as your sister; you shall be our dearest, best, and nearest friend. You do not know how good he is. Owen, will you not tell me that you will love me as a brother loves?'

'No!' and the sternness of his face was such that it was dreadful to look on it. 'I will tell you nothing that is false.'

'And would that be false?'

'Yes, false as hell! What, sit by at his hearth-stone and see you leaning on his bosom! Sleep under his roof while you were in his arms! No, Lady Clara, that would not be possible. That virtue, if it be virtue, I cannot possess.'

'And you must go from me in anger? If you knew what I am suffering you would not speak to me so cruelly.'

'Cruel! I would not wish to be cruel to you; certainly not now, for we shall not meet again; if ever, not for many years. I do not think that I have been cruel to you.'

'Then say one word of kindness before you go!'

'A word of kindness! Well; what shall I say? Every night, as I have lain in my bed, I have said words of kindness to you, since—since—since longer than you will remember; since I first knew you as a child. Do you ever think of the day when you walked with me round by the bridge?'

'It is bootless thinking of that now.'

'Bootless! yes, and words of kindness are bootless. Between you and me, such words should be full of love, or they would have no meaning. What can I say to you that shall be both kind and true?'

'Bid God bless me before you leave me.'

'Well, I will say that. May God bless you, in this world and in the next! And now, Lady Clara Desmond, good-bye!' and he tendered to her his hand.

She took it, and pressed it between both of hers, and looked up into his face, and stood so, while the fast tears ran down her face. He must have been more or less than man had he not relented then. 'And Owen,' she said, 'dear Owen, may God in his mercy bless you also, and make you happy, and give you some one that you can love, and—and—teach you in your heart to forgive the injury I have done you.' And then she stooped down her head and pressed her lips upon the hand which she held within her own.

'Forgive you! Well—I do forgive you. Perhaps it may be right that we should both forgive; though I have not wittingly brought unhappiness upon you. But what there is to be forgiven on my side, I do forgive. And—and I hope that you may be happy.' They were the last words that he spoke; and then leading her back to her seat, he placed her there, and without turning to look at her again, he left the room.

He hurried down into the court, and called for his horse. As he stood there, when his foot was in the stirrup, and his hand on the animal's neck, Lord Desmond came up to him. 'Good-bye, Desmond,' he said. 'It is all over; God knows when you and I may meet again.' And without waiting for a word of reply he rode out under the porch, and putting spurs to his horse, galloped fast across the park. The earl, when he spoke of it afterwards to his mother, said that Owen's face had been as it were a thundercloud.

CHAPTER XXXIX.

FOX-HUNTING IN SPINNY LANE.

I THINK it will be acknowledged that Mr. Prendergast had said
no word throughout the conversation recorded in a late chapter
as having taken place between him and Herbert Fitzgerald over
their wine, which could lead Herbert to think it possible that he
might yet recover his lost inheritance; but nevertheless during
the whole of that evening he held in his pocket a letter, received
by him only that afternoon, which did encourage him to think
that such an event might at any rate be possible. And, indeed,
he held in his pocket two letters having a tendency to the same
effect, but we shall have nothing now to say as to that letter
from Mr. Somers of which we have spoken before.

It must be understood that up to this time certain inquiries
had been going on with reference to the life of Mr. Matthew
Mollett, and that these inquiries were being made by agents
employed by Mr. Prendergast. He had found that Mollett's
identity with Talbot had been so fully proved as to make it, in
his opinion, absolutely necessary that Herbert and his mother
should openly give up Castle Richmond. But, nevertheless,
without a hope, and in obedience solely to what he felt that
prudence demanded in so momentous a matter, he did prosecute
all manner of inquiries;—but prosecuted them altogether in vain.
And now, O thou most acute of lawyers, this new twinkling
spark of hope has come to thee from a source whence thou least
expectedst it!

Quod minime reris Graiâ pandetur ab urbe.

And then, as soon as Herbert was gone from him, crossing one
leg over the other as he sat in his easy chair, he took it from his
pocket and read it for the third time. The signature at the end
of it was very plain and legible, being that of a scholar no less
accomplished than Mr. Abraham Mollett. This letter we will
have entire, though it was not perhaps as short as it might have
been. It ran as follows:—

45 Tabernacle row London.
April—1847.

'Respectit Sir—

    'In hall them doings about the Fitsjerrals at Carsal Rich-
mon I halways felt the most profound respict for you because

you wanted to do the thing as was rite wich was what I halways wanted to myself only coodent becase of the guvnor. "Let the right un win, guvnor," said I, hover hand hover agin; but no, he woodent. And what cood the likes of me do then seeing as ow I was obligated by the forth comanment to honor my father and mother, wich however if it wasent that she was ded leving me a horphand there woodent av been none of this trobbel. If she ad lived Mr. Pindargrasp Ide av been brot hup honest, and thats what I weps for. But she dide and my guvnor why hes been a gitten the rong side of the post hever sins that hunfortunate day. Praps you knows Mr. Pindargrasp what it is to lose a mother in your herly hinfantsey. But I was at the guvnor hovers and hovers agin, but hall of no yuse. "He as stumpt hoff with my missus and now he shall stump hup the reddy." Them was my guvnors hown words halways. Well, Mr. Pindargrasp; what does I do. It warnt no good my talking to him he was for going so confounedly the rong side of the post. But I new as how Appy ouse Fitsjerral was the orse as ort to win. Lecstways I thawt I new it, and so you thawt too Mr. Pindargrasp only we was both running the rong cent. But what did I do when I was so confounedly disgusted by my guvnor ankring after the baronnites money wich it wasnt rite nor yet onest. Why I went meself to Appy ouse as you noes Mr. Pindargrasp, and was the first to tel the Appy ouse gent hall about it. But wat dos he do. Hoh, Mr. Pindargrasp, I shal never forgit that faitel day and only he got me hunewairs by the scruf of the nek Im has good a man as he hevery day of the week. But you was ther Mr. Pindargrasp and noes wat I got for befrindin the Appy ouse side wich was agin the guvnor and he as brot me to the loest pich of distress in the way of rino seein the guvnor as cut of my halowence becase I wint agin his hinterest.

' And now Mr. Pindargrasp I ave a terrible secret to hunraffel wich will put the sadel on the rite orse at last and as I does hall this agin my own guvnor wich of corse I love derely I do hope Mr. Pindargrasp you wont see me haltoogether left in the lerch. A litel something to go on with at furst wood be very agrebbel for indeed Mr. Pindargrasp its uncommon low water with your umbel servant at this presant moment. And now wat I has to say is this—Lady Fits warnt niver my guvnors wife hat all becase why hed a wife alivin has I can pruv and will and shes alivin now number 7 Spinny lane Centbotollfs intheheast. Now I do call that noos worse a Jews high Mr. Pindargrasp and I opes youll see me honestly delt with sein as how I coms forward and tels it hall without any haskin and cood keep it all to miself and no one coodent be the wiser only I chews to do the thing as is rite.

'You may fine out hall about it hall at number 7 Spinny lane and I advises you to go there immejat. Missus Mary Swan thats what she calls herself but her richeous name his Mollett—and why not seein who is er usban. So no more at presence but will com forward hany day to pruv hall this agin my guvnor becase he arnt doing the thing as is rite and I looks to you Mr. Pindargrasp to see as I gits someat ansum sein as ow I coms forward agin the Appy ouse gent and for the hother party oos side you is a bakkin.

'I ham respictit Sir

'Your umbel servant to command,

'ABM. MOLLETT.'

I cannot say that Mr. Prendergast believed much of this terribly long epistle when he first received it, or felt himself imbued with any great hope that his old friend's wife might be restored to her name and rank, and his old friend's son to his estate and fortune. But nevertheless he knew that it was worth inquiry. That Aby Mollett had been kicked out of Hap House in a manner that must have been mortifying to his feelings, Mr. Prendergast had himself seen; and that he would, therefore, do anything in his power to injure Owen Fitzgerald, Mr. Prendergast was quite sure. That he was a viler wretch even than his father, Mr. Prendergast suspected,—having been led to think so by words which had fallen from Sir Thomas, and being further confirmed in that opinion by the letter now in his hand. He was not, therefore, led into any strong opinion that these new tidings were of value. And, indeed, he was prone to disbelieve them, because they ran counter to a conviction which had already been made in his own heart, and had been extensively acted on by him. Nevertheless he resolved that even Aby's letter deserved attention, and that it should receive that attention early on the following morning.

And thus he had sat for the three hours after dinner, chatting comfortably with his young friend, and holding this letter in his pocket. Had he shown it to Herbert, or spoken of it, he would have utterly disturbed the equilibrium of the embryo law student, and rendered his entrance in Mr. Die's chambers absolutely futile. 'Ten will not be too early for you,' he had said. 'Mr. Die is always in his room by that hour.' Herbert had of course declared that ten would not be at all too early for him; and Mr. Prendergast had observed that after leaving Mr. Die's chambers, he himself would go on to the City. He might have said beyond the City, for his intended expedition was to Spinny Lane, at St. Botolph's in the East.

When Herbert was gone he sat musing over his fire with Aby's letter still in his hand. A lawyer has always a sort of affection for a scoundrel,—such affection as a hunting man has for a fox. He loves to watch the skill and dodges of the animal, to study the wiles by which he lives, and to circumvent them by wiles of his own, still more wily. It is his glory to run the beast down; but then he would not for worlds run him down, except in conformity with certain laws, fixed by old custom for the guidance of men in such sports. And the two-legged vermin is adapted for pursuit as is the fox with four legs. He is an unclean animal, leaving a scent upon his trail, which the nose of your acute law hound can pick up over almost any ground. And the more wily the beast is, the longer he can run, the more trouble he can give in the pursuit, the longer he can stand up before a pack of legal hounds, the better does the forensic sportsman love and value him. There are foxes of so excellent a nature, so keen in their dodges, so perfect in their cunning, so skilful in evasion, that a sportsman cannot find it in his heart to push them to their destruction unless the field be very large so that many eyes are looking on. And the feeling is I think the same with lawyers.

Mr. Prendergast had always felt a tenderness towards the Molletts, father and son,—a tenderness which would by no means have prevented him from sending them both to the halter had that been necessary, and had they put themselves so far in his power. Much as the sportsman loves the fox, it is a moment to him of keen enjoyment when he puts his heavy boot on the beast's body,—the expectant dogs standing round demanding their prey—and there both beheads and betails him. 'A grand old dog,' he says to those around him. 'I know him well It was he who took us that day from Poulnarer, through Castlecor, and right away to Drumcollogher.' And then he throws the heavy carcass to the hungry hounds. And so could Mr. Prendergast have delivered up either of the Molletts to be devoured by the dogs of the law; but he did not the less love them tenderly while they were yet running.

And so he sat with the letter in his hand, smiling to think that the father and son had come to grief among themselves; smiling also at the dodge by which, as he thought most probable, Aby Mollett was striving to injure the man who had kicked him, and raise a little money for his own private needs. There was too much earnestness in that prayer for cash to leave Mr. Prendergast in any doubt as to Aby's trust that money would be forthcoming. There must be something in the dodge, or Aby would not have had such trust.

And the lawyer felt that he might perhaps be inclined to give some little assistance to poor Aby in the soreness of his needs. Foxes will not do well in any country which is not provided with their natural food. Rats they eat, and if rats be plentiful it is so far good. ' But one should not begrudge them occasional geese and turkeys, or even break one's heart if they like a lamb in season. A fox will always run well when he has come far from home seeking his breakfast.

Poor Aby, when he had been so cruelly treated by the 'gent of Appy ouse,' whose side in the family dispute he had latterly been so anxious to take, had remained crouching for some hour or two in Owen's kitchen, absolutely mute. The servants there for a while felt sure that he was dying; but in their master's present mood they did not dare to go near him with any such tidings. And then when the hounds were gone, and the place was again quiet, Aby gradually roused himself, allowed them to wash the blood from his hands and face, to restore him to life by whisky and scraps of food, and gradually got himself into his car, and so back to the Kanturk Hotel, in South Main Street, Cork.

But, alas! his state there was more wretched by far than it had been in the Hap House kitchen. That his father had fled was no more than he expected. Each had known that the other would now play some separate secret game. But not the less did he complain loudly when he heard that 'his guvnor' had not paid the bill, and had left neither money nor message for him. How Fanny had scorned and upbraided him, and ordered Tom to turn him out of the house 'neck and crop;' how he had squared at Tom, and ultimately had been turned out of the house 'neck and crop,'—whatever that may mean—by Fanny's father, needs not here to be particularly narrated. With much suffering and many privations—such as foxes in their solitary wanderings so often know—he did find his way to London; and did, moreover, by means of such wiles as foxes have, find out something as to his 'guvnor's' whereabouts, and some secrets also as to his 'guvnor' which his 'guvnor' would fain have kept to himself had it been possible. And then, also, he again found for himself a sort of home—or hole rather—in his old original gorse covert of London; somewhere among the Jews we may surmise, from the name of the row from which he dated; and here, setting to work once more with his usual cunning industry,—for your fox is very industrious,—he once more attempted to build up a slender fortune by means of the 'Fitsjerral' family. The grand days in which he could look for the hand of the fair Emmeline were all gone by; but still the property had been too good not to leave something for which he might grasp. Properly worked, by

himself alone, as he said to himself, it might still yield him some
comfortable returns, especially as he should be able to throw
over that 'confouned old guvnor of his.'

He remained at home the whole of the day after his letter was
written, indeed for the next three days, thinking that Mr. Prendergast would come to him, or send for him; but Mr. Prendergast did neither the one nor the other. Mr. Prendergast took
his advice instead, and putting himself into a Hansom cab, had
himself driven to ' Centbotollfs intheheast.'

Spinny Lane, St. Botolph's in the East, when at last it was
found, was not exactly the sort of place that Mr. Prendergast had
expected. It must be known that he did not allow the cabman
to drive him up to the very door indicated, nor even to the lane
itself; but contented himself with leaving the cab at St. Botolph's
church. The huntsman in looking after his game is as wily as
the fox himself. Men do not talk at the covert side—or at any
rate they ought not. And they should stand together discreetly at the non-running side. All manner of wiles and silences
and discretions are necessary, though too often broken through
by the uninstructed,—much to their own discomfort. And so in
hunting his fox, Mr. Prendergast did not dash up loudly into
the covert, but discreetly left his cab at the church of St. Botolph's.

Spinny Lane, when at last found by intelligence given to him
at the baker's,—never in such unknown regions ask a lad in the
street, for he invariably will accompany you, talking of your
whereabouts very loudly, so that people stare at you, and ask
each other what can possibly be your business in those parts.
Spinny Lane, I say, was not the sort of locality that he had expected. He knew the look of the half-protected, half-condemned
Alsatias of the present-day rascals, and Spinny Lane did not at
all bear their character. It was a street of small new tenements,
built, as yet, only on one side of the way, with the pavement
only one third finished, and the stones in the road as yet unbroken and untrodden. Of such streets there are thousands now
round London. They are to be found in every suburb, creating
wonder in all thoughtful minds as to who can be their tens of
thousands of occupants. The houses are a little too good for arti-
sans, too small and too silent to be the abode of various lodgers,
and too mean for clerks who live on salaries. They are as dull-
looking as Lethe itself, dull and silent, dingy and repulsive.
But they are not discreditable in appearance, and never have that
Mohawk look which by some unknown sympathy in bricks and
mortar attaches itself to the residences of professional ruffians.

Number seven he found to be as quiet and decent a house as

any in the row, and having inspected it from a little distance he walked up briskly to the door, and rang the bell. He walked up briskly in order that his advance might not be seen; unless, indeed, as he began to think not, impossible, Aby's statement was altogether a hoax.

'Does a woman named Mrs. Mary Swan live here?' he asked of a decent-looking young woman of some seven or eight and twenty, who opened the door for him. She was decent looking, but poverty stricken and wan with work and care, and with that heaviness about her which perpetual sorrow always gives. Otherwise she would not have been ill-featured; and even as it was she was feminine and soft in her gait and manner. 'Does Mrs. Mary Swan live here?' asked Mr. Prendergast in a mild voice.

She at once said Mrs. Mary Swan did live there; but she stood with the door in her hand by no means fully opened, as though she did not wish to ask him to enter; and yet there was nothing in her tone to repel him. Mr. Prendergast at once felt that he was on the right scent, and that it behoved him at any rate to make his way into that house; for if ever a modest-looking daughter was like an immodest-looking father, that young woman was like Mr. Mollett senior.

'Then I will see her, if you please,' said Mr. Prendergast, entering the passage without her invitation. Not that he pushed in with roughness; but she receded before the authority of his tone, and obeyed the command which she read in his eye. The poor young woman hesitated as though it had been her intention to declare that Mrs. Swan was not within; but if so, she had not strength to carry out her purpose, for in the next moment Mr. Prendergast found himself in the presence of the woman he had come to seek.

'Mrs. Mary Swan?' said Mr. Prendergast, asking a question as to her identity.

'Yes, sir, that is my name,' said a sickly-looking elderly woman, rising from her chair.

The room in which the two had been sitting was very poor; but nevertheless it was neat, and arranged with some attention to appearance. It was not carpeted, but there was a piece of drugget some three yards long spread before the fireplace. The wall had been papered from time to time with scraps of different coloured paper, as opportunity offered. The table on which the work of the two women was lying was very old and somewhat rickety, but it was of mahogany; and Mrs. Mary Swan herself was accommodated with a high-backed arm-chair, which gave some appearance of comfort to her position. It was now spring;

but they had a small, very small fire in the small grate, on which a pot had been placed in hopes that it might be induced to boil. All these things did the eye of Mr. Prendergast take in; but the fact which his eye took in with its keenest glance was this,— that on the other side of the fire to that on which sat Mrs. Mary Swan, there was a second arm-chair standing close over the fender, an ordinary old mahogany chair, in which it was evident that the younger woman had not been sitting. Her place had been close to the table-side, where her needles and thread were still lying. But the arm-chair was placed idly away from any accommodation for work, and had, as Mr. Prendergast thought, been recently filled by some idle person.

The woman who rose from her chair as she declared herself to be Mary Swan was old and sickly looking, but nevertheless there was that about her which was prepossessing. Her face was thin and delicate and pale, and not hard and coarse; her voice was low, as a woman's should be, and her hands were white and small. Her clothes, though very poor, were neat, and worn as a poor lady might have worn them. Though there was in her face an aspect almost of terror as she owned to her name in the stranger's presence, yet there was also about her a certain amount of female dignity, which made Mr. Prendergast feel that it behoved him to treat her not only with gentleness, but also with respect.

'I want to say a few words to you,' said he, 'in consequence of a letter I have received; perhaps you will allow me to sit down for a minute or two.'

'Certainly, sir, certainly. This is my daughter, Mary Swan; do you wish that she should leave the room, sir?' And Mary Swan, as her mother spoke, got up and prepared to depart quietly.

'By no means, by no means,' said Mr. Prendergast, putting his hand out so as to detain her. ' I would much rather that she should remain, as it may be very likely that she may assist me in my inquiries. You will know who I am, no doubt, when I mention my name; Mr. Mollett will have mentioned me to you—I am Mr. Prendergast.'

'No, sir, he never did,' said Mrs. Swan.

'Oh!' said Mr. Prendergast, having ascertained that Mr. Mollett was at any rate well known at No. 7 Spinny Lane. 'I thought that he might probably have done so. He is at home at present, I believe?'

' Sir?' said Mary Swan senior.

'Your father is at home, I believe?' said Mr. Prendergast, turning to the young woman.

' Sir?' said Mary Swan junior. It was clear at any rate that the women were not practised liars, for they could not bring themselves on the spur of the moment to deny that he was in the house.

Mr. Prendergast did not wish to be confronted at present with Matthew Mollett. Such a step might or might not be desirable before the termination of the interview; but at the present moment he thought that he might probably learn more from the two women as they were than he would do if Mollett were with them.

It had been acknowledged to him that Mollett was living in that house, that he was now at home, and also that the younger woman present before him was the child of Mollett and of Mary Swan the elder. That the young woman was older than Herbert Fitzgerald, and that therefore the connection between Mollett and her mother must have been prior to that marriage down in Dorsetshire, he was sure; but then it might still be possible that there had been no marriage between Mollett and Mary Swan. If he could show that they had been man and wife when that child was born, then would his old friend Mr. Die lose his new pupil.

'I have a letter in my pocket, Mrs. Swan, from Abraham Mollett—' Mr. Prendergast commenced, pulling out the letter in question.

'He is nothing to me, sir,' said the woman, almost in a tone of anger. 'I know nothing whatever about him.'

'So I should have supposed from the respectability of your appearance, if I may be allowed to say so.'

'Nothing at all, sir; and as for that, we do try to keep ourselves respectable. But this is a very hard world for some people to live in. It has been very hard to me and this poor girl here.'

'It is a hard world to some people, and to some honest people, too,—which is harder still.'

'We've always tried to be honest,' said Mary Swan the elder.

'I am sure you have; and permit me to say, madam, that you will find it at the last to be the best policy; at the last, even as far as this world is concerned. But about this letter—I can assure you that I have never thought of identifying you with Abraham Mollett.'

'His mother was dead, sir, before ever I set eyes on him or his father; and though I tried to do my——' and then she stopped herself suddenly. Honesty might be the best policy, but, nevertheless, was it necessary that she should tell everything to this stranger?

'Ah, yes; Abraham's mother was dead before you were mar-

ried,' said Mr. Prendergast, hunting his fox ever so craftily,—
his fox whom he knew to be lying in ambush up stairs. It was
of course possible that old Mollett should slip away out of the
back door and over a wall. If foxes did not do those sort of
things they would not be worth half the attention that is paid to
them. But Mr. Prendergast was well on the scent; all that a
sportsman wants is good scent. He would rather not have a
view till the run comes to its close. 'But,' continued Mr.
Prendergast, 'it is necessary that I should say a few words to
you about this letter. Abraham's mother was, I suppose, not
exactly an—an educated woman?'

'I never saw her, sir.'

'She died when he was very young?'

'Four years old, sir.'

'And her son hardly seems to have had much education?'

'It was his own fault, sir; I sent him to school when he came
to me, though, goodness knows, sir, I was short enough of
means of doing so. He had better opportunities than my own
daughter there; and though I say it myself, who ought not to say
it, she is a good scholar.'

'I'm sure she is,—and a very good young woman too, if I can
judge by her appearance. But about this letter. I am afraid
your husband has not been so particular in his way of living as
he should have been.'

'What could I do, sir? a poor weak woman!'

'Nothing; what you could do, I'm sure you did do.'

'I've always kept a house over my head, though it's very
humble, as you see, sir. And he has had a morsel to eat and a
cup to drink of when he has come here. It is not often that he
has troubled me this many years past.'

'Mother,' said Mary Swan the younger, 'the gentleman won't
care to know about—about all that between you and father.'

'Ah, but it is just what I do care to know.'

'But, sir, father perhaps mightn't choose it.'

The obedience of women to men—to those men to whom they
are legally bound—is, I think, the most remarkable trait in
human nature. Nothing equals it but the instinctive loyalty of
a dog. Of course we hear of gray mares, and of garments worn
by the wrong persons. Xanthippe doubtless did live, and the
character from time to time is repeated; but the rule, I think,
is as I have said.

'Mrs. Swan,' said Mr. Prendergast, 'I should think myself dishonest were I to worm your secrets out of you, seeing that you
are yourself so truthful and so respectable.' Perhaps it may be
thought that Mr. Prendergast was a little late in looking at the

matter in this light. 'But it behoves me to learn much of the
early history of your husband, who is now living with you here,
and whose name, as I take it, is not Swan, but Mollett. Your
maiden name probably was Swan?'

'But I was honestly married, sir, in the parish church at Putney, and that young woman was honestly born.'

'I am quite sure of it. I have never doubted it. But as I
was saying, I have come here for information about your husband, and I do not like to ask you questions off your guard,'—
oh, Mr. Prendergast!—'and therefore I think it right to tell
you, that neither I nor those for whom I am concerned have any
wish to bear more heavily than we can help upon your husband,
if he will only come forward with willingness to do that which
we can make him do either willingly or unwillingly.'

'But what was it about Abraham's letter, sir?'

'Well, it does not so much signify now.'

'It was he sent you here, was it, sir? How has he learned
where we are, Mary?' and the poor woman turned to her daughter.
'The truth is, sir, he has never known anything of us for these
twenty years; nor we of him. I have not set eyes on him for
more than twenty years,—not that I know of. And he never
knew me by any other name than Swan, and when he was a
child he took me for his aunt.'

'He hasn't known then that you and his father were husband
and wife?'

'I have always thought he didn't, sir. But how—'

Then after all the young fox had not been so full of craft as
the elder one, thought Mr. Prendergast to himself. But nevertheless he still liked the old fox best. There are foxes that
run so uncommonly short that you can never get a burst after
them.

'I suppose, Mrs. Swan,' continued Mr. Prendergast, 'that you
have heard the name of Fitzgerald?'

The poor woman sat silent and amazed, but after a moment the
daughter answered him. 'My mother, sir, would rather that
you should ask her no questions.'

'But, my good girl, your mother, I suppose, would wish to
protect your father, and she would not wish to answer these
questions in a court of law.'

'Heaven forbid!' said the poor woman.

'Your father has behaved very badly to an unfortunate lady
whose friend I am, and on her behalf I must learn the truth.'

'He has behaved badly, sir, to a great many ladies,' said Mrs.
Swan, or Mrs. Mollett as we may now call her.

'You are aware, are you not, that he went through a form of

marriage with this lady many years ago?' said Mr. Prendergast, almost severely.

'Let him answer for himself,' said the true wife. 'Mary, go up stairs, and ask your father to come down.'

CHAPTER XL.

THE FOX IN HIS EARTH.

MARY SWAN the younger hesitated a moment before she executed her mother's order, not saying anything, but looking doubtfully up into her mother's face. 'Go, my dear,' said the old woman, 'and ask your father to come down. It is no use denying him.'

'None in the least,' said Mr. Prendergast; and then the daughter went.

For ten minutes the lawyer and the old woman sat alone, during which time the ear of the former was keenly alive to any steps that might be heard on the stairs or above head. Not that he would himself have taken any active measures to prevent Mr. Mollett's escape, had such an attempt been made. The woman could be a better witness for him than the man, and there would be no fear of her running. Nevertheless, he was anxious that Mollett should, of his own accord, come into his presence.

'I am sorry to keep you so long waiting, sir,' said Mrs. Swan.

'It does not signify. I can easily understand that your husband should wish to reflect a little before he speaks to me. I can forgive that.'

'And, sir—'

'Well, Mrs. Mollett?'

'Are you going to do anything to punish him, sir? If a poor woman may venture to speak a word, I would beg you on my bended knees to be merciful to him. If you would forgive him now I think he would live honest, and be sorry for what he has done.'

'He has worked terrible evil,' said Mr. Prendergast solemnly. 'Do you know that he has harassed a poor gentleman into his grave?'

'Heaven be merciful to him!' said the poor woman. 'But, sir, was not that his son? Was it not Abraham Mollett who did that? Oh, sir, if you will let a poor wife speak, it is he that has been worse than his father.'

Before Mr. Prendergast had made up his mind how he would answer her, he heard the sound of footsteps slowly descending upon the stairs.   They were those of a person who stepped heavily and feebly, and it was still a minute before the door was opened.

'Sir,' said the woman. 'Sir,' and as she spoke she looked eagerly into his face—' " Forgive us our trespasses as we forgive them that trespass against us." We should all remember that, sir.'

'True, Mrs. Mollett, quite true;' and Mr. Prendergast rose from his chair as the door opened.

It will be remembered that Mr. Prendergast and Matthew Mollett had met once before, in the room usually occupied by Sir Thomas Fitzgerald. On that occasion Mr. Mollett had at any rate entered the chamber with some of the prestige of power about him. He had come to Castle Richmond.as the man having the whip hand; and though his courage had certainly fallen somewhat before he left it, nevertheless he had not been so beaten down but what he was able to say a word or two for himself. He had been well in health and decent in appearance, and even as he left the room had hardly realized the absolute ruin which had fallen upon him.

But now he looked as though he had realized it with sufficient clearness. He was lean and sick and pale, and seemed to be ten years older then when Mr. Prendergast had last seen him. He was wrapped in an old dressing-gown, and had a nightcap on his head, and coughed violently before he got himself into his chair. It is hard for any tame domestic animal to know through what fire and water a poor fox is driven as it is hunted from hole to hole and covert to covert. It is a wonderful fact, but no less a fact, that no men work so hard and work for so little pay as scoundrels who strive to live without any work at all, and to feed on the sweat of other men's brows. Poor Matthew Mollett had suffered dire misfortune, had encountered very hard lines, betwixt that day on which he.stole away from the Kanturk Hotel in South Main Street, Cork, and that other day on which he presented himself, cold and hungry and almost sick to death, at the door of his wife's house in Spinny Lane, St. Botolph's in the East.

He never showed himself there unless when hard pressed indeed, and then he would skulk in, seeking for shelter and food, and pleading with bated voice his husband right to assistance and comfort. Nor was his plea ever denied him.

On this occasion he had arrived in very bad plight indeed; he had brought away from Cork nothing but what he could carry on his body, and had been forced to pawn what.he could pawn in order that he might subsist. And then he had been taken with ague, and with the fit strong on him had crawled away to Spinny Lane, and had there been nursed by the mother and daughter whom he had ill used, deserted, and betrayed. 'When the devil was sick the devil a monk would be;' and now his wife, credulous as all women are in such matters, believed the devil's protestations. A time may perhaps come when even————But stop!—or I may chance to tread on the corns of orthodoxy. What I mean to insinuate is this; that it was on the cards that Mr. Mollett would now at last turn over a new leaf.

'How do you do, Mr. Mollett?' said Mr. Prendergast. 'I am sorry to see you looking so poorly.'

'Yes, sir. I am poorly enough certainly. I have been very ill since I last had the pleasure of seeing you, sir.'

'Ah, yes, that was at Castle Richmond; was it not? Well, you have done the best thing that a man can do; you have come home to your wife and family now that you are ill and require their attendance.'

Mr. Mollett looked up at him with a countenance full of unutterable woe and weakness. What was he to say on such a subject in such a company? There sat his wife and daughter, his veritable wife and true-born daughter, on whom he was now dependent, and in whose hands he lay, as a sick man does lie in the hands of women: could he deny them? And there sat the awful Mr. Prendergast, the representative of all that Fitzgerald interest which he had so wronged, and who up to this morning had at any rate believed the story with which he, Mollett, had pushed his fortunes in county Cork. Could he in his presence acknowledge that Lady Fitzgerald had never been his wife? It must be confessed that he was in a sore plight. And then remember his ague!

'You feel yourself tolerably comfortable, I suppose, now that you are with your wife and daughter,' continued Mr. Prendergast, most inhumanly.

Mr. Mollett continued to look at him so piteously from beneath his nightcap. 'I am better than I was, thank you, sir,' said he.

'There is nothing like the bosom of one's family for restoring one to health; is there, Mrs. Mollett;—or for keeping one in health?'

'I wish you gentlemen would think so,' said she, drily.

'As for me I never was blessed with a wife. When I am sick I have to trust to hired attendance. In that respect I am not s fortunate as your husband: I am only an old bachelor.'

'Oh, ain't you, sir?' said Mrs. Mollett; 'and perhaps it's best so. It ain't all married people that are the happiest.'

The daughter during this time was sitting intent on her work, not lifting her face from the shirt she was sewing. But an observer might have seen from her forehead and eye that she

was not only listening to what was said, but thinking and meditating on the scene before her.

'Well, Mr. Mollett,' said Mr. Prendergast, 'you at any rate
are not an old bachelor.' Mr. Mollett still looked piteously at
him, but said nothing. It may be thought that in all this Mr.
Prendergast was more cruel than necessary, but it must be
remembered that it was incumbent on him to bring the poor
wretch before him down absolutely on his marrow-bones. Mollett
must be made to confess his sin, and own that this woman before
him was his real wife; and the time for mercy had not commenced till that had been done.

And then his daughter spoke, seeing how things were going
with him. 'Father,' said she, 'this gentleman has called because
he has had a letter from Abraham Mollett; and he was speaking
about what Abraham has been doing in Ireland.'

'Oh dear, oh dear!' said poor Mollett. 'The unfortunate
young man; that wretched, unfortunate, young man! He will
bring me to the grave at last—to the grave at last.'

'Come, Mr. Mollett,' said Mr. Prendergast, now getting up and
standing with his back to the fire, 'I do not know that you and
I need beat about the bush much longer. I suppose I may speak
openly before these ladies as to what has been taking place in
county Cork.'

'Sir!' said Mr. Mollett, with a look of deprecation about his
mouth that ought to have moved the lawyer's heart.

'I know nothing about it,' said Mrs. Mollett, very stiffly.

'Yes, mother, we do know something about it; and the gentleman may speak out if it so pleases him. It will be better,
father, for you that he should do so.'

'Very well, my dear,' said Mr. Mollett, in the lowest possible
voice; 'whatever the gentleman likes—only I do hope—' and
he uttered a deep sigh, and gave no further expression to his
hopes or wishes.

'I presume, in the first place,' began Mr. Prendergast, 'that
this lady here is your legal wife, and this younger lady your
legitimate daughter? There is no doubt I take it as to that?'

'Not—any—doubt—in the world, sir,' said Mrs. Mollett, who
claimed to be so de jure. 'I have got my marriage lines to show,
sir. Abraham's mother was dead just six months before we came
together; and then we were married just six months after that.'

'Well, Mr. Mollett, I suppose you do not wish to contradict
that?'

'He can't, sir, whether he wish it or not,' said Mrs. Mollett.

'Could you show me that—that marriage certificate?' asked
Mr. Prendergast.

Mrs. Mollett looked rather doubtful as to this. It may be, that much as she trusted in her husband's reform, she did not wish to let him know where she kept this important palladium of her rights.

'It can be forthcoming, sir, whenever it may be wanted,' said Mary Mollett the younger; and then Mr. Prendergast, seeing what was passing through the minds of the two women, did not press that matter any further.

'But I should be glad to hear from your own lips, Mr. Mollett, that you acknowledge the marriage, which took place at—at Fulham, I think you said, ma'am?'

'At Putney, sir; at Putney parish church, in the year of our Lord eighteen hundred and fourteen.'

'Ah, that was the year before Mr. Mollett went into Dorsetshire.'

'Yes, sir. He didn't stay with me long, not at that time. He went away and left me; and then all that happened, that you know of—down in Dorsetshire, as they told me. And afterwards when he went away on his keeping, leaving Aby behind, I took the child, and said that I was his aunt. There were reasons then; and I feared——But never mind about that, sir; for anything that I was wrong enough to say then to the contrary, I am his lawful wedded wife, and before my face he won't deny it. And then when he was sore pressed and in trouble he came back to me, and after that Mary here was born; and one other, a boy, who, God rest him, has gone from these troubles. And since that it is not often that he has been with me. But now, now that he is here, you should have pity on us, and give him another chance.'

But still Mr. Mollett had said nothing himself. He sat during all this time, wearily moving his head to and fro, as though the conversation were anything but comfortable to him. And, indeed, it cannot be presumed to have been very pleasant. He moved his head slowly and wearily to and fro; every now and then lifting up one hand weakly, as though deprecating any recurrence to circumstances so decidedly unpleasant. But Mr. Prendergast was determined that he should speak.

'Mr. Mollett,' said he, 'I must beg you to say in so many words, whether the statement of this lady is correct or is incorrect. Do you acknowledge her for your lawful wife?'

'He daren't deny me, sir,' said the woman, who was, perhaps, a little too eager in the matter.

'Father, why don't you behave like a man and speak?' said his daughter, now turning upon him. 'You have done ill to all of us;—to so many; but now—'

'And are you going to turn against me, Mary?' he whined out, almost crying.

'Turn against you! no, I have never done that. But look at mother. Would you let that gentleman think that she is—what I won't name before him? Will you say that I am not your honest-born child? You have done very wickedly, and you must now make what amends is in your power. If you do not answer him here he will make you answer in some worse place than this.'

'What is it I am to say, sir?' he whined out again.

'Is this lady here your legal wife?'

'Yes, sir,' said the poor man, whimpering.

'And that marriage ceremony which you went through in Dorsetshire with Miss Wainwright was not a legal marriage?'

'I suppose not, sir.'

'You were well aware at the time that you were committing bigamy?'

'Sir!'

'You knew, I say, that you were committing bigamy; that the child whom you were professing to marry would not become your wife through that ceremony. I say that you knew all this at the time? Come, Mr. Mollett, answer me, if you do not wish me to have you dragged out of this by a policeman and taken at once before a magistrate.'

'Oh, sir! be merciful to us; pray be merciful to us,' said Mrs. Mollett, holding up her apron to her eyes.

'Father, why don't you speak out plainly to the gentleman? He will forgive you, if you do that.'

'Am I to criminate myself, sir?' said Mr. Mollett, still in the humblest voice in the world, and hardly above his breath.

After all, this fox had still some running left in him, Mr. Prendergast thought to himself. He was not even yet so thoroughly beaten but what he had a dodge or two remaining at his service. 'Am I to criminate myself, sir?' he asked, as innocently as a child might ask whether or no she were to stand longer in the corner.

'You may do as you like about that, Mr. Mollett,' said the lawyer; 'I am neither a magistrate nor a policeman; and at the present moment I am not acting even as a lawyer. I am the friend of a family whom you have misused and defrauded most outrageously. You have killed the father of that family—'

'Oh, gracious!' said Mrs. Mollett.

'Yes, madam, he has done so; and nearly broken the heart of that poor lady, and driven her son from the house which is his own. You have done all this in order that you might swindle them out of money for your vile indulgences, while you left your own wife and your own child to starve at home. In the whole course of my life I never came across so mean a scoundrel; and now you chaffer with me as to whether or no you shall criminate yourself! Scoundrel and villain as you are—a double-dyed scoundrel, still there are reasons why I shall not wish to have you gibbeted, as you deserve.'

'Oh, sir, he has done nothing that would come to that!' said the poor wife.

'You had better let the gentleman finish,' said the daughter. 'He doesn't mean that father will be hung.'

'It would be too good for him,' said Mr. Prendergast, who was now absolutely almost out of temper. 'But I do not wish to be his executioner. For the peace of that family which you have so brutally plundered and ill used, I shall remain quiet,—if I can attain my object without a public prosecution. But, remember, that I guarantee nothing to you. For aught I know you may be in gaol before the night is come. All I have to tell you is this, that if by obtaining a confession from you I am able to restore my friends to their property without a prosecution, I shall do so. Now you may answer me or not, as you like.'

'Trust him, father,' said the daughter. 'It will be best for you.'

'But I have told him everything,' said Mollett. 'What more does he want of me?'

'I want you to give your written acknowledgment that when you went through that ceremony of marriage with Miss Wainwright in Dorsetshire, you committed bigamy, and that you knew at that time that you were doing so.'

Mr. Mollett, as a matter of course, gave him the written document, and then Mr. Prendergast took his leave, bowing graciously to the two women, and not deigning to cast his eyes again on the abject wretch who crouched by the fire.

'Don't be hard on a poor creature who has fallen so low,' said Mrs. Mollett, as he left the room. But Mary Mollett junior followed him to the door and opened it for him. 'Sir,' she said, addressing him with some hesitation as he was preparing to depart.

'Well, Miss Mollett; if I could do anything for you it would gratify me, for I sincerely feel for you,—both for you and for your mother.'

'Thank you, sir; I don't know that there is anything you can do for us—except to spare him. The thief on the cross was forgiven, sir.'

'But the thief on the cross repented.'

'And who shall say that he does not repent? You cannot tell of his heart by scripture word, as you can of that other one. But our Lord has taught us that it is good to forgive the worst of sinners. Tell that poor lady to think of this when she remembers him in her prayers.'

'I will, Miss Mollett; indeed, indeed I will;' and then as he left her he gave her his hand in token of respect. And so he walked away out of Spinny Lane.

CHAPTER XLI.

THE LOBBY OF THE HOUSE OF COMMONS.

MR. PRENDERGAST as he walked out of Spinny Lane, and back to St. Botolph's church, and as he returned thence again to Blooms-bury Square in his cab, had a good deal of which to think. In the first place it must be explained that he was not altogether self-satisfied with the manner in which things had gone. That he would have made almost any sacrifice to recover the property for Herbert Fitzgerald, is certainly true; and it is as true that he would have omitted no possible effort to discover all that which he had now discovered, almost without necessity for any effort. But nevertheless he was not altogether pleased; he had made up his mind a month or two ago that Lady Fitzgerald was not the lawful wife of her husband; and had come to this con-clusion on, as he still thought, sufficient evidence. But now he was proved to have been wrong; his character for shrewdness and discernment would be damaged, and his great ally and chum Mr. Die, the Chancery barrister, would be down on him with unmiti-gated sarcasm. A man who has been right so frequently as Mr. Prendergast, does not like to find that he is ever in the wrong. And then, had his decision not have been sudden, might not the life of that old baronet have been saved?

Mr. Prendergast could not help feeling this in some degree as he drove away to Bloomsbury Square; but nevertheless he had also the feeling of having achieved a great triumph. It was with him as with a man who has made a fortune when he has declared to his friends that he should infallibly be ruined. It piques him to think how wrong he has been in his prophecy; but still it is very pleasant to have made one's fortune.

When he found himself at the top of Chancery Lane in Holborn, he stopped his cab and got out of it. He had by that time made up his mind as to what he would do; so he walked briskly down to Stone Buildings, and nodding to the old clerk, with whom he was very intimate, asked if he could see Mr. Die. It was his second visit to those chambers that morning, seeing that he had been there early in the day, introducing Herbert to his new

Gamaliel. 'Yes, Mr. Die is in,' said the clerk, smiling, and so Mr. Prendergast passed on into the well-known dingy temple of the Chancery god himself.

There he remained for full an hour, a message in the meanwhile having been sent out to Herbert Fitzgerald, begging him not to leave the chambers till he should have seen Mr. Die; 'and your friend Mr. Prendergast is with him,' said the clerk. 'A very nice gentleman is Mr. Prendergast, uncommon clever too; but it seems to me that he never can hold his own when he comes across our Mr. Die.'

At the end of the hour Herbert was summoned into the sanctum, and there he found Mr. Die sitting in his accustomed chair, with his body much bent, nursing the calf of his leg, which was always enveloped in a black, well-fitting close pantaloon, and smiling very blandly. Mr. Prendergast had in his countenance not quite so sweet an aspect. Mr. Die had repeated to him, perhaps once too often, a very well-known motto of his; one by the aid of which he professed to have steered himself safely through the shoals of life—himself and perhaps some others. It was a motto which he would have loved to see inscribed over the great gates of the noble inn to which he belonged: and which, indeed, a few years since might have been inscribed there with much justice. 'Festinâ lentè,' Mr. Die would say to all those who came to him in any sort of hurry. And then when men accused him of being dilatory by premeditation, he would say no, he had always recommended despatch. 'Festinâ,' he would say; 'festinâ' by all means; but 'festinâ lentè.' The doctrine had at any rate thriven with the teacher, for Mr. Die had amassed a large fortune.

Herbert at once saw that Mr. Prendergast was a little fluttered. Judging from what he had seen of the lawyer in Ireland, he would have said that it was impossible to flutter Mr. Prendergast; but in truth greatness is great only till it encounters greater greatness. Mars and Apollo are terrible and magnificent gods till one is enabled to see them seated at the foot of Jove's great throne. That Apollo, Mr. Prendergast, though greatly in favour with the old Chancery Jupiter, had now been reminded that he had also on this occasion driven his team too fast, and been nearly as indiscreet in his own rash offering.

'We are very sorry to keep you waiting here, Mr. Fitzgerald,' said Mr. Die, giving his hand to the young man, without, however, rising from his chair; 'especially sorry, seeing that it is your first day in harness. But your friend Mr. Prendergast thinks it as well that we should talk over together a piece of business which does not seem as yet to be quite settled.'

Herbert of course declared that he had been in no hurry to go away; he was, he said, quite ready to talk over anything; but to his mind at that moment nothing occurred more momentous than the nature of the agreement between himself and Mr. Die. There was an honorarium which it was presumed Mr. Die would expect, and which Herbert Fitzgerald had ready for the occasion.

'I hardly know how to describe what has taken place this morning, since I saw you,' said Mr. Prendergast, whose features told plainly that something more important than the honorarium was now on the tapis.

'What has taken place?' said Herbert, whose mind now flew off to Castle Richmond.

'Gently, gently,' said Mr. Die; 'in the whole course of my legal experience,—and that now has been a very long experience,—I have never come across so,—so singular a family history as this of yours, Mr. Fitzgerald. When our friend Mr. Prendergast here, on his return from Ireland, first told me the whole of it, I was inclined to think that he had formed a right and just decision—'

'There can be no doubt about that,' said Herbert.

'Stop a moment, my dear sir; wait half a moment—a just decision, I say—regarding the evidence of the facts as conclusive. But I was not quite so certain that he might not have been a little—premature perhaps may be too strong a word—a little too assured in taking those facts as proved.'

'But they were proved,' said Herbert.

'I shall always maintain that there was ample ground to induce me to recommend your poor father so to regard them,' said Mr. Prendergast, stoutly. 'You must remember that those men would instantly have been at work on the other side; indeed, one of them did attempt it.'

'Without any signal success, I believe,' said Mr. Die.

'My father thought you were quite right, Mr. Prendergast,' said Herbert, with a tear forming in his eye; 'and though it may be possible that the affair hurried him to his death, there was no alternative but that he should know the whole.' At this Mr. Prendergast seemed to wince as he sat in his chair. 'And I am sure of this,' continued Herbert, 'that had he been left to the villanies of those two men, his last days would have been much less comfortable than they were. My mother feels that quite as strongly as I do.' And then Mr. Prendergast looked as though he were somewhat reassured.

'It was a difficult crisis in which to act,' said Mr. Prendergast, 'and I can only say that I did so to the best of my poor judgment.'

'It was a difficult crisis in which to act,' said Mr. Die, assenting.

'But why is all this brought up now?' asked Herbert.

'Festinâ lentè,' said Mr. Die; 'lentè, lentè, lentè; always lentè. The more haste we make in trying to understand each other, with the less speed shall we arrive at that object.'

'What is it, Mr. Prendergast?' again demanded Herbert, who was now too greatly excited to care much for the Chancery wisdom of the great barrister. 'Has anything new turned up about—about those Molletts?'

'Yes, Herbert, something has turned up—'

'Remember, Prendergast, that your evidence is again incomplete.'

'Upon my word, sir, I do not think it is: it would be sufficient for any intellectual jury in a Common Law court,' said Mr. Prendergast, who sometimes, behind his back, gave to Mr. Die the surname of Cunctator.

'But juries in Common Law courts are not always intelligent. And you may be sure, Prendergast, that any gentleman taking up the case on the other side would have as much to say for his client as your counsel would have for yours. Remember, you have not even been to Putney yet.'

'Been to Putney!' said Herbert, who was becoming uneasy.

'The onus probandi would lie with them,' said Mr. Prendergast. 'We take possession of that which is our own till it is proved to belong to others.'

'You have already abandoned the possession.'

'No; we have done nothing already: we have taken no legal step; when we believed—'

'Having by your own act put yourself in your present position, I think you ought to be very careful before you take up another.'

'Certainly we ought to be careful. But I do maintain that we may be too punctilious. As a matter of course I shall go to Putney.'

'To Putney!' said Herbert Fitzgerald.

'Yes, Herbert, and now if Mr. Die will permit, I will tell you what has happened. On yesterday afternoon, before you came to dine with me, I received that letter. No, that is from your cousin, Owen Fitzgerald. You must see that also by-and-by. It was this one,—from the younger Mollett, the man whom you saw that day in your poor father's room.'

Herbert anxiously put out his hand for the letter, but he was again interrupted by Mr. Die. 'I beg your pardon Mr. Fitzgerald, for a moment. Prendergast, let me see that letter again, will you?' And taking hold of it, he proceeded to read it very carefully, still nursing his leg with his left hand, while he held the letter with his right.

'What's it all about?' said Herbert, appealing to Prendergast almost in a whisper.

'Lentè, lentè, lentè, my dear Mr. Fitzgerald,' said Mr. Die, while his eyes were still intent upon the paper. 'If you will take advantage of the experience of gray hairs, and bald heads,'— his own was as bald all round as a big white stone—'you must put up with some of the disadvantages of a momentary delay. Suppose now, Prendergast, that he is acting in concert with those people in—what do you call the street?'

'In Spinny Lane.'

'Yes; with his father and the two women there.'

'What could they gain by that?'

'Share with him whatever he might be able to get out of you.'

'The man would never accuse himself of bigamy for that. Besides, you should have seen the women, Die.'

'Seen the women! Tsh—tsh—tsh; I have seen enough of them, young and old, to know that a clean apron and a humble tone and a down-turned eye don't always go with a true tongue and an honest heart. Women are now the most successful swindlers of the age! That profession at any rate is not closed against them.'

'You will not find these women to be swindlers; at least I think not.'

'Ah! but we want to be sure, Prendergast;' and then Mr. Die finished the letter, very leisurely, as Herbert thought.

When he had finished it, he folded it up and gave it back to Mr. Prendergast. 'I don't think but what you've a strong primâ facie case; so strong that perhaps you are right to explain the whole matter to our young friend here, who is so deeply concerned in it. But at the same time I should caution him that the matter is still enveloped in doubt.'

Herbert eagerly put out his hand for the letter. 'You may trust me with it,' said he: 'I am not of a sanguine temperament, nor easily excited; and you may be sure that I will not take it for more than it is worth.' So saying, he at last got hold of the letter, and managed to read it through much more quickly than Mr. Die had done. As he did so he became very red in the face, and too plainly showed that he had made a false boast in speaking of the coolness of his temperament. Indeed, the stakes were so high that it was difficult for a young man to be cool while he was playing the game: he had made up his mind to lose, and to

that he had been reconciled; but now again every pulse of his
heart and every nerve of his body was disturbed. 'Was never
his wife,' he said out loud when he got to that part of the letter.
'His real wife living now in Spinny Lane! Do you believe that,
Mr. Prendergast?'

'Yes, I do,' said the attorney,

'Lentè, lentè, lentè,' said the barrister, quite oppressed by his
friend's unprofessional abruptness.

'But I do believe it,' said Mr. Prendergast: 'you must
always understand, Herbert, that this new story may possibly
not be true—'

'Quite possible,' said Mr. Die, with something almost approaching to a slight laugh.

'But the evidence is so strong,' continued the other, 'that I
do believe it heartily. I have been to that house, and seen the
man, old Mollett, and the woman whom I believe to be his wife,
and a daughter who lives with them. As far as my poor judgment goes,' and he made a bow of deference towards the barrister, whose face, however, seemed to say that in his opinion
the judgment of his friend Mr. Prendergast did not always go
very far—'As far as my poor judgment goes, the women are
honest and respectable. The man is as great a villain as there is
unhung—unless his son be a greater one; but he is now so
driven into a corner, that the truth may be more serviceable to
him than a lie.'

'People of that sort are never driven into a corner,' said Mr.
Die; 'they may sometimes be crushed to death.'

'Well, I believe the matter is as I tell you. There at any
rate is Mollett's assurance that it is so. The woman has been
residing in the same place for years, and will come forward at
any time to prove that she was married to this man before he
ever saw—before he went to Dorsetshire: she has her marriage
certificate; and as far as I can learn there is no one able or willing to raise the question against you. Your cousin Owen certainly will not do so.'

'It will hardly do to depend upon that,' said Mr. Die, with
another sneer. 'Twelve thousand a year is a great provocative
to litigation.'

'If he does we must fight him; that's all. Of course steps
will be taken at once to get together in the proper legal form all
evidence of every description which may bear on the subject, so
that should the question ever be raised again, the whole matter
may be in a nutshell.'

'You'll find it a nutshell very difficult to crack in five-and
twenty years' time,' said Mr. Die.

' And what would you advise me to do?' asked Herbert.

That after all was now the main question, and it was discussed between them for a long time, till the shades of evening came upon them, and the dull dingy chambers became almost dark as they sat there. Mr. Die at first conceived that it would be well that Herbert should still stick to the law. What indeed could be more conducive to salutary equanimity in the mind of a young man so singularly circumstanced, than the study of Blackstone, of Coke, and of Chitty? as long as he remained there, at work in those chambers, amusing himself occasionally with the eloquence of the neighbouring courts, there might be reasonable hope that he would be able to keep his mind equally poised, so that neither success nor failure, as regarded his Irish inheritance, should affect him injuriously. Thus at least argued Mr. Die. But at this point Herbert seemed to have views of his own : he said that in the first place he must be with his mother; and then, in the next place, as it was now clear that he was not to throw up Castle Richmond—as it would not now behove him to allow any one else to call himself master there—it would be nis duty to reassume the place of master. ' The onus probandi will now rest with them,' he said, repeating Mr. Prendergast's words ; and then he was ultimately successful in persuading even Mr. Die to agree that it would be better for him to go to Ireland than to remain in London, sipping the delicious honey of Chancery buttercups.

' And you will assume the title, I suppose?' said Mr. Die.

' Not at any rate till I get to Castle Richmond,' he said, blushing. He had so completely abandoned all thought of being Sir Herbert Fitzgerald, that he had now almost felt ashamed of saying that he should so far presume as to call himself by that name.

And then he and Mr. Prendergast went away and dined together, leaving Mr. Die to complete his legal work for the day. At this he would often sit till nine or ten, or even eleven in the evening, without any apparent ill results from such effects, and then go home to his dinner and port wine. He was already nearly seventy, and work seemed to have no effect on him. In what Medea's caldron is it that the great lawyers so cook themselves, that they are able to achieve half an immortality, even while the body still clings to the soul? Mr. Die, though he would talk of his bald head, had no idea of giving way to time. Superannuated! The men who think of superannuation at sixty are those whose lives have been idle, not they who have really buckled themselves to work. It is my opinion that nothing seasons the mind for endurance like hard work. Port wine should perhaps be added.

It was not till Herbert once more found himself alone that he fully realized this new change in his position. He had dined with Mr. Prendergast at that gentleman's club, and had been specially called upon to enjoy himself, drinking as it were to his own restoration in large glasses of some special claret, which Mr. Prendergast assured him was very extraordinary.

'You may be as satisfied as that you are sitting there that that's 34,' said he ; ' and I hardly know anywhere else that you'll get it.'

This assertion Herbert was not in the least inclined to dispute. In the first place, he was not quite clear what 34 meant, and then any other number, 32 or 36, would have suited his palate as well. But he drank the 34, and tried to look as though he appreciated it.

'Our wines here are wonderfully cheap,' said Mr. Prendergast, becoming confidential ; ' but nevertheless we have raised the price of that to twelve shillings.   We'll have another bottle.'

During all this Herbert could hardly think of his own fate and fortune, though, indeed, he could hardly think of anything else. He was eager to be alone, that he might think, and was nearly broken-hearted when the second bottle of 34 made its appearance. Something, however, was arranged in those intercalary moments between the raising of the glasses.   Mr. Prendergast said that he would write both to Owen Fitzgerald and to Mr. Somers ; and it was agreed that Herbert should immediately return to Castle Richmond, merely giving his mother time to have notice of his coming.

And then at last he got away, and started by himself for a night walk through the streets of London.   It seemed to him now to be a month since he had arrived there ; but in truth it was only on the yesterday that he had got out of the train at the Euston Station.   He had come up, looking forward to live in London all his life, and now his London life was over,—unless, indeed, those other hopes should come back to him, unless he should appear again, not as a student in Mr. Die's chamber, but as one of the council of the legislature assembled to make laws for the governance of Mr. Die and of others.   It was singular how greatly this episode in his life had humbled him in his own esteem.   Six months ago he had thought himself almost too good for Castle Richmond, and had regarded a seat in Parliament as the only place which he could fitly fill without violation to his nature.   But now he felt as though he should hardly dare to show himself within the walls of that assembly.   He had been so knocked about by circumstances, so rudely toppled from his high place,—he had found it necessary to put himself so completely into the hands of other people, that his self-pride had all left him. That it would in fact return might be held as certain, but the lesson which he had learned would not altogether be thrown away upon him.

At this moment, as I was saying, he felt himself to be completely humbled. A lie spoken by one of the meanest of God's creatures had turned him away from all his pursuits, and broken all his hopes; and now another word from this man was to restore him,—if only that other word should not appear to be the greater lie! and then that there should be such question as to his mother's name and fame—as to the very name by which she should now be called! that it should depend on the amount of infamy of which that wretch had been guilty, whether or no the woman whom in the world he most honoured was entitled to any share of respect from the world around her! That she was entitled to the respect of all good men, let the truth in these matters be where it might, Herbert knew, and all who heard the story would acknowledge. But respect is of two sorts, and the outer respect of the world cannot be parted with conveniently.

He did acknowledge himself to be a humbled man,—more so than he had ever yet done, or had been like to do, while conscious of the loss which had fallen on him. It was at this moment when he began to perceive that his fortune would return to him, when he became aware that he was knocked about like a shuttlecock from a battledore, that his pride came by its first fall. Mollett was in truth the great man,—the Warwick who was to make and unmake the kings of Castle Richmond. A month ago, and it had pleased Earl Mollett to say that Owen Fitzgerald should reign; but there had been a turn upon the cards, and now he, King Herbert, was to be again installed.

He walked down all alone through St. James's Street, and by Pall Mall and Charing Cross, feeling rather than thinking of all this. Those doubts of Mr. Die did not trouble him much: He fully believed that he should regain his title and property; or rather that he should never lose them. But he thought that he could never show himself about the country again as he had done before all this was known. In spite of his good fortune he was sad at heart, little conscious of the good that all this would do him.

He went on by the Horse Guards and Treasury Chambers into Parliament Street, and so up to the new Houses of Parliament, and sauntered into Westminster Hall; and there, at the privileged door between the lamps on his left hand, he saw busy men going in and out, some slow and dignified, others hot, hasty, and anxious, and he felt as though the regions to and from which they passed must be far out of his reach. Could he aspire to pass those august lamp-posts, he whose very name depended on what in truth might have been the early doings of a low scoundrel who was now skulking from the law?

And then he went on, and mounting by the public stairs and anterooms found his way to the lobby of the house. There he stood with his back to the ginger-beer stall, moody and melancholy, looking on as men in the crowd pushed forward to speak to members whom they knew; or, as it sometimes appeared, to members whom they did not know. There was somewhat of interest going on in the house, for the throng was thick, and ordinary men sometimes jostled themselves on into the middle of the hall—with impious steps; for on those centre stones none but legislators should presume to stand.

'Stand back, gentlemen, stand back; back a little, if you please, sir,' said a very courteous but peremptory policeman, so moving the throng that Herbert, who had been behind, in no way anxious for a forward place, or for distinguishing nods from passing members, found himself suddenly in the front rank, in the immediate neighbourhood of a cluster of young senators who were cooling themselves in the lobby after the ardour of the debate.

'It was as pretty a thing as ever I saw in my life,' said one, 'and beautifully ridden.' Surely it must have been the Spring Meeting and not the debate that they were discussing.

'I don't know much about that,' said another, and the voice sounded on Herbert's ears as it might almost be the voice of a brother. 'I know I lost the odds. But I'll have a bottle of soda-water. Hallo, Fitzgerald! Why—;' and then the young member stopped himself, for Herbert Fitzgerald's story was rife about London at this time.

'How do you do, Moulsey?' said Herbert, very glumly, for he did not at all like being recognized. This was Lord Moulsey, the eldest son of the Earl of Hampton Court, who was now member for the River Regions, and had been one of Herbert's most intimate friends at Oxford.

'I did not exactly expect to see you here,' said Lord Moulsey, drawing him apart. 'And upon my soul I was never so cut up in my life as when I heard all that. Is it true?'

'True! why no;—it was true, but I don't think it is. That is to say—upon my word I don't know. It's all unsettled— Good evening to you.' And again nodding his head at his old friend in a very sombre manner, he skulked off and made his way out of Westminster Hall.

'Do you know who that was?' said Lord Moulsey going back to his ally. 'That was young Fitzgerald, the poor fellow who has been done out of his title and all his property. You have heard about his mother, haven't you?'

'Was that young Fitzgerald?' said the other senator, apparently more interested in this subject than he had even been about the pretty riding. 'I wish I'd looked at him. Poor fellow! How does he bear it?'

'Upon my word then, I never saw a fellow so changed in my life. He and I were like brothers, but he would hardly speak to me. Perhaps I ought to have written to him. But he says it's not settled.'

'Oh, that's all gammon. It's settled enough. Why they've given up the place. I heard all about it the other day from Sullivan O'Leary. They are not even making any fight Sullivan O'Leary says they are the greatest fools in the world.'

'Upon my word I think young Fitzgerald was mad just now. His manner was so very odd.'

'I shouldn't wonder. I know I should go mad if my mother turned out to be somebody else's wife.' And then they both sauntered away.

Herbert was doubly angry with himself as he made his way down into the noble old hall,—angry that he had gone where there was a possibility of his being recognized, and angry also that he had behaved himself with so little presence of mind when he was recognized. He felt that he had been taken aback, that he had been beside himself, and unable to maintain his own dignity; he had run away from his old intimate friend because he had been unable to bear being looked on as the hero of a family tragedy. 'He would go back to Ireland,' he said to himself, 'and he would never leave it again. Perhaps he might teach himself there to endure the eyes and voices of men around him. Nothing at any rate should induce him to come again to London.' And so he went home to bed in a mood by no means so happy as might have been expected from the result of the day's doings. And yet he had been cheerful enough when he went to Mr. Die's chambers in the morning.

CHAPTER XLII.

ANOTHER JOURNEY.

On the following day he did go back to Ireland, stopping a night in Dublin on the road, so that his mother might receive his letter, and that his cousin and Somers might receive those written by Mr. Prendergast. He spent one night in Dublin, and then went on, so that he might arrive at Castle Richmond after dark. In his present mood he dreaded to be seen returning, even by his own people about the place.

At Buttevant he was met by his own car and by Richard, as he had desired; but he found that he was utterly frustrated as to that method of seating himself in his vehicle which he had promised to himself. He was still glum and gloomy enough when the coach stopped, for he had been all alone, thinking over many things—thinking of his father's death and his mother's early life—of all that he had suffered and might yet have to suffer, and above all things dreading the consciousness that men were talking of him and staring at him. In this mood he was preparing to leave the coach when he found himself approaching near to that Buttevant stage; but he had more to go through at present than he expected.

'There's his honour—Hurrah! God bless his sweet face that's come among us agin this day! Hurrah for Sir Herbert, boys! hurrah! The rail ould Fitzgerald 'll be back agin among us, glory be to God and the Blessed Virgin! Hurrah for Sir Herbert!' and then there was a shout that seemed to be repeated all down the street of Buttevant.

But that was nothing to what was coming. Herbert, when he first heard this, retreated for a moment back into the coach. But there was little use in that. It was necessary that he should descend, and had he not done so he would have been dragged out. He put his foot on the steps, and then found himself seized in the arms of a man outside, and pressed and embraced as though he had been a baby.

'Ugh, ugh, ugh!' exclaimed a voice, the owner of which intended to send forth notes of joy; but so overcome was he by the intensity of his own feelings that he was in nowise able to moderate his voice either for joy or sorrow. 'Ugh, ugh, ugh! Eh! Sir Herbert! but it's I that am proud to see yer honour this day,—wid yer ouwn name, wid yer ouwn name. Glory be to God; oh dear! oh dear! And I knew the Lord 'd niver forgit us that way, and let the warld go intirely wrong like that. For av you weren't the masther, Sir Herbert, as you are, the Lord presarve you to us, divil a masther 'd iver be able to hould a foot in Castle Richmond, and that's God's ouwn thruth.'

'And that's thrue for you, Richard,' said another, whom Herbert in the confusion could not recognize, though his voice was familiar to him. ''Deed and the boys had it all made out. But what matthers now Sir Herbert's back?'

'And God bless the day and the hour that he came to us!' And then leaving his master's arm and coat to which he had still stuck, he began to busy himself loudly about the travelling gear. 'Coachman, where's Sir Herbert's portmantel? Yes; that's Sir Herbert's hat-box. 'Deed, an' I ought to know it well. And the black bag; yes, that'll be Sir Herbert's, to be sure,' and so on.

Nor was this all. The name seemed to run like wildfire through all the Buttevantians there assembled; and no sound seemed to reach our hero's name but that of Sir Herbert, Sir Herbert. Everybody took hold of him, and kissed his hand, and pulled his skirts, and stroked his face. His hat was knocked off, and put on again amid thousands of blessings. It was nearly dark, and his eyes were dazed by the coach lanterns which were carried about, so that he could hardly see his friends; but the one sound which was dinned into his ears was that of Sir Herbert, Sir Herbert.

Had he thought about it when starting from Dublin early that morning he would have said that it would have killed him to have heard himself so greeted in the public street, but as it was he found that he got over it very easily. Before he was well seated on his car it may be questioned whether he was not so used to his name, that he would have been startled to hear himself designated as Mr. Fitzgerald. For half a minute he had been wretched, and had felt a disgust at poor Richard which he thought at the moment would be insuperable; but when he was on the car, and the poor fellow came round to tuck the apron in under his feet, he could not help giving him his hand, and fraternizing with him.

'And how is my mother, Richard?'

'' Deed then, Sir Herbert, me lady is surprising—very quiet-like; but her leddyship was always that, and as sweet to them as comes nigh her as flowers in May; but sure that's nathural to her leddyship.'

'And, Richard—'

'Yes, Sir Herbert.'

'Was Mr. Owen over at Castle Richmond since I left?'

'Sorrow a foot, Sir Herbert. Nor no one ain't heard on him, nor seen him. And I will say this on him—'

'Don't say anything against him, Richard.'

'No, surely not, seeing he is yer honour's far-away cousin, Sir Herbert. But what I war going to say warn't agin Mr. Owen at all, at all. For they do say that cart-ropes wouldn't have dragged him to Castle Richmond; and that only yer honour has come back to yer own,—and why not?—there wouldn't have been any masther in Castle Richmond at all, at all. That's what they do say.'

'There's no knowing how it will go yet, Richard.'

''Deed, an' I know how it 'll go very well, Sir Herbert, and so does Mr. Somers, God bless him! 'Twas only this morning he tould me. An', faix, it's he has the right to be glad.'

'He is a very old friend.'

'So is we all ould frinds, an' we're all glad—out of our skins wid gladness, Sir Herbert. 'Deed an' I thought the eend of the warld had come when I heerd it, for my head went round and round and round as I stood in the stable, and only for the fork I had a hould of, I'd have been down among the crathur's legs.'

And then it struck Herbert that as they were going on he heard the footsteps of some one running after the car, always at an equal distance behind them. 'Who's that running, Richard?'

'Sure an' that's just Larry Carson, yer honour's own boy, that minds yer honour's own nag, Sir Herbert. But, faix, I suppose ye'll be having a dozen of 'em now.'

'Stop and take him up; you've room there.'

'Room enough, Sir Herbert an' yer honour's so good. Here, Larry, yer born fool, Sir Herbert, says ye're to get up. He would come over, Sir Herbert, just to say he'd been the first to see your honour.'

'God—bless—yer honour—Sir Herbert,' exclaimed the poor fellow, out of breath, as he took his seat. It was his voice that Sir Herbert had recognized among the crowd, angry enough at that moment. But in future days it was remembered in Larry Carson's favour, that he had come over to Castle Richmond to see his master, contented to run the whole road back to Castle Richmond behind the car. A better fate, however, was his, for he made one in the triumphal entry up the avenue.

When they got to the lodge it was quite dark—so dark that even Richard, who was experienced in night-driving, declared that a cat could not see. However, they turned in at the great gates without any accident, the accustomed woman coming out to open them.

'An' is his honour there thin?' said the woman; 'and may God bless you, Sir Herbert, and ye're welcome back to yer own; so ye are!'

And then a warm large hand was laid upon his leg, and a warm voice sounded greeting in his ear. 'Herbert, my boy. how are you? This is well, is it not?' It was Mr. Somers, who had been waiting there for him at the lodge gate.

Upon the whole he could not but acknowledge to himself that it was well. Mr. Somers got up beside him on the car, so that by this time it was well laden. 'And how does my mother take it?' Herbert asked.

'Very quietly. Your Aunt Letty told me that she had spent most of her time in prayer since she heard it. But Miss Letty seems to think that on your account she is very full of joy.'

'And the girls?'

'Oh! the girls—what girls? Well, they must answer for themselves; I left them about half an hour ago, and now you hear their voices in the porch.'

He did hear the voices in the porch plainly, though he could not distinguish them, as the horse's feet and the car wheels rattled over the gravel. But as the car stopped at the door with somewhat of a crash, he heard Emmeline say, 'There's Herbert,' and then as he got down they all retreated in among the lights in the hall.

'God bless your honour, Sir Herbert. An' it's you that are welcome back this blessed night to Castle Richmond.' Such and such like were the greetings which met him from twenty different voices as he essayed to enter the house. Every servant and groom about the place was there, and some few of the nearest tenants,—of those who had lived near enough to hear the glad tidings since the morning. A dozen, at any rate, took his hands as he strove to make his way through them; and though he was never quite sure about it, he believed that one or two had kissed him in the dark. At last he found himself in the hall, and even then the first person who got hold of him was Mrs. Jones.

'And so you've come back to us after all, Mr. Herbert—Sir Herbert I should say, begging your pardon, sir; and it's all right about my lady. I never thought to be so happy again, never—never—never.' And then she retreated with her apron up to her eyes, leaving him in the arms of Aunt Letty.

'The Lord giveth, and the Lord taketh away. Blessed be the name of the Lord. Oh! Herbert, my darling boy. I hope this may be a lesson and a warning to you, so that you may flee from the wrath to come.' Aunt Letty,—had time been allowed to her, would certainly have shown that the evil had all come from tampering with papistical abominations; and that the returning prosperity of the house of Castle Richmond was due to Protestant energy and truth. But much time was not allowed to Aunt Letty, as Herbert hurried on after his sisters.

As he had advanced they had retreated, and now he heard them in the drawing-room. He began to be conscious that they were not alone,—that they had some visitor with them, and began to be conscious also who that visitor was. And when he got himself at last into the room, sure enough there were three girls there, two running forward to meet him from the fireplace to which they had retreated, and the other lingering a little in their rear.

'Oh, Herbert!' and 'oh Herbert!' and then their arms were thrown about his neck, and their warm kisses were on his cheeks —kisses not unmixed with tears; for of course they began to cry immediately that he was with them, though their eyes had been dry enough for the two or three hours before. Their arms were about his neck, and their kisses on his cheeks, I have said,— meaning thereby, the arms and kisses of his sisters, for the third young lady still lingered a little in the rear.

'Was it not lucky Clara was here when the news came to us this morning?' said Mary.

'Such difficulty as we have had to get her,' said Emmeline. 'It was to have been her farewell visit to us; but we will have no more farewells now; will we, Clara?'

And now at last he had his arm round her waist, or as near to that position as he was destined to get it on the present occasion. She gave him her hand, and let him hold that fast, and smiled on him through her soft tears, and was gracious to him with her sweet words and pleasant looks; but she would not come forward and kiss him boldly as she had done when last they had met at Desmond Court. He attempted it now; but he could get his lips no nearer to hers than her forehead; and when he tried to hold her she slipped away from him, and he continually found himself in the embraces of his sisters,—which was not the same thing at all. 'Never mind,' he said to himself; 'his day would soon come round.'

'You did not expect to find Clara here, did you?' asked Emmeline.

'I hardly know what I have expected, or not expected, for the last two days. No, certainly, I had no hope of seeing her to-night.'

'I trust I am not in the way,' said Clara.

Whereupon he made another attempt with his arm, but when

he thought he had caught his prize, Emmeline was again within his grasp.

'And my mother?' he then said. It must be remembered that he had only yet been in the room for three minutes, though his little efforts have taken longer than that in the telling.

'She is up stairs, and you are to go to her. But I told her that we should keep you for a quarter of an hour, and you have not been here half that time yet.'

'And how has she borne all this?'

'Why, well on the whole. When first she heard it this morning, which she did before any of us, you know——'

'Oh, yes, I wrote to her.'

'But your letter told her nothing. Mr. Somers came down almost as soon as your letter was here. He had heard also—from Mr. Prendergast, I think it was, and Mr. Prendergast said a great deal more than you did.'

'Well?'

'We thought she was going to be ill at first, for she became so very pale,—flushing up sometimes for half a minute or so; but after an hour or two she became quite calm. She has seen nobody since but us and Aunt Letty.'

'She saw me,' said Clara.

'Oh, yes, you; you are one of us now,—just the same as ourselves, isn't she, Herbert?'

Not exactly the same, Herbert thought. And then he went up stairs to his mother.

This interview I will not attempt to describe. Lady Fitzgerald had become a stricken woman from the first moment that she had heard that that man had returned to life, who in her early girlhood had come to her as a suitor. Nay, this had been so from the first moment that she had expected his return. And these misfortunes had come upon her so quickly that, though they had not shattered her in body and mind as they had shattered her husband, nevertheless they had told terribly on her heart. The coming of those men, the agony of Sir Thomas, the telling of the story as it had been told to her by Mr. Prendergast, the resolve to abandon everything—even a name by which she might be called, as far as she herself was concerned, the death of her husband, and then the departure of her ruined son, had, one may say, been enough to destroy the spirit of any woman. Her spirit they had not utterly destroyed. Her powers of endurance were great,—and she had endured, still hoping. But as the uttermost malice of adversity had not been able altogether to depress her, so neither did returning prosperity exalt her,—as far as she herself was concerned. She rejoiced for her children greatly, thanking God that she had not entailed on them an existence without a name. But for herself, as she now told Herbert, outside life was all over. Her children and the poor she might still have with her, but beyond, nothing in this world;—to them would be confined all her wishes on this side the grave.

But nevertheless she could be warm in her greetings to her son. She could understand that though she were dead to the world he need not be so,—nor indeed ought to be so. Things that were now all ending with her were but beginning with him. She had no feeling that taught her to think that it was bad for him to bo a man of rank and fortune, the head of his family, and the privileged one of his race. It had been perhaps her greatest misery that she, by her doing, had placed him in the terrible position which he had lately been called upon to fill.

'Dearest mother, it did not make me unhappy,' he said, caressing her.

'You bore it like a man, Herbert, as I shall ever remember. But it did make me unhappy,—more unhappy than it should have done, when we remember how very short is our time here below.'

He remained with his mother for more than an hour, and then returned to the drawing-room, where the girls were waiting for him with the tea-things arranged before them.

'I was very nearly coming up to fetch you,' said Mary, 'only that wo knew how much mamma must have to say to you.'

'We dined early because we are all so upset,' said Emmeline; 'and Clara must be dying for her tea.'

'And why should Clara die for tea any more than any one else?' asked Lady Clara herself.

I will not venture to say what hour it was before they separated for bed. They sat there with their feet over the fender, talking about things gone and things coming,—and there were so many of such things for them to discuss! Even yet, as one of the girls remarked, Lady Desmond had not heard of the last change, or if she had so heard, had had no time to communicate with her daughter upon the subject.

And then Owen was spoken of with the warmest praise by them all, and Clara explained openly what had been the full tenor of his intended conduct.

'That would have been impossible,' said Herbert.

'But it was not the less noble in him, was it?' said Clara, eagerly. But she did not tell how Owen Fitzgerald had prayed that her love might be given back to him, as his reward for what he wished to do on behalf of his cousin. Now, at least, at this moment it was not told; yet the day did come when all that was described,—a day when Owen in his absence was regarded by them both among the dearest of their friends.

But even on that night Clara resolved that he should have some meed of praise. 'Has he not been noble?' she said, appealing to him who was to be her husband; 'has he not been very noble?'

Herbert, too happy to be jealous, acknowledged that it was so.

CHAPTER XLIII.

PLAYING ROUNDERS.

MY story is nearly at its close, and all readers will now know how it is to end. Those difficulties raised by Mr. Die were all made to vanish; and though he implored Mr. Prendergast over and over again to go about this business with a moderated eagerness, that gentleman would not consent to let any grass grow under his heels till he had made assurance doubly sure, and had seen Herbert Fitzgerald firmly seated on his throne. All that the women in Spinny Lane had told him was quite true. The register was found in the archives of the parish of Putney, and Mr. Prendergast was able to prove that Mr. Matthew Mollett, now of Spinny Lane, and the Mr. Matthew Mollett then designated as of Newmarket in Cambridgeshire, were one and the same person; therefore Mr. Mollett's marriage with Miss Wainwright was no marriage, and therefore, also, the marriage between Sir Thomas Fitzgerald and that lady was a true marriage; all which things will now be plain to any novel-reading capacity, mean as such capacity may be in respect to legal law.

And I have only further to tell in respect to this part of my story, that the Molletts, both father and son, escaped all punishment for the frauds and villanies related in these pages—except such punishment as these frauds and villanies, acting by their own innate destructive forces and poisons, brought down upon their unfortunate heads. For so allowing them to escape I shall be held by many to have been deficient in sound teaching. 'What!' men will say, 'not punish your evil principle! Allow the prevailing evil genius of your book to escape scot free, without administering any of that condign punishment which it would have been so easy for you to allot to them! Had you not treadmills to your hand, and all manner of new prison disciplines? Should not Matthew have repented in the sackcloth of solitary confinement, and Aby have munched and crunched between his teeth the bitter ashes of prison bread and water? Nay, for such offences as those did you wot of no penal settlements? Were not Portland and Spike Islands gaping for them? Had you no memory of Dartmoor and the Bermudas?'

Gentle readers, no; not in this instance shall Spike Island or the Bermudas be asked to give us their assistance. There is a sackcloth harsher to the skin than that of the penal settlement, and ashes more bitter in the crunching than convict rations. It would be sad indeed if we thought that those rascals who escape the law escape also the just reward of their rascality. May it not rather be believed that the whole life of the professional rascal is one long wretched punishment, to which, if he could but know it, the rations and comparative innocence of Bermuda would be so preferable? Is he not always rolling the stone of Sisyphus, gyrating on the wheel of Ixion, hankering after the waters of Tantalus, filling the sieves of the daughters of Danaüs? He pours into his sieve stolen corn beyond measure, but no grain will stay there. He lifts to his lips rich cups, but Rhadamanthus the policeman allows him no moment for a draught. The wheel of justice is ever going, while his poor hanging head is in a whirl. The stone which he rolls never perches for a moment at the top of the hill, for the trade which he follows admits of no rest. Have I not said truly that he is hunted like a fox, driven from covert to covert with his poor empty craving belly? prowling about through the wet night, he returns with his prey, and finds that he is shut out from his lair; his bloodshot eye is ever over his shoulder, and his advanced foot is ever ready for a start; he stinks in the nostrils of the hounds of the law, and is held by all men to be vermin.

One would say that the rascal, if he but knew the truth, would look forward to Spike Island and the Bermudas with impatience and raptures. The cold, hungry, friendless, solitary doom of unconvicted rascaldom has ever seemed to me to be the most wretched phase of human existence,—that phase of living in which the liver can trust no one, and be trusted by none; in which the heart is ever quailing at the policeman's hat, and the eye ever shrinking from the policeman's gaze. The convict does trust his gaoler, at any rate his master gaoler, and in so doing is not all wretched. It is Bill Sikes before conviction that I have ever pitied. Any man can endure to be hanged; but how can any man have taken that Bill Sikes' walk and have lived through it.?

To such punishments will we leave the Molletts, hoping of the elder one, that under the care of those ministering angels in Spinny Lane, his heart may yet be softened; hoping also for the younger one that some ministering angel may be appointed also for his aid. 'Tis a grievous piece of work though, that of a ministering angel to such a soul as his. And now, having seen them so far on their mortal career, we will take our leave of both of them.

Mr. Prendergast's object in sparing them was of course that of saving Lady Fitzgerald from the terrible pain of having her name brought forward at any trial. She never spoke of this, even to Herbert, allowing those in whom she trusted to manage those things for her without an expression of anxiety on her own part; but she was not the less thankful when she found that no public notice was to be taken of the matter.

Very shortly after Herbert's return to Castle Richmond, it was notified to him that he need have no fear as to his inheritance; and it was so notified with the great additional comfort of an assuring opinion from Mr. Die. He then openly called himself Sir Herbert, took upon himself the property which became his by right of the entail, and issued orders for the preparation of his marriage settlement. During this period he saw Owen Fitzgerald; but he did so in the presence of Mr. Somers, and not a word was then said about Lady Clara Desmond. Both the gentlemen, Herbert and Mr. Somers, cordially thanked the master of Hap House for the way in which he had behaved to the Castle Richmond family, and in reference to the Castle Richmond property during the terrible events of the last two months; but Owen took their thanks somewhat haughtily. He shook hands warmly enough with his cousin, wishing him joy on the arrangement of his affairs, and was at first less distant than usual with Mr. Somers; but when they alluded to his own conduct, and expressed their gratitude, he declared that he had done nothing for which thanks were due, and that he begged it to be understood that he laid claim to no gratitude. Had he acted otherwise, he said, he would have deserved to be kicked out of the presence of all honest men; and to be thanked for the ordinary conduct of a gentleman was almost an insult. This he said looking chiefly at Mr. Somers, and then turning to his cousin, he asked him if he intended to remain in the country.

'Oh, certainly,' said Herbert.

'I shall not,' said Owen; 'and if you know any one who will take a lease of Hap House for ten or twelve years, I shall be glad to find a tenant.'

'And you, where are you going?'

'To Africa in the first instance,' said he; 'there seems to be some good hunting there, and I think that I shall try it.'

The new tidings were not long in reaching Desmond Court, and the countess was all alone when she first heard them. With very great difficulty, taking as it were the bit between her teeth, Clara had managed to get over to Castle Richmond that she might pay a last visit to the Fitzgerald girls. At this time Lady Desmond's mind was in a terribly distracted state. The rumour was rife about the country that Owen had refused to accept the property; and the countess herself had of course been made aware that he had so refused. But she was too keenly awake to the affairs of the world to suppose that such a refusal could continue long in force; neither, as she knew well, could Herbert accept of that which was offered to him. It might be that for some years to come the property might be unenjoyed; the rich fruit might fall rotten from the wall; but what would that avail to her or to her child? Herbert would still be a nameless man, and could never be master of Castle Richmond.

Nevertheless Clara carried her point, and went over to her friends, leaving the countess all alone. She had now permitted her son to return to Eton, finding that he was powerless to aid her. The young earl was quite willing that his sister should marry Owen Fitzgerald; but he was not willing to use any power of persuasion that he might have, in what his mother considered a useful or legitimate manner. He talked of rewarding Owen for his generosity; but Clara would have nothing to do either with the generosity or with the reward. And so Lady Desmond was left alone, hearing that even Owen, Owen himself, had now given up the quest, and feeling that it was useless to have any further hope. 'She will make her own bed,' the countess said to herself, 'and she must lie on it.'

And then came this rumour that after all Herbert was to be the man. It first reached her ears about the same time that Herbert arrived at his own house; but it did so in such a manner as to make but little impression at the moment. Lady Desmond had but few gossips, and in a general way heard but little of what was doing in the country. On this occasion the Caleb Balderston of her house came in, making stately bows to his mistress, and with low voice, and eyes wide open, told her what a gossoon running over from Castle Richmond had reported in the kitchen of Desmond Court. 'At any rate, my lady, Mr. Herbert is expected this evening at the house;' and then Caleb Balderston, bowing stately again, left the room. This did not make much impression, but it made some.

And then on the following day Clara wrote to her; this she did after deep consideration and much consultation with her friends. It would be unkind, they argued, to leave Lady Desmond in ignorance on such a subject; and therefore a note was written very guardedly, the joint production of the three, in which, with the expression of many doubts, it was told that perhaps after all Herbert might yet be the man. But even then the countess did not believe it.

But during the next week the rumour became a fact through the country, and everybody knew, even the Countess of Desmond, that all that family history was again changed. Lady Fitzgerald, whom they had all known, was Lady Fitzgerald still, and Herbert was once more on his throne. When rumours thus became a fact, there was no longer any doubt about the matter. The country-side did not say that, ' perhaps after all so and so would go in such and such a way,' or that ' legal doubts having been entertained, the gentlemen of the long robe were about to do this and that.' By the end of the first week the affair was as surely settled in county Cork as though the line of the Fitzgeralds had never been disturbed; and Sir Herbert was fully seated on his throne.

It was well then for poor Owen that he had never assumed the regalia of royalty : had he done so his fall would have been very dreadful; as it was, not only were all those pangs spared to him, but he achieved at once an immense popularity through the whole country. Everybody called him poor Owen, and declared how well he had behaved. Some expressed almost a regret that his generosity should go unrewarded, and others went so far as to give him his reward: he was to marry Emmeline Fitzgerald, they said at the clubs in Cork, and a considerable slice of the property was destined to give additional charms to the young lady's hand and heart. For a month or so Owen Fitzgerald was the most popular man in the south of Ireland; that is, as far as a man can be popular who never shows himself.

And the countess had to answer her daughter's letter. ' If this be so,' she said, ' of course I shall be well pleased. My anxiety has been only for your welfare, to further which I have been willing to make any possible sacrifice.' Clara when she read this did not know what sacrifice had been made, nor had the countess thought as she wrote the words what had been the sacrifice to which she had thus alluded, though her heart was ever conscious of it, unconsciously. And the countess sent her love to them all at Castle Richmond. ' She did not fear,' she said, ' that they would misinterpret her. Lady Fitzgerald, she was sure, would perfectly understand that she had endeavoured to do her duty by her child.' It was by no means a bad letter, and, which was better, was in the main a true letter. According to her light she had striven to do her duty, and her conduct was not misjudged, at any rate at Castle Richmond.

'You must not think harshly of mamma,' said Clara to her future mother-in-law.

'Oh no,' said Lady Fitzgerald. 'I certainly do not think harshly of her. In her position I should probably have acted as she has done.' The difference, however, between them was this, that it was all but impossible that Lady Fitzgerald should not sympathize with her children, while it was almost impossible that the Countess of Desmond should do so.

And so Lady Desmond remained all alone at Desmond Court, brooding over the things as they now were. For the present it was better that Clara should remain at Castle Richmond, and nothing therefore was said of her return on either side. She could not add to her mother's comfort at home, and why should she not remain happy where she was? She was already a Fitzgerald in heart rather than a Desmond; and was it not well that she should be so? If she could love Herbert Fitzgerald, that was well also. Since the day on which he had appeared at Desmond Court, wet and dirty and wretched, with a broken spirit and fortunes as draggled as his dress, he had lost all claim to be a hero in the estimation of Lady Desmond. To her those only were heroes whose pride and spirit were never draggled; and such a hero there still was in her close neighbourhood.

Lady Desmond herself was a woman of a mercenary spirit; so at least it will be said and thought of her. But she was not altogether so, although the two facts were strong against her that she had sold herself for a title, and had been willing to sell her daughter for a fortune. Poverty she herself had endured upon the whole with patience; and though she hated and scorned it from her very soul, she would now have given herself in marriage to a poor man without rank or station,—she, a countess, and the mother of an earl; and that she would have done with all the romantic love of a girl of sixteen, though she was now a woman verging upon forty!

Men and women only know so much of themselves and others as circumstances and their destiny have allowed to appear. Had it perchance fallen to thy lot, O my forensic friend, heavy laden with the wisdom of the law, to write tales such as this of mine, how charmingly might not thy characters have come forth upon the canvas—how much more charmingly than I can limn them! While, on the other hand, ignorant as thou now tellest me that I am of the very alphabet of the courts, had thy wig been allotted to me, I might have gathered guineas thick as daisies in summer, while to thee perhaps they come no faster than snowdrops in the early spring. It is all in our destiny. Chance had thrown that terrible earl in the way of the poor girl in her early youth, and she had married him. She had married him, and all idea of love had flown from her heart. All idea of love, but not all the capacity——as now within this last year or two she had learned, so much to her cost.

Long months had passed since she had first owned this to herself, since she had dared to tell herself that it was possible even for her to begin the world again, and to play the game which women love to play, once at least before they die. She could have worshipped this man, and sat at his feet, and endowed him in her heart with heroism, and given him her soft brown hair to play with when it suited her Hercules to rest from his labours. She could have forgotten her years, and have forgotten too the children who had now grown up to seize the world from beneath her feet—to seize it before she herself had enjoyed it. She could have forgotten all that was past, and have been every whit as young as her own daughter. If only—!

It is so, I believe, with most of us who have begun to turn the hill. I myself could go on to that common that is at this moment before me, and join that game of rounders with the most intense delight. 'By George! you fellow, you've no eyes; didn't you see that he hadn't put his foot in the hole? He'll get back now that long-backed, hard-hitting chap, and your side is done for the next half-hour!' But then they would all be awestruck for a while; and after that, when they grew to be familiar with me, they would laugh at me because I loomed large in my running, and returned to my ground scant of breath. Alas, alas! I know that it would not do. So I pass by, imperious in my heavy manhood, and one of the lads respectfully abstains from me though the ball is under my very feet.

But then I have had my game of rounders. No horrible old earl with gloating eyes carried me off in my childhood and robbed me of the pleasure of my youth. That part of my cake has been eaten, and, in spite of some occasional headache, has been digested not altogether unsatisfactorily. Lady Desmond had as yet been allowed no slice of her cake. She had never yet taken her side in any game of rounders. But she too had looked on and seen how jocund was the play; she also had acknowledged that that running in the ring, that stout hitting of the ball, that innocent craft, that bringing back by her own skill and with her own hand of some long-backed fellow, would be pleasant to her as well as to others. If only she now could be chosen in at that game! But what if the side that she cared for would not have her?

But *tempus edax rerum*, though it had hardly nibbled at her heart or wishes, had been feeding on the freshness of her brow and the bloom of her lips. The child with whom she would have

loved to play kept aloof from her too, and would not pick up the
ball when it rolled to his feet. All this, if one thinks of it, is
hard to bear. It is very hard to have had no period for rounders,
not to be able even to look back to one's games, and to talk of
them to one's old comrades! ' But why then did she allow herself to be carried off by the wicked wrinkled earl with the gloating eyes?' asks of me the prettiest girl in the world, just turned
eighteen. Oh heavens! Is it not possible that one should have
one more game of rounders? Quite impossible, O my fat friend!
And therefore I answer the young lady somewhat grimly. ' Take
care that thou also art not carried off by a wrinkled earl. Is thy
heart free from all vanity? Of what nature is the heroism that
thou worshippest?' 'A nice young man!' she says, boldly,
though in words somewhat different. ' If so it will be well for
thee; but did I not see thine eyes hankering the other day after
the precious stones of Ophir, and thy mouth watering for the
flesh-pots of Egypt? Was I not watching thee as thou sattest at
that counter, so frightfully intent? Beware!' 'The grumpy
old fellow with the bald head!' she said shortly afterwards to her
bosom friend, not careful that her words should be duly inaudible.

Some idea that all was not yet over with her had come upon
her poor heart,—upon Lady Desmond's heart, soon after Owen
Fitzgerald had made himself familiar in her old mansion. We
have read how that idea was banished, and how she had ultimately resolved that that man whom she could have loved herself
should be given up to her own child when she thought that he
was no longer poor and of low rank. She could not sympathize
with her daughter,—love with her love, and rejoice with her
joy; but she could do her duty by her, and according to her
lights she endeavoured so to do.

But now again all was turned and changed and altered. Owen
of Hap House was once more Owen of Hap House only, but still
in her eyes heroic, as it behoved a man to be. He would not
creep about the country with moaning voice and melancholy
eyes, with draggled dress and outward signs of wretchedness.
He might be wretched, but he would still be manly. Could it
be possible that to her should yet be given the privilege of
soothing that noble, unbending wretchedness? By no means
possible, poor, heart-laden countess; thy years are all against
thee. Girls whose mouths will water unduly for the flesh-pots
of Egypt must in after life undergo such penalties as these. Art
thou not a countess?

But not so did she answer herself. Might it not be possible?
Ah, might it not be possible? And as the question was even
then being asked, perhaps for the ten thousandth time, Owen

Fitzgerald stood before her. She had not yet seen him since the new news had gone abroad, and had hardly yet conceived how it might be possible that she should do so. But now as she thought of him there he was. They two were together,—alone together; and the door by which he had entered had closed upon him before she was aware of his presence.

'Owen Fitzgerald!' she said, starting up and giving him both her hands. This she did, not of judgment, nor yet from passion, but of impulse. She had been thinking of him with such kindly thoughts, and now he was there it became natural that her greeting should be kindly. It was more so than it had ever been to any but her son since the wrinkled, gloating earl had come and fetched her.

'Yes, Owen Fitzgerald,' said he, taking the two hands that were offered to him, and holding them a while; not pressing them as a man who loved her, who could have loved her, would have done. 'After all that has gone and passed between us, Lady Desmond, I cannot leave the country without saying one word of farewell to you.'

'Leave the country!' she exclaimed. 'And where are you going?'

As she looked into his face with her hands still in his,—for she did not on the moment withdraw them, she felt that he had never before looked so noble, so handsome, so grand. Leave the country! ah yes; and why should not she leave it also? What was there to bind her to those odious walls in which she had been immolated during the best half of her life?

'Where are you going?' she asked, looking almost wildly up at him.

'Somewhere very far a-field, Lady Desmond,' he said; and then the hands dropped from him. 'You will understand at any rate that Hap House will not be a fitting residence for me.'

'I hate the whole country,' said she, 'the whole place hereabouts. I have never been happy here. Happy! I have never been other than unhappy. I have been wretched. What would I not give to leave it also?'

'To you it cannot be intolerable as it will be to me. You have known so thoroughly where all my hopes were garnered, that I need not tell you why I must go from Hap House. I think that I have been wronged, but I do not desire that others should think so. And as for you and me, Lady Desmond, though we have been enemies, we have been friends also.'

'Enemies!' said she, 'I hope not.' And she spoke so softly, so unlike her usual self, in the tones so suited to a loving, clinging woman, that though he did not understand it, he was startled at her tenderness. 'I have never felt that you were my enemy, Mr. Fitzgerald; and certainly I never was an enemy to you.'

'Well; we were opposed to each other. I thought that you were robbing me of all I valued in life; and you, you thought—'

'I thought that Clara's happiness demanded rank and wealth and position. There; I tell you my sins fairly. You may say that I was mercenary if you will,—mercenary for her. I thought that I knew what would be needful for her. Can you be angry with a mother for that?'

'She had given me a promise! But never mind. It is all over now. I did not come to upbraid you, but to tell you that I now know how it must be, and that I am going.'

'Had you won her, Owen,' said the countess, looking intently into his face, 'had you won her, she would not have made you happy.'

'As to that it was for me to judge—for me and her. I thought it would, and was willing to peril all in the trial. And so was she—willing at one time. But never mind; it is useless to talk of that.'

'Quite useless now.'

'I did think—when it was as they said in my power to give him back his own,—I did think;—but no, it would have been mean to look for payment. It is all over, and I will say nothing further; not a word. I am not a girl to harp on such a thing day after day, and to grow sick with love. I shall be better away. And therefore I am going, and I have now come to say good-bye, because we were friends in old days, Lady Desmond.'

Friends in old days! They were old days to him, but they were no more than the other day to her. It was as yet hardly more than two years since she had first known him, and yet he looked on the acquaintance as one that had run out its time and required to be ended. She would so fain have been able to think that the beginning only had as yet come to them. But there he was, anxious to bid her adieu, and what was she to say to him?

'Yes, we were friends. You have been my only friend here I think. You will hardly believe with how much true friendship I have thought of you when the feud between us—if it was a feud—was at the strongest. Owen Fitzgerald, I have loved you through it all.'

Loved him? She was so handsome as she spoke, so womanly, so graceful, there was still about her so much of the charm of beauty, that he could hardly take the word when coming from her mouth as applicable to ordinary friendship. And yet he did so take it. They had all loved each other—as friends should love- -and now that he was going she had chosen to say as much.

He felt the blood tingle his cheek at the sound of her words; but he was not vain enough to take it in its usual sense. 'Then we will part as friends,' said he—tamely enough.

'Yes, we will part,' she said. And as she spoke the blood mantled deep on her neck and cheek and forehead, and a spirit came out of her eye, such as never had shone there before in his presence. 'Yes, we will part,' and she took up his right hand, and held it closely, pressed between both her own. 'And as we must part I will tell you all. Owen Fitzgerald, I have loved you with all my heart,—with all the love that a woman has to give. I have loved you, and have never loved any other. Stop, stop,' for he was going to interrupt her. 'You shall hear me now to the last,—and for the last time. I have loved you with such love—such love as you perhaps felt for her, but as she will never feel. But you shall not say, nay you shall not think that I have been selfish. I would have kept you from her when you were poor as you are now,—not because I loved you. No; you will never think that of me. And when I thought that you were rich, and the head of your family, I did all that I could to bring her back for you. Did I not, Owen?'

'Yes, I think you did,' he muttered between his teeth, hardly knowing how to speak.

'Indeed, indeed I did so. Others may say that I was selfish for my child, but you shall not think that I was selfish for myself. I sent for Patrick, and bade him go to you. I strove as mothers do strive for their children. I taught myself,—I strove to teach myself to forget that I had loved you. I swore on my knees that I would love you only as my son,—as my dear, dear son. Nay, Owen, I did: on my knees before my God.'

He turned away from her to rub the tears from his eyes, and in doing so he dragged his hand away from her. But she followed him, and again took it. 'You will hear me to the end now,' she said; 'will you not? you will not begrudge me that? And then came these other tidings, and all that scheme was dashed to the ground. It was better so, Owen; you would not have been happy with the property—'

'I should never have taken it.'

'And she, she would have clung closer to him as a poor man than ever she had done when he was rich. She is her mother's daughter there. And then—then—but I need not tell you more. You will know it all now. If you had become rich, I would have ceased to love you; but I shall never cease now that you are again poor,—now that you are Owen of Hap House again, as you sent us word yourself that day.'

And then she ceased, and bending down her head bathed his

hand with her tears. Had any one asked him that morning, he would have said that it was impossible that the Countess of Desmond should weep. And now the tears were streaming from her eyes as though she were a broken-hearted girl. And so she was. Her girlhood had been postponed and marred,—not destroyed and made away with, by the wrinkled earl with the gloating eyes.

She had said all now, and she stood there, still holding his hand in hers, but with her head turned from him. It was his turn to speak now, and how was he to answer her? I know how most men would have answered;—by the pressure of an arm, by a warm kiss, by a promise of love, and by a feeling that such love was possible. And then most men would have gone home, leaving the woman triumphant, and have repented bitterly as they sat moody over their own fires, with their wine-bottles before them. But it was not so with Owen Fitzgerald. His heart was to him a reality. He had loved with all his power and strength, with all the vigour of his soul,—having chosen to love. But he would not now be enticed by pity into a bastard feeling, which would die away when the tenderness of the moment was no longer present to his eye and touch. His love for Clara had been such that he could not even say that he loved another.

'Dear Lady Desmond,' he began.

'Ah, Owen; we are to part now, part for ever,' she said; 'speak to me once in your life as though we were equal friends. Cannot you forget for one minute that I am Countess of Desmond?'

Mary, Countess of Desmond; such was her name and title. But so little familiar had he been with the name by which he had never heard her called, that in his confusion he could not remember it. And had he done so, he could not have brought himself to use it. 'Yes,' he said; 'we must part. It is impossible for me to remain here.'

'Doubly impossible now,' she replied, half reproaching him.

'Yes; doubly impossible now. Is it not better that the truth should be spoken?'

'Oh, yes. I have spoken it—too plainly.'

'And so will I speak it plainly. We cannot control our own hearts, Lady Desmond. It is, as you say, doubly impossible now. All the love I have had to give she has had,—and has. Such being so, why should I stay here? or could you wish that I should do so?'

'I do not wish it.' That was true enough. The wish would have been to wander away with him.

'I must go, and shall start at once. My very things are packed

for my going. I will not be here to have the sound of their
marriage bells jangling in my ears. I will not be pointed at as
the man who has been duped on every side.'

'Ah me, that I was a man too,—that I could go away and
make for myself a life!'

'You have Desmond with you.'

'No, no. He will go too; of course he will go. He will go,
and I shall be utterly alone. What a fool I am,—what an ass,
that by this time I have not learned to bear it!'

'They will always be near you at Castle Richmond.'

'Ah, Owen, how little you understand! Have we been friends
while we lived under the same roof? And now that she is there,
do you think that she will heed me? I tell you that you do not
know her. She is excellent, good, devoted; but cold as ice.
She will live among the poor, and grace his table; and he will
have all that he wants. In twelve months, Owen, she would
have turned your heart to a stone.'

'It is that already I think,' said he. 'At any rate, it will be
so to all others. Good-bye, Lady Desmond.'

'Good-bye, Owen; and God bless you. My secret will be safe
with you.'

'Safe! yes, it will be safe.' And then, as she put her cheek
up to him, he kissed it and left her.

He had been very stern. She had laid bare to him her whole
heart, and he had answered her love by never a word. He had
made no reply in any shape,—given her no thanks for her heart's
treasure. He had responded to her affection by no tenderness.
He had not even said that this might have been so, had that
other not have come to pass. By no word had he alluded to her
confession,—but had regarded her delusion as monstrous, a thing
of which no word was to be spoken.

So at least said the countess to herself, sitting there all alone
where he had left her. 'He regards me as old and worn. In
his eyes I am wrinkled and ugly.' 'Twas thus that her thoughts
expressed themselves; and then she walked across the room
towards the mirror, but when there she could not look in it: she
turned her back upon it without a glance, and returned to her
seat by the window. What mattered it now? It was her doom
to live there alone for the term of life with which it might still
please God to afflict her.

And then looking out from the window her eyes fell upon Owen
as he rode slowly down across the park. His horse was walking
very slowly, and it seemed as though he himself were unconscious
of the pace. As long as he remained in sight she did not take
her eyes from his figure, gazing at him painfully as he grew

dimmer and more dim in the distance. Then at last he turned behind the bushes near the lodge, and she felt that she was all alone. It was the last that she ever saw of Owen Fitzgerald.

Unfortunate girl, marred in thy childhood by that wrinkled earl with the gloating eyes; or marred rather by thine own vanity! Those flesh-pots of Egypt! Are they not always thus bitter in the eating?

CHAPTER XLIV.

CONCLUSION.

AND now my story is told; and were it not for the fashion of the thing, this last short chapter might be spared. It shall at any rate be very short.

Were it not that I eschew the fashion of double names for a book, thinking that no amount of ingenuity in this respect will make a bad book pass muster, whereas a good book will turn out as such though no such ingenuity be displayed, I might have called this 'A Tale of the Famine Year in Ireland.' At the period of the year to which the story has brought us—and at which it will leave us—the famine was at its very worst. People were beginning to believe that there would never be a bit more to eat in the land, and that the time for hope and energy was gone. Land was becoming of no value, and the only thing regarded was a sufficiency of food to keep body and soul together. Under such circumstances it was difficult to hope.

But energy without hope is impossible, and therefore was there such an apathy and deadness through the country. It was not that they did not work who were most concerned to work. The amount of conscientious work then done was most praiseworthy. But it was done almost without hope of success, and done chiefly as a matter of conscience. There was a feeling, which was not often expressed but which seemed to prevail everywhere, that ginger would not again be hot in the mouth, and that in very truth the time for cakes and ale in this world was all over. It was this feeling that made a residence in Ireland at that period so very sad.

Ah me! how little do we know what is coming to us! Irish cakes and ale were done and over for this world, we all thought. But in truth the Irish cakes were only then a-baking, and the Irish ale was being brewed. I am not sure that these good things are yet quite fit for the palates of the guest;—not as fit as a little more time will make them. The cake is still too new, —cakes often are; and the ale is not sufficiently mellowed. But of this I am sure, that the cakes and ale are there;—and the ginger, too, very hot in the mouth. Let a committee of Irish landlords say how the rents are paid now, and what amount of arrears was due through the country when the famine came among them. Rents paid to the day: that is the ginger hot in the mouth which best pleases the palate of a country gentleman.

But if one did in truth write a tale of the famine, after that it would behove the author to write a tale of the pestilence; and then another, a tale of the exodus. These three wonderful events, following each other, were the blessings coming from Omniscience and Omnipotence by which the black clouds were driven from the Irish firmament. If one, through it all, could have dared to hope, and have had from the first that wisdom which has learned to acknowledge that His mercy endureth for ever! And then the same author going on with his series would give in his last set,—Ireland in her prosperity.

Of all those who did true good conscientious work at this time, none exceeded in energy our friend Herbert Fitzgerald after his return to Castle Richmond. It seemed to him as though some thank-offering were due from him for all the good things that Providence had showered upon him, and the best thank-offering that he could give was a devoted attention to the interest of the poor around him. Mr. Somers soon resigned to him the chair at those committee meetings at Berryhill and Gortnaclough, and it was acknowledged that the Castle Richmond arrangements for soup-kitchens, out-door relief, and labour-gangs, might be taken as a model for the south of Ireland. Few other men were able to go to the work with means so ample and with hands so perfectly free. Mr. Carter even, who by this time had become cemented in a warm trilateral friendship with Father Barney and the Rev. Æneas Townsend, was obliged to own that many a young English country gentleman might take a lesson from Sir Herbert Fitzgerald in the duties peculiar to his position.

His marriage did not take place till full six months after the period to which our story has brought us. Baronets with twelve thousand a year cannot be married off the hooks, as may be done with ordinary mortals. Settlements of a grandiose nature were required, and were duly concocted. Perhaps Mr. Die had something to say to them, so that the great maxim of the law was brought into play. Perhaps also, though of this Herbert heard no word, it was thought inexpedient to hurry matters while any further inquiry was possible in that affair of the Mollett connection. Mr. Die and Mr. Prendergast were certainly going about, still drawing all coverts far and near, lest their fox might not have been fairly run to his last earth. But, as I have said, no tidings as to this reached Castle Richmond. There, in Ireland, no man troubled himself further with any doubt upon the subject; and Sir Herbert took his title and received his rents, by the hands of Mr. Somers, exactly as though the Molletts, father and son, had never appeared in those parts.

It was six months before the marriage was celebrated, but during a considerable part of that time Clara remained a visitor at Castle Richmond. To Lady Fitzgerald she was now the same as a daughter, and to Aunt Letty the same as a niece. By the girls she had for months been regarded as a sister. So she remained in the house of which she was to be the mistress, learning to know their ways, and ingratiating herself with those who were to be dependent on her.

'But I had rather stay with you, mamma, if you will allow me,' Clara had said to her mother when the countess was making some arrangement with her that she should return to Castle Richmond. 'I shall be leaving you altogether so soon now!' And she got up close to her mother's side caressingly, and would fain have pressed into her arms and kissed her, and have talked to her of what was coming, as a daughter loves to talk to a loving mother. But Lady Desmond's heart was sore and sad and harsh, and she preferred to be alone.

'You will be better at Castle Richmond, my dear: you will be much happier there, of course. There can be no reason why you should come again into the gloom of this prison.'

'But I should be with you, dearest mamma.'

'It is better that you should be with the Fitzgeralds now; and as for me—I must learn to live alone. Indeed I have learned it, so you need not mind for me.' Clara was rebuffed by the tone rather than the words, but she still looked up into her mother's face wistfully. 'Go, my dear,' said the countess—'I would sooner be alone at present.' And so Clara went. It was hard upon her that even now her mother would not accept her love.

But Lady Desmond could not be cordial with her daughter. She made more than one struggle to do so, but always failed. She could,—she thought that she could, have watched her child's happiness with contentment had Clara married Owen Fitzgerald—Sir Owen, as he would then have been. But now she could only remember that Owen was lost to them both, lost through her child's fault. She did not hate Clara: nay, she would have made any sacrifice for her daughter's welfare; but she could not take her lovingly to her bosom. So she shut herself up alone, in her prison as she called it, and then looked back upon the errors of her life. It was as well for her to look back as to look forward, for what joy was there for which she could dare to hope?

In the days that were coming, however, she did relax some-thing of her sternness. Clara was of course married from Des-mond Court, and the very necessity of making some preparations for this festivity was in itself salutary. But indeed it could hardly be called a festivity,—it was so quiet and sombre. Clara had but two bridesmaids, and they were Mary and Emmeline Fitzgerald. The young earl gave away his sister, and Aunt Letty was there, and Mr. Prendergast, who had come over about the settlements; Mr. Somers also attended, and the ceremony was performed by our old friend Mr. Townsend. Beyond these there were no guests at the wedding of Sir Herbert Fitzgerald.

The young earl was there, and at the last the wedding had been postponed a week for his coming. He had left Eton at Mid-summer in order that he might travel for a couple of years with Owen Fitzgerald before he went to Oxford. It had been the lad's own request, and had been for a while refused by Owen. But Fitzgerald had at last given way to the earl's love, and they had started together for Norway.

'They want me to be home,' he had said one morning to his friend.

'Ah, yes; I suppose so.'

'Do you know why?' They had never spoken a word about Clara since they had left England together, and the earl now dreaded to mention her name.

'Know why!' replied Owen; 'of course I do. It is to give away your sister. Go home, Desmond, my boy; when you have returned we will talk about her. I shall bear it better when I know that she is his wife.'

And so it was with them. For two years Lord Desmond travelled with him, and after that Owen Fitzgerald went on upon his wanderings alone. Many a long year has run by since that, and yet he has never come back to Hap House. Men of the county Cork now talk of him as one whom they knew long since. He who took his house as a stranger is a stranger no longer in the country, and the place that Owen left vacant has been filled. The hounds of Duhallow would not recognize his voice, nor would the steed in the stable follow gently at his heels. But there is yet one left who thinks of him, hoping that she may yet see him before she dies.

THE END.